Pieces of Her

Karin Slaughter is one of the world's most popular and acclaimed storytellers. Published in 120 countries with more than 35 million copies sold across the globe, her 19 novels include the Grant County and Will Trent books, as well as the Edgar-nominated *Cop Town* and the instant *Sunday Times* bestselling novels *Pretty Girls*, *The Good Daughter*, and *Pieces of Her*. Slaughter is the founder of the Save the Libraries project—a nonprofit organization established to support libraries and library programming. A native of Georgia, Karin Slaughter lives in Atlanta. Her standalone novels *Pieces of Her*, *The Good Daughter* and *Cop Town* are in development for film and television.

For more information visit KarinSlaughter.com
f /AuthorKarinSlaughter
🐦 @SlaughterKarin

Also by Karin Slaughter

Blindsighted
Kisscut
A Faint Cold Fear
Indelible
Faithless
Triptych
Skin Privilege
Fractured
Genesis
Broken
Fallen
Criminal
Unseen
Cop Town
Pretty Girls
The Kept Woman
The Good Daughter

EBOOK ORIGINALS
Snatched
Cold, Cold Heart
Busted
Blonde Hair, Blue Eyes
Last Breath

NOVELLAS AND STORIES
Like a Charm (Editor)
Martin Misunderstood

Karin Slaughter
Pieces of Her

HarperCollins*Publishers*

HarperCollins*Publishers* Ltd
1 London Bridge Street,
London SE1 9GF

www.harpercollins.co.uk

This paperback edition 2019
1

First published in Great Britain in 2018 by HarperCollins*Publishers*

A catalogue record for this book is available from the British Library

ISBN: 978-0-00-815085-3 (PB b-format)
ISBN: 978-0-00-815087-7 (PB a-format)

Set in Sabon by Palimpsest Book Production Limited, Falkirk, Stirlingshire

Printed and bound in the UK by CPI Group (UK) Ltd, Croydon CR0 4YY

This ... paper

Fo... n

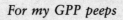

For my GPP peeps

I'm Nobody! Who are you?
Are you—Nobody—Too?
Then there's a pair of us!
Don't tell! they'd advertise—you know!

How dreary—to be—Somebody!
How public—like a Frog—
To tell one's name—the livelong June—
To an admiring Bog!

—Emily Dickinson

PROLOGUE

For years, even while she'd loved him, part of her had hated him in that childish way that you hate something you can't control. He was headstrong, and stupid, and handsome, which gave him cover for a hell of a lot of the mistakes he continually made—the same mistakes, over and over again, because why try new ones when the old ones worked so well in his favor?

He was charming, too. That was the problem. He would charm her. He would make her furious. Then he would charm her back again so that she did not know if he was the snake or she was the snake and he was the handler.

So he sailed along on his charm, and his fury, and he hurt people, and he found new things that interested him more, and the old things were left broken in his wake.

Then, quite suddenly, his charm had stopped working. A trolley car off the tracks. A train without a conductor. The mistakes could not be forgiven, and eventually, the second same mistake would not be overlooked, and the third same mistake had dire consequences that had ended with a life being taken, a death sentence being passed, then—almost—resulted in the loss of another life, her life.

How could she still love someone who had tried to destroy her?

When she had been with him—and she was decidedly with

him during his long fall from grace—they had raged against the system: The group homes. The emergency departments. The loony bin. The mental hospital. The squalor. The staff who neglected their patients. The orderlies who ratcheted tight the straightjackets. The nurses who looked the other way. The doctors who doled out the pills. The urine on the floor. The feces on the walls. The inmates, the fellow prisoners, taunting, wanting, beating, biting.

The spark of rage, not the injustice, was what had excited him the most. The novelty of a new cause. The chance to annihilate. The dangerous game. The threat of violence. The promise of fame. Their names in lights. Their righteous deeds on the tongues of schoolchildren who were taught the lessons of change.

A penny, a nickel, a dime, a quarter, a dollar bill . . .

What she had kept hidden, the one sin that she could never confess to, was that she had ignited that first spark.

She had always believed—vehemently, with great conviction—that the only way to change the world was to destroy it.

2

August 20, 2018

1

"Andrea," her mother said. Then, in concession to a request made roughly one thousand times before, "Andy."

"Mom—"

"Let me speak, darling." Laura paused. "Please."

Andy nodded, preparing for a long-awaited lecture. She was officially thirty-one years old today. Her life was stagnating. She had to start making decisions rather than having life make decisions for her.

Laura said, "This is my fault."

Andy felt her chapped lips peel apart in surprise. "What's your fault?"

"Your being here. Trapped here."

Andy held out her arms, indicating the restaurant. "At the Rise-n-Dine?"

Her mother's eyes traveled the distance from the top of Andy's head to her hands, which fluttered nervously back to the table. Dirty brown hair thrown into a careless ponytail. Dark circles under her tired eyes. Nails bitten down to the quick. The bones of her wrists like the promontory of a ship. Her skin, normally pale, had taken on the pallor of hot dog water.

The catalog of flaws didn't even include her work outfit. The navy-blue uniform hung off Andy like a paper sack. The stitched silver badge on her breast pocket was stiff, the Belle Isle palm

5

tree logo surrounded by the words POLICE DISPATCH DIVISION. Like a police officer, but not actually. Like an adult, but not really. Five nights a week, Andy sat in a dark, dank room with four other women answering 911 calls, running license plate and driver's license checks, and assigning case numbers. Then, around six in the morning, she slinked back to her mother's house and spent the majority of what should've been her waking hours asleep.

Laura said, "I never should have let you come back here."

Andy pressed together her lips. She stared down at the last bits of yellow eggs on her plate.

"My sweet girl." Laura reached across the table for her hand, waited for her to look up. "I pulled you away from your life. I was scared, and I was selfish." Tears rimmed her mother's eyes. "I shouldn't have needed you so much. I shouldn't have asked for so much."

Andy shook her head. She looked back down at her plate.

"Darling."

Andy kept shaking her head because the alternative was to speak, and if she spoke, she would have to tell the truth.

Her mother had not asked her to do anything.

Three years ago, Andy had been walking to her shitty Lower East Side fourth-floor walk-up, dreading the thought of another night in the one-bedroom hovel she shared with three other girls, none of whom she particularly liked, all of whom were younger, prettier and more accomplished, when Laura had called.

"Breast cancer," Laura had said, not whispering or hedging but coming straight out with it in her usual calm way. "Stage three. The surgeon will remove the tumor, then while I'm under, he'll biopsy the lymph nodes to evaluate—"

Laura had said more, detailing what was to come with a degree of detached, scientific specificity that was lost on Andy, whose language-processing skills had momentarily evaporated. She had heard the word "breast" more than "cancer," and thought instantly of her mother's generous bosom. Tucked beneath her modest one-piece swimsuit at the beach. Peeking

6

over the neckline of her Regency dress for Andy's Netherfield-themed sixteenth birthday party. Strapped under the padded cups and gouging underwires of her LadyComfort Bras as she sat on the couch in her office and worked with her speech therapy patients.

Laura Oliver was not a bombshell, but she had always been what men called very well put together. Or maybe it was women who called it that, probably back in the last century. Laura wasn't the type for heavy make-up and pearls, but she never left the house without her short gray hair neatly styled, her linen pants crisply starched, her underwear clean and still elasticized.

Andy barely made it out of the apartment most days. She was constantly having to double back for something she had forgotten like her phone or her ID badge for work or, one time, her sneakers because she'd walked out of the building wearing her bedroom slippers.

Whenever people in New York asked Andy what her mother was like, she always thought of something Laura had said about her own mother: *She always knew where all the tops were to her Tupperware.*

Andy couldn't be bothered to close a Ziploc bag.

On the phone, eight hundred miles away, Laura's stuttered intake of breath was the only sign that this was difficult for her. "Andrea?"

Andy's ears, buzzing with New York sounds, had zeroed back in on her mother's voice.

Cancer.

Andy tried to grunt. She could not make the noise. This was shock. This was fear. This was unfettered terror because the world had suddenly stopped spinning and everything—the failures, the disappointments, the horror of Andy's New York existence for the last six years—receded like the drawback wave of a tsunami. Things that should've never been uncovered were suddenly out in the open.

Her mother had cancer.

She could be dying.

7

She could die.

Laura had said, "So, there's chemo, which will by all accounts be very difficult." She was used to filling Andy's protracted silences, had learned long ago that confronting her on them was more likely to end up in a fight than a resumption of civil conversation. "Then I'll take a pill every day, and that's that. The five-year survival rate is over seventy percent, so there's not a lot to worry about except for getting through it." A pause for breath, or maybe in hopes that Andy was ready to speak. "It's very treatable, darling. I don't want you to worry. Just stay where you are. There's nothing you can do."

A car horn had blared. Andy had looked up. She was standing statue-like in the middle of a crosswalk. She struggled to move. The phone was hot against her ear. It was past midnight. Sweat rolled down her back and leached from her armpits like melted butter. She could hear the canned laughter of a sitcom, bottles clinking, and an anonymous piercing scream for help, the likes of which she had learned to tune out her first month living in the city.

Too much silence on her end of the phone. Finally, her mother had prompted, "Andrea?"

Andy had opened her mouth without considering what words should come out.

"Darling?" her mother had said, still patient, still generously *nice* in the way that her mother was to everyone she met. "I can hear the street noises, otherwise I'd think we'd lost the connection." She paused again. "Andrea, I really need you to acknowledge what I'm telling you. It's important."

Her mouth was still hanging open. The sewer smell that was endemic to her neighborhood had stuck to the back of her nasal passages like a piece of overcooked spaghetti slapped onto a kitchen cabinet. Another car horn blared. Another woman screamed for help. Another ball of sweat rolled down Andy's back and pooled in the waistband of her underwear. The elastic was torn where her thumb went when she pulled them down.

Andy still could not recall how she'd managed to force herself out of her stupor, but she remembered the words she had finally said to her mother: "I'm coming home."

There had not been much to show for her six years in the city. Andy's three part-time jobs had all been resigned from by text. Her subway card was given to a homeless woman who had thanked her, then screeched that she was a fucking whore. Only the absolutely necessary things went into Andy's suitcase: favorite T-shirts, broken-in jeans, several books that had survived not just the trip from Belle Isle, but five different moves into progressively shittier apartments. Andy wouldn't need her gloves or her puffy winter coat or her earmuffs back home. She didn't bother to wash her sheets or even take them off the old Chesterfield sofa that was her bed. She had left for LaGuardia at the crack of dawn, less than six hours after her mother's phone call. In the blink of an eye, Andy's life in New York was over. The only thing the three younger, more accomplished roommates had to remember her by was the half-eaten Filet-O-Fish sandwich Andy had left in the fridge and her part of the next month's rent.

That had been three years ago, almost half as many years as she had lived in the city. Andy didn't want to, but in low moments she checked in with her former cohabitants on Facebook. They were her yardstick. Her truncheon. One had reached middle management at a fashion blog. The other had started her own bespoke sneaker design company. The third had died after a cocaine binge on a rich man's yacht and still, some nights when Andy was answering calls and the person on the end of the line was a twelve-year-old who thought it was funny to call 911 and pretend he was being molested, she could not help but think that she remained the least accomplished of them all.

A yacht, for chrissakes.

A *yacht*.

"Darling?" her mother rapped the table for attention. The lunch crowd had thinned out. A man seated at the front gave her an angry look over his newspaper. "Where are you?"

Andy held out her arms again, indicating the restaurant, but

9

the gesture felt forced. They knew exactly where she was: less than five miles from where she had started.

Andy had gone to New York City thinking she would find a way to shine and ended up emitting the equivalent amount of light you'd find in an old emergency flashlight left in a kitchen drawer. She hadn't wanted to be an actor or a model or any of the usual clichés. Stardom was never her dream. She had yearned to be star-adjacent: the personal assistant, the coffee fetcher, the prop wrangler, the scenery painter, the social media manager, the support staff that made the star's life possible. She wanted to bask in the glow. To be in the middle of things. To know people. To have connections.

Her professor at the Savannah College of Art and Design had seemed like a good connection. She had dazzled him with her passion for the arts, or at least that's what he'd claimed. That they were in bed when he'd said this only mattered to Andy after the fact. When she'd broken off the affair, the man had taken as a threat her idle chatter about wanting to focus on her career. Before Andy knew what was happening, before she could explain to her professor that she wasn't trying to leverage his gross inappropriateness into career advancement, he had pulled some strings to get her a job as an assistant to the assistant scenery designer in an off-Broadway show.

Off-Broadway!

Just down the street from *on Broadway!*

Andy was two semesters away from earning her degree in technical theater arts. She had packed her suitcase and barely did more than toss a wave over her shoulder as she headed to the airport.

Two months later, the show had closed under crushingly bad reviews.

Everyone on the crew had quickly found other jobs, joined other shows, except for Andy, who had settled into a real New York life. She was a waitress, a dog walker, a sign painter, a telephone debt collector, a delivery person, a fax machine monitor, a sandwich maker, a non-unionized copier paper feeder, and finally, the loser bitch who had left a half-eaten Filet-O-Fish in the fridge and one month's rent on the counter and run off to Buttfuck, Georgia, or wherever the hell it was that she was from.

Really, all Andy had brought home with her was one tiny shred of dignity, and now she was going to waste it on her mother.

She looked up from the eggs.

"Mom." She had to clear her throat before she could get out the confession. "I love you for saying that, but it's not your fault. You're right that I wanted to come home to see you. But I stayed for other reasons."

Laura frowned. "What other reasons? You loved New York."

She had hated New York.

"You were doing so well up there."

She had been drowning.

"That boy you were seeing was so into you."

And every other vagina in his building.

"You had so many friends."

She had not heard from one of them since she'd left.

"Well." Laura sighed. The list of encouragements had been short if not probing. As usual, she had read Andy like a book. "Baby, you've always wanted to be somebody different. Someone special. I mean in the sense of someone with a gift, an unusual talent. Of course you're special to me and Dad."

Andy's eyes strained to roll up in her head. "Thanks."

"You *are* talented. You're smart. You're better than smart. You're *clever*."

Andy ran her hands up and down her face as if she could erase herself from this conversation. She knew she was talented and smart. The problem was that in New York, everyone else had been talented and smart, too. Even the guy working the counter at the bodega was funnier, quicker, more clever than she was.

Laura insisted, "There's nothing wrong with being normal. Normal people have very meaningful lives. Look at me. It's not selling out to enjoy yourself."

11

Andy said, "I'm thirty-one years old, I haven't gone on a real date in three years, I have sixty-three thousand dollars in student debt for a degree I never finished and I live in a one-room apartment over my mother's garage." Air strained through Andy's nose as she tried to breathe. Verbalizing the long list had put a tight band around her chest. "The question isn't what else can I do. It's what else am I going to fuck up?"

"You're not fucking up."

"Mom—"

"You've fallen into the habit of feeling low. You can get used to anything, especially bad things. But the only direction now is up. You can't fall off the floor."

"Have you ever heard of basements?"

"Basements have floors, too."

"That's the ground."

"But *ground* is just another word for *floor*."

"Ground is like, six feet under."

"Why do you always have to be so morbid?"

Andy felt a sudden irritation honing her tongue into a razor. She swallowed it back down. They couldn't argue about curfew or make-up or tight jeans anymore, so these were the fights that she now had with her mother: That basements had floors. The proper direction from which toilet paper should come off the roll. Whether forks should be placed in the dishwasher tines up or tines down. If a grocery cart was called a cart or a buggy. That Laura was pronouncing it wrong when she called the cat "Mr. Perkins" because his name was actually Mr. Purrkins.

Laura said, "I was working with a patient the other day, and the strangest thing happened."

The cliffhanger-change-of-subject was one of their well-worn paths to truce.

"So strange," Laura baited.

Andy hesitated, then nodded for her to continue.

"He presented with Broca's Aphasia. Some right-side paralysis." Laura was a licensed speech pathologist living in a coastal retirement community. The majority of her patients had experienced some form of debilitating stroke. "He was an IT guy in his previous life, but I guess that doesn't matter."

"What happened that was strange?" Andy asked, doing her part.

Laura smiled. "He was telling me about his grandson's wedding, and I have no idea what he was trying to say, but it came out as 'blue suede shoes.' And I had this flash in my head, this sort of memory, to back when Elvis died."

"Elvis Presley?"

She nodded. "This was '77, so I would've been fourteen years old, more Rod Stewart than Elvis. But anyway. There were these very conservative, beehived ladies at our church, and they were bawling their eyes out that he was gone."

Andy grinned the way you grin when you know you're missing something.

Laura gave her the same grin back. Chemo brain, even this far out from her last treatment. She had forgotten the point of her story. "It's just a funny thing I remembered."

"I guess the beehive ladies were kind of hypocritical?" Andy tried to jog her memory. "I mean, Elvis was really sexy, right?"

"It doesn't matter." Laura patted her hand. "I'm so grateful for you. The strength you gave me while I was sick. The closeness we still have. I cherish that. It's a gift." Her mother's voice started to quiver. "But I'm better now. And I want you to live your life. I want you to be happy, or, failing that, I want you to find peace with yourself. And I don't think you can do it here, baby. As much as I want to make it easier for you, I know that it'll never take unless you do it all on your own."

Andy looked up at the ceiling. She looked out at the empty mall. She finally looked back at her mother.

Laura had tears in her eyes. She shook her head as if in awe. "You're magnificent. Do you know that?"

Andy forced out a laugh.

"You are magnificent because you are so uniquely you." Laura pressed her hand to her heart. "You are talented, and you are beautiful, and you'll find your way, my love, and it will be the right way, no matter what, because it's the path that you set out for yourself."

Andy felt a lump in her throat. Her eyes started to water. There was a stillness around them. She could hear the sound of her own blood swooshing through her veins.

"Well." Laura laughed, another well-worn tactic for lightening an emotional moment. "Gordon thinks I should give you a deadline to move out."

Gordon. Andy's father. He was a trusts and estates lawyer. His entire life was deadlines.

Laura said, "But I'm not going to give you a deadline, or an ultimatum."

Gordon loved ultimatums, too.

"I'm saying if this is your life"—she indicated the police-like, adult-ish uniform—"then embrace it. Accept it. And if you want to do something else"—she squeezed Andy's hand—"do something else. You're still young. You don't have a mortgage or even a car payment. You have your health. You're smart. You're free to do whatever you like."

"Not with my student loan debt."

"Andrea," Laura said, "I don't want to be a doomsayer, but if you continue listlessly spinning around, pretty soon you'll be forty and find yourself very tired of living inside of a cartwheel."

"Forty," Andy repeated, an age that seemed less decrepit every year it drew closer.

"Your father would say—"

"Shit or get off the pot." Gordon was always telling Andy to move, to make something of herself, to *do something*. For a long time, she had blamed him for her lethargy. When both of your parents were driven, accomplished people, it was a form of rebellion to be lazy, right? To stubbornly and consistently take the easy road when the hard road was just so . . . hard?

"Dr. Oliver?" an older woman said. That she was invading a quiet mother–daughter moment seemed to be lost on her. "I'm Betsy Barnard. You worked with my father last year. I just wanted to say thank you. You're a miracle worker."

14

Laura stood up to shake the woman's hand. "You're very sweet to say that, but he did the work himself." She slipped into what Andy thought of as her Healing Dr. Oliver Mode, asking open-ended questions about the woman's father, clearly not quite remembering who he was but making a passable effort so that the woman was just as clearly fooled.

Laura nodded toward Andy. "This is my daughter, Andrea."

Betsy duplicated the nod with a passing interest. She was beaming under Laura's attention. Everyone loved her mother, no matter what mode she was in: therapist, friend, business owner, cancer patient, mother. She had a sort of relentless kindness that was kept from being too sugary by her quick, sometimes acerbic wit.

Occasionally, usually after a few drinks, Andy could show these same qualities to strangers, but once they got to know her, they seldom stuck around. Maybe that was Laura's secret. She had dozens, even hundreds, of friends, but not one single person knew all of the pieces of her.

"Oh!" Betsy practically shouted. "I want you to meet my daughter, too. I'm sure Frank told you all about her."

"Frank sure did." Andy caught the relief on Laura's face; she really had forgotten the man's name. She winked at Andy, momentarily switching back into Mom Mode.

"Shelly!" Betsy frantically waved over her daughter. "Come meet the woman who helped save Pop-Pop's life."

A very pretty young blonde reluctantly shuffled over. She tugged self-consciously at the long sleeves of her red UGA T-shirt. The white bulldog on her chest was wearing a matching red shirt. She was obviously mortified, still at that age when you didn't want a mother unless you needed money or compassion. Andy could remember what that push-pull felt like. Most days, she wasn't as far removed from it as she wanted to be. It was a truth universally acknowledged that your mother was the only person in the world who could say, "Your hair looks nice," but what you heard was, "Your hair always looks awful except for this one, brief moment in time."

"Shelly, this is Dr. Oliver." Betsy Barnard looped a possessive arm through her daughter's. "Shelly's about to start UGA in the fall. Isn't that right, sweetie?"

Laura said, "I went to UGA, too. Of course, this was back when we took notes on stone tablets."

Shelly's mortification amped up a few degrees as her mother laughed a little too loudly at the stale joke. Laura tried to smooth things over, politely questioning the girl on her major, her dreams, her aspirations. This was the type of prying you took as a personal affront when you were young, but as an adult, you realized these were the only types of questions adults knew how to ask you.

Andy looked down at her half-filled coffee cup. She felt unreasonably tired. Night shifts. She couldn't get used to them, only handled them by stringing together naps, which meant that she ended up stealing toilet paper and peanut butter from her mother's pantry because she never made time to go to the grocery store. That was probably why Laura had insisted they have a birthday lunch today instead of a birthday breakfast, which would've allowed Andy to return to her cave over the garage and fall asleep in front of the TV.

She drank the last of her coffee, which was so cold it hit the back of her throat like crushed ice. She looked for the waitress. The girl had her nose buried in her phone. Her shoulders were slouched. She was smacking gum.

Andy suppressed the wave of bitchiness as she stood up from the table. The older she got, the harder it was to resist the urge to become her mother. Though, in retrospect, Laura had often had good advice: Stand up straight or your back will hurt when you're thirty. Wear better shoes or you'll pay for it when you're thirty. Establish sensible habits or you'll pay for it when you're thirty.

Andy was thirty-one. She was paying so much that she was practically bankrupt.

"You a cop?" The waitress finally looked up from her phone.

"Theater major."

The girl wrinkled her nose. "I don't know what that means."

"You and me both."

Andy helped herself to more coffee. The waitress kept giving her sideways glances. Maybe it was the police-like uniform. The girl looked like the type who would have some Molly or at least a bag of weed stashed in her purse. Andy was wary of the uniform, too. Gordon had gotten her the job. She figured he was hoping she would eventually join the force. At first, Andy had been repulsed by the idea because she'd had it in her head that cops were bad guys. Then she had met some actual cops and realized they were mostly decent human beings trying to do a really shitty job. Then she had worked dispatch for a year and started to hate the entire world, because two thirds of the calls were just stupid people who didn't understand what an emergency was.

Laura was still talking with Betsy and Shelly Barnard. Andy had seen this same scene play out countless times. They didn't quite know how to gracefully exit and Laura was too polite to move them along. Instead of returning to the table, Andy walked over to the plate glass window. The diner was in a prime location inside the Mall of Belle Isle, a corner unit on the bottom floor. Past the boardwalk, the Atlantic Ocean roiled from a coming storm. People were walking their dogs or riding their bikes along the flat stretch of packed sand.

Belle Isle was neither belle nor, technically, an isle. It was basically a man-made peninsula created when the Army Corps of Engineers had dredged the port of Savannah back in the eighties. They had intended the new landmass to be an uninhabited, natural barrier against hurricanes, but the state had seen dollar signs on the new beachfront. Within five years of the dredging, more than half the surface area was covered in concrete: beach villas, townhouses, condos, shopping malls. The rest was tennis courts and golf courses. Retired Northerners played in the sun all day, drank martinis at sunset and called 911 when their neighbors left their trash cans by the street too long.

"Jesus," somebody whispered, low and mean, but with a tinge of surprise, all at the same time.

The air had changed. That was the only way to describe it. The fine hairs on the back of Andy's neck stood up. A chill went down her spine. Her nostrils flared. Her mouth went dry. Her eyes watered.

There was a sound like a jar popping open.

Andy turned.

The handle of the coffee cup slipped from her fingers. Her eyes followed its path to the floor. White ceramic shards bounced off the white tiles.

There had been an eerie silence before, but now there was chaos. Screaming. Crying. People running, ducked down, hands covering their heads.

Bullets.

Pop-pop.

Shelly Barnard was lying on the floor. On her back. Arms splayed. Legs twisted. Eyes wide open. Her red T-shirt looked wet, stuck to her chest. Blood dribbled from her nose. Andy watched the thin red line slide down her cheek and into her ear.

She was wearing tiny Bulldog earrings.

"No!" Betsy Barnard wailed. "N—"

Pop.

Andy saw the back of the woman's throat vomit out in a spray of blood.

Pop.

The side of Betsy's skull snapped open like a plastic bag.

She fell sideways onto the floor. On top of her daughter. Onto her dead daughter.

Dead.

"Mom," Andy whispered, but Laura was already there. She was running toward Andy with her arms out, knees bent low. Her mouth was open. Her eyes were wide with fear. Red dots peppered her face like freckles.

The back of Andy's head slammed into the window as she

was tackled to the ground. She felt the rush of air from her mother's mouth as the wind was knocked out of her. Andy's vision blurred. She could hear a cracking sound. She looked up. The glass above her had started to spiderweb.

"Please!" Laura screamed. She had rolled over, was on her knees, then her feet. "Please, stop."

Andy blinked. She rubbed her fists into her eyes. Grit cut into her eyelids. Dirt? Glass? Blood?

"Please!" Laura shouted.

Andy blinked again.

Then again.

A man was pointing a gun at her mother's chest. Not a cop's gun, but the kind with a cylinder like in the Old West. He was dressed the part—black jeans, black shirt with pearl buttons, black leather vest and black cowboy hat. Gunbelt hanging low on his hips. One holster for the gun, a long leather sheath for a hunting knife.

Handsome.

His face was young, unlined. He was Shelly's age, maybe a little older.

But Shelly was dead now. She would not be going to UGA. She would never be mortified by her mother again because her mother was dead, too.

And now the man who had murdered them both was pointing a gun at her mother's chest.

Andy sat up.

Laura only had one breast, the left one, over her heart. The surgeon had taken the right one and she hadn't gotten reconstructive surgery yet because she couldn't stand the thought of going to yet another doctor, having another procedure, and now this murderer standing in front of her was going to put a bullet in it.

"Mm—" The word got caught in Andy's throat. She could only think it—

Mom.

"It's all right." Laura's voice was calm, controlled. She had

19

her hands out in front of her like they could catch the bullets. She told the man, "You can leave now."

"Fuck you." His eyes darted to Andy. "Where's your gun, you fucking pig?"

Andy's whole body cringed. She felt herself tightening into a ball.

"She doesn't have a gun," Laura said, her voice still composed. "She's a secretary at the police station. She's not a cop."

"Get up!" he screamed at Andy. "I see your badge! Get up, pig! Do your job!"

Laura said, "It's not a badge. It's an emblem. Just stay calm." She patted her hands down the same way she used to tuck Andy into bed at night. "Andy, listen to me."

"Listen to *me*, you fucking bitches!" Saliva flew from the man's mouth. He shook the gun in the air. "Stand up, pig. You're next."

"No." Laura blocked his way. "I'm next."

His eyes turreted back to Laura.

"Shoot me." Laura spoke with unmistakable certainty. "I want you to shoot me."

Confusion broke the mask of anger that was his face. He hadn't planned for this. People were supposed to be terrified, not volunteer.

"Shoot me," she repeated.

He peered over Laura's shoulder at Andy, then looked back.

"Do it," Laura said. "You only have one bullet left. You know that. There are only six bullets in the gun." She held up her hands showing four fingers on her left hand, one on her right. "It's why you haven't pulled the trigger yet. There's only one bullet left."

"You don't know—"

"Only one more." She waved her thumb, indicating the sixth bullet. "When you shoot me, my daughter will run out of here. Right, Andy?"

What?

"Andy," her mother said. "I need you to run, darling."

What?

20

"He can't reload fast enough to hurt you."

"Fuck!" the man screamed, trying to get his rage back. "Be still! Both of you."

"Andy." Laura took a step toward the gunman. She was limping. A tear in her linen pants was weeping blood. Something white stuck out like bone. "Listen to me, sweetheart."

"I said don't move!"

"Go through the kitchen door." Laura's voice remained steady. "There's an exit in the back."

What?

"Stop there, bitch. Both of you."

"You need to trust me," Laura said. "He can't reload in time."

Mom.

"Get up." Laura took another step forward. "I said, get up."

Mom, no.

"Andrea Eloise." She was using her Mother voice, not her Mom voice. "Get up. Now."

Andy's body worked of its own volition. Left foot flat, right heel up, fingers touching the ground, a runner at the block.

"Stop it!" The man jerked the gun toward Andy, but Laura moved with it. He jerked it back and she followed the path, blocking Andy with her body. Shielding her from the last bullet in the gun.

"Shoot me," Laura told the man. "Go ahead."

"Fuck this."

Andy heard a *snap*.

The trigger pulling back? The hammer hitting the bullet?

Her eyes had squeezed closed, hands flew to cover her head.

But there was nothing.

No bullet fired. No cry of pain.

No sound of her mother falling dead to the ground.

Floor. Ground. Six feet under.

Andy cringed as she looked back up.

The man had unsnapped the sheath on the hunting knife.

He was slowly drawing it out.

Six inches of steel. Serrated on one side. Sharp on the other.

He holstered the gun, tossed the knife into his dominant hand. He didn't have the blade pointing up the way you'd hold a steak knife but down, the way you'd stab somebody.

Laura asked, "What are you going to do with that?"

He didn't answer. He showed her.

Two steps forward.

The knife arced up, then slashed down toward her mother's heart.

Andy was paralyzed, too terrified to ball herself up, too shocked to do anything but watch her mother die.

Laura stuck out her hand as if she could block the knife. The blade sliced straight into the center of her palm. Instead of collapsing, or screaming, Laura's fingers wrapped around the hilt of the knife.

There was no struggle. The murderer was too surprised.

Laura wrenched the knife away from his grip even as the long blade was still sticking out of her hand.

He stumbled back.

He looked at the knife jutting out of her hand.

One second.

Two seconds.

Three.

He seemed to remember the gun on his hip. His right hand reached down. His fingers wrapped around the handle. The silver flashed on the muzzle. His left hand swung around to cup the weapon as he prepared to fire the last bullet into her mother's heart.

Silently, Laura swung her arm, backhanding the blade into the side of his neck.

Crunch, like a butcher cutting a side of beef.

The sound had an echo that bounced off the corners of the room.

The man gasped. His mouth fished open. His eyes widened.

The back of Laura's hand was still pinned to his neck, caught between the handle and the blade.

Andy saw her fingers move.

22

There was a clicking sound. The gun shaking as he tried to raise it.

Laura spoke, more growl than words.

He kept lifting the gun. Tried to aim.

Laura raked the blade out through the front of his throat.

Blood, sinew, cartilage.

No spray or mist like before. Everything gushed out of his open neck like a dam breaking open.

His black shirt turned blacker. The pearl buttons showed different shades of pink.

The gun dropped first.

Then his knees hit the floor. Then his chest. Then his head.

Andy watched his eyes as he fell.

He was dead before he hit the ground.

2

When Andy was in the ninth grade, she'd had a crush on a boy named Cletus Laraby, who went by Cleet, but in an ironic way. He had floppy brown hair and he knew how to play the guitar and he was the smartest guy in their chemistry class, so Andy tried to learn how to play the guitar and pretended to be interested in chemistry, too.

This was how she ended up entering the school's science fair: Cleet signed up, so Andy did, too.

She had never spoken a word to him in her life.

No one questioned the wisdom of giving a drama club kid who barely passed earth sciences access to ammonium nitrate and ignition switches, but in retrospect, Dr. Finney was probably so pleased Andy was interested in something other than mime arts that she had looked the other way.

Andy's father, too, was elated by the news. Gordon took Andy to the library where they checked out books on engineering and rocket design. He filled out a form for a loyalty card from the local hobby shop. Over the dinner table, he would read aloud from pamphlets from the American Association for Rocketry.

Whenever Andy was staying at her dad's house, Gordon worked in the garage with his sanding blocks, shaping the fins and nose cone shoulders, while Andy sat at his workbench and sketched out designs for the tube.

Andy knew that Cleet liked the Goo Goo Dolls because he had a sticker on his backpack, so she started out thinking the tube of the rocket would look like a steampunk telescope from the video for "Iris," then she thought about putting wings on it because "Iris" was from the movie *City of Angels*, then she decided that she would put Nicolas Cage's face on the side, in profile, because he was the angel in the movie, then she decided that she should paint Meg Ryan instead because this was for Cleet and he would probably think that Meg Ryan was a lot more interesting than Nicolas Cage.

A week before the fair, Andy had to turn in all of her notes and photographs to Dr. Finney to prove that she had actually done all of the work herself. She was laying out the dubious evidence on the teacher's desk when Cleet Laraby walked in. Andy had to clasp together her hands to keep them from trembling when Cleet stopped to look at the photos.

"Meg Ryan," Cleet said. "I dig it. Blow up the bitch, right?"

Andy felt a cold slice of air cut open her lips.

"My girlfriend loves that stupid movie. The one with the angels?" Cleet showed her the sticker on his backpack. "They wrote that shitty song for the soundtrack, man. That's why I keep this here, to remind me never to sell out my art like those faggots."

Andy didn't move. She couldn't speak.

Girlfriend. Stupid. Shitty. Man. Faggots.

Andy had left Dr. Finney's classroom without her notes or her books or even her purse. She'd walked through the cafeteria, then out the exit door that was always propped open so the lunch ladies could smoke cigarettes behind the Dumpster.

Gordon lived two miles away from the school. It was June. In Georgia. On the coast. By the time she reached his house, Andy was badly sunburned and soaked in her own sweat and tears. She took the Meg Ryan rocket and the two Nicolas Cage test rockets and threw them in the outdoor trash can. Then she soaked them with lighter fluid. Then she threw a match into the can. Then she woke up on her back in Gordon's driveway because a neighbor was squirting her down with the garden hose.

The *whoosh* of fire had singed off Andy's eyebrows, eyelashes, bangs and nose hairs. The sound of the explosion was so intense that Andy's ears had started to bleed. The neighbor started screaming in her face. His wife, a nurse, came over and was clearly trying to tell Andy something, but the only thing she could hear was a sharp tone, like when her chorus teacher blew a single note on her pitch pipe—

Eeeeeeeeeeee . . .

Andy heard The Sound, and nothing but The Sound, for four whole days.

Waking. Trying to sleep. Bathing. Walking to the kitchen. Sitting in front of the television. Reading notes her mother and father furiously scratched out on a dry erase board.

We don't know what's wrong.

Probably temporary.

Don't cry.

Eeeeeeeeeeee . . .

That had been almost twenty years ago. Andy hadn't thought much about the explosion until now, and that was only because The Sound was back. When it returned, or when she became aware of the return, she was standing in the diner by her mother, who was seated in a chair. There were three dead people on the floor. On the ground. The murderer, his black shirt even blacker. Shelly Barnard, her red shirt even redder. Betsy Barnard, the bottom part of her face hanging by strands of muscle and sinew.

Andy had looked up from the bodies. People were standing outside the restaurant. Mall shoppers with Abercrombie and Juicy bags and Starbucks coffees and Icees. Some of them had been crying. Some of them had been taking pictures.

Andy had felt pressure on her arm. Laura was struggling to turn the chair away from the gawkers. Every movement had a stuttering motion to Andy's eye, like she was watching a stop-action movie. Laura's hand shook as she tried to wrap a tablecloth around her bleeding leg. The white thing sticking out was not a bone but a shard of broken china. Laura was right-handed, but the knife jutting from her left hand made wrapping her leg impossible. She was talking to Andy, likely asking for help, but all Andy could hear was The Sound.

"Andy," Laura had said.

Eeeeeeeeeeee . . .

"Andrea."

Andy stared at her mother's mouth, wondering if she was hearing the word or reading the word on her lips—so familiar that her brain processed it as heard rather than seen.

"Andy," Laura repeated. "Help me."

That had come through, a muffled request like her mother was speaking through a long tube.

"Andy," Laura had grabbed both of Andy's hands in her own. Her mother was bent over in the chair, obviously in pain. Andy had knelt down. She'd started knotting the tablecloth.

Tie it tight—

That's what Andy would have said to a panicked caller on the dispatch line: *Don't worry about hurting her. Tie the cloth as tight as you can to stop the bleeding.*

It was different when your hands were the ones tying the cloth. Different when the pain you saw was registered on your own mother's face.

"Andy." Laura had waited for her to look up.

Andy's eyes had trouble focusing. She wanted to pay attention. She needed to pay attention.

Her mother had grabbed Andy by the chin, given her a hard shake to knock her out of her stupor.

She had said, "Don't talk to the police. Don't sign a statement. Tell them you can't remember anything."

What?

"Promise me," Laura had insisted. "Don't talk to the police."

Four hours later, Andy still hadn't talked to the police, but that was more because the police had not talked to her. Not at the diner, not in the ambulance and not now.

Andy was waiting outside the closed doors to the surgical

suite while the doctors operated on Laura. She was slumped in a hard plastic chair. She had refused to lie down, refused to take the nurse up on the offer of a bed, because nothing was wrong with her. Laura needed the help. And Shelly. And Shelly's mother, whose name Andy could not now remember.

Who was Mrs. Barnard, really, if not a mother to her child?

Andy sat back in the chair. She had to turn a certain way to keep the bruise on her head from throbbing. The plate glass window overlooking the boardwalk. Andy remembered her mother tackling her to the ground. The pounding at the back of her head as her skull cracked against the window. The spider-webbing glass. The way Laura quickly scrambled to stand. The way she had looked and sounded so calm.

The way she had held up her fingers—four on the left hand, one on the right—as she explained to the shooter that he only had one bullet left out of the six he had started with.

Andy rubbed her face with her hands. She did not look at the clock, because looking up at the clock every time she wanted to would make the hours stretch out interminably. She ran her tongue along her fillings. The metal ones had been drilled out and replaced with composite, but she could still remember how The Sound had made them almost vibrate inside her molars. Into her jaw. Up into her skull. A vise-like noise that made her brain feel as if it was going to implode.

Eeeeeeeeeeee . . .

Andy squeezed her eyes shut. Immediately, the images started scrolling like one of Gordon's vacation slide shows.

Laura holding up her hand.

The long blade slicing into her palm.

Wrenching the knife away.

Backhanding the blade into the man's neck.

Blood.

So much blood.

Jonah Helsinger. That was the murderer's name. Andy knew it—she wasn't sure how. Was it on the dispatch radio when she rode in the ambulance with her mother? Was it on the news

28

blaring from the TV when Andy was led into the triage waiting room? Was it on the nurses' lips as they led her up to the surgical wing?

"*Jonah Helsinger*," someone had whispered, the way you'd whisper that someone had cancer. "*The killer's name is Jonah Helsinger.*"

"Ma'am?" A Savannah police officer was standing in front of Andy.

"I don't—" Andy tried to recall what her mother had told her to say. "I can't remember."

"Ma'am," the officer repeated, which was weird because she was older than Andy. "I'm sorry to bother you, but there's a man. He says he's your father, but—"

Andy looked up the hall.

Gordon was standing by the elevators.

She was up and running before she could think about it. Gordon met her halfway, grabbing her in a bear hug, holding her so close that she could feel his heart pounding in his chest. She pressed her face into his starched white shirt. He had been at work, dressed in his usual three-piece suit. His reading glasses were still on top of his head. His Montblanc pen was tucked into his shirt pocket. The metal was cold against the tip of her ear.

Andy had been losing her shit in little pieces since the shooting began, but in her father's arms, finally safe, she completely lost it. She started to cry so hard that she couldn't support her own weight. Gordon half lifted, half dragged her to a set of chairs against the wall. He held onto her so tightly that she had to take shallow breaths to breathe.

"I'm here," he told her, again and again. "I'm here, baby. I'm here."

"Daddy," she said, the word coming out around a sob.

"It's okay." Gordon stroked back her hair. "You're safe now. Everybody's safe."

Andy kept crying. She cried so long that she began to feel self-conscious, like it was too much. Laura was alive. Bad things

29

had happened, but Laura was going to be okay. Andy was going to be okay. She *had* to be okay.

"It's okay," Gordon murmured. "Just let it all out."

Andy sniffed back her tears. She tried to regain her composure. And tried. Every time she thought she might be all right, she remembered another detail—the sound of the first gunshot, like a jar popping open, the thwack as her mother lodged the knife into flesh and bone—and the tears started to fall again.

"It's all right," Gordon said, patiently stroking her head. "Everybody's okay, sweetheart."

Andy wiped her nose. She took a shaky breath. Gordon leaned up in the chair, still holding onto her, and pulled out his handkerchief.

Andy blotted away her tears, blew her nose. "I'm sorry."

"You have nothing to apologize for." Gordon pushed her hair back out of her eyes. "Were you hurt?"

She shook her head. Blew her nose again until her ears popped. The Sound was gone.

She closed her eyes, relief taking hold.

"All right?" Gordon asked. His hand was warm against her back. She felt anchored again. "You okay?"

Andy opened her eyes. Her nerves still felt raw, but she had to tell her father what had happened. "Mom—she had a knife, and this guy, she mur—"

"Shhh," he hushed, pressing his fingers to her lips. "Mom's okay. We're all okay."

"But—"

He put his finger back to her lips to keep her quiet. "I talked to the doctor. Mom's in recovery. Her hand is going to be fine. Her leg is fine. It's all fine." He raised an eyebrow, tilted his head slightly to the right where the cop was standing. The woman was on the phone, but she was clearly listening.

Gordon asked Andy, "You sure you're okay? Did they check you out?"

She nodded.

"You're just tired, baby. You were up all night working. You saw something horrible happen. Your life was in danger. Your mother's life was in danger. It's understandable you're in shock. You need some rest, give your memories some time to piece themselves together." His tone was measured. Andy realized that Gordon was coaching her. "All right?"

She nodded because he was nodding. Why was he telling her what to say? Had he talked to Laura? Was her mother in trouble?

She had killed a man. Of course she was in trouble.

The police officer said, "Ma'am, do you mind giving me some basic information? Full name, address, birthdate, that kind of thing."

"I'll provide that, Officer." Gordon waited for the woman to pull out her pen and notebook before he complied.

Andy tucked herself back underneath his protective arm. She swallowed so hard that her throat clicked.

And then she made herself look at the situation as a human being out in the world rather than a terrified spectator.

This wasn't one drug dealer shooting another drug dealer in the streets, or an abusive spouse finally crossing the last line. A white kid had shot two white women, then was killed by another white woman, in one of the most affluent malls in the state.

News trucks would probably come down from Atlanta and Charleston. Lawyers would intervene for the families, the victims, the mall management, the city, the county, maybe even the feds. An array of police forces would descend: Belle Isle, Savannah, Chatham County, the Georgia Bureau of Investigation. Witness statements. Forensics. Photographs. Autopsies. Evidence collection.

Part of Andy's job in radio dispatch was to assign case numbers for crimes on a far smaller scale, and she often tracked their progress over the months, sometimes years, it took for a case to go to trial. She of all people should have known that her mother's actions would be scrutinized at every single level of the criminal justice system.

As if on cue, there was a loud ding from the elevator. The cop's leather gunbelt made a squeaking noise as she adjusted it on her hips. The doors slid open. A man and a woman walked into the hallway. Both in wrinkled suits. Both with tired looks on their faces. The guy was bald and bloated with patches of peeling sunburn on his nose. The woman was around Andy's height, at least ten years older, with olive skin and dark hair.

Andy started to stand, but Gordon kept her in the chair.

"Ms. Oliver." The woman took out her badge and showed it to Andy. "I'm Detective Sergeant Lisa Palazzolo. This is Detective Brant Wilkes. We're with the Savannah Police Department. We're assisting Belle Isle with the investigation." She tucked her badge back into her jacket pocket. "We need to talk to you about what happened this morning."

Andy's mouth opened, but again, she couldn't remember what her mother had told her to say, or what Gordon had coached her to say, so she reverted to her default response which was to close her mouth and stare blankly at the person who had asked the question.

Gordon said, "This isn't a good time, Detectives. My daughter is in shock. She's not yet ready to give her statement."

Wilkes huffed a disapproving grunt. "You're her father?"

Andy always forgot Gordon was black and she was white until someone else pointed it out to her.

"Yes, Detective. I'm her father." Gordon's tone was patient. He was used to this. Over the years, he'd smoothed the nerves of anxious teachers, concerned store clerks, and aggressively racist store security. "I'm Gordon Oliver, Laura's ex-husband. Andrea's adoptive father."

Wilkes twisted his mouth to the side as he silently scrutinized the story.

Palazzolo said, "We're real sorry about what happened, Mr. Oliver, but we need to ask Andrea some questions."

Gordon repeated, "As I said, she isn't prepared at the moment to discuss the incident." He crossed his legs, casual, as if this was all a formality. "Andrea is a dispatch operator, which I'm sure you can tell from her uniform. She worked a night shift. She's bone-tired. She witnessed a terrible tragedy. She's not in any shape to give a statement."

"It *was* a terrible tragedy," Palazzolo agreed. "Three people are dead."

"And my daughter could've been the fourth." Gordon kept a protective arm around Andy's shoulders. "We'd be happy to make an appointment to come to the station tomorrow."

"This is an active murder investigation."

"The suspect is dead," Gordon reminded her. "There's no clock on this, Detective. One more day won't make a difference."

Wilkes grunted again. "How old are you?"

Andy realized he was talking to her.

Gordon said, "She's thirty-one. Her birthday is today."

Andy suddenly remembered Gordon's voicemail this morning, an off-key version of "Happy Birthday" in his deep baritone.

Wilkes said, "She's a little old to let her *daddy* talk for her."

Palazzolo rolled her eyes, but said, "Ms. Oliver, we'd really like it if you helped us get the chain of events down on paper. You're the only witness who hasn't given a statement."

Andy knew that wasn't true, because Laura was still coming round from the anesthesia.

Gordon said, "Detectives, if—"

"You her daddy or her fucking lawyer?" Wilkes demanded. "Because we can remove you from—"

Gordon stood up. He was at least a foot taller than Wilkes. "I happen to be a lawyer, Mr. Wilkes, and I can either school you on my daughter's constitutional right to refuse this interrogation or I can file a formal complaint with your superiors."

Andy could see the man's eyes shifting back and forth, his mouth itching to put Gordon in his place.

Palazzolo said, "Brant, take a walk."

Wilkes didn't move.

"Brant, come on. Meet me in the cafeteria. Get something to eat."

Wilkes glared at Gordon like an unneutered pitbull before stomping away.

Palazzolo said, "Mr. Oliver, I understand your daughter's been through a lot today, but even though Savannah's not what you'd

33

call a sleepy town, we're unaccustomed to triple homicides. We really need to get your daughter's statement down. We need to know what happened."

Gordon corrected, "Double homicide."

"Right." There was a moment of hesitation before Palazzolo spoke again. "Can we do this sitting down?" She offered Andy a conciliatory smile. "I work the night shift, too. I've been up eighteen hours straight with no end in sight." She was dragging over a chair before Gordon could stop her. "Look, I'll tell you what I know, and then if Andrea feels like it, she can tell me what she knows. Or not. Either way, you get to see our side of this thing." She indicated the other chairs. "That's a good deal, Mr. Oliver. I hope you'll consider taking it."

Andy looked up at her father. Triple homicide? Two people wounded? Why did it feel like the detective was not counting Laura among the injured?

"Mr. Oliver?" Palazzolo tapped the back of her chair, but didn't sit. "What about it?"

Gordon looked down at Andy.

She had seen that look a thousand times before: *Remember what I told you.*

Andy nodded. She was, if anything, extraordinarily good at keeping her mouth shut.

"Great." Palazzolo sat down with a sharp groan.

Gordon nudged Andy down so that he would be the one who was directly across from Palazzolo.

"Okay." Palazzolo took out her notebook, but not her pen. She flipped through the pages. "The shooter's name is Jonah Lee Helsinger. Eighteen years old. High school senior. Early acceptance into Florida State University. The young girl was Shelly Anne Barnard. She was at the diner with her mother, Elizabeth Leona Bernard; Betsy. Jonah Lee Helsinger is—was—the ex-boyfriend of Shelly. Her father says Shelly broke up with Helsinger two weeks ago. Wanted to do it before going to college next month. Helsinger didn't take it well."

Gordon cleared his throat. "That's quite an understatement."

She nodded, ignoring the sarcasm. "Unfortunately, law enforcement has had a lot of these cases to study over the years. We know that spree killings aren't usually spur of the moment. They're well-planned, well-executed operations that tend to get worked over in the back of the killer's mind until something— an event like a break-up or an impending life change like going off to college—jumpstarts the plan. The first victim is generally a close female, which is why we were relieved to find Helsinger's mother was out of town this morning. Business in Charleston. But the way Helsinger was dressed—the black hat, the vest and gunbelt he bought on Amazon six months ago—all that tells us that he put a lot of thought into how this was going to go down. The spark came when Shelly broke up with him, but the idea of it, the planning, was in his head for months."

Spree killings.

The two words bounced around inside Andy's head.

Gordon asked, "His victims were all women?"

"There was a man sitting in the restaurant. He was struck in the eye by shrapnel. Not sure if he'll lose it or not. The eye." She went back to Jonah Helsinger. "What we also know about spree killers is, they tend to plant explosive devices in their homes for maximum casualties. That's why we got the state bomb squad to clear Helsinger's bedroom before we went in. He had a pipe bomb wired to the doorknob. Faulty set-up. Probably got it off the internet. Nothing went boom, thank God."

Andy opened her mouth so she could breathe. She had come face-to-face with this guy. He had almost killed Laura. Almost killed Andy. Murdered people. Tried to blow them up.

He had probably attended Belle Isle High School, the same as Andy.

"Helsinger," Gordon said. "That name sounds familiar."

"Yeah, the family's pretty well known up in Bibb County. Anyway—"

"Well known," Gordon repeated, but the two words were weighted in a way that Andy could not decipher.

Palazzolo obviously got their meaning. She held Gordon's gaze for a moment before she continued, "Anyway—Jonah Helsinger left some school notebooks on his bed. Most of them were filled with drawings. Disturbing images, weird stuff. He had four more handguns, an AR-15 and a shotgun, so he chose to take the six-shooter and the knife for a reason. We think we know the reason. There was a file on his laptop called 'Death Plan' that contained two documents and a PDF."

Andy felt a shudder work its way through her body. While she was getting ready for work last night, Jonah Helsinger was probably lying in bed, psyching himself up for his killing spree.

Palazzolo continued, "The PDF was a schematic of the diner, sort of like what you'd see an architect draw. One of the docs was a timeline, like a bullet point: wake up at this time, shower at this time, clean gun here, fill up car with gas there. The other doc was sort of like a diary entry where Helsinger wrote about how and why this was going to go down." She referred to her notebook again. "His first targets were going to be Shelly and her mother. Apparently, they had a standing lunch date every Monday at the Rise-n-Dine. Shelly wrote about it on Facebook, Snapchatted her food or whatever. Mr. Barnard told us the lunches are something his wife and daughter decided to do together over the summer before college."

"*Were* something they decided to do," Gordon mumbled, because everything in the two women's lives was past tense now.

"Were. Yeah," Palazzolo said. "Helsinger planned to kill both of them. He blamed the mother for the break-up. He said in his diary that it was Betsy's fault, that she was always pushing Shelly, blah blah blah. Crazy talk. It doesn't matter, because we all know it's Jonah Helsinger's fault, right?"

"Right," Gordon said, his voice firm.

Palazzolo held his gaze in that meaningful way again before she referred back to her notes. "This was his plan: after he killed Betsy and Shelly, Helsinger was going to take hostage whoever was left in the diner. He had a time noted—1:16, not the actual time but a notation of timing." She looked up at Andy, then

Gordon. "See, we think that he did a dry run. Last week, at approximately the same time as the shooting today, somebody threw a rock through the plate glass window that faces the boardwalk. We're waiting for the security feed. The incident was filed with burglary division. It took the first mall cop about one minute, sixteen seconds, to get to the diner."

The mall cops weren't the usual rent-a-cops, but off-duty police officers hired to protect the high-end stores. Andy had seen the guns on their hips and never given it a second thought.

Palazzolo told them, "In Helsinger's predicted timeline of the shooting, he allowed that he would have to kill at least one other bystander to let the cops know that he was serious. Then he was going to let the cops kill him. Helsinger must have thought his plan was fast-forwarded when he saw your uniform and assumed that you were law enforcement." Palazzolo was talking directly to Andy now. "We gather from the other witnesses that he wanted you to shoot him. Suicide by cop."

Except Andy was not a cop.

Get up! Do your job!

That's what Helsinger had screamed at Andy.

Then Andy's mother had said, "*Shoot me.*"

"He's a really bad guy. Was a bad guy. This Helsinger kid." Palazzolo was still focused on Andy. "We've got it all in his notes. He planned this out meticulously. He knew he was going to murder people. He hoped that he would murder even more people when somebody opened his bedroom door. He packed screws and nails into that pipe bomb. If the wiring hadn't been switched on the doorknob end, the whole house would be gone, along with whoever happened to be inside. We would've found nails two blocks away buried in God knows who or what."

Andy wanted to nod but she felt immobilized. Screws and nails flying through the air. What did it take to build such a device, to pack in all those projectiles in hopes that they would maim or kill people?

"You're lucky," Palazzolo told Andy. "If your mom hadn't

37

been there, he would've killed you. He was just a really bad guy."

Andy felt the woman looking at her, but she kept her eyes directed toward the floor.

Bad guy.

Palazzolo kept repeating the phrase, like it was okay that Helsinger was dead. Like he had gotten what he deserved. Like whatever Laura had done was completely justified because Jonah Lee Helsinger was a *bad guy*.

Andy worked at a police station. Most of the people who got murdered would fall into the bad guy category, yet she had never heard any of the detectives harp on the fact that the victim was a *bad guy*.

"Mr. Oliver," Palazzolo had turned to Gordon. "Has your wife had any military training?"

Gordon did not answer.

Palazzolo said, "Her background is pretty bland." Again, she flipped through the pages in her notebook. "Born in Providence, Rhode Island. Attended the University of Rhode Island. Master's and PhD from UGA. She's lived in Belle Isle for twenty-eight years. House is paid off, which, congratulations. She could sell it for a bag of money—but, I get it, where would she go? One marriage, one divorce. No large outstanding debts. Pays her bills on time. Never left the country. Got a parking ticket three years ago that she paid online. She must've been one of the first people to buy here." Palazzolo turned back toward Andy. "You were raised here, right?"

Andy stared at the woman. She had a mole near her ear, just under her jawline.

"You went to school on the Isle, then SCAD for college?"

Andy had spent the first two years of her life in Athens while Laura was finishing her doctorate, but the only thing she remembered about UGA was being scared of the neighbor's parakeet.

"Ms. Oliver." Palazzolo's voice sounded strained. She was apparently used to having her questions answered. "Did your mother ever take any self-defense classes?"

Andy studied the mole. There were some short hairs sticking out of it.

"Yoga? Pilates? Tai chi?" Palazzolo waited. And waited. Then she closed her notebook. She put it back into her pocket. She reached into her other pocket. She pulled out her phone. She tapped at the screen. "I'm showing you this because it's already on the news." She swiped at the screen. "One of the patrons in the diner decided that it was more important to record what was happening on his cell phone than to call 911 or run for his life."

She turned the phone around. The image was paused. Jonah Helsinger stood at the entrance to the restaurant. The lower half of his body was obscured by a trash can. The mall was empty behind him. From the angle, Andy knew the waitress standing in the back had not taken the video. She wondered if it was the man with the newspaper. The phone had been tilted just over the salt and pepper shakers, like he was trying to hide the fact that he was recording the weird kid who was dressed like the villain from a John Wayne movie.

Objectively, the hat was ridiculous; too large for Helsinger's head, stiff on the top and curled up almost comically.

Andy might have filmed him, too.

Palazzolo said, "This is pretty graphic. They're blurring the images on the news. Are you okay to see this?" She was talking to Gordon because, obviously, Andy had already seen it.

Gordon smoothed down his mustache with his finger and thumb as he considered the question. Andy knew he could handle it. He was asking himself if he really wanted to see it.

He finally decided. "Yes."

Palazzolo snaked her finger around the edge of the phone and tapped the screen.

At first, Andy wondered if the touch had registered because Jonah Helsinger was not moving. For several seconds, he just stood there behind the trash can, staring blankly into the restaurant, his ten-gallon hat high on his shiny-looking forehead.

Two older women, mall walkers, strutted behind him. One

of them clocked the western attire, elbowed the other, and they both laughed.

Muzak played in the background. Madonna's 'Dress You Up'.

Someone coughed. The tinny sound vibrated into Andy's ears, and she wondered if she had registered any of these noises when they happened, when she was in the restaurant telling the waitress she was a theater major, when she was staring out the window at the waves cresting in the distance.

On the screen, Helsinger's head moved to the right, then the left, as if he was scanning the restaurant. Andy knew there was not much to see. The place was half-empty, a handful of patrons enjoying a last cup of coffee or glass of tea before they did errands or played golf or, in Andy's case, went to sleep.

Helsinger stepped away from the garbage can.

A man's voice said, "Jesus."

Andy remembered that word, the lowness and meanness to it, the hint of surprise.

The gun went up. A puff of smoke from the muzzle. A loud *pop*.

Shelly was shot in the back of the head. She sank to the floor like a paper doll.

Betsy Barnard started screaming.

The second bullet missed Betsy, but a loud cry said that it had hit someone else.

The third bullet came sharp on the heels of the second.

A cup on the table exploded into a million pieces. Shards flew through the air.

Laura was turning away from the shooter when one of the pieces lodged into her leg. The wound did not register in her mother's expression. She started to run, but not away. She was closer to the mall entrance than to the back of the restaurant. She could've ducked under a table. She could've escaped.

Instead, she ran toward Andy.

Andy saw herself standing with her back now turned toward the window. Video-Andy dropped her coffee mug. The ceramic splintered. In the foreground, Betsy Barnard was being murdered. Bullet four was fired into her mouth, the fifth into her head. She fell on top of her daughter.

Then Laura tackled Andy to the ground.

There was a blink of stillness before Laura jumped up.

She patted her hands down the same way she used to tuck Andy into bed at night. The man in black, Jonah Lee Helsinger, had a gun pointed at Laura's chest. In the distance, Andy could see herself. She was curled into a ball. The glass behind her was spiderwebbing. Chunks were falling down.

Sitting in the chair beside Gordon, Andy reached up and touched her hair. She pulled out a piece of glass from the tangles.

When she looked back down at Detective Palazzolo's phone, the angle of the video had changed. The image was shaky, taken from behind the shooter. Whoever had made the recording was lying on the ground, just beyond an overturned table. The position afforded Andy a completely different perspective. Instead of facing the shooter, she was behind him now. Instead of watching her mother's back, she could see Laura's face. Her hands holding up six digits to indicate the total number of bullets. Her thumb wagging to show the one live round left in the chamber.

Shoot me.

That's what Laura had told the kid who had already murdered two people—*shoot me*. She had said it repeatedly. Andy's brain echoed the words each time Laura said them on the video.

Shoot me, I want you to shoot me, shoot me, when you shoot me, my daughter will run—

When the killing spree had first started, every living person in the restaurant had screamed or ducked or run away or all three.

Laura had started counting the number of bullets.

"What?" Gordon mumbled. "What's he doing?"

Snap.

41

On the screen, Helsinger was unsnapping the sheath hanging from his gunbelt.

"That's a knife," Gordon said. "I thought he used a gun."

The gun was holstered. The knife was gripped in Helsinger's fist, blade angled down for maximum carnage.

Andy wanted to close her eyes, but just as badly, she wanted to see it again, to watch her mother's face, because right now, at this moment on the video when Helsinger was holding the menacing-looking hunting knife, Laura's expression was almost placid, like a switch inside of her had been turned off.

The knife arced up.

Gordon sucked in air between his teeth.

The knife arced down.

Laura lifted her left hand. The blade sliced straight through the center of her palm. Her fingers wrapped around the handle. She wrenched it from his grasp, then, the knife still embedded in her hand, backhanded the blade into the side of his neck.

Thunk.

Helsinger's eyes went wide.

Laura's left hand was pinned to the left side of his neck like a message tacked to a bulletin board.

There was a slight pause, no more than a few milliseconds.

Laura's mouth moved. One or two words, her lips barely parting.

Then she crossed her right arm underneath her trapped left.

She braced the heel of her right hand near Helsinger's right shoulder.

Her right hand pushed his shoulder.

Her left hand jerked the knife blade straight out of the front of his throat.

Blood.

Everywhere.

Gordon's mouth gaped open.

Andy's tongue turned into cotton.

Right hand pushing, left hand pulling.

From the video, it looked like Laura had willfully pulled the knife out of Helsinger's throat.

42

Not just killing him.

Murdering him.

"She just—" Gordon saw it, too. "She—"

His hand went to his mouth.

On the video, Helsinger's knees hit the floor. His chest. His face.

Andy saw herself in the distance. The whites of her eyes were almost perfect circles.

In the foreground, Laura's expression remained placid. She looked down at the knife that pierced her hand straight through, turning it to see—first the palm, then the back—as if she had found a splinter.

That's where Palazzolo chose to pause the video.

She waited a beat, then asked, "Do you want to see it again?"

Gordon swallowed so hard that Andy saw his Adam's apple bob.

"Mr. Oliver?"

He shook his head, looked down the hallway.

Palazzolo clicked off the screen. She returned the phone to her pocket. Without Andy noticing, she had angled her chair away from Gordon. Palazzolo leaned forward, hands resting on her legs. There was only two inches of space between her knees and Andy's. She said, "It's pretty horrific. It must be hard seeing it again."

Gordon shook his head. He thought the detective was still talking to him.

Palazzolo said, "Take all the time you need, Ms. Oliver. I know this is hard. Right?" She was talking to Andy again, leaning in closer; so close that it was making Andy feel uncomfortable.

One hand pushing, one hand pulling.

Pushing his shoulder. Pulling the knife through his neck.

The calm expression on Laura's face.

I'll tell you what I know, and then if Andrea feels like it, she can tell me what she knows.

The detective had not told them anything, or shown them

43

anything, that probably was not already on the news. And now she was crowding Andy without seeming to crowd her, taking up a section of her personal space. Andy knew this was an interview technique because she had read some of the training textbooks during slow times at work.

Horton's Annotations on the Police Interview: Witness Statements, Hostile Witness Interrogations and Confessions.

You were supposed to make the subject feel uncomfortable without them knowing why they were feeling uncomfortable.

And the reason Palazzolo was trying to make Andy uncomfortable was because she was not taking a statement. She was interrogating her.

Palazzolo said, "You're lucky your mom was there to save you. Some people would call her a hero."

Some people.

Palazzolo asked, "What did your mother say to Jonah before he died?"

Andy watched the space between them narrow. Two inches turned into one.

"Ms. Oliver?"

Laura had seemed too calm. That was the problem. She had been too calm and methodical the whole time, especially when she'd raised her right hand and placed it near Jonah's right shoulder.

One hand pushing, one hand pulling.

Not scared for her life.

Deliberate.

"Ms. Oliver?" Palazzolo repeated. "What did your mother say?"

The detective's unspoken question filled that tiny inch of uncomfortable space between them: If Laura really was that calm, if she really was that methodical, why hadn't she used the same hand to take away Helsinger's gun?

"Andrea?" Palazzolo rested her elbows on her knees. Andy could smell coffee on the detective's breath. "I know this is a difficult time for you, but we can clear this up really fast if you just tell me what your mom said before Helsinger died." She waited a beat. "The phone didn't pick it up. I guess we could send the video to the state lab, but it would be easier if you just told—"

"The father," Gordon said. "We should pray for the father."

Palazzolo didn't look at him, but Andy did. Gordon was not the praying kind.

"I can't imagine . . ." he paused. "I can't imagine what it feels like, to lose your family like that." He had snapped his fingers together on the last word, but close to his face, as if to wake himself from the trance that the video had put him in. "I'm so glad your mother was there to protect you, Andrea. And herself."

Andy nodded. For once, she was a few steps ahead of her father.

"Look, guys," Palazzolo finally sat back in her chair. "I know you're thinking I'm not on your side, but there are no sides here. Jonah Helsinger was a bad guy. He had a plan. He wanted to murder people, and that's exactly what he did. And you're right, Mr. Oliver. Your wife and daughter could've been his third and fourth victims. But I'm a cop, and it's my job to ask questions about what really happened in that diner this afternoon. All I'm after is the truth."

"Detective Palazzolo." Gordon finally sounded like himself again. "We've both been on this earth long enough to know that the truth is open to interpretation."

"That's true, Mr. Oliver. That's very true." She looked at Andy. "You know, I've just realized that you haven't said one word this whole time." Her hand went to Andy's knee with almost sisterly affection. "It's all right, honey. Don't be afraid. You can talk to me."

Andy stared at the mole on the woman's jawline because it was too hard to look her in the eye. She wasn't afraid. She was confused.

Was Jonah Helsinger still a threat when Laura had killed him?

45

Because you could legally kill someone who was threatening you, but if they weren't threatening you and you killed them, that meant you weren't defending yourself anymore.

You were just killing them.

Andy tried to think back to this morning, to fill in the blanks with the video. Could Laura have left the knife in Jonah Helsinger's throat, taken away his gun, and then . . . *what?*

The police would've come. Dispatch would've radioed in an ambulance, not a coroner, because the fact was that, even with a knife sticking Herman Munster-like from the side of his neck, Jonah Helsinger had not been dead. No blood had coughed from his mouth or sneezed from his nose. He had still been capable of moving his arms and legs, which meant his carotid, his jugular, were likely intact. Which meant he had the chance to remain alive until Laura had killed him.

So, what would've happened next?

The EMTs could've stabilized him for the ride to the hospital and the surgeons could've worked to safely remove the knife, but none of that had happened because Laura had braced her right hand near Jonah Helsinger's right shoulder and ended his life.

"Ms. Oliver," Palazzolo said. "I find the lack of communication on your part very troubling. If nothing's wrong, then why aren't you talking to me?"

Andy made herself look the detective in the eye. She had to speak. This was her time to say that Laura had no other choice. *My mother was acting in self-defense. You weren't there but I was and I will swear on a stack of Bibles in front of any jury that my mother had no other choice but to kill Jonah Lee Helsinger.*

"Laura?" Gordon said.

Andy turned, finally breaking out of Palazzolo's vortex. She had expected to see her mother lying in yet another hospital bed, but Laura was sitting up in a wheelchair.

"I'm all right," Laura said, but her face was contorted in pain. She was dressed in a white gown. Her arm was strapped to her waist in a Velcro sling. Her fingers were held stiff by something that looked like a biker's glove with the tips cut off. "I need to change, then I'm ready to go home."

Gordon opened his mouth to protest, but Laura cut him off.

"Please," she said. "I've already told the doctor I'm going to sign myself out. She's getting together the paperwork. Can you pull up the car?" She looked annoyed, especially when Gordon didn't move. "Gordon, can you please pull up your car?"

"Dr. Oliver," Palazzolo said. "Your surgeon told me you would need to stay overnight, maybe longer."

Laura didn't ask the woman who she was or why she was talking to the surgeon. "Gordon, I want to go home."

"Ma'am," Palazzolo tried again. "I'm Detective Lisa Palazzolo with the Savannah—"

"I don't want to talk to you." She looked up at Gordon. "I want to go home."

"Ma'am—"

"Are you hard of hearing?" Laura asked. "This man is a lawyer. He can advise you of my legal rights if you're unfamiliar with them."

Palazzolo frowned. "Yeah, we've already do-si-doed that two-step, but I want to get this straight with you, on the record: you're refusing to be interviewed?"

"For now," Gordon intervened, because nothing made him stand more firmly by Laura's side than to have a stranger challenge her. "My office will call you to schedule an appointment."

"I could detain her as a material witness."

"You could," Gordon agreed. "But then she could stay here under doctor's orders and you'd be denied access to her anyway."

Laura tried, "I was under anesthesia. I'm not competent to—"

"You're making this worse. You realize that, right?" Palazzolo had let the helpful, we're-on-the-same-team façade drop. She was clearly pissed off. "The only people who are quiet are the ones who have something to hide."

Gordon said, "My office will be in touch when she's ready to talk."

The hinge of Palazzolo's jaw stuck out like a bolt on the side of her face as she gritted her teeth. She gave a curt nod, then walked off, her jacket swinging as she made her way toward the elevator.

Gordon told Laura, "You should stay in the hospital. She won't bother you. I'll get a restraining order if I—"

"Home," Laura said. "Either get your car or I'll call a taxi."

Gordon looked to the orderly behind the wheelchair for help.

The man shrugged. "She's right, bro. Once she signs that paperwork, we can't keep her here if she doesn't wanna stay."

Gordon knelt down in front of the chair. "Honey, I don't think—"

"Andrea." Laura squeezed Andy's hand so hard that the bones moved. "I don't want to be here. I can't be in a hospital again. Not overnight. Do you understand?"

Andy nodded, because that much, at least, she understood. Laura had spent almost a year in and out of the hospital because of complications from her surgery, two bouts of pneumonia and a case of C. *difficile* that was persistent enough to start shutting down her kidneys.

Andy said, "Dad, she wants to go home."

Gordon muttered something under his breath. He stood up. He tucked his hand into his pocket. His keys jangled. "You're sure?" He shook his head, because Laura wasn't given to making statements she wasn't sure about. "Get changed. Sign your paperwork. I'll be out front."

Andy watched her father leave. She felt a familiar guilt ebb into her chest because she had chosen her mother's demands over her father's wishes.

"Thank you." Laura loosened her grip on Andy's hand. She asked the orderly, "Could you find a T-shirt or something for me to change into?"

He bowed out with a nod.

"Andrea." Laura kept her voice low. "Did you say anything to that detective?"

Andy shook her head.

"You were talking to her when I was being wheeled up the hall."

"I wasn't—" Andy wondered at her mother's sharp tone. "She asked questions. I didn't tell her anything." Andy added, "I didn't speak. At all."

"Okay." Laura tried to shift in the chair but, judging by the wince on her face, the pain was too much. "What we were discussing before, in the diner. I need you to move out. Tonight. You have to go."

What?

"I know I said I wasn't going to give you a deadline, but I am, and it's now." Laura tried to shift in the chair again. "You're an adult, Andrea. You need to start acting like one. I want you to find an apartment and move out. Today."

Andy felt her stomach go into free fall.

"Your father agrees with me," Laura said, as if that carried more weight. "I want you out of the house. The garage. Just get out, okay? You can't sleep there tonight."

"Mom—"

Laura hissed in air between her teeth as she tried again to find a comfortable position. "Andrea, please don't argue with me. I need to be alone tonight. And tomorrow, and—you just need to go. I've looked after you for thirty-one years. I've earned the right to be alone."

"But—" Andy didn't know what the *but* was.

But people are dead.

But you could've died.

But you killed somebody when you didn't have to.

Didn't you?

Laura said, "My mind is made up. Go downstairs and make sure your father knows the right entrance to pull up to."

Gordon had picked them up at the hospital before. "Mom—"

"Andrea! Can't you just for once do something I tell you to do?"

Andy wanted to cover her ears. She had never in her life felt this much coldness from her mother. There was a giant, frozen gulf between them.

Laura's teeth were clenched. "Go."

Andy turned on her heel and walked away from her mother. Tears streamed down her face. She had heard that same edge to her mother's voice twice today, and each time, her body had responded before her mind could shut her down.

Gordon was nowhere in sight, but Detective Palazzolo was waiting for the elevator. The woman opened her mouth to speak. Andy kept walking. She took the stairs. Her feet stumbled over the treads. She was numb. Her head was spinning. Tears rolled like rain.

Move out? Tonight?

As in now? As in forever?

Andy bit her lip so that she would stop crying. She had to keep it together at least until she saw her dad. Gordon would fix this. He would make it better. He would have a plan. He would be able to explain what the hell had happened to her kind, caring mother.

Andy picked up the pace, practically flinging herself down the stairs. The anvil on her chest lifted the tiniest bit. There had to be a reason Laura was acting like this. Stress. Anesthesia. Grief. Fear. Pain. Any one of these things could bring out the worst in a person. All of them wrapped together could make them go crazy.

That was it.

Laura just needed time.

Andy felt her breathing start to calm. She rounded the stairs at the next landing. Her sweaty hand slipped on the railing. One foot hit sideways on the tread, the other foot slipped out from under her and she found herself flat on her ass.

Fuck.

Andy put her head in her hands. Something wet slid down the back of her fingers that was too thick to be sweat.

Fuck!

Her knuckle was bleeding. She put it in her mouth. She could feel her hands trembling. Her brain was spinning inside her head. Something weird was happening with her heartbeat.

50

Above her, a door opened, then closed, then there were scuffling footsteps on the stairs.

Andy tested her ankle, which, remarkably, was fine. Her knee felt wonky but nothing was sprained or broken. She stood up, ready to head down to the ground floor, but a wave of nausea spun up her throat.

Above her, the footsteps were getting closer.

It was bad enough to vomit in a public place. The only thing worse was having a witness. Andy had to find a bathroom. At the next landing, she pushed open the door and sprinted down another hallway until she found the toilets.

She had to run to make it to the stall in time. She opened her mouth and waited to throw up but now that she was here, squatting in front of the toilet bowl, the only thing that came up was bile.

Andy horked out as much as she could before flushing the toilet. She sat down on the closed lid. She used the back of her hand to wipe her mouth. Sweat dripped down her neck. She was breathing like she'd run a marathon.

"Andrea?"

Fuck.

Her legs retracted like a roller shade, heels hooked onto the edge of the toilet bowl, as if drawing herself into a ball would make her invisible.

"Andrea?" Palazzolo's chunky police-issue shoes thumped across the tiles. She stopped directly in front of Andy's stall.

Andy stared at the door. A faucet was dripping. She counted off six drops before—

"Andrea, I know you're in there."

Andy rolled her eyes at the stupidity of the situation.

"I gather you don't like to talk," Palazzolo said. "So maybe you could just listen?"

Andy waited.

"Your mom might be in a lot of trouble." Palazzolo waited another beat. "Or not."

Andy's heart leapt at the possibility of the *not*.

"What she did—I get that. She was protecting her daughter. I've got a kid. I would do anything for the little guy. He's my baby."

Andy bit her bottom lip.

"I can help you with this. Help you both get out of this."

Andy waited again.

"I'm going to leave my card here on the counter."

Andy kept waiting.

"You call me, anytime, day or night, and together, you and I can figure out what you need to say to make this problem go away." She paused. "I'm offering to help your mom, Andrea. That's all I want to do—help."

Andy rolled her eyes again. She had learned a long time ago that one of the prices of prolonged silence was people assumed that you were simple-minded or outright stupid.

"But here's the thing: if you really want to help your mom," Palazzolo tried. "First you have to tell me the truth. About what happened."

Andy almost laughed.

"Then we'll go from there. All right?" Another weighted pause. "Right?"

Right.

"Card's on the counter, doll. Day or night."

Andy listened to the drips from the faucet.

One drip . . . two drips . . . three . . . four . . . five . . . six . . .

"You wanna make a gesture, like flush the toilet to let me know you heard me?"

Andy held up her middle finger to the back of the stall door.

"All right," Palazzolo said. "Well, I'm just going to assume you heard. The thing is, sooner rather than later, okay? We don't wanna have to drag your mom down to the station, open a formal interview, all that stuff. Especially since she's been hurt. Right?"

Andy had this flash in her head, the image of herself standing from the toilet, kicking open the stall, and telling the woman to go fuck herself.

52

Then she realized that the stall door opened in, not out, so she couldn't really kick it open, so she waited on the toilet, hands wrapped around her legs, head buried between her knees, until the detective went away.

3

Andy waited on the toilet so long that her knee popped when she finally uncurled from her perch. Her hamstrings jangled like ukulele strings. She pulled open the stall door. She walked to the sink. She ignored the detective's card with its shiny gold shield as she washed her face with cold water. The blood on her knuckle ran fresh. She wrapped a paper towel around her finger, then tentatively opened the bathroom door.

She checked the hallway. No Detective Palazzolo. Andy started to leave, but at the last minute, she grabbed the detective's card off the counter. She would give it to her father. She would tell him what had happened. The cops were not supposed to question you when you had a lawyer. Anybody who watched *Law & Order* knew that.

There was a crowd in front of the elevator. Again, no Detective Palazzolo, but Andy used the stairs anyway. She walked carefully this time. Her knuckle had stopped bleeding. She threw the napkin into a trash can outside the stairwell. The air in the hospital's main waiting room was tinged with chemicals and vomit. Andy hoped that the vomit smell wasn't coming from her. She looked down at her shirt to check.

"My Lord," someone muttered. "My good Lord."

The TV.

A sudden understanding hit Andy like a punch to the face.

Every single person in the waiting room, at least twenty people, was watching the diner video play on CNN.

"Holy crap," someone else said.

On the television, Laura's hands were showing five fingers and a thumb for six bullets.

Helsinger was standing in front of her. Cowboy hat. Leather vest. Gun still out.

A banner rolled across the bottom of the TV warning people that they were about to see graphic content.

A woman asked, "What's he doing?"

Helsinger was drawing his knife from the sheath on his hip.

"What the—"

"Oh, shit!"

The crowd went silent as they watched what came next.

There were gasps, a shocked scream, like they were inside a movie theater instead of a hospital waiting room.

Andy was as transfixed as everyone else. The more she watched it, the more she was able to see it happening outside of herself. Who was that woman on the television? What had Laura become while Andy was cowering against the broken window pane?

Someone joked, "Like some kinda ninja granny."

"Grambo."

There was uncomfortable laughter.

Andy couldn't listen to it. She couldn't be in this room, in this hospital, in this emotional turmoil where the tether that had always linked her back to her mother had been broken.

She turned around and slammed right into a man who was standing too close behind her.

"Sorry." He tipped his Alabama baseball cap at her.

Andy wasn't in the mood for chivalry. She stepped to the left as he stepped to the right. The opposite happened when she stepped to the right.

He laughed.

She glared at him.

"My apologies." Alabama took off his hat and made a sweeping gesture, indicating that she could pass.

Andy walked so quickly that the sliding doors didn't have time to fully open. She slapped her hand against the frame.

"Bad day?" Alabama had followed her outside. He stood at a respectful distance, but even that felt too close. "You all right?"

Andy glared at him again. Had he not just seen what was on television? Did he not understand that Andy was the useless girl whose mother had faced down a cold-blooded murderer?

And then turned into a murderer herself?

"Is something wrong, Officer?" Alabama kept smiling at Andy.

She looked down at her police-like uniform. The stupid silver badge that was stitched on like a Girl Scout patch—but with far less meaning, because Girl Scouts had to at least do something for those patches. All Andy did was answer phones and walk terrified people through performing CPR or turning off their car engines after a crash.

Jonah Lee Helsinger had thought that she was a cop.

He had thought that she would kill him. Murder him. In cold blood.

Andy looked down at her own hands. They would not stop shaking. She was going to start crying again. Why did she keep crying?

"Here." Alabama offered her a handkerchief.

Andy stared at the folded white cloth. She thought Gordon was the only man who still carried a handkerchief.

"Just trying to help a lady in need," he grinned, still holding out the cloth.

Andy did not take it. For the first time, she really looked at the man. He was tall and fit, probably close to forty. Jeans and sneakers. His white button-down shirt was open at the collar, long sleeves neatly rolled up. He looked like he had forgotten to shave this morning, or maybe that was part of his look.

A thought occurred to her that was so startling she blurted it out. "Are you a reporter?"

He laughed and shook his head. "I make my living the honest way."

56

"You're a cop?" she tried. "Detective?" When he did not immediately answer, she told him, "Please leave me alone."

"Whoa, porcupine." He held up both his hands in surrender. "I was just making small talk."

Andy did not want to talk. She scanned the drive for Gordon's white BMW.

Where was her father?

Andy took out her cell phone. The home screen was filled with text alerts and missed calls. *Mindy Logan. Sarah Ives. Alice Blaedel. Danny Kwon.* In the last few hours, the smattering of band, chorus and drama geeks Andy had been friends with in high school had all suddenly remembered her phone number.

She dismissed the notices, then pulled up DAD and texted: *hurry.*

Alabama finally seemed to realize that she wasn't open to small talk. He tucked his handkerchief back into his jeans pocket. He walked over to one of the benches and sat down. He pulled out his phone. His thumbs worked across the screen.

Andy glanced behind her, wondering what was taking Laura so long. Then she scanned the front parking area for Gordon. Her father was probably in the parking deck, which meant he would be at least twenty minutes because the woman working the booth had to talk to every single person who handed her a ticket to get out.

All she could do was sit down on a bench three down from Alabama. Every muscle in Andy's body felt like an overstretched rubber band. Her head throbbed. Her stomach was sour. She checked her phone to see if Gordon had texted back, but he would never look at his phone while he was driving because it was dangerous.

The sliding doors opened. Andy felt relief, then trepidation, upon seeing her mother. The orderly pushed the wheelchair to a stop beside the curb. Laura was wearing a cotton candy pink Belle Isle Medical Center T-shirt that was too big for her slender frame. She was clearly in pain. Her face was the color of notebook paper. Her good hand was wrapped around the arm of the chair in a death grip.

Andy asked, "Didn't they give you anything?"

Laura said nothing, so the orderly volunteered, "The surgery meds are wearing off. The doc offered her a script but she wouldn't take it."

"Mom—" Andy didn't know what to say. Laura wouldn't even look at her. "Mother."

"I'm fine," Laura insisted, though her teeth were gritted. She asked the orderly, "Do you have a cigarette?"

"You don't smoke," Andy said, just as her mother reached for a Marlboro from the pack that the orderly pulled from his shirt pocket.

The man cupped his hand as he flicked the lighter.

Andy stepped away from the smell.

Laura didn't seem to notice. She took a deep drag, then coughed out white puffs of smoke. She held the cigarette awkwardly, pinched between her thumb and forefinger the way a junkie would.

"I'm all right," Laura said, her voice a raspy whisper. "I just need some space."

Andy took her at her word. She stepped farther away, putting distance between herself and her mother. She looked at the parking deck, willing Gordon to hurry. She started to cry again, but quietly. She didn't know what to do. None of this made any sense.

Laura said, "There are some boxes at your father's house."

Andy's lips trembled. Silence eluded her. She had to have answers. "What did I do wrong?"

"You didn't do anything wrong." Laura smoked the cigarette. "I just need to stop coddling you. You need to learn to stand on your own two feet."

"By moving in with Dad?" She needed this to make sense. Laura always made sense. "Mom, please—"

Laura took a last hit from the cigarette, then handed it to the orderly to finish. She told Andy, "Pack what you need for the night. Your dad won't let you stay with him forever. You'll work out a budget. You'll see what you can afford. You could move to Atlanta, or even back to New York." She looked up at Andy from her chair. "You have to go, Andrea. I want to be alone now. I've earned the right to be alone."

"I didn't . . ." the words got tangled in Andy's mouth. "I never—"

"Stop," Laura said. She had never talked to Andy this way. It was as if she hated her. "Just stop."

Why?

"Thank God," Laura muttered as Gordon's BMW glided to a stop in front of the wheelchair ramp.

"Help me up." Laura held out her hand for the orderly, but the guy in the Alabama hat was suddenly at her side.

He said, "Happy to be of service, ma'am."

If Andy hadn't been watching closely, she would've missed the look that flashed across her mother's face. Panic? Fear? Disgust?

He said, "Up you go."

"Thank you." Laura let him lift her to standing.

Gordon came around the car and opened the door. He told Alabama, "I've got it from here."

"No problem, big guy." Alabama didn't relinquish his hold. He guided Laura down to the front seat, then gently lifted her legs as she turned to face the front. "Take care, now."

Gordon said, "Thank you."

"My pleasure." Alabama offered Gordon his hand. "I'm sorry for the situation your wife and daughter are in."

"Uh—yes." Gordon was too polite to correct him about his marital status, let alone refuse to shake his hand. "Thank you."

Alabama tipped his hat at Andy as she got into the back of the car. He shut the door before she could slam it in his face.

Gordon got behind the wheel. He sniffed the air with visible distaste. "Have you been smoking?"

"Gordon, just drive."

He waited for her to look at him. She did not. He put the car in gear. He drove away from the portico, past the entrance to the parking garage, then pulled over and parked the car. He turned to Laura. His mouth opened. Nothing came out.

"No," she said. "Not here. Not now."

He shook his head slowly back and forth.

"Andy doesn't need to hear this."

Gordon didn't seem to care. "The kid's father was Bobby Helsinger. Did you know that?"

Laura's lips pursed. Andy could tell she knew.

Gordon said, "He was the sheriff of Bibb County before a bank robber blew off his head with a shotgun. This was six months ago, around the same time the detective says Jonah Helsinger started weaponizing."

The vest and gunbelt.

Palazzolo had told them that Jonah bought it off Amazon six months ago.

Gordon said, "I looked up the obituary on my phone. Jonah's got three uncles who are cops, two cousins who are in the military. His mother used to work at the district attorney's office in Beaufort before she went private. The family's practically law enforcement royalty." He waited for Laura to say something. "Did you hear me? Do you understand what I'm saying to you?"

Laura took a sharp breath before speaking. "His family royalty does not negate the fact that he murdered two people."

"He didn't just murder them. He planned it. He knew exactly what he was doing. He had maps and—" Gordon shook his head, like he could not believe how stupid she was. "Do you think the family's going to believe their little boy is a sadistic murderer, or do you think they're going to say he had some kind of mental problem because his hero daddy was murdered by a bank robber and all of this was a cry for help?"

"They can say what they want."

"That's the first thing you've said that makes any fucking sense," Gordon snapped. "The Helsingers are going to say

60

exactly what they want—that yeah, this poor, heart-broken, dead cop's son deserved to go to prison for what he did, but he didn't deserve to be viciously murdered."

"That's not—"

"They're going to take you down harder than him, Laura. You did that kid a favor. This is all going to be about what *you* did, not what *he* did."

Laura kept silent.

Andy stopped breathing.

Gordon asked, "Do you know there's a video?"

Laura did not answer, though she must have seen the TV when the orderly wheeled her through the waiting room.

"That detective showed—" Gordon had to stop to swallow. "The look on your face when you killed him, Laura. The serenity. The everyday-ness. How do you think that's going to stack up against a mentally troubled, fatherless teenage boy?"

Laura turned her head and looked out the window.

"Do you know what that detective kept asking? Over and over again?"

"The pigs always ask a lot of questions."

"Stop fucking around, Laura. What did you say before you killed him?" Gordon waited, but she did not respond. "What did you say to Helsinger?"

Laura continued to stare out the window.

"Whatever you said—that's motivation. That's the difference between maybe—just maybe—being able to argue justifiable homicide and the death penalty."

Andy felt her heart stop.

"Laura?" He banged his hand on the steering wheel. "God dammit! Answer me. Answer me or—"

"I am not a fool, Gordon." Laura's tone was cold enough to burn. "Why do you think I refused to be interviewed? Why do you think I told Andrea to keep her mouth shut?"

"You want our daughter to lie to a police detective? To perjure herself in court?"

"I want her to do what she always does and keep her mouth

61

shut." Her tone was quiet but her anger was so palpable that Andy felt like the air was vibrating with rage.

Why wasn't her mother arguing that Gordon was wrong? Why wasn't she saying that she didn't have a choice? That she was saving Andy? That it was self-defense? That she was horrified by what she had done? That she had panicked or just reacted or was terrified and she was sorry—so sorry—that she had killed that troubled kid?

Andy slid her hand into her pocket. The detective's card was still wet from the bathroom counter.

Palazzolo tried to talk to me again. She wanted me to turn on you. She gave me her card.

Gordon said, "Laura, this is deadly serious."

She fake-laughed. "That's an interesting choice of words."

"Cops protect their own. Don't you know that? They stick together no matter what. That brotherhood bullshit is not just some urban legend you hear on TV." Gordon was so angry that his voice broke. "This whole thing will turn into a crusade just by virtue of the kid's last name."

Laura inhaled, then slowly shushed it out. "I just—I need a moment, Gordon. All right? I need time alone to think this through."

"You need a criminal litigator to do the thinking for you."

"And you need to stop telling me what to do!" She was so furious that she screeched out the words. Laura covered her eyes with her hand. "Has hectoring me ever worked? Has it?" She wasn't looking for an answer. She turned to Gordon, roaring at him, "This is why I left you! I had to get away from you, to get you out of my life, because you have no idea who I am. You never have and you never will."

Each word was like a slap across her father's face.

"Jesus." Laura grabbed the handle above the door, tried to shift her weight off her injured leg. "Will you drive the fucking car?"

Andy waited for her father to say Laura was welcome to walk home, but he didn't. He faced forward. He pushed the gear into drive. He glanced over his shoulder before hitting the gas.

The car lurched toward the main road.

Andy didn't know why, but she found herself turning to look out the back window.

Alabama was still standing under the portico. He tipped his hat one last time.

The look on her mother's face—panic? Fear? Disgust?

Is something wrong, Officer?

Alabama stood rooted in place as Gordon took a left out of the hospital drive. He was still standing there, head turning to follow their progress, when they drove down the street.

Andy watched him watching the car until he was just a speck in the distance.

I'm sorry for the situation your wife and daughter are in.

How had he known that Gordon was her father?

Andy stood under the shower until the hot water ran out. Manic thoughts kept flitting around inside of her head like a swarm of mosquitos. She could not blink without remembering a stray detail from the diner, from the video, from the police interview, the car.

None of it made sense. Her mother was a fifty-five-year-old speech therapist. She played bridge, for chrissakes. She didn't kill people and smoke cigarettes and rail against the pigs.

Andy avoided her reflection in the bathroom mirror as she dried her hair. Her skin felt like sandpaper. There were tiny shards of glass embedded in her scalp. Her chapped lips had started bleeding at the corner. Her nerves were still shaky. At least she thought it was her nerves. Maybe it was lack of sleep that was making her feel so jumpy, or the absence of adrenaline, or the desperation she felt every time she replayed the last thing that Laura had said to Andy before she went into the house—

I'm not going to change my mind. You need to leave tonight.

Andy's heart felt so raw that a feather could've splayed it open.

She rummaged through the clean clothes pile and found a pair of lined running shorts and a navy-blue work shirt. She dressed quickly, walking to the window as she did up the buttons. The garage was detached from the house. The apartment was her cave. Gray walls. Gray carpet. Light-blocking shades. The ceiling sloped with the roofline, only made livable by two tiny dormers.

Andy stood at the narrow window and looked down at her mother's house. She could not hear her parents arguing, but she knew what was happening the same way that you knew you had managed to give yourself food poisoning. She was seized by that awful, clammy feeling that something just wasn't right.

The death penalty.

Where had her mother even learned to catch a knife like that? Laura had never been in the military. As far as Andy knew, she hadn't taken any self-defense classes.

Almost every day of her mother's life for the last three years had been spent either trying not to die from cancer or enduring all the horrible indignities that cancer treatment brought with it. There had not been a hell of a lot of free time to train for hand-to-hand combat. Andy was surprised her mother had been able to raise her arm so quickly. Laura struggled to lift a grocery bag, even with her good hand. The breast cancer had invaded her chest wall. The surgeon had removed part of her pectoral muscle.

Adrenaline.

Maybe that was the answer. There were all kinds of stories about mothers lifting cars off their trapped babies or performing other tremendous physical feats in order to protect their children. Sure, it wasn't common, but it happened.

But that still didn't explain the look on Laura's face when she pulled the knife through. Blank. Almost workman-like. Not panicked. Not afraid. She could've just as easily been sitting at her desk reviewing a patient's chart.

Andy shivered.

Thunder rumbled in the distance. The sun would not go down

64

for another hour, but the clouds were dark and heavy with the promise of rain. Andy could hear waves throwing themselves onto the beach. Seagulls hashing out dinner plans. She looked down at her mother's tidy bungalow. Most of the lights were on. Gordon was pacing back and forth in front of the kitchen window. Her mother was seated at the table, but all that Andy could make out was her hand, the one that wasn't strapped to her waist, resting on a placemat. Laura's fingers occasionally tapped, but otherwise she was still.

Andy saw Gordon throw his hands into the air. He walked toward the kitchen door.

Andy stepped back into the shadows. She heard the door slam closed. She chanced another look outside the window.

Gordon walked down the porch stairs. The motion detector flipped on the floodlights. He looked up at them, shielding his eyes with his hand. Instead of heading toward her apartment, he stopped on the bottom riser and sat down. He rested his forehead on the heels of his hands.

Her first thought was that he was crying, but then she realized that he was probably trying to regain his composure so that Andy wouldn't be even more worried when she saw him.

She had seen Gordon cry once, and only once, before. It was at the beginning of her parents' divorce. He hadn't let go and sobbed or anything. What he had done was so much worse. Tears had rolled down his cheeks, one long drip after another, like condensation on the side of a glass. He'd kept sniffing, wiping his eyes with the back of his hand. He had left for work one morning assuming his fourteen-year marriage was solid, then before lunchtime had been served with divorce papers.

"*I don't understand,*" he had told Andy between sniffles. "*I just don't understand.*"

Andy couldn't remember the man who was her real father, and even thinking the words *real father* felt like a betrayal to Gordon. *Sperm donor* felt too overtly feminist. Not that Andy wasn't a feminist, but she didn't want to be the kind of feminist that men hated.

Her *birth father*—which sounded strange but kind of made

sense because adopted kids said birth mother—was an optometrist whom Laura had met at a Sandals resort. Which was weird, because her mother hated to travel anywhere. Andy thought they'd met in the Bahamas, but she was told the story so long ago that a lot of details were lost.

These were the things she knew: That her birth parents had never married. That Andy was born the first year they were together. That her birth father, Jerry Randall, had died in a car accident while on a trip home to Chicago when Andy was eighteen months old.

Unlike Laura's parents, who had both died before Andy was born, Andy still had grandparents on her birth father's side—Laverne and Phil Randall. She had an old photo somewhere of herself, no more than two, sitting in their laps, balanced between each of their knees. There was a painting of the beach on the wood-paneled wall behind them. The couch looked scruffy. They seemed like kind people, and maybe they were in some ways, but they had completely cut off both Laura and Andy when Gordon had entered their lives.

Gordon—of all people. A Phi Beta Sigma who had graduated Georgetown Law while working as a volunteer coordinator at Habitat for Humanity. A man who played golf, loved classical music, was the president of his local wine-tasting society and had chosen for his vocation one of the most boring areas of the law, helping wealthy people figure out how their money would be spent after they died.

That Andy's birth grandparents had balked at the dorkiest, most uptight black man walking the planet simply because of the color of his skin was enough to make Andy glad she didn't have any contact with them.

The kitchen door opened. Andy watched Gordon stand up. He tripped the floodlights again. Laura handed him a plate of food. Gordon said something Andy could not hear. Laura slammed the door in lieu of response.

Through the kitchen window, she saw her mother making her way back to the table, gripping the counter, the doorjamb, the back of a chair—anything she could find to take the pressure off of her leg.

Andy could've helped her. She could've been down there making her mother tea or helping her wash off the hospital smell the way she'd done so many times before.

I've earned the right to be alone.

The TV by Andy's bed caught her attention. The set was small, formerly taking up space on her mother's kitchen counter. By habit, Andy had turned it on when she walked through the door. The sound was muted. CNN was showing the diner video again.

Andy closed her eyes, because she knew what the video showed.

She breathed in.

Out.

The air-conditioner hummed in her ears. The ceiling fan wah-wahed overhead. She felt cold air curl around her neck and face. She was so tired. Her brain was filled with slow-rolling marbles. She wanted to sleep, but she knew she could not sleep here. She would have to stay at Gordon's tonight and then, first thing tomorrow morning, her father would require she make some kind of a plan. Gordon always wanted a plan.

A car door opened and closed. Andy knew it was her father because the McMansions along her mother's street, all of them so huge that they literally blocked out the sun, were always vacant during the most extreme heat of the summer.

She heard scuffling feet across the driveway. Then Gordon's heavy footsteps were on the metal stairs to the apartment.

Andy grabbed a trashbag out of the box. She was supposed to be packing. She opened the top drawer of her dresser and dumped her underwear into the bag.

"Andrea?" Gordon knocked on the door, then opened it.

He glanced around the room. It was hard to tell whether Andy had been robbed or a tornado had hit. Dirty clothes carpeted the floor. Shoes were piled on top of a flat box that contained two unassembled Ikea shoe racks. The bathroom door hung open. Her period panties from a week ago hung stiffly from the towel rod.

"Here." Gordon offered the plate that Laura had given him. PB&J, chips and a pickle. "Your mom said to make sure you eat something."

What else did she say?

"I asked for a bottle of wine, but got this." He reached into his jacket pocket and pulled out a pint-sized bottle of Knob Creek. "Did you know your mother keeps bourbon in the house?"

Andy had known about her mother's stash since she was fourteen.

"Anyway, I thought this might help tamp down some nerves. Take the edge off." He broke the seal on the top. "What are the chances that you have some clean glasses in this mess?"

Andy put the plate on the floor. She felt underneath the sofa bed and found an open pack of Solo cups.

Gordon scowled. "I guess that's better than passing the bottle back and forth like a couple of hobos."

What did Mom say?

He poured two fingers of bourbon into the deep cup. "Eat something before you have a drink. Your stomach's empty and you're tired."

Belle Isle Andy hadn't had a drink since she'd returned home. She wasn't sure whether or not she wanted to break the streak. Still, she took a cup and sat cross-legged on the floor so that her dad could sit in the chair.

He sniffed at the chair. "Did you get a dog?"

Andy sucked down a mouthful of bourbon. The 100 proof made her eyes water.

He said, "We should toast your birthday."

She pressed together her lips.

He held up the cup. "To my beautiful daughter."

Andy held up her drink, too. Then she took another sip.

Gordon didn't imbibe. He dug into his suit pocket and retrieved a white mailing envelope. "I got you these. I'm sorry I didn't have time to wrap them in something pretty."

Andy took the envelope. She already knew what was inside. Gordon always bought her gift cards because he knew the stores she liked, but he had no idea what she liked from those stores. She dumped the contents onto the floor. Two $25 gas cards for the station down the street. Two $25 iTunes cards. Two $25 Target gift cards. One $50 gift card to Dick Blick for art supplies. She picked up a piece of paper. He had printed out a coupon for a free sandwich at Subway when you bought one of equal or lesser value.

He said, "I know you like sandwiches. I thought we could go together. Unless you want to take someone else."

"These are great, Dad. Thank you."

He swished around the bourbon but still did not drink. "You should eat."

Andy bit into the sandwich. She looked up at Gordon. He was touching his mustache again, smoothing it down the same way he stroked Mr. Purrkins' shoulders.

He said, "I have no idea what's going through your mother's mind."

Andy's jaw made a grinding noise as she chewed. She might as well have been eating paste and cardboard.

He said, "She told me to let you know that she's going to pay off your student loans."

Andy choked on the bite.

"That was my response, too." Her student loans were a sore point with Gordon. He had offered to refinance the debt in order to help Andy get out from under $800's worth of interest a month, but for reasons known only to her id, she had passed his deadline for gathering all the paperwork.

He said, "Your mother wants you to move back to New York City. To pursue your dreams. She said she'd help you with the move. Financially, I mean. Suddenly, she's very free with her money."

Andy worked peanut butter off the roof of her mouth with her tongue.

"You can stay with me tonight. We'll work out something

69

tomorrow. A plan. I—I don't want you going back to New York, sweetheart. You never seemed happy up there. I felt like it took a piece of you; took away some of your Andy-ness."

Andy's throat made a gulping sound as she swallowed.

"When you moved back home, you were so good taking care of Mom. So good. But maybe that was asking too much. Maybe I should've helped more or . . . I don't know. It was a lot for you to take on. A lot of pressure. A lot of stress." His voice was thick with guilt, like it was his fault that Laura got cancer. "Mom's right that you need to start your life. To have a career and maybe, I don't know, maybe one day a family." He held up his hand to stop her protest. "Okay, I know I'm getting ahead of myself, but whatever the problem is, I just don't think going back to New York is the answer."

Gordon's head turned toward the television. Something had caught his eye. "That's—from high school. What's her—"

Motherfucker.

CNN had identified Alice Blaedel, one of Andy's friends from high school, as a *Close Friend of the Family.*

Andy found the remote and unmuted the sound.

"—always the cool mom," Alice, who had not spoken to Andy in over a decade, was telling the reporter. "You could, you know, talk to her about your problems and she'd, like, she wouldn't judge, you know?" Alice kept shrugging her shoulder every other word, as if she was being electrocuted. "I dunno, it's weird to watch her on the video because, you're like, wow, that's Mrs. Oliver, but it's like in *Kill Bill* where the mom is all normal in front of her kid but she's secretly a killing machine."

Andy's mouth was still thick with peanut butter, but she managed to push out the words, "Killing machine?"

Gordon took the remote from Andy. He muted the sound. He stared at Alice Blaedel, whose mouth was still moving despite not knowing a goddamn thing.

Andy poured more bourbon into her empty cup. Alice had walked out on *Kill Bill* because she'd said it was stupid and now she was using it as a cultural touchstone.

70

Gordon tried, "I'm sure she'll regret her choice of words."

Like she'd regretted getting genital warts from Adam Humphrey.

He tried again. "I didn't realize you had reconnected with Alice."

"I haven't. She's a self-serving bitch." Andy swallowed the bourbon in one go. She coughed at the sudden heat in her throat, then poured herself some more.

"Maybe you should—"

"They lift cars," Andy said, which wasn't exactly what she meant. "Mothers, I mean. Like, the adrenaline, when they see that their kids are trapped." She raised her hands to indicate the act of picking up an overturned automobile.

Gordon stroked his mustache with his fingers.

"She was so calm," Andy said. "In the diner."

Gordon sat back in the chair.

Andy said, "People were screaming. It was terrifying. I didn't see him shoot—I didn't see the first one. The second one, I saw that." She rubbed her jaw with her hand. "You know that phrase people say in the movies, 'I'm gonna blow your head off'? That happens. It literally happens."

Gordon crossed his arms.

"Mom came running toward me." Andy saw it all happening again in her head. The tiny red dots of blood freckling Laura's face. Her arms reaching out to tackle Andy to the ground. "She looked scared, Dad. With everything that happened, that's the only time I ever saw her look scared."

He waited.

"You watched the video. You saw what I did. Didn't do. I was panicked. Useless. Is that why . . ." She struggled to give voice to her fear. "Is that why Mom's mad at me? Because I was a coward?"

"Absolutely not." He shook his head, vehement. "There's no such thing as a coward in that kind of situation."

Andy wondered if he was right, and more importantly, if her mother agreed with him.

71

"Andrea—"

"Mom killed him." Saying the words put a burning lump of coal in her stomach. "She could've taken the gun out of his hand. She had time to do that, to reach down, but instead she reached up and—"

Gordon let her speak.

"I mean—did she have time? Is it right to assume she was capable of making rational choices?" Andy did not expect an answer. "She looked calm in the video. Serene, that's what you said. Or maybe we're both wrong, because, really, she didn't have an expression. Nothing, right? You saw her face. Everydayness."

He nodded, but let her continue.

"When it was happening, I didn't see it from the front. I mean, I was behind her, right? When it was happening. And then I saw the video from the front and it—it looked different." Andy tried to keep her muddled brain on track. She ate a couple of potato chips, hoping the starch would absorb the alcohol.

She told her father, "I remember when the knife was in Jonah's neck and he was raising the gun—I remember being really clear that he could've shot somebody. Shot me. It doesn't take much to pull a trigger, right?"

Gordon nodded.

"But from the front—you see Mom's face, and you wonder if she did the right thing. If she was thinking that, yes, she could take away the gun, but she wasn't going to do that. She was going to kill the guy. And it wasn't out of fear or self-preservation but it was like . . . a conscious choice. Like a killing machine." Andy couldn't believe she had used Alice Blaedel's spiteful words to describe her mother. "I don't get it, Daddy. Why didn't Mom talk to the police? Why didn't she tell them it was self-defense?"

Why was she letting everyone believe that she had deliberately committed murder?

"I don't get it," Andy repeated. "I just don't understand."

Gordon stroked his mustache again. It was becoming a nervous habit. He didn't answer her at first. He was used to carefully considering his words. Everything felt especially dangerous right now. Neither one of them wanted to say something that could not be taken back.

Your mother is a murderer. Yes, she had a choice. She chose to kill that boy.

Eventually, Gordon said, "I have no idea how your mother was able to do what she did. Her thought process. The choices she made. Why she behaved the way she did toward the police." He shrugged, his hands out in the air. "One could hazard that her refusal to talk about it, her anger, is post-traumatic stress, or perhaps it triggered something from her childhood that we don't know about. She's never been one to discuss the past."

He stopped again to gather his thoughts.

"What your mother said in the car—she's right. I don't know her. I can't comprehend her motivations. I mean, yes, I do get that she had the instinct to protect you. I'm very glad that she did. So grateful. But *how* she did it . . ." He let his gaze travel back to the television. More talking heads. Someone was pointing to a diagram of the Mall of Belle Isle, explaining the route Jonah Helsinger had taken to the diner. "Andrea, I just don't know." Gordon said it again: "I just don't know."

Andy had finished her drink. Under her father's watchful eye, she poured another one.

He said, "That's a lot of alcohol on an empty stomach."

Andy shoved the rest of the sandwich into her mouth. She chewed on one side so she could ask, "Did you know that guy at the hospital?"

"Which guy?"

"The one in the Alabama hat who helped Mom into the car."

He shook his head. "Why?"

"It seemed like Mom knew him. Or maybe was scared of him. Or—" Andy stopped to swallow. "He knew you were my dad, which most people don't assume."

Gordon touched the ends of his mustache. He was clearly trying to recall the exchange. "Your mother knows a lot of

73

people in town. She has a lot of friends. Which, hopefully, will help her."

"You mean legally?"

He did not answer the question. "I put in a call to a criminal defense lawyer I've used before. He's aggressive, but that's what your mother needs right now."

Andy sipped the bourbon. Gordon was right: the edge was coming off. She felt her eyes wanting to close.

He said, "When I first met your mom, I thought she was a puzzle. A fascinating, beautiful, complex puzzle. But then I realized that no matter how close I got to her, no matter what combination I tried, she would never really open up to me." He finally drank some bourbon. Instead of gulping it like Andy, he let it roll down his throat.

He told her, "I've said too much. I'm sorry, sweetheart. It's been a troubling day, and I haven't done much to help the situation." He indicated a box filled with art supplies. "I assume you want this to go tonight?"

"I'll get it tomorrow."

Gordon gave her a careful look. As a kid, she would freak out whenever her art supplies were not close at hand.

Andy said, "I'm too tired to do anything but sleep." She did not tell him that she had not held a charcoal pencil or a sketchpad in her hands since her first year in New York. "Daddy, should I talk to her? Not to ask her if I can stay, but to ask her why."

"I don't feel equipped to offer you advice."

Which probably meant she shouldn't.

"Sweetheart." Gordon sensed her melancholy. He leaned over and put his hands on her shoulders. "Everything will work itself out. We'll discuss your future at the end of the month, all right? That gives us eleven days to formulate a plan."

Andy chewed her lip. Gordon would formulate a plan. Andy would pretend like she had a lot of time to think about it until the tenth day, then she would panic.

He said. "For tonight, we'll take your toothbrush, your comb,

74

whatever you absolutely need, then we'll pack everything else tomorrow. And get your car. I assume it's still at the mall?"

Andy nodded. She had forgotten all about her car. Laura's Honda was there, too. They were probably both clamped or towed by now.

Gordon stood up. He closed her art supply box and put it on the floor out of the way. "I think your mother just needs some time alone. She used to take her drives, remember?"

Andy remembered.

On weekends, Andy and Gordon would be doing a project, or Gordon would be doing the project and Andy would be nearby reading a book, and suddenly Laura would burst in, keys in her hand, and announce, "I'm going to be gone for the day."

Oftentimes she would bring back chocolate for Andy or a nice bottle of wine for Gordon. Once, she'd brought a snowglobe from the Tubman Museum in Macon, which was two and a half hours away. Whenever they asked Laura where she had gone and why, she would say, "Oh, you know, just needed to be somewhere besides here."

Andy looked around the cramped, cluttered room. Suddenly, it felt less like a cave and more like a hovel.

Before Gordon could say it, she told him, "We should go."

"We should. But I'm leaving this on your mother's porch." Gordon pocketed the bourbon. He hesitated, then added, "You know you can always talk to me, sweetie. I just wish you didn't have to get tipsy to do it."

"Tipsy." Andy laughed at the silly-sounding word because the alternative was to cry, and she was sick of crying. "Dad, I think—I think I want some time alone, too."

"O-kay," he drew out the word.

"Not, like, forever. I just think maybe it would be good if I walked to your house." She would need another shower, but something about being enveloped by the sweltering, humid night was appealing. "Is that okay?"

"Of course it's okay. I'll tell Mr. Purrkins to warm your bed for you." Gordon kissed the top of her head, then grabbed the plastic garbage bag she had filled with underwear. "Don't dawdle too long. The app on my phone says it's going to start raining in half an hour."

"No dawdling," she promised.

He opened the door but did not leave. "Next year will be better, Andrea. Time puts everything into perspective. We'll get through what happened today. Mom will be herself again. You'll be standing on your own two feet. Your life will be back on track."

She held up her crossed fingers.

"It'll be better," Gordon repeated. "I promise."

He closed the door behind him.

Andy heard his heavy footsteps on the metal stairs.

She didn't believe him.

4

Andy rolled over in bed. She brushed something away from her face. In her sleeping brain, she told herself it was Mr. Purrkins, but her half-awake brain told her that the item was way too malleable to be Gordon's chubby calico. And that she couldn't be at her father's house because she had no recollection of walking there.

She sat up too fast and fell back from dizziness.

An involuntary groan came out of Andy's mouth. She pressed her fingers into her eyes. She could not tell if she was tipsy from the bourbon or had crossed into legit hungover, but the headache she'd had since the shooting was like a bear's teeth gnawing at her skull.

The shooting.

It had a name now, an *after* that calved her life away from the *before*.

Andy let her hand fall away. She blinked her eyes, willing them to adjust to the darkness. Lowlight from a soundless television. The wah-wah noise of a ceiling fan. She was still in her apartment, splayed out on the pile of clean clothes that she stored on the sofa bed. The last thing she remembered was searching for a clean pair of socks.

Rain pelted the roof. Lightning zigzagged outside the tiny dormer windows.

Crap.

She had dawdled after promising her father that she would not dawdle, and now her choices were to either beg him to pick her up or walk through what sounded like a monsoon.

With great care, she slowly sat back up. The television pulled Andy's attention. CNN was showing a photo of Laura from two years ago. Bald head covered in a pink scarf. Tired smile on her face. The Breast Cancer Awareness Walk in Charleston. Andy had been cropped out of the image, but her hand was visible on Laura's shoulder. Someone—maybe a friend, maybe a stranger—had taken that private, candid moment and exploited it for a photo credit.

Laura's details appeared on one side of the screen, a résumé of sorts:

—55-Year-Old Divorcee.
—One Adult Child.
—Speech Pathologist.
—No Formal Combat Training.

The image changed. The diner video started to play, the ubiquitous scroll warning that some viewers might find it graphic.

They're going to take you down harder than him, Laura. This is all going to be about what you *did, not what he* did.

Andy couldn't bear to watch it again; didn't really need to because she could blink and see it all happening live in her head. She stumbled out of bed. She found her phone in the bathroom. 1:18 a.m. She'd been asleep for over six hours. Gordon hadn't texted, which was some kind of miracle. He was probably as wiped out as Andy. Or maybe he thought that Laura and Andy had made amends.

If only.

She tapped on the text icon and selected DAD. Her eyes watered. The light from the screen was like a straight razor. Andy's brain was still oscillating in her skull. She dashed off an apology in case her father woke up, found her bed empty and freaked: *fell asleep almost there don't worry I've got an umbrella*.

The part about the umbrella was a lie. Also the part about

78

being almost there. And that he shouldn't worry, because she could very well get struck by lightning.

Actually, considering how her day had gone, the odds that Andy would be electrocuted seemed enormously high.

She looked out the dormer window. Her mother's house was dark but for the light in her office window. It seemed very unlikely that Laura was working. During her various illnesses, she had slept in the recliner in the living room. Maybe Laura had accidentally left the light on and couldn't bring herself to limp across the foyer to turn it off.

Andy turned away from the window. The television pulled her back in. Laura backhanding the knife into Jonah Helsinger's neck.

Thwack.

Andy had to get out of here.

There was a floor lamp by the chair but the bulb had blown weeks ago. The overhead lights would be like a beacon in the night. Andy used the flashlight app on her phone to search for an old pair of sneakers that could get ruined in the rain and a poncho she'd bought at a convenience store because it seemed like an adult thing to have in case of an emergency.

Which is why she had left it in the glove box of her car, because why would she go out in the rain unless she got caught without an umbrella in her car?

Lightning illuminated every corner of the room.

Crap.

Andy pulled a trashbag from the box. Of course she didn't have any scissors. She used her teeth to rip out a hole approximately the circumference of her head. She held up the phone to gauge her progress.

The screen flickered, then died.

The last thing Andy saw were the words LO BAT.

She found the charger stuck in an outlet. The cable was in her car. Her car was two and a half miles away parked in front of the Zegna menswear store.

Unless it had already been towed.

"Fuck!" She said the word with heartfelt conviction. She pushed her head through the trashbag hole and stepped outside. Rain slid down her back. Within seconds, her clothes were soaked so that the homemade poncho turned into cling wrap.

Andy kept walking.

The rain had somehow amplified the day's heat. She felt hot needles stabbing into her face as she turned onto the road. Streetlights did not exist in this part of the city. People bought houses on Belle Isle because they wanted an authentic, old-fashioned, southern coastal town experience. At least as old-fashioned as you could get when the cheapest mansion off the beach ran north of two million dollars.

Nearly three decades ago, Laura had paid $118,000 for her beachside bungalow. The closest grocery store had been the Piggly Wiggly outside of Savannah. The gas station sold live bait and pickled pigs' feet in large jars by the cash register. Now, Laura's house was one of only six original bungalows left in Belle Isle. The land itself was worth literally twenty times the house.

A bolt of lightning licked down from the sky. Andy's arms flew up as if she could stop it. The rain had intensified. Visibility was around five feet. She stopped in the middle of the road. Another flash of lightning stuttered the raindrops. She couldn't decide whether or not to turn around and wait for a lull in the storm or keep heading toward her father's.

Standing in the street like an idiot seemed like the worst of her options.

Andy jumped over the curb onto the sidewalk. Her sneakers made a satisfying splash. She made another splash. She picked up her feet and lengthened her strides. Soon, Andy had pushed herself into a light jog. Then she went faster. And faster.

Running was the only thing that Andy ever felt she did well. It was hard to continually throw one foot after the other. Sweating. Heart pounding. Blood racing through your ears. A lot of people couldn't do it. A lot of people didn't want to, especially in the summer when there were heat advisories warning people not to go outside because they could literally die.

Andy could hear the rhythmic slap of her sneakers over the shushing rain. She detoured away from the road that led to Gordon's, not ready to stop. The boardwalk was thirty yards ahead. The beach just beyond. Her eyes started to sting from the salt air. She couldn't hear the waves, but she somehow absorbed their velocity, the relentless persistence to keep pushing forward no matter how hard gravity pulled at your back.

She took a left onto the boardwalk, fighting an inelegant battle between the wind and the trashbag before she managed to tear off the plastic and slam it into the nearest recycling bin. Her shoes *thudded* on the wooden planks. Hot rain drilled open her pores. She wasn't wearing socks. A blister rubbed on her heel. Her shorts were bunched up. Her shirt was glued down. Her hair was like resin. She sucked in a great big gulp of wet air and coughed it back out.

The spray of blood coming from Betsy Barnard's mouth.

Shelly already dead on the floor.

Laura with the knife in her hand.

Thwack.

Her mother's face.

Her face.

Andy shook her head. Water flew like a dog sloughing off the sea. Her fingernails were cutting into her palms. She loosened her hands out of the tight fists they'd clawed into. She swiped hair away from her eyes. She imagined her thoughts receding like the low tide. She pulled air into her lungs. She ran harder, legs pumping, tendon and muscle working in tandem to keep her upright during what was nothing more than a series of controlled falls.

Something clicked inside of her head. Andy had never achieved a runner's high, not even back when she kept to something like a schedule. She just got to a place where her body didn't hurt so much that she wanted to stop, but her brain was occupied enough by that pain to keep her thoughts floating along the surface rather than diving down into the darkness.

Left foot. Right foot.

Breathe in. Breathe out.

Left. Right. Left.

Breathe.

Tension slowly drained from her shoulders. Her jaw unclenched. The bear-teeth headache turned from a gnawing to a more manageable nibble. Andy's thoughts started to wander. She listened to the rain, watched the drops fall in front of her face. What would it feel like to open her box of art supplies? To take out her pencil and sketchbook? To draw something like a puddle splattering up from her ruined sneakers? Andy visualized lines and light and shadows, the impact of her sneaker inside a puddle, the jerk of her shoestring caught mid-step.

Laura had almost died during her cancer treatments. It wasn't just the toxic mixture of drugs, but the other problems that treatment brought with it. The infections. The *C. difficile.* Pneumonia. Double pneumonia. Staph infections. A collapsed lung.

And now they could add to the list: Jonah Helsinger. Detective Palazzolo. Needing Gordon to butt out of her life. Needing space from her only daughter.

They were going to survive Laura's coldness the same way they had survived the cancer.

Gordon was right about time putting things in perspective. Andy knew all about waiting—for the surgeon to come out, for the films to be read for the biopsy to be cultured for the chemo and the antibiotics and the pain meds and the anti-nausea shot and the clean sheets and the fresh pillows and finally, blissfully, for the cautious smile on the doctor's face when she had told Laura and Andy that the scan was clear.

All that Andy had to do now was wait for her mother to come back around. Laura would fight her way out of the dark place she was in until eventually, finally, in a month or six months or by Andy's next birthday, she would be looking back at what had happened yesterday as if through a telescope rather than through a magnifying glass.

The boardwalk ran out sooner than Andy had expected. She

jumped back onto the one-way road that skirted the beachfront mansions. The asphalt felt solid beneath her feet. The roar of the sea began to fade behind the giant houses. The shore along this stretch bent around the tip of the Isle. Her mother's bungalow was another half mile away. Andy hadn't meant to go back home. She started to turn around but then remembered—

Her bicycle.

Andy saw the bike hanging from the ceiling every time she went into the garage. The trip back to Gordon's would be faster on two wheels. Considering the lightning, having a set of rubber tires between herself and the asphalt seemed like a good idea.

She slowed down to a jog, then a brisk walk. The intensity of the rain dialed back. Fat water drops slapped against the top of her head, made divots in her skin. Andy slowed her walk when she saw the faint glow of light from Laura's office. The house was at least fifty yards away, but this time of year, all the McMansions in the vicinity were unoccupied. Belle Isle was mostly a snowbird town, a respite for Northerners during the harsh winter months. The other homeowners were chased away by the August heat.

Andy glanced into Laura's office window as she walked down the driveway. Empty, at least as far as she could tell. She used the side entrance to the garage. The glass panes rattled in the door as she closed it. The shushing sound of the rain was amplified in the open space. Andy reached for the garage door opener to turn on the light, but caught herself at the last minute because the light only came on when the door rolled up and the rackety sound could wake the dead. Fortunately, the glow from Laura's office reached through the glass in the side door. Andy had just enough light to squint by.

She walked to the back, leaving a Pig-Pen-like trail of rain puddles in her wake. Her bike hung upside down from two hooks Gordon had screwed into the ceiling. Andy's shoulders screamed with pain as she tried to lift the Schwinn's tires from the hooks. Once. Twice. Then the bike was falling and she almost toppled backward trying to turn it right side up before it hit the ground.

Which was why she hadn't wanted to hang the fucking thing from the ceiling in the first place, Andy would never, ever say to her father.

One of the pedals had scraped her shin. Andy didn't worry about the trickle of blood. She checked the tread, expecting dry rot, but found the tires were so new they still had the little alveoli poking out of the sides. Andy sensed her father's handiwork. Over the summer, Gordon had repeatedly suggested they resume their weekend bike rides. It was just like him to make sure everything would be ready on the off-chance that Andy said yes.

She started to lift her leg, but stopped mid-air. There was a distinct, jangly noise from above. Andy cocked her head like a retriever. All she could make out was the white noise of the rain. She was trying to think of a Jacob Marley joke when the jangle happened again. She strained to listen, but there was nothing more than the constant *shush* of water falling.

Great. She was a proven coward. She literally did not know when to come in out of the rain, and now, apparently, she was paranoid.

Andy shook her head. She had to get moving again. She sat on the bike and wrapped her fingers around the handlebars.

Her heart jumped into her throat.

A man.

Standing outside the door. White. Beady eyes. Dark hoodie clinging to his face.

Andy froze.

He cupped his hands to the glass.

She should scream. She should be quiet. She should look for a weapon. She should walk the bike back. She should hide in the shadows.

The man leaned closer, peering into the garage. He looked left, then right, then straight ahead.

Andy flinched, drawing in her shoulders like she could fold herself into obscurity.

He was staring right at her.

She held her breath. Waited. Trembled. He could see her. She was certain that he could see her.

Slowly, his head turned away, scanning left, then right, again. He took one last look directly at Andy, then disappeared.

She opened her mouth. She drew in a thimbleful of air. She leaned over the handlebars and tried not to throw up.

The man at the hospital—the one in the Alabama hat. Had he followed them home? Had he been lying in wait until he thought the coast was clear?

No. Alabama had been tall and slim. The guy at the garage door, Hoodie, was stocky, muscle-bound, about Andy's height but three times as wide.

The jangling noise had been Hoodie walking down the metal stairs.

He had checked to make sure the apartment was vacant.

He had checked to make sure the garage was empty.

And now he was probably going to break into her mother's house.

Andy furiously patted her pockets, even as she realized that her phone was upstairs, dead where she had left it. Laura had gotten rid of the landline last year. The mansions on either side probably didn't have phones, either. The bike ride back to Gordon's would take ten minutes at least and by then her mother could be—

Andy's heart jerked to a stop.

Her bladder wanted to release. Her stomach was filled with thumbtacks. She carefully stepped off the bike. She leaned it against the wall. The rain was a steady snare drum now. All that she could hear over the *shush-shush-shush* was her teeth chattering.

She made herself walk to the door. She reached out, wrapped her hand around the doorknob. Her fingers felt cold. Was Hoodie waiting on the other side of the door, back pressed to the garage, arms raised with a bat or a gun or just his giant hands that could strangle the life out of her?

Andy tasted vomit in her mouth. The water on her skin felt frozen. She told herself that the man was cutting through to the beach, but nobody cut through to the beach here. Especially in the rain. And lightning.

Andy opened the door. She bent her knees low, then peered out into the driveway. The light was still on in Laura's office. Andy saw no one—no shadows, no tripped floodlights, no man in a hoodie waiting with a knife beside the garage or looking through the windows to the house.

Her mother could take care of herself. She *had* taken care of herself. But that was with both hands. Now, one arm was strapped to her waist and Laura could barely walk across the kitchen on her injured leg without grabbing onto the counter for support.

Andy gently closed the garage door. She cupped her hands to the glass, the same as Hoodie. She looked into the dark space. Again, she could see nothing—not her bike, not the shelves of emergency food and water.

Her relief was only slight, because Hoodie had not walked up the driveway when he'd left. He had turned toward the house.

Andy brushed her fingers across her forehead. She was sweating underneath all the rain. Maybe the guy hadn't gone inside the bungalow. Why would a burglar choose the smallest house on the street, one of the smallest in the entire city? The surrounding mansions were filled with high-end electronics. Every Friday night, dispatch got at least one call from someone who had driven down from Atlanta expecting to enjoy a relaxing weekend and found instead that their TVs were gone.

Hoodie had been upstairs in the apartment. He had looked in the garage.

He hadn't taken anything. He was looking for something.

Someone.

Andy walked along the side of the house. The motion detector was not working. The floodlights were supposed to trip. She felt glass crunch under her sneaker. Broken lightbulbs? Broken motion detector? She stood on tiptoe, peered through the kitchen

86

window. To the right, the office door was ajar, but just slightly. The narrow opening cast a triangle of white light onto the kitchen floor.

Andy waited for movement, for shadows. There were none. She stepped back. The porch steps were to her left. She could enter the kitchen. She could turn on the lights. She could surprise Hoodie so that he turned around and shot her or stabbed her the same way that Jonah Helsinger had tried to do.

The two things had to be connected. That was the only thing that made sense. This was Belle Isle, not Atlantic City. Guys in hoodies didn't case bungalows in the pouring rain.

Andy walked to the back of the house. She shivered in the stiff breeze coming off the ocean. She carefully opened the door to the screened porch. The squeak of the hinge was drowned out by the rain. She found the key inside the saucer under the pansies.

Two French doors opened onto her mother's bedroom. Again, Andy cupped her hand to glass. Unlike the garage, she could see clear to the corners of the room. The nightlight was on in the bathroom. Laura's bed was made. A book was on the nightstand. The room was empty.

Andy pressed her ear to the glass. She closed her eyes, tried to focus all of her senses on picking up sounds from inside—feet creaking across the floor, her mother's voice calling for help, glass breaking, a struggle.

All she heard were the rocking chairs swaying in the wind.

Over the weekend, Andy had joined her mother on the porch to watch the sun rise.

"Andrea Eloise." Laura had smiled over her cup of tea. "Did you know that when you were born, I wanted to name you Heloise, but the nurse misunderstood me and she wrote down 'Eloise,' and your father thought it was so beautiful that I didn't have the heart to tell him she'd spelled it wrong?"

Yes, Andy knew. She had heard the story before. Every year, on or around her birthday, her mother contrived a reason to tell her that the *H* had been dropped.

Andy listened at the glass for another moment before forcing herself to move. Her fingers felt so thick she could barely slide the key into the lock. Tears filled her eyes. She was so scared. She had never been this terrified. Not even at the diner, because during the shooting spree, there was no time to think. Andy was reacting, not contemplating. Now, she had plenty of time to consider her actions and the scenarios reeling through her mind were all horrifying.

Hoodie could injure her mother—again. He could be inside, waiting for Andy. He could be killing Laura right now. He could rape Andy. He could kill her in front of her mother. He could rape them both and make one watch or he could kill them then rape them or—

Andy's knees nearly buckled as she walked into the bedroom. She pulled the door closed, cringing when the latch clicked. Rainwater puddled onto the carpet. She slipped out of her sneakers. Pushed back her wet hair.

She listened.

There was a murmuring sound from the other side of the house.

Conversational. Not threatening, or screaming, or begging for help. More like Andy used to hear from her parents after she went to bed.

"Diana Krall's going to be at the Fox next weekend."

"Oh, Gordon, you know jazz makes me nervous."

Andy felt her eyelids flutter like she was going to pass out. Everything was shaking. Inside her head, the sound of her heartbeat was like a gymnasium full of bouncing basketballs. She had to press her palm to the back of her leg to make herself walk.

The house was basically a square with a hallway that horse-shoed around the interior. Laura's office was where the dining room had been, off the front of the kitchen. Andy walked up the opposite side of the hallway. She passed her old bedroom, now a guest room, ignored all of the family photos and school drawings hanging on the walls.

"—do anything," Laura said, her tone firm and clear.

Andy stood in the living room. Only the foyer separated her from Laura's office. The pocket doors had been pulled wide open. The layout of the room was as familiar to Andy as her garage apartment. Couch, chair, glass coffee table with a bowl of potpourri, desk, desk chair, bookcase, filing cabinet, reproduction of the *Birth of Venus* on the wall beside two framed pages taken from a textbook called *Physiology and Anatomy for Speech-Language Pathology*.

A framed snapshot of Andy on the desk. A bright green leather blotter. A single pen. A laptop computer.

"Well?" Laura said.

Her mother was sitting on the couch. Andy could see part of her chin, the tip of her nose, her legs uncrossed, one hand resting on her thigh while the other was strapped to her waist. Laura's face was tilted slightly upward, looking at the person sitting in the leather chair.

Hoodie.

His jeans were soaked. A puddle spread out on the rug at his feet.

He said, "Let's think about our options here." His voice was deep. Andy could feel his words rattle inside her chest. "I could talk to Paula Koontz."

Laura was silent, then said, "I hear she's in Seattle."

"Austin." He waited a moment. "But good try."

There was silence, long and protracted.

Then Laura said, "Hurting me won't get you what you need."

"I'm not going to hurt you. I'm just going to scare the shit out of you."

Andy felt her eyelids start to flutter again. It was the way he said it—with conviction, almost with glee.

"Is that so?" Laura forced out a fake-sounding laugh. "You think I can be scared?"

"Depends on how much you love your daughter."

Suddenly, Andy was standing in the middle of her old bedroom. Teeth chattering. Eyes weeping. She couldn't remember

89

how she had gotten there. Her breath was huffing out of her lungs. Her heart had stopped beating, or maybe it was beating so fast that she couldn't feel it anymore.

Her mother's phone would be in the kitchen. She always left it to charge overnight.

Leave the house. Run for help. Don't put yourself in danger.

Andy's legs were shaky as she walked down the hall toward the back of the house. Involuntarily, her hand reached out, grabbed onto the doorjamb to Laura's bedroom, but Andy compelled herself to continue toward the kitchen.

Laura's phone was at the end of the counter, the section that was closest to her office, the part that was catching a triangle of light from the partially open door.

They had stopped talking. Why had they stopped talking?

Depends on how much you love your daughter.

Andy swung around, expecting to see Hoodie, finding nothing but the open doorway to her mother's bedroom.

She could run. She could justify leaving because her mother would want her to leave, to be safe, to get away. That's all Laura had wanted in the diner. That's all that she would want now.

Andy turned back toward the kitchen. She was inside of her body but somehow outside of it at the same time. She saw herself walking toward the phone at the end of the counter. The cold tile cupped her bare feet. Water was on the floor by the side entrance, probably from Hoodie. Andy's vision tunneled on her mother's cell phone. She gritted her teeth to keep them from clicking. If Hoodie was still sitting in the chair, all that separated him from Andy was three feet and a thin wooden door. She reached for the phone. Gently pulled out the charging cord. Slowly walked backward into the shadows.

"Tell me," Hoodie said, his voice carrying into the kitchen. "Have you ever had one of those dreams where you're being buried alive?" He waited. "Like you're suffocating?"

Andy's mouth was spitless. The pneumonia. The collapsed lung. The horrible wheezing sounds. The panicked attempts to breathe. Her mother had been terrified of suffocating. She was so obsessed with the fear of choking to death on the fluids from her lungs that the doctors had to give her Valium to make her sleep.

Hoodie said, "What I'm going to do is, I'm going to put this bag over your head for twenty seconds. You're going to feel like you're dying, but you're not." He added, "Yet."

Andy's finger trembled as she pressed the *home* button on her mother's phone. Both of their fingerprints were stored. Touching the button was supposed to unlock the screen, but nothing happened.

Hoodie said, "It's like dry waterboarding. Very effective."

"Please . . ." Laura choked on the word. "You don't have to do this."

Andy wiped her finger on the wall, trying to dry it.

"Stop!" her mother shouted so loudly that Andy almost dropped the phone. "Just listen to me. Just for a moment. Just listen to me."

Andy pressed *home* again.

Hoodie said, "I'm listening."

The screen unlocked.

"You don't have to do this. We can work something out. I have money."

"Money's not what I want from you."

"You'll never get it out of me. What you're looking for. I'll never—"

"We'll see."

Andy tapped the text icon. Belle Isle dispatch had adopted the Text-to-911 system six months ago. The alerts flashed at the top of their monitors.

"Twenty seconds," the man said. "You want me to count them for you?"

Andy's fingers worked furiously across the keyboard:

419 Seaborne Ave armed man imminent danger pls hurry

"The street's deserted," Hoodie said. "You can scream as loud as you need to."

Andy tapped the arrow to send.

"Stop—" Laura's voice rose in panic. "Please." She had started to cry. Her sobs were muffled like she was holding something to her mouth. "Please," she begged. "Oh, God, plea—"

Silence.

Andy strained to hear.

Nothing.

Not a cry or a gasp or even more pleading.

The quiet was deafening.

"One," Hoodie counted. "Two." He paused. "Three."

Clank. The heavy glass on the coffee table. Her mother was obviously kicking. Something *thumped* onto the carpet. Laura only had one hand free. She could barely lift a shopping bag.

"Four," Hoodie said. "Try not to wet yourself."

Andy opened her mouth wide, as if she could breathe for her mother.

"Five." Hoodie was clearly enjoying this. "Six. Almost halfway there."

Andy heard a desperate, high-pitched wheezing, the exact same sound her mother had made in the hospital when the pneumonia had collapsed her lung.

She grabbed the first heavy object she could find. The cast iron frying pan made a loud screech as she lifted it off the stove. There was no chance of surprising Hoodie now, no going back. Andy kicked open the door. Hoodie was standing over Laura. His hands were wrapped around her neck. He wasn't choking her. His fingers were sealing the clear plastic bag that encased her mother's head.

Hoodie turned, startled.

Andy swung the frying pan like a bat.

In the cartoons, the flat bottom of the pan always hit the coyote's head like the clapper on a bell, rendering him stunned.

In real life, Andy had the pan turned sideways. The cast iron edge wedged into the man's skull with a nauseatingly loud crack.

Not a ringing, but like the sound a tree limb makes when it breaks off.

92

The reverberations were so strong that Andy couldn't hold onto the handle.

The frying pan banged to the floor.

At first, Hoodie didn't respond. He didn't fall. He didn't rage. He didn't strike out. He just looked at Andy, seemingly confused.

She looked back.

Blood slowly flushed into the white of his left eye, moving through the capillaries like smoke, curling around the cornea. His lips moved wordlessly. His hand was steady as he reached up to touch his head. The temple was crushed at a sharp angle, a perfect match to the edge of the frying pan. He looked at his fingers.

No blood.

Andy's hand went to her throat. She felt like she had swallowed glass.

Was he okay? Was he going to be okay? Enough to hurt her? Enough to suffocate her mother? To rape them? To kill them both? To—

A trilling noise came from his throat. His mouth fell open. His eyes started to roll up. He reached for the chair, knees bent, trying to sit down, but he missed and fell to the floor.

Andy jumped back like she might get scalded.

He had fallen on his side, legs twisted, hands clutching his stomach.

Andy could not stop staring, waiting, trembling, panicking.

Laura said, "Andrea."

Andy's heart flickered like a candle. Her muscles were stone. She was fixed in position, cast like a statue.

Laura screamed, "Andrea!"

Andy was jolted out of her trance. She blinked. She looked at her mother.

Laura was trying to lean up on the couch. The whites of her eyes were dotted with broken blood vessels. Her lips were blue. More broken blood vessels pinpricked her cheeks. The plastic bag was still tied around her neck. Deep gouge marks ringed her skin. She had clawed the bag open with her fingers the same way Andy had chewed through the poncho trashbag.

"Hurry." Laura's voice was hoarse. "See if he's breathing."

Andy's vision telescoped. She felt dizzy. She heard a whistling sound as she tried to draw air into her lungs. She was starting to hyperventilate.

"Andrea," Laura said. "He has my gun in the waist of his jeans. Give it to me. Before he wakes up."

What?

"Andrea, snap out of it." Laura slid off the couch onto the floor. Her leg was bleeding again. She used her good arm to edge across the carpet. "We need to get the gun. Before he comes round."

Hoodie's hands moved.

"Mom!" Andy fell back against the wall. "Mom!"

Laura said, "It's okay, he's—"

Hoodie gave a sudden, violent jerk that knocked over the leather chair. His hands started moving in circles, then the circles turned into tremors that quaked into his shoulders, then head. His torso. His legs. Within seconds, his entire body convulsed into a full-blown seizure.

Andy heard a wail come out of her mouth. He was dying. He was going to die.

"Andrea," Laura said, calm, controlled. "Go into the kitchen."

"Mom!" Andy cried. The man's back arched into a half-circle. His feet kicked into the air. What had she done? What had she done?

"Andrea," Laura repeated. "Go into the kitchen."

He started to make a grunting noise. Andy covered her ears, but nothing could block the sound. She watched in horror as his fingers curved away from his hands. His mouth foamed. His eyes rolled wildly.

"Go into the—"

"He's dying!" Andy wailed.

The grunting intensified. His eyes had rolled up so far in his head that it looked like cotton had been stuffed into the sockets. Urine spread out from the crotch of his jeans. His shoe flew off. His hands scratched at the air.

94

"Do something!" Andy screamed. "Mom!"

Laura grabbed the frying pan. She lifted it over her head.

"No!" Andy leapt across the room. She wrenched the frying pan away from her mother. Laura's arm snaked around her waist before Andy could get away. She pulled her close, pressed her mouth to Andy's head. "Don't look, baby. Don't look."

"What did I do?" Andy keened. "What did I do?"

"You saved me," Laura said. "You saved me."

"I d-d-d . . ." Andy couldn't get out the words. "Mom . . . he's . . . I c-can't . . ."

"Don't look." Laura tried to cover Andy's eyes, but she pushed her mother's hand away.

There was total silence.

Even the rain had stopped tapping against the window.

Hoodie had gone still. The muscles in his face were relaxed. One eye stared up at the ceiling. The other looked toward the window. His pupils were solid black dimes.

Andy felt her heart tumble back down her throat.

The waist of the man's hoodie had slipped up. Above the white waistband of his underwear, Andy could see a tattoo of a smiling dolphin. It was cresting out of the water. The word *Maria* was written in an ornate script underneath.

"Is he—" Andy couldn't say the words. "Mom, is he—"

Laura did not equivocate. "He's dead."

"I k-k-k . . ." Andy couldn't get the word out. "K-kill . . . k-kill—"

"Andy?" Laura's tone had changed. "Do you hear sirens?" She turned to look out the window. "Did you call the police?"

Andy could only stare at the tattoo. Was Maria his girlfriend? His wife? Had she killed someone's dad?

"Andy?" Laura pushed herself back along the carpet. She reached under the couch with her hand. She was searching for something. "Darling, quickly. Get his wallet out of his pants."

Andy stared at her mother.

"Get his wallet. Now."

Andy did not move.

95

"Look under the couch, then. Come here. Now." Laura snapped her fingers. "Andy, come here. Do as I say."

Andy crawled toward the couch, not sure what she was supposed to do.

"Back corner," Laura told her. "Inside the batting on top of the spring. Reach up. There's a make-up bag."

Andy leaned down on her elbow so she could reach into the innards of the couch. She found a vinyl make-up bag, black with a brass zipper. It was heavy, packed tight.

How had it gotten here?

"Listen to me." Laura had the man's wallet. She pulled out the cash. "Take this. All of it. There's a town called Carrollton in West Georgia. It's on the state line. Are you listening to me?"

Andy had unzipped the bag. Inside was a flip phone with a charging cable, a thick stack of twenty-dollar bills, and a white, unlabeled keycard like you'd use to get into a hotel room.

"Andy," Laura was reaching for the framed photo on her desk. "You want the Get-Em-Go storage facility. Can you remember? G-e-t-e-m-g-o."

What?

"Take his wallet. Throw it in the bay."

Andy looked down at the leather wallet that her mother had tossed onto the floor. The driver's license showed through a plastic sleeve. Her eyes were so swollen from crying that she couldn't see the words.

Laura said, "Don't use the credit cards, all right? Just use the cash. Close your eyes." She broke the picture frame against the side of her desk. Glass splintered. She picked away the photo. There was a small key inside, the kind you'd use to open a padlock. "You'll need this, okay? Andy, are you listening? Take this. Take it."

Andy took the key. She dropped it into the open bag.

"This, too." Laura wedged the wallet into the make-up bag alongside the cash. "Unit one-twenty. That's what you need to remember: One-twenty. Get-Em-Go in Carrollton." She searched the man's pockets, found his keys. "This is for a Ford. He

96

probably parked in the cul-de-sac at the end of Beachview. Take it."

Andy took the keys, but her mind would not register what she was holding.

"Unit one-twenty. There's a car inside. Take that one, leave his Ford. Unhook the battery cables. That's very important, Andy. You need to cut the power to the GPS. Can you remember that, baby? Unhook the battery cables. Dad showed you what the battery looks like. Remember?"

Andy slowly nodded. She remembered Gordon showing her the parts of a car.

"The unit number is your birthday. One-twenty. Say it."

"One-twenty," Andy managed.

"The sirens are getting closer. You have to leave," Laura said. "I need you to leave. Now."

Andy was incapacitated. It was too much. Way too much.

"Darling." Laura cupped Andy's chin with her hand. "Listen to me. I need you to run. Now. Go out the back. Find the man's Ford. If you can't find it, then take Daddy's car. I'll explain it to him later. I need you to head northwest. Okay?" She gripped Andy's shoulder as she struggled to stand. "Andy, please. Are you listening?"

"Northwest," Andy whispered.

"Try to make it to Macon first, then buy a map, an actual paper map, and find Carrollton. Get-Em-Go is near the Walmart." Laura pulled Andy up by the arm. "You need to leave your phone here. Don't take anything with you." She shook Andy again. "Listen to me. Don't call Daddy. Don't make him lie for you."

"Lie for—"

"They're going to arrest me for this." She put her finger to Andy's lips to stop her protest. "It's okay, darling. I'll be okay. But you have to leave. You can't let Daddy know where you are. Do you understand? If you contact him, they'll know. They'll trace it back and find you. Telephone calls, email, anything. Don't reach out to him. Don't try to call me. Don't call any of your friends, or anyone you've ever had contact with, okay? Do you understand me? Do you hear what I'm saying?"

Andy nodded because that's what her mother wanted her to do.

"Keep heading northwest after Carrollton." Laura walked her through the kitchen, her arm tight around Andy's waist. "Somewhere far away, like Idaho. When it's safe, I'll call you on the phone that's in the bag."

Safe?

"You're so strong, Andrea. Stronger than you know." Laura was breathing hard. She was clearly trying not to cry. "I'll call you on that phone. Don't come home until you hear from me, okay? Only respond to my voice, my actual voice, saying these exact words: 'It's safe to come home.' Do you understand? Andy?"

The sirens were getting closer. Andy could hear them now. At least three cruisers. There was a dead man in the house. Andy had killed him. She had murdered a man and the cops were almost here.

"Andrea?"

"Okay," Andy breathed. "Okay."

"Get-Em-Go. One-twenty. Right?"

Andy nodded.

"Out the back. You need to run." Laura tried to push her toward the door.

"Mom." Andy couldn't leave without knowing. "Are you—are you a spy?"

"A what?" Laura looked bewildered.

"Or an assassin, or government agent, or—"

"Oh, Andy, no," Laura sounded as if she wanted to laugh. "I'm your mother. All I've ever been is your mother." She pressed her palm to the side of Andy's face. "I'm so proud of you, my angel. The last thirty-one years have been a gift. You are the reason I am alive. I would've never made it without you. Do you understand me? You are my heart. You are every ounce of blood in my body."

The sirens were close, maybe two streets over.

"I'm so sorry." Laura could no longer hold back her tears. Yesterday, she had killed a man. She had been stabbed, cut, almost suffocated. She had pushed away her family and not a tear had dropped from her eyes until this moment. "My angel. Please forgive me. Everything I've ever done is for you, my Andrea Heloise. Everything."

The sirens were out front. Tires screeched against pavement.

"Run," Laura begged. "Andy, please, my darling, please—run."

5

Wet sand caked into the insides of Andy's sneakers as she ran along the shore. She had the make-up bag clutched to her chest, fingers holding together the top because she dared not take the time to zip it. There was no moon, no light from the McMansions, nothing but mist in her face and the sounds of sirens at her back.

She looked over her shoulder. Flashlights were skipping around the outside of her mother's house. Shouting traveled down the beach.

"Clear on the left!"

"Clear in the back!"

Sometimes, when Andy stayed on a 911 call, she would hear the cops in the background saying those same words.

"It's okay to hang up now," she would tell the caller. *"The police will take care of you."*

Laura wouldn't tell the cops anything. She would probably be sitting at the kitchen table, mouth firmly closed, when they found her. Detective Palazzolo wouldn't be making any deals after tonight. Laura would be arrested. She would go to jail. She would appear in front of a judge and jury. She would go to prison.

Andy ran harder, like she could get away from the thought of her mother behind bars. She bit her lip until she tasted the metallic tang of blood. The wet sand had turned into concrete inside her shoe. There was a tiny bit of karmic retribution about the pain.

Hoodie was dead. She had killed him. She had murdered a man. Andy was a murderer.

She shook her head so hard that her neck popped. She tried to get her bearings. Seaborne extended three tenths of a mile before it dead-ended into Beachview. If she missed the turn-off, she would find herself in a more inhabited area of the Isle where someone might glance out the window and call the police.

Andy tried to count her footsteps, pacing off two hundred yards, then three hundred, then finally veering left away from the ocean. All of the McMansions had security gates to keep strangers from wandering in off the beach. City code forbade any permanent fences in front of the sand dunes, so people had erected flimsy wooden slats hanging from barbed wire to serve as a deterrent. Only some of the gates were alarmed, but all of them were marked with warnings that a siren would go off if they were opened.

Andy stopped at the first gate she came to. She ran her hand along the sides. Her fingers brushed against a plastic box with a wire coming out of it.

Alarmed.

She ran to the next gate and went through the same check.

Alarmed.

Andy cursed, knowing the fastest way to the street would be to climb over the dunes. She gingerly pushed the wooden slats with her foot. The wire bowed. Some unseen anchor slipped from the sand so that the fence fell low enough to step over. She lifted her leg, careful not to snag her shorts on the barbed wire. Sea oats crushed under her feet as she traversed the steep slope. She cringed at the destruction she was causing. By the time she made it to a stone path, she was limping.

Andy leaned her hand against the wall, stopped to take a breath. Her throat was so dry that she went into a coughing attack. She covered her mouth, waiting it out. Her eyes watered. Her lungs ached. When the coughing had finally passed, she let her hand drop. She took a step that might as well have been on glass. The sand in her sneakers had the consistency of clumping cat litter. Andy took them off, tried to shake them out. The synthetic mesh had turned into a cheese grater. Still, she tried to cram her feet back into the sneakers. The pain was too much. She was already bleeding.

Andy walked barefoot up the path. She thought about all of the clues that Detective Palazzolo would find when she arrived at the bungalow: Laura's face, especially her bloodshot eyes, still showing signs of suffocation. The plastic bag around her neck with the dead man's fingerprints on it. The dead man lying in the office by the overturned coffee table. The side of his head caved in. Urine soaking his pants. Foam drying on his lips. His eyes pointing in two different directions. Blood from Laura's leg streaked across the carpet. Andy's fingerprints on the handle of the frying pan.

In the driveway: broken glass from the floodlights. The lock on the kitchen door probably jimmied. The puddles on the kitchen tiles showing the path Hoodie had taken. More water showing Andy's route from the bedroom to the hall to the guest room to the living room and back again.

On the beach: Andy's footprints carved into the wet sand. Her destructive path up the dunes. Her blood, her DNA, on the stone path where she now stood.

Andy clamped her teeth closed and groaned into the sky. Her neck strained from the effort. She leaned over, elbows on her knees, bowed over by the impact of her horrible actions. None of this was right. Nothing made sense.

What was she supposed to do?

What *could* she do?

She needed to talk to her father.

Andy started to walk toward the road. She would go to Gordon's house. She would ask him what to do. He would help her do the right thing.

Andy stopped walking.

She knew what her father would do. Gordon would let Laura

take the blame. He would not allow Andy to turn herself in. He would not risk the possibility that she could go to prison for the rest of her life.

But then Palazzolo would find Andy's wet footprints inside Laura's house, more footprints in the sand, her DNA between the McMansions, and she would charge Gordon with lying to a police officer and accomplice to murder after the fact.

Her father could go to prison. He could lose his license to practice.

Don't make him lie for you.

Andy remembered the tears in her mother's eyes, her insistence that everything she'd done was for Andy. At a basic level, Andy had to trust that Laura was telling her to do the right thing. She continued up the driveway. Laura had guessed that the man's Ford would be in the Beachview Drive cul-de-sac. She had also said to run, so Andy started to run again, holding her sneakers in one hand and the make-up bag in the other.

She was rounding the corner when a bright light hit her face. Andy ducked back onto the stone path. Her first thought was that a police cruiser had hit her with the spotlight. Then she chanced a look up and realized she had triggered the motion detector on the floodlights.

Andy ran up the driveway. She kept to the middle of the street away from the motion detectors on the houses. She did not look back, but her peripheral vision had caught the distant rolling of the red and blue lights. It looked like every Belle Isle police cruiser had responded to the emergency text. Andy probably had minutes, possibly seconds, before someone in charge told them to fan out and search the area.

She got to the end of the one-way street. Beachview Drive dead-ended into Seaborne Avenue. There was a little dog-leg at the other end that served as beach access for emergency vehicles. Laura had guessed that the dead man's car would be there.

There was no Ford in sight.

Shit.

A pair of headlights approached from Beachview. Andy

panicked, running left, then right, then circling back and diving behind a palm tree as a black Suburban drove by. There was a giant, springy antenna on the bumper that told Andy the car belonged to law enforcement.

Andy looked back up Beachview Drive. There was an unpaved driveway halfway up, weeds and bushes overgrown at the entrance. One of the six remaining bungalows on Belle Isle was owned by the Hazeltons, a Pennsylvania couple who'd stopped coming down years ago.

Andy could hide there, try to figure out what to do next.

She checked Seaborne in case any cars were driving up the wrong way. She scanned Beachview for headlights. Then she jogged up the road, her bare feet slapping the asphalt, until she reached the Hazeltons' long, sandy driveway.

There was something off.

The overgrown tangle of bushes had been tamped down.

Someone had recently driven up to the house.

Andy skirted the bushes, heading into the yard instead of down the driveway. Her feet were bleeding so badly that the sand created a second layer of sole. She kept moving forward, crouching down to make herself less visible. No lights were on inside the Hazelton house. Andy realized she could sort of see in the darkness. It was later—or earlier—than she'd thought. Not exactly sunrise, but Andy recalled there was a sciencey explanation about how the rays bounced against the ocean surface and brought the light to the beach before you could see the sun.

Whatever the phenomenon, it allowed her to make out the Ford truck parked in the driveway. The tires were bigger than normal. Black bumpers. Tinted windows. Florida license plate.

There was another truck parked beside it—smaller; a white Chevy, probably ten years old but otherwise nondescript. The license plate was from South Carolina, which wasn't unusual this close to Charleston, but as far as Andy knew, the Hazeltons were still based in Pennsylvania.

Andy carefully approached the Chevy, crouching to look

inside. The windows were rolled down. She saw the key was in the ignition. There was a giant lucky rabbit's foot dangling from the keychain. Fuzzy dice hung from the mirror. Andy had no idea whether or not the truck belonged to the Hazeltons, but leaving the keys inside seemed like something the older couple would do. And the dice and giant rabbit's foot keychain was right up their grandson's alley.

Andy considered her options.

No GPS in the Chevy. No one to report it stolen. Should she take this instead? Should she leave the dead man's truck behind?

Andy let Laura do the thinking for her. Her mother had said to take the dead man's truck so she was going to take the dead man's truck.

Andy approached the Ford cautiously. The dark windows were rolled tight. The doors were locked. She found Hoodie's keys in the make-up bag. The ring had a can opener and the Ford key. No house keys, but maybe they were inside the truck.

Instead of pressing the remote, Andy used the actual key to unlock the door. Inside, she smelled a musky cologne mingled with leather. She tossed the make-up bag onto the passenger's seat. She had to brace her hands on the sides of the cab to pull herself up into the driver's seat.

The door gave a solid *thunk* when she closed it.

Andy stuck the key into the ignition. She turned it slowly, like the truck would blow up or self-destruct with the wrong move. The engine gave a deep purr. She put her hand on the gear. She stopped, because something was wrong.

There should have been light coming from the dash, but there was nothing. Andy pressed her fingers to the console. Construction paper, or something that felt like it, was taped over the display. She turned her head. The dome light had not come on, either.

Andy thought about Hoodie sitting in the truck blacking out all the light then parking it at the Hazeltons.

And then she thought about the light in her mother's office. The only light Laura had left on in the house. Andy had assumed her mother had forgotten to turn it off, but maybe Laura had not been sleeping in the recliner. Maybe she had been sitting on the couch in her office waiting for someone like Hoodie to break in.

He has my gun in the waistband of his jeans.

Not *a* gun, but *my* gun.

Andy felt her mouth go dry.

When had her mother bought a gun?

A siren whooped behind her. Andy cringed, but the cruiser rolled past rather than turning down the driveway. She moved the gear around, slowly letting her foot off the brake, testing each notch until she found reverse.

There was no seeing out the dark windows as she backed out of the driveway. Tree limbs and thorny bushes scraped at the truck. She hit Beachview Drive sideways, the truck wheels bumping off the hard edge of the curb.

Andy performed the same trick with the gear until she found drive. The headlights were off. In the pre-dawn darkness, she had no way of finding the dial to turn them on. She kept both hands tight on the wheel. Her shoulders were up around her ears. She felt like she was about to roll off a cliff.

She drove past the road to Gordon's house. The flashing lights of a police cruiser were at the end of his street. Andy accelerated before she could be seen. And then she realized that she could not be seen because all of the lights were off, not just the interior lights and the headlights. She glanced into the rearview mirror as she tapped the brakes. The taillights did not come on, either.

This was not good.

It was one thing to cover all of your lights when you were on the way to doing something bad, but when you were leaving the bad thing, when the road was crawling with police officers, driving without your lights was tantamount to writing the word GUILTY on your forehead.

There was one bridge in and out of Belle Isle. The Savannah police would be streaking down one side while Andy, illuminated by the sun reflecting off the water, would be trying to sneak out of town on the other.

106

She pulled into the parking lot of what happened to be the Mall of Belle Isle. She jumped out of the truck and walked around to the back. Some kind of thick black tape covered the taillights. She picked at the edge and found that it wasn't tape, but a large magnetic sheet. The other light had the same.

The corners were rounded off. The sheets were the exact size needed to cover both the brake lights and the back-up lights.

Andy's brain lacked the ability to process why this mattered. She tossed the magnets into the back of the truck and got behind the wheel. She peeled away the construction paper on the console. Like the magnets, the paper was cut to the exact size. More black paper covered the radio and lighted buttons on the console.

She found the knob for the headlights. She drove away from the mall. Her heart was thumping against the side of her neck as she approached the bridge. She held her breath. She crossed the bridge. No other cars were on the road. No other cars were on the turn-off.

As she accelerated toward the highway, she caught a glimpse of three Savannah cruisers rushing toward the bridge, lights rolling, sirens off.

Andy let out the breath she'd been holding.

There was a sign by the road:

MACON 170

ATLANTA 248

Andy checked the gas gauge. The tank was full. She would try to make the over four-hour trip to Atlanta without stopping, then buy a map at the first gas station she found. Andy had no idea how far Carrollton was from there, or how she'd find the Get-Em-Go storage facility near the Walmart.

The unit number is your birthday. One-twenty. Say it.

"One-twenty," Andy spoke the numbers aloud, suddenly confused.

Her birthday was yesterday, August twentieth.

Why had Laura said that she was born in January?

107

6

Andy drove up and down what seemed like the city of Carrollton's main drag. She had easily found the Walmart, but unlike the Walmart, the Get-Em-Go storage facility did not have a gigantic, glowing sign that you could see from the interstate.

The bypass into Atlanta had been tedious and—worse—unnecessary. Andy had been tempted to use the truck's navigation system, but in the end decided to follow Laura's orders. She'd bought a folding map of Georgia once she was inside the Atlanta city limits. The drive from Belle Isle to Carrollton should have been around four and a half hours. Because Andy had driven straight through Atlanta during morning rush hour, six hours had passed before she'd finally reached the Walmart. Her eyelids had been so heavy that she'd been forced to take a two-hour nap in the parking lot.

How did people locate businesses before they had the internet?

The white pages seemed like an obvious source, but there were no phone booths in sight. Andy had already asked a Walmart security guard for directions. She sensed it was too dangerous to keep asking around. Someone might get suspicious. Someone might call a cop. She did not have her driver's license or proof of insurance. Her rain-soaked hair had dried in crazy, unkempt swirls. She was driving a stolen truck with Florida plates and dressed like a teenager who had woken up in the wrong bed during spring break.

Andy had been in such a panicked hurry to get to Carrollton that she hadn't bothered to wonder why her mother was sending her here in the first place. What was inside the storage facility? Why did Laura have a hidden key and a flip phone and money and what was Andy going to find if she ever located the Get-Em-Go?

The questions seemed pointless after over an hour of searching. Carrollton wasn't a Podunk town, but it wasn't a buzzing metropolis, either. Andy had figured her best bet was to aimlessly drive around in search of her destination, but now she was worried that she would never find it.

The library.

Andy felt the idea hit her like an anvil. She had passed the building at least five times, but she was just now making the connection. Libraries had computers and, more importantly, anonymous access to the internet. At the very least, she would be able to locate the Get-Em-Go.

Andy swerved a massive U-turn and got into the turning lane for the library. The big tires bumped over the sidewalk. She had her choice of parking spaces, so she drove to the far end. There were only two other cars, both old clunkers. She assumed they belonged to the library staff. The branch was small, probably the size of Laura's bungalow. The plaque beside the front door said the building opened at 9 a.m.

Eight minutes.

She stared at the squat building, the crisp edges of the red brick, the grainy pores in the mortar. Her vision was oddly sharp. Her mouth was still dry, but her hands had stopped shaking and her heart no longer felt like it was going to explode. The stress and exhaustion from the last few days had peaked around Macon. Andy was numb to almost everything now.

She felt no remorse.

Even when she thought about the horrible last few seconds of Hoodie's life, she could not summon an ounce of pity for the man who had tortured her mother.

What Andy did feel was guilt over her lack of remorse.

She remembered years ago one of her college friends proclaiming that everyone was capable of murder. At the time, Andy had silently bristled at the generalization, because if everyone were truly capable of murder, there would be no such thing as rape. It was the kind of stupid *what if* question that came up at college parties—what if you had to defend yourself? Could you kill someone? Would you be able to do it? Guys always said yes because guys were hardwired to say yes to everything. Girls tended to equivocate, maybe because statistically they were a billion times more likely to be attacked. When the question invariably came round to Andy, she had always joked that she would do exactly what she'd ended up doing at the diner: cower and wait to die.

Andy hadn't cowered in her mother's kitchen. Maybe it was different when someone you loved was being threatened. Maybe it was genetic.

Suicides ran in families. Was it the same with killing?

What Andy really wanted to know was what had her face looked like. In that moment, as she kicked open the office door and swung the pan, she had been thoughtless, as in, there was not a single thought in her mind. Her brain was filled with the equivalent of white noise. There was a complete disconnect between her head and her body. She was not considering her own safety. She was not thinking about her mother's life or death. She was just acting.

A killing machine.

Hoodie had a name. Andy had looked at his driver's license before she'd thrown the wallet into the bay.

Samuel Godfrey Beckett, resident of Neptune Beach, Florida, born October 10, 1981.

The Samuel Beckett part had thrown her off, because Hoodie's existence outside Laura's office had taken shape with the name. He'd had a parent who was a fan of Irish avant-garde poetry. That somehow made his life more vivid than the *Maria* tattoo. Andy could picture Hoodie's mother sitting on her back porch watching the sunrise, asking her son, "Do you know who I named you after?" the same way that Laura always told Andy the story about how the *H* got dropped from her middle name.

Andy pushed away the image.

She had to remind herself that Samuel Godfrey Beckett was, in Detective Palazzolo's parlance, a *bad guy*. There were likely a lot of bad things Samuel or Sam or Sammy had done in his lifetime. You didn't darken all the interior lights in your truck and cover your taillights on a whim. You did these things deliberately, with malice aforethought.

And someone probably paid you for your expertise.

Nine a.m. A librarian unlocked the door and waved Andy in.

Andy waved back, then waited until the woman went inside before retrieving the black make-up bag from under the seat. She opened the brass zip. She checked the phone to make sure the battery was full. No calls registered on the screen. She closed the phone and shoved it back into the bag alongside the keycard, the padlock key, the thick bundle of twenties.

She had counted the stash in Atlanta. There was only $1,061 to get Andy through however many days she needed to get through before the phone rang and her mother said it was safe to come home.

Andy felt stricken by the thought that she would have to devise some kind of budget. A Gordon budget. Not an Andy budget, which consisted of praying that cash would appear from the ether. She had no way of making more money. She couldn't get a job without using her social security number and even then, she had no idea how long she'd need the job for. And she especially did not know what kind of job she could possibly be qualified to do in Idaho.

Keep heading northwest after Carrollton . . . Somewhere far away, like Idaho.

Where the hell had her mother gotten that idea? Andy had only ever been to Georgia, New York, Florida and the Carolinas. She knew nothing about Idaho except that there was probably a lot of snow and undoubtedly a lot of potatoes.

$1,061.

Gas, meals, hotel rooms.

Andy zipped the bag closed. She got out of the truck. She pulled down the ridiculously small T-shirt, which was as flattering as Saran Wrap on a waffle fry. Her shorts were stiff from the salt air. Her feet hurt so badly that she was limping. There was a cut on her shin that she did not remember getting. She needed a shower. She needed Band-Aids, better shoes, long pants, shirts, underwear . . . that thousand bucks and change would probably not last more than a few days.

She tried to do the math in her head as she walked toward the library. She knew from one of her former roommates that the driving distance between New York City and Los Angeles was almost three thousand miles. Idaho was somewhere in the upper left part of the United States—Andy sucked at geography—but it was definitely northwest.

If she had to guess, Andy would assume the driving time was about the same from Georgia to Idaho as from New York to California. The trip from Belle Isle to Macon was right under two hundred miles, which took about two and a half hours to drive, so basically she was looking at around twelve days of driving, eleven nights in cheap motels, three meals a day, gas to get there, whatever supplies she needed in the immediate . . .

Andy shook her head. Would it take twelve days to get to Idaho?

She really sucked at math, too.

"Good morning," the librarian said. "Coffee's ready in the corner."

"Thanks," Andy mumbled, feeling guilty because she wasn't a local taxpayer and shouldn't technically be able to use all of this stuff for free. Still, she poured herself a cup of coffee and sat down at a computer.

The glowing screen made her feel oddly at ease. She had been without her phone or iPad all night. Andy had not realized how much time she wasted listening to Spotify or checking Instagram and Snapchat and reading blogs and doing Hogwarts house sorting quizzes until she lacked the means to access them.

112

She stared at the computer screen. She drank her coffee. She thought about emailing her father. Or calling him. Or sending him a letter.

If you contact him, they'll know. They'll trace it back and find you.

Andy put down her cup. She typed *Get-Em-Go Carrollton GA* into the browser, then clicked on the map.

She almost laughed.

The storage facility was just over one hundred yards behind the library. She knew this because the high school's football field separated the two. Andy could've walked to it. She checked the hours on the Get-Em-Go website. The banner across the top said that the facilities were open twenty-four hours, but then it also said that the office was open from 10 a.m. to 6 p.m.

Andy looked at the clock. She had fifty minutes.

She opened MapQuest on the computer and pulled up driving directions from Georgia to Idaho. Two thousand three hundred miles. Thirty hours of driving, not twelve days, which was why Andy had been forced to take Algebra twice. She had selected PRINT before her brain could tell her not to. Andy clicked CANCEL. The library charged ten cents a page, but money wasn't the issue. She would have to walk up to the counter and ask for the pages, which meant the librarian would see that she was driving to Idaho.

Which meant if somebody else, maybe a guy like Hoodie who had magnets on his taillights and construction paper on his dashboard, asked the librarian where Andy was heading, then the librarian would know.

They'll trace it back and find you. Telephone calls, email, anything.

Andy silently mulled over Laura's warning in her head. Obviously, *they* were the ones who'd hired Hoodie, aka Samuel Godfrey Beckett. But what exactly had *they* hired him to do? Hoodie had told Laura that he wasn't going to kill her. At least not instantly. He'd said that he was going to scare the shit out of her by suffocating her with the plastic bag. Andy's knowledge of torture came mostly from Netflix. If you weren't a torturer in a sadistic, *Saw* kind of way, then you were a torturer in the badass *Jack Reacher* way, which meant you wanted information.

What information did a fifty-five-year-old divorced speech pathologist have that was worth hiring a goon to torture it out of her?

Better yet, during what period of her life had Laura accumulated this torturable information?

Everything Detective Palazzolo had said about Laura's past, from being born in Rhode Island to attending UGA to buying the house on Belle Isle tracked with what Andy knew to be true. There was no unexplained gap in Laura's history. She had never been out of the country. She never even took vacations because she already lived right on the beach.

So what did Laura know that *they* wanted to torture out of her?

And what was so important that Laura would endure torture rather than give it up?

Andy fluttered out air between her lips. She could spend the rest of her life circling down this rabbit hole.

She located the scratch paper and pencils beside the computer. She took several sheets and began to transcribe the directions to Idaho: *75S to 84E to 80E, NE2E, 1-29S, I70E . . .*

Andy stared at the jumble of numbers and letters. She would need to buy another map. There would be a rest stop at the Georgia/Alabama border. First, she would go to the storage facility, change out the truck for the car Laura had said would be there, then head northwest.

She fluttered her lips again.

She was taking a hell of a lot on her mother's word. Then again, following her own instincts would've meant that Andy would be at the funeral home right now sobbing on Gordon's shoulder while he worked out burial arrangements for her mother.

Andy's fingers returned to the keyboard. She looked over her shoulder. The librarians had disappeared, probably to log in the returned books or practice shushing people.

Andy clicked on PREFERENCES under the Google tab. She set the browser to Incognito Mode to mask her browsing history. She probably should've done this first thing. Or maybe it was overkill. Or maybe she should stop berating herself for acting paranoid and just accept the fact that she *was* paranoid for a very damn good reason.

The first site she went to was the *Belle Isle Review*.

The front page was devoted to Laura Oliver, local speech pathologist and killing machine. They didn't actually call her a killing machine, but they'd quoted Alice Blaedel in the first paragraph, which was the same as.

Andy scanned the article. There was no mention of a man in a hoodie found with a frying-pan-shaped indentation in his head. There wasn't even a stolen vehicle report on the black truck. She clicked through the other stories and gave them a quick read.

Nothing.

She sat back in her chair, perplexed.

Behind her, the door opened. An old man shuffled in, heading straight for the coffee as he launched into a political tirade.

Andy didn't know who the tirade was for, but she tuned out the rant and pulled up CNN.com. The site led with the *Killing Machine* quote in the headline. Gordon was right about a lot of things, but Andy knew her father would not be pleased to be proven correct about the focus of the news stories. The patheticness of Jonah Lee Helsinger's life was highlighted in the second paragraph:

Six months ago, Helsinger's sheriff father, a war veteran and local hero, was tragically killed in a stand-off with a gunman, around the same time police believe young Helsinger's thoughts turned to murder.

Andy checked FoxNews.com, the *Savannah Reporter*, the *Atlanta Journal-Constitution*.

All of the stories were focused on Laura Oliver and what she had done at the Rise-n-Dine. There was no mention of Samuel Godfrey Beckett, or even an unidentified murder victim in a hoodie.

Had Laura managed to move the body? That didn't seem possible. Andy supposed her mother could've refused the police entry into the house, but the 911 text sent from Laura's phone was probable cause for entry. Even if Laura managed to turn away the Belle Isle cops, the person in that unmarked black Suburban would not have taken no for an answer.

Andy tapped her finger on the mouse as she tried to think it through.

Someone with a lot of connections was keeping a tight lid on the story.

They?

The same people who had sent Hoodie? The same people Laura was terrified would track down Andy?

She felt her heart bang against the base of her throat. Half the police force would have been outside Laura's bungalow. Probably Palazzolo, maybe even the Georgia Bureau of Investigation. That would mean *they* had some kind of pull with the governor, maybe even the feds.

Andy checked behind her.

The old man was leaning on the check-in desk, trying to engage one of the librarians in a political discussion.

Andy looked at the time on the computer again, watched the seconds turn into minutes.

The unit number is your birthday. One-twenty.

Andy put down the coffee. She typed in January 20, 1987.

January 20, 1987, was a Tuesday. People born on this day are Aquarius. Ronald Reagan was president. "Walk Like an Egyptian" by the Bangles was on the radio. Critical Condition *starring Richard Pryor topped the box office.* Tom Clancy's Red Storm Rising *was #1 on the* New York Times *bestseller list.*

Andy counted back nine months in her head and entered *April 1986 news* into the search. Instead of a month-specific timeline, she got a general overview of the year:

US bombs Libya. Iran–Contra. Chernobyl nuclear disaster. Perestroika. Halley's Comet. Challenger explosion. Swedish Prime Minister murdered. Oslo G-FAB assassination. Pan-Am 73

116

hijacked. Explosion on TWA jet over Greece. Mercantile bombing. FBI Miami bank shoot-out. Oprah Winfrey Show *debuts. 38,401 cases of AIDS worldwide.*

Andy stared at the words, only some of which seemed familiar. She could spend all day backtracking the events, but the fact was, you couldn't find something if you didn't know what you were looking for.

Paula Koontz.

The name had been edging around Andy's thoughts for the last few hours. She had never, ever heard her mother mention a woman named Paula. As far as Andy knew, all of Laura's friends were in Belle Isle. She never talked to anyone else on the phone. She wasn't even on Facebook because she claimed there was no one back in Rhode Island she wanted to keep in touch with.

I could talk to Paula Koontz.

I hear she's in Seattle.

Austin. But good try.

Laura had tried to fake out Hoodie. Or maybe she was testing him? But testing him for what?

Andy searched for *Paula Koontz Austin TX.*

Nothing Austin-specific came back, but apparently, Paula Koontz was a popular name for real estate agents in the northeast.

"Koontz," Andy whispered the word aloud. It didn't sound right to her ears. She had been thinking more like Dean Koontz when Hoodie had said it more like "koontz-ah."

She tried *koontze, koontzee, khoontzah* . . .

Google asked: *do you mean koontah?*

Andy clicked the suggested search. Nothing, but Google offered *khoontey* as an alternative. She kept clicking through the *do you means*. Several iterations later brought up a faculty directory for the University of Texas at Austin.

Paula Kunde was currently teaching *Introduction to Irish Women's Poetry and Feminist Thought* on Mondays, Wednesdays and Fridays. She was head of the women's studies department.

Her book, *The Madonna and Madonna: Like a Virgin from Jesus Christ to Ronald Reagan*, was available in paperback from IndieBound.

Andy enlarged the woman's photo, which had been taken in an unflattering side profile. Black and white, but that didn't help matters. It was hard to tell how old Paula was because she'd obviously spent way too much time in the sun. Her face was worn and craggly. She was at least Laura's age, but she did not look like any of her mother's usual friends, who wore Eileen Fisher and sunscreen every time they left the house.

Paula Kunde was basically a washed-out old hippie. Her hair was a mixture of blonde and gray with an unnatural-looking dark streak in the bangs. Her shirt, or dress, or whatever she was wearing, had a Native American pattern.

The sunken look to her cheeks reminded Andy of Laura during chemo.

Andy scrolled through Kunde's credentials. Publications in *Feminist Theory and Exposition*, several keynote speaker slots at feminist conferences. Kunde had earned her undergrad at the University of California, Berkeley, and her master's at Stanford, which explained the hippie vibe. Her doctorate came from a state college in western Connecticut, which seemed weird because Bryn Mawr or Vassar would've better suited her field of study, especially with a Stanford master's, which was to Andy's unfinished technical theater arts degree as diamonds were to dog shit.

More importantly, there was nothing in Paula Kunde's résumé that indicated she would ever cross paths with Laura. Feminist theory did not overlap with speech therapy in any way that Andy could think of. Laura was more likely to ridicule an old hippie than befriend one. So why had her mother recognized this woman's name smack in the middle of being tortured?

"Hey, hon." The librarian smiled down at Andy. "Sorry, but we're gonna have to ask you not to drink coffee around the computers." She nodded toward the old guy, who was glaring

118

at Andy over his own steaming cup of coffee. "Rules have to apply to everybody."

"I'm sorry," Andy said, because it was her nature to apologize for everything in her orbit. "I was leaving anyway."

"Oh, you don't have to—" the woman tried, but Andy was already getting up.

"I'm sorry." Andy stuffed the scribbled directions to Idaho into her pocket. She tried to smile at the old man as she left. He did not return the gesture.

Outside, the intense sunlight made her eyes water. Andy had to find some sunglasses before she went blind. She guessed Walmart would be the best place to go. She would also need to purchase some essentials like underwear and jeans and another T-shirt, plus maybe a jacket in case Idaho was cold this time of year.

Andy stopped walking. Her knees went wobbly.

Someone was looking inside the truck. Not just glancing as he walked by but looking with his hands pressed to the glass the same way Hoodie had peered through the garage door a few hours ago. The man was wearing a blue baseball cap, jeans and a white T-shirt. His face was cast in shadow under the brim of his hat.

Andy felt a scream get caught up in her throat. Her heart boxed at her ribs as she walked backward, which was stupid because the guy could turn around any minute and see her. But he did not, even as Andy darted around the back of the building, her throat straining from the scream that she could not let out.

She ran into the woods, frantically trying to summon up the Google Earth view, the high school behind the library, the squat storage facility with its rows of metal buildings. The relief she felt when she saw the high fence around the football field was only dampened by the fear that she was being followed. With every step, Andy tried to talk herself out of her paranoia. The guy in the hat hadn't seen her. Or maybe it didn't matter if he had. The black truck was nice. Maybe the guy was looking to buy one. Or maybe he was looking to see how to break in. Or maybe he was looking for Andy.

You think I can be scared?

Depends on how much you love your daughter.

The Get-Em-Go office lights were off. A sign on the door read CLOSED. A chain-link fence, even taller than the one at the high school, ringed around the storage units. The low one-story buildings with metal roll-up doors looked like something you'd see in a *Mad Max* movie. There was a gate across the driveway. A keypad was at car-window height, but it didn't have numbers, just a black plastic square with a red light.

She unzipped the make-up bag. She found the white, unlabeled keycard. She pressed it to the black square. The red light turned green. The gate screeched as it moved back on rubber tires.

Andy closed her eyes. She tried to calm herself. She had a right to be here. She had a keycard. She had a unit number. She had a key.

Still, her legs felt shaky as she walked into the compound. There would be answers inside the storage unit. Andy would find out something about her mother. Maybe something that she did not want to know. That Laura did not want her to know—not until now, because *they* were after her.

Andy wiped sweat from the back of her neck. She checked behind her to make sure she was not being followed. There was no way of knowing whether or not she was safe. The complex was huge. She counted at least ten buildings, all of them about fifty feet long with rolled doors like dirty teeth. Andy checked the signs until she found building one hundred. She paced down the aisle and stopped in front of unit one-twenty.

Her birthday.

Not the one she'd had all of her life, but the one Laura told her was real.

"Christ," Andy hissed.

She wasn't sure what was real anymore.

The padlock looked new, or at least it wasn't rusted like the other ones. Andy reached into the make-up bag and retrieved the tiny key. She could not keep the tremble out of her hands as she opened the padlock.

The smell was the first thing she noticed: clean, almost sanitized. The concrete floor looked like it had been poured last week. There were no cobwebs in the corners. No scuffs or fingerprints on the walls. Empty particleboard shelves lined the back. A tiny metal desk with a lamp was shoved into the corner.

A dark blue station wagon was parked in the middle of the space.

Andy found the light switch. She closed the rolling door behind her. Instantly, the heat started to swelter, but she thought about the man looking inside the truck—not her truck, but the dead man's truck—and figured she had no choice.

The first thing she checked out was the car, which was so boxy it looked like something Fred Flintstone would drive. The paint was pristine. The tires had to be brand new. A sticker on the windshield said the oil had been changed four months ago. As with everything else inside the unit, there was no dust, no grime. The car could have been sitting on a showroom floor.

Andy peered inside the open driver's side window. There were rolly things, like actual cranks that you had to turn to open and close the windows. The seats were dark blue vinyl, one long bench, no center console. The radio had thick white punch-buttons. There were big silver knobs and slider controls. The gearshift was on the steering wheel. The dash had stickers on the flat parts to simulate woodgrain. The odometer showed only 22,184 miles.

Andy didn't recognize the logo on the steering wheel, a pentagon with a star inside, but there were raised metal letters on the outside of the car that read RELIANT K FRONT WHEEL DRIVE.

She went around to the other side and reached in to open the glove box. Andy reeled back. A gun had fallen out; a revolver, the same type that Jonah Helsinger had pointed at Laura's chest. There were scratch marks on the side where the serial number had been shaved off. Andy stared at the nasty-looking weapon sitting on the floorboard, waiting, like it might suddenly twitch.

It did not.

She found the owner's manual.

1989 Plymouth Reliant SE Wagon.

She flipped through the pages. The graphics were old, the illustrations clearly placed by hand. A twenty-nine-year-old car with barely any miles on it. Two years younger than Andy. Stored in a place that Andy did not know about in a town that she had never heard of before her mother told her to go there.

So many questions.

Andy started to walk around the back of the car, but stopped. She turned around and stood by the closed door. She listened to make sure a car hadn't pulled up, or a man wasn't standing on the other side. Just to be extra paranoid, she lay down on her stomach. She looked under the crack to the door.

Nothing.

Andy pushed herself up. She wiped her hands on her shorts. She continued her walk around the station wagon to check the license plate.

Canada. The plate design was as boxy as the car; blue on white with a crown between the letters and numbers, the words *Yours To Discover* at the bottom. The emissions sticker read 18 DEC, which meant that the registration was current.

Andy knew from her work at dispatch that the NCIC, the National Crime Information Center, shared information with Canada. The thing was, the system only checked for stolen vehicles. If a cop pulled over this car, all they'd be able to verify was that the registered owner's name matched the driver's license.

Which meant that for the last twenty-nine years, her mother had kept a secret, untraceable car hidden from the world.

From Andy.

She opened the wagon's hatch. The springs worked silently. She rolled back the vinyl cover obscuring the cargo area. Navy-blue sleeping bag, a pillow, an empty cooler, a box of Slim Jims, a case of water, a white beach tote filled with paperbacks, batteries, a flashlight, a first aid kit.

Underneath it was a light blue Samsonite suitcase. Fake leather. Gold zippers. Carry-on size. Not the kind with wheels but the kind you had to carry. The bag had a top and a bottom clam-shell design. Andy opened the top first. She found three of everything: jeans, white silk panties, matching white bras, socks, white button-up shirts with polo ponies on the front, and a tan Members Only jacket.

None of the clothes looked like anything her mother would wear. Maybe that was the point. Andy slipped off her shorts and pulled on the underwear. She preferred cotton, but anything was better than the shorts. The jeans were loose at the waist, but again, she was in no position to complain. She removed the twenties from the make-up bag and shoved them into the back pocket. She changed out of her shirt but kept her bra because Laura was two cups bigger. At least she used to be.

Which meant that her mother had packed this bag before the cancer diagnosis three years ago.

Andy turned the suitcase over. She unzipped the other side.

Holy shit.

Stacks of money. Twenties again, each bundle wrapped with a lavender strap that said $2,000. The bill design looked like the old kind before all the new security features had been added. Andy counted the stacks. Ten across, three wide, four deep.

Two hundred and forty thousand dollars.

She zipped up the bag, pulled the vinyl cargo cover over everything, then closed the hatch.

Andy leaned against the car for a moment, her mind reeling. Was it worth it to wonder where her mother had gotten all of this money? She would be better served wondering how many unicorns were left in the forest.

The shelves behind the car were empty but for two jugs of bleach, a scrub brush and a folded pile of white cleaning rags. An upside down mop and broom were in the corner. Andy ran her hand along the particleboard shelves. No dust. Her mother, who was not a neat freak, had scrubbed this place top to bottom.

Why?

Andy sat down at the desk in the corner. She turned on the lamp. She checked the drawers. A box of pens. Two pencils. A legal pad. A leather folio. The keys to the Plymouth. The file drawer was packed with empty hanging files. Andy pushed them aside. She reached into the back and found a small shoebox with the lid taped on.

Andy put the box on the desk.

She opened the leather folio. Two pockets. One held a car registration receipt from the Province of Ontario for a blue 1989 Plymouth Reliant. The owner's name was listed as Daniela Barbara Cooper. The original registration date was August 20, the day Andy had always thought was her birthday, but two years from her birth, 1989. The annual car tag receipt was clipped to the corner. The printout listed the date it was processed as May 12, 2017.

Last year.

There was no calendar to confirm, but the date had to be around Mother's Day. Andy tried to think back. Had she picked up her mother from the airport before taking her to lunch? Or was that the year before? Laura didn't often leave Belle Isle, but at least once a year, she attended a professional conference. This had been going on since Andy's childhood and she'd never bothered to look up the events because why would she?

What she did know was that the annual pilgrimage was very important to her mother. Even when Laura was sick from the chemo treatments, she had made Andy drive her to the Savannah airport so she could attend a speech pathologist thing in Houston.

Had she really gone to Houston? Or had she skipped over to Austin to see her old friend Professor Paula Kunde?

Once Andy dropped her off at the airport, she had no idea where Laura went.

Andy dug around inside the other folio pocket. Two laminated cards. The first was a light blue Ontario, Canada, enhanced driver's license.

The *enhanced* part meant the license could be used for sea and land US border crossings. So, no taking an airplane to Canada, but a car could get through.

The photo on the license showed Laura before the cancer had taken some of the roundness from her cheeks. The expiration date was in 2024. Her mother was listed by the same name as the owner of the Reliant, Daniela Barbara Cooper, born December 15, 1964, which was wrong because Laura's birthdate was April 9, 1963, but what the hell did that matter because her mother, as far as Andy knew, was not currently residing in apartment 20 at 22 Adelaide Street West in Toronto, Ontario.

D.B. Cooper.

Andy wondered if the name was some kind of joke, but given where she was sitting, maybe it wasn't crazy to wonder if Laura was the famous hijacker who'd parachuted out of a plane with millions of dollars and never been heard from again.

Except Cooper was a man, and in the seventies Laura was still a teenager.

This was '77, so I would've been fourteen years old, more Rod Stewart than Elvis.

Andy pulled out the other card. Also from Ontario, also with Daniela Cooper's name and birthdate. This one said HEALTH • SANTE. Andy had taken Spanish in high school. She had no idea what *sante* meant, but she wondered why the hell her mother hadn't used Canada's national insurance program instead of depleting most of her retirement savings to pay for her cancer treatments in the United States.

Which brought her to the shoebox. Taped closed, hidden in a desk drawer inside a locked, secret storage facility. The logo on the outside was from Thom McAn. The box was small, definitely not for adult-sized shoes. When Andy was little, Laura always took her to the Charleston mall to buy shoes before school started.

Whatever was inside was lightweight, but felt like a bomb.

Or maybe it was more like Pandora's box, containing all the evils of Laura's world. Andy knew the rest of the myth, that once you let out the evil, all that was left was hope, but she doubted very seriously that anything inside the box would give her hope.

Andy picked at the tape. The tacky side had turned to dust. She had no problem slipping off the lid.

Photographs—not many, some in black and white, some in faded color.

A bundle of Polaroids was held together by an old rubber band. Andy chose those first because she had never seen her mother look so young.

The rubber band broke off in her hands.

Laura must have been in her early twenties when the pictures were taken. The 1980s were on full display, from her blue eyeshadow to her pink lipstick to the blush strafing up her cheeks like a bird's wings. Her normally dark brown hair was shockingly blonde and over-permed. Giant shoulder pads squared off her short-sleeved white sweater. She could've been about to tell everybody who shot J.R. Ewing.

The only reason Andy wasn't smiling was that it was clear from the photo that someone had repeatedly punched her mother in the face.

Laura's left eye was swollen shut. Her nose was askew. There were deep bruises around her neck. She stared into the camera, expressionless. She was somewhere else, being someone else, while her injuries were documented.

Andy knew that look.

She shuffled to the next Polaroid. The white sweater was lifted to show bruises on Laura's abdomen. The next photo showed a gash on the inside of her thigh.

Andy had seen the horrible-looking scar during one of her mother's hospital stays. Three inches long, pink and jagged even after all of this time. Andy had actually gasped at the sight of it.

"*Ice skating*," Laura had said, rolling her eyes like those two words explained everything.

Andy picked up the next stack of pictures, which were jarring, but only in their differentness. Not Polaroids, but regular printed snapshots of a toddler dressed in pink winter clothing. The date stamped on the back was January 4, 1989. The series captured the little girl rolling around in the snow, throwing snowballs, making angels, then a snowman, then destroying the snowman. Sometimes there was an adult in the photo—a disembodied hand hanging down or a leg sticking out below a heavy wool coat.

Andy recognized the toddler as herself. She had always had the same distinctive almond shape to her eyes, a feature she had inherited from her mother.

Going by the date on the back, toddler Andy would've been almost two years old when the series of photos was taken. That was the same time period that Andy and Laura had lived at UGA while Laura finished her PhD.

That kind of snow did not happen in Athens and especially not in Belle Isle. Andy had no recollection from her youth of ever taking a trip up north. Nor had Laura ever told her about one. Actually, when Andy revealed her plans to move to New York City, the first thing Laura had said was, "*Oh, darling, you've never been that far away from home before.*"

The last two photos in the box were paperclipped together.

Phil and Laverne Randall, her birth father's parents, were sitting on a couch. A painting of the beach hung on the wood-paneled wall behind them. There was something very familiar about the expressions on their faces, how they were sitting, even the shadow of a floor lamp that was cast along the back of the couch.

Andy slid away the paperclip to reveal the second photo.

Same people, same expressions, same postures, same shadows— but this time Andy, maybe six months old, was sitting in the Randalls' laps, balanced on one knee each.

She traced her finger along the thick outline of her baby self.

In school, Andy had learned to use Photoshop to, among other things, superimpose one image onto another. She had forgotten that, before computers, people had to alter images by hand. What you did was take an X-Acto knife and carefully cut someone out of a photo, then you sprayed the back with mounting adhesive, then positioned the cut-out piece onto a different photo.

Once you were happy with the result, you had to take another photograph of the overlaid images, and even then it didn't always turn out right. Shadows were wrong. The positioning looked unnatural. The whole process was painstakingly delicate.

Which made Laura's skill that much more impressive.

During Andy's early teens, she had often stared longingly at the photo of her Randall grandparents. Usually, she was mad at Laura, or worse, at Gordon. Sometimes, she would search the Randalls' features, trying to divine why their hatred and bigotry were more important to them than having contact with their dead son's only child.

Andy had never really focused on the section of the photo that her baby self was in. Which was too bad. If she'd made even a cursory study, she would have noticed that she was not actually sitting in the Randalls' lap.

Hovering would be a better word to describe it.

The racist Randalls were a difficult subject that Andy did not bring up to her mother, the same way she did not bring up Laura's own parents, Anne and Bob Mitchell, who had died before Andy was born. Nor did she ask about Jerry Randall, her father, who had been killed in a car accident long before Andy could establish any memories of him. They had never visited his grave in Chicago. They had never visited anyone's grave.

"*We should meet in Providence,*" Andy had told Laura her first year in New York. "*You can show me where you grew up.*"

"*Oh, darling,*" Laura had sighed. "*Nobody wants to go to Rhode Island. Besides, it was so long ago I'm sure I can't remember.*"

There were all kinds of photographs at home—an abundance of photos. From hiking trips and Disney World vacations and beach picnics and first days of schools. Only a handful showed Laura alone because she hated having her picture taken. There was nothing from the time before Andy was born. Laura had just one picture of Jerry Randall, the same photo Andy had found online in the *Chicago Sun Times* obituary archives.

Jerome Phillip Randall, 28 yrs old; optometrist and avid Bears fan; survived by a daughter, Andrea, and parents Phillip and Laverne.

Andy had seen other documents, too: her father's birth certificate and death certificate, both issued in Cook County, Illinois. Laura's various diplomas, her birth certificate from Rhode Island, her social security card, her driver's license. Andrea Eloise Mitchell's record of live birth dated August 20, 1987. The deed to the Belle Isle house. Immunization records. Marriage license. Divorce decree. Car titles. Insurance cards. Bank statements. Credit card statements.

Daniela Barbara Cooper's driver's license. The Ontario car registration. The HEALTH card. The Plymouth station wagon with a gun in the glove box and supplies and money in the trunk that was waiting in a storage facility in an anonymous town.

The make-up bag hidden inside the couch in Laura's office. The padlock key taped behind the framed photo of Andy.

Everything I've ever done is for you, my Andrea Heloise. Everything.

Andy spread out the Polaroids of her mother on the desk. The gash in her leg. The black eye. The bruised neck. The pummeled abdomen. The broken nose.

Pieces of a woman she had never known.

July 26, 1986

They tried to bury us.
They didn't know we were seeds.
—Mexican Proverb

7

Martin Queller's children were spoiled in that quintessential American way. Too much money. Too much education. Too much travel. Too much too much, so that the abundance of things had left them empty.

Laura Juneau found the girl in particular painful to watch. Her eyes furtively darting around the room. The nervous way she kept twitching her fingers as if they were floating across invisible keys. Her need to connect was reminiscent of an octopus blindly extending its tendrils in search of nourishment.

As for the boy—well, he had charm, and a lot could be forgiven of a charming man.

"Excuse me, madam?" The *politi* was lean and tall. The rifle hanging from his neck reminded Laura of her youngest son's favorite toy. "Have you misplaced your conference badge?"

Laura gave him an apologetic look as she leaned into her walking cane. "I had planned to check in before my panel."

"Shall I escort you?"

She had no choice but to follow. The additional security was neither unexpected nor without cause. Protestors were picketing outside the Oslo conference center—the usual mix of anarchists, anti-fascists, skinheads and trouble-makers alongside some of Norway's Pakistani immigrants, who were angry about recent immigration policy. The unrest had found its way inside, where

133

there were lingering suspicions around Arne Treholt's trial the previous year. The former labor party politician was serving a twenty-year term for high treason. There were those who believed the Russians had more spies planted within the Norwegian government. There were still more who feared that the KGB was spreading Hydra-like into the rest of Scandinavia.

The *politi* turned to ensure Laura was following. The cane was a hindrance, but she was forty-three, not ninety-three. Still, he cut a channel for her through the crowd of stodgy old men in boxy suits, all wearing badges that identified them by name, nationality, and field of expertise. There were the expected scions from top universities—MIT, Harvard, Princeton, Cal Tech, Stanford—alongside the usual suspects: Exxon, Tenneco, Eastman Kodak, Raytheon, DuPont and, in a nod to keynote speaker Lee Iacocca, a healthy smattering of senior executives from the Chrysler Motor Company.

The check-in table was beneath a large banner reading WELCOME TO G-FAB. As with everything else at the Global Finance and Business Consortium, the words were written in English, French, German and, in deference to the conference hosts, Norwegian.

"Thank you," Laura told the officer, but the man would not be dismissed. She smiled at the woman sitting behind the table, and delivered the well-practiced lie: "I'm Dr. Alex Maplecroft with the University of California at Berkeley."

The woman thumbed through a card catalog and pulled the appropriate credentials. Laura had a moment of relief when she thought that the woman would simply hand over the badge, but she said, "Your identification, please, madam."

Laura rested her cane against the table. She unzipped her purse. She reached for her wallet. She willed the tremble out of her fingers.

She had practiced for this, too; not formally, but in her mind, Laura had walked herself through the steps of approaching the check-in table, pulling out her wallet and showing the fake ID that identified her as Alexandra Maplecroft, Professor of Economics.

I'm very sorry but could you hurry? My panel starts in a few minutes.

"Madam." The woman behind the table looked not at Laura's eyes, but at her hair. "Could you kindly remove your identification from your wallet?"

Another layer of scrutiny Laura had not anticipated. She again found her hands trembling as she tried to work the card from beneath the plastic sleeve. According to the forger in Toronto, the ID was perfect, but then the man's vocation was deception. What if the girl behind the table found a flaw? What if a photo of the real Alex Maplecroft had somehow been scrounged? Would the *politi* drag Laura away in handcuffs? Would the last six months of careful planning fall apart for want of a simple plastic card?

"Dr. Maplecroft!"

They all turned to locate the source of the yelling.

"Andrew, come meet Dr. Maplecroft!"

Laura had always known Nicholas Harp to be breathtakingly handsome. In fact, the woman behind the table inhaled sharply as he approached.

"Dr. Maplecroft, how lovely to see you again." Nick shook her hand with both of his. The wink he offered was clearly meant to reassure her, but Laura would find no reassurance from this point forward. He said, "I was in your econ 401 at Berkeley. Racial and Gender Disparities in Western Economies. I can't believe I finally remembered."

"Yes." Laura was always taken aback by the ease with which Nick lied. "How lovely to see you again, Mister—"

"Harp. Nicholas Harp. Andrew!" He waved over another young man, handsome but less so, similarly dressed in chinos and a button-down, light blue polo. Future captains of industry, these young men. Their sun-bleached hair just so. Skin tanned a healthy bronze. Stiff collars upturned. No socks. Pennies stuck into the slots on the top of their loafers.

Nick said, "Andy, be quick. Dr. Maplecroft doesn't have all day."

135

Andrew Queller seemed flustered. Laura could understand why. The plan had dictated that they all stay anonymous and separate from one another. Andrew glanced at the girl behind the table, and in that moment, seemed to understand why Nick had risked breaking cover. "Dr. Maplecroft, you're on Father's two p.m. panel, I believe? 'Socio-Political Ramifications of the Queller Correction.'"

"Yes, that's right." Laura tried to force some naturalness into her tone. "You're Andrew, Martin's middle child?"

"Guilty." Andrew smiled at the girl. "Is there a problem, miss?"

His sense of entitlement was communicable. The woman handed Laura the badge for Dr. Alex Maplecroft, and like that, Laura was legitimized.

"Thank you," Nick told the girl, who beamed under his attention.

"Yes, thank you." Laura's hands were considerably more steady as she pinned the badge to the breast of her navy-blue blazer.

"Madam." The *politi* took his leave.

Laura found her cane. She wanted to get away from the table.

"Not so fast, Dr. Maplecroft." Nick, ever the showman, clapped together his hands. "Shall we buy you a drink?"

"It's very early," Laura said, though in fact she could use something to calm her nerves. "I'm not sure what time it is."

"Just shy of one," Andrew provided. He was using a hand-kerchief to wipe his already red nose. "Sorry, I caught a stinking cold on the flight."

She tried to keep the sadness out of her smile. Laura had wanted to mother him from the beginning. "You should find some soup."

"I should." He tucked the handkerchief back into his pocket. "We'll see you in an hour, then? Your panel will be in the Raufoss ballroom. Father was told to get there ten minutes ahead of time."

"You might want to freshen up before that." Nick nodded

toward the ladies room. He was giddy with the deception. "It's a wonder they even bothered to open it, Dr. Maplecroft. The wives have all gone on a shopping excursion to Storo. It appears you're the only woman slated to speak at the conference."

"Nick," Andrew cautioned. "'It's such a fine line between stupid and clever.'"

"Ouch, old boy. I know it's time to go when you start quoting *Spinal Tap*." Nick gave Laura another wink before allowing Andrew to lead him away. The river of suited old men turned as the two young bucks, so full of life and possibility, rode in their wake.

Laura pursed her lips and drew in a shallow breath. She feigned interest in locating an item inside of her handbag as she tried to regain her equilibrium.

As was often the case when she was around Nick and Andrew, Laura was reminded of her eldest son. On the day he was murdered, David Juneau was sixteen years old. The fuzz along his jaw had started to form into the semblance of a beard. His father had already shown him at the bathroom mirror how much shaving cream to use, how to draw the blade down his cheek and up his neck. Laura could still recall that crisp fall morning, their last morning, how the sun had teased its fingers through the fine hairs on David's chin as she had poured orange juice into his glass.

"Dr. Maplecroft?" The voice was hesitant, the vowels rounded in that distinctively Scandinavian way. "Dr. Alex Maplecroft?"

Laura furtively glanced for Nick to save her again.

"Dr. Maplecroft?" The Scandinavian had persuaded himself that he had the right person. There was nothing more validatory than a plastic conference badge. "Professor Jacob Brundstad, *Norges Handelshøyskole*. I was eager to discuss—"

"It's my pleasure to meet you, Professor Brundstad." Laura gave his hand a firm shake. "Shall we speak after my panel? It's in less than an hour and I need to collect my notes. I hope you understand."

He was too polite to argue. "Of course."

"I look forward to it." Laura stabbed her cane into the floor as she turned away.

She inserted herself into the crowd of white-haired men with pipes and cigarettes and briefcases and rolled sheaths of paper in their hands. That she was being stared at was undeniable. She propelled herself forward, head held high. She had studied Dr. Alex Maplecroft enough to understand that the woman's arrogance was legend. Laura had watched from the back of packed classes as Maplecroft eviscerated the slower students; overheard her chastising colleagues for not reaching the point quickly enough.

Or maybe it wasn't arrogance so much as the wall Maplecroft had built in order to protect herself from the stares of angry men. Nick was correct when he said that the renowned economics professor was the only woman slated to speak at the conference. The accusatory looks— *Why isn't that waitress wearing a uniform? Why isn't she emptying our ashtrays?* —were doubly warranted.

Laura hesitated. She was walking straight into nothing; a blank wall with a poster advertising Eastern Airline's Moonlight Special flights. Under such withering examination, she felt she could not reverse course. She took a sharp right and found herself standing at the closed glass door leading into the bar.

Blessedly, Laura found the door unlocked.

Stale smoke with an undertone of expensive bourbon shrouded the bar. There was a wooden dance floor with a darkened disco ball. The booths were low to the floor. Darkened mirrors hung from the ceiling. Laura's watch was turned to Toronto time, but she gathered from the empty room that it was still too early to have a proper drink.

After today, Dr. Maplecroft's reputation would be the least of her worries.

Laura could hear the tinkling of keys on the piano as she took her place at the end of the bar. She rested her cane against the wall. Her hand was reliably steady as she found the pack of Marlboros in her purse. There was a box of matches on top

138

of the glass ashtray. The flash of nicotine catching fire soothed her jangling nerves.

The bartender came through the swinging door. He was stout and starched with a white apron wrapped around his thick waist. "Madam?"

"Gin and tonic," she said, her voice soft, because the cacophonous notes from the piano had turned into a familiar melody; not Rossini or even, given the locale, Edvard Grieg, but a slow tune that escalated into a familiar verve.

Laura smiled as she blew out a plume of smoke.

She recognized the song from the radio. A-ha, the Norwegian singing group with the funny cartoon video. "Take On Me" or "Take Me On" or some variation of those words repeated *ad nauseam* over a relentlessly chirpy electric keyboard.

When Laura's daughter was still alive, the same type of candy synthpop had recurrently blared from Lila's record player or Walkman or even her mouth while she was in the shower. Every car trip, no matter how short, began with her daughter tuning the radio dial to The Quake. Laura was not shy with her daughter when she explained why the silly songs grated on her nerves. The Beatles. The Stones. James Brown. Stevie Wonder. *Those* were artists.

Laura had never felt so old as when Lila had made her watch a Madonna video on MTV. The only semi-positive comment Laura could muster was, "What a bold choice to wear her underwear on the outside."

Laura retrieved a pack of tissues from her purse and wiped her eyes.

"Madam." The bartender pronounced the word as an apology, gently placing her drink on a cocktail napkin.

"May I join you?"

Laura was stunned to find Jane Queller suddenly at her elbow. Andrew's sister was a complete stranger and meant to stay that way. Laura struggled to keep the recognition out of her expression. She had only ever seen the girl in photographs or from a great distance. Up close, she looked younger than her twenty-three years. Her voice, too, was deeper than Laura had imagined.

Jane said, "Please forgive the interruption." She had seen Laura's tears. "I was just sitting over there wondering if it's too early to drink alone."

Laura quickly recovered. "I think it is. Won't you join me?"

Jane hesitated. "You're sure?"

"I insist."

Jane sat, nodding for the same from the bartender. "I'm Jane Queller. I think I saw you talking to my brother, Andrew."

"Alex Maplecroft." For the first time in this entire enterprise, Laura regretted a lie. "I'm on a panel with your father in"—she checked the clock on the wall—"forty-five minutes."

Jane worked artlessly to mask her reaction to the news. Her eyes, as was so often the case, went to Laura's hairline. "Your photo wasn't in the conference directory."

"I'm not much for photographs." Laura had heard Alex Maplecroft say the same thing at a lecture in San Francisco. Along with shortening her first name, the doctor felt hiding the fact of her womanhood was the only way to make sure that her work was taken seriously.

Jane asked, "Has Father ever met you in person?"

Laura found the phrasing odd—not asking if she'd met Martin Queller, but whether or not Martin Queller had met her. "No, not that I can recall."

"I think I'll actually enjoy attending one of the old man's panels, then." Jane picked up her glass as soon as the bartender set it down. "I'm sure you're aware of his reputation."

"I am." Laura raised her own glass in a toast. "Any advice?"

Jane's nose wrinkled in thought. "Don't listen to the first five words he says to you, because none of them will make you feel good about yourself."

"Is that a general rule?"

"It's carved into the family coat of arms."

"Is that before or after the '*arbeit macht frei*'?"

Jane choked out a laugh, spitting gin and tonic onto the bar.

She used the cocktail napkin to wipe up the mess. Her long, elegant fingers looked incongruous to the task. "Could I bum one off you?"

She meant the cigarettes. Laura slid the pack over, but warned, "They'll kill you."

"Yes, that's what Dr. Koop tells us." Jane held the cigarette between her lips. She picked open the box of matches, but ended up scattering them across the bar. "God. I'm so sorry." Jane looked like a self-conscious child as she gathered the matches. "Clumsy Jinx strikes again."

The phrase had a practiced tone. Laura could imagine Martin Queller had found unique and precise ways to remind his children that they would never be perfect.

"Madam?" The bartender had appeared with a light.

"Thank you." Rather than cup her hands to his, Jane leaned toward the match. She inhaled deeply, her eyes closed like a cat enjoying a sunbeam. When she found Laura watching, she laughed out puffs of smoke. "Sorry, I've been in Europe for three months. It's good to have an American cigarette."

"I thought all of you young expats enjoyed smoking Gauloises and arguing about Camus and the tragedy of the human condition?"

"If only." Jane coughed out another cloud of dark smoke.

Laura felt a sudden maternal rush toward the girl. She wanted to snatch the cigarette from her hand, but she knew the gesture would be pointless. At twenty-three, Laura had been desperate for the years to come more quickly, to firmly step into her adulthood, to establish herself, to become someone. She had not yet felt the desire to claw back time as you would a piece of wet muslin clinging to your face; that one day her back might ache as she climbed the stairs, that her stomach could sag from childbirth, that her spine might become misshapen from a cancerous tumor.

"Disagree with him." Jane held the cigarette between her thumb and forefinger, the same way as her brother. "That's my advice to you on Father. He can't stomach people contradicting him."

"I've staked my reputation on contradicting him."

"I hope you're prepared for battle." She indicated the conference buzzing outside the barroom door. "Was it Jonah or Daniel who was in the lion's den?"

"Jonah was in the belly of a whale. Daniel was in the lions' den."

"Yes, of course. God sent an angel to close the lions' mouths."

"Is your father really that bad?" Laura realized too late the pointedness of her question. All three Queller children had found their own particular way to live in their father's shadow.

Jane said, "I'm sure you can hold your own against the Mighty Martin. You weren't invited here on a whim. Just keep in mind that once he's locked onto something, he won't back down. All or none is the Queller way." She didn't seem to expect a reply. Her eyes kept finding the mirror behind the bar as she scanned the empty room. Here was the octopus from the lobby, the one who was desperately in search of something, anything, that would render her whole.

Laura asked, "You're Martin's youngest?"

"Yes, then Andrew, then there's our older brother, Jasper. He's given up glory in the Air Force to join the family business."

"Economic advisory?"

"Oh, God, no. The money-making side. We're all terribly proud of him."

Laura disregarded the sarcasm. She knew full well the details of Jasper Queller's ascendancy. "Was that you just now on the piano?"

Jane offered a self-deprecating eye-roll. "Grieg seemed too aphoristic."

"I saw you play once." The shock of truthfulness brought an image to Laura's mind: Jinx Queller at the piano, the entire audience held rapt as her hands floated across the keyboard. Squaring that remarkably confident performer with the anxious young girl beside her—the nails bitten to the quick, the furtive glances at the mirror—was an unwieldy task.

Laura asked, "You don't go by Jinx anymore?"

Another eye-roll. "An unfortunate cross I bore from my childhood."

Laura knew from Andrew that Jane abhorred the family nickname. It felt wrong to know so much about the girl when she knew nothing of Laura, but this was how the game had to be played. "Jane suits you more, I think."

"I like to think so." She silently tapped ash off of her cigarette. The fact that Laura had seen her perform was clearly bothersome. Had Jane been rendered in paint, lines of anxiety would have radiated from her body. She finally asked, "Where did you see me play?"

"The Hollywood Bowl."

"Last year?"

"Eighty-four." Laura worked to keep the melancholy out of her tone. The concert had been a last-minute invitation from her husband. They had eaten dinner at their favorite Italian restaurant. Laura had drunk too much chianti. She could remember leaning into her husband as they walked to the parking lot. The feel of his hand on her waist. The smell of his cologne.

Jane said, "That was part of the Jazz Bowl before the Olympics. I sat in with the Richie Reedie Orchestra. There was a Harry James tribute and"—she squinted her eyes in memory—"I fell out of time during 'Two O'Clock Jump.' Thank God the horns came in early."

Laura hadn't noticed any slips, just that the crowd had been on its feet by the end. "Do you only remember your performances by their mistakes?"

She shook her head, but there was more to the story. Jane Queller had been a world-class pianist. She had sacrificed her youth to music. She had given up classical for jazz, then jazz for studio work. Between them all, she had performed in some of the most venerated halls and venues.

And then she had walked away.

"I read your paper on punitive taxation." Jane lifted her chin toward the bartender, silently requesting another drink. "If you're

143

wondering, Father expects us to keep up with his professional life. Even from nearly six thousand miles away."

"How edifying."

"I'd say it's more alarming than edifying. He sneaks his clippings into my mother's letters to save postage. 'Dear Daughter, we attended supper with the Flannigans this weekend and please be prepared to answer questions pertaining to the enclosed abstract on macroeconomic variables in Nicaragua.'" Jane watched the gin fall from the bottle. The bartender was being more generous with the alcohol than he'd been with Laura, but beautiful young women always got more.

Jane said, "Your passage about the weaponization of financial policy against minorities really made me think about government in a different way. Though, to hear my father tell it, your type of social engineering will ruin the world."

"Only for men like him."

"Be careful." This was a serious warning. "My father does not like to be contradicted. Especially by women." She met Laura's gaze. "Especially by women who look like you."

Laura remembered something her mother had told her a long time ago. "Men never have to be uncomfortable around women. Women have to be uncomfortable around men all of the time."

Jane gave a rueful laugh as she stubbed her cigarette into the ashtray.

Laura motioned for another gin and tonic, though the first one sat sourly in her stomach. She needed her hands to stop shaking, her heart to stop pattering like a frightened rabbit.

The clock gave her only thirty minutes to prepare herself.

In the best of circumstances, Laura had never been a comfortable public speaker. She was a watcher by nature, preferring to blend with the crowd. Behind Iacocca's keynote, the Queller panel was expected to be the most well-attended of the conference. The ticket supply had been exhausted within a day of the announcement. There were two other men who would join them, a German analyst from the RAND Corporation, and a Belgian executive from Royal Dutch Shell,

144

but the focus of the eight hundred attendees would be squarely on the two Americans.

Even Laura had to admit that Martin Queller's C.V. could draw a crowd: former president of Queller Healthcare, professor emeritus at the Queller School of Economics, Long Beach, former advisor to the governor of California, current member of the President's Council on Economic Development, at the top of the shortlist to replace James Baker as Secretary of the Treasury, and, most importantly, progenitor of the Queller Correction.

It was the Correction that had brought them all here. While Alex Maplecroft had managed to distinguish herself first at Harvard, then Stanford and Berkeley, she would have likely lived in academic obscurity but for her writings and publications accomplishing something that no man dared: vehemently questioning the morality of not just the Queller Correction, but Martin Queller himself.

Given Martin's standing in the economic and business community, this was tantamount to nailing the Ninety-Five Theses on the church doors.

Laura gladly counted herself among Maplecroft's converts.

In a nutshell, the Queller Correction posited that economic expansion has historically been underpinned by an undesirable minority or immigrant working class that is kept in check by nativistic corrections.

The progress of many on the backs of an *other*.

Irish immigrants erecting New York's bridges and skyscrapers. Chinese laborers building the transcontinental railroad. Italian workers fueling the textile industry. Here was the so-called nativistic correction: Alien Land Laws. No Irish, No Blacks, No Dogs. The Emergency Quota Act. The Literacy Act. *Dred Scott v. Sandford*. The Chinese Exclusion Act. Jim Crow. *Plessy v. Ferguson*. The Bracero Programs. Poll taxes. Operation Wetback.

The research behind Martin's theory was well substantiated. One might even call it a summation of facts rather than an actual theory. The problem—at least according to Alex Maplecroft—was that the Queller Correction was being used not as an academic term to describe a historical phenomenon but as a justification for setting current monetary and social policy. A sort of "history repeats itself," but without the usual irony.

Here were some of the more recent Queller Corrections: less AIDS funding to thin out the homosexual population, harsher sentences for African American crack users, regressive penalties for post-conviction felons, mandatory life sentences for repeat offenders, the for-profit privatization of prisons and mental health facilities.

In a *Los Angeles Times* op-ed, Alex Maplecroft derided the thinking that went into the Queller Correction with this inflammatory line: "*One wonders if Hermann Göring swallowed that cyanide capsule after all.*"

"Doctor?" Jane pulled Laura out of her thoughts. "Do you mind if—"

The girl wanted another cigarette. Laura shook two out of the pack.

This time, the bartender had a light for both of them.

Laura held in the smoke. She watched Jane watching the mirror. She asked, "Why did you give up performing?"

At first, Jane did not answer. She must have been asked the same question dozens of times. Maybe she was preparing to give Laura the same pat answer, but something altered in her expression as she turned in her seat. "Do you know how many famous women pianists there are?"

Laura was no musical expert—that had been her husband's hobby—but she had the tickling of a memory. "There's a Brazilian woman, Maria Arruda, or . . .?"

"Martha Argerich, from Argentina, but well done." Jane smiled without humor. "Name another."

Laura shrugged. She had not technically named one.

Jane said, "I was backstage at Carnegie, and I looked around and realized I was the only woman there. Which had happened before, many times, but this was the first time that I had really noticed. And that people noticed *me*." She rolled the ash off of her cigarette. "So then my teacher dropped me." The sudden appearance of tears at the corners of her eyes indicated the girl was still stung by the loss. "I'd trained with Pechenikov from the age of eight, but he told me that he had taken me as far as I could go."

Laura felt the need to ask, "Can you not find another teacher?"

"No one will take me on." She puffed the cigarette. "Pechenikov was the best, so I went to the second best. Then the third. By the time I worked my way down to the junior high band directors, I realized that they were using the same code." She held Laura's gaze with a knowing expression. "When they said, 'I don't have time to take on a new student,' what they meant was, 'I'm not going to waste my talent and effort on a silly girl who's going to give it all up once she falls in love.'"

"Ah," Laura said, because that was really all she could say.

"It's easier in some ways, I suppose. I've been devoting three or four hours a day, every day of my life, to practicing. Classical is so exact. You have to play every note as written. Your dynamics matter almost more than touch. With jazz, there's a melodic expression you can bring to the piece. And rock—do you know The Doors?"

Laura had to shift her thinking in a different direction. "Jim Morrison?"

Jane tapped her fingers on the bar top. At first, Laura only heard a frantic rapping, but then, remarkably—

"'Love Me Two Times.'" Laura laughed at the neat trick.

Jane said, "Manzarek played both the keyboard part and the bass part at the same time. It's amazing how he pulled it off, as if each hand worked completely independent of the other. A split personality, almost, but people don't concentrate on the technical aspects. They just love the sound." She kept tapping out the song as she spoke. "If I can't play music that people appreciate, then I want to play music that people love."

"Good for you." Laura let the beats play in the silence for a moment before asking, "You've been in Europe for the last three months, you said?"

147

"Berlin." Jane's hands finally wound down. "I was filling in as a session pianist at Hansa Tonstudio."

Laura shook her head. She had never heard of it.

"It's a recording studio by the Wall. They have a space, the Meistersaal, which has the most beautiful acoustics for every type of music—classical, chamber, pop, rock. Bowie recorded there. Iggy Pop. Depeche Mode."

"Sounds like you've met some famous people."

"Oh, no. My part's done by the time they roll in. That's the beauty of it. It's just me and my performance in isolation. No one knows who's behind the keyboard. No one cares if you're a woman, or a man, or a French poodle. They just want you to feel the music, and that's what I'm good at—feeling where the notes go." A glow of excitement enhanced her natural beauty. "If you love music—really, truly, love music—then you play it for yourself."

Laura felt herself nodding. She had no musical point of reference, but she understood that the pure love of something could not only give you strength but propel you forward.

Still, she said, "It's a lot to give up."

"Is it?" Jane seemed genuinely curious. "How can I give up something that was never really offered to me because of what's between my legs?" She gave a hard laugh. "Or *not* between my legs, or what might come out from between my legs at some point in the future."

"Men can always reinvent themselves," Laura said. "For women, once you're a mother, you're always a mother."

"That's not terribly feminist of you, Dr. Maplecroft."

"No, but you understand this because you're a chameleon like me. If you can't play the music people appreciate, then you play the music that they love." Laura hoped that one day that might change. Then again, she hoped every morning when she woke up that she would hear Lila's awful music on the radio, watch Peter run around the living room looking for his shoes, and find David talking low into the telephone because he did not want his mother to know that he had a girlfriend.

"You should go." Jane pointed to the clock. The forty-five minutes were almost up.

Laura wanted to keep talking, but she knew she had no choice. She reached into her purse for her wallet.

"It's on me," Jane offered.

"I couldn't—"

"I should say it's on the Queller family tab."

"All right," Laura agreed. She slid from the stool, stifling a wince from the pain as she put weight back on her leg. Her cane was where she had left it. She gripped the silver knob in her hand. She looked at Jane and wondered if this was the last person she would have a normal conversation with. If that turned out to be the case, she was glad.

She told the girl, "It's been a pleasure talking to you."

"You, too." Jane offered, "I'll be on the front row if you need a friendly face."

Laura felt enormously sad at the news. Uncharacteristically, she reached out and covered Jane's hand with her own. She could feel the coolness of the girl's skin. Laura wondered how long it had been since she had touched another human being for comfort.

She blurted out the words, "You are a magnificent person."

"Gosh." Jane blushed.

"It's not because you're talented, or beautiful, though you certainly are both. It's because you're so uniquely you." Laura said the words that she wished she'd had time to tell her own daughter: "Everything about you is amazing."

The blush reddened as Jane struggled for a pithy response.

"No." Laura would not let the girl's sarcasm ruin the moment. "You'll find your way, Jane, and it will be the right way, no matter what, because it's the path that you set out for yourself." She squeezed the girl's hand one last time. "That's my advice."

Laura felt Jane's eyes follow her progress as she slowly walked across the room. She had sat at the bar too long. Her foot was numb. The bullet lodged inside of her back felt as if it was a living, breathing thing. She cursed the shard of metal, no larger

149

than the nail on her pinky finger, that sat dangerously close to her spinal cord.

Just this once, this last time, she wanted to move quickly, to recapture some of her former agility, and complete the task before Jane could find her seat on the front row.

The lobby had emptied of important men, but their cigarette and pipe smoke lingered. Laura pushed open the door to the ladies room.

Empty, as Nick had predicted.

She walked to the last stall. She opened and closed the door. She struggled with the lock. The sliding bolt would not fit into the slot. She banged it twice, the metal singing against metal, then finally got it to stay closed.

Laura was overcome by a sudden dizziness. She pressed her hands to the walls. She took a few moments to stabilize. The two drinks on top of her jet lag had been a mistake, but she could be forgiven her fatalistic choices on today of all days.

The toilet was old-fashioned, the tank mounted high on the wall. She reached behind it. Her heart fluttered as she blindly searched. She felt the tape first. Her panic ebbed only slightly as her fingers traced their way up to the paper bag.

The door opened.

"*Hej-hej*?" a man said.

Laura froze, heart stopped.

"Hello?" The man was dragging something heavy across the floor. "Cleaner here. Hello?"

"Just a moment," Laura called back, the words choking in her throat.

"Cleaner," he repeated.

"*Nej*," she said, more stridently. "Occupied."

He gave a vexed sigh.

She waited.

Another sigh.

Another moment.

Finally, he dragged whatever he had brought into the toilets back across the floor. He closed the door so hard that the stall door slipped its flimsy lock and creaked open.

Laura felt the sliding bolt press its finger into the small of her back.

Improbably, a laugh tickled the back of her throat. She could only imagine what she looked like, skirt rucked up, standing with a leg on either side of the toilet bowl, her hand up the back of the tank.

All that was missing was the sound of a passing train and Michael Corleone.

Laura pulled down the paper bag. She shoved it into her purse. She went to the sink. She checked her hair and lipstick in the mirror. She studied her reflection as she washed her trembling hands.

The eyeshadow was jarring. She had never really worn make-up in her normal life. Her hair was normally worn back off her face. She normally wore jeans and one of her husband's shirts and a pair of her son's sneakers that he normally left by the door.

Normally, she had a camera swung around her neck.

Normally, she was frantically running around, trying to book sessions, working sessions, planning recitals and rehearsals and practice and meals and time to cook and time to read and time to love.

But normal wasn't normal anymore.

Laura dried her hands on a paper towel. She put on fresh lipstick. She bared her white teeth to the mirror.

The cleaner was waiting outside the ladies room. He was smoking, leaning against a large trash can that had spray bottles looped around the sides.

Laura suppressed the urge to apologize. She checked the paper bag in her purse. She pulled closed the zipper. The dizziness returned, but she managed to shake it. There was nothing to do about the churning in her stomach. Her heart was a metronome at the base of her throat. She could feel the blood pulsing through her veins. Her vision sharpened to the point of a tack.

"Dr. Maplecroft?" A flustered young woman in a floral dress

151

approached from nowhere. "Follow me, please. Your panel will start soon."

Laura tried to keep up with the girl's brisk, almost panicked walk. They were halfway down the hall when Laura realized she was getting winded. She slowed down, letting her hand rest longer on the cane. She had to remain calm. What she was about to do could not be rushed.

"Madam," the young girl pleaded, motioning for Laura to hurry.

"They won't start without me," Laura said, though she wasn't certain, given Martin Queller's reputation, that the man would wait. She found the pack of tissues in her purse. She wiped the sweat from her forehead.

A door flew open.

"Young lady." Martin Queller was snapping his fingers as if to call a dog. "Where is Maplecroft?" He glanced at Laura. "Coffee, two sugars."

The girl tried, "Doctor—"

"Coffee," Martin repeated, visibly annoyed. "Are you deaf?"

"I'm Dr. Maplecroft."

He did a double-take. Twice. "*Alex* Maplecroft?"

"Alexandra." She offered her hand. "I'm glad for this opportunity to meet in person."

A group of colleagues had congregated behind him. Martin had no choice but to shake her hand. His eyes, as was the case with so many before him, went to her hair. That's what gave it away. Laura's skin tone was closer to her white mother's, but she had the distinctive, kinky hair of her black father.

Martin said, "I understand you now. You've let your anecdotal experiences color your research."

Laura gazed down at the stark white hand she was holding. "Color is such an interesting choice of words, Martin."

He corrected her, "It's Dr. Queller."

"Yes, I heard about you while I was at Harvard." Laura turned toward the man on Martin's right; the German, judging by the sharp gray suit and thin navy tie. "Dr. Richter?"

152

"Friedrich, please. It is my pleasure." The man could hardly be bothered to hide his smile. He pulled over another man, gray-haired but wearing a fashionable, teal-colored jacket. "May I introduce you to our fellow panelist, Herr Dr. Maes?"

"So good to meet you." Laura shook the Belgian's hand, feeding off Martin's obvious disdain. She turned to the young woman. "Are we ready to begin?"

"Certainly, madam." The girl escorted them across the hall to the stage entrance.

The introductions had already begun. The lights were darkened in the wings. The girl used a flashlight to show the way. Laura could hear the rumble of male voices from the audience. Another man, the announcer, was speaking into a microphone. His French was too rapid for Laura to follow. She was grateful when he switched to English.

"And now, enough of my babbling, hey? Without further ado, we must welcome our four panelists."

The applause shook the floor beneath Laura's feet. Butterflies flipped inside her stomach. Eight hundred people. The house lights had gone up. Just past the curtain, she could see the right side of the auditorium. The audience, most all of them men, was standing, their hands clapping, waiting for the show to begin.

"Doctor?" Friedrich Richter murmured.

Her fellow panelists were waiting for Laura to lead the way. Even Martin Queller had the basic manners to not walk out ahead of a woman. This was the moment Laura had waited for. This was what had forced her out of her hospital bed, pushed her to complete the excruciating therapies, propelled her onto the four airplanes she'd taken to get here.

And yet, Laura felt herself frozen in place, momentarily lost in what she was about to do.

"For Godsakes." Martin quickly grew impatient. He strode onto the stage.

The crowd roared at his appearance. Feet were stamped. Hands were waved. Fists were pumped.

153

Friedrich and Maes performed a Laurel and Hardy-like panto-mime of who would have the honor of letting Laura precede them.

She had to go. She had to do this.

Now.

The air grew suffocatingly close as she walked onto the stage. Despite the howl of cheers and applause, Laura was conscious of the hard tap of her cane across the wooden boards. She felt her shoulders roll in. Her head bowed. The urge to make herself smaller was overpowering.

She looked up.

More lights. A fugue of cigarette smoke hung in the rafters.

She turned toward the audience—not to see the crowd, but to find Jane. She was in the front row, as promised. Andrew was to her left, Nick to her right, but it was Jane who held Laura's attention. They exchanged private smiles before Laura turned back to the stage.

She had to start this so that she could end it.

Microphones pointed rifle-like at four chairs that were sepa-rated by small side tables. Laura had not been part of any discussion regarding seating, so she stopped at the first chair. Beads of sweat broke out onto her upper lip. The harsh lights might as well have been lasers. She realized too late that this was the part she should have practiced. The chair was typical Scandinavian design: beautiful to look at, but low to the ground with not much support in the back. Worse yet, it appeared to swivel.

"Doctor?" Maes grabbed the back of the adjacent chair, holding it still for her. So, Laura was meant to go in the middle. She lowered herself into the low chair, the muscles in her shoul-ders and legs spasming with pain.

"Yes?" Maes offered to lay her cane on the floor.

"Yes." Laura clutched her purse in her lap. "Thank you."

Maes took the chair on her left. Friedrich walked to the far end, leaving the chair beside Laura empty.

She looked past the pointed end of the microphones into the

154

crowd. The clapping was tapering off. People were starting to take their seats.

Martin Queller was not quite ready to let them settle. He stood with his hand high in the air as he saluted the audience. Poor optics, given Maplecroft's line about Göring. As was the slight bow he gave before finally taking the chair center stage.

Now the audience began to settle. The last of the stray claps died down. The house lights lowered. The stage lights came up.

Laura blinked, momentarily blinded. She waited for the inevitable, which was for Martin Queller to adjust the microphone to his satisfaction and begin speaking.

He said, "On behalf of my fellow panelists, I'd like to thank you for your attendance. It is my fervent hope that our discourse remain lively and civil and, most importantly, that it lives up to your expectations." He looked to his left, then right, as he reached into his breast pocket and pulled out a stack of index cards. "Let's begin with what Comrade General Secretary Gorbachev has dubbed the 'Era of Stagnation.'"

There was laughter from the crowd.

"Dr. Maes, let's let you take this one." Martin Queller was, it must be said, a man who could command a room. He was clearly putting on a show, teasing around the edges of the topic they had all come to see debated. In his youth, he'd likely been considered attractive in that way that money makes a boring man suddenly interesting. Age had agreed with him. Laura knew he was sixty-three, but his dark hair was only slightly peppered with gray. The aquiline nose was less pronounced than in his photographs, which had likely been chosen for their ability to garner respect rather than physical admiration. People often mistook personality for character.

"What of Chernenko, Herr Richter?" Martin's voice boomed without the aid of a microphone. "Is it likely we'll see the full implementation of Andropov's arguably modest reforms?"

"Well," Friedrich began. "As perhaps the Russians would tell us, 'When money speaks, the truth keeps silent.'"

There was another smattering of laughter.

Laura shifted in the chair as she tried to relieve the pain radiating down her leg. Her sciatic nerve sang like the strings of a harp. Instead of listening to Friedrich's densely academic answer, she stared off to the side of the audience. There was a bank of lights hanging from a metal pole. A man stood on a raised platform working a shoulder-mounted Beta Movie video camera. His hand manually twisted around the lens. The lighting had likely thrown off the auto-focus.

Laura looked down at her own hand. The thumb and two of her fingers were still calloused from years of adjusting the focus ring on her Hasselblad.

The month before Lila had died, she'd told Laura that she wanted to take photography lessons, just not from her mother. Laura had been hurt. She was, after all, a professional photographer. But then a friend had reminded Laura that teenage girls were finished learning from their mothers until they had children of their own, and Laura had decided to bide her time.

And then time had run out.

All because of Martin Queller.

"—the juxtaposition of social policy and economics," Martin was saying. "So, Dr. Maplecroft, while you might disagree with what you call the 'atavistic tone' of the Queller Correction, I merely sought to put a name to a statistically occurring phenomenon."

Laura saw his chest rise as he took a breath to continue, so she jumped in. "I wonder, Dr. Queller, if you understand that your policies have real-world implications."

"They are not policies, dear. They are theories assigned to what you yourself have described as tribal morality."

"But, Doctor—"

"If you find my conclusions cold, then I would warn you that statistics are, in fact, a cold mistress." He seemed to enjoy the turn of phrase. It had appeared in many of his editorials and essays. "Using emotion or hysterics to interpret the datum opens up the entire field to ridicule. You might as well ask a janitor

156

to explain how the volcanic eruption at Beerenberg will influence weather patterns in Guam."

He seemed very smug about the pronouncement. Laura yearned to be the one who slapped that self-satisfied grin off of his face. She said, "You say that your theories are not policies, but in fact, your economic theories have been used to affect policy."

"You flatter me," he said, though in a way that indicated the flattery was warranted.

"Your work influenced the Lanterman-Petris-Short Act in '67."

Martin scowled at the comment, but then turned to the audience and said, "For the benefit of the Europeans, you should explain that the Patients' Bill of Rights was a landmark piece of legislation in the state of California. Among other things, it helped end the practice of institutionalizing people in mental hospitals against their will."

"Didn't the bill also cut funding to state mental hospitals?"

The smirk on his lips said he knew where this was going. "The funding cuts were temporary. Then-governor Reagan reinstated the funds the following year."

"To previous levels?"

"You've spent your life in front of a chalkboard, Maplecroft. It's different in the real world. The turning of government policy is as the turning of a battleship. You need a lot of room to make corrections."

"Some would call them mistakes rather than corrections." Laura held up her hand to stop his retort. "And another *correction* was that the following year, the criminal justice system saw twice as many mentally ill people entering into, and staying in, the criminal justice system."

"Well—"

"The overcrowding of the California penal system has given rise to violent gangs, led to the re-incarceration of thousands and helped incubate an explosion of HIV cases." Laura turned to the audience. "Churchill told us that 'those who fail to learn

157

from history are doomed to repeat it.' My colleague seems to be saying, 'Repeating our history is the only way we can stay in power.'"

"Patients!" He said the word so loudly that it echoed against the back wall.

In the ensuing silence, Laura asked, "Sir?"

"Doctor." Martin smoothed down his tie. He visibly worked to control his temper. "This law that you're talking about was rightly called a Patients' Bill of Rights. Those who left state mental hospitals were either moved into group homes or received out-patient treatment so that they could become useful members of society."

"Were they capable of being useful?"

"Of course they were. This is the problem with socialists. You believe the government's job is to coddle man from cradle to grave. That's the very type of faulty reasoning that has turned half of America into a welfare state." He leaned forward, addressing the audience. "I believe—and most Americans believe—every man deserves a chance to stand on his own two feet. It's called the American Dream, and it's available to anyone who's willing to work for it."

Laura indicated her cane. "What if they can't stand on their own two feet?"

"For God's sake, woman. It's a figure of speech." He turned back to the audience. "The group home setting allows—"

"What group homes? The ones run by Queller Healthcare Services?"

That threw him off, but only for a moment. "The company is privately held in a blind trust. I have no say over any of the decisions made."

"Are you not aware that Queller Healthcare derives upwards of thirty percent of its annual profits from the management of group homes for the mentally ill?" She held up her hands in an open shrug. "What a wonderful coincidence that your position as an economic advisor to the state allowed you to advocate that government money should be diverted into the private, for-profit healthcare industry which has been the source of so much of your family's wealth."

Martin sighed. He gave a dramatic shake of his head.

"Your company is about to go public, is it not? You took on some very high-level investors going into the offering to make sure your numbers were up." This was the reason behind the *now* of it all, why there was no turning back. "Your family's fortune will grow considerably when the Queller model is expanded to the rest of the United States. Isn't that right?"

Martin sighed again, shook his head again. He glanced at the crowd as if to pull them to his side. "I feel you have hijacked this panel with your own agenda, Maplecroft. It matters not one lick what I say. You seem to have your mind made up. I'm an evil man. Capitalism is an evil system. We'd all be better off if we picked flowers and braided them into our hair."

Laura said the words she had lied for, stolen for, kidnapped for and finally flown nearly six thousand miles to say to Martin Queller's face: "Robert David Juneau."

Again, Martin was caught off guard, but he made an adroit recovery, once more addressing the audience. "For those of you who do not read the newspapers in northern California, Robert David Juneau was a black construction worker who—"

"Engineer," Laura interrupted.

He turned, seemingly stunned that she had corrected him.

"Juneau was an engineer. He studied at Cal Tech. He was not a construction worker, though he was black, if that's the point you're making."

He started to wag his finger at her. "Let's remember that you're the one who keeps bringing race into this."

She said, "Robert Juneau was injured while visiting a construction site in downtown San Francisco." Laura turned to the crowd. She tried to keep the quiver out of her voice when she told the story. "One of the workers made a mistake. It happens. But Juneau was in the wrong place at the wrong time. A steel beam struck his head here—" She pointed to her own head, and for a moment, her fingers could feel the rough scar on Robert's scalp. "His brain started to swell. He experienced a series of strokes during the surgery to relieve the swelling. The doctors were unsure of his recovery, but he managed to walk again, to speak, to recognize his children and his wife."

"Yes," Martin snapped. "There's no need to over-dramatize the story. There was severe damage in the frontal lobe. The man's personality was permanently altered by the accident. Some call it Jekyll and Hyde Syndrome. Juneau was a competent family man before the injury. Afterward, he became violent."

"You like to draw straight lines across a crooked world, don't you?" Laura was repulsed by his cavalier assessment. She finally let her gaze find Jane in the front row. Laura spoke to the girl because she wanted her to know the truth. "Robert Juneau was a good man before he got hurt. He fought for his country in Vietnam. He earned his degree on the GI Bill. He paid taxes. He saved his money, bought a house, paid his bills, took care of his family, reached out with both hands for the American Dream, and . . ." Laura had to pause to swallow. "And when he couldn't stand on his own two feet anymore, when it came time for his country to take care of him—" She turned back to Martin. "Men like you said no."

Martin heaved a pained sigh. "That's a tragic tale, Maplecroft, but who's going to write a check for twenty-four-hour, supervised medical care? That's three doctors on call, at least five nursing staff, the facilities, the infrastructure, the insurance billing, the secretaries, the janitors, the cafeteria staff, the bleach, the Mop & Glo, multiplied by however many seriously mentally ill people there are in America. Do you want to pay eighty percent of your income in taxes as they do in our host country? If your answer is yes, feel free to move. If the answer is no, then tell me, where do we get the money?"

"We are the richest country in the—"

"Because we don't squander—"

"From you!" she yelled. There was a stillness in the audience that transferred to the stage. She said, "How about we get the money from you?"

He snorted by way of answer.

"Robert Juneau was kicked out of six different group homes managed by Queller Healthcare. Each time he returned, they contrived a different reason to send him away."

"I had nothing to do with—"

"Do you know how much money it costs to bury three children?" Laura could still see her babies on that crisp fall day. David whispering to some girl on the phone. Lila upstairs listening to the radio as she dressed for school. Peter running around the living room looking for his shoes.

Pow.

A single shot to the head brought down her youngest son.

Pow-pow.

Two bullets tore open David's chest.

Pow-pow.

Lila had slipped as she was running down the stairs. Two bullets went into the top of her head. One of them exited out of her foot.

The other was still lodged in Laura's spine.

She'd hit her head on the fireplace as she fell to the ground. There were six shots in the revolver. Robert had brought it back from his tunnel-rat duty in Vietnam.

The last thing Laura had seen that day was her husband pressing the muzzle of the gun underneath his chin and pulling the trigger.

She asked Martin Queller, "How much do you think those funerals cost? Coffins, clothes, shoes—you have to put them in shoes—Kleenex, burial space at the cemetery, headstones, hearse rental, pallbearers, and a preacher to bless a dead sixteen-year-old boy, a dead fourteen-year-old girl, and a dead five-year-old little boy?" She knew that she was the only person in this room who could answer that question because she had written the check. "What were their lives worth, Martin? Were they worth more to society than the cost of keeping a sick man hospitalized? Were those three babies nothing more than a goddamn *correction*?"

Martin seemed at a loss for words.

"Well?" she waited. Everyone was waiting.

Martin said, "He served. The Veterans' Hospital—"

"Was overcrowded and underfunded," she told him. "Robert was on a year-long waiting list at the VA. There was no state mental hospital to go to because there was no state funding. The regular hospital had barred him. He'd already attacked a nurse and hurt an orderly. They knew he was violent, but they moved him to a group home because there was nowhere else to warehouse him." She added, "A Queller Healthcare-managed group home."

"You," Martin said, because the well-respected thinker had finally figured her out. "You're not Alex Maplecroft."

"No." She reached into her purse. She found the paper bag. Dye packs.

That was what was supposed to be inside the bag.

Back in California, they had all agreed on the red dye packs, flat and slim, less than the size and thickness of a pager. Banks hid the exploding dye inside stacks of paper money so that would-be bank robbers would be indelibly stained when they tried to count their loot.

The plan was to see Martin Queller humiliated on the world stage, stained by the proverbial blood of his victims.

Laura had lost faith in proverbs when her children were murdered by their father.

She took a deep breath. She located Jane again.

The girl was crying. She shook her head, silently mouthed the words her father would never say: *I'm sorry.*

Laura smiled. She hoped that Jane remembered what Laura had told her in the bar. She *was* magnificent. She *would* find her own path.

The next part went quickly, perhaps because Laura had watched it play out so many times in her head—that is, when she wasn't trying to conjure memories of her children; the way David's feet had smelled when he was a baby, the soft whistle that Peter's lips made when he colored with his crayons, the wrinkle in Lila's brow when she studied how to frame a photograph. Even Robert sometimes haunted her thoughts. The man before the accident who had danced to Jinx Queller on the piano at the Hollywood Bowl. The patient who had wanted so desperately to get well. The violent inmate at the hospital. The trouble-maker who'd been kicked out of so many group homes. The homeless man who'd been arrested time and time again for theft, assault, public intoxication, aggressive panhandling, public nuisance, loitering, suicidal tendencies, making terroristic threats, willfully threatening to commit bodily harm.

"*In some ways you were lucky,*" Laura's oncologist had told her after the shooting. "*If the bullet had entered your back three centimeters lower, the scan would've never found the cancer.*"

Laura reached into the paper bag.

She had known the moment she pulled it from behind the toilet tank that she was not holding the agreed-upon dye packs, but something better.

A six-shot revolver, just like the one her husband had used.

First, she shot Martin Queller in the head.

Then she pressed the muzzle of the gun beneath her chin and killed herself.

August 21, 2018

8

Andy felt numb as she drove through Alabama in her mother's secret Reliant K station wagon filled with secret money toward a destination that Laura had seemed to pull from thin air. Or maybe she hadn't. Maybe her mother knew exactly what she was doing, because you didn't have a covert storage facility filled with everything you needed to completely restart your life unless you had a hell of a lot of things to hide.

The fake IDs. The revolver with the serial number shaved off. The photos of Andy in snow that she could not ever recall seeing, holding the hand of a person she could not remember.

The Polaroids.

Andy had shoved them into the beach tote in the back of the Reliant. She could've spent the rest of her day staring at them, trying to pick apart the terrible things that had happened to the young woman in the pictures. Beaten. Punched. Bitten—that was what the gash on her leg looked like, as if an animal had taken a bite of her flesh.

That young woman had been her mother.

Who had done all of those awful things to Laura? Was it the *they* who had sent Hoodie? Was it the *they* who were probably tracking Andy?

Andy wasn't doing a great job of eluding them. She had made it as far as Birmingham before she remembered that she hadn't unhooked the battery cables in the dead man's truck. Laura had told her that she had to make sure the GPS wasn't working. Did GPS work without the engine running? Coordinating with a satellite seemed like something the on-board computer would do, which meant the computer had to be awake, which meant the car had to be on.

Right?

The LoJack vehicle recovery system had its own battery. Andy knew this from working stolen car reports through dispatch. She also knew Ford had a Sync system, but you had to register for the real-time monitoring service, and Andy didn't think that a guy who went to the trouble of blocking out all the lights on his vehicle would give up his anonymity just so he could use voice commands to locate the nearest Mexican restaurant.

Right?

What would happen if the truck was found? Andy played out the investigation in her mind, the same as she had while running away from her mother's house.

First up, the police would have to ID Hoodie, aka Samuel Godfrey Beckett. Considering the guy's vocation, he was more than likely in the system, so a fingerprint scan was all it would take to get his name. Once they had his name, they would find the truck registration, then they would put out an APB on the wire, which would create an alert that would show up on the screen of every squad car in the tri-state area.

Of course, this assumed that what was supposed to happen was what actually happened. There were tons of APBs all the time. Even the high-priority ones were missed by a lot of the patrol officers, who had maybe a billion things to do on their shifts, including trying not to get shot, and stopping to read an alert was often not a high priority.

That did not necessarily mean Andy was in the clear. If the cops didn't find the truck, the librarians, or more likely the grumpy old guy with the political rants, would probably report the abandoned vehicle. Then the cops would roll up. The officer would run the plates and VIN, see there was an APB, notify

Savannah, then the forensic techs would find Andy's shoes and work shirt and her fingerprints and DNA all over the interior.

Andy felt her stomach pitch.

Her fingerprints on the frying pan could be explained away— Andy cooked eggs in her mother's kitchen all of the time—but stealing the dead man's truck and crossing state lines put her squarely in special circumstances territory, meaning if Palazzolo charged Andy with the murder of Hoodie, the prosecutor could seek the death penalty.

The death penalty.

She opened her mouth to breathe as a wave of dizziness took hold. Her hands were shaking again. Big, fat tears rolled down her face. The trees blurred outside the car windows. Andy should turn herself in. She shouldn't be running away. She had dropped her mother in a pile of shit. It didn't matter that Laura had told Andy to leave. She should've stayed. At least that way Andy wouldn't be so alone right now.

The truth brought a sob to her mouth.

"Get it together," she coaxed herself. "Stop this."

Andy gripped the steering wheel. She blinked away her tears. Laura had told her to go to Idaho. She needed to go to Idaho. Once Andy was there, once she crossed the state line, she could break down and cry every single day until the phone rang and Laura told her it was safe to come home. Following Laura's orders was the only way she would get through this.

Laura had also told her to unhook the Ford's battery.

"Fuck," Andy muttered, then, channeling Gordon, Andy told herself, "What's done is done." The finality of the proclamation loosened the tight bands around Andy's chest. There was also the benefit of it being true. Whether or not the Ford was found or what the cops did with it was completely out of Andy's control.

This was the question she needed to worry about: during her computer searches at the library, at what point exactly had she turned on the Google Incognito Mode? Because once the cops found the truck, they would talk to the librarians, and the librarians would tell them that Andy had used the computer. While she felt certain that the librarians would put up a fight—as a group, they were mostly First Amendment badasses—a warrant to search the computer would take maybe an hour and then a tech would need five seconds to find Andy's search history.

She was certain the Incognito Mode was on before she looked up Paula Kunde of Austin, Texas, but was it on before or after she searched for directions to Idaho?

Andy could not recall.

Second worrisome thing: what if it wasn't the cops who asked the librarians these questions? What if Laura's omniscient *they* found someone to look for Hoodie's truck, and *they* talked to the librarians, and *they* searched the computer?

Andy wiped her nose with her arm. She backed down on the speed because the Reliant started to shake like a bag of cat treats if she went over fifty-five.

Had she put other people's lives at risk by abandoning the truck? Had she put her own life at risk by looking up the directions to Idaho? Andy tried again to mentally walk through the morning. Entering the library. Pouring the coffee. Sitting down at the computer. She had looked up the *Belle Isle Review* first, right? And then clicked to private browsing?

She was giving Google Incognito Mode a lot of credit. It seemed very unlikely that something so standard could fool a forensic computer whiz. Andy probably should've cleared out the cache and wiped the history and erased all the cookies the way she had learned to do after that horrible time Gordon had accidentally seen the loop of erotic *Outlander* scenes Andy had accessed from his laptop.

Andy wiped her nose again. Her cheeks felt hot. She saw a road sign.

FLORENCE 5 MI

Andy guessed she was heading in the right direction, which was somewhere in the upper left corner of Alabama. She hadn't stopped to buy a new map to plot the route to Idaho. Once she'd left the storage unit, her only goal was to get as far away from Carrollton as possible. She had her highway and interstate scribbles from the library, but she was mostly relying on the back of the Georgia map, which had ads for other maps. There was a small rendering of *The Contiguous United States of America* available for $5.99 plus postage and handling. Andy had grown up looking at similar maps, which was why she was in her twenties before she'd understood how Canada and New York State could share Niagara Falls.

This was her plan: after Alabama, she'd cut through a corner of Tennessee, a corner of Arkansas, Missouri, a tiny piece of Kansas, left at Nebraska, then Wyoming, then she would literally fucking kill herself if she wasn't in Idaho by then.

Andy leaned forward, resting her chin on the shaky steering wheel. The vertebrae in her lower back had turned into prickly pears. The trees started to blur again. She wasn't crying anymore, just exhausted. Her eyelids kept fluttering. She felt like they were weighted down with paste.

She made herself sit up straight. She punched the thick white buttons on the radio. She twisted the dial back and forth. All she found were sermons and farm reports and country music, but not the good kind; the kind that made you want to stab a pencil into your ear.

Andy opened her mouth and screamed as loud as she could.

It felt good, but she couldn't scream for the rest of her life.

At some point, she would have to get some sleep. The five-and-a-half-hour drive from Belle Isle had been draining enough. So far, the drive from Carrollton had added another four and a half hours because of traffic, which Andy seemed pre-ordained to find no matter which route she took. It was almost three p.m. Except for zonking out for a few hours in her apartment and the catnap in the Walmart parking lot, she hadn't really slept since she got up for her dispatch shift two days ago. During that time, Andy had survived a shooting, watched her mother get injured, agonized outside of the surgical suite, freaked out over a police interrogation and killed a man, so as these things

171

went, it was no wonder that she felt like she wanted to vomit and yell and cry at the same time.

Not to mention that her bladder was a hot-water bottle sitting inside of her body. She had stopped only once since leaving the storage unit, pulling onto the shoulder of the highway, hiding between the open front and back car doors, waiting for traffic to clear, then squatting down to relieve herself in the grass because she was terrified to leave the Reliant unattended.

$240,000

Andy couldn't leave that kind of cash in the car while she ran into Burger King, and taking the suitcase inside would be like carrying a neon sign for somebody to rob her. What the hell was Laura doing with that kind of cash? How long had it taken for her to save it?

Was she a bank robber?

The question was only a little crazy. Being a bank robber would explain the money, and it jibed with the D.B. Cooper joke on the Canada ID and maybe even the gun in the glove box.

Andy's heart pinged at the thought of the gun.

Here was the problem: bank robbers seldom got away with their crimes. It was a very high risk for a very low reward, because the FBI was in charge of all investigations that had to do with federally insured funds. Andy thought the law's origins had something to do with Bonnie and Clyde or John Dillinger or the government just basically making sure that people knew their money was safe.

Anyway, she couldn't see her mother pulling on a ski mask and robbing a bank.

Then again, before the shooting at the diner, she couldn't see her mom knifing a kid in the neck.

Then again—again—Andy could not see her reliable, sensible mother doing a lot of the crazy shit that Laura had done in the last thirty-six hours. The hidden make-up bag, the key behind the photograph, the storage unit, the Thom McAn box.

Which brought Andy to the photo of toddler Andy in the snow.

172

Here was the Lifetime Movie question: Had Andy been kidnapped as a child? Had Laura seen a baby left alone in a shopping cart or unattended on a playground and decided to take her home?

Andy glanced in the rearview mirror. The shape of her eyes, the same shape as Laura's, told her that Laura was her mother.

The Polaroids showed Laura so badly beaten that her bottom lip was split open. Maybe Jerry Randall was an awful man. Maybe back in 1989, he was beating Laura, and she snapped and took Andy on the run with her, and Jerry had been looking for them ever since.

Which was a Julia Roberts movie. Or a Jennifer Lopez movie. Or Kathy Bates. Or Ashley Judd, Keri Russell, Ellen Page . . .

Andy snorted.

There were a lot of movies about women getting pissed off about men beating the shit out of them.

But the Polaroids showed that her mother had in fact had the shit beaten out of her, so maybe that wasn't so far off base.

Andy found herself shaking her head.

Laura hadn't said *he* can trace you. She'd said *they*.

Going by the movies, *they* generally meant evil corporations, corrupt presidents or power-hungry tech billionaires with unlimited funds. Andy tried to play out each scenario with her mother at the center of some vast conspiracy. And then she decided she should probably stop using Netflix as a crime sourcebook.

The Florence exit was up. Andy couldn't squat on the highway again. She hadn't had lunch because she couldn't bear to eat another hamburger in another car. The part of her brain that was still capable of thinking told her that she could not make the thirty-hour drive straight through to Idaho without sleep. Eventually, she would have to stop at a hotel.

Which meant that, eventually, she would have to figure out what to do with the money.

Her hand had pushed down the blinker before she could stop it. She glided off the Florence exit. Adrenaline had kept Andy going for so long that there was hardly anything left to move her. There were signs off the exit for six different hotels. She took a right at the light because it was easier. She coasted to the first motel because it was the first motel. Worrying about safety and cleanliness were luxuries from her former life.

Still, her heart started pounding as she got out of the Reliant. The motel was two stories, a squat, concrete design from the seventies with an ornate balcony railing around the top floor. Andy had backed crookedly into the parking space so that the rear of the station wagon never left her sight. She clutched the make-up bag in her hand as she walked into the lobby. She checked the flip phone. Laura had not called. Andy had depleted the battery by half from constantly checking the screen.

There was an older woman at the front desk. High hair. Tight perm. She smiled at Andy. Andy glanced back at the car. There were huge windows all around the lobby. The Reliant was where she had left it, unmolested. She didn't know if she looked weird or normal swiveling her head back and forth, but at this point, Andy didn't care about anything but falling into a bed.

"Hey there," the woman said. "We got some rooms on the top floor if you want."

Andy felt the vestiges of her waking brain start to slip away. She'd heard what the woman had said, but there was no sense in it.

"Unless you want something on the bottom floor?" The woman sounded dubious.

Andy was incapable of making a decision. "Uh—" Her throat was so dry that she could barely speak. "Okay."

The woman took a key from a hook on the wall. She told Andy, "Forty bucks for two hours. Sixty for the night."

Andy reached into the make-up bag. She peeled off a few twenties.

"Overnight, then." The woman handed back one of the bills. She slid the guestbook across the counter. "Name, license plate, make and model." She was looking over Andy's shoulder at the car. "Boy, haven't seen one of those in a long time. They make those new in Canada? Looks like you just drove it off the lot."

Andy wrote down the car's information. She had to look at the license plate three times before she got the correct combination of numbers and letters.

"You okay, sweetheart?"

Andy smelled French fries. Her stomach grumbled. There was a diner connected to the motel. Red vinyl booths, lots of chrome. Her stomach grumbled again.

What was more important, eating or sleeping?

"Hon?"

Andy turned back around. She was clearly expected to say something.

The woman leaned across the counter. "You okay, sugar?"

Andy struggled to swallow. She couldn't be weird right now. She didn't need to make herself memorable. "Thank you," was the first thing that came out. "Just tired. I came from . . ." She tried to think of a place that was far from Belle Isle. She settled on, "I've been driving all day. To visit my parents. In I-Iowa."

She laughed. "Honey, I think you overshot Iowa by about six hundred miles."

Shit.

Andy tried again. "It's my grandmother's car." She searched her brain for a compelling lie. "I mean, I was at the beach. The Alabama beach. Gulf. In a town called Mystic Falls." Christ, she was crazy-sounding. Mystic Falls was from the *Vampire Diaries.* She said, "My grandmother's a snowbird. You know, people who—"

"I know what a snowbird is." She glanced down at the name Andy had written in the guestbook. "Daniela Cooper. That's pretty."

Andy stared, unblinking. Why had she written down that name?

"Sweetheart, maybe you should get some rest." She pushed the key across the counter. "Top floor, corner. I think you'll feel safer there."

"Thank you," Andy managed. She was in tears again by the time she climbed behind the wheel of the Reliant. The diner was so close. She should get something to eat. Her stomach was doing that thing where it hurt so bad she couldn't tell if it was from being hungry or being sick.

Andy got back out of the car. She held the make-up bag in both hands as she walked the twenty feet to the diner. The sun beat down on the top of her head. The heat brought out a thick layer of sweat. She stopped at the door. She looked back at her car. Should she get the suitcase? How would that look? She could take it to her room, but then how could she leave the suitcase in her room when—

The diner was empty when she walked in, a lone waitress reading a newspaper at the bar. Andy went to the ladies room first because her bladder gave her no other choice. She was in such a hurry that she didn't wash her hands. The car was still there when she came out of the bathroom. No one in a blue baseball cap and blue jeans was peering into the windows. No one was running away with a 1989 Samsonite suitcase in their hand.

She found a booth by the window overlooking the parking lot. She kept the make-up bag between her legs. The menu was giant, filled with everything from tacos to fried chicken. Her eyes saw the words but by the time they made it into her consciousness, she was stymied. She would never be able to make a choice. She could order a bunch of things, but that would only draw even more attention. She should probably leave, drive up another few exits and find a different motel where she didn't act like an idiot. Or she could just put her head in her hands and stay here, in the air-conditioning, for a few minutes while she tried to get her thoughts in order.

"Honey?"

Andy jerked up from the table, disoriented.

"You're beat, ain't you?" the woman from the motel said. "Poor thing. I told them to let you sleep."

Andy felt her stomach drop. She had fallen asleep again. In

176

public—again. She looked down. The make-up bag was still between her legs. There was drool on the table. She used a napkin to wipe it up. She used her hand to wipe her mouth. Everything was vibrating. Her brain felt like it was being squished onto the point of a juice grinder.

"Hon?" the woman said. "You should probably go to your room now. It's getting a little busy in here."

The restaurant had been empty when Andy walked in, but now it was filling with people.

"I'm sorry," she said.

"It's all right." The woman patted Andy's shoulder. "I asked Darla to put a plate aside for you. You want it here or do you wanna take it to your room?"

Andy stared at her.

"Take it to your room," the woman said. "That way you can go right back to sleep when you're finished."

Andy nodded, grateful that someone was telling her what to do.

Then she remembered the money.

Her neck strained as she turned to look for the car. The blue Reliant was still parked in front of the motel office. Had someone opened the trunk? Was the suitcase still there?

"Your car is fine." The woman handed her a Styrofoam box. "Take your food. Your room's the last one on the top floor. I don't like to put young women on the ground floor. Old gals like me, we'd welcome a strange man knocking at our door, but you . . ." She gave a husky chuckle. "Just keep to yourself and you'll be fine."

Andy took the box, which weighed the equivalent of a cement block. She put the make-up bag on top. Her legs were wobbly when she stood. Her stomach rumbled. She ignored the people staring at her as she walked back into the parking lot. She fumbled with the keys to open the hatch. She couldn't decide what to take inside, so she loaded herself up like a pack mule, slinging the tote bag over her shoulder, tucking the sleeping bag into her armpit, grabbing the handle of the

177

suitcase and balancing the make-up bag/take-out Jenga with her free hand.

Andy made it as far as the stairway landing before she had to stop to readjust her load. Her shoulders felt boneless. Either she was still exhausted or she'd lost all of her muscle mass from sitting in the car for almost ten hours.

She scanned the numbers as she walked along the narrow balcony on the top floor. There were burned-out hibachi grills and empty beer cans and greasy pizza boxes in front of some of the doors. The smell of cigarettes was strong. It brought back the memory of Laura bumming a smoke off the orderly in front of the hospital.

Andy longed for the time when her biggest concern was that her mother held a cigarette between her finger and thumb like a junkie.

Behind her, a door opened. A disembodied hand dropped an empty pizza box on the concrete balcony. The door slammed shut.

Andy tried to calm her heart, which had detonated inside her throat when the door opened. She took a deep breath and let it go. She readjusted the sleeping bag under her arm. She mentally summoned her father and tried to make a list of things she would need to stop doing. One, stop panicking every time she heard a noise. Two, stop falling asleep in public places. That seemed a hell of a lot easier than it was proving to be. Three, figure out what to do with all of the money. Four, locate another library so she could read the *Belle Isle Review*. Five, stop being weird, because right now, if the cops happened to follow her trail, the first person any of the potential witnesses would think of was Andy.

Then they'd get Daniela Cooper's name, and the car details, and that would be it.

Andy looked out at the road. There was a bar across the street. Neon signs filled the windows. The parking lot was packed with trucks. She could hear the faint clink of honky-tonk music. In that moment, she wanted a drink so badly that her body strained toward the bar like a plant reaching up to the sun.

She put down the suitcase and used the key to open the door to her room. It was the kind of cheap place Laura used to book for vacations when Andy was little. The single window looked out at the parking lot. The air-conditioner rattled below. There were two queen-sized beds with sticky-looking bedspreads and a plastic dining table with two chairs. Andy gladly put the heavy take-out box on the table. The chest of drawers had a place for a suitcase. She lugged the Samsonite on top. She dropped the tote bag and make-up bag and the sleeping bag on the bed. She lowered the blind on the window and dragged closed the flimsy blackout curtain. Or at least tried to. The curtain rod stopped an inch before the window did. Light bled in around the edge.

A flat-screen television was mounted on the wall. The cords hung down like tendrils. Out of habit, Andy found the remote and turned on the TV.

CNN. The weatherman was standing in front of a map. Andy had never been so relieved to see a hurricane warning.

She muted the sound. She sat down at the table. She opened the Styrofoam box.

Fried chicken, mashed potatoes, green beans, a cornbread muffin. She should've been disgusted, but her stomach sent up a noise like the Hallelujah Chorus.

There was no silverware, but Andy was no stranger to this dilemma. She used the chicken leg to eat the mashed potatoes, then she ate the chicken, then she used her fingers to go after the green beans, then she used the cornbread like a sponge to clean up any edible pieces of fried chicken skin or green bean juice that she had missed. It wasn't until she closed the empty box that she considered how filthy her hands were. The last time they'd been washed was in the shower of her apartment. The cleanest thing she'd touched since then was probably the desk in Laura's secret storage unit.

She looked up at the television. As if on cue, the story had switched from the hurricane to her mother. The diner video was paused on Laura holding up her hands to show Jonah Helsinger the number of bullets.

So weird, the way she was doing it—four fingers on the left hand, one on her right. Why not hold up just one hand to show five fingers for five bullets?

Suddenly, the image switched to a photograph. Andy felt her heart do a weird flip at the sight of Laura. She was wearing her standard going-out-to-parties outfit of a simple black dress with a colorful silk scarf. Andy knelt in front of the TV so she could study the details. Laura's chest was flat on one side. Her hair was short. There was a lighted star behind her, the topper on a Christmas tree. The hand on her waist must have belonged to Gordon, though he'd been cropped out of the image. The photo was probably from Gordon's most recent office Christmas party, which Laura had never missed, even when they'd wanted to kill each other. She smiled at the camera, her expression slightly guarded in what Andy always thought of as her mother's Gordon's Wife Mode.

She unmuted the sound.

". . . on the off-chance that it might happen. Ashleigh?"

Andy had missed the story. The camera cut to Ashleigh Banfield, who said, "Thanks, Chandra. We have breaking news about a shooting in Green County, Oregon."

Andy pressed the mute button again. She sat on the edge of the bed. She watched Ashleigh Banfield's face go into a split scene beside a run-down looking house that was surrounded by a SWAT team. The banner said: *Man kills own mother, two kids, holding injured wife hostage, demanding pizza and beer.*

Another shooting.

Andy flipped the channels. She wanted to see the photo of Laura again, or even to glimpse Gordon's hand. MSNBC. Fox. The local news stations. All of them were showing the live stand-off with the man who wanted pizza after murdering most of his family.

Was that a good or bad thing—not the man killing people, but the news stations covering it live? Did that mean they'd moved on from covering Laura? Would there be another *killing machine* to profile?

Andy's head was shaking even before she asked herself the obvious question: where was the story about the body of Samuel Godfrey Beckett being found in Laura Oliver's beachside bungalow? That was big news. The victim had been felled by a frying pan, ostensibly by a woman who had hours before killed a police officer's son.

And yet, the scroll at the bottom of the screen contained the usual headlines: another senator resigning, probably because of sexual harassment, another gunman shot by cops, interest rates going up, healthcare costs on the rise, stock market drops.

Nothing about Hoodie.

Andy felt her eyebrows furrow. None of this made sense. Had Laura somehow managed to keep the police out of the house? How would she even do that? The 911 text Andy had sent provided legal cause for them to break down the door. So why wasn't *Killing Machine Strikes Again* being shouted about all over the news? Even with the SWAT stand-off happening in Oregon, the last photo of Laura should have been her mugshot or, worse, video of her entering the jail in handcuffs, not a photo from a Christmas celebration.

Andy's brain was overloaded with all the *whats* and *whys*.

She let herself fall back onto the bed. She closed her eyes. When she opened them again, there was no light coming from around the closed curtain. She looked at the clock: nine thirty in the evening.

She should go back to sleep, but her eyes refused to stay closed. She stared at the brown spots on the popcorn-textured ceiling. What was her mother doing right now? Was she at home? Was she talking to Gordon on a jail phone with a thick piece of glass between them? Andy turned her head to look at the television. Still the SWAT story, even this many hours later. Her nostrils flared. The bedspread smelled like a bear had slept on it. Andy sniffed under her arms.

Ugh.

She was the bear.

She checked the lock on the door. She closed the hotel latch.

She wedged one of the chairs underneath the doorknob. Someone could still break the large window to get in, but if someone broke the window to get in, she was fucked anyway. Andy peeled off the jeans and polo shirt and underwear. Her bra was disgusting. The underwire had rubbed the skin raw underneath her armpit. She threw it into the sink and turned on the cold water.

The hotel soap was the size of a pebble and smelled like the last vestiges of a dying bouquet of flowers. She took it into the shower and between the soap and the shampoo, the tiny bathroom took on the scent of a whore house. At least what Andy thought a whore house might smell like.

She turned off the shower. She dried herself with the hotel towel, which had the consistency of notebook paper. The soap came apart in her hands as she tried to clean the stink out of her bra. She spread the crappy hotel lotion on her body as she walked into the bedroom. Then she wiped her hands on the towel to get the lotion off, then she washed her hands at the sink to remove the fuzz from the towel.

She unrolled the sleeping bag on the bed. She unzipped the side. The material was thick, filled with some kind of synthetic down, and with a nylon, waterproof outer layer. Flannel liner. Not the kind of thing you'd ever need in Belle Isle, so maybe Laura hadn't pulled Idaho out of thin air after all.

Andy opened the suitcase and picked off the top row of twenties. Ten across, three wide, times $2,000 was . . . a lot of money to hide inside of a sleeping bag.

She laid the stacks out in a flat row along the bottom of the bag. She smoothed down the nylon and pulled up the zipper. She started to roll the sleeping bag from the bottom, but the money bunched into a lump. Andy took a deep breath. She unrolled the bag again. She reached into the bottom and pulled the stacks to the center. She rolled the bag carefully from the top, secured it with the Velcro strap, then stood back to judge her work.

It looked like a sleeping bag.

Andy hefted the weight. Heavier than a sleeping bag, but not so that you'd become alarmed and think there was a small fortune inside.

She turned back to the suitcase. A third of the money was left. Bad guys in movies always ended up in train stations, which had lockers, which made it easy for them to hide money. Andy doubted there were any train stations in Florence, Alabama.

The best solution was to split it up. She should probably hide some of it in the car. There would be space inside the spare tire well under the trunk. That way, if she got separated from the sleeping bag, she could jump in the car and still have some cash. For the same reason, she could put some of the cash in her purse. Except that her purse was back in her apartment.

Andy found the hotel notepad. She wrote *purse* at the top, then *soap, lotion, bra*.

She dumped out the white tote bag. Flashlight. Batteries. Three paperbacks, unread, the titles popular approximately eleven billion years ago. The plastic first aid kit had some Band-Aids. Andy covered the scrape on her shin, which she suddenly remembered was caused by the pedal on her bike. She used the alcohol wipes to clean her blisters. It would take more than Band-Aids to get her feet into something more than Crocs. There was a cut on the side of her foot that looked pretty bad. She slapped on another Band-Aid and prayed for the best.

The Ace bandage gave her an idea. She could wrap some of the cash around her waist and secure it with the bandage. Driving would be uncomfortable, but it wasn't a bad idea to keep some of the money as close to her as possible.

Or was it? Andy remembered an NPR story about cops in rural areas pulling people over and confiscating their cash. Civil forfeiture. The Canada license plate would make her the proverbial sitting duck.

Andy unzipped the make-up bag. She opened the phone. No calls.

She pulled the Daniela Cooper driver's license from the black vinyl bag. Andy had taken the Canadian ID, health insurance card and car registration with her when she left the storage unit. She studied her mother's photograph. They had always looked like mother and daughter. Even strangers had commented on it. The eyes were a dead giveaway, but their faces were both heart-shaped and their hair was the same color brown. Andy had forgotten how dark her mother used to keep her hair. Post-cancer treatments, it had grown out in a shockingly beautiful gray. Laura wore it fashionably short now, but the Laura in the driver's license photo wore her hair down to her shoulders. Andy's hair was the same length, but she always kept it in a ponytail because she was too lazy to style it.

She looked at the mirror across from the bed. Her face was ragged. Dark circles were under her eyes. Mirror Andy looked older than her thirty-one years, that was for damn sure, but could she pass for the woman in the photo? Andy held up the driver's license. She let her eyes go back and forth. She scrunched her wet hair. She pulled down the bangs. Did that help or hinder Andy's ability to look twenty-four years older than she actually was?

There was one way to get an honest appraisal.

Andy rinsed her bra in the sink. The hotel soap had made it smell like Miss Havisham's asshole, but that was actually an improvement. Patting it dry with the towel transferred white fuzz onto the material. She used the hairdryer until the bra was only slightly damp. Then she dried her hair messier than usual, pulling it forward, styling it close to the way Laura wore hers in the Canada license photo. She put on another pair of jeans, another white polo shirt. Andy cringed as her feet slid into the Crocs again. She needed socks and real shoes. And she needed an actual written list to keep track of everything.

She grabbed a $2,000 brick of twenties, split it in two and shoved one half into each of her back pockets. The jeans were old, from a time when manufacturers actually sewed usable pockets into women's wear. Still, the bills stuck out like large cell phones. She transferred some layers into her front pocket. She looked at herself in the mirror. It worked.

Andy scooped up more handfuls of strapped twenties and hid some between the mattress and boxspring. Others got folded into her wet towel, which she artfully arranged on the bathroom floor. The rest lined the bottom of the tote bag. She put the paperbacks on top along with the first aid kit and make-up bag.

All of her machinations had left one row of bills on the bottom of the suitcase. Ten across, three wide, times $2,000 was . . . a lot of money to have in a suitcase. There was nothing to do but zip it closed and leave it out in the open. If someone broke into the room, they hopefully would be excited enough by the cash in the Samsonite to not look for the rest of the money.

Andy slung the tote bag over her shoulder as she walked out of the room. The night air slapped her face like the sudden blast of heat from an oven door. She scanned the parking lot as she walked down the stairs. There were a few Serv-Pro vans, a red truck with a Trump sticker on one side and a Confederate flag on the other, and a Mustang from the 1990s that had the front bumper held on with duct tape.

The diner was closed. The motel office lights were still on. Andy guessed it was about ten in the evening. The clerk behind the desk had his nose in his phone.

She got behind the wheel of the Reliant and moved the car to the far end of the parking lot. There were security lights on the building, but several bulbs were out. Andy walked to the back of the station wagon and opened the hatch. She checked to make sure no one was watching, then pried open the bottom of the cargo area.

Jesus.

More money, this time hundreds, stacked all around the spare tire.

Andy quickly pressed the floor cover back into place. She closed the hatch. She kept her hand pressed to the back of the car. Her heart was jackrabbiting against her ribs.

Should she feel good that her mother had split up the money the same way Andy had intended to, or should she be freaked the hell out that Laura had so carefully thought out an escape plan that there was over half a million bucks stashed in the trunk of her untraceable car?

This was the part where Andy wondered where she would've fit into Laura's disappearance, because everything Andy had found so far pointed to only one person being on the lam.

So Andy had to wonder: which Laura was her real mother—the one who'd told Andy to leave her alone or the one who'd said that everything she'd done in her life was for Andy?

"Okay," Andy mumbled, acknowledging the question had finally been asked, but fully prepared not to do any more thinking about it.

The new Andy who did math and planned driving routes and considered consequences and dealt with money problems was wearing the hell out of the old Andy, who desperately needed a drink.

She carried the tote like a purse as she walked toward the bar across the road from the motel. Half a dozen pick-up trucks were in the parking lot. All of them had signs on their sides—Joe's Plumbing, Bubba's Locksmith Services, Knepper's Knippers. Andy took a closer look at the last one, which apparently belonged to a gardener. The logo on the side, a mustachioed grasshopper holding a pair of shears, promised, *We'll knip your lawn into shape!*

Every set of eyes inside the place looked up when Andy walked through the front door. She tried to pretend like she belonged, but it was hard, considering she was the only woman. A television was blaring in the corner. Some kind of sports show. Most of the guys were sitting one or two to a booth. Two men were standing around the pool table. They had both stopped, pool sticks in the air, to watch her progress through the room.

There was only one customer sitting at the bar, but his attention was squarely focused on the television. Andy took a seat as far away from him as possible, her ass hanging off the stool, the tote bag wedged between her arm and the wall.

The bartender ambled over, throwing a white towel over his shoulder. "Whatcha want, babydoll?"

Not to be called babydoll.

"Vodka rocks," she requested, because for the first time since college, her student loan debt didn't dictate her drinking habits.

"Gottan ID?"

She found Laura's license in the make-up bag and slid it over.

He gave it a quick glance. "Vodka rocks, eh?"

Andy stared at him.

He mixed the drink in front of her, using a lot more ice than Andy would've liked.

She picked one of the twenties off the brick in her back pocket. She waited for him to leave, then tried not to set on the vodka like a wildebeest. "Personality shots," her roommates used to call the first drinks of the night. Liquid courage. Whatever you called it, the point was to turn off the voice in your head that reminded you of everything wrong in your life.

Andy tossed back the drink. The fiery sensation of the alcohol sliding down her throat made the muscles of her shoulders relax for the first time in what felt like decades.

The bartender was back with her change. She left it on the bar, nodded toward the glass. He poured another, then leaned against the bar to watch TV. Some half-bald guy in a suit was talking about the possibility of a football coach getting fired.

"Bullshit," the man at the end of the bar mumbled. He rubbed his jaw, which was rough with stubble. For some reason, Andy's gaze found his hand. The fingers were long and lean, like the rest of him. "I can't believe what that moron just said."

The bartender asked, "Want me to turn it?"

"Well, hell yeah. Why would I want to keep listening to that crap?" The guy took off his burgundy-colored baseball cap and threw it onto the bar. He ran his fingers through his thick hair. He turned to Andy and her jaw dropped open in shock.

Alabama.

From the hospital.

She was certain of it.

"I know you." His finger was pointing at her. "Right? Don't I know you?"

Fear snapped her jaw shut.

What was he doing here? Had he followed her?

"You were at the—" He stood up. He was taller than she remembered, leaner. "Are you following me?" He swiped his hat off the bar as he walked down to her end of the bar.

She looked at the door. He was in her way. He was getting closer. He was standing right in front of her.

"You're the same gal, right?" He waited for an answer that Andy could not give. "From the hospital?"

Andy's back was to the wall. She had nowhere else to go.

His expression changed from annoyed to concerned. "You okay?"

Andy could not answer.

"Hey, buddy," Alabama called to the bartender. "What'd you give her?"

The bartender looked insulted. "What the hell are you—"

"Sorry." Alabama held up his hand, but his eyes stayed on Andy. "What are you doing here?"

She couldn't swallow, let alone speak.

"Seriously, lady. Did you follow me?"

The bartender was listening now. "She's from Canada," he said, like that might help clear things up.

"Canada?" Alabama had his arms crossed. He looked uneasy. "This is some kind of weird freaking coincidence." He told the bartender, "I saw this same gal yesterday down in Savannah. I told you my granny was poorly. Had to drive down to see her. And now here's this lady right in front of me that I saw outside of the hospital the day I left. Weird, right?"

The bartender nodded. "Weird."

Alabama asked Andy, "Are you going to talk to me or what?"

"Yeah," the bartender echoed. "What's up, little bit? You stalking this guy?" He told Alabama, "You could be stalked by worse, bro."

"Not funny, man." Alabama told Andy, "Explain yourself, porcupine. Or should I call the cops?"

"I—" Andy couldn't let him call the police. "I don't know."

She realized that wasn't enough. "I was visiting," she said. "My mother. And—" *Fuck, fuck, fuck.* What could she say? How could she turn this around?

Her mental Gordon offered the solution: she could turn it around.

Andy tried to make her voice strong. "What are *you* doing here?"

"Me?"

She tried to sound indignant. "I was just passing through. Why are *you* following *me*?"

"What?" he seemed taken aback by the question.

"You," she said, because his presence made about as much sense as hers did. "I'm on my way back from visiting my parents. That's why I'm here." She squared her shoulders. "What's your reason? Why are *you* here?"

"Why am I here?" He reached behind his back.

Andy braced herself for a police badge or, worse, a gun.

But he took out his wallet. There was no badge, just his Alabama driver's license. He held it up to her face. "I live here."

Andy scanned the name.

Michael Benjamin Knepper.

He introduced himself. "Mike Knepper. The *K* is silent."

"Mi'e?" The joke came out before she could stop it.

He gave a startled laugh. His face broke out into a grin. "Holy shit, I can't believe I've gone thirty-eight years with nobody ever making that joke."

The bartender was laughing, too. They clearly knew each other, which made sense because they were roughly the same age. In a town this small, they'd probably gone to school together.

Andy felt some of the tension leave her chest. So, this was a coincidence.

Was it?

She hadn't looked closely at the photo on his license. She hadn't looked to see what town he was from.

"You're a funny lady." Mike was already tucking his wallet back into his pocket. "What're you drinking?"

The bartender said, "Vodka."

Mike held out two fingers as he sat down on the stool beside her. "How's your mom doing?"

"My—" Andy suddenly felt tipsy from the alcohol. This didn't feel completely right. She probably shouldn't drink anything else.

"Hello?" Mike said. "You still in there?"

Andy said, "My mother is fine. Just needs rest."

"I bet." He was scratching his jaw again. She tried not to look at his fingers. He looked like a man, was the thing that kept drawing her attention. Andy had only ever dated guys who looked like guys. Her last sort-of almost boyfriend had shaved once a week and needed a trigger warning anytime Andy talked about calls that came in through dispatch.

"Here ya go." The bartender placed a Sam Adams in front of Mike and a new glass of vodka in front of Andy. This one had less ice and more alcohol. He gave Mike a salute before walking to the far end of the bar.

"To coincidences." Mike raised his beer.

Andy tapped her glass against his bottle. She kept her gaze away from his hands. She took a drink before she remembered not to.

Mike said, "You cleaned up nice."

Andy felt a blush work its way up her neck.

"Seriously," Mike said. "What are you doing in Muscle Shoals?"

She sipped some vodka to give herself time to think. "I thought this was Florence?"

"Same difference." His smile was crooked. There were flecks of umber in his brown eyes. Was he flirting with her? He couldn't be flirting with her. He was too good-looking and Andy had always looked too much like somebody's kid sister.

He said, "You gonna tell me why you're here or do I have to guess?"

Andy could have cried with relief. "Guess."

He squinted at her like she was a crystal ball. "People either

190

come here for the book warehouse or the music, but you got a rock-n-roll thing going with your hair, so I'm gonna say music."

She liked the hair compliment, though she was completely clueless about his guess. "Music is right."

"You gotta book appointments to tour the studios." He kept looking at her mouth in a very obvious way. Or maybe it wasn't obvious. Maybe she was imagining the sparkle in his beautiful eyes, because in her long history of being Andy, no man had ever openly flirted with her like this.

Mike said, "Nobody really plays on weeknights, but there's a bar over near the river—"

"Tuscumbia," the bartender volunteered.

"Right, anyway, a lot of musicians, they'll go out to the clubs and work on new material. You can check online to see who's gonna be where." He took his phone out of his back pocket. She watched him dial in the code, which was all 3s. He said, "My mom's got this story. Back when she was a kid, she saw George Michael working a live set trying out that song, 'Careless Whisper.' You know it?"

Andy shook her head. He was just being nice. He wasn't flirting. She was the only woman here, and he was the best-looking guy, so it followed that he'd be the one talking with her.

But should she be talking back? He had been at the hospital. Now he was here. That couldn't be right. Andy should go. But she didn't want to go.

Every time the pendulum of doubt swung her away, he managed to charm it back in his direction.

"Here we go." Mike put his phone on the bar so she could see the screen. He'd pulled up a website that listed a bunch of names she had never heard of alongside clubs she would never go to.

To be polite, Andy pretended to read the list. Then she wondered if he was waiting for her to suggest they go to a club together, then she wondered how embarrassing it would be if she asked Mike to go and he said no, then she was finishing her drink in one gulp and motioning for another.

191

Mike asked, "So, where're you heading to from here?"

Andy almost told him, but she still had a bit of sanity underneath the all-consuming flattery of his attention. "What happened to your head?" She hadn't noticed before, but he had those weird clear strips holding together a not insignificant cut on his temple.

"Weedeater kicked a rock in my face. Does it look bad?"

Nothing could make him look bad. "How did you know he was my father?"

The crooked grin was back. "The weedeater?"

"The guy with us. Driving the car. At the hospital yester—The day before, or whenever." Andy had lost track. "You told my dad you were sorry his family was going through this. How did you know he was my father?"

Mike rubbed his jaw again. "I'm kind of nosey." He spoke with a mixture of embarrassment and pride. "I blame my three older sisters. They were always keeping things from me, so I just kind of got nosey as a way of self-preservation."

"I haven't drunk so much that I didn't notice that you didn't answer the question." Andy never articulated her thoughts this way, which should have been a warning, but she was sick of feeling terrified all of the time. "How did you know he was my dad?"

"Your cell phone," he admitted. "I saw you pull up the text messages and it said DAD at the top, and you texted 'hurry.'" He pointed to his eyes. "They just go where they want to go." As if to prove the point, he looked down at her mouth again.

Andy used her last bit of common sense to turn back toward the bar. She rolled her glass between her hands. She had to stop being stupid with this man. Mike was flirting with her when nobody ever flirted with her. He had been at the hospital and now he was hundreds of miles away in a town whose name Andy had never even heard of before she saw it on the exit sign. Setting aside her criminal enterprises, it was just damn creepy that he was here. Not just *here*, but smiling at her, looking at her mouth, making her feel sexy, buying her drinks.

But Mike lived here. The bartender knew him. And his explanations made sense, especially about Gordon. She remembered Mike hovering at her elbow in front of the hospital while she wrote the text. She remembered the glare that sent him to the bench on the opposite side of the doors.

She asked, "Why did you stay?"

"Stay where?"

"Outside the hospital." She watched his face, because she wanted to see if he was lying. "You backed off, but you didn't go back inside. You sat down on the bench outside."

"Ah." He drank a swig of beer. "Well, I told you that my granny was sick. She's not a nice person. Which is hard, because, well, as my granny herself used to say, when somebody dies, you forget they're an asshole. But at that point when you saw me outside, she wasn't dead yet. She was still alive and disapproving of me and my sisters—especially my sisters—so I just needed a break." He took another drink. He gave her a sideways glance. "Okay, that's not completely truthful."

Andy felt like an idiot, because she had bought the entire story until he'd told her not to.

Mike said, "I saw the news and . . ." He lowered his voice. "I don't know, it's kind of weird, but I saw you in the waiting room and I recognized you from the video, and I just wanted to talk to you."

Andy had no words.

"I'm not a creep." He laughed. "I understand that's what a creep would say, but this thing happened when I was a kid, and . . ." He was leaning closer to her, his voice lower. "This guy broke into our house, and my dad shot him."

Andy felt her hand go to her throat.

"Yeah, it was pretty bad. I mean, shit, I was a kid, so I didn't realize how bad it really was. Plus it turned out to be the guy he shot was dating one of my sisters, but she had broken up with him, and he had all this shit on him like handcuffs and a gag and a knife, and, anyway—" he waved all of that off. "After it happened, I had this sick feeling in my gut all of the time.

Like, on the one hand, this guy was going to kidnap my sister and probably hurt her really bad. On the other hand, my dad had killed somebody." He shrugged. "I saw you and I thought, well, hey, there's somebody who knows what it feels like. For, like, the first time in my life."

Andy tilted the vodka to her lips but she did not drink. The story was too good. Somewhere in the back of her head, she could hear warning bells clanging. This was too much of a coincidence. He had been at the hospital. He was here. He had a story that was similar to her own.

But he had the driver's license. And the truck outside. And this was obviously his local bar, and coincidences happened, otherwise there wouldn't be a word called *coincidences*.

Andy stared at the clear liquid in her glass. She needed to get out of here. It was too risky.

"—doesn't make sense," Mike was saying. "If you look at the part where—"

"What?"

"Here, let me show you." He stood up. He turned Andy's barstool so that she was facing him. "So, I'm the bad guy with the knife in his neck, right?"

Andy nodded, only now realizing that he was talking about the video from the Rise-n-Dine.

"Put the back of your left hand here at the left side of my neck like your mom." He had already picked up her left hand and placed it in position. His skin was hot against the back of her hand. "So, she's got her left hand trapped at his neck, and she crosses her other arm underneath and puts her right hand here." He picked up Andy's right hand and placed it just below his right shoulder. "Does that make sense, crossing all the way underneath to put your hand there?"

Andy considered the position of her hands. It was awkward. One arm was twisted under the other. The heel of her palm barely reached into the meaty part of his shoulder.

One hand pushing, one hand pulling.

The calm expression on Laura's face.

194

"Okay," Mike said. "Keep your left hand where it is, pinned to my neck. Push me with your right hand."

She pushed, but not hard, because her right arm was mostly already extended. His right shoulder barely twinged back. The rest of his body did not move. Her left hand, the one at his neck, had stayed firmly at his neck.

"Now here." He moved her right hand to the center of his chest. "Push."

It was easier to push hard this time. Mike took a step back. If she'd had a knife sticking through the back of her left hand, it would've come straight out of his neck.

Mike said, "Right?"

Andy mentally ran through the motions, saw Laura with the knife, pushing and pulling—but maybe not.

Mike said, "No offense, but we both know your mom knew what she was doing. You don't catch a knife like that, then your next move is to tweak the guy on the shoulder. If you're gonna kill him, you're gonna shove him hard, center mass."

Andy nodded. She was starting to see it now. Laura had not been pushing Jonah away. Her right hand had reached for his shoulder. She was trying to grab onto it.

Mike asked, "Have you looked at her feet in the video?"

"Her feet?"

"You'd step forward, right? If you were planning on yanking out that knife, you'd counterbalance the movement with one foot in front, the other in back. Basic Einstein. But that's not what she does."

"What does she do?"

"She steps her foot out to the side, like this." He slid his feet shoulder-width apart, like a boxer, or like someone who does not want to lose their balance because they are trying to keep another person from moving.

Mike said, "It's Helsinger who starts to step back. Watch the video again. You can see him lift his foot, clear as day."

Andy hadn't noticed any of this. She had assumed that her mother was some kind of cold-blooded killing machine when

195

in fact, her right hand had gone to Jonah Helsinger's shoulder to keep him from moving, not aid in his violent murder.

She asked, "You're sure he was stepping back on his own? Not stepping back to catch himself?"

"That's what it looks like to me."

Andy replayed the familiar sequence in her head. Had Jonah really stepped back? He'd written a suicide note. He'd clearly had a death wish. But was an eighteen-year-old kid really capable of stepping back from the knife, knowing what a horrific death he would be giving himself?

Mike asked, "She said something, right?"

Andy almost answered.

Mike shrugged it off. "The geeks will figure it out. But what I'm saying is, everybody's been watching the faces in the video when they should've been watching the feet."

Andy's head was reeling as she tried to process it in her mind's eye. Was he right? Or was he some kind of Belle Isle truther trying to spread conspiracy theories, and Andy believed him because she so desperately wanted another explanation?

Mike said, "Hey, listen, I gotta go see a man about a dog."

Andy nodded. She wanted time to think about this. She needed to see the video again.

Mike joked, "Don't follow me this time."

Andy didn't laugh. She watched him head to the back of the bar and disappear down a hallway. The men's room door squeaked open and banged closed.

Andy rubbed her face with her hands. She was more than tipsy after all of those stupid gulps from the glass. She needed to think about what Mike had said about the diner video. And consider her own guilt, because she had assumed that her mother was a killer. No one, not Andy, not Gordon, had thought for a moment that Laura was trying to do the right thing.

So why hadn't Laura told that to the cops? Why had she acted so guilty? And where the hell had Hoodie come from? What about the storage unit?

Every time Andy thought something made sense, the world went sideways again.

Andy started to reach for her drink.

Mike had left his phone on the bar.

She had seen his passcode. Six 3s.

The bartender was watching television. The pool players were arguing about a shot. The long hallway was still empty. She would hear the door when Mike came out of the bathroom. She had heard it when he went in.

Andy picked up the phone. She dialed in the 3s. The home screen had a photo of a cat behind it, and weirdly, she thought a man who had his cat on his phone could not be that bad. Andy tapped Safari. She pulled up the *Belle Isle Review*. The front page had the new photo of Laura at the party, the one she'd seen on CNN. Gordon was not cropped out this time. Andy scanned the story, which was basically the same one that had been there the day before.

She scrolled down for other news. She was more relieved than startled when she saw the headline:

BODY FOUND UNDER YAMACRAW BRIDGE

Andy skimmed the details. Head injury. No ID. Jeans and a black hoodie. Dolphin tattoo on his hip. Found by fishermen. No foul play suspected. Police asking people to come forward with information.

She heard the bathroom door open. Andy closed the browser page. She tapped back to the home screen. She clicked the phone off and had it back on the bar by the time Mike appeared in the hallway.

Andy sipped the vodka.

Unidentified body?

Head injury?

No foul play?

Mike groaned as he sat back on the stool. "Had to lift about sixteen thousand pounds of boulders today."

Andy murmured in sympathy, but the new story was her focus now. The Yamacraw Bridge spanned the Tugaloo River. How had Hoodie's body gotten there? Laura couldn't have taken him herself. Even without the police watching, she only had one good arm and one good leg.

What the hell was going on?

"Hello?" Mike was rapping his knuckles on the bar again, this time for Andy's attention. "Past my bedtime. I gotta big job to start tomorrow. Want me to walk you to your car?"

Andy didn't think it was a good idea to stay in the bar alone. She looked around for the bartender.

"He'll put it on my tab." Mike tucked his phone into his pocket. He indicated Andy should go ahead of him. He kept his distance until she got to the door, then he reached ahead to hold it open.

Outside, the heat was only slightly less awful than before. Andy would take another shower before she went to bed. Maybe she would crank down the a/c and climb into the sleeping bag. Or maybe she would climb into the Reliant because wasn't it still weird that she had met Mike here, of all places? And that he was telling her things that she wanted to hear? And that he had walked her out of the bar, which meant he would know where she was going next?

Knepper Knippers. There was lawn equipment in the back of the truck—a weedeater, a leaf blower, some rakes and a shovel. Streaks of dirt and grass were on the side panels. Mike had been in the bar when she got there, not the other way around. His truck was clearly used for lawncare purposes. He had a driver's license with his name on it. He had a tab at the bar, for the love of God. Either he was a clairvoyant psychopath or Andy was losing her mind.

He patted the truck. "This is me."

She said, "I like the grasshopper."

"You're beautiful."

Andy was taken off guard.

He laughed. "That was weird, right? I just met you. I mean, really met you. And we flirted with each other in a bar and it was nice but it's still kind of strange that we're both here at the same time, right?"

198

"You keep saying things that I'm thinking in my head, but you say them like they're normal instead of something I should be worried about." Andy wanted to clap her hands over her mouth. She had not meant to say any of that out loud. "I should go."

"All right."

She didn't go. Why had he called her beautiful?

"You've got—" he reached to pick something out of her hair. A piece of fuzz from the cheap motel towel.

Andy wrapped her hand around his, because apparently, Hand-fetish Andy was also a hell of a lot bolder than normal Andy.

"You really are so damn beautiful." He said it like he was in awe. Like he meant it.

Andy leaned her head into his hand. His palm was rough against her cheek. The neon lights from the bar caught the umber in his eyes. She wanted to melt into him. It felt so damn good to be looked at, to be touched, by somebody. By this body. By this weird, attractive man.

And then he kissed her.

Mike was tentative at first but then her fingers were in his hair and the kissing got deeper and suddenly all of Andy's nerves went collectively insane. Her feet left the ground. He backed her into the truck, pressed hard against her. His mouth was on her neck, her breasts. Every single inch of Andy's body wanted him. She had never been so overcome with lust. She reached down to stroke him with her hand, and—

"Keychain," he said.

He was laughing, so Andy laughed, too. She'd felt up the keychain in his front pocket.

Her feet went back to the ground. They were both breathing hard.

She leaned in to kiss him again, but Mike turned away.

He said, "I'm sorry."

Oh, God.

"I'm just—" His voice was rough. "I—"

199

Andy wanted to disappear into the ether. "I should—"

He pressed his fingers to her mouth to stop her. "You really are so beautiful. All I could think about in there was kissing you." His thumb traced across her lips. He looked like he was going to kiss her again, but he took a step back and tucked his hand into his pocket instead. "I'm really attracted to you. I mean, obviously, I'm attracted to you, but—"

"Please don't."

"I need to say this," he told her, because his feelings were the most important thing right now. "I'm not that guy. You know, the one who picks up women in bars and takes them to the parking lot and—"

"I wasn't going to," Andy said, but that was a lie because she'd been about to. "I didn't—"

"Could you—"

Andy waited.

Mike didn't finish his sentence. He just shrugged and said, "I should go."

She kept waiting for more because she was stupid.

"Anyway." He pulled his keys out of his pocket and looped the keychain around his fingers. And then he laughed.

Please don't make a joke about me giving your keychain a handjob.

He said, "I could—I mean, I should walk you to—"

Andy left. Her face was on fire as she crossed the road. He was watching her leave again the same way he had watched her leave outside of the hospital. "Idiot, idiot, idiot," Andy whispered, then, "What the fuck? What the *fuck*?"

She felt disgusted with herself as she climbed the stairs to the motel. Mike's truck was pulling onto the road. He was looking up at her as she walked across the balcony. Andy wished for a bazooka to blow him away. Or a gun to kill herself with. She had never hooked up with a stranger. Not even in college. What the hell was wrong with her? Why was she making such stupid decisions? She was a criminal on the run. No one could be trusted. So what if Mike had an Alabama driver's license? Laura

200

had one from Ontario, for fucksakes. She had a fake car. Mike could have a fake truck. The sign with the grasshopper was magnetized, not permanently stuck on. The bartender could've been friendly with Mike because bartenders are always friendly with their customers.

Andy jammed the key in the lock and threw open the door to her room. She was so upset that she barely noted the suitcase and sleeping bag were where she'd left them.

She sat on the bed, head in her hands, and tried not to burst into tears.

Had Mike played her? For what purpose? Was he some freak who was interested in Andy because he saw her on the diner video? He'd sure as hell spent a lot of time figuring out what had happened between Laura and Jonah Helsinger. At least what he thought had happened. He probably had a conspiracy blog. He probably listened to those crazy shows on the radio.

But he had called her beautiful. And he was right about being excited. Unless somehow between opening the front door of the bar and walking to his truck he'd shoved a can of Coke down his pants.

"Christ!"

That stupid keychain.

Andy stood up. She had to pace. She had to go through every single fucking stupid thing she had done. Kissed him too deeply? Too much saliva? Not enough tongue? Maybe her breasts were too small. Or, God, no—

She smelled her bra, which carried the scent of the disgusting hotel soap.

Did guys care about that kind of thing?

Andy covered her eyes with her hands. She sank back to the bed.

The memory of her fingers stroking that stupid keychain in his pocket made her cheeks radiate with heat. He had probably been insulted. Or maybe he hadn't wanted to take advantage of someone who was so painfully inept. What kind of idiot thought a rabbit's foot keychain was a man's penis?

But what kind of grown-ass man kept a giant rabbit's foot in his pocket?

That guy.

What the hell did that even mean—*that guy?*

Andy dropped her hands from her face.

She felt her mouth gape open.

The truck.

Not Mike's grasshopper truck or the dead man's truck, but the beat-up old Chevy she had seen parked in the Hazeltons' driveway early this morning.

This morning—

After Andy had killed a man. After she had run down the beach looking for the dead man's Ford because Laura had told her to.

There had been two trucks parked in the Hazeltons' driveway, not one.

The windows had been rolled down. Andy had looked inside the cab. She had considered stealing the old Chevy instead of taking the Ford. It would've been easy, because the key was in the ignition. She had seen it clearly in the pre-dawn light.

It was attached to a rabbit's foot keychain, just like the one that Mike Knepper had taken out of his pocket and looped around his fingers.

July 31, 1986

FIVE DAYS AFTER THE OSLO SHOOTING

9

Jane Queller woke in a cold sweat. She had been crying in her sleep again. Her nose was raw. Her body ached. She started shaking uncontrollably. Panic made her heart shiver inside of her chest. In the semi-darkness, she thought she was back in Berlin, then in the Oslo hotel room, then she realized that she was in her childhood bedroom inside the Presidio Heights house. Pink wallpaper. Satin pink duvet and pillows. More pink in the rug, on the couch, the desk chair. Posters and stuffed animals and dolls.

Her mother had decorated the room because Jane did not have time to do it herself. From the age of six, almost every waking moment of Jane's life had been spent in front of the piano. Tinkering. Practicing. Playing. Learning. Performing. Touring. Judging. Failing. Recovering. Coaxing. Succeeding. Mastering.

In the early days, Martin would stand behind Jane while she played, his eyes following the notes, his hands on her shoulders, gently pressing when she made a mistake. Pechenikov had requested Martin abandon his post as a condition of taking on Jane as a student, but the tension of Martin's presence had shadowed her career. Her life. Her triumphs. Her failures. Whether she was in Tokyo or Sydney or New York, or even during her three months of isolation in Berlin, Jane could always feel an invisible Martin hovering behind her.

Jane shivered again. She glanced behind her, as if Martin might be there. She sat up and pressed her back against the headboard. She pulled the sheets around her.

What had they done?

Nick would argue that they hadn't done anything. Laura Juneau was the one who'd pulled the trigger. The woman had been visibly at peace with the decision. She could've walked away at any time. That she had murdered Martin, then herself, was an act of bravery, and also an act that she had committed alone.

But for the first time in the six years that Jane had known Nicholas Harp, she found herself incapable of believing him.

They had all put Laura on that stage with Martin—Jane, Andrew, Nick, the other cells in the other cities. By Nick's design, they were each a cog in a decentralized machine. A mysterious man on the inside had helped Chicago infiltrate the company that produced the red dye packs that were supposed to be inside the brown paper bag. New York had worked with the document forger in Toronto. San Francisco had paid for airline tickets, hotel rooms, taxi rides and meals. Like Martin's shadow behind Jane, they had all stood invisible behind Laura Juneau as she pulled the revolver from her purse and twice squeezed the trigger.

Was this crazy?

Were they all insane?

Every morning for the last eighteen months Jane had found herself waking up with doubt on her mind. Her emotions would violently swing like the clapper inside a bell. One moment, she would think that they were acting like lunatics—running drills, practicing escapes and learning how to use weapons. Wasn't that ridiculous? Why did Jane have to learn hand-to-hand combat? Why did she need to memorize safe house locations and understand diagrams of false panels and secret compartments? They were just a handful of people, all of them under the age of thirty, believing that they had the wherewithal, the power, to pull off extraordinary acts of opposition.

206

Wasn't that the very definition of delusional?

But then the next moment, Nick would start speaking and Jane would be convinced beyond a shadow of a doubt that everything they were doing made perfect sense.

Jane put her head in her hands.

She had helped a woman murder her own father. She had planned for his death. She had known it was going to happen and said nothing.

Oslo had taken away the ridiculousness. The skepticism. Everything was real now. All of it was happening.

Jane was losing her mind.

"There you are." Nick came into the room with a mug in one hand and a newspaper in the other. He was wearing his boxer shorts and nothing else. "Drink all of this."

Jane took the mug. Hot tea and bourbon. The last time she'd had a drink was with Laura Juneau in the bar. Jane's heart had been pounding then as it pounded now. Laura had called Jane a chameleon. And she had been right. The woman had no idea that Jane was part of the group. They had talked like strangers, then intimates, then Laura was gone.

You are a magnificent person, she had told Jane before leaving. *You are magnificent because you are so uniquely you.*

"More G-men just pulled up." Nick was at the window looking down on the motorcourt. "I'm guessing FBI by the shitty car." He flashed Jane a crooked grin, as if the presence of more feds on top of the CIA, NSA, Interpol, Revenue Agents and Secret Service men they'd already spoken to was a trifle. "You be Bonnie and I'll be Clyde."

Jane gulped the tea. She barely tasted the hot liquid as it scorched into her stomach. Martin had been murdered five days ago. His funeral was tomorrow. Nick seemed to be feeding off the stress, almost giddy during the interviews that more and more felt like interrogations. Jane wanted to scream at him that this was real, that they had murdered someone, that what they were planning next could land them all in prison for the rest of their lives—or worse.

Instead, she whispered, "I'm scared, Nicky."

"Darling." He was on the bed, holding her, before she could ask. His lips were at her ear. "You'll be okay. Trust me. I've been through a hell of a lot worse than this. It makes you stronger. It reminds you why we're doing this."

Jane closed her eyes as she tried to absorb his words. She had lost the point of doing this. Why was she grieving her father? For so many years, she'd truly believed that any love she'd had for Martin had been beaten out of her. So why was Jane so racked with guilt? Why did it hurt every time she remembered that Martin was gone?

"Stop." Nick could always tell when she was troubled. He told her, "Think of something else. Something good."

Jane shook her head. She did not have Nick's talent of compartmentalization. She couldn't even close her eyes without seeing Martin's head exploding. He'd been shot in the temple. Brain and tissue and bone had splattered Friedrich Richter like mud from a car wheel. Then Laura had pulled the trigger again and the top of her head had sprayed up into the ceiling.

I'm sorry, Jane had mouthed to the woman seconds before.

Had Laura even known why Jane was apologizing?

"Come on," Nick said, giving Jane a squeeze on the shoulder to bring her back to the present. "Do you remember the first time I met you?"

Jane shook her head again, but only to try to clear the violent images from her mind. The gun. The explosions. The splatter and spray.

"Come on, Jinx," Nick coaxed. "Have you forgotten about the first time we met? It'll be six years in December. Did you know that?"

Jane wiped her nose. Of course she knew. The moment she first saw Nick was etched into every fiber of her being: Andrew and Nick home from college, pushing and shoving each other like schoolboys in the front hall. Jane had stormed out of the parlor to complain about the racket. Nick had smiled at her,

208

and she'd felt her heart fill like a hot-air balloon that threatened to float out of her chest.

"Jinx?"

She knew that he wouldn't give up unless she played along, so she played along, saying, "You barely noticed me."

"You were barely legal."

"I was seventeen." She hated when he treated her like she was a child. Like Andrew, he was only three years her senior. "And you ignored me the entire weekend because you and Andy were chasing after those trashy girls from North Beach."

He laughed. "You would've never given me a chance if I'd fallen all over myself like the other fools."

There were no other fools. No one had ever fallen all over themselves for Jane. Men had looked at her with either awe or boredom, as if she was a doll inside of a glass case. Nick was the first of Andrew's friends who had seen her as a woman.

He stroked back her hair. His mouth went to her ear. He always whispered when he told her the important things. "I didn't ignore you the *entire* weekend."

Jane could not stop her heart from doing the floaty thing again. Even now in this horrible moment, she could still remember the thrill of Nick surprising her in the kitchen. She was reading a magazine when he'd wandered in. Jane had said something flinty to make him go away, and he'd kissed her, wordlessly, before backing out of the room and closing the door.

Nick said, "I was practically an orphan when I met you. I didn't have anybody. I was completely alone. And then I had you." His hand held the back of her neck. He was suddenly serious. "Tell me you're still with me. I have to know."

"Of course." He'd done this in Oslo, then again on the plane home, then their first night back in San Francisco. He seemed terrified that the three months they'd spent apart had somehow weakened her resolve. "I'm with you, Nick. Always."

He searched her eyes for a sign, some indication that she was lying to him the way that everyone else had in his life.

"I am yours," she repeated, firmly. "Every part of me is yours."

"Good girl." His smile was hesitant. He had been hurt by so many people before.

Jane wanted to hold him, but he hated when she got clingy. Instead, she tilted up her face so that he would kiss her. Nick obliged, and for the first time in days, Jane could breathe again.

"My darling," he whispered into her ear. His hands slid under her camisole. His mouth moved to her breasts. Jane was finally able to wrap her arms around him. She didn't want sex, but she knew telling him no again would hurt his feelings. What she craved most was the after. When he held her. When he told her that he loved her. When he made her feel like everything was going to be okay.

That would be the moment to tell him.

As Nick laid her back on the bed, Jane felt all the words she had silently practiced over the last month rush to her lips—*I'm sorry, terrified, ecstatic, overjoyed, anxious, panicky, elated, so scared that you'll leave me because—*

I'm pregnant.

"Hello?"

They both sat back up. Jane gripped the sheets around her neck.

"You guys awake?" Andrew knocked on the door before peering into the room. "Everyone decent?"

"Never," Nick said. He still held one of her breasts underneath the sheet. Jane tried to pull away, but Nick snaked his arm around her waist so that she could not. He stroked the small of her back, his eyes on Andrew.

Nick said, "Two more agents pulled into the front drive."

"I saw." Andrew wiped his nose with his sleeve. He was still fighting off the cold from Norway. He told Nick what Jane dared not. "Don't be aggressive with them, Nicky. Please."

They all looked at each other. Nick's hand stroked lower down Jane's back. She felt a flush of heat work its way up her neck and into her face. She hated when he did this sort of thing in front of Andrew.

Nick said, "I feel like we should be touching the sides of our noses like they did in *The Sting*."

"This is real life." Andrew's tone was strident. They were all terrified that the house was bugged. The last few days had been like tiptoeing around the sharp end of a needle. "Our father has been murdered. A woman has been kidnapped. You need to take this seriously."

"I'll at least take it cleanly." Nick bit Jane's shoulder before marching into the bathroom.

Jane pulled the sheets tighter around her neck. She stared at the closed bathroom door. She wanted to go after him, to beg him to listen to Andrew, but she had always lacked the ability to tell Nick that he was wrong about anything.

Andrew said, "Jane—"

She motioned for him to turn around so she could get dressed.

He obliged, saying, "Mother was asking for you."

Jane rolled on a pair of pantyhose. The waist felt tight when she stood. "Was that Ellis-Anne you were on the phone with this morning?"

Andrew did not answer. The subject of his ex-girlfriend was somehow off limits now.

Still, she tried, "You were together for two years. She's just—"

"Jane," Andrew repeated, his voice low. He'd been trying to talk to her about Martin since they got home, but Jane was too afraid that speaking to him would open something inside of her that could not be closed.

She told him, "You should go to the doctor." Her fingers fumbled with the tiny pearl buttons on her blouse. She yanked a pair of slacks off the hanger.

"I feel—" His head slowly moved from side to side. "I feel like something is missing inside of me. Like an organ has been taken away. Is that strange?"

Jane tried to zip up the side of her slacks. Her fingers felt clumsy. She had to wipe the sweat off her hands. The pants

211

were tight. Everything was tight because she was pregnant and they had killed their father and they were probably going to kill more people by the time this was over.

"Andy, I can't—" her words were cut off by a sob.

I can't talk to you. I can't listen to you. I can't be around you because you're going to say what I've been thinking and it will end up tearing us to shreds.

How had Laura Juneau done it?

Not the physical act—Jane had been there, she had witnessed every single detail of the actual murder and suicide—but how had Laura flipped that switch inside of herself that turned her into a cold-blooded killer? How could the kind, interesting woman whom Jane had smoked with in the conference center bar be the same woman who had taken a gun from her purse and murdered a man, then herself?

Jane kept coming back to the expression of absolute serenity on Laura Juneau's face. It was the slight smile on the woman's lips that had given her away. Clearly, Laura had been totally at peace with her actions. There was no hesitation. Not a moment of second thought or doubt. When Laura's hand had reached into her purse to find the revolver, she might as well have been looking for a pack of chewing gum.

"Jinx?" Andrew had turned back around. There were tears in his eyes, which made Jane cry even harder. "Let me help with this."

She watched him tug up the zipper on the side of her slacks. His breath had a sickly smell. His skin looked clammy. She said, "You've lost weight."

"Here it is." He playfully pinched the new roll of fat ringing her waist. "Nick said we'll get through this, right? And Nick's always right, isn't he?"

They smiled, but neither one of them laughed out loud, because they didn't know whether or not Nick was listening on the other side of the door.

"We should try to pull ourselves together." Jane found some tissue. She handed it to Andrew, then took some for herself.

They both blew their noses. Andrew coughed. The rattle in his chest was like marbles clicking together.

She put her hand to his forehead. "You need to go to the doctor."

He shrugged, asking, "When?"

The bathroom door opened. Nick came out, naked, toweling his hair dry. "What'd I miss?"

Andrew offered, "I'll go downstairs before Jasper comes looking for us."

"You go, too," Nick told Jane. "Wear the boots. They're more intimidating."

Jane found a pair of black socks in the drawer. She slipped them on over her pantyhose. She held up a few pairs of boots before Nick nodded that she'd found the right ones. She was leaning over to do up the buckles when she felt Nick pressing behind her. He talked to Andrew as his hands rubbed her lower back. "Jane's right. You should make time to go to the doctor. We can't have you sick for the—the funeral."

Jane felt bile slide up her throat as she finished buckling her riding boots. She didn't know if it was the awful morning sickness or the fear. From the beginning, Nick had been playing these unnecessary verbal games. Jane knew he got a thrill out of picturing an FBI agent sitting in a surveillance van down the street, hanging on his every word.

He put his mouth to her ear again. "Knock them out, my darling."

She nodded, telling Andrew, "Ready."

Nick slapped her ass as she left the room. Jane felt the same deep flush of embarrassment from before. It was pointless to ask him to stop because begging only made him worse.

Andrew let Jane precede him down the front stairs. She worked to cool the heat in her face. She knew that Nick had grown up unloved, that it was important to him that people understood he belonged, but she hated when he treated her like a hunting trophy.

"Okay?" Andrew asked.

Jane realized she'd put her hand to her stomach. She had not told Andrew or anyone else about the baby. At first, she'd persuaded herself that it was because she wanted Nick to be the first to know, but as the weeks had passed, she'd realized that she was terrified that he would not want the baby and she would have to explain to everyone why she was no longer pregnant.

Next time, he'd told her the last time. *We'll keep it next time.*

"Miss Queller?" a man was waiting for them in the front hallway. He had his wallet open to a gold shield. "I'm Agent Barlow with the FBI. This is Agent Danberry."

Danberry was standing inside the parlor with his hands clasped behind his back. He looked like a lesser version of Barlow: less hair, less confidence, less teeth, even, because he appeared to be missing an upper cuspid. He had been talking to Jasper, who was dressed in his Air Force Reserve uniform. Medals and colorful bars lined her brother's chest. Jasper was twelve years older than Jane, the over-protective brother who had always been her anchor. He had attended her concerts and asked about her schoolwork and taken her to the prom when no one else would. Jane had always seen him as a miniature adult, a heroic figure who played with his toy soldiers and read military history books but could reliably be depended upon to scare the hell out of any boy who dared hurt her feelings or to give her cash so she could buy lipstick.

"Miss Queller?" Agent Barlow repeated.

"I'm sorry," Jane apologized, taking a tissue from the box on the coffee table.

Barlow seemed chastened. "My condolences on your loss."

Jane wiped her eyes as she looked in the mirror behind the couch. Her skin felt raw. Her eyes were swollen. Her nose was bright red. She had been crying for almost five days straight.

"Take your time," Barlow offered, but he seemed anxious to begin.

Jane blew her nose as quietly as she could.

Nick had made them practice their statements for hours, but

nothing could prepare Jane for the stress of being interviewed. The first time, she had sobbed uncontrollably, panicked that she would say the wrong thing. In subsequent interviews, Jane had realized that the tears were a godsend, because crying was what was expected of her. Andrew, too, seemed to have figured out a strategy. When a tough question was put to him, he would sniff and wipe his eyes and turn his head away while he considered his answer.

It was Nick who made them nervous—not just Jane and Andrew, but anyone who happened to be in the room. He seemed to get a perverse pleasure from taunting the agents, going right up to the line, then inventing an innocent explanation that pulled them back from the brink.

Watching him with the Secret Service agents yesterday, Jane had wondered if he was suicidal.

"Jinx?" Jasper said.

They were all waiting for her to sit down. She perched on the edge of the couch. Andrew sat beside her. Barlow sat on the couch opposite with his hands on his knees. Only Jasper and Danberry remained standing, one to pace and the other, seemingly, to inspect the room. Instead of asking a question, Danberry opened an onyx box on one of the bookshelves and peered inside.

Across from her, Barlow took a notebook out of his breast pocket and thumbed through the pages. His eyes moved back and forth as he silently read through the notes.

Jane looked at Andrew, then Jasper, who shrugged.

This was new. The other agents had started with small talk, asked about the house, the decorations. It was Andrew who usually gave them the rundown. The parlor, like the rest of the house, was a gothic-beaux-arts mishmash, with spindly furniture and velvet wallpaper between the dark mahogany panels. The twin chandeliers had belonged to some ancient Queller who'd worked with Mr. Tiffany on the design. The coffee table was from sequoias felled by her mother's side of the family. A grown man could stand comfortably inside the fireplace. Rumor had

215

it that the rug was gotten off a Japanese family who'd been sent to an internment camp during the war.

Andrew shifted on the couch. Jasper resumed pacing.

Barlow turned a page in his notebook. The noise was like sandpaper in the silence. Danberry had tilted his head to the side so he could read the titles on the spines of books.

Jane had to do something with her hands. She found a pack of cigarettes on the coffee table. Andrew struck a match for her. He was staying only partially still beside her. He kept randomly tapping his foot. Jane wondered how it would look if she reached over to still his leg. Or if she asked Barlow to please begin. Or if she screamed as loud as she could until everyone left and she could go back upstairs and find Nick.

This was a manipulation tactic, obviously. Barlow and Danberry were ramping up everyone's nerves so that they would make stupid mistakes.

Silently, Jane went through the questions that all the other agents had asked.

Have you ever met the real Alexandra Maplecroft? What did Laura Juneau say to you at the conference? Why didn't you know she was an imposter? Where do you think the real Dr. Alexandra Maplecroft is?

Kidnapped.

The answer to the last question was common knowledge. The ransom note had been printed on the front page of yesterday's *San Francisco Chronicle—*

We have Dr. Alexandra Maplecroft, a tool of the fascist regime . . .

"Miss Queller?" Barlow was finally looking up from his notebook. "I'm just going to sum up what we already know from the other interviews you've given."

Jane could barely manage a nod. Her body had gone rigid with tension. Something was different about these two men. With their wrinkled suits and stained ties and missing teeth and bad haircuts, they looked like TV parodies of G-men, but they would not be here if they were second or third string.

"Here we go," Barlow said. "You'd never met Laura Juneau before the conference. You might've recognized her name from before, when her husband killed their children, because the story was in the newspapers. You were in Berlin to fill in for a friend at a studio for two months. You—"

"Three," Jasper corrected.

"Right, three months. Thank you, Major Queller." Barlow kept his focus on Jane as he continued, "You've never met Dr. Alexandra Maplecroft before and you've only heard her name in relation to your father, because she was a rival who—"

"No," Jasper said. "In order to be rivals, you have to be equals. Maplecroft was a nuisance."

"Thank you again, Major." Barlow clearly wanted Jasper to shut up, but instead, he continued, "Miss Queller, first, I'd like to talk about your discussion with Mrs. Juneau at the bar."

Jane blinked, and she could see the delighted look on Laura's face when she recognized Jane tapping out "Love Me Two Times" on the bar top.

Barlow asked, "Did you approach Mrs. Juneau or did she approach you?"

Jane's throat felt so tight that she had to cough before she could speak. "I did. I was on the piano, playing the piano, when she walked in. I assumed she was American because of—"

"The way she was dressed," Barlow finished. "You wanted to speak to an American after being in Germany for so long."

Jane felt a sick kind of dizziness. Why had he finished the sentence for her? Was he trying to prove that he'd talked to the other agents, that they'd all compared notes, or was he just trying to get her to move along?

Or, most terrifying of all, had Nick made them practice too much? Were their word choices, their gestures, their comments, so rehearsed that they'd managed to throw up flags?

Jane parted her lips. She tried to pull air into her lungs.

Barlow asked, "What did you and Mrs. Juneau talk about?"

Jane felt a pressing weight on her chest. The room suddenly felt stifling. She put the cigarette in the ashtray, worked to line

217

it up in the groove. Her hand was trembling again. She didn't know what to do, so she told them the truth. "She'd seen me play a few years back. We talked about the performance. And about music in general."

"So, Bach, Beethoven, Mozart?" Barlow seemed to be plucking names from thin air. "Chopin? Chacopsky?"

Tchaikovsky, Jane almost corrected, but she caught herself at the last moment because—was it a trick? Had she told another agent something else?

Andrew coughed again. He picked up the cigarette that Jane had left smoldering in the ashtray.

Barlow prompted, "Miss Queller?"

Jane found the tissues and blew her nose. She willed the panic back down.

Stick to the truth, Nick had coached them. *Just make sure it's not the whole truth.*

"Well . . ." Jane tried not to rush her words. "We spoke about Edvard Grieg, because he's Norwegian. A-ha, the pop music group, also Norwegian. Martha Argerich, from Argentina. I'm not sure why she came up, but she did."

"Did you see Juneau go into the bathroom?" Barlow studied Jane closely as she shook her head. "Were you in the bathroom at any point before the shooting?"

"It was a long conference. I'm sure I was." Jane was aware that her voice was shaking. Was that a good thing? Did it make her story sound more believable? She looked at Danberry. He'd been circling the room like a shark. Why wasn't he asking any questions?

Barlow said, "There was tape residue behind one of the toilet tanks. We think the gun was hidden there."

"Fantastic," Jasper said. "Then you'll have fingerprints. Case closed."

"They wore gloves." Barlow asked Jane, "So, what we've been told is, before the murder, you'd heard about Laura and Robert Juneau. What about Maplecroft?"

"Juneau and Maplecroft in the front parlor," Nick bellowed,

218

choosing this moment to make his appearance. "Good God, they sound like characters from the Canadian version of Clue. Which one had the candlestick?"

Everyone had turned to look at Nick standing in the entryway. He had somehow managed to take all of the air out of the room. Jane had seen him do this countless times before. He could bring the tone up or down like a deejay turning the knob on a record player.

"Mr. Harp," Barlow said. "Nice that you can join us."

"My pleasure." Nick walked into the room with a self-satisfied grin on his face. Jane kept her eyes on Barlow, who was taking in Nick's fine features. The agent's expression was neutral, but she could feel his distaste. Nick's good looks and charm either worked for him or against him. There was never any in between.

"Now, gentlemen." Nick put a proprietary arm behind Jane as he wedged himself between Jane and Andrew on the couch. "I'm assuming you've already been told that none of us knew either Maplecroft or Juneau before Martin was murdered?" His fingers combed through the back of Jane's hair. "Poor girl has been broken up about it. I don't see how anyone could have that many tears inside of them."

Barlow held Nick's gaze for just a moment before turning to Andrew, asking, "Why weren't you and Mr. Harp on the same flight out of San Francisco?"

"Nick left a day ahead of me." Andrew took out his hand-kerchief and wiped his nose. "He had business in New York, I believe."

"What kind of business?"

Andrew looked puzzled, because Barlow wasn't asking Nick these questions.

"Major Queller." Barlow made a point of turning his head toward Jasper. "How is it that your family knows Mr. Harp?"

"Nick's been with us for years." Jasper's tone was even, which was surprising because he had never cared for Nick. "We've taken him on vacations, spent holidays together. That sort of thing."

Andrew added, "His family lives on the East Coast. Nick was sort of orphaned out here. Mother and Father welcomed him as one of the family."

Barlow asked, "He was sent out here at the age of fifteen, wasn't he?" He waited, but no one spoke. "Got into some trouble with the police back home? Mother shipped him across the country to live with his granny?"

"Nick told us all about it." Andrew glanced nervously at Nick. "It was a tough road, but he still managed to get into Stanford."

"Right." Barlow looked back at his notes. They were doing the silent thing again.

Nick affected indifference. He brushed imaginary lint from his trousers. He gave Jane a quick wink. Only she could feel the tension inside his body. His arm behind her shoulders had gone taut. She could feel his fingers digging into her skin.

Was he mad at her? Should she be defending him? Should she tell the agents that Nick was a good man, that he'd managed to pull himself up from the gutter, that they had no right to treat him this way because he was—

Losing.

Nick didn't see it now, but he had lost the game the minute he'd walked into the room. He had been making fun of the government agents for days, railing against their stupidity, bragging about his own cleverness. He had not realized that they were just as capable of putting on an act as he was.

Jane took a stuttered breath. She had started to cry again. Nothing was more terrifying than watching him try to punch his way out of a tight spot.

"Mr. Queller." Barlow looked up at Andrew. "Did Mr. Harp mention to you that he attended one of Dr. Maplecroft's lectures?"

Andrew shot Jane a frightened look that mirrored her own feelings: *What should they say? What did Nick want?*

"I can answer that one," Nick offered. "If you'd like me to?"

"Why not?" Barlow sat back on the couch.

Behind him, Danberry opened and closed another box.

Nick made them wait.

He reached for the cigarette in the ashtray. He inhaled audibly, then blew out a stream of smoke. He tapped off some ash. He lined the cigarette up with the groove in the marble ashtray. He leaned back against the couch. His arm went behind Jane.

Finally, he looked up, pretending to be surprised that they were all waiting on him. "Oh, you want my answer now?"

Danberry crossed his arms.

Jane swallowed back a flood of bile that rushed up her throat.

Nick asked Barlow, "Do you have a record of my attendance at this lecture?"

"According to her assistant, Dr. Maplecroft didn't believe in keeping attendance."

"Pity."

"We'll be talking to other students this week."

"That must be quite an undertaking," Nick said. "How many kids are at Berkeley now? Thirty, forty thousand?"

Barlow gave a heavy sigh. He opened his notebook again. He resumed the game, directing his words toward Andrew. "At the conference, when Mr. Harp approached Laura Juneau, who was at that time posing as Dr. Maplecroft, Mr. Harp mentioned attending one of Dr. Maplecroft's lectures. The police officer and the girl working the check-in table both heard him say the same thing."

Andrew said, "I wasn't there for that part of the conversation, but I'm sure Nick can—"

"Are you aware that Mr. Harp has a drug conviction?"

Nick snapped, "Are you aware that Mr. Queller does?"

"Christ," Jasper muttered.

"Just making sure they have the facts," Nick said. "It's a felony to lie to an FBI agent. Isn't that correct, Mr. Danberry?"

Danberry kept silent, but Jane could tell he'd picked up on the fact that Nick had not been here when the agents had introduced themselves. Jane could've told him that he was likely

221

listening at the top of the stairs. She had learned the hard way that Nick was a stealthy eavesdropper.

Andrew volunteered, "Two years ago, I was convicted for possession of cocaine. I performed community service in exchange for my record being expunged."

Nick added, "That kind of thing doesn't stay a secret in times like these, does it?"

Barlow quipped, "It does not."

Jane tried not to wince as Nick ran his fingers roughly through her hair. He told Barlow, "I met Laura Juneau in the KLM lounge at Schiphol. We were both en route to Oslo. She approached me. She asked if the seat next to me was taken. I said no. She introduced herself as Dr. Alexandra Maplecroft. She said she recognized me from one of her lectures, which could be true, but honestly, gentlemen, I was stoned out of my mind during most of my classes, so I'm hardly a reliable witness."

"Hardly," Barlow echoed.

Danberry still said nothing. He'd made it to the Bösendorfer Imperial Concert Grand on the other side of the room. Jane tried not to bristle when he soundlessly glided his fingers over the extra bass keys.

Barlow said, "So, Mr. Harp, as far as you can recall, you met Dr. Maplecroft for the first time at the Amsterdam airport, then you met her for the second time in Oslo?"

"That's right," Nick agreed. Jane could have cried with relief when he returned to the script. "In order to be polite, I pretended to recognize the woman whom I thought was Dr. Maplecroft. Then I saw her again at the conference and again pretended in order to be polite." His shoulder went up in a shrug. "I think the operative word here is 'pretend,' gentlemen. She pretended to know me. I pretended to know her. Only one of us had darker intentions."

Barlow made a mark in his notepad.

Andrew picked up his part. "At the conference, Nick introduced me to the Juneau woman as Dr. Maplecroft. I recognized

222

the name, if not the face. There aren't many photographs of Maplecroft in circulation, as I'm sure you've realized now that you're searching for her. I believe I said something to the fake Maplecroft about being on Father's panel. She didn't have a badge, so I asked if there was a problem with the check-in." He shrugged the exact same way that Nick had shrugged. "That was the extent of my interaction with the woman. The next time I saw her, she was murdering my father."

Jane flinched. She couldn't help it.

Barlow said, "That's a very tidy explanation."

Nick said, "Most explanations are. The ones that are complicated are the ones I'd look out for." He smoothed out the leg of his trousers. "But you know, gentlemen, it seems to me that I've already told this to your compatriots. We all have, endlessly. So, I think I'll make my exit."

Neither agent moved to stop him.

Nick hesitated only slightly before he kissed Jane on the mouth, then crossed the room in long strides. Jane felt her heart drop when he took a left instead of a right. He wasn't going upstairs to wait for her.

He was leaving.

The front door opened and closed. She felt the sound reverberate like a knife to her heart. She had to part her lips again to take in breath. She was torn between relief to have him gone and fear that she would never see him again.

"I'm sorry Nick is such an ass," Jasper told Barlow. "But he does have a point. We can't keep doing this. The answers are not going to change."

Barlow said, "This is an active investigation. The people who orchestrated the Oslo assassination still have Dr. Maplecroft."

"Which is a tragedy," Jasper said. "However, there's nothing my family can do about it."

Barlow said, "The ransom note for Dr. Maplecroft asked for an admission of guilt from your father's company. They blame him for Robert Juneau's murderous spree."

"It's the family's company." Jasper had been sensitive about this since taking over last year. "The kidnappers also asked for one million dollars, which is preposterous. We can't take responsibility for the actions of a madman. Do you know how many homes Queller Healthcare runs? Just in the Bay Area?"

"Fifteen," Andrew answered, but only Jane heard him.

Barlow said, "The kidnappers are calling themselves the Army of the Changing World. You've never heard of them?"

Both Jane and Andrew shook their heads.

Across the room, Danberry closed the fallboard on the piano.

Jane felt her heart lurch. The ivory would yellow without sunlight.

Jasper picked up on her distress. He asked her, "Shouldn't that be up?"

She shook her head. Nick would tell her to let the keys yellow. To skip practice. To stop pushing herself so hard. Martin could not punish her from the grave.

"Major Queller?" Barlow was waiting. "Have you heard of the Army of the—"

"Of course not." Jasper edged close to losing his cool, but brought himself back quickly. "I don't have to tell you how damaging those lies are to the company. We were meant to go public this week. We've got some very powerful investors who are getting very antsy about this mess. The charges the kidnappers made are ludicrous. We don't torture sick people, for Chrissakes. This isn't Soviet Russia."

Danberry tried, "Major Queller—"

"My father was a good man," Jasper insisted. "He made some controversial statements, I'll admit, but he always had the good of the family, the good of the country, in his mind. He was a patriot. His mission in life was to serve others, and that's what got him killed."

"No one here is disagreeing with that."

"Look." Jasper moderated his tone. "Laura Juneau obviously had a screw loose. We may never know why she—"

"The why is pretty clear." Andrew spoke quietly, but they were all listening. "Robert Juneau was kicked out of half a dozen Queller group homes. He should've been hospitalized, but there was no hospital to go to. You can say the system failed him, but we're the system, Jasper. Queller is the system. Ergo—"

"Ergo, shut the hell up, Andy." He glared at Andrew, fire in his eyes. "The company could be ruined by this idiotic bullshit. The investors could pull out completely. Do you understand that?"

"I need some air." Jane stood up. Andrew and Barlow did the same. She felt dizzy. Her stomach flipped. She had to look down at the floor as she walked away. Her boots might as well have been crossing a spinning wheel. She wanted to go to the bathroom and throw up or cry or just sit there, alone, and try to figure out what was happening.

Where had Nick gone?

Was he mad at Jane? Had she made a mistake? Had she been silent when Nick wanted her to defend him? Would he be angry? Would he shut her out again?

Jane couldn't be shut out again. She couldn't take it. Not now.

Not when she was carrying his child.

Instead of going into the bathroom or stopping in the kitchen to leave a desperate message on Nick's answering machine, she walked to the back of the house and went outside.

She stood on the patio with her eyes closed and tried to breathe. The fresh air made her feel like the band around her chest was loosening. She looked up at the cloudy sky. She could see a tiny sliver of sun behind the Golden Gate Bridge. Morning fog still laced the Marin Headlands. There was a chill in the air, but Jane didn't want to go back inside for her sweater.

She saw signs on the wrought iron table that her mother had been here: Annette's lipstick-stained teacup, a full ashtray, the newspaper held down by a cut glass paperweight.

Jane's eyes scanned the front page of the *Chronicle*, though she knew the ransom letter by heart. Nick had bragged about its cleverness, even as Jane worried that it made them sound like evil super villains in a cartoon—

This is a direct communication from the Army of the Changing World. We have kidnapped Dr. Alexandra Maplecroft, a tool of the fascist regime, a pawn in the dangerous game played by Martin Queller and his so-called healthcare company. We demand an apology for the part that Martin Queller played in the genocide of the Juneau family and other families across the greater California area. Queller Healthcare must be stopped. They have systematically exploited, tortured and beaten patients in their institutions. More lives will be lost if—

"Nice digs."

Jane startled.

"Sorry." Agent Danberry was standing in the doorway. He had an unlit cigarette in his mouth. He stared at the view with open admiration. "My apartment, I can see the alley I share with my neighbor. If I open the window, I get to smell the puke from the junkies sleeping it off."

Jane didn't know what to say. Her heart was hammering so hard that she was sure he could see it moving beneath her blouse.

"They closed it a few years ago," he said. "The bridge. Wind gusts." He took the cigarette out of his mouth. "That piano in there—probably could pay off my car, right?"

The Bösendorfer could likely buy him fifty new cars, but he wasn't here to talk about pianos.

"What're the extra keys for?" He waited.

And waited.

Jane wiped her eyes. She couldn't just stand here crying. She had to say something—anything—about the bridge, the fog, the view, but her mind was so filled with panic that even the most innocuous observation could not make its way to her mouth.

Danberry nodded, as if this was expected. He lit his cigarette. He stared past the trees at the bridge. The distant bray of foghorns floated up from the rocks.

Jane looked up at the bridge, too. She thought of the first time she'd stood with Nick in the backyard to watch the fog roll in. It wasn't until that moment that Jane had realized that she'd taken the view for granted. Only Nick had understood how lucky they were.

Danberry said, "I saw you play once."

Jane knew what he was doing—trying to steer her to something familiar, to make her comfortable.

"My wife dragged me to a club on Vallejo. Keystone Korner. This was a long time ago. They've moved across the Bay, I heard." He pulled out a chair for Jane. She had no choice but to sit. He said, "I know this is hard for you."

Jane wiped her eyes with her fingers. The skin felt burned by her tears.

He took a seat without being asked. "What were you doing in Germany?"

Jane knew the answer to the question, at least the one she was supposed to give.

"Miss Queller?"

She forced out the word, "Working." Her voice was barely more than a whisper. She had to pull herself together. They had practiced this. It was just like a performance. All the notes were in her head. She just had to coax them out with her fingers.

She rubbed her throat to relax the muscles. She said, "It was meant to be temporary. I was filling in for a friend in Berlin as a session pianist."

"West Berlin, I hope."

He smiled, so Jane smiled.

He told her, "I know what you're thinking: we know what you did over there. We know where you lived. We know where you worked, where you ate lunch, that you went to the East sometimes. We also know your flight to Oslo was out of East Berlin, which isn't unusual over there, right? The fares are cheaper." He looked back at the house. "Not that you need to save money, but who can pass up a bargain?"

Jane felt the panic start to return. Did he really know everything, or was this a trick?

He asked, "How was East Germany?"

She tried to see past his question. Did they think she was a communist? A spy?

He said, "I hear everybody watches you. Like, what you're doing, who you're talking to, what you're saying." He tapped his cigarette into the overfull ashtray. "Kind of like me right now, huh?"

He smiled again, so Jane smiled again.

Danberry asked, "They let them listen to music over there?"

Jane chewed her lip. She heard Nick's voice in her head: *If they try to make you comfortable, let them think they're making you comfortable.*

Danberry said, "A little Springsteen, maybe some Michael Jackson?"

She pushed out the well-rehearsed words, "Popular music is frowned upon, but it's not completely *verboten*."

"Music is freedom, right?"

Jane shook her head. There was no script for this.

"It's like—" He held out his hands, fingers splayed. "It moves people. Inspires them. Makes them wanna dance or grab a gal and have a good time. It's got power."

Jane felt herself nodding, because that was exactly how she'd felt watching the impromptu concerts the students had put on in Treptow Park. She'd wanted desperately to tell Nick about them, but she had to be careful about Germany because she didn't want him to feel left out.

Danberry asked, "You political?"

She shook her head. She had to play the game.

They'll know you've never voted.

She told the agent, "I've never even voted."

"You do a lot of volunteering, though. Soup kitchens. Homeless shelters. Even that AIDS ward they set up over at UCSF. Not afraid you'll catch it?"

Jane watched him smoke his cigarette.

He said, "Rock Hudson shocked the hell out of me. Never would've thought he was one of them." He stared up at the Golden Gate, asking, "Was your dad playing matchmaker?"

Don't answer the question if you don't understand it.

Danberry explained, "You went away to Germany for three months. Your boyfriend stayed here catting around with your brother." He glanced at her, then looked back at the bridge. "Ellis-Anne MacMillan said the break-up with Andrew was very unexpected. But they usually are."

Don't let them surprise you into reacting.

He asked, "So, the old man flies Mr. Harp to Norway for what? To get you two kids back together?"

Just give them the facts. Don't over-explain.

She told him, "Nick and I were never apart. I was in Berlin for a job. He had to stay here for work." Jane knew she should stop talking, but she could not. "Father gave him the job at Queller. He probably wanted Nick in Oslo for himself. The panel with Maplecroft was a big deal. Nick's very charming, very easy to be around. People have always liked him. They're drawn to him. Father was no exception. He wanted to help Nick up the ladder."

"Guys like that always fall up."

Jane chewed the tip of her tongue. She had to look away so that he did not catch the anger in her eyes. She had never been able to abide anyone running down Nick. He'd suffered so much as a child. People like Danberry would never understand that.

"He's got charisma, right?" Danberry put out the cigarette on the bottom of his shoe and tossed the butt into the ashtray. "The pretty face. The quick wit. The cool clothes. But it's more than that, right? He's got that thing some guys have. Makes you want to listen to them. Follow them."

The wind picked up, rustling the edges of the *Chronicle*. Jane folded the paper closed. She saw the garish headline: $1,000,000 RANSOM OR PROF DIES!

A ridiculous headline for a ridiculous manifesto. Nick had made them all sound unhinged.

Danberry said, "'Death to the fascist insect that preys on the life of the people.'"

Jane didn't recognize the line from the ransom note. She pretended to skim the paper.

Danberry said, "It's not in there. I was talking about the Patty Hearst kidnapping. That's how the Symbionese Liberation Army signed all of their screeds—'Death to the fascist insect that preys on the life of the people.'" He studied her face. "Your family has another house near the Hearsts, right? Up in Hillsborough?"

"I was a kid when it happened."

His laugh said that he thought she still was a kid. "Carter couldn't free the hostages, but he got Patty Hearst out of lock-up."

"I told you I don't follow politics."

"Not even in college?" He said, "My old man told me everybody's a socialist until they start paying taxes."

She mirrored his smile again.

"Do you know where the word 'symbionese' comes from?"

Jane waited.

"The SLA's leader, Donald DeFreeze—the jackass didn't know the word 'symbiotic,' so he made up the word 'symbionese.'" Danberry leaned back in the chair, crossed his ankle over his knee. "The newspapers called them terrorists, and they committed acts of terror, but all terror cells are basically cults, and all cults usually have one guy at the center who's driving the bus. Your Manson or your Jim Jones or your Reverend Moon."

They'll seem almost nonchalant the closer they get to the point.

"DeFreeze was a black fella, an escaped con doing five-to-life for rolling a hooker, and like a lot of cons, he had a lot of charisma, and the kids who followed him—all of them white, middle class, most of them in college—well, they weren't stupid. They were worse. They were true believers. They felt sorry for him because he was this poor black guy in prison and they were spoiled white kids with everything, and they really believed all the shit that came out of his mouth about fascist insects and

230

everybody living together all Kumbaya. Like I said, he had that thing. Charisma."

Pay attention to the words they repeat because that's the point of the story.

Danberry said, "He had everybody in his circle convinced he was smarter than he actually was. More clever than he was. Fact is, he was just another con man running another cult so he could bed the pretty girls and play God with all the boys. He knew when people were pulling away. He knew how to bring them back on side." Danberry looked at the bridge. His shoulders were relaxed. "They were like yo-yos he could snap back with a flick of his wrist."

Make eye contact. Don't look nervous.

"So, anyway." Danberry clasped his hands together and rested them on his stomach. "What happened was, most of the kids following him ended up shot in the head or burned to death. And I have to tell you, that's not uncommon. These anarchist groups think they're doing the right thing, right up until they end up in prison or flat on their backs in the morgue."

Jane wiped her eyes. She could see everything he was doing, but felt helpless to stop him.

What would Nick do? How would he throw it back in Danberry's face?

"Miss Queller," Danberry said, then, "Jinx." He leaned forward, his knees almost touching her leg.

They'll get in your space to try to intimidate you.

He said, "Look, I'm on your side here. But your boyfriend—"

"Have you ever seen someone shot in the head?" The stunned look on his face told Jane she'd found the right mark. Like Nick, she let herself draw power from his mistake. "You were so cavalier when you said those kids ended up getting shot in the head. I'm just wondering if you know what that looks like."

"I didn't—" He reeled back. "What I meant—"

"There's a hole, a black hole no larger than the size of a dime, right here"—she pointed to her own temple where Martin Queller was shot—"and on the opposite side, where the bullet exits, you see this bloody pulp, and you realize that everything that makes up that person, everything that makes them so who they are, is splattered onto the floor. Something a janitor will mop up and toss down the drain. Gone. Forever."

"I—" His mouth opened and closed. "I'm sorry, Miss Queller. I didn't—"

Jane stood. She went back into the house and slammed the door behind her. She used her hand to wipe her nose as she walked down the hallway. She couldn't keep up this façade much longer. She had to get out of here. To find Nick. To tell him what was going on.

Her purse was on the sideboard. Jane rummaged for her keys, and then she realized that Nick had taken them.

Where had he gone?

"Jinx?" Jasper was still in the parlor. He was sitting on the couch beside Andrew. They both had drinks in their hands. Even Agent Barlow, standing by the fireplace, had a glass of whisky.

"What is it?" Jasper stood up when she entered the room.

"Are you okay?" Andrew was standing, too. They both looked alarmed, almost angry. Neither one of them had ever been able to abide seeing her upset.

"I'm all right," she patted her hands in the air to calm them. "Please, could I just have someone's keys?"

"Take mine." Jasper gave Andrew his keys. "Andy, you drive her. She's in no condition."

Jane tried, "I'm not—"

"Where do you want to go?" Andrew was already heading to the closet for their jackets.

Jasper had his hand in his pocket. "Do you need some money?"

"No." Jane didn't have the strength to fight both of her brothers. "I need to find—" She was aware that Barlow was listening. "Air. I need some air."

Barlow asked, "Not enough of it in the backyard?"

Jane turned away from him. She did not wait for Andrew. She grabbed her purse off the table. She walked out the front door, down the front steps. Jasper's Porsche was parked beside the garage.

"I've got it." Andrew had jogged to catch up with her. He reached down to open the door.

"Andy—" Jane grabbed his arm. Her knees felt weak. She could barely stand.

"It's okay," he said, trying to help her into the car. "Just play it cool."

"No," she said. "You don't understand. They know."

10

They were too afraid to speak openly in the car. Jasper was not a part of this, but only they knew that. The FBI or CIA or NSA or whoever could have planted bugs in any of the crevices inside the Porsche. Even the car phone could be tapped.

Before Oslo, before every branch of law enforcement had swept down on the Presidio Heights house, before Agent Danberry had cornered Jane in the backyard, it had felt ridiculously paranoid when Nick had told them to assume that every familiar place was monitored, that someone was always going to be listening. To speak openly, they were supposed to find a park or a random café. They had to sneak down alleys and walk through buildings and say the passwords and know the interrogation techniques and practice self-defense and drill themselves over and over again so that they had their stories right.

The stories had been too right.

Jane could see that now. As she replayed all the conversations with all the agents over the last five days, she could see how their interrogators had registered certain phrases, certain gestures, in their notepads, to compare later.

I pretended to recognize the woman whom I thought was Dr. Maplecroft.

Only one of us had darker intentions.

I wanted to speak to an American after being in Germany for so long.

"Pull over," Jane told Andrew, fear twisting her stomach into knots. She pushed open the door before the car fully stopped. Her boots skipped across the pavement. They were inside the city proper. There was no grass, just concrete. Jane had no choice but to vomit on the sidewalk.

I met Laura Juneau at the KLM lounge at Schiphol.

I could tell she was an American by the way she was dressed.

Jane retched so hard that she was on her knees. Her stomach clenched out dark bile. She hadn't been able to eat more than toast and eggs since the murder. The tea that Nick had given her this morning tasted like bark as it burned its way up her throat.

Nick. She had to find Nick so he could explain how they were all going to be fine.

"Jinx." Andrew's hand was on her shoulder. He was kneeling beside her.

Jane sat back on her heels. She wiped her mouth. There was a tremble in her fingers that she could not get rid of. It was as if the bones were vibrating beneath her skin.

Theyknowtheyknowtheyknow . . .

Andrew asked, "Are you okay?"

Her laugh had an edge of uncontrollability.

"Jane—"

"None of us is okay." Saying the words inserted some sanity into this madness. "It's all closing in on us. They talked to Ellis-Ann."

"I kept her out of this. She doesn't know anything."

"*They* know everything." How could he not see this? "My God, Andy. They think we're in a cult."

He laughed. "Like the People's Temple? The Manson Family?"

Jane wasn't laughing. "What are we going to do?"

"Stick to the plan," he said, his voice low. "That's what it's there for. When in doubt, just let the plan lead the way."

"The plan," Jane repeated, but not with his reverence.

The stupid fucking plan. So carefully plotted, so relentlessly discussed and strategized.

So wrong.

"Come on," Andrew said. "We'll find a café and—"

"No." Jane had to find Nick. He could solve this for them. Or maybe he already had. Just the thought of Nick taking control immediately soothed some of her jagged nerves. Maybe what had happened with Danberry and Barlow was part of a larger, secret plan. Nick did that sometimes—made them all think they were about to walk into the path of an oncoming train, only to reveal at the last minute that he was the cunning conductor braking at the last possible moment to keep them out of harm's way. He tested them like this all of the time. Even in Berlin, Nick had asked Jane to do things, to put herself in danger, just to make sure she would obey.

He had so much trouble trusting people. Everyone in his family had turned their backs on him. He had been forced to live on the streets. He had managed to pull himself up entirely on his own. Time and again, he had trusted people who had hurt him. It was no wonder that Jane had to repeatedly prove herself.

They were like yo-yos he could snap back with a flick of his wrist.

"Jane," Andrew said.

She felt Danberry's words echoing in her head. Was she like a yo-yo? Was Nick a con man? A cult leader? How different was he from Jim Jones? The People's Temple had started out doing wonderful things. Feeding the homeless. Taking care of the elderly. Working to eradicate racism. And then a decade later, over nine hundred people, many of them children, were killed by cyanide-laced Kool-Aid.

Why?

"Jane, come on," Andrew said. "The pigs don't *know* anything. Not for certain."

Jane shook her head, trying to banish the dark thoughts. Nick had said that the police would try to separate them, that their

236

psyches would be poked and prodded in the hope that they would eventually turn on each other.

If nobody speaks, then no one will know.

Did Nick really believe the crazy-sounding things that came out of his mouth, or was this how he pulled Jane back in? She had spent six years of her life chasing after him, pleasing him, loving him, fighting with him, breaking up with him. She always went back. No matter what, she always found her way back.

Snap.

"Come on. Let's get out of here."

Jane let Andrew help her up. "Take me to Nick's apartment."

"He won't be there."

"We'll wait for him." Jane got back into the car. She searched her purse for some tissue. Her mouth felt like it was rotting from the inside. Maybe it was. Maybe everything was rotting, even the child they had made.

She anticipated Nick's wry reaction—*problem solved.*

"It's going to be okay," Andrew turned the key. The Porsche fishtailed as he pulled away from the curb. "We just need to drive a bit. Maybe we'll swing by Nick's?"

Jane was confused by his avuncular tone, but then she realized that Andrew was talking for the bug that might be in the car.

She told him, "Danberry compared Nick to Donald DeFreeze."

"Field Marshal Cinque?" Andrew gave her a careful look. He instantly got the portent of Danberry's observation. "Does that make you Patricia Hearst?"

She said it again, "They think we're in a cult."

"Do Hare Krishnas drive Porsches?" Andrew didn't realize that she wanted a real answer. He was still speaking for the benefit of a phantom listener. "Come on, Jinx. This is crazy. The pigs don't like Nick, which is understandable. He's being an asshole for no reason. Once they figure out he's playing them, they'll move on to investigating the real bad guys."

Jane wondered if Andrew had accidentally hit on the truth. Why did Nick have to constantly play games? They were supposed to be taking this seriously—and since Oslo, everything had become deadly serious. What they were about to do in San Francisco, Chicago, and New York would bring the full weight of the federal government down on them. Nick couldn't keep flying so close to the sun. They would all end up plummeting into prison cells.

"It's nothing," Andrew said. "We're not a cult, Jinx. Nick has been my best friend for seven years. He's been your boyfriend for six. Those agents are focused on him because they have to focus on someone. There always has to be a boogeyman with those people. Even David Berkowitz blamed his neighbor's dog."

Jane felt no relief from his cavalier words. "What if they don't move on?"

"They'll have to. Our father was murdered in front of our eyes."

Jane winced.

"The FBI won't fail us. Jasper won't let that happen. They'll catch whoever did this."

She shook her head. Tears streamed down her cheeks.

That was exactly what she was worried about.

The car banked around a steep curve.

Jane put her hand to her throat. The sickness threatened to return. She looked out the window and watched the houses blur by. She thought about Nick because that was the only thing that kept her from breaking down. Jane had to stop questioning him, even if only in her mind. The one thing Nick could not abide was disloyalty. That was the reason for his tests while she was in Berlin—sending Jane to a biker bar near the Bornholmer checkpoint, airmailing her a dime-bag of cocaine to sell to a university student, sending her into the police station to report a stolen bike that had never existed.

Nick had told her at the time that he was helping Jane practice, honing her ability to adapt to dangerous situations. That she could've been raped in the bar, arrested for the coke or charged with making a false police report had never occurred to him.

Or maybe it had.

Jane took a deep breath as Andrew steered into another curve. She held onto the strap. She watched him weave in and out of traffic with barely a glance over his shoulder.

Evasive maneuvers.

They had driven repeatedly to San Luis Obispo and back, three or four cars at a time, working on their driving skills. Nick, predictably, had been the best of all of them, but Andrew was a close second. They were both naturally competitive. They both shared a dangerous disregard for life that allowed them to speed and swerve with moral impunity.

Andrew coughed into the crook of his elbow so he wouldn't have to take his hands off the wheel. They were going deeper into the city. His eyes were trained on the road. In the sunlight, she could see the faint line of a scar along his neck where he'd tried to hang himself. This was three years ago, after he'd taken too many pills but before he'd shot up enough heroin to stop his heart. Jasper had found him hanging in the basement. The rope was thin, a clothesline, really, with a metal wire that had gouged out a slice of Andrew's skin.

Jane was overwhelmed with a mixture of grief and regret every time she saw the scar. The truth was that, at the time of the attempt, she had hated her brother. Not because Andrew was older or because he teased her about her knobby knees and social awkwardness, but because, for most of his life, Andrew had been a drug addict, and there was nothing he would not do in service of his addiction. Robbing Annette. Fighting with Jasper. Stealing from Martin. Relentlessly dismissing Jane.

Cocaine. Benzodiazepine. Heroin. Speed.

She was twelve years old when it became clear that Andrew was an addict, and like most twelve-year-olds, she only saw his misery through her own lens of deprivation. As she got older, Jane had been forced to accept that the shape of her life would always bend around her brother. To understand that the entire family would forever be held hostage to what Martin called Andrew's weakness. The arrests, the treatment facilities, the court appearances, the favors called in, the money handed under

239

the table, the political donations—continually sucked away all of her parents' attention. Jane had never had a normal life, but Andrew took away any hope of a peaceful, sometimes ordinary existence.

By the time she'd turned sixteen, Jane had lost track of the family meetings about Andrew's problem, the screaming and blame-laying and accusations and beatings and haranguing and hope—that was the worst part of it all—the hope. Maybe this time he'll quit. Maybe this birthday or Thanksgiving or Christmas he'll show up sober.

And maybe, just maybe, this concert or performance that was so important to Jane; the first one where she had been allowed to choose her own music, the special one to which she had devoted thousands of hours of practice, would not be overshadowed by another overdose, another suicide attempt, another hospitalization, another family meeting where Martin railed and Jasper glowered and Jane sobbed while Andrew pleaded for more chances and Annette drank herself into a blameless stupor.

Then, suddenly, Nick had gotten Andrew clean.

The arrest on the cocaine possession two years ago had been an eye-opener for both of them, but not in the expected, relentlessly hoped for, way. They had been arrested by an Alameda County sheriff's deputy, otherwise Martin would have as usual made the charge go away. The Alameda deputy had dealt with too many spoiled rich kids before. He was determined to see the case through the court system. He'd threatened to go to the newspapers if some kind of justice was not meted out.

Which was how Andrew and Nick had ended up living at the Queller Bayside Home, the last group home that Robert Juneau had been kicked out of.

That was where Laura had found Nick. Nick had introduced her to Andrew. Then Nick had formulated a plan, and that plan had finally given Andrew a cause that urgently demanded his sobriety.

The Porsche screeched to a halt. They were outside Nick's

apartment complex, a squat, low building with a wobbly metal railing around the upper-floor balcony. He didn't live in the best area, but it wasn't the worst the city had to offer, either. The place was clean. The homeless people were kept at bay. Still, Jane hated that Nick couldn't live at the Presidio Heights house with the rest of them.

Except that now he could.

Right?

"I'll go check," Andrew said. "You stay here."

Jane opened the car door before Andrew could stop her. A sense of urgency overwhelmed her. All of the doubts she'd had for the last half hour would be wrapped up in Nick's arms and explained away. The sooner she was with him, the better she would feel.

"Jinx," Andrew called, trailing behind her. "Jinx, wait up."

She started to run, tripping over the sidewalk, heading up the rusty metal stairs. Her boots were stiff and hurt her feet but Jane did not care. She could feel that Nick was inside his apartment. That he was waiting. That he might be wondering what had taken them so long, that maybe they no longer cared about him, had lost their faith in him.

She *had* lost faith. She *had* doubted him.

She wasn't a fool. She was a monster.

Jane ran harder. Every step felt like it was taking her farther away. Andrew jogged behind her, calling her name, telling her to slow down, to stop, but Jane could not.

She had let Agent Danberry get into her head. Nick was not a con man or a cultist. He was a survivor. His first memory was of watching his mother screw a police officer, still in uniform, who paid her in heroin. He'd never known his father. A series of pimps had beaten and abused him. He'd attended dozens of schools by the time he hitchhiked across the country to find his grandmother. She'd hated him on sight, woke him up in the middle of the night kicking and screaming at him. He'd been forced into the streets, then lived in a homeless shelter, while he finished school. That Nick had managed to get into Stanford

241

despite all of these hardships proved that he was smarter, more clever, than anybody had ever given him credit for.

Especially Agent Danberry with his missing tooth and cheap suit.

"Jinx," Andrew called from the other end of the balcony. He was walking slowly because he couldn't run anymore. She could hear his coughing from thirty feet away.

Jane reached into her purse for the key—not the one she kept on the chain, but the one for emergencies that she kept in the zippered pocket. Her hands were shaking so hard that she dropped the key. She bent down to get it. Sweat covered her palms.

"Jinx." Andrew was leaning over, hands on his knees, wheezing.

Jane opened the door.

She felt her world tilt off center.

Nick wasn't there.

Worse, his stuff wasn't there. The apartment was almost empty. All of his cherished things—the leather couch he'd spent hours thinking about, the tasteful glass side tables, the hanging lamp, the plush brown carpet—all of it was gone. There was just a large, overstuffed chair facing the back wall. The beautiful brass and glass kitchen table set was gone. The big television. The stereo with its giant speakers. His record collection. The walls were bare; all of his cherished art was gone, even the pieces that Andrew had drawn for him.

She almost fell to her knees. Her hand went to her chest as she felt her heart tear in two.

Had Nick abandoned them?

Abandoned her?

She put her hand to her mouth so that she wouldn't start screaming. She walked on shaky legs into the middle of the room. None of his magazines, his books, his shoes left by the balcony door. Each missing item was like an arrow piercing her heart. Jane was so terrified that she almost felt numb. All of the worst thoughts spun through her head—

He had left her. He knew that she was doubting him. That she had stopped believing in him, if just for a moment. He had disappeared. He had overdosed. He had found someone else.

He had tried to kill himself.

Jane's knees buckled as she tried to walk down the hall. Nick had threatened to kill himself more than once and the thought of losing him was so wrenching to Jane that each time she had cried out like a child, begging him to please stay with her.

I can't live without you. I need you. You are the breath in my body. Please never leave me.

"Jane?" Andrew had made it to the door. "Jane, where are you?"

Nick's bedroom door was closed. She had to brace herself against the wall as she made her way down the hallway. Past the bathroom—toothbrush, toothpaste, no cologne, no shaving set, no brush and comb.

More arrows slicing open her heart.

Jane stopped outside the bedroom. Her hand could barely grip the doorknob. There was not enough air to fill her lungs. Her heart had stopped its steady beat.

She pushed open the door.

A strangled sound came from her throat.

No bed with its puffy duvet. No side tables with matching lamps. No antique chest of drawers Nick had lovingly refinished. Only a sleeping bag was rolled out on the bare floor.

The closet door was open.

Jane started crying again, almost sobbing from relief, when she saw that his clothes were still hanging on the rack. Nick loved his clothes. He would never leave without them.

"Jinx?" Andrew was beside her, holding her up.

"I thought—" Her knees finally sunk to the floor. She felt sick again. "I thought he—"

"Come back through here." Andrew lifted her to standing and practically carried her out of the room.

Jane leaned into him as they walked up the hallway, her feet dragging across the bare floor. He took her into the living room.

He flipped the light switch. Jane squinted from the glare. Even the light fixtures were missing. Bare bulbs hung from the sockets. Except for the massive chair that looked like it belonged on the street, everything that Nick had ever cared for was gone.

His clothes were still in the closet. He would not leave his clothes.

Would he?

"Is—" she couldn't say the words. "Andrew, where—"

Andrew put his finger to his lips, indicating that there might be someone listening.

Jane shook her head. She couldn't play this game anymore. She needed words, assurances.

"It's all right." Andrew gave her that careful look again, like she was missing something important.

Jane looked around the room, desperate for some kind of understanding. What could she be missing in this bare space?

The bare space.

Nick had gotten rid of his things. He had either sold them or given them away. Was he cleverly foiling the police so they didn't have anywhere to plant their listening devices?

Jane couldn't stand any more. She sat on the floor, tears of relief flooding from her eyes. That had to be the answer. Nick hadn't left them. He was fucking with the pigs. The almost-empty apartment was just another one of Nick's games.

"Jinx?" Andrew was clearly concerned.

"I'm all right." She wiped her tears. She felt foolish for making such a scene. "Please don't tell Nick I was so upset. Please."

Andrew opened his mouth to respond, but a cough came out instead. Jane winced at the wet, congested sound. He coughed again, then again, and finally walked into the kitchen where he found a glass drying by the sink.

Jane wiped her nose with the back of her hand. She looked around the room again, noticing a small cardboard box beside the hideous chair. Her heart fluttered at the sight of the framed photo resting on the top.

Nick had given away almost everything but this—

Jane and Nick last Christmas at the Hillsborough house. Smiling for the camera, but not for each other, despite the proprietary arm Nick had draped over her shoulders. Jane had been out on tour for the previous three weeks. She had come back to find Nick antsy and distracted. He had kept insisting there was nothing wrong. Jane had kept begging him to speak. It had gone on like that for hours, sunset to sunrise, until finally, Nick had told Jane about meeting Laura Juneau.

He had been smoking a cigarette outside the front gates of the Queller Bayside Home. This was after the cocaine bust in Alameda County. Both he and Andrew were serving their court-mandated sentence. That Nick had met Laura was pure happenstance. For months, she'd been looking for a way into Queller. She had approached countless patients and staff in search of someone, anyone, who could help find proof that her husband had been screwed over by the system.

In Nick, Laura had found a truly sympathetic listener. For most of his life, he had been told by those in authority that he didn't matter, that he wasn't smart enough or from the right family or that he did not belong. Pulling in Andrew must have been even easier. Her brother had spent most of his life focused on his own wants and needs. Directing that attention toward another person's tragedy was his way out of the darkness.

I felt so selfish when I heard her story, Andrew had told Jane. *I thought I was suffering, but I had no idea what true suffering really is.*

Jane wasn't sure at what point Nick had brought in other people. That's what he did best—collected stragglers, outsiders, people like him who felt that their voices were not being heard. By that Christmas night at the Hillsborough house when Nick had finally told Jane about the plan, there were dozens of people in other cities who were ready to change the world.

Was it Laura who'd first come up with the idea? Not just Oslo, but San Francisco, Chicago, and New York?

Queller Healthcare was one company in one state doing bad things to good people, but going public would infuse the company with enough cash to take their program of neglect nationwide. The competition was clearly working from the same business plan. Nick had told Jane stories about treatment facilities in Georgia and Alabama that were kicking patients out into the streets. An institution in Maryland had been caught dropping mentally incapacitated patients at bus stops in the harshest cold of winter. Illinois had a waitlist that effectively denied coverage for years.

As Nick had explained, Martin would be the first target, but meaningful change required meaningful acts of resistance. They had to show the rest of the country, the rest of the world, what was happening to these poor, abandoned people. They had to take a page from ACT UP, the Weather Underground, the United Freedom Front, and shake these corrupt institutions to their very foundations.

Which was fantastical.

Wasn't it?

The truth was that Nick was always either outraged or excited about something. He wrote to politicians demanding action. Mailed angry letters to the editors of the *San Francisco Gate*. Volunteered alongside Jane at homeless shelters and AIDS clinics. He was constantly drawing ideas for incredible inventions, or scribbling notes about new business ventures. Jane always encouraged him because Nick following through on these ideas was another matter entirely. Either he thought the people who could help him were too stupid or too intransigent, or he would grow bored and move on to another thing.

She had assumed that Laura Juneau was one of the things Nick would move on from. When she'd realized that this time was different, that Andrew was involved, too, that they were both deadly serious about their fantastical plans, Jane couldn't back out. She was too afraid that Nick would go on without her. That she would be left behind. A niggling voice inside of Jane always reminded her that she needed Nick far more than he needed her.

"Jinx." Andrew was waiting for her attention. He was holding the Christmas photograph in his hands. He opened the back of the frame. A tiny key was taped to the cardboard.

Jane caught herself before she could ask what he was doing. She glanced nervously around the room. Nick had told them cameras could be hidden in lamps, tucked inside potted plants or secreted behind air-conditioning vents.

She realized now that Nick had removed all the vents. Nothing was left but the open mouths of the ducts that had been cut into the walls.

It's only paranoia if you're wrong.

Andrew handed Jane the key. She slipped it into her back pocket. He returned the photo to its place on the cardboard box.

As quietly as possible, he pushed the heavy, overstuffed chair over onto its side.

"What—" the word slipped out before she could catch it. Jane stared her curiosity into her brother.

What the hell is going on?

Andrew's only response was to yet again put his finger to his lips.

A groan escaped from his mouth as he got down on his knees. He yanked away the material along the bottom of the chair. Jane strangled back the questions that wanted to come. Instead, she watched her brother take apart the chair. He bent back a section of the metal springs. He reached deep into the foam and pulled out a rectangular metal box that was about four inches thick and as tall and wide as a sheet of legal paper.

Jane felt her muscles tense as she thought about all the things that could be inside the box: weapons, explosives, more photographs, all sorts of things that Jane did not want to see because Nick didn't hide something unless he did not want it to be found.

Andrew put the box on the floor. He sat back on his heels. He was trying to catch his breath, though all he'd done was tip over a chair. The harsh lights did his complexion no favors. He looked even sicker now. The dark circles under his eyes were rimmed with tiny dots of broken blood vessels. The wheeze in his breath had not abated.

"Andy?"

He tucked the box under his arm. "Let's go."

"What if Nick—"

"Now."

He shoved the chair back onto its legs. He waited for Jane to walk ahead of him, then he waited for her to lock the door.

Jane kept her mouth closed as she crossed the balcony. She could hear their heavy footsteps against the concrete, the sharp click of her boots, the hard clap of Andrew's loafers. His wheezing was more pronounced. Jane tried to keep the pace slow. They were on the first landing to the stairs when he put out his hand to stop her.

Jane looked up at her brother. The wind rustled his hair. Sunlight cut a fine line across his forehead. She wondered how he was managing to stay upright. His face had taken on the pallor of a dead person.

She felt safe to ask, "What are we doing, Andrew? I don't understand why we had to leave. Shouldn't we wait for Nick?"

He asked, "Back at the house, did you hear Jasper telling those feds what a good man Father was?"

Jane couldn't joke about Jasper right now. She was terrified that he'd somehow get pulled into this thing that none of them could control. "Andrew, please, will you tell me what's going on?"

"Jasper defended Father because he's just like him."

Jane wanted to roll her eyes. She couldn't believe he was doing this now. "Don't be so cruel. Jasper loves you. He always has."

"It's you he loves. And that's fine. It's good that he looks after you."

"I'm not a child who needs a minder." Jane couldn't keep the peevishness out of her tone. They had fought about Jasper since they were little. Andrew always saw the worst in him. Jane saw him as her savior. "Do you know how many times Jasper took me to dinner when Father was in one of his moods, or helped me pick out something to wear when Mother was too drunk, or tried to talk to me about music or listened to me cry about boys or—"

"I get it. He's a saint. You're his perfect baby sister." Andrew sat down on the stairs. "Sit."

Jane begrudgingly sat on the step below him. There were so many things she could say about Jasper that would only hurt Andrew, like the way that, every time Andrew overdosed or disappeared or ended up in the hospital, it was Jasper who made sure that Jane was okay.

Andrew said, "Give me the key."

She retrieved it from her pocket and handed it over. Jane studied his face as he worked the key in the lock. He was still breathing hard, sweating profusely despite the cool breeze.

"Here." Andrew finally opened the lid on the metal box.

Jane saw that it was filled with file folders. She recognized the Queller Healthcare logo printed along the bottoms.

"Look at these." Andrew handed her a stack of files. "You know Father got Nick a job at corporate."

Jane chewed her tongue so she didn't snap that of course she knew that her boyfriend was working for her father's company. She scanned the forms inside the folders, trying to understand why they were important enough for Nick to hide. She easily recognized the patient packets with billing codes and intake forms. Martin routinely brought them home in his briefcase, then Jasper started doing the same when he joined the business.

Andrew said, "Nick's been snooping around."

This, too, was not news. Nick was their man on the inside, as he liked to say. Jane flipped through the forms. Patient names, social security numbers, addresses, billing codes, correspondences with the state, with medical professionals, with accounting. Queller Bayside Home. Queller Hilltop House. Queller Youth Facility.

She told Andrew, "We've seen these before. They're part of the plan. Nick is sending them to the newspapers."

Andrew flipped through the folders until he found what he was looking for. "Read this one."

Jane opened the file. She immediately recognized the name on the admitting form.

ROBERT DAVID JUNEAU.

She shrugged. They knew that Robert Juneau had been at Bayside. Everyone knew. It was the place where all of this had started.

He said, "Look at the admitting dates."

She read aloud: "April 1–22, 1984; May 6–28, 1984; June 21–July 14, 1984." She looked back up at Andrew, confused, because they knew all of this, too. Queller had been gaming the system. Patients who stayed at the facilities for longer than twenty-three days were considered long-term patients, which meant that the state paid a lower daily rate for their care. Martin's way around the lowered rate was to kick out patients before they could hit the twenty-three-day mark, then re-admit them a few days later.

Jane said, "This is going to be released after Chicago and New York. Nick has the envelopes ready to go to the newspapers and the FBI field offices."

Andrew laughed. "Can you really see Nick sitting around stuffing almost one hundred envelopes? Licking stamps and writing out addresses?" He pointed to the file in Jane's hands. "Look at the next page."

She was too stressed and exhausted to play these games, but she turned the form over anyway. She saw more dates and summed them up for Andrew. "Twenty-two days in August, again in September, then in . . . Oh."

Jane stared at the numbers. The revulsion she had felt for her father became magnified.

Robert Juneau had murdered his children, then killed himself, on September 9, 1984. According to the information in his file, he'd continued to be admitted and re-admitted to various facilities for the next six months.

Queller facilities.

Her father had not just exploited Robert Juneau's injuries for profit. He had kept the profit rolling in even after the man had committed mass murder and suicide.

Jane had to swallow before she could ask, "Did Laura know that Father did this? I mean, did she know before Oslo?" She looked up at Andrew. "Laura saw these?"

He nodded.

Her hands were shaking when she looked back down. "I feel like a fool," she said. "I was guilty—feeling guilty—this morning. Yesterday. I kept remembering these stupid moments when Father wasn't a monster, but he was—"

"He was a monster," Andrew said. "He exploited the misery of thousands of people, and when the company went public, he would've exploited hundreds of thousands of more, all for his own financial gain. We had to stop him."

Nothing that Nick had said over the last five days had made Jane feel more at peace with what they had done.

She paged to the back of Robert Juneau's file. Queller had made hundreds of thousands of dollars off of Robert Juneau's death. She found paid invoices and billing codes and proof that the government had continued to pay for the treatment of a patient who'd never needed a clean bed or medication or meals.

Andrew said, "Turn to—"

Jane was already looking for the Intervening Report. A senior executive had to sign off on all multiple re-admissions so that an advisory board could convene to discuss the best course of action to get the patient the help that he needed. At least, that was what was supposed to happen because Queller Healthcare was allegedly in the business of helping people.

Jane scanned down to the senior executive's name. Her heart fell into her stomach. She knew the signature as well as she knew her own. It had appeared on school forms and blank checks that she took to the mall to buy clothes or when she got her hair cut or needed gas money.

Jasper Queller.

Her eyes filled with tears. She held up the form to the light. "It must be forged or—"

"You know it's not. That's his signature, Jinx. Probably signed with his special fucking Montblanc that Father got him when he left the Air Force."

Jane felt her head start to shake. She could see where this was going. "Please, Andrew. He's our brother."

"You need to accept the facts. I know you think that Jasper's your guardian angel, but he's been part of it the whole time. Everything Father was doing, he was doing, too."

Jane's head kept shaking, even though she had the proof right in front of her. Jasper had known that Robert Juneau was dead. He'd talked to Jane about the newspaper stories. He'd been just as horrified as Jane that Queller had so spectacularly failed a patient.

And then he had helped the company make money off of it.

Jane grabbed the other files, checked the signatures, because she was certain this had been some kind of mistake. The more she looked, the more desperate she felt.

Jasper's signature was on every single one.

She worked to swallow down her devastation. "Are all of these patients dead?"

"Most of them. Some moved out of state. Their patient credentials are still being used to charge for treatment." Andrew explained, "Jasper and Father were running up the numbers. The investors were getting antsy that the public offering wasn't going to be as much."

The investors. Martin had taken them on a few years ago so he could buy out the competition. Jasper was obsessed with the group, as if they were some sort of all-seeing monolith who could destroy them on a whim.

Andrew said, "Jasper has to be stopped. If the company goes public, he'll be sitting on millions of dollars in blood money. We can't let that happen."

Jane felt a quiver of panic. This was exactly how it had started with Martin. One bad revelation had followed another bad revelation and then suddenly Laura Juneau was shooting him in the head.

Andrew said, "I know you want to defend him, but this is indefensible."

"We can't—" Jane had to stop. This was too much. All of this was too much. "I won't hurt him, Andy. Not like Father. I don't care what you say."

"Jasper's not worth the bullet. But he has to pay for this."

"Who are we to play—" She stopped herself again, because they had played God in Oslo and none of them had blinked until the second it was over. "What are you going to do?"

"Release it to the newspapers."

Jane grabbed his arm. "Andy, please. I'm begging you. I know Jasper hasn't been the perfect brother to you, but he loves you. He loves both of us."

"Father would've said the same thing."

His words were like a slap. "You know that's different."

Andrew's jaw was set. "There's a finite amount of money in the system to take care of these people, Jinx. Jasper stole those resources to keep the investors happy. How many more Robert Juneaus are out there because of what our brother did?"

She knew he was right, but this was Jasper. "We can't—"

"It's no use arguing, Jinx. Nick's already put it into play. That's why he told me to come here first."

"First?" she repeated, alarmed. "First before what?"

Instead of answering, Andrew rubbed his face with his hands, the only sign that any of this was bothering him.

"Please." She could not stop saying the word. Her tears were on an endless flow.

Think of what destroying Jasper will do to me, she wanted to say. *I can't hurt anyone else. I can't turn off that switch that makes me feel responsible.*

Andrew said, "Jinx, you've got to know that this decision is not up to us."

She understood what he was telling her. Nick wanted revenge—not just for the bad things that Jasper had done, but for snubbing him at the dinner table, looking down his nose at

253

Nick, asking pointed questions about his background, making it clear that he was not *one of us*.

Andrew reached into the metal box again. Jane cringed when he pulled out a bundle of Polaroid photos. Andrew took off the rubber band and snapped it around his wrist.

She whispered, "Don't."

He ignored her, carefully studying each photo, a catalog of the beating that Jane had endured. "I'll never forgive Father for doing this to you." He showed her the close-up of her pummeled stomach.

The first time, not the last time, that Jane had been pregnant.

"Where was Jasper when this happened, Jane?" Andrew's anger had sparked. He could not be talked down. "I own my part. I was stoned. I didn't give a shit about myself, let alone anybody else. But Jasper?"

Jane looked into the parking lot. Her tears kept falling.

"Jasper was home when this happened, wasn't he? Locked in his room? Ignoring the screaming?"

They had all ignored the screaming when it was happening to someone else.

"Jesus." Andrew studied the next photo, the one that showed the deep gash in her leg. "Every time over the last few months, if I felt my nerve slipping, Nick would take these out to remind us both of what Father did to you." He showed Jane the close-up of her swollen eye. "How many times did Father hit you? How many black eyes did we ignore at the breakfast table? How many times did Mother laugh or Jasper kid you about being so uncoordinated?"

She tried to make light of it, saying her family nickname, "Clumsy Jinx."

Andrew said, "I will never let anyone hurt you again. Ever."

Jane was so tired of crying, but she seemed incapable of stopping herself. She had cried for Laura Juneau's broken family. She had cried for Nick. She had cried, inexplicably, for Martin, and now she cried from shame.

Andrew sniffed loudly. He put the rubber band back around

the Polaroids and dropped them into the box. "I'm not going to ask you if you knew about the gun."

Jane smoothed together her lips. She kept her gaze steady on the parking lot. "I'm not going to ask you, either."

He took in a wheezy, labored breath. "So, Nick—"

"Please don't say it." Jane's hand was pressed flat to her stomach again. She longed for Laura Juneau's serenity, her righteousness of cause.

Andrew said, "Laura had a choice. She could've left when she found the gun in the bag."

The same words from Nick had not brought Jane any comfort. She knew that Laura would never have backed out. The woman was determined, totally at peace with her choice. Maybe even glad of it. There was something to be said for being the master of your own fate. Or, as Nick had said, taking out a bastard with you.

Jane said, "She seemed nice."

Andrew made himself busy closing the lid on the box, checking the lock.

She repeated, "She just seemed really, really nice."

He cleared his throat several times. "She was a wonderful person."

His tone spoke to his anguish. Nick had put Andrew in charge of handling Laura. He was her sole point of contact for the group. It was Andrew who'd walked Laura through the details, given her the money, relayed information on flights, where to meet the forger in Toronto, how to present herself, what secret words would open this door or close the other.

He asked Jane, "Why did you talk to her? In Oslo?"

Jane shook her head. She could not answer the question. Nick had warned them that anonymity was their only protection if things went sideways. Jane, ever-eager to follow his orders, had been hiding in the bar when Laura Juneau walked in. There was less than an hour before the panel. It was too early to drink and Jane knew she shouldn't be drinking anyway. The piano had always worked to soothe her nerves, but for some inexplicable reason, she'd been drawn to Laura sitting alone at the bar.

"We should go," Andrew said.

Jane didn't argue. She just followed him silently down the steps and to the car.

She held the metal box in her lap as he started the engine and headed deeper into the city.

Jane struggled to keep her thoughts away from Jasper. Neither could she ask Andrew where they were going. It wasn't just the possibility of hidden listening devices that was keeping her brother silent. Her gut told her that there was something else going on. Jane's time in Berlin had somehow managed to remove her from the circle. She had noticed it in Oslo and it was especially obvious now that they were all back home. Nick and Andrew had been going for long walks, lurking in corners, their voices quickly dying down when Jane appeared.

At first she had thought they were managing her guilt, but now she wondered if there were other things that they didn't want her to know about.

Were there more hidden boxes?

Who else was Nick planning to hurt?

The car crested a hill. Jane closed her eyes against the sudden, bright sunlight. She let her mind wander back to Laura Juneau. Jane wanted to figure out what had motivated her to approach the woman in the bar. It was exactly the wrong thing to do. Nick had repeatedly warned Jane that she needed to stay far away from Laura, that interacting with her would only make the pigs look at Jane more carefully.

He'd been right.

She had known he was right when she was doing it. Maybe Jane had been rebelling against Nick. Or maybe she had been drawn to Laura's clarity of purpose. Andrew's coded letters had been filled with reverence for the woman. He'd told Jane that, out of all of them, Laura was the one who never seemed to waver.

Why?

"Look for a space," Andrew said.

256

They had already reached the Mission District. Jane was familiar with the area. As a student, she used to sneak down here to listen to punk bands at the old fire station. Around the corner were a homeless shelter and a soup kitchen where she often volunteered. The area had been a focal point for fringe activities as far back as when the Franciscan Friars built the first Mission in the late 1700s. Bear fighting and duels and horse races had given way to impoverished students and homeless people and drug addicts. There was a violent energy emanating from the abandoned warehouses and dilapidated immigrant housing. Anarchist graffiti was everywhere. Trash littered the street. Prostitutes stood on corners. It was the middle of the morning, but everything had the dark, dingy tint of sundown.

She said, "You can't park Jasper's Porsche here. Someone will steal it."

"They've never touched it before."

Before, Jane thought. *You mean all of those times the brother you claim to hate drove down here in the middle of the night to rescue you?*

Andrew tucked into a space between a motorcycle and a burned-out jalopy. He started to get out of the car, but Jane put her hand over his. His skin felt rough. There was a patch of dry skin on his wrist just under his watch. She started to comment on it, but she did not want words to intrude on this moment.

They had not been alone together since before they'd left the house. Since Laura Juneau had fired that last bullet into her skull. Since the *politi* had rushed both Jane and Nick from the auditorium.

The policemen had mistaken Nick for Andrew, and by the time they had figured out why Jane was screaming for her brother, Andrew was banging his fists on the door.

He'd looked almost deranged. Blood had stained the front of his shirt, dripped from his hands, soaked his trousers. Martin's blood. While everyone was running away from the stage, Andrew had run toward it. He had pushed aside the security. He had fallen to his knees. The next day, Jane would see a photograph of this moment in a newspaper: Andrew holding in his lap what was left of their father's head, his eyes raised to the ceiling, his mouth open as he screamed.

"It's funny," Andrew said now. "I didn't remember that I loved him until I saw her pointing the gun at his head."

Jane nodded, because she had felt it, too—a wrenching of her heart, a sweaty, cold second-guessing.

When Jane was a girl, she used to sit on Martin's knee while he read to her. He had placed Jane in front of her first piano. He had sought out Pechenikov to hone her studies. He had attended recitals and concerts and performances. He had kept a notebook in the breast pocket of his suit jacket in which he recorded her mistakes. He had punched her in the back when she slumped at the keyboard. He had switched her legs with a metal ruler when she didn't practice enough. He had kept her awake so many nights, screaming at her, telling her she was worthless, squandering her talent, doing everything wrong.

Andrew said, "I had all of these things I wanted to say to him."

Jane yet again found herself helpless to stop her tears.

"I wanted him to be proud of me. Not now, I knew it couldn't be now, but one day." Andrew turned to face her. He had always been lean, but now, in his grief, his cheeks were so hollow she could see the shape of the bones underneath. "Do you think that would've ever happened? That Father would've been proud of me, eventually?"

Jane knew the truth, but she answered, "Yes."

He looked back into the street. He told her, "There's Paula."

Jane felt the fine hairs on her arms and neck stand on end.

Paula Evans, dressed in her usual combat boots, dirty shift and fingerless gloves, fit in perfectly with the scenery. Her curly hair was frizzed wild. Her lips were bright red. For reasons unknown, she'd blackened under her eyes with a charcoal pencil. She saw the Porsche and flipped them off with both hands. Instead of heading toward the car, she stomped toward the warehouse.

258

Jane told Andrew, "She scares me. There's something wrong with her."

"Nick trusts her. She would do anything he asked."

"That's what scares me." Jane shuddered as she watched Paula disappear into the warehouse. If Nick was playing Russian roulette with their futures, Paula was the single bullet in the gun.

Jane got out of the car. The air had a greasy stench that reminded her of East Berlin. She left the metal box on the seat so she could slide on her jacket. She found her leather gloves and her scarf in her purse.

Andrew tucked the box under his arm as he locked the car. He told Jane, "Stay close."

They walked into the warehouse, but only to get through to the back. Jane hadn't been here for three months, but she knew the route by heart. They all did, because Nick had made them study diagrams, run up and down alleys, dart into backyards and even slide behind sewer grates.

Which had felt unhinged until now.

Paranoia seized Jane as she made her way down the familiar path. An alley took them through to the next street over. They blended in here, despite their expensive clothes. Thrift stores and dilapidated apartments were filled with students from nearby San Francisco State. Wadded-up newspapers had been shoved into broken windows. Trash cans overflowed with debris. Jane could smell the sickly-sweet odor of a thousand joints being lit to welcome the new morning.

The safe house was on 17th and Valencia, a block from Mission. At some point, it had been a single-family Victorian, but now it was chopped up into five one-bedroom apartments that appeared to be inhabited by a drug dealer, a group of strippers and a young couple with AIDS who had lost everything but each other. As with a lot of structures in this area, the house had been condemned. As with a lot of structures in the area, the inhabitants did not care.

They both climbed the wobbly front steps to the front door.

For the hundredth time, Andrew glanced over his shoulder before going in. The front hall was narrow enough that he had to turn his shoulders sideways to walk through to the open kitchen door. The backyard contained an old shed-like structure that had been converted into living space. An orange extension cord that draped from the house to the shed served as electrical service. There was no plumbing. The top floor balanced precariously on what was originally meant to be a storage area. Music throbbed against the closed windows. Pink Floyd's screechy "Bring the Boys Back Home."

Andrew looked up at the second floor, then looked back over his shoulder yet again. He knocked twice on the door. He paused. He knocked one last time and the door flew open.

"Idiots!" Paula grabbed Andrew by his shirt and yanked him inside. "What the fuck were you thinking? We all said dye packs. Who put that fucking gun in the bag?"

Andrew straightened his shirt. The metal box had fallen to the floor. He tried, "Paula, we—"

The air went cold.

Paula said, "What did you call me?"

Andrew didn't respond for a moment. In the silence, all Jane could hear was the record playing upstairs. She dropped her purse on the floor in case she had to help her brother. Paula's fists were clenched. Nick had told them only to use their code names, and as with everything else that came out of his mouth, Paula had taken his order as gospel.

"Sorry," Andrew said. "I meant Penny. As in, Penny, we can talk about this later?"

Paula did not back down. "Are you in charge now?"

"Penny," Jane said. "Stop this."

Paula reeled on her. "Don't you—"

Quarter cleared his throat.

Jane startled at the noise. She hadn't seen him when they'd walked in. He was sitting at the table. A red apple was in his hand. He lifted his chin toward Jane, then Andrew, by way of solidarity. He told Paula, "What's done is done."

260

"Are you fucking kidding me?" Paula's hands went to her hips. "This is murder, you fucking idiots. Do you know that? We're all part of a conspiracy to commit murder."

"In Norway," Quarter said. "Even if they manage to extradite us, we'll get seven years, tops."

Paula snorted in disgust. "You think the United States government is going to let us stand trial in a foreign country? It was you, wasn't it?" Paula was pointing her finger at Jane. "You put the gun in the bag, you dumb bitch."

Jane refused to be bullied by this festering asshole. "Are you pissed at me because Nick didn't tell you about the gun or because Nick is fucking me instead of you?"

Quarter chuckled.

Andrew sighed as he leaned down to pick up the metal box. Then he froze.

They all froze.

Someone was outside. Jane heard feet stamping. She held her breath as she waited for the secret knock—twice, then a pause, then another knock.

Nick?

Jane felt her heart leap at the possibility, but still, she was racked with anxiety until she opened the door and saw the smile on his face.

"Hello, gang." Nick gave Jane a kiss on the cheek. His mouth was at her ear. He whispered, "Switzerland."

Jane felt a rush of love for him.

Switzerland.

Their dreamed-about little flat in Basel, surrounded by students in a country that had no formal extradition treaty with the United States. Nick had talked about Switzerland that same Christmas night that he had revealed the plan. Jane had been shocked that he'd been able to focus so acutely not just on the mayhem they would cause, but on how they would extricate themselves from the fallout.

My darling, he had whispered in her ear. *Don't you know I've thought of everything?*

261

"Now." Nick clapped together his hands. He addressed the group. "All right, troops? How are we doing?"

Quarter pointed to Paula. "This one was freaking out."

"I was not," Paula insisted. "Nick, what happened in Norway was—"

"Exceptional!" He grabbed her by the arms, his excitement flowing through the room like a ray of light. "It was tremendous! Absolutely the single most important thing that has happened to an American in this century!"

Paula blinked, and Jane could see her mind instantly shift to Nick's way of thinking.

Nick clearly noted the change, too. He said, "Oh, Penny, if only you had been there to witness the act. The room was shocked. Laura pulled the revolver right as Martin was waxing poetic about the costs of floor cleaner. Then"—he made a gun of his fingers and thumb—"Pow. A gunshot heard around the world. Because of us." He winked at Jane, then expanded his arms to include the group. "My God, troops. What we've done, what we are about to do, is nothing short of heroic."

"He's right." As usual, Andrew rushed in to back him up. "Laura had a choice. We all had a choice. She decided to do what she did. We decided to do what we're doing. Right?"

"Right," Paula said, eager to be the first to agree. "We all knew what we were getting into."

Nick looked at Jane, waited for her to nod.

Quarter grunted, but his loyalty was never in question. He asked Nick, "What's going on with the pigs?"

Jane tried, "Agent Danberry—"

"It's not just the pigs," Nick interrupted. "It's every federal agency in the country. And Interpol." He seemed delighted by the last part. "It's what we wanted, gang. The eyes of the world are upon us. What we're doing now—in New York, Chicago, Stanford, what's already happened in Oslo—we're going to change the world."

"That's right," Paula said, a congregant calling back to the preacher.

262

"Do you know how rare it is to make change?" Nick's eyes were still glowing with purpose. It was infectious. They were all leaning toward him, a physical manifestation of hanging on his every word.

Nick asked, "Do each of you know how truly, genuinely rare it is that simple people like us are able to make a difference in the lives of—well, it'll be the lives of millions, won't it? Millions of people who are sick, others who have no idea that their tax dollars are being used to line the coffers of soulless corporations while real people, everyday people who need help, are left behind."

He looked around the room and made eye contact with every single one of them. This was what Nick fed off, knowing that he was inspiring all of them to reach toward greatness.

He said, "Penny, your work in Chicago is going to shock the world. Schoolchildren will be taught about your integral part in this. They will know that you stood for something. And Quarter, your logistical help—it's unfathomable that we'd be here without you. Your Stanford plans are the linchpin of this entire operation. And Andrew, our dear Dime. My God, how you handled Laura, how you put together all the pieces. Jane—"

Paula snorted again.

"Jane." Nick rested his hands on Jane's shoulders. He pressed his lips to her forehead and she felt awash with love. "You, my darling. You give me strength. You make it possible for me to lead our glorious troops toward greatness."

Paula said, "We're gonna get caught." She no longer seemed furious about the prospect. "You guys know that, right?"

"So what?" Quarter had taken out his knife. He was peeling the apple. "Are you afraid now? All your big-talk bullshit and now—"

"I'm not afraid," Paula said. "I'm in this. I said I was in this, so I'm in it. You can always count on me, Nick."

"Good girl." Nick rubbed Jane's back. She almost curled into him like a kitten. It was that easy for him. All he had to do was put his hand in the right place, say the right word, and she was firmly back at his side.

Was Jane a yo-yo?

Or was she a true believer, because what Nick was saying was right? They had to wake people up. They could not sit idly by while so many people were suffering. Inaction was unconscionable.

Nick said, "All right, troops. I know the gun in Oslo was a surprise, but can't you see how fantastic things are for us now? Laura did us a tremendous favor by pulling that trigger and sacrificing her life. Her words resonate far more now than if she'd been shouting them from behind prison bars. She is a martyr—a celebrated martyr. And what we do next, the steps we take, will make people realize that they can't just run along like sheep anymore. Things will have to change. People will have to change. Governments will have to change. Corporations will have to change. Only we can make that happen. We're the ones who have to wake up everyone else."

They were all beaming at him, his willing acolytes. Even Andrew was glowing under Nick's praise. Maybe their blind devotion was what allowed Jane's anxiety to keep seeping back in.

Things had changed while she was away in Berlin. The energy in the room was more kinetic.

Almost fatalistic.

Had Paula cleaned out her apartment, too?

Had Quarter gotten rid of all of his most prized possessions?

Andrew had broken things off with Ellis-Ann. He was visibly unwell, yet he kept refusing to go to the doctor.

Was their blind devotion another form of sickness?

All of them but Jane had been in one psychiatric facility or another. Nick had purloined their files at Queller, or in the instances of the other members of the cells, found someone who would give them access. He knew about their hopes and fears and breakdowns and suicide attempts and eating disorders and criminal histories and, most importantly, Nick knew how to exploit this information for effect.

Yo-yos unraveling or rolling back up at Nick's whim.

"Let's do this." Quarter reached into his pocket. He slapped a quarter on the table beside the peeled apple. He said, "The Stanford Team is ready."

Manic depression. Schizoid tendencies. Violent recidivism.

Paula fell into a chair as she placed a penny on the table. "Chicago's been ready for a month."

Anti-social behavior. Kleptomania. Anorexia nervosa. Akiltism.

Nick flipped a nickel into the air. He caught it in his hand and dropped it onto the table. "New York is raring to go."

Sociopathy. Impulse control disorder. Cocaine addiction.

Andrew looked at Jane again before reaching into his pocket. He placed a dime with the other change and sat down. "Oslo is complete."

Anxiety disorder. Depression. Suicidal ideation. Drug-induced psychosis.

They all turned to Jane. She reached into her jacket pocket, but Nick stopped her.

"Take this upstairs, would you, darling?" He handed Jane the apple that Quarter had peeled.

"I can do it," Paula offered.

"Can you be quiet?" Nick was not telling her to shut up. He was asking a question.

Paula sat back down.

Jane took the apple. The fruit made a wet spot on her leather glove. She felt around on the secret panel until she found the button to push. One of Nick's clever ideas. They wanted to make it as hard as possible for anyone to find the stairs. Jane pulled back the panel, then used the hook to close it firmly behind her.

There was a sharp click as the release mechanism went back in place.

She climbed the stairs slowly, trying to make out what they were saying. The Pink Floyd song blaring from a tinny speaker was doing too good a job. Only Paula's raised voice could be heard over the soaring instrumental of "Comfortably Numb."

"Fuckers," she kept saying, obviously trying to impress Nick

265

with her rabid devotion. "We'll show those stupid mother-fuckers."

Jane could feel an almost animalistic excitement rising through the floorboards as she reached the top of the stairs. There was incense burning inside the locked room. She could smell lavender. Paula had likely brought one of her voodoo talismans to keep the spirits at peace.

Laura Juneau had kept lavender in her house. This was one of the many stray details that Andrew had managed to relay in his coded letters. Like that Laura enjoyed pottery. That, like Andrew, she was a fairly good painter. That she had just come from the garden outside her house and was on her knees in the living room looking for a vase in the cupboard when Robert Juneau had used his key to unlock the front door.

A single shot to the head of a five-year-old.

Two bullets into a sixteen-year-old's chest.

Two more bullets into the body of a fourteen-year-old girl.

One of those bullets lodged into Laura Juneau's spine.

The last bullet, the final bullet, had entered Robert Juneau's skull from beneath his chin.

Thorazine. Valium. Xanax. Round-the-clock care. Doctors. Nurses. Accountants. Janitors. Mop & Glo.

"Do you know how much it costs to commit a man full-time?" Martin had demanded of Jane. They were sitting at the breakfast table. The newspaper was spread in front of them, garish headlines capturing the horror of a mass murder: MAN MURDERS FAMILY THEN SELF. Jane was asking her father how this had happened—why Robert Juneau had been kicked out of so many Queller Homes.

"Almost one hundred thousand dollars a year." Martin was stirring his coffee with an antique Liberty & Company silver spoon that had been gifted to a distant Queller. He asked Jane, "Do you know how many trips to Europe that represents? Cars for your brothers? How many road trips and tours and lessons with your precious Pechenikov?"

Why did you give up performing?

Because I could no longer play with blood on my hands.

Jane found the key on a hook and pushed it into the deadbolt lock. On the other side of the door, the record had reached the part where David Gilmour took over the chorus—

There is no pain, you are receding . . .

Jane walked into the room. The smell of lavender enveloped her. A glass vase held fresh cut flowers. Incense burned on a metal tray. Jane realized these were not meant to ward off bad spirits, but to cover the odor of shit and piss in the bucket by the window.

When I was a child, I had a fever . . .

There were only two windows in the small space, one facing the Victorian in the front, the other facing the house that was on the street behind them. Jane opened both, hoping the cross-breeze would alleviate some of the odor.

She stood in the middle of the room holding the peeled apple. She let the song play through to the guitar solo. She followed the notes in her head. Visualized her fingers on the strings. She had played guitar for a while, then the violin, cello, mandolin and, just for the sheer joy of it, a steel-stringed fiddle.

Then Martin had told her that she had to choose between being good at many things or perfect at one.

Jane lifted the needle from the record.

She heard them downstairs. First, Andrew's coughing with its worrisome rattle. Nick's pithy little asides. Quarter told them all to keep their voices down, but then Paula started another *fucking pigs will pay* diatribe that drowned them all out.

"Come now," Nick spoke in a teasing tone. "We're so close. Do you know how important we're going to be when this is all over?"

When this is all over . . .

Jane put her hand to her stomach as she walked across the room.

Would this ever be over?

Could they go on after this? Could they bring a child into this world that they were trying to create? Was there really a flat waiting for them in Switzerland?

Jane reminded herself again: Nick had sold his furniture. Stripped away the fixtures in his apartment. He was sleeping on the floor. Was that a man who thought there was a future?

Was that a man who could be a father to their child?

Jane kneeled beside the bed.

She lowered her voice a few octaves, warning, "Don't say a word."

She pulled down the gag from the woman's mouth.

Alexandra Maplecroft started screaming.

August 23, 2018

11

Andy hefted a heavy box of old sneakers out of the back of the Reliant. Fat drops of rain smacked the cardboard. Steam came off the asphalt. The sky had opened after days of punishing heat, so now in addition to the punishing heat she had to deal with getting wet. She sprinted back and forth between the hatch and the open storage unit, head cowed every time a bolt of lightning slipped between the afternoon clouds.

She had taken a page from her mother and rented two different storage units in two different facilities in two different states to hide the gazillion dollars of cash inside the Reliant. Actually, Andy had done Laura one better. Instead of just piling the money on the floor of the unit like she was Skyler in *Breaking Bad*, she had cleaned out the back room of a Salvation Army store in Little Rock, then hidden the stacks of cash underneath old clothes, camping gear and a bunch of broken toys.

That way, anyone watching would think Andy was doing what most Americans did and paying to store a bunch of crap they didn't want instead of donating it to people who could actually use it.

Andy ran back to the Reliant and grabbed another box. Rain splashed inside her brand-new sneakers. Her new socks took on the consistency of quicksand. Andy had stopped at another Walmart after leaving the first storage facility on the Arkansas side of Texarkana. She was finally wearing clothes that were not from the 1980s. She'd bought a messenger bag and a $350 laptop. She had sunglasses, underwear that didn't sag around her ass, and, weirdly, a sense of purpose.

I want you to live your life, Laura had said back at the diner. *As much as I want to make it easier for you, I know that it'll never take unless you do it all on your own.* Andy was certainly on her own now. But what had changed? She couldn't quite articulate even to herself why she felt so different. She just knew that she was sick of floating between disaster points like an amoeba inside a petri dish. Was it the realization that her mother was a spectacular liar? Was it the feeling of shame for being such a gullible believer? Was it the fact that a hired gun had followed Andy all the way to Alabama, and instead of listening to her gut and taking off, she had tried to hook up with him?

Her face burned with shame as she slid another box out of the back of the Reliant.

Andy had stayed in Muscle Shoals long enough to watch Mike Knepper's truck drive past the motel twice in the space of two hours. She had waited through the third hour and into the fourth to make certain that he wasn't coming back, then she'd packed up the Reliant and hit the road again.

She had been shaky from the outset, loaded with caffeine from McDonald's coffee, still terrified to pull over to go to the restroom because, at that point, she still had the cash hidden inside of the car. The drive to Little Rock, Arkansas, had taken five hours, but every single one of them had weighed on her soul.

Why had Laura lied to her? Who was she so afraid of? Why had she told Andy to go to Idaho?

More importantly, why was Andy still blindly following her mother's orders?

Andy's inability to answer any of these questions had not been helped by lack of sleep. She had stopped in Little Rock because it was a town she had heard of, then she had stopped at the first hotel with an underground parking deck because she figured she should hide the Reliant in case Mike was somehow following her.

Andy had backed the station wagon into a space so that any would-be thieves would have trouble accessing the hatch. Then she had gotten back into the car and pulled forward so that she could take the sleeping bag and the beach tote out of the trunk. Then she had backed into the space again, then she had checked into the hotel, where she had slept for almost eighteen hours straight.

The last time she had slept that long, Gordon had taken her to the doctor because he was afraid she had narcolepsy. Andy thought of the Arkansas sleep as therapeutic. She was not gripping a steering wheel. She was not screaming or sobbing into the empty car. She was not checking Laura's cell phone every five minutes. She was not fretting about all the money that tethered her to the Reliant. She was not worrying that Mike had followed her because she had actually crawled under the car and checked for any GPS tracking devices.

Mike.

With his stupid *K* in his last name and his stupid grasshopper on his truck and his stupid kissing her in the parking lot like some kind of psychopath because he was clearly there to follow Andy, or torture her, or do something horrible, and instead he had seduced her.

Worse, she had let him.

Andy grabbed the last box from the back of the car and approximated a walk of shame into the unit. She dropped the box onto the floor. She sat down on a wooden stool with a wobbly third leg. She rubbed her face. Her cheeks were on fire.

Idiot, she silently admonished herself. *He saw right through you.*

The painful truth was, there was not much of a story to tell about Andy's sex life. She would always trot out the affair with her college professor as a way to sound sophisticated, but she left out the part where they'd had sex only three and a half times. And that the guy was a pothead. And mostly impotent.

And that they usually ended up sitting on his couch while he got high and Andy watched *Golden Girls* reruns.

Still, he was better than her high school boyfriend. They had met in drama club, which should have been a giant freaking clue. But they were best friends. And they had both decided that their first times should be with each other.

Afterward, Andy had been underwhelmed, but lied to make him feel better. He had been just as underwhelmed, but failed to extend her the same courtesy.

You get too wet, he had told her, shuddering dramatically, and even though he admitted he was probably gay in the next sentence, Andy had carried that debilitating criticism with her for the ensuing decade and a half.

Too wet. She mulled the phrase in her mind as she stared at the wall of rain outside the storage unit. There were so many things she would say to that jackass now if he would just accept her friend request on Facebook.

Which brought her to her New York boyfriend. Andy had thought that he was so gentle and kind and considerate and then Andy had been in the bathroom at a friend's apartment when she'd overheard him talking to his buddies.

She's like the ballerina in a jewelry box, he had confided. *The second you bend her over, the music stops.*

Andy shook her head like a dog. She ran back to the car, got the light blue Samsonite suitcase, and dragged it into the unit. With the door closed, she changed into dry clothes. There was nothing she could do about her sneakers but at least she had socks that weren't peeling at her already sore feet. By the time she rolled the door up, the rain had tapered off, which was the first good luck she'd had in days.

Andy used one of her Walmart padlocks on the latch. Instead of a key, she had chosen a combination lock that used letters rather than numbers. The Texarkana code was FUCKR because she was feeling particularly hostile when she programmed it. For the Hook 'Em & Store outside of Austin, Texas, she'd gone with the more obvious KUNDE, as in —

I could talk to Paula Kunde.

I hear she's in Seattle.

Austin. But good try.

Andy had decided back in Little Rock that she was not going to amoeba her way to Idaho like Laura had told her to. If she could not get answers from her mother, then maybe she could get them from Professor Paula Kunde.

She reached up to close the hatch on the wagon. The sleeping bag and beach tote were still loaded up with cash, but she figured she might as well keep them in the car. She should probably put the little cooler and the box of Slim Jims in the storage unit, but Andy was antsy to get back on the road.

The Reliant's engine made a whirly Chitty-Chitty-Bang-Bang sound when she pulled away. Instead of heading toward the interstate, she took the next right into McDonald's. She used the drive-thru to order a large coffee and get the Wi-Fi password.

Andy chose a parking space close to the building. She dumped the coffee out the window because she was pretty sure her heart would explode if she drank any more caffeine. She got her new laptop out of the messenger bag and logged onto the network.

She stared at the flashing cursor on the search bar.

As usual, she had a moment of indecision about whether or not to create a fake Gmail account and send something to Gordon. Andy had composed all kinds of drafts in her mind, pretending to be a Habitat for Humanity coordinator or a fellow Phi Beta Sigma, contriving some kind of coded message that let her father know that she was okay.

Just asking if you saw that great Subway coupon offering two-for-one?

Saw a story about Knob Creek bourbon I thought you might enjoy!

As usual, Andy decided against it. There wasn't a hell of a lot she trusted about her mother right now, but even the slightest chance of putting Gordon in harm's way was too much of a risk.

She typed in the web address for the *Belle Isle Review*.

The photo of Laura and Gordon at the Christmas party was still on the front page.

Andy studied her mother's face, wondering how the familiar woman smiling at the camera could be the same woman who'd deceived her only daughter for so many years. Then she zoomed in closer, because Andy had never given the bump in her mother's nose a second thought. Had it been broken at some point and healed crookedly?

The Polaroids from her mother's storage unit told Andy that the explanation was possible.

Would she ever know the truth?

Andy scrolled down the page. The article about the body that had washed up under the Yamacraw Bridge had not changed, either. Still no identity on the man in the hoodie. No report of his stolen vehicle. Which meant that Laura had not only kept a battalion of police officers out of her house, she had somehow managed to drag an almost two hundred pound man to her Honda, then dump him in the river twenty miles away.

With one arm strapped to her chest and barely a set of legs to walk on.

Her mother was a criminal.

That was the only explanation that made sense. Andy had been thinking of Laura as passive and reactionary when all of the evidence pointed to her being logical and devious. The almost one million bucks in cash had not come from helping stroke patients work on their diction. The fake IDs were scary enough, but Andy had walked that back a step and realized that Laura not only had a fake ID, she had a contact—a forger—who could make documents for her. Every time Laura had crossed into Canada to renew the license or the car tag, she had broken federal law. Andy doubted the IRS knew about the cash, which broke all kinds of other federal laws. Laura wasn't afraid of the police. She knew that she could refuse an interrogation. She had a preternatural coolness around law enforcement. That didn't come from Gordon, which meant that Laura had learned it on her own.

Which meant that Laura Oliver was not a *good guy*.

Andy closed the laptop and returned it to the messenger bag. There wasn't enough memory on the machine to start listing all the things that her mother needed to explain. At this point, how Laura had disposed of Hoodie's dead body wasn't even in the top three.

Rain tapped at the windshield. Dark clouds had rolled in. Andy backed out of the space and followed the signs toward UT-AUSTIN. The sprawling campus took up forty acres of prime real estate. There was a medical school and hospital, a law school, all kinds of liberal arts programs and, despite not having its own football team, countless Texas Longhorns flags and bumper stickers.

According to the class schedule on the school's website, Dr. Kunde had taught a morning class called Feminist Perspectives on Domestic Violence and Sexual Assault followed by an hour set aside for student advisory. Andy checked the time on the radio. Even assuming Paula's sessions had run long or she'd stopped for lunch, or maybe met a colleague for another meeting, she was probably home by now.

Andy had tried to do more research on the woman's background, but there wasn't a hell of a lot about Paula Kunde on the internet. The UT-Austin site listed tons of academic papers and conferences, but nothing about her personal life. ProfRatings. com gave her only one half of a star, but when Andy dug into the student reviews, she saw they were mostly whining about bad grades that Dr. Kunde refused to change or offering long, adverb-riddled diatribes about how Dr. Kunde was a harsh bitch, which was basically the hallmark of her generation's contribution to higher education.

The only easy part of the investigoogling was finding the professor's home address. Austin's tax records were online. All Andy had to do was enter Paula Kunde's name and not only was she able to see that the property taxes had been paid consistently for the last ten years, she was able to click onto Google Street View and see for herself the low-slung one-story house in a section of the city called Travis Heights.

Andy checked her map again as she turned down Paula's street. She had studied the street on her laptop, like she was some kind of burglar casing the joint, but the images had been taken in the dead of winter when all the shrubs and trees lay dormant—nothing like the lush, overflowing gardens she passed now. The neighborhood had a trendy feel, with hybrids in the driveways and artistic yard ornaments. Despite the rain, people were out jogging. The houses were painted in their own color schemes, regardless of what their neighbors chose. Old trees. Wide streets. Solar panels and one very strange-looking miniature windmill in front of a dilapidated bungalow.

She was so intent on looking at the houses that she drove past Paula's on the first go. She went down to South Congress and turned back around. This time, she looked at the street numbers on the mailboxes.

Paula Kunde lived in a craftsman-style house, but with a kind of funkiness to it that wasn't out of touch with the rest of the neighborhood. An older model white Prius was parked in front of the closed garage door. Andy saw dormers stuck into the garage roof. She wondered if Paula Kunde had a daughter in her apartment that she couldn't get rid of, too. That would be a good opening line, or at least a second or a third, because the onus was going to be on Andy to talk her way into the house.

This could be it.

All the questions she'd had about Laura might be answered by the time Andy got back into the Reliant.

The thought made her knees rubbery when she stepped out of the car. Talking had never been her forte. Amoebas didn't have mouths. She threw her new messenger bag over her shoulder. She checked the contents to give her brain something else to concentrate on as she walked toward the house. There was some cash in there, the laptop, Laura's make-up bag with the burner phone, hand lotion, eye drops, lip gloss—just enough to make her feel like a human woman again.

Andy searched the windows of the house. All of the lights were off inside, at least from what she could see. Maybe Paula

278

wasn't home. Andy had only guessed by the online schedule. The Prius could belong to a tenant. Or Mike could've changed out his truck.

The thought sent a shiver down her spine as she navigated the path to the front door. Leggy petunias draped over wooden planters. Dead patches in the otherwise neatly trimmed yard showed where the Texas sun had burned the ground. Andy glanced behind her as she climbed the porch stairs. She felt furtive, but wasn't sure whether or not the feeling was justified.

I'm not going to hurt you. I'm just going to scare the shit out of you.

Maybe that's why Mike had kissed Andy. He knew that threats had not worked against Laura, so he'd figured he would do something awful to Andy and use that for leverage.

"Who the fuck are you?"

Andy had been so caught up in her own thoughts that she hadn't noticed the front door had opened.

Paula Kunde gripped an aluminum baseball bat between her hands. She was wearing dark sunglasses. A scarf was tied around her neck. "Hello?" She waited, the bat still reared back like she was ready to swing it. "What do you want, girl? Speak up."

Andy had practiced this in the car, but the sight of the baseball bat had erased her mind. All she could get out was a stuttered, "I-I-I—"

"Jesus Christ." Paula finally lowered the bat and leaned it inside the doorframe. She looked like her faculty photo, but older and much angrier. "Are you one of my students? Is this about a grade?" Her voice was scratchy as a cactus. "Trigger warning, dumbass, I'm not going to change your grade, so you can dry your snowflake tears all the way back to community college."

"I—" Andy tried again. "I'm not—"

"What the hell is wrong with you?" Paula tugged at the scarf around her neck. It was silk, too hot for the weather, and didn't match her shorts and sleeveless shirt. She looked down her long nose at Andy. "Unless you're going to talk, get your ass—"

"No!" Andy panicked when she started to shut the door. "I need to talk to you."

"About what?"

Andy stared at her. She felt her mouth trying to form words. The scarf. The glasses. The scratchy voice. The bat by the door. "About you getting suffocated. With a bag. A plastic bag."

Paula's lips pressed into a thin line.

"Your neck." Andy touched her own neck. "You're wearing the scarf to hide the scratch marks and your eyes probably have—"

Paula took off her sunglasses. "What about them?"

Andy tried not to gawk. One of the woman's eyes was milky white. The other was streaked with red as if she had been crying, or strangled, or both.

Paula asked, "Why are you here? What do you want?"

"To talk—my mother. I mean, do you know her? My mother?"

"Who's your mother?"

Good question.

Paula watched a car drive past her house. "Are you going to say something or stand there like a little fish with your mouth gaping open?"

Andy felt her resolve start to evaporate. She had to think of something. She couldn't give up now. Suddenly, she remembered a game they used to play in drama, an improv exercise called *Yes, And . . .* You had to accept the other person's statement and build on it in order to keep the conversation going.

She said, "Yes, and I'm confused because I've recently found out some things about my mother that I don't understand."

"I'm not going to be part of your *bildungsroman*. Now cheese it or I'll call the police."

"Yes." Andy almost screamed. "I mean, yes, call the police. And then they'll come."

"That's kind of the point of calling the police."

"Yes," Andy repeated. She could see where the game really required two people. "And they'll ask lots of questions. Questions you don't want to answer. Like about why your eye has petechiae."

Paula looked over Andy's shoulder again. "Is that your car in my driveway, the one that looks like a box of maxi pads?"

"Yes, and it's a Reliant."

"Take off your shoes if you're going to come inside. And stop that '*Yes, And*' bullshit, Jazz Hands. This isn't drama club."

Paula left her at the door.

Andy felt weirdly terrified and excited that she had managed to get this far.

This was it. She was going to find out about her mother.

She dropped the messenger bag on the floor. She rested her hand on the hall table. A glass bowl of change clicked against the marble top. She slipped off her sneakers and left them in front of the aluminum baseball bat. Her wet socks went inside the shoes. She was so nervous that she was sweating. She pulled at the front of her shirt as she stepped down into Paula's sunken living room.

The woman had a stark sense of design. There was nothing craftsman inside the house except some paneling on the walls. Everything had been painted white. The furniture was white. The rugs were white. The doors were white. The tiles were white.

Andy followed the sound of a chopping knife down the back hall. She tried the swinging door, pushing it just enough to poke her head in. She found herself looking in the kitchen, surrounded by still more white: countertops, cabinets, tiles, even light fixtures. The only color came from Paula Kunde and the muted television on the wall.

"Come in already." Paula waved her in with a long chef's knife. "I need to get my vegetables in before the water boils off."

Andy pushed open the door all the way. She walked into the room. She smelled broth cooking. Steam rose off a large pot on the stove.

Paula sliced broccoli into florets. "Do you know who did it?"

"Did . . ." Andy realized she meant Hoodie. She shook her head, which was only partially lying. Hoodie had been sent by somebody. Somebody who was clearly known to Laura. Somebody who might be known to Paula Kunde.

"He had weird eyes, like . . ." Paula's voice trailed off. "That's all I could tell the pigs. They wanted to set me up with a sketch artist, but what's the point?"

"I could—" Andy's ego cut her off. She had been about to offer to draw Hoodie, but she hadn't drawn anything, even a doodle, since her first year in New York.

Paula snorted. "Good Lord, child. If I had a dollar bill every time you left a sentence hanging, I sure as shit wouldn't be living in Texas."

"I was just—" Andy tried to think of a lie, but then she wondered if Hoodie had really come here first. Maybe Andy had misunderstood the exchange in Laura's office. Maybe Mike had been sent to Austin and Hoodie had been sent to Belle Isle.

She told Paula, "If you've got some paper, maybe I could do a sketch for you?"

"Over there." She used her elbow to indicate a small desk area at the end of the counter.

Andy opened the drawer. She was expecting to find the usual junk—spare keys, a flashlight, stray coins, too many pens—but there were only two items, a sharpened pencil and a pad of paper.

"So, art's your thing?" Paula asked. "You get that from someone in your family?"

"I—" Andy didn't have to see the look on Paula's face to know that she'd done it again.

Instead, she flipped open the notebook, which was filled with blank pages. Andy didn't give herself time to freak out about what she was about to do, to question her talents or to talk herself out of having the hubris to believe she still had any skills left in her hands. Instead, she knocked the sharp point off the pencil and sketched out what she remembered of Hoodie's face.

"Yep." Paula was nodding before she'd finished. "That looks like the bastard. Especially the eyes. You can tell a lot about somebody from their eyes."

Andy found herself looking into Paula's blank left eye.

Paula asked, "How do you know what he looks like?"

Andy didn't answer the question. She turned to a fresh page. She drew another man, this one with a square jaw and an Alabama baseball cap. "What about this guy? Have you ever seen him around here?"

Paula studied the image. "Nope. Was he with the other guy?"

"Maybe. I'm not sure." She felt her head shaking. "I don't know. About anything, actually."

"I'm getting that."

Andy had to buy herself some time to think. She returned the pad and pencil to the drawer. This whole conversation was going sideways. Andy wasn't so stupid that she didn't know she was being played. She'd come here for answers, not more questions.

Paula said, "You look like her."

Andy felt a bolt of lightning shoot from head to toe.

You-look-like-her-you-look-like-her-you-look-like-your-mother.

Slowly, Andy turned around.

"The eyes, mostly." Paula used the point of a large chef's knife to indicate her eyes. "The shape of your face, like a heart."

Andy felt frozen in place. She kept playing back Paula's words in her head because her heart was pounding so loudly that she could barely hear.

The eyes . . . The shape of your face . . .

Paula said, "She was never as timid as you. Must get that from your father?"

Andy didn't know because she didn't know anything except that she had to lean against the counter and lock her knees so she didn't fall down.

Paula resumed chopping. "What do you know about her?"

"That . . ." Andy was having trouble speaking again. Her stomach had filled with bees. "That she's been my mother for thirty-one years."

Paula nodded. "That's some interesting math."

"Why?"

"Why indeed."

283

The sound of the knife *thwapping* the chopping board resonated inside of Andy's head. She had to stop reacting. She needed
to ask her questions. She'd made a whole list of them in her
head on the seven-hour drive and now—

"Could you—"

"Dollar bill, kid. Could I what?"

Andy felt dizzy. Her body was experiencing the odd numbness
of days before. Her arms and legs wanted to float up toward
the ceiling, her brain had disconnected from her mouth. She
couldn't fall back into old patterns. Not now. Not when she
was so close.

"Can—" Andy tried a third time, "How do you know her?
My mother?"

"I'm not a snitch."

Snitch?

Paula had looked up from her chopping. Her expression was
unreadable. "I'm not trying to be a bitch. Though, admittedly,
being a bitch is kind of my thing." She diced together a bundle
of celery and carrots. The pieces were all identical in size. The
knife moved so fast that it looked still. "I learned how to cook
in the prison kitchen. We had to be fast."

Prison?

"I always wanted to learn." Paula scooped the vegetables into
her hands and walked over to the stove. She dropped everything
into a stew pot as she told Andy, "It took over a decade for me
to earn the privilege. They only let the older gals handle the
knives."

Over a decade?

Paula asked, "I gather you didn't see that when you googled
me."

Andy realized her tongue was stuck to the roof of her mouth.
She was too astonished to process all of these revelations.

Snitch. Prison. Over a decade.

Andy had been telling herself for days that Laura was a criminal. Hearing the theory confirmed was like a punch to her gut.

"I pay to keep that out of the top searches. It's not cheap, but—" She shrugged, her eyes on Andy again. "You *did* google me, right? Found my address through the property tax records. Saw my course schedule, read my shitty student reviews?" She was smiling. She seemed to like the effect she was having. "Then, you looked at my CV, and you asked yourself, UC-Berkeley, Stanford, West Connecticut State. Which one of those doesn't belong? Right?"

Andy could only nod.

Paula started chopping up a potato. "There's a women's federal corrections facility near West Conn. Danbury—you probably know it from that TV show. They used to let you do a higher ed program. Not so much anymore. Martha Stewart was a guest, but that was after my two dimes."

Two dimes?

Paula glanced up at Andy again. "People at the school know. It's not a secret. But I don't like to talk about it, either. My revolutionary days are over. Hell, at my age, pretty much most of my life is over."

Andy looked down at her hands. The fingers felt like cat whiskers. What awful thing did a person have to do to be sentenced to a federal prison for twenty years? Should Laura have been in prison for the same amount of time, only she had stolen a bunch of money, run away, created a new life, while Paula Kunde was counting the days until she was old enough to work in the prison kitchen?

"I should—" Andy's throat was so tight she could barely draw air. She needed to think about this, but she couldn't do that in this stuffy kitchen under this woman's watchful eye. "Leave, I mean. I should—"

"Calm down, Bambi. I didn't meet your mother in prison, if that's what you're freaking out about." She started on another potato. "Of course, who knows what you're thinking, because you're not really asking me any questions."

Andy swallowed the cotton in her throat. She tried to remember her questions. "How—how do you know her?"

"What's her name again?"

285

Andy didn't understand the rules of this cruel game. "Laura Oliver. Mitchell, I mean. She got married, and now—"

"I know how marriage works." Paula sliced open a bell pepper. She used the sharp tip of the blade to pick out the seeds. "Ever hear of QuellCorp?"

Andy shook her head, but she answered, "The pharmaceutical company?"

"What's your life like?"

"My li—"

"Nice schools? Fancy car? Great job? Cute boyfriend who's gonna do a YouTube video when he proposes to you?"

Andy finally picked up on the hard edge to the woman's tone. She wasn't being matter-of-fact anymore. The smile on her face was a sneer.

"Uh—" Andy started to edge toward the door. "I really should—"

"Is she a good mother?"

"Yes." The answer came easy when Andy didn't think about it.

"Chaperoned school dances, joined the PTA, took pictures of you at the prom?"

Andy nodded to all of this, because it was true.

"I saw her murdering that kid on the news." Paula turned her back on Andy as she washed her hands at the sink. "Though they're saying she's cleared now. She was trying to save him. Please don't move."

Andy stood perfectly still. "I wasn't—"

"I'm not saying 'Please don't move' to you, kid. 'Please' is a patriarchal construct designed to make women apologize for their vaginas." She wiped her hands on a kitchen towel. "I was talking about what your mother said before she murdered that boy. It's all over the news."

Andy looked at the muted television on the wall. The diner video was showing again. Laura was holding up her hands in that strange way, four fingers raised on her left, one on her right, to show Jonah Helsinger how many bullets he had left.

The closed captioning scrolled, but Andy was incapable of processing the information.

"The experts have weighed in," Paula said. "They claim to know what your mother said to Helsinger—*Please don't move*, as in *Please don't move or the inside of your throat will splat onto the floor.*"

Andy put her hand to her own neck. Her pulse tapped furiously against her fingers. She should be relieved that her mother was in the clear, but every bone in her body was telling her to leave this house. No one knew she was here. Paula could gut her like a pig and no one would be the wiser.

"It's funny, isn't it?" Paula leaned her elbows on the counter. She pinned Andy with her one good eye. "Your sweet little ol' mother kills a kid in cold blood, but walks because she thought to say *Please don't move* instead of *Hasta la vista*. Lucky Laura Oliver." Paula seemed to roll the phrase around on her tongue. "Did you see the look on her face when she did it? Gal didn't look bothered to me. Looked like she knew exactly what she was doing, right? And that she was a-okay with it. Just like always."

Andy was frozen again, but not from fear. She wanted to hear what Paula had to say.

"Cool as a cucumber. Never cries over spilled milk. Trouble rolls off her like water off a duck's back. That's what we used to say about her. I mean, those of us who said anything. You know Laura Oliver, but you don't *know* her. There's only the surface. Still waters don't run deep. Have you noticed?"

Andy wanted to shake her head, but she was paralyzed.

"I hate to say it kid, but your mother is full of the worst type of bullshit. That dumb bitch has always been an actress playing the role of her life. Haven't you noticed?"

Andy finally managed to shake her head, but she was thinking—*Mom Mode. Healing Dr. Oliver Mode. Gordon's Wife Mode.*

"Stay here." Paula left the room.

Andy could not have followed if she'd wanted to. She felt like her bare feet were glued to the tiled floor. Nothing this scary stranger had said about Laura was new information, but Paula had framed it in such a way that Andy was beginning to understand that the different facets of her mother weren't pieces of a whole; they were camouflage.

You have no idea who I am. You never have and you never will.

"Are you still there?" Paula called from the other side of the house.

Andy rubbed her face. She had to forget what Paula had said for now and get the hell out of here. The woman was still dangerous. She was clearly working some kind of angle. Andy should never have come here.

She opened the desk drawer. She ripped the drawings of Hoodie and Mike out of the pad, shoved them into her back pocket, then pushed open the kitchen door.

She was met by Paula Kunde pointing a shotgun at her chest.

"Jesus Christ!" Andy fell back against the swinging door.

"Hold up your hands, you dimwit."

Andy's hands went up.

"Are you wired?"

"What?"

"Bugged. Mic'd." Paula patted the front of Andy's shirt first, then her pockets, down her legs and back up. "Did she send you here to trap me?"

"What?"

"Come on." Paula pressed the muzzle into Andy's sternum. "Speak, you little monkey. Who sent you?"

"N-n-body."

"Nobody." Paula snorted. "Tell your mother your stupid deer in the headlights act almost got me. But if I ever see you again, I'll pull the trigger on this thing until it's empty. And then I'll reload and come after her."

Andy almost lost control of her bladder. Every part of her body was shaking. She kept her hands up, her eyes on Paula, and walked backward down the hallway. She stumbled on the stair down into the sunken living room.

Paula rested the shotgun on her shoulder. She glared at

Andy for another few seconds, then walked back into the kitchen.

Andy choked back bile as she turned to run. She sprinted past the couch, up the single stair to the foyer, and stumbled again on the tile floor. Pain shot into her knee, but she caught herself on the side table. Change spilled out of the glass bowl and tapped against the floor. Every nerve in her body was trapped inside the teeth of a bear trap. She could barely wedge her foot into her shoe. Then she realized the fucking socks were wadded up inside. She checked over her shoulder as she jammed the socks into her messenger bag and shoved her feet into the sneakers. Her hand was so sweaty she almost couldn't turn the knob to open the front door.

Fuck.

Mike was standing on the front porch.

He grinned at Andy the same way he'd grinned at her when they were outside the bar in Muscle Shoals.

He said, "What a strange coinci—"

Andy grabbed the baseball bat.

"Whoa-whoa-whoa!" Mike's hands shot into the air as she cocked the bat over her shoulder. "Come on, beautiful. Let's talk this—"

"You shut the fuck up, you fucking psycho." Andy gripped the bat so tight that her fingers were cramping. "How did you find me?"

"Well, that's a funny story."

Andy jerked the bat higher.

"Wait!" he said, his voice raking up. "Hit me here"—he pointed down at his side—"you can fracture a rib, easy. I'll probably drop like a flaming sack of shit. Or punch it into the center of my chest. There's no such thing as the solar plexus but—"

Andy swung the bat, but not hard, because she wasn't trying to hit him.

Mike easily caught the end of the bat with his hand. He had to step back to do it. His legs were about a shoulder-width apart. Or a foot's width, which Andy soon found out when she kicked him in the nuts as hard as she could.

He dropped to the ground like a flaming sack of shit.

"Fuh—" He coughed, then coughed again. He was squeezing his hands between his legs, rolling on the front porch. Foam came out of his mouth, the same as Hoodie, but this time was different because he wasn't going to die, he was just going to suffer.

"Well done."

Andy jumped.

Paula Kunde was standing behind her. The shotgun was still resting against her shoulder. She said, "That's the guy from the second drawing, right?"

Andy's fear of Paula was overridden by her rage at Mike. She was sick of people treating her like a crash-test dummy. She patted his pockets. She found his wallet, his stupid rabbit's foot keychain. He put up absolutely no resistance. He was too busy clutching his balls.

"Wait," Paula said. "Your mother didn't send you here, did she?"

Andy shoved the wallet and keys into her messenger bag. She stepped over Mike's writhing body.

"I said wait!"

Andy stopped. She turned around and gave Paula the most hateful look she could muster.

"You'll need this." Paula dug around to the bottom of the change bowl and found a folded dollar bill. She handed it to Andy. "Clara Bellamy. Illinois."

"What?"

Paula slammed the door so hard that the house shook.

Who the hell was Clara Bellamy?

Why was Andy listening to a fucking lunatic?

She crammed the dollar bill into her pocket as she walked down the steps. Mike was still huffing like a broken muffler. Andy did not want to feel guilty for hurting him, but she felt guilty. She felt guilty as she got into the Reliant. She felt guilty as she pulled away from the house. She felt guilty as she turned onto the next street. She felt guilty right up until she saw Mike's white truck parked around the corner.

Motherfucker.

He had changed the magnetic sign on the side of the door.

LAWN CARE BY GEORGE

Andy jerked the Reliant to a stop in front of the truck. She popped the hatch. She found the box of Slim Jims and ripped it open. Nothing but Slim Jims. She opened the little cooler, something she hadn't done since she'd found it back at Laura's storage unit.

Idiot.

There was a tracker taped to the underside of the cooler lid. Small, jet black, about the size of an old iPod. The red light was blinking, sending back the coordinates of her location to a satellite somewhere in space. Mike must've put it there while Andy was passed out in the Muscle Shoals motel.

She chucked the cooler lid across the street like a Frisbee. She reached into the hatch and pulled out the sleeping bag and beach tote. She threw both into the front of Mike's truck. Then she grabbed two weedeaters and a set of trimmers from the back and dropped them onto the sidewalk. The magnetic signs easily peeled off the doors. She slapped them onto the hood of the Reliant. Andy thought about leaving him the key, but fuck that. All the money was sitting in storage units. He could drive around in the Maxi-Pad box for a while.

She got into Mike's truck. Her messenger bag went onto the seat beside her. The steering wheel had a weird fake leather wrap. A pair of dice hung from the rearview mirror. Andy jammed the key into the ignition. The engine roared to life. Dave Matthews warbled through the speakers.

Andy pulled away from the curb. Her brain summoned up a map as she drove toward the university. She figured she had about one thousand miles ahead of her, which was around twenty hours of driving, or two full days if she broke it up the right way. Dallas first, then straight up to Oklahoma, then Missouri, then Illinois, where she hoped like hell she could find a person or thing named Clara Bellamy.

July 31, 1986

12

Alexandra Maplecroft's screams were like a siren pitching higher and higher. The sirens from a police car. From the FBI. From the prison van.

Jane knew that she should do something to stop the wailing, but she could only stand there listening to the woman's desperate pleas for help.

"Jane!" Andrew called from downstairs.

The sound of her brother's voice broke Jane from her trance. She struggled to put the gag back in place. Maplecroft started thrashing in the bed, pulling at the restraints around her wrist and ankles. Her head jerked back and forth. The blindfold slipped up. One eye spun desperately around before she found Jane. Suddenly, one of the woman's hands was loose, then a foot. Jane leaned over to hold her down, but she wasn't fast enough.

Maplecroft punched Jane so hard in the face that she fell back onto the floor, literal stars dancing in front of her eyes.

"Jane!" Andrew screamed. She could hear footsteps pounding up the stairs.

Maplecroft heard it too. She struggled so hard against the ropes that the metal bed frame tipped over onto the floor. She worked furiously to untie her other hand while her leg jerked back and forth to work away the bindings.

Jane tried to stand. Her legs felt wonky. Her feet would not find purchase. Blood was streaming down her face, gagging her throat. She somehow found the strength to push herself up. All she could think to do was throw her body on top of Maplecroft's and pray that she could hold her down long enough for help to arrive.

Seconds later, it did.

"Jane!" The door flew open. Andrew reached her first. He pulled Jane up, wrapped his arm around her.

Maplecroft was standing, too. She was in the middle of the floor, fists up like a boxer, one ankle still tied to the bed. Her clothes were torn, her eyes wild, her hair matted to her skull with filth and sweat. She screamed unintelligibly as she moved back and forth between her feet.

Paula snorted a laugh. She was blocking the door. "Give it up, bitch."

"Let me go!" Maplecroft screamed. "I won't tell anyone. I won't—"

"Stop her," Nick said.

Jane didn't know what he meant until she saw Quarter raise his knife.

"No—" she yelled, but it happened too fast.

Quarter slashed down. The blade flashed in the sunlight.

Jane stood helpless, watching the knife arc down.

But then it stopped.

Maplecroft had caught the knife in her hand.

The blade pierced the center of her palm.

The effect hit them all like a stun grenade. No one could speak. They were too shocked.

Except for Maplecroft.

She had known exactly what she was going to do. While they all stood transfixed, she wrenched her arm across her body, preparing to backhand the blade in Jane's direction.

Nick's fist snaked out, punching Maplecroft square in the face.

Blood shot out of her nose. The woman spun in a half-circle, wildly slicing the air with the blade that pierced her hand.

Nick punched her again.

Jane heard the sharp *snap* of her nose breaking.

Maplecroft stumbled. The bed frame dragged back with her foot.

"Nick—" Jane tried.

He punched her a third time.

Maplecroft's head jerked back on her neck. She started to fall, but her pinned leg pulled her sideways. Her temple bounced against the metal edge of the bed frame with a sickening *pop* before she hit the floor. A pool of blood flowered from beneath her, rolled across the wood, seeped into the cracks between the boards.

Her eyes were wide. Her lips gaped apart. Her body was still.

They all stared at her. No one could speak until—

"Jesus," Andrew whispered.

Paula asked, "Is she dead?"

Quarter knelt down to check, but he leapt back when Alexandra Maplecroft's eyes blinked.

Jane screamed once before she could cover her mouth with both hands.

"Christ," Paula whispered.

Urine puddled from between the woman's legs. They could almost hear the sound of her soul leaving her body.

"Nick," Jane breathed. "What have you done? What have you done?"

"She—" Nick looked scared. He never looked scared. He told Jane, "I didn't mean—"

"You killed her!" Jane screamed. "You punched her, and she fell, and she—"

"It was me," Quarter said. "I'm the one who put the knife in her."

"Because Nick told you to!"

"I didn't—" Nick tried. "I said to stop her, not to—"

"What have you done?" Jane felt her head shaking furiously side to side. "What have we done? What have we done?" She couldn't ask the question enough. This had crossed the line of

297

insanity. They were all psychotic. Every single one of them. "How could you?" she asked Nick. "How could you—"

"He was protecting you, dumb bitch," Paula said, unable or unwilling to keep the derision out of her voice. "This is your fault."

"Penny," Andrew said.

Nick tried, "Jinx, you have to believe—"

"You punched—you killed—" Jane's throat felt strangled. They had all watched it happen. She didn't have to give them a replay. Maplecroft had been spinning out of control after the first hit. Nick could've grabbed her arm, but he had punched her two more times and now her blood was sliding along the cracks in the floor.

Paula told Jane, "You're the one who let her get untied. So much for our ransom demand. That's our leverage pissing on her own grave."

Jane walked to the open back window. She tried to pull air into her lungs. She couldn't witness this, couldn't be here. Nick had crossed the line. Paula was making excuses for him. Andrew was keeping his mouth shut. Quarter had been willing to murder for him. They had all completely lost their senses.

Nick said, "Darling—"

Jane braced her hands on the windowsill. She looked at the back of the house across the alley because she couldn't bear to look at Nick. A pair of pink sheers wistfully furled in the late morning breeze. She wanted to be back home in her bed. She wanted to take back Oslo, to rewind the last two years of her life and leave Nick before he had pulled them all into the abyss.

"Jane," Andrew said. He was using his patient voice.

She turned around, but not to look at her brother. Her eyes automatically found the woman lying on the floor. "Don't," she begged Andrew. "Please don't tell me to calm—"

Maplecroft blinked again.

Jane didn't scream like the first time, because the more this kept happening, the more it felt normal. That's how Nick had gotten them. The drills and the rehearsals and the constant state

298

of paranoia had all hypnotized them into believing that what they were doing was not just reasonable, but necessary.

Paula broke the silence this time. "We have to finish it."

Jane could only stare at her.

Paula said, "Put the pillow over her head, or just use your hands to cover her mouth and pinch her nose closed. Unless you want to try to stab her in the heart? Drown her in that bucket of piss?"

Jane felt bile stream up her throat. She turned, but not quickly enough. Vomit spewed onto the floor. She pressed her hands against the wall. She opened her mouth and tried not to wail.

How could she bring a child into this terrible, violent world?

"Christ," Paula said. "You can watch your own daddy being shot, but a gal bumps her head—"

"Penny," Andrew cautioned.

"Jinx," Nick tried to put his hand on Jane's back, but she shrugged him off. "I didn't mean to do it. I just—I wasn't thinking. She hurt you. She was still trying to hurt you."

"It's moot." Quarter was pressing two fingers to the woman's neck. "She doesn't have a pulse."

"Well, fuck," Paula mumbled. "What a surprise."

"It doesn't matter," Andrew said. "What's done is done." He, too, was looking at Jane. "It's all right. I mean, no, of course it's not all right, but it was an accident, and we have to get past it because there are more important things at play here."

"He's right," Quarter said. "We still have Stanford, Chicago, New York."

Paula said, "You know I'm still in. I'm not like little Miss Princess here. You should've stuck to your volunteer work with the other rich ladies. I knew you'd wimp out the second things got messy."

Jane finally allowed herself to look at Nick. His chest was heaving. His fists were still clenched. The skin along the back of his knuckles was torn where he'd punched Alexandra Maplecroft in the face.

Who was this man?

"I can't—" Jane started, but she could not say the words.

"You can't what?" Nick wiped the back of his hand on his pants. Blood smeared across like dirty fingerprints. There was more blood on the sleeve of his shirt. Jane looked down at her trousers. Red slashes crossed her legs. Speckles dotted her blouse.

"I can't—" she tried again.

"Can't what?" Nick asked. "Jinx, talk to me. What can't you do?"

Do this, be a part of this, hurt more people, live with the secrets, live with the guilt, give life to your child because I will never, ever be able to explain to her that you are her father.

"Jinxie?" Nick had recovered from his shock. He was giving her his half grin. He wrapped his hands around her arms. He pressed his lips to her forehead.

She wanted to resist. She told herself to resist. But her body moved toward his and then he was holding her and she was letting herself take comfort from the warmth of his embrace.

The yo-yo flipping back on itself.

Andrew said, "Let's go downstairs and—"

Suddenly, Quarter made a gulping sound.

His entire body jerked, his arms flying into the air. Blood burst from his chest.

A millisecond later, Jane heard the loud crack of a rifle firing, the sound of glass breaking in the window pane.

She was already lying flat on the floor when she realized what was happening.

Someone was shooting at them.

Jane could see the crazy red dots from rifle scopes slipping along the walls as if they were in an action movie. The police had found them. They had tracked Jasper's car or someone in the neighborhood had reported them or they had followed Andrew and Jane and none of that mattered now because Quarter was dead. Maplecroft was dead. They were all going to die in this horrible room with the bucket of shit and piss and Jane's vomit on the floor.

Another bullet broke out the rest of the glass. Then another

300

zinged around the room. Then another. Then they were suddenly completely swallowed by the sharp percussion of gunfire.

"Move!" Nick yelled, upending the mattress to block the front window. "Let's go, troops! Let's go!"

They had trained for this. It had seemed preposterous at the time, but Nick had made them drill for this exact scenario.

Andrew ran in a crouch toward the open door at the top of the stairs. Paula crawled on her hands and knees toward the back window. Jane started to follow, but a bullet pinged past her head. She flattened back to the floor. The vase of flowers shattered. Holes pierced the flimsy walls, lines of sunlight creating a disco effect.

"Over here!" Paula was already at the window.

Jane started to crawl again, but she stopped, screaming as Quarter's body bucked into the air. They were shooting him. She heard the sickening suck of bullets punching into his dead flesh. Maplecroft's head cracked open. Blood splattered everywhere. Bone. Brain. Tissue.

Another explosion downstairs; the front door blowing open.

"FBI! FBI!" The agents screamed over each other like a crescendo building. Jane heard their boots stomping through the lower floor, fists banging on the walls, looking for the stairs.

"Don't wait for me!" Andrew had already closed the door. Jane watched him heft up the heavy post that fit into the brackets on either side of the jamb.

"Jane, hurry!" Nick shouted. He was helping Paula guide the extension ladder out the back window. It was too heavy for just one person to manage. They knew this from the training exercise. Two people on the ladder. One person barring the door. Mattress against the window.

Duck and run, move fast, don't stop for anything.

Paula was first out the window. The rickety ladder clanged as she crawled on hands and knees to the house on the other side of the alley. The distance between the two windows was fifteen feet. Below was a pile of rotting garbage filled with needles and broken glass. No one would willingly go into the pit. Not unless the ladder broke and they plummeted twenty feet down.

"Go-go-go!" Nick yelled. The pounding downstairs was getting louder. The agents were still looking for the stairs. Wood started to splinter as they used the butts of their shotguns on the walls.

"Fuck!" a man yelled. "Get the fucking sledgehammer!"

Jane went on the ladder next. Her hands were wet with sweat. The cold metal rungs dug into her knees. There was a vibration in the ladder from a sledgehammer pounding into the walls below.

"Hurry!" Paula kept looking down at the pile of garbage. Jane chanced a peek and saw that there were three FBI agents in blue jackets swarming around the pile, trying to find a way in.

A gunshot rang out—not from the agents, but from Nick. He was leaning out the window, giving Andrew cover as he made his way across the ladder. The going was slower for her brother. The metal box was clutched under his arm. He could only use one hand. Jane couldn't even remember him bringing the box up the stairs.

"Fuckers!" Paula screeched as she shook her fist at the agents on the ground. She was drawing a sick sort of excitement from the carnage. "Fascist fucking pig cunts!"

Andrew slipped on the ladder. Jane gasped. She heard him curse. He'd almost dropped the box.

"Please," she whispered, begged, pleaded.

Forget the box. Forget the plan. Just get us out of this. Make us sane again.

"Nickel!" Paula yelled. "Throw it to me!"

She meant the gun. Nick tossed it across the fifteen-foot span. Paula caught it with both hands just as Andrew was coming off the ladder.

Jane had her arms around him before his feet hit the floor.

"Fuckers!" Paula started shooting at the FBI agents. Her eyes were closed. Her mouth was open. She was yelling like a madwoman because of course she was mad. They were all

302

deranged, and if they died here today that was exactly what they deserved.

"Take my hand!" Andrew reached out to Nick, yanking him across the last few feet. They both fell back onto the floor.

Jane stood at the window. She looked across at the shed. The stairs had been found. The snipers had stopped firing. There was an agent, an older man cut from Danberry and Barlow's same cloth, standing directly across from her.

He raised his gun and pointed it at Jane's chest.

"Idiot!" Paula pulled Jane down into a crouch just as the gun fired. She reached up with both hands to push the ladder off the edge of the windowsill.

They heard the metal bang against the house, then clatter into the debris.

"This way." Andrew took the lead, crouching as he ran across the room. They were down the stairs, on the main floor, when they heard cars pull up in the street outside, which was fine, because leaving by the front door had never been the plan.

Andrew felt along the wall with his fingers. He found another secret button, accessed another secret panel, and revealed the steps to the basement.

This was why Nick had chosen the two-story shed after months of searching. He'd told the group that they needed a safe place to keep Alexandra Maplecroft, but they also needed a safe route of escape. There were very few basements in the Mission District, at least as far as the city knew. The water table was too high, the sand too swampy. The shallow basement under the Victorian was one of the city's many remnants from the original Armory. Soldiers had hidden in the dungeons when the Mission was under siege. Nick knew about the passages from his homeless days. There was a tunnel connecting the house to a warehouse one street over.

Nick clicked the panel closed behind them. Jane felt a chill as the temperature dropped. At the bottom of the stairs, Andrew was trying to push away the bookcase that covered the tunnel entrance.

Nick had to help him. The bookcase slid across the concrete. Jane saw scrapes across the floor and prayed like hell the FBI would not see them until it was too late.

Paula slapped a flashlight into Jane's hand and pushed her into the tunnel. Nick helped Andrew tug on the rope that pulled the bookcase back into its spot. Quarter was supposed to pull the rope. He was the carpenter of the group, the one who had turned all of Nick's sketches into actual working designs.

And now he was dead.

Jane switched on the flashlight before the bookcase sent them into complete darkness. Her job was to lead them through the tunnel. Nick had made her run through dozens of times, sometimes with a working flashlight, sometimes without. Jane had not been down here in three months, but she still remembered all the irregular rocks that could snag against a shoe or cause a bone-breaking fall.

Like the one Alexandra Maplecroft had experienced.

"Stop dawdling," Paula hissed, shoving Jane hard in the back. "Move."

Jane tripped over a stone she knew was there. None of the practice runs mattered. Adrenaline could not be faked. The deeper they went underground, the more claustrophobic she felt. The dome of light was too narrow. The darkness was overpowering. She felt a scream bubbling into her throat. Water from Mission Creek seeped in from every crevice, splashed up under their shoes. The tunnel was forty-eight feet long. Jane put her hand on the wall to steady herself. Her heart was pushing into her throat. She felt the need to vomit again but dared not stop. Now that she was out of Nick's embrace, away from his calming influence, the same question kept darting around inside of her head—

What the hell were they doing?

"Move it." Paula pushed Jane again. "Hurry."

Jane picked up the pace. She reached out in front of her, because she knew that they had to be close. Finally, the flashlight picked out the wooden back of the second bookcase. Jane didn't

304

ask for help. She made an opening that was wide enough for them to squeeze through.

They all blinked in the sudden light. There were windows high in the basement walls. Jane could see feet shuffling past. She ran up the stairs, some sort of internal autopilot clicking on. She took a right because she had trained to take a right. Thirty yards later, she took a left because she had trained to take a left. She pushed open a door, climbed through a break in the wall, and found the van parked in a cavernous bay that smelled of black pepper from the building's previous life as a spice storage facility.

Paula ran ahead of Jane, because the first person to reach the van was the person who got to drive. Jane was second, so she pulled back the side door. Nick was already heading toward the bay door. There was a combination lock.

8-4-19.

They all knew the combination.

Andrew threw the metal box into the van. He tried to get in, but he started to fall backward. Jane grabbed at his arm, desperate to get him inside. Nick rolled up the bay door. He sprinted back to the van. Jane closed the sliding door behind him.

Paula was already driving out of the warehouse. She had tied up her hair and stuck a brown hat on her head. A matching brown jacket covered the top of her shift dress. The sunlight razored through the windshield. Jane squeezed her eyes shut. Tears slid down the side of her face. She was on her back, lying between Nick and Andrew. They were on a futon mattress, but every bump and pothole in the road reverberated into her bones. She craned her neck, trying to see out the window. They were on Mission within seconds, then turning deeper into the city, when they heard the sirens whizzing past.

"Keep cool," Nick whispered. He was holding Jane's hand. Jane was holding Andrew's. She could not remember when this had happened, but she was so grateful to be safely between them, to be alive, that she could not stop weeping.

They all lay there on their backs, clinging to each other, until Paula told them they had reached the 101.

"Chicago is thirty hours away." Paula had to shout to be heard over the road noise that echoed like a dentist's drill inside the van. "We'll stop in Idaho Falls to let them know we're on the way to the safe house."

Safe house.

A farm just outside of Chicago with a red barn and cows and horses and what did it matter because they were never going to be safe again?

Paula said, "We'll change drivers in Sacramento after we drop Nick at the airport. We'll follow the speed limit. We'll obey all traffic laws. We'll make sure to not draw attention to ourselves." She was mimicking Nick's instructions. They were all mimicking Nick's instructions because he claimed to always know what he was doing, even when everything was out of control.

This was madness. It was absolute madness.

"Je-sus Christ, that was close." Nick sat up, stretching his arms into the air. He gave Jane one of his rakish grins. He had that internal switch, too—the one that Laura Juneau had when she murdered Martin, then herself. Jane could see it so clearly now. For Nick, everything that had happened in the shed was behind him.

Jane could not look at him. She studied Andrew, still lying beside her. His face was ashen. Streaks of blood crisscrossed his cheeks. Jane could not begin to know the source. When she thought of the shed, she could only see death and carnage and bullets ricocheting around like mosquitos.

Andrew coughed into the crook of his arm. Jane reached out to touch his face. His skin had the texture of cotton candy.

Nick said, "Glad you practiced now, aren't you, troops?" Like Andrew, his face was splattered with blood. His hair had fallen into his left eye. He had that familiar look of exhilaration, as if everything was perfect. "Imagine going over that ladder for the first time without having your training to—"

Jane sat up. She should have gone to Nick, but she leaned

her back against the hump over the tire. Could she call Jasper? Could she find a telephone, beg him for help, and wait for her big brother to swoop in and save them all? How would she tell him that she had been responsible for helping to kill their father? How could she look him in the eye and say that everything they had done until this point was not the result of some form of collective derangement?

A cult.

"Jinx?" Nick asked.

She shook her head, but not at Nick. Even Jasper could not save her now. And how would she reward him if he tried, by being part of a plot to send him to prison for healthcare fraud?

Nick crawled on his knees to the locked box that Quarter had bolted to the floor. He dialed in the combination on the lock—

6-12-32.

They all knew the combination.

Jane watched him push up the lid. He removed a blanket, a Thermos filled with water. All part of the escape plan. There were Slim Jims, a small cooler, various emergency supplies and, secreted beneath a false bottom, $250,000 in cash.

Nick poured some water into the cup of the Thermos. He found the handkerchief in his back pocket and cleaned his face, then leaned over and wiped at Andrew's cheeks until they turned ruddy.

Jane watched her lover clean blood from her brother's face. *Maplecroft's? Quarter's?*

She said, "We don't even know his real name."

They both looked at her.

"Quarter," she said. "We don't know his name, where he lives, who his parents are, and he's dead. We watched him die, and we don't even know who to tell."

Nick said, "His name was Leonard Brandt. No children. Never married. He lived alone at 1239 Van Duff Street. He worked as a carpenter over in Marin. Of course I know who he is, Jinx. I know everyone who is involved in this because I

307

am responsible for their lives. Because I will do whatever it takes to try to protect all of you."

Jane couldn't tell whether or not he was lying. His features were blurred by the tears streaming from her eyes.

Nick put the cup back on the Thermos, telling him, "You don't look so good, old pal."

Andrew tried to muffle a cough. "I don't feel so good."

Nick grabbed Andrew's shoulders. Andrew grabbed Nick's arms. They could've been in a football scrimmage.

"Listen," Nick said. "We've had a hard time, but we're back on track. You'll rest at the safe house, you and Jane. I'll be back from New York as soon as I can, and we'll watch the world fall down together. Yes?"

Andrew nodded. "Yes."

Jesus.

Nick patted Andrew's cheek. He slid across the van toward Jane, because it was her turn for the rousing pep talk that pulled her back on side.

"Darling." His arm looped around her waist. His lips brushed her ear. "It's okay, my love. Everything is going to be okay."

Jane's tears came faster. "We could've died. All of us could've—"

"Poor lamb." Nick pressed his lips to the top of her head. "Can't you believe me when I tell you that we're all going to be okay?"

Jane's mouth opened. She tried to pull breath into her shaking lungs. She wanted so desperately to believe him. She told herself the only things that mattered right now in this moment: Nick was safe. Andrew was safe. The baby was safe. The ladder had saved them. The tunnel had saved them. The van had saved them.

Nick had saved them.

He'd made Jane keep up her training while she was in Berlin. So far away from everything, Jane had thought it was silly to go through the movements every morning, her hands whipping past each other, fists boxing out, as if she expected to go to war.

The thing that had driven her most back in San Francisco was the pleasure of kicking Paula's ass every time they sparred. With Paula gone, and in truth with Nick gone, Jane had found herself slipping—away from her resolve, away from the plan, away from Nick.

What have you been up to, my darling? he would ask across the scratchy, international telephone line.

Nothing, she would lie. *I miss you too much to do more than sulk and mark the days off the calendar.*

Jane did miss him, but only a certain part of him. The part that was charming. That was loving. That was pleased with her. That didn't willfully, almost hedonistically, push everything to the breaking point. ·

What Jane had not realized until she was safely tucked away in Berlin was that for as long as she had been conscious of being alive, she had always had a ball of fear that slept inside of her stomach. For years, she had told herself that being neurotic was the bane of a solo artist's success, but in truth, the thing that kept her walking carefully, self-censoring her words, conforming her emotions, was the heavy presence of the two men in her life. Sometimes Martin would wake her fear. Sometimes Nick. With their words. With their threats. With their hands. And sometimes, occasionally, with their fists.

In Berlin, for the first time in her memory, Jane had experienced what it was to live a life without fear.

She went to clubs. She danced with lanky, stoned German guys with tattoos on their hands. She attended concerts and art openings and underground political meetings. She sat in cafés arguing about Camus and smoking Gauloises and discussing the tragedy of the human condition. At a distance, Jane would sometimes catch a glimpse of what her life was supposed to be like. She was a world-class performer. She had worked for two decades to get to this place, this exalted position, and yet—

She had never been a child. She had never been a teenager. She had never been a young woman in her twenties. She had never really been single. She had belonged to her father, then Pechenikov and then Nick.

In Berlin, she had belonged to no one.

"Hey." Nick snapped his fingers in front of her face. "Come back to us, my darling."

Jane realized that they'd all been having a conversation without her.

Nick said, "We were talking about when to release Jasper's files. After Chicago? After New York?"

Jane shook her head. "We can't," she told Nick. "Please. Enough people have been hurt."

"Jane," Andrew said. "We're not doing this on a whim. People have been hurt, have died, over this. We can't back out because we've lost our nerve. Not when they took a bullet for us."

"Literally," Nick said, as if Jane needed to be reminded. "Two people. Two bullets. Laura and Quarter really believed in what we're doing. How can we let them down now?"

"I can't," she told them both. There was nothing more to add. She just couldn't anymore.

"You're exhausted, my love." Nick tightened his arm around Jane's waist, but he didn't tell her what she wanted to hear: that they were going to stop now, that Jasper's files would be destroyed, that they would find their way to Switzerland and try to atone for the damage they had done.

He said, "We should take turns sleeping." Then he raised his voice so that Paula could hear. "I'll fly to New York from Chicago. It's too hot for me to go out of Sacramento. Paula, you'll stay with your team and make sure they're set for Chicago. We'll coordinate times when we get to the safe house."

Jane waited for Paula to chime in, but she was uncharacteristically silent.

"Jinx?" Andrew asked. "Are you okay?"

She nodded, but he could tell that she was lying. "I'm okay," she repeated, unable to keep her voice from wavering.

Nick told Andrew, "Go sit with Penny. Keep her awake. Jane and I will sleep, then we'll take the next shift."

Jane wanted to tell him no, that Andrew should go first, but she hadn't the energy and besides, Andrew was already struggling to his knees.

She watched her brother crawl to the front of the van. He sat beside Paula. Jane heard a groan come out of his mouth as he reached toward the radio. The news station was at a low murmur. They should've listened to it, but Andrew turned the knob until he found an oldies station.

Jane turned to Nick. "He needs a doctor."

"We've got bigger problems than that."

Jane knew instantly the problem he was talking about—not that things had gone sideways, but that Nick knew she was doubting him.

He said, "I told you what happened to Maplecroft was an accident." His voice was so low that only Jane could hear him. "I went crazy when I saw what she'd done to your beautiful face."

Jane touched her nose. The pain was instantaneous. So much had happened since that awful moment that she had forgotten about Maplecroft punching her.

Nick said, "I know I should've just grabbed her, or—something else. I don't know what happened to me, darling. I just felt so angry. But I wasn't out of control. Not completely. I promised you that I would never let that happen again."

Again.

Jane tried not to think about the baby growing inside of her.

"Darling," Nick said. "Tell me it's okay. We're okay. Tell me, please."

Jane reluctantly nodded. She lacked the energy to argue otherwise.

"My love."

He kissed her on the mouth with a surprising passion. She found herself unable to summon any desire as their tongues touched. Still, she wrapped her arms around him because she desperately needed to feel normal. They hadn't made love in Oslo, even after three months of separation. They'd both been

311

too anxious, then the shooting had happened and they were terrified of saying or doing the wrong thing, then they were back in San Francisco and he had left her alone until this morning. Jane hadn't wanted him then, either, but she remembered keenly craving the *after*. To be held in his arms. To press her ear to his chest and listen to the steady, content beat of his heart. To tell him about the baby. To see the happiness in his expression.

He hadn't been happy the first time.

"Come on, love." Nick gave her a chaste kiss on the forehead. "Let's get some sleep."

Jane let him pull her down to the futon mattress. His mouth went to her ear again, but only to brush his lips against her skin. He wrapped his body around hers. Legs intertwined, arms holding her close. He made a pillow for her head out of the crook of his elbow. Instead of feeling the usual sense of peace, Jane felt like she was trapped in place by an octopus.

She stared up at the ceiling of the van. She had no thoughts in her mind. She was too exhausted. Her body felt numb, but in a different way from before. She wasn't being shot at or fretting about Danberry's interrogation or mourning Martin or worrying that they would all get caught. She was looking at her future and realizing that she was never going to get out of this. Even if every facet of Nick's plan worked, even if they managed to escape to Switzerland, Jane was always going to be living inside of a cartwheel.

Nick's breathing started to slow. She could feel his body relax. Jane thought to slide out from his grasp, but she hadn't the strength. Her eyelids began to flutter. She could almost taste every beat of her heart. She let herself give in to it, falling asleep for what she thought was just a moment, but they both woke up when Paula stopped at a gas station just inside the Nevada state line.

They were the only customers. The attendant inside barely glanced up from the television when they all climbed out of the van.

"Snacks?" Paula asked. No one answered, so she loped off to the store with her hands stuck into the pockets of the brown jacket.

Andrew worked the gas pump. He closed his eyes and leaned against the van as the tank started to fill.

Nick didn't speak to anyone. He didn't clap together his hands and try to rally the troops. He walked a few yards away from them. His hands were in his back pockets. He stared out at the road. Jane watched him look up at the sky, then out at the vast, brown landscape.

Everyone was subdued. Jane couldn't tell if it was from shellshock or debilitating fatigue. There was an almost tangible feel among them that they had reached a point of no return. The giddy high they had foolishly experienced when they'd talked about being on the lam from the law, as if they were gangsters in a James Cagney movie, had been eviscerated by reality.

Nick was the only one who could reliably pull them out of free fall. Jane had seen it happen so many times before. Nick could walk into a room and instantly make everything better. She had witnessed it this morning at the shed. Andrew and Jane were quarreling with Paula, who was about to kill them all, then Nick had somehow turned them all into a single, working group again. Everyone looked to him for his strength, his surety of purpose.

His charisma.

Nick turned away from the road. His eyes skipped over Jane as he walked toward the bathrooms on the side of the building. His shoulders were slumped. His feet dragged across the asphalt. Her heart broke at the sight of him. Jane had only seen him like this a handful of times before, so stuck in a fugue of depression that he could barely lift his head.

It was her fault.

She had doubted him, the one betrayal that Nick could not abide. He was a man, not an all-seeing god. Yes, what had happened in the shed was terrible, but they were still alive. Nick had made

313

that happen. He had designed drills and made sketches to map out their escape. He had insisted they practice until their arms and legs felt weak. To keep them safe. To keep them on track. To keep their spirits up and their minds focused and their hearts motivated. No one else had the ability to do all of those things.

And no one, especially Jane, had stopped to think what a toll these responsibilities were taking on him.

She followed Nick's path to the men's bathroom. She didn't think about what she would find when she pushed open the door, but she felt sick with her own complicity when she saw Nick.

His hands were braced on the sink. His head was bent. When he looked up at Jane, tears were streaming from his eyes.

"I'll be out in a minute." He turned away, grabbing a handful of paper towels. "Maybe you could help Penny with—"

Jane wrapped her arms around him. She pressed her face to his back.

He laughed, but only at himself. "I seem to be falling apart."

Jane squeezed him as tight as she dared.

His chest heaved as he took a shuddered breath. His arms covered hers. He shifted his weight into her and Jane held him up because that was what she did best.

"I love you," she told him, kissing the back of his neck.

He misread her intentions. "Afraid I'm not up for any hijinks, my Jinx, but it means the world to me that you're offering."

She loved him even more for trying to sound like his old, confident self. She made him turn around. She put her hands on his shoulders the same way he always did with everyone else. She put her mouth to his ear the same way he only did with her. She said the three words that mattered most to him, not *I love you*, but—

"I'm with you."

Nick blinked, then he laughed, embarrassed by his obvious swell of emotion. "Really?"

"Really." Jane kissed him on the lips, and inexplicably, everything felt right. His arms around her. His heart beating against hers. Even standing in the filthy men's room felt right.

314

"My love," she said. Over and over again. "My only love."

Andrew was fast asleep in the passenger's seat when they got back to the van. Paula was too wired to do anything but keep driving. Nick helped Jane into the back. He did the same thing as before, wrapping his arms and legs around her as they lay on the futon. This time, Jane curled into him. Instead of closing her eyes to sleep, she started talking—mundane nonsense at first, like the feeling of joy the first time she had nailed a performance, or the excitement of a standing ovation. She wasn't bragging. She was giving Nick context because nothing compared to the absolute elation Jane had experienced the first time Nick had kissed her, the first time they had made love, the first time she'd realized that he belonged to her.

Because Nick did belong to her, just as surely as Jane belonged to him.

She told him how her heart had floated up like a hot-air balloon when she'd first seen him roughhousing with Andrew in the front hall. How her spirits had soared when Nick had walked into the kitchen, kissed her, then backed away like a thief. Then she told Nick how much she had ached for him in Berlin. How she had missed the taste of his mouth. How nothing she did could chase away the longing she'd had for his touch.

Then they were in Wyoming, then Nebraska, then Iowa, then finally Illinois.

Over the twenty-eight remaining hours it took to drive to the outskirts of Chicago, Jane spent almost every waking moment telling Nick how much she loved him.

She was a yo-yo. She was Patricia Hearst. She had drunk the Kool-Aid. She was taking orders from her neighbor's dog.

Jane did not care if she was in a cult or if Nick was Donald DeFreeze. Actually, she no longer cared about the plan. Her part was over, anyway. The other cell members were on the frontlines now. Of course, she still felt outraged by the atrocities committed by her father and older brother. She mourned Laura and Robert Juneau's loss. She felt bad for what had happened to Quarter and Alexandra Maplecroft in the shed. But Jane did not really have to believe in what they were doing or why.

All she had to do was believe in Nick.

"Turn left up here," Paula said. She was kneeling behind the driver's seat. She put her hand on Jane's shoulder, which was alarming because Paula never touched except to hurt. "Look for a driveway on the right. It's kind of hidden in the trees."

Jane saw the driveway a few yards later. She put on the turn signal even though the van was the only vehicle for miles.

Paula punched Jane's arm. "Dumb bitch."

Jane listened to her disappear into the back of the van. Paula's mood had lifted because Nick's mood had lifted. The same had happened with Andrew. The effect was magical. The moment they had seen Nick's easy grin, any feelings of worry or doubt had vanished.

Jane had made that happen.

"Jinx?" Andrew stirred in the passenger's seat as the tires bumped onto the gravel driveway.

"We're here." Jane let out a slow sigh of relief as they cleared the stand of trees. The farm was just as she had pictured it from Andrew's coded letters. Cows grazed in the pasture. A huge, red barn loomed over a quaint, one-story house that was painted a matching color. Daisies were planted in the yard. There was a small patch of grass and a white picket fence. This was the sort of happy place you could raise a child.

Jane rested her hand on her stomach.

"Okay?" Andrew asked.

She looked at her brother. The sleep had done him no good. Improbably, he looked worse than before. "Should I be worried?"

"Absolutely not." His smile was unconvincing. He told her, "We'll be able to rest here. To be safe."

"I know," Jane said, but she would not feel safe until Nick returned from New York.

The front tire hit a rut in the gravel drive. Jane winced as tree limbs lashed the side of the van. She almost said a prayer of thanks when she finally parked beside two cars in front of the barn.

"Hello, Chicago!" Nick called as he slid open the side door. He jumped to the ground. He stretched his arms and arched his back, his face looking up at the sky. "My God, it's good to be out of that tin box."

"No shit." Paula groaned as she tried to stretch. She was only a few years older than Nick, but rage had curled her body in on itself.

Jane sighed again as her feet touched solid ground. The air was sharp, the temperature considerably lower than what they had left in California. She rubbed her arms to warm them as she looked out at the horizon. The sun hung heavy over the treetops. She guessed it was around four o'clock in the afternoon. She didn't know what day it was, where they were exactly, or what was going to happen next, but she was so relieved to be out of the van that she could've cried.

"Stay here." Paula stomped toward the house. Her boots kicked up a cloud of dust. She had taken off her fingerless gloves, wiped the black charcoal from under her eyes. The back of her hair corkscrewed into a cowlick. The hem of her shift was filthy. Like the rest of them, she had slashes of blood on her clothes.

Jane looked past her to the farmhouse. She wasn't going to think about the blood anymore. She was either with Nick or she wasn't.

All or none; the Queller way.

The front door opened. A small woman stood with a shawl wrapped around her narrow shoulders. Beside her, a tall man with long hair and an elaborate, handlebar mustache held a shotgun in his hands. He saw Paula, but did not lower the gun until she placed a penny in the palm of the woman's open hand.

This was Nick's idea. Penny, nickel, quarter, dime—each representing a cell, each cell using the coins as a way of indicating to each other that it was safe to talk. Nick delighted in the play on their name, the Army of the Changing World. He'd made them all dress in black, even down to their underwear, and stand in a line like soldiers as he placed a coin in each of their hands to designate their code names.

The jackass didn't know the word 'symbiotic,' so he made up the word 'symbionese.'

Jane gritted her teeth as she banished Danberry's words from her mind.

She had made her choice.

"I don't know about you, troops, but I'm starving." Nick looped his arm around Andrew's shoulders. "Andy, what about you? Is it feed a cold and starve a fever, or the other way around?"

"I think it's give them both whisky and sleep in a real bed." Andrew trudged toward the house, Nick beside him. They were both noticeably exhausted, but Nick's energy was carrying them through, just as it always did.

Jane did not follow them toward the house. She wanted to stretch her legs and look at the farm. The thought of a moment alone in the silence appealed to her. She had grown up in the city. The Hillsborough house was too close to the airport to be called the country. While other girls Jane's age learned horseback riding and attended Girl Scout retreats, she was sitting in front of her piano for five and six hours at a time, trying to sharpen the fine motor movements of her fingers.

Her hand, as always, found its way to her stomach.

Would her daughter play the piano?

Jane wondered how she was so certain that the child was a girl. She wanted to name her something wonderful, not plain Jane or silly Jinx or the cartoony Janey that Nick sometimes called her. She wanted to give the girl all of her strengths and none of her weaknesses. To make sure that she did not pass on that sleeping ball of fear to her precious child.

She stopped at the wooden fence. Two white horses were grazing in the field. She smiled as they nuzzled each other.

Andrew and Jane would be here for at least a week, maybe more. When Nick got back from New York, they would lie low for another week before crossing into Canada. Switzerland was their dream, but what would it feel like to raise her baby on a farm like this one? To walk her to the end of the driveway and wait for the school bus? Hide Easter eggs in bales of hay? Take the horses out into the field and lay a picnic—Jane, her baby, and Nick.

Next time, Nick told her the last time. *We'll keep it next time.*

"Hello." The thin woman with the shawl called to Jane. She was making her way past the barn. "I'm sorry to bother you. They're asking for you. Tucker can move the van into the barn. Spinner and Wyman are already inside."

Jane gave a solemn nod. The lieutenants in each cell had all been assigned code names from past Secretaries of the United States Treasury. When Nick had first told Jane the idea, she had struggled not to laugh. Now, she could see that the cloak and dagger had been for a reason. The identities of the Stanford cell had died with Quarter.

"Oh," the woman had stopped in her tracks, her mouth rounded in surprise.

Jane was just as shocked to see the familiar face. They had never met before, but she knew Clara Bellamy from magazines and newspapers and posters outside the State Theater at Lincoln Center. She was a *prima ballerina*, one of Balanchine's last shining stars, until a debilitating knee injury had forced her into retirement.

"Well now." Clara resumed walking toward Jane with a grin on her face. "You must be Dollar Bill."

Another necessary part of spycraft. She told Clara, "We decided calling me 'DB' is easier than Dollar Bill. Penny thinks it stands for 'Dumb Bitch.'"

"That's Penny for you." Clara had easily picked up on Paula's prickliness. "Nice to meet you, DB. They call me Selden."

Jane shook the woman's hand. Then she laughed to let her know she recognized that the two of them meeting on a secluded farm outside of Chicago was wild.

"It's a funny old world, isn't it?" Clara looped her arm through

319

Jane's as they slowly headed toward the farmhouse. There was a slight limp to her walk. "I saw you at Carnegie three years ago. Brought me to tears. Mozart's Concerto Number 24 in C Minor, I believe."

Jane felt her lips curve into a smile. She loved it when people really loved music.

Clara said, "That green dress was amazing."

"I thought the shoes were going to kill me."

She smiled in commiseration. "I remember it was right after Horowitz's Japan concert. To see a man who's so accomplished fail so spectacularly—you must've been on pins and needles when you walked onto that stage."

"I wasn't." Jane was surprised by her own honesty, but someone like Clara Bellamy would understand. "Every note I played came with this sense of déjà vu, as if I had already played it perfectly."

"A fait accompli." Clara nodded her understanding. "I lived for those moments. They never happened often enough. Makes you understand drug addicts, doesn't it?" She had stopped walking. "That was your last classical performance, wasn't it? Why did you give it up?"

Jane was too ashamed to answer. Clara Bellamy had stopped dancing because she had no choice. She wouldn't understand choosing to walk away.

Clara offered, "Pechenikov put it around that you lacked ambition. They always say that about women, but that can't be the truth. I saw your face when you performed. You weren't just playing the music. You *were* the music."

Jane looked past Clara's shoulder to the house. She had wanted to keep her spirits up for Nick, but the reminder of her lost performing life brought back her tears. She had loved playing classical, then she had loved the energy of jazz, then she'd had to find a way to love being alone inside a studio with no feedback from anyone but the chain-smoking man on the other side of the soundproofed glass.

"Jane?"

She shook her head, dismissing her grief as a foolish luxury. As usual, she told a version of the truth that the listener could relate to. "I used to think my father was proud of me when I played. Then one day, I realized that everything I did, every award and gig and newspaper or magazine story reflected well on him. That's what he got out of it. Not admiration for me, but admiration for himself."

Clara nodded her understanding. "I had a mother like that. But you won't give it up for long." Without warning, she pressed her palm to Jane's round belly. "You'll want to play for her."

Jane felt a narrowing in her throat. "How did—"

"Your face." She stroked Jane's cheek. "It's so much fuller than in your photos. And you have this bump in your belly, of course. You're carrying high, which is why I assumed it was a girl. Nick must be—"

"You can't tell him." Jane's hand flew to her mouth as if she could claw back the desperation in her tone. "He doesn't know yet. I need to find the right time."

Clara seemed surprised, but she nodded. "I get it. What you guys are going through, it's not easy. You want some space around it before you tell him."

Jane forced a change in subject. "How did you get involved with the group?"

"Edwin—" Clara laughed, then corrected herself. "Tucker, I mean. He met Paula while they were both at Stanford. He was in law school. She was in poly-sci. Had a bit of a fling, I expect. But he's mine now."

Jane tried to hide her surprise. She couldn't see Paula as a student, let alone having a fling. "He's handling any legal issues that come up?"

"That's right. Nick is lucky to have him. Tucker dealt with some nasty contract problems for me when my knee blew out. We kind of hit it off. I've always been a sucker for a man with interesting facial hair. Anyway, Paula introduced Tucker to Nick, I mean, Nickel. Tucker introduced Nickel to me, and, well, you know how it is when you meet Nick. You believe every word

321

that comes out of his mouth. It's a good thing he didn't try to sell me a used car."

Jane laughed because Clara laughed.

Clara said, "I'm not a true believer. I mean, yeah, I get what you're doing and of course it's important, but I'm a big chicken when it comes to putting myself on the line. I'd rather write some checks and provide safe harbor."

"Don't dismiss what you're doing. Your contributions are still important." Jane felt like she was channeling Nick, but they all had to do their part. "More important, actually, because you keep us safe."

"Lord, you do sound like him."

"Do I?" Jane knew that she did. This was the cost of giving herself to Nick. She was starting to become him.

"I want lots of babies," Clara said. "I couldn't when I was dancing, but now"—she indicated the farm—"I bought this so I can raise my kids here. To let them grow up happy, and safe. Edwin's learning to take care of the cows. I'm learning to cook. That's why I'm helping Nick. I want to help make a better place for my children. Our children."

Jane studied the woman's face for a tell-tale grin.

"I really believe that, Jane. I'm not just blowing smoke up your ass. It's exciting to be a part of it, even on the periphery. And I'm not taking a big risk, but there's still a risk. One or all of you could end up in an interrogation room. Imagine the kind of press you could get for pointing the finger at me." She gave a startled laugh. "Do you know, I'm sort of jealous, because I think you're more famous than I am, so I'm already hating you for hogging all of the press."

Jane didn't laugh because she had been in the spotlight long enough to know that the woman was not really joking.

"Edwin thinks we'll be okay. I set great store by his opinion."

"Do you—" Jane stopped herself, because she had been about to say the exact wrong thing.

Do you know that Quarter got shot? That Maplecroft was killed? What if the buildings aren't really empty? What if we

322

kill a security guard or a policeman? What if what we're doing is wrong?

"Do I what?" Clara asked.

"Cough medicine," Jane said, the first thing that came to mind. "Do you have any? My brother—"

"Poor Andy. He's really gone downhill, hasn't it?" Clara frowned in sympathy. "It's come as quite a shock. But we've both seen it happen so many times before, haven't we? You can't be in the arts without knowing dozens of extraordinary men who are infected."

Infected?

"Jinx?" Nick was standing at the open front door. "Are you coming in? You need to see this. Both of you."

Clara hastened her step.

Jane could barely find the strength to lift her legs.

Her mouth had gone dry. Her heart was jerking inside of her chest. She struggled to maintain the forward momentum. Up the front walk. The stairs to the porch. To the front door. Into the house.

Infected?

Inside, Jane had to lean against the wall, to lock her knees so that she did not collapse. The numbness was back. Her muscles were liquid.

We've both seen it happen so many times before.

Jane had known so many young, vigorous men who had coughed like Andrew was coughing. Who had looked sick the same way that Andrew looked sick. Same pale skin tone. Same heavy droop to his eyelids. A jazz saxophonist, a first chair cellist, a tenor, an opera singer, a dancer, another dancer, and another—

All dead.

"Come, darling." Nick waved Jane into the room.

They were all gathered around the television. Paula was on the couch beside the man who was probably Tucker. The two others, Spinner and Wyman, a woman and man respectively, sat in folding chairs. Clara sat on the floor because dancers always sat on the floor.

"Andrew's asleep." Nick was on his knees, adjusting the volume on the set. "It's amazing, Jinx. Apparently, they've been doing special reports for the last two days."

Jane saw his mouth move, but it was as if the sound was traveling through water.

Nick sat back on his heels, elated by their notoriety.

Jane watched because everyone else was watching.

Dan Rather was reporting on the events in San Francisco. The camera cut to a reporter standing outside the Victorian house that fronted the shed.

The man said, "According to sources from the FBI, listening devices helped them ascertain that Alexandra Maplecroft had already been murdered by the conspirators. The likely culprit is their leader, Nicholas Harp. Andrew Queller was joined by a second woman who helped them escape through an adjacent building."

Jane flinched when she saw first Nick's face, then Andrew's, flash up. Paula was represented by a shadowy outline with a question mark in the center. Jane closed her eyes. She summoned the photo of Andrew that she had just seen. One year ago, at least. His cheeks were ruddy. A jaunty scarf was tied around his neck. A birthday party, or some kind of celebration? He looked happy, vibrant, alive.

She opened her eyes.

The television reporter said, "The question now is whether Jinx Queller is another hostage or a willing accomplice. Back to you in New York, Dan."

Dan Rather stacked together his papers on the top of his news desk. "William Argenis Johnson, another conspirator, was shot by snipers while trying to escape. A married father of two who worked as a graduate student at Stanford Uni—"

Nick turned off the volume. He did not look at Jane.

"William Johnson." She whispered the words aloud because she did not understand.

His name was Leonard Brandt. No children. Never married. He lived alone at 1239 Van Duff Street. He worked as a carpenter over in Marin.

"A fucking question mark?" Paula demanded. "That's all I rate is a fucking question mark?" She stood up, started to pace. "Meanwhile, poor Jinx Queller gets off scot fucking free. How about I write them a fucking letter and tell them you're fucking willing and able and ready? Would that make you happy, Dumb Bitch?"

"Penny," Nick said. "We don't have time for this. Troops, listen to me. We have to move everything up. This is bigger than even I had hoped for. Where are we with Chicago?"

"The bombs are ready," Spinner said, as if she was telling them that she'd just put dinner on the table. "All we have to do is plant them in the underground parking garage, then be within fifty feet of the building when we press the button on the remote."

"Fantastic!" Nick clapped together his hands. He was bouncing on the toes of his feet, amping them all back up again. "It should be the same with the explosives in New York. I'll rest here a few hours, then start driving. Even without my photo on the news, the FBI will heighten security at the airports. I'm not sure my ID will hold up to that kind of scrutiny."

Wyman said, "The forger in Toronto—"

"Is expensive. We blew our wad on Maplecroft's credentials because none of this would've mattered without Laura getting into that conference." Nick rubbed his hands together. Jane could almost see his brain working. This was the part he had always loved, not the planning, but holding them all rapt. "Nebecker and Huston are waiting for me at the safe house in Brooklyn. We'll drive the van into the city after rush hour, plant the devices, then go back the following morning and set them off."

Paula asked, "When do you want my team to set up?"

"Tomorrow morning." Nick watched their faces as realization set in. "Don't set up, *do it*. Plant the explosives first thing in the morning before anyone shows up for work, get as far away as you can, then blow the motherfucker down."

"Fuck yeah!" Paula raised her fist into the air. The others joined in.

"We're doing this, troops!" Nick shouted to be heard over the din. "We're going to make them stand up and take notice! We have to tear down the system before we can make it better."

"Damn right!" Wyman shouted.

"Hell yeah!" Paula was still pacing. She was like an animal ready to break out of her cage. "We're gonna show those mother-fucking pigs!"

Jane looked around the room. They were all wound up the same way, clapping their hands, stomping their feet, whooping as if they were watching a football game.

Tucker said, "Hey! Listen! Just listen!" He'd stood up, hands raised for attention. This was Edwin, Clara's lover. With his handlebar mustache and wavy hair, he looked more like Friedrich Nietzsche than a lawyer, but Nick trusted him, so they all trusted him.

He said, "Remember, you have a legal right to refuse to answer any and all questions from law enforcement. Ask the pigs, 'Am I under arrest?' If they say no, then walk away. If they say yes, shut your mouth—not just to the pigs, but to everybody, especially on the phone. Make sure you have my number memorized. You have a legal right to call your lawyer. Clara and I will be in the city standing by in case I need to go to the jail."

"Good man, Tuck, but it's not going to come to that. And fuck taking a rest. I'm leaving now!"

There was another round of whooping and cheering.

Nick was grinning like a fool. He told Clara, "Go wake up Dime. I'll need someone to help swap out the driving. It's only twelve hours, but I think—"

"No," Jane said. But she hadn't said it. She had shouted it.

The ensuing silence felt like a needle scratching off a record. Jane had ruined the game. No one was smiling anymore.

"Christ," Paula said. "Are you going to start whining again?"

Jane ignored her.

Nick was all that mattered. He looked confused, probably because he'd never heard Jane say *no* before.

"No," she repeated. "Andrew can't. You can't ask him to do

326

anything more. He did his part. Oslo was our part, and it's over and—" She was crying again, but this was different from the last week of crying. She wasn't grieving over something that had already happened. She was grieving over something that was going to happen very soon.

Jane saw it so clearly now—every sign she had missed in the months, the days, before. Andrew's sudden chills. The exhaustion. The weakness. The sores in his mouth that he'd mentioned in passing. The stomach aches. The weird rash on his wrist.

Infection.

"Jinx?" Nick was waiting. They were all waiting.

Jane walked down the hallway. She'd never been in the house before, so she had to open and close several doors before she finally found the bedroom where Andrew was sleeping.

Her brother was lying face-down in bed, fully clothed. He hadn't bothered to undress or get under the covers or even take off his shoes. Jane put her hand to his back. She waited for the up and down of his breathing before she allowed herself to take in her own breath.

She gently slid off his shoes. Carefully rolled him onto his back.

Andrew groaned, but didn't wake. His breath was raspy through his chapped lips. His skin was the color of paper. She could see the blue and red of his veins and arteries as easily as if she had been looking at a diagram. She unbuttoned his shirt partway down and saw the deep purple lesions on his skin. Kaposi's sarcoma. There were probably more lesions in his lungs, his throat, maybe even his brain.

Jane sat down on the bed.

She had lasted no more than six months volunteering at UCSF's AIDS ward. Watching so many men walk through the doors knowing that they would never walk out had proven to be too overwhelming. Jane had thought that the rattle in their chests as they gasped for their last breaths would be the worst sound that she would ever hear.

Until now, when she heard the same sounds coming from her brother.

Jane carefully buttoned his shirt back up.

There was a blue afghan on the back of a rocking chair. She draped it over her brother. She kissed his forehead. He felt so cold. His hands. His feet. She tucked the afghan around his body. She stroked the side of his pale face.

Jane had been seventeen years old when she'd found the old cigar box in the glove box of Andrew's car. She'd thought she'd caught him stealing Martin's cigars, but then she had opened the lid and gasped out loud. A plastic cigarette lighter. A bent silver teaspoon from one of her mother's precious sets. Stained cotton balls. The bottom of a Coke can. A handful of filthy Q-tips. A tube of skin cream squeezed in the middle. A length of rubber tubing for a tourniquet. Insulin syringes with black dots of blood staining the tips of the sharp needles. Tiny rocks of debris that she recognized from her years backstage as tar heroin.

Andrew had given it up eighteen months ago. After meeting Laura. After Nick had developed a plan.

But it was too late.

"Jinx?" Nick was standing in the doorway. He nodded for her to come into the hall.

Jane walked past Nick and went into the bathroom. She wrapped her arms around her waist, shivering. The room was large and cold. A cast iron tub was underneath the leaky window. The toilet was the old-fashioned type with the tank mounted high above the bowl.

Just like the one in Oslo.

"All right." Nick closed the door behind him. "What's got you so worked up, Ms. Queller?"

Jane looked at her reflection in the mirror. She saw her face, but it wasn't her face. The bridge of her nose was almost black. Dried blood caked the nostrils. What was she feeling? She couldn't tell anymore.

Uncomfortably numb.

"Jinx?"

She turned away from the mirror. She looked at Nick. His face, but not his face. Their connection, but not really a connection.

He had lied about knowing Quarter's name. He had lied about their future. He had lied every time that he had pretended that her brother was not dying.

And now, he had the audacity to look at his watch. "What is it, Jinx? We haven't much time."

"Time?" she had to repeat the word to truly understand the cruelty. "You're worried about time?"

"Jane—"

"You robbed me." Her throat felt so tight that she could barely speak. "You stole from me."

"Love, what are you—"

"I could've been here with my brother, but you sent me away. Thousands of miles away." Jane clenched her hands. She knew what she was feeling now: rage. "You're a liar. Everything that comes out of your mouth is a lie."

"Andy was—"

She slapped him hard across the face. "He's sick!" She screamed the words so loud that her throat ached. "My brother has AIDS, and you sent me to fucking Germany."

Nick touched his fingers to his cheek. He looked down at his open hand.

He'd been slapped before. Over the years, he'd told Jane about the abuse he'd suffered as a child. The prostitute mother. The absent father. The violent grandmother. The year of homelessness. The disgusting things people had wanted him to do. The self-loathing and hate and the fear that it would happen no matter how hard he tried to run away.

Jane understood the emotions all too well. From the age of eight, she had known what it was like to desperately want to run away. From Martin's hand clamping over her mouth in the middle of the night. From all the times he grabbed the back of her head and pressed her face into the pillow.

Which Nick had known about.

Which is why his stories were so effective. Jane saw it happen over and over again with every person he met. He mirrored your darkest fear with stories of his own.

329

That's how Nick got you: he inserted himself into the common ground.

Now, he simply asked, "What do you want me to say, Jinx? Yes, Andy has AIDS. Yes, I knew about it when you left for Berlin."

"Is Ellis-Anne . . ." Jane's voice trailed off. Andrew's girlfriend of two years. So sweet and devoted. She had called every day since Oslo. "Is she positive, too?"

"She's fine. She took the ELISA test last month." Nick's tone was filled with authority and reason, the same as it had been when he'd lied about Quarter's real name.

He told Jane, "Listen, you're right about all of this. And it's horrible. I know Andrew is close to the end. I know that having him out here is likely causing him to spiral down faster. And I've been so worried about him, but I have the whole group depending on me, expecting me to lead them and—I can't let myself think about it. I have to look ahead, otherwise I'd just curl into a useless ball of grief. I can't do that, and neither can you, because I need you, darling. Everyone thinks I'm so strong, but I'm only strong when you're standing beside me."

Jane could not believe he was giving her one of his rallying speeches. "You know how they die, Nick. You've heard the stories. Ben Mitchell—do you remember him?" Jane's voice lowered as if she was saying a sacrament. "I took care of him on the ward, but then his parents finally said it was okay for him to come home to die. They took him to the hospital and none of the nurses would touch him because they were afraid of getting infected. Do you remember me telling you about it? They wouldn't even give him morphine. Do you remember?"

Nick's face was impassive. "I remember."

"He suffocated on the fluid inside his lungs. It took almost eight agonizing minutes for him to die, and Ben was awake for every single second of it." She waited, but Nick said nothing. "He was terrified. He kept trying to scream, clawing at his neck, begging people to help. No one would help him. His own mother

330

had to leave the room. Do you remember that story, Nick? Do you?"

He only said, "I remember."

"Is that what you want for Andrew?" She waited, but again, he said nothing. "He's coughing the same way Ben did. The same way Charlie Bray did. The same thing happened to him. Charlie went home to Florida and—"

"You don't have to give me a play-by-play, Jinx. I told you: I remember the stories. Yes, how they died was horrible. All of it was horrible. But we don't have a choice."

She wanted to shake him. "Of course we have a choice."

"It was Andy's idea to send you to Berlin."

Jane knew he was telling the truth, just as she knew that Nick was a surgeon when it came to transplanting his ideas onto other people's tongues.

Nick said, "He thought if you knew he was sick, that you would . . . I don't know, Jinx. Do something stupid. Make us stop. Make everything stop. He believes in this thing that we're doing. He wants us to finish it. That's why I'm taking him to Brooklyn. You can come too. Take care of him. Keep him alive long enough to—"

"Stop." She couldn't listen to his bullshit. "I am not going to let my brother suffocate to death in the back of that filthy van."

"It's not about his life anymore," Nick insisted. "It's about his legacy. This is how Andy wants to go out. On his own terms, like a man. That's what he's always wanted. The overdoses, the hanging, the pills and needles, showing up in places he shouldn't be, hanging out with the wrong people. You know what hell his life has been. He got clean for this thing that we're doing— that we're all doing. This is what gave him the strength to stop using, Jane. Don't take that away from him."

She gripped her fists in frustration. "He's doing it for you, Nick. All it would take is one word from you and he'd go to the hospital where he can die in peace."

"You know him better than me?"

"I know *you* better. Andy wants to please you. They all want

331

to please you. But this is different. It's cruel. He'll suffocate like—"

"Yes, Jane, I get it. He'll suffocate on the fluids in his lungs. He'll have eight minutes of agonizing terror, and that's—well, agonizing—but you need to listen to me very carefully, darling, because this part is very important," Nick said. "You have to choose between him or me."

What?

"If Andy can't make the trip with me, then you need to go with me in his place."

What?

"I can't trust you anymore." Nick's shoulder went up in a shrug. "I know how your mind works. The minute I leave, you'll take Andy to the hospital. You'll stay with him because that's what you do, Jinx. You stay with people. You've always been loyal, sitting with homeless men down at the shelter, helping serve soup at the mission, wiping spittle from the mouths of dying men at the infection ward. I won't say you're a good little dog, because that's cruel. But your loyalty to Andrew will land us all in prison, because the moment you walk into the hospital, the police will arrest you, and they'll know we're in Chicago, and I can't let that happen."

She felt her mouth gape open.

"I'll only give you this one chance. You have to choose right here, right now: him or me."

Jane felt the room shift. This couldn't be happening.

He looked at her coldly, as if she was a specimen under glass. "You must have known it would come to this, Jane. You're naïve, but you're not stupid." Nick waited a moment. "Choose."

She had to rest her hand on the sink so that she wouldn't slide to the floor. "He's your best friend." Her voice was no more than a whisper. "He's my brother."

"I need your decision."

Jane heard a high-pitched sound in her ears, as if her skull had been struck by a tuning fork. She didn't know what was happening. Panic made her words brim with fear. "Are you leaving me? Breaking up with me?"

332

"I said me or him. It's your choice, not mine."

"Nick, I can't—" She didn't know how to finish the sentence. Was this a test? Was he doing what he always did, gauging her loyalty? "I love you."

"Then choose me."

"I—you know you're everything to me. I've given up—" She held out her arms, indicating the world, because there was nothing left that she had not abandoned for him. Her father. Jasper. Her life. Her music. "Please, don't make me choose. He's dying."

Nick stared at her, icy cold.

Jane felt a wail come out of her mouth. She knew how Nick looked when he was finished with a person. Six years of her life, her heart, her love, was evaporating in front of her eyes. How could he so easily throw it all away? "Nicky, please—"

"Andrew's impending death should make your choice easy. A few more hours with a dying man or the rest of your life with me." He waited. "Choose."

"Nick—" Another sob cut her off. She felt like she was dying. He couldn't leave her. Not now. "It's not just a few more hours. It's hours of terror, or—" Jane couldn't think about what Andrew would go through if he was abandoned. "You can't mean this. I know you're just testing me. I love you. Of course I love you. I told you I'm with you."

Nick reached for the door.

"Please!" Jane grabbed him by the front of his shirt. He turned away his head when she tried to kiss him. Jane pressed her face to his chest. She was crying so hard that she could barely speak. "Please, Nicky. Please don't make me choose. You know that I can't live without you. I'm nothing without you. Please!"

"Then you'll go with me?"

She looked up at him. She had cried so hard for so long that her eyelids felt like barbed wire.

"I need you to say it, Jane. I need to hear your choice."

"I c-can't—" she stuttered out the word. "Nick, I can't—"

"You can't choose?"

"No." The realization almost stopped her heart. "I can't leave him."

Nick's face gave nothing away.

"I—" Jane could barely swallow. Her mouth had gone dry. She was terrified, but she knew that what she was doing was right. "I will not let my brother die alone."

"All right." Nick reached for the door again, but then something changed his mind.

For just a moment, she thought that he was going to tell her it was okay.

But he didn't.

His hands shot out. He shoved Jane across the room. Her head whipped back, broke the glass out of the window.

She was dumbstruck. She felt the back of her head, expecting to find blood. "Why did—"

Nick punched her in the stomach.

Jane collapsed to her knees. Bile erupted from her mouth. She tasted blood. Her stomach spasmed so hard that she doubled over, her forehead touching the floor.

Nick grabbed her hair, jerked her head back up. He was kneeling in front of her. "What did you think would happen after we did this, Janey, that we would run off to a little flat in Switzerland and raise our baby?"

The baby—

"Look at me." His fingers wrapped around her neck. He shook her like a doll. "Were you stupid enough to think I'd let you keep it? That I'd turn into some fat old man who reads the Sunday paper while you do the dishes and we talk about Junior's class project?"

Jane couldn't breathe. Her fingernails dug into his wrists. He was choking her.

"Don't you understand that I know everything about you, Jinx? We've never been whole people. We only make sense when we're together." He tightened his grip with both hands. "Nothing can come between us. Not a whining baby. Not your dying brother. Nothing. Do you hear me?"

She clawed at him, desperate for air. He banged her head against the wall.

"I'll kill you before I let you leave me." He looked her in the eye, and Jane knew that this time, Nick was telling the truth. "You belong to me, Jinx Queller. If you ever try to leave me, I will scorch the earth to get you back. Do you understand?" He shook her again. "Do you?"

His hands were too tight. Jane felt a darkness edging around her vision. Her lungs shuddered. Her tongue would not stay inside of her mouth.

"Look at me." Nick's face was glowing with sweat. His eyes were on fire. He was smiling his usual self-satisfied grin. "How does it feel to suffocate, darling? Is it everything you imagined?"

Her eyelids started to flutter. For the first time in days, Jane's vision was clear. There were no more tears left.

Nick had taken them away, just like he had taken everything else.

August 26, 2018

13

Andy sat at a booth in the back of a McDonald's outside of Big Rock, Illinois. She had been so happy to be out of Mike's truck after two and a half monotonous days of driving that she'd treated herself to a milkshake. Worrying about her cholesterol and lack of exercise was a problem for Future Andy.

Present Andy had enough problems already. She was no longer an amoeba, but there were some obsessive tendencies that she had to accept were baked into her DNA. She had spent the first day of the trip freaking out over all of the mistakes she had made and was probably still making: that she had never checked the cooler in the Reliant for a GPS tracker, that she had left the unregistered revolver in the glove box for Mike to find, that she had possibly broken his testicles and actually stolen his wallet and was committing a felony by taking a stolen vehicle across multiple state lines.

This was the really important one: had Mike heard Paula tell Andy to look for Clara Bellamy in Illinois, or had he been too concerned that his nuts were imploding?

Future Andy would find out eventually.

She chewed the straw on her milkshake. She watched the screensaver bounce around the laptop screen. She would have to save her neurosis about Mike for when she was trying to fall asleep and needed something to torment herself over. For now, she had to figure out what the hell had landed Paula Kunde in prison for twenty years and why she so clearly held a grudge against Laura.

Andy had so far been stymied in her computer searches. Three nights spent in three different motels with the laptop propped open on her belly had resulted in nothing more than an angry red rectangle of skin on her stomach.

The easiest route to finding shit on people was always Facebook. The night Andy had left Austin, she'd created a fake account in the name of Stefan Salvatore and used the Texas Longhorns' logo as her profile photo. Unsurprisingly, Paula Kunde was not on the social media site. ProfRatings.com let Andy use her Facebook credentials to log in as a user. She went onto Paula's review page with its cumulative half-star rating. She sent dozens of private messages to Paula's most vocal critics, the texts all saying the same thing:

DUDE!!! Kunde in FEDERAL PEN 20 yrs?!?!?! MUST HAVE DEETS!!! Bitch won't change my grade!!!

Andy hadn't heard back much more than *Fuck that fucking bitch I hope you kill her*, but she knew that eventually, someone would get bored and do the kind of deep dive that took knowing the number off your parents' credit card.

A toddler screamed on the other side of the McDonald's.

Andy watched his mother carry him toward the bathroom. She wondered if she had ever been to this McDonald's with her mother. Laura hadn't just pulled Chicago, Illinois, out of her ass for Jerry Randall's birth and death place.

Right?

Andy slurped the last of the milkshake. Now was not the time to dive into the silly string of her mother's lies. She studied the scrap of paper at her elbow. The second that Andy was safe enough outside of Austin, she had pulled over to the side of the road and scribbled down everything she could remember about her conversation with Paula Kunde.

—Twenty years in Danbury?

—QuellCorp?

—Knew Hoodie, but not Mike?

—31 years—interesting math?

—Laura full of the worst type of bullshit?

—Shotgun? What made her change her mind—Clara Bellamy???

Andy had started with the easiest searches first. The Danbury Federal Penitentiary's records were accessible through the BOP. gov inmate locator, but Paula Kunde was not listed on the site. Nor was she listed on the UC-Berkeley, Stanford or West Connecticut University alumni pages. The obvious explanation was that Paula had at some point gotten married and, patriarchal constructs aside, changed her last name.

I know how marriage works.

Andy had already checked marriage and divorce records in Austin, then in surrounding counties, then done the same in Western Connecticut and Berkeley County and Palo Alto, then Andy had decided that she was wasting her time because Paula could've flown to Vegas and gotten hitched and actually, why did Andy believe that a shotgun-wielding lunatic had told her the truth about being in prison in the first place?

Snitch and *two dimes* were basically in every prison show ever. All it took was saying them with attitude, which Paula Kunde had plenty of.

Regardless, the BOP search was a dead end.

Andy tapped her fingers on the table as she studied the list. She tried to think back to the conversation inside of Paula's kitchen. There had been a definite before and after. Before, meaning when Paula was talking to her, and after, meaning when she'd gone to fetch her shotgun and told Andy to get the hell out.

Andy couldn't think of what she'd said wrong. They had been talking about Laura, and how she was full of bullshit—the worst type of bullshit—

And then Paula had told Andy to wait and then threatened to shoot her.

Andy could only shake her head, because it still didn't make sense.

Even more puzzling was the after-after, because Paula hadn't given up Clara Bellamy's name until after Andy had kicked the shit out of Mike. Andy could take it at face value and assume that Paula had been impressed by the violence, but something told her she was on the wrong track. Paula was fucking smart. You didn't go to Stanford if you were an idiot. She had played Andy like a fiddle from the moment she'd opened the front door. She was very likely playing Andy even now, but trying to figure out a maniac's end game was far beyond Andy's deductive skills.

She looked back at her notes, focusing on the item that still niggled most at her brain:

—31 years—interesting math?

Had Paula gone to prison thirty-one years ago while a pregnant Laura ran off with nearly one million bucks and a fake ID to live her fabulous life on the beach for thirty-one years until suddenly the diner video appeared on the national news, pointing the bad guys to her location?

Hoodie had strangled both Laura and Paula, so obviously both women had information that someone else wanted.

The mysterious *they* who could track Andy's emails and phone calls?

Andy returned to the laptop and tried QuellCorp.com again, because all she could do now was go back and see if she'd missed anything the last twenty times she had looked at the website.

The splash page offered a Ken Burns-effect photo slowly zooming onto a young, multicultural group of lab-coated scientists staring intently at a beaker full of glowing liquid. Violins played in the background like Leonardo da Vinci had just discovered the cure for herpes.

Andy muted the sound.

She was familiar with the pharmaceutical company the same way everybody was familiar with Band-Aids. QuellCorp made everything from baby wipes to erectile dysfunction pills. The only information Andy could find under HISTORY was that a guy named Douglas Paul Queller had founded the company in the 1920s, then his descendants had sold out in the 1980s, then by the early 2000s QuellCorp had basically swallowed the world, because that's what evil corporations did.

They could certainly be an evil corporation. That was the plot of almost every sci-fi movie Andy had seen, from *Avatar* to all of the *Terminator*s.

She closed the QuellCorp page and pulled up the wiki for Clara Bellamy.

If it was strange that Laura knew Paula Kunde, it was downright shocking that Paula Kunde knew a woman like Clara Bellamy. She had been a *prima ballerina*, which according to another wiki page was an honor only bestowed on a handful of women. Clara had danced for George Balanchine, a choreographer whose name even Andy recognized. Clara had toured the world. Danced on the most celebrated stages. Been at the top of her field. Then a horrific knee injury had forced her to retire.

Because Andy had had nothing better to do after driving all day, she had seen almost every video of Clara Bellamy that YouTube had to offer. There were countless performances and interviews with all kinds of famous people, but Andy's favorite was from what she believed was the first Tchaikovsky Festival ever staged by the New York City Ballet.

Since Andy was a theater nerd, the foremost thing she'd noticed about the video was that the set was spectacular, with weird translucent tubes in the background that made everything look like it was encased in ice. She had assumed that it would be boring to watch tiny women spinning on their toes to old-people music, but there was something almost hummingbird-like about Clara Bellamy that made her impossible to look away from. For a woman Andy had never heard of, Clara had been extraordinarily famous. *Newsweek* and *Time* had both featured her on the cover. She was constantly showing up in the *New York Times Magazine* or highlighted in the *New Yorker*'s "Goings On About Town" section.

That was where Andy's searches had hit a wall. Or, to be more exact, a pay wall. She was only allowed a certain number of articles on a lot of the websites, so she had to be careful about what she clicked on. It wasn't like she could just pull out a credit card and buy more access.

As far as she could tell, Clara had disappeared from public life around 1983. The last photo in the *Times* showed the woman with her head down, tissue held to her nose, as she left George Balanchine's funeral.

As with Paula, Andy assumed that Clara Bellamy had been married at some point and changed her name, though why anybody would work so hard to create a famous name, then change it, was hard to fathom. Clara had no Facebook page, but there was a closed appreciation group and a public thinspo one that was grossly obsessed with her weight.

Andy had not been able to locate any marriage or divorce documents for Clara Bellamy in New York, or Chicago's Cook County or the surrounding areas, but she had found an interesting article in the *Chicago Sun Times* about a lawsuit that had taken place after Clara's knee injury.

The *prima ballerina* had sued a company called EliteDream BodyWear for payment on an endorsement contract. The lawyer who'd represented her was not named in the article, but the accompanying photo showed Clara leaving the courthouse with a lanky, mustachioed man who looked to Andy like the perfect embodiment of a hippie lawyer, or a hipster Millennial trying to look like one. More importantly, when the photographer had clicked the button to take the photo, Hippie Lawyer was looking directly at the camera.

Andy had taken several photography classes at SCAD. She knew how unusual it was to have a candid where someone wasn't blinking or moving their lips in a weird way. Hippie Lawyer had defied the odds. Both of his eyes were open. His lips were slightly parted. His ridiculously curled handlebar mustache was on center. His silky, long hair rested square on his shoulders. The image was so clear that Andy could even see the tips of his ears sticking out from his hair like tiny pistachios.

Andy had to assume that Hippie Lawyer had not changed

that much over the years. A guy who in his thirties took his facial hair grooming cues from Wyatt Earp did not suddenly wake up in his sixties and realize his mistake.

She entered a new search: *Chicago+Lawyer+Mustache+Hair*.

Within seconds, she was looking at a group called the Funkadelic Fiduciaries, a self-described "hair band." They played every Wednesday night at a bar called the EZ Inn. Each one had some weird facial hair going on, whether it was devilish Van Dykes or Elvis sideburns, and there were enough man-buns to start an emo colony. Andy zoomed in on each face in the eight-member group and spotted the familiar curl of a handlebar mustache on the drummer.

Andy looked down at his name.

Edwin Van Wees.

She rubbed her eyes. She was tired from driving all day and staring at computer screens all night. It couldn't be that easy.

She found the old photo from the newspaper to do a comparison. The drummer was a little plumper, a lot less hairy and not as handsome, but she knew that she had the right guy.

Andy looked out the window, taking a moment to acknowledge her good luck. Was finding Edwin, who might know how to find Clara Bellamy, really that easy?

She opened another browser window.

As with Clara, Edwin Van Wees did not have his own Facebook page, but she was able to find a homemade-looking website that listed him as partially retired but still available for speaking gigs and drum solos. She clicked on the *about* tab. Edwin was a Stanford-trained, former ACLU lawyer with a long, successful career of defending artists and anarchists and rabble-rousers and revolutionaries who had happily posted photos of themselves grinning beside the lawyer who'd kept them out of prison. Even some of the ones who'd ended up going to jail still had glowing things to say about him. It made perfect sense that a guy like Edwin would know a crazy bitch like Paula Kunde.

My revolutionary days are over.

Andy believed with all of her heart that Edwin Van Wees still knew how to get in touch with Clara Bellamy. It was the familiar way she was touching his arm in the courthouse photo. It was also the nasty look Edwin was giving the man behind the lens. Maybe Andy was reading too much into it, but if the professor from Andy's Emotions of Light in Black and White Photography class had tasked her with finding a photo of a fragile woman holding onto her strong protector, this was the picture Andy would've chosen.

The toddler started screaming again.

His mother snatched him up and took him to the bathroom again.

Andy closed the laptop and shoved it into her messenger bag. She tossed her trash and got back into Mike's truck. Stone Temple Pilots' "Interstate Love Song" was still playing. Andy reached down to turn it off, but she couldn't. She hated that she loved Mike's music. All of his mix-CDs were awesome, from Dashboard Confessional to Blink 182 and a surprising amount of J-Lo.

Andy checked the time on the McDonald's sign as she pulled onto the road. Two twelve in the afternoon. Not the worst time to drop by unannounced. On his website, Edwin Van Wees had listed his office address at a farm about an hour and a half drive from Chicago. She assumed that meant he worked from home, which made it highly likely that he would be there when Andy pulled up. She had mapped out the directions on Google Earth, zooming in and out of the lush farmlands, locating Edwin's big red barn and matching house with its bright metal roof.

From the McDonald's, it took her ten minutes to find the farm. She almost missed the driveway because it was hidden in a thick stand of trees. Andy stopped the truck just shy of the turn. The road was deserted. The floorboard vibrated as the engine idled.

She didn't feel the same nervousness she'd felt when she walked toward Paula's house. Andy understood now that there was no guarantee that finding a person meant that the person was going to tell you the truth. Or even that the person was not going to shove a shotgun in your chest. Maybe Edwin Van Wees would do the same thing. It kind of made sense that Paula Kunde would send Andy to someone who would not be happy to see her. The drive from Austin had given Paula plenty of time to call ahead and warn Clara Bellamy that Laura Oliver's kid might be looking for her. If Edwin Van Wees was still close to Clara, then Clara could've called Edwin and—

Andy rubbed her face with her hands. She could spend the rest of the day doing this stupid dance or she could go find out for herself. She turned the wheel and drove down the driveway. The trees didn't clear for what felt like half a mile, but soon she saw the top of the red barn, then a large pasture with cows, then the small farmhouse with a wide porch and sunflowers planted in the front yard.

Andy parked in front of the barn. There were no other cars in sight, which was a bad sign. The front door to the house didn't open. There was no fluttering of curtains or furtive faces in the windows. Still, she wasn't too much of an imbecile to leave without knocking on the door.

Andy started to climb out of the truck, but then she remembered the burner phone that Laura was supposed to call her on when the coast was clear. In truth, she had lost hope around Tulsa that it would ever ring. The *Belle Isle Review* had provided the salient facts: Hoodie's body remained unidentified. After analyzing the video from the diner, the police had reached the same conclusion as Mike. Laura had tried to stop Jonah Helsinger from killing himself. She would not be charged with his murder. The kid's family was still making noises, but police royalty or not, public sentiment had turned away from them, and the local prosecutor was a political weathervane of the vilest kind. In short, whatever lurking danger was keeping Andy away from home was either unrelated or simply another part of Laura's colossal web of lies.

Andy unzipped the make-up bag and checked the phone to make sure the battery was full before slipping it into her back pocket. She saw Laura's Canada license and health card. Andy studied the photo of her mother, trying to ignore the pang of longing that she did not want to feel. Instead, she looked at her own reflection in the mirror. Maybe it was Andy's crappy diet or lack of sleep or the fact that she had started wearing her hair down, but as each day passed, she had started to look more and more like her mother. The last three hotel clerks had barely glanced up when Andy had used the license to check in.

She shoved it back into her messenger bag beside a black leather wallet.

Mike's wallet.

For the last two and a half days, Andy had been studiously avoiding opening the wallet and staring at Mike's handsome face, especially when she was lying in bed at night and trying not to think about him because he was a psychopath and she was pathetic.

She looked up at the farmhouse, then checked the driveway, then opened the wallet.

"Oh for fucksakes," she muttered.

He had four different driver's licenses, each of them pretty damn good forgeries: Michael Knepper from Alabama; Michael Davey from Arkansas; Michael George from Texas; Michael Falcone from Georgia. There was a thick flap of leather dividing the wallet. Andy picked it open.

Holy shit.

He had a fake United States marshal badge. Andy had seen the real thing before, a gold star inside of a circle. It was a good replica, as convincing as all of the fake IDs. Whoever his forger was had done a damn good job.

There was a tap at the window.

"Fuck!" Andy dropped the wallet as her hands flew up.

Then her mouth dropped open, because the person who had knocked on the window looked a hell of a lot like Clara Bellamy.

"You," the woman said, a bright smile to her lips. "What are you doing sitting out here in this dirty truck?"

Andy wondered if her eyes were playing tricks, or if she had looked at so many YouTube videos that she was seeing Clara

Bellamy everywhere. The woman was older, her face lined, her long hair a peppered gray, but undoubtedly Andy was looking at the real-life person.

Clara said, "Come on, silly. It's chilly out here. Let's go inside."

Why was she talking to Andy like she knew her?

Clara pulled open the door. She held out her hand to help Andy down.

"My goodness," Clara said. "You look tired. Has Andrea been keeping you up again? Did you leave her at the hotel?"

Andy opened her mouth, but there was no way to answer. She looked into Clara's eyes, wondering who the woman saw staring back at her.

"What is it?" Clara asked. "Do you need Edwin?"

"Uh—" Andy struggled to answer. "Is he—is Edwin here?"

She looked at the area in front of the barn. "His car isn't here."

Andy waited.

"I just put Andrea down for a nap," she said, as if she hadn't two seconds ago asked if Andrea was at the hotel.

Did she mean Andrea as in Andy, or someone else?

Clara said, "Should we have some tea?" She didn't wait for an answer. She looped her arm through Andy's and led her back toward the farmhouse. "I have no idea why, but I was thinking about Andrew this morning. What happened to him." She put her hand to the base of her throat. She had started to cry. "Jane, I'm so very sorry."

"Uh—" Andy had no idea what she was talking about, but she felt a strange desire to cry, too.

Andrew? Andrea?

Clara said, "Let's not talk about depressing things today. You've got enough of that going on in your life right now." She pushed open the front door with her foot. "Now, tell me how you've been. Are you all right? Still having trouble sleeping?"

"Uh," Andy said, because apparently that's all she was capable of coming up with. "I've been . . ." She tried to think of something to say that would keep this woman talking. "What about you? What have you been up to?"

"Oh, so much. I've been clipping magazine photos with ideas for the nursery and working on some scrapbooks from my glory years. The worst kind of self-aggrandizement, but you know, it's such a strange thing—I've forgotten most of my performances. Have you?"

"Uh . . ." Andy still didn't know what the hell the woman was talking about.

Clara laughed. "I bet you remember every single one. You were always so sharp that way." She pushed open a swinging door with her foot. "Have a seat. I'll make us some tea."

Andy realized she was in another kitchen with another stranger who might or might not know everything about her mother.

"I think I have some cookies." Clara started opening cupboards.

Andy took in the kitchen. The space was small, cut off from the rest of the house, and probably not much changed since it was built. The metal cabinets were painted bright teal. The countertops were made from butcher's blocks. The appliances looked like they belonged on the set of *The Partridge Family*.

There was a large whiteboard on the wall by the fridge. Someone had written:

Clara: it's Sunday. Edwin will be in town from 1–4pm. Lunch is in the fridge. Do not use the stove.

Clara turned on the stove. The starter clicked several times before the gas caught. "Chamomile?"

"Uh—sure." Andy sat down at the table. She tried to think of some questions to ask Clara, like what year it was or who was the current president, but none of that was necessary because you don't put notes on a board like that unless a person has memory problems.

Andy felt an almost overwhelming sadness that was quickly chased by a healthy dose of guilt, because if Clara had early-onset Alzheimer's, then what had happened to her last week was gone, but what had happened to her thirty-one years ago was probably close to the surface.

350

Andy asked, "What colors were you thinking of for the nursery?"

"No pinks," Clara insisted. "Maybe some greens and yellows?"

"That sounds pretty." Andy tried to keep her talking. "Like the sunflowers outside."

"Yes, exactly." She seemed pleased. "Edwin says we'll try as soon as this is over, but I don't know. It seems like we should start now. I'm not getting any younger." She put her hand to her stomach as she laughed. There was something so beautiful about the sound that Andy felt it pull at her heart.

Clara Bellamy exuded kindness. To try to trick her felt dirty.

Clara asked, "How are you feeling, though? Are you still exhausted?"

"I'm better." Andy watched Clara pour cold water into two cups. She hadn't heated the kettle. The flame flickered high on the stove. Andy stood up to turn it off, asking, "Do you remember how we met? I was trying to recall the details the other day."

"Oh, so horrible." Her fingers went to her throat. "Poor Andrew."

Andrew again.

Andy sat back down at the table. She wasn't equipped for this kind of subterfuge. A smarter person would know how to get information out of this clearly troubled woman. Paula Kunde would likely have her singing like a bird.

Which gave Andy an idea.

She tried, "I saw Paula a few days ago."

Clara rolled her eyes. "I hope you didn't call her that."

"What else would I call her?" Andy tried. "Bitch?"

Clara laughed as she sat down at the table. She had put tea bags in the cold water. "I wouldn't say that to her face. Penny would probably just as soon see us all dead right now."

Penny?

Andy mulled the word around in her head. And then she remembered the dollar bill that Paula Kunde had shoved into her hand. Andy was wearing the same jeans from that day. She

351

dug into her pocket and found the bill wadded into a tight ball. She smoothed it out on the table. She slid it toward Clara.

"Ah." Clara's lips turned up mischievously. "Dumb Bitch, reporting for duty."

Another spectacular success.

Andy had to stop being subtle. She asked, "Do you remember Paula's last name?"

Clara's eyebrow went up. "Is this some sort of test? Do you think I can't remember?"

Andy tried to decipher Clara's suddenly sharp tone. Was she irritated? Had Andy ruined her chances?

Clara laughed, breaking the tension. "Of course I remember. What's gotten into you, Jane? You're acting so strange."

Jane?

Clara said the name again. "Jane?"

Andy played with the string on her tea bag. The water had turned orange. "I've forgotten, is the problem. She's using a different name now."

"Penny?"

Penny?

"I just—" Andy couldn't keep playing these games. "Just tell me, Clara. What's her last name?"

Clara reeled back at the demand. Tears seeped from her eyes.

Andy felt like an asshole. "I'm sorry. I shouldn't have snapped at you."

Clara stood up. She walked to the refrigerator and opened it. Instead of getting something out, she just stood there.

"Clara, I'm so—"

"It's Evans. Paula Louise Evans."

Andy's elation was considerably tempered by her shame.

"I'm not completely bonkers." Clara's back was stiff. "I remember the important things. I always have."

"I know that. I'm so sorry."

Clara kept her own counsel as she stared into the open fridge.

Andy wanted to slide onto the floor and grovel for forgiveness. She also wanted to run outside and get her laptop, but she needed internet access to look up Paula Louise Evans. She hesitated, but only slightly, before asking Clara, "Do you know the—" She stopped herself, because Clara probably had no idea what Wi-Fi was, let alone knew the password.

Andy asked, "Is there an office in the house?"

"Of course." Clara closed the fridge and turned around, the warm smile back in place. "Do you need to make a phone call?"

"Yes," Andy said, because agreeing was the quickest way forward. "Do you mind?"

"Is it long-distance?"

"No."

"That's good. Edwin's been grousing at me about the phone bill lately." Clara's smile started to falter. She had lost her way in the conversation again.

Andy said, "When I finish my phone call in the office, we could talk some more about Andrew."

"Of course." Clara's smile brightened. "It's this way, but I'm not sure where Edwin is. He's been working so hard lately. And obviously the news has made him very upset."

Andy didn't ask what news because she couldn't bear to risk setting the woman off again.

She followed Clara back through the house. Even with the bad knee, the dancer's walk was breathtakingly graceful. Her feet barely touched the floor. Andy couldn't fully appreciate watching her move because so many questions flooded her mind: Who was Jane? Who was Andrew? Why did Clara cry every time she said the man's name?

And why did Andy feel the desire to protect this fragile woman she had never met before?

"Here." Clara was at the end of the hall. She opened the door to what had likely been a bedroom at some point, but was now a tidy office with a wall of locked filing cabinets, a roll-top desk and a MacBook Pro on the arm of a leather couch.

Clara smiled at Andy. "What did you need?"

Andy hesitated again. She should go back to the McDonald's and use their Wi-Fi. There was no reason to do this here. Except that she still wanted to know answers. What if Paula Louise Evans wasn't online? And then Andy would have to drive back, and Edwin Van Wees would probably be home by then, and he would probably not want Clara talking to Andy.

Clara asked, "Can I help you with something?"

"The computer?"

"That's easy. They're not as scary as you think." Clara sat on the floor. She opened the MacBook. The password prompt came up. Andy expected her to struggle with the code, but Clara pressed her finger to the Touch ID and the desktop was unlocked.

She told Andy, "You'll have to sit here, otherwise the light from the window blacks out the screen."

She meant the giant window behind the couch. Andy could see Mike's truck parked in front of the red barn. She could still leave. Edwin would be home in less than an hour. Now would be the time to go.

Clara said, "Come, Jane. I can show you how to use it. It's not terribly complicated."

Andy sat down on the floor beside Clara.

Clara put the open laptop on the seat of the couch so they could both see it. She said, "I've been looking at videos of myself. Does that make me terribly vain?"

Andy looked at this stranger sitting so close beside her, who kept talking to her like they had been friends for a long time, and said, "I watched your videos, too. Almost all of them. You were—are—such a beautiful dancer, Clara. I never thought I liked ballet before, but watching you made me understand that it's lovely."

Clara touched her fingers to Andy's leg. "Oh, darling, you're so sweet. You know I feel the same about you."

Andy did not know what to say. She reached up to the laptop. She found the browser. Her fingers fumbled on the keyboard. She was sweaty and shaky for no reason. She squeezed her hands into fists in an attempt to get them back under control. She rested her fingers on the keyboard. She slowly typed.

PAULA LOUISE EVANS.

Andy's pinky finger rested on the ENTER key but did not press it. This was the moment. She would find out something—at least one thing—about the horrible woman who had known her mother thirty-one years ago.

Andy tapped ENTER.

Motherfucker.

Paula Louise Evans had her own Wikipedia page.

Andy clicked on the link.

The warning at the top of the page indicated the information was not without controversy. Which made sense, because Paula struck Andy as a woman who loved controversy.

She felt a nervous energy take hold as she skimmed the contents, scrolling through an extensive bio that listed everything from the hospital where Paula had been born to her inmate number at Danberry Federal Penitentiary for Women.

Raised in Corte Madera, California . . . Berkeley . . . Stanford . . . murder.

Andy's stomach dropped.

Paula Evans had murdered a woman.

Andy looked up at the ceiling for a moment. She thought about Paula pointing the shotgun at her chest.

Clara said, "There's so much information about her. Is it horrible that I'm a bit jealous?"

Andy scrolled down to the next section:

INVOLVEMENT WITH THE ARMY OF THE CHANGING WORLD.

There was a blurry photo of Paula. The date underneath read "July 1986."

Thirty-two years ago.

Andy could remember doing the math back in Carrollton at the library computer. She had been looking for events that had taken place around the time she would've been conceived.

Bombings and plane hijackings and shoot-outs at banks.

Andy studied the photo of Paula Evans.

She was wearing a weird dress that looked like a cotton slip. Thick, black lines of make-up were smeared beneath her eyes.

Fingerless gloves were on her hands. Combat boots were on her feet. She was wearing a beret. A cigarette dangled from her mouth. She had a revolver in one hand and a hunting knife in the other. It would've been funny except for the fact that Paula had murdered someone.

And been involved in a conspiracy to bring down the world, apparently.

"Jane?" Clara had pulled a blue afghan around her shoulders. "Should we have some tea?"

"In a moment," Andy said, doing a search for the word *JANE* on Paula's Wikipedia page.

Nothing.

ANDREW.

Nothing.

She clicked on the link that took her to the wiki page for THE ARMY OF THE CHANGING WORLD.

Starting with the assassination of Martin Queller in Oslo . . .

"QuellCorp," Andy said.

Clara made a hissing sound. "Aren't they awful?"

Andy skipped down the page. She saw a photo of their leader, a guy who looked like Zac Efron with Charles Manson's eyes. The Army's crimes were bullet-pointed past the Martin Queller assassination. They had kidnapped and murdered a Berkeley professor. Been involved in a shoot-out, a nationwide manhunt. Their crazy-ass leader had written a manifesto, a ransom note that had appeared on the front page of the *San Francisco Chronicle*.

Andy clicked on the note.

She read the first part about the fascist regime and then her eyes started to glaze over.

It was like something Calvin and Hobbes would concoct during a meeting of G.R.O.S.S. to get back at Susie Derkins.

Andy returned to the Army page and found a section called MEMBERS. Most of the names were in blue hyperlinks amid the sea of black text. Dozens of people. How had Andy never seen a Dateline or Lifetime movie about this insane cult?

William Johnson. Dead.

Franklin Powell. Dead.

Metta Larsen. Dead.

Andrew Queller—

Andy's heart flipped, but Andrew's name was in black, which meant he didn't have a page. Then again, you didn't have to be Scooby-Doo to link him back to QuellCorp and its assassinated namesake.

She scrolled back up to Martin Queller and clicked his name. Apparently, there were a lot more famous Quellers out there that Andy didn't know about. His wife, Annette Queller, née Logan, had a family line that would take hours to explore. Their eldest son, Jasper Queller, was hyperlinked, but Andy already knew the asshole billionaire who kept trying and failing to run for president.

The cursor drifted over the next name: Daughter, Jane "Jinx" Queller.

"Jane?" Clara asked, because she had Alzheimer's and her mind was trapped in a time over thirty years ago when she knew a woman named Jane who looked just like Andy.

Just as Andy looked like the Daniela B. Cooper photo in the fake Canada driver's license.

Her mother.

Andy started to cry. Not just cry, but sob. A wail came out of her mouth. Tears and snot rolled down her face. She leaned over, her forehead on the seat of the couch.

"Oh, sweetheart." Clara was on her knees, her arms wrapped around Andy's shoulders.

Andy shook with grief. Was Laura's real name Jane Queller? Why did this one lie matter so much more than the others?

"Here, let me." Clara slid the laptop over and started to type. "It's okay, my darling. I cry when I watch mine sometimes, too, but look at this one. It's perfect."

Clara slid the laptop back to the center.

Andy tried to wipe her eyes. Clara put a tissue in her hand. Andy blew her nose, tried to stanch her tears. She looked at the laptop.

Clara had pulled up a YouTube video.

!!!RARE!!! JINX QUELLER 1983 CARNEGIE HALL!!!

What?

"That green dress!" Clara's eyes glowed with excitement. She clicked the icon for full screen. "A fait accompli."

Andy did not know what to do but watch the video as it autoplayed. The recording was fuzzy and weirdly colored, like everything else from the eighties. An orchestra was already on stage. A massive, black grand piano was front and center.

"Oh!" Clara unmuted the sound.

Andy heard soft murmurs from the crowd.

Clara said, "This was my favorite part. I always peeked out to feel their mood."

For some reason, Andy held her breath.

The audience had gone silent.

A very thin woman in a dark green evening gown walked out of the wings.

"So elegant," Clara murmured, but Andy barely registered the comment.

The woman crossing the stage was young-looking, maybe eighteen, and obviously uncomfortable walking in such dressy shoes. Her hair was bleached almost white, permed within an inch of its life. The camera swept to the audience. They were giving her a standing ovation before she even turned to look at them.

The camera zoomed in on the woman's face.

Andy felt her stomach clench.

Laura.

In the video, her mother performed a slight bow. She looked so cool as she stared into the faces of thousands of people. Andy had seen that look before on other performers' faces. Absolute certainty. She had always loved watching an actor's transformation from the wings, had been in awe that they could walk out in front of all of those judgmental strangers and so believably pretend to be someone else.

Like her mother had pretended for all of Andy's life.

The worst type of bullshit.

358

The cheering started to die down as Jinx Queller sat down in front of the piano.

She nodded to the conductor.

The conductor raised his hands.

The audience abruptly silenced.

Clara turned up the volume as loud as it would go.

Violins strummed. The low vibration tickled her eardrums. Then the tempo bounced, then calmed, then bounced again.

Andy didn't know music, especially classical. Laura never listened to it at home. The Red Hot Chili Peppers. Heart. Nirvana. Those were the groups that Laura played on the radio when she was driving around town or doing chores or working on patient reports. She knew the words to "Mr. Brightside" before anyone else did. She had downloaded "Lemonade" the night it dropped. Her eclectic taste made her the cool mom, the mom that everyone could talk to because she wouldn't judge you.

Because she had played Carnegie Hall and she knew what the fuck she was talking about.

In the video, Jinx Queller was still waiting at the piano, hands resting in her lap, eyes straight ahead. Other instruments had joined the violins. Andy didn't know which ones because her mother had never taught her about music. She had discouraged Andy from joining the band, winced every time Andy picked up the cymbals.

Flutes. Andy could see the guys in front pursing their lips.

Bows moved. Oboe. Cello. Horns.

Jinx Queller still patiently awaited her turn at the grand piano.

Andy pressed her palm to her stomach as if to calm it. She was sick with tension for the woman in the video.

Her mother.

This stranger.

What was Jinx Queller thinking while she waited? Was she wondering how her life would turn out? Did she know that she would one day have a daughter? Did she know that she had only four years left before Andy came along and somehow took her away from this amazing life?

359

At 2:22, her mother finally raised her hands.

There was an appreciable tension before her fingers lightly touched the keys.

Soft at first, just a few notes, a slow, lazy progression.

The violins came back in, then her hands moved faster, floating up and down the keyboard, bringing out the most beautiful sound that Andy had ever heard.

Flowing. Lush. Rich. Exuberant.

There weren't enough adjectives in the world to describe what Jinx Queller coaxed from the piano.

Swelling—that's what Andy felt. A swelling in her heart.

Pride. Joy. Confusion. Euphoria.

Andy's emotions matched the look on her mother's face as the music went from solemn to dramatic to thrilling, then back again. Every note seemed to be reflected in Jane's expression, her eyebrows lifting, her eyes closing, her lips curled up in pleasure. She was absolutely enraptured. Confidence radiated off the grainy video like rays from the sun. There was a smile on her mother's lips, but it was a secret smile that Andy had never seen before. Jinx Queller, still so impossibly young, had the look of a woman who was exactly where she was meant to be.

Not in Belle Isle. Not at a parent–teacher conference or on the couch in her office working with a patient, but on stage, holding the world in the palm of her hand.

Andy wiped her eyes. She could not stop crying. She did not understand how her mother had not cried every day for the rest of her life.

How could anyone walk away from something so magical?

Andy sat completely transfixed for the entire length of the video. She could not take her eyes off the screen. Sometimes her mother's hands flicked up and down the length of the piano, other times they seemed to be on top of each other, the fingers moving independently across the white and black keys in a way that reminded Andy of Laura kneading dough in the kitchen.

The smile never left her face right up until the ebullient last notes.

Then it was over.

Her hands floated to her lap.

The audience went crazy. They were on their feet. The clapping turned into a solid wall of sound, more like the constant shush of a summer rain.

Jinx Queller stayed seated, hands in her lap, looking down at the keys. Her breath was heavy from physical exertion. Her shoulders had rolled in. She started nodding. She seemed to be taking a moment with the piano, with herself, to absorb the sensation of absolute perfection.

She nodded once more. She stood up. She shook the conductor's hand. She waved to the orchestra. They were already standing, saluting her with their bows, furiously clapping their hands.

She turned to the audience and the cheering swelled. She bowed stage left, then right, then center. She smiled—a different smile, not so confident, not so joyful—and walked off the stage.

That was it.

Andy closed the laptop before the next video could play.

She looked up at the window behind the couch. The sun was bright against the blue sky. Tears dripped down into the collar of her shirt. She tried to think of a word to describe how she was feeling—

Astonished? Bewildered? Overcome? Dumbfounded?

Laura had been the one thing that Andy had wanted to be close to all of her life.

A star.

She studied her own hands. She had normal fingers—not too long or thin. When Laura was sick and unable to take care of herself, Andy had washed her mother's hands, put lotion on them, rubbed them, held them. But what did they really look like? They had to be graceful, enchanted, imbued with an otherworldly sort of grace. Andy should have felt sparks when she massaged them, or spellbound, or—*something*.

Yet they were the same normal hands that had waved for Andy to hurry up or she'd be late for school. Dug soil in the

361

garden when it was time to plant spring flowers. Wrapped around the back of Gordon's neck when they danced. Pointed at Andy in fury when she did something wrong.

Why?

Andy blinked, trying to clear the tears from her eyes. Clara had disappeared. Maybe she hadn't been able to handle Andy's grief, or the perceived pain that Jane Queller experienced when she watched her younger self playing. The two women had clearly discussed the performance before.

That green dress!

Andy reached into her back pocket for the burner phone.

She dialed her mother's number.

She listened to the phone ring.

She closed her eyes against the sunlight, imagining Laura in the kitchen. Walking over to her phone where it was charging on the counter. Seeing the unfamiliar number on the screen. Trying to decide whether or not to answer it. Was it a robocall? A new client?

"Hello?" Laura said.

The sound of her voice cracked Andy open. She had longed for nearly a week to have her mother call, to hear the words that it was safe to come back home, but now that she was on the phone, Andy was incapable of doing anything but crying.

"Hello?" Laura repeated. Then, because she had gotten similar calls before, "Andrea?"

Andy lost what little shit she had managed to keep together. She leaned over her knees, head in her hand, trying not to wail again.

"Andrea, why are you calling me?" Laura's tone was clipped. "What's wrong? What happened?"

Andy opened her mouth, but only to breathe.

"Andrea, please," Laura said. "I need you to acknowledge that you can hear me." She waited. "Andy—"

"Who are you?"

Laura did not make a sound. Seconds passed, then what felt like a full minute.

Andy looked at the screen, wondering if they had been disconnected. She pressed the phone back to her ear. She finally heard the gentle slap of waves from the beach. Laura had walked outside. She was on the back porch.

"You lied to me," Andy said.

Nothing.

"My birthday. Where I was born. Where we lived. That fake picture of my fake grandparents. Do you even know who my father is?"

Laura still said nothing.

"You used to be somebody, Mom. I saw it online. You were on stage at-at-at Carnegie Hall. People were worshipping you. It must've taken years to get that good. All of your life. You were somebody, and you walked away from it."

"You're wrong," Laura finally said. There was no emotion in her tone, just a cold flatness. "I'm nobody, and that's exactly who I want to be."

Andy pressed her fingers into her eyes. She couldn't take any more of these fucking riddles. Her head was going to explode.

Laura asked, "Where are you?"

"I'm nowhere."

Andy wanted to close the phone, to give Laura the biggest silent *fuck you* she could, but the moment was too desperate for hollow gestures.

She asked Laura, "Are you even my real mother?"

"Of course I am. I was in labor for sixteen hours. The doctors thought they were going to lose both of us. But they didn't. We didn't. We survived."

Andy heard a car pulling into the driveway.

Fuck.

"An-Andrea," Laura struggled to get out her name. "Where are you? I need to know you're safe."

Andy knelt on the couch and looked out the window. Edwin Van Wees with his stupid handlebar mustache. He saw Mike's truck and practically fell out of his car as he scrambled toward the front door.

"Clara!" he yelled. "Clara, where—"

Clara answered, but Andy couldn't make out the words.

Laura must have heard something. She asked, "Where are you?"

Andy listened to heavy boots pounding down the hallway.

"Andrea," Laura said, her tone clipped. "This is deadly serious. You need to tell me—"

"Who the fuck are you?" Edwin demanded.

Andy turned around.

"Shit," Edwin muttered. "Andrea."

"Is that—" Laura said, but Andy pressed the phone to her chest.

She asked the man, "How do you know me?"

"Come away from the window." Edwin motioned Andy out of the office. "You can't be here. You need to go. Now."

Andy didn't move. "Tell me how you know me."

Edwin saw the phone in her hand. "Who are you talking to?"

When Andy didn't answer, he wrenched the phone out of her hand and put it to his ear.

He said, "Who is—fuck." Edwin turned his back to Andy, telling Laura, "No, I have no idea what Clara told her. You know she's been unwell." He started nodding, listening. "I didn't tell her—no. Clara doesn't know about that. It's privileged information. I would never—" He stopped again. "Laura, you need to calm down. No one knows where it is except for me."

They knew each other. They were arguing the way old friends argued. Edwin had known Andy by sight. Clara had thought she was Jane, who was really Laura . . .

Andy's teeth had started to chatter. She could hear them clicking inside of her head. She rubbed her arms with her hands. She felt cold, almost frozen.

"Laura, I—" Edwin leaned down his head and looked out the window. "Listen, you just need to trust me. You know I would never—" He turned around and looked at Andy. She watched his anger soften into something else. He smiled at her the same way Gordon smiled at her when she fucked up but he still wanted her to know that he loved her.

Why was a man she had never met looking at her like her father?

Edwin said, "I will, Laura. I promise I'll—"

There was a loud *crack*.

Then another.

Then another.

Andy was on the floor, the same as the last time she had heard a sudden burst of gunfire.

Everything was exactly the same.

Glass broke. Papers started to fly. The air filled with debris.

Edwin took the brunt of the bullets, his arms jerking up, his skull almost vaporizing, bone and chunks of his hair splattering against the couch, the walls, the ceiling.

Andy was flat on her belly, hands covering her head, when she heard the nauseating *thunk* of his body hitting the floor.

She looked at his face. Nothing but a dark hole with white shards of skull stared back. His mustache was still curled up at the ends, held in place with a thick wax.

Andy tasted blood in her mouth. Her heart felt like it was beating inside of her eardrums. She thought that she had lost her hearing, but there was nothing to hear.

The shooter had stopped.

Andy scanned the room for the burner phone. She saw it fifteen feet away in the hall. She had no idea if it was still working, but she heard her mother's voice as clear as if she was in the room—

I need you to run, darling. He can't reload fast enough to hurt you.

Andy tried to stand. She could barely get to her knees before throwing up from the pain. The McDonald's milkshake was pink with blood. Every time she heaved, it felt like fire was ripping down her left side.

Footsteps. Outside. Getting closer.

Andy forced herself up onto her hands and knees. She crawled toward the door, her palms digging into broken glass, her knees sliding across the floor. She made it as far as the hallway before the searing pain made her stop. She fell over onto her hip. She pushed herself up to sitting. Pressed her back to the wall. Her skull was filled with a high-pitched whining noise. Shards of glass porcupined from her bare arms.

Andy listened.

She heard a strange sound from the other side of the house. *Click-click-click-click.*

The cylinder spinning in the revolver?

She looked at the burner phone. The screen had been shattered.

There was nowhere to go. Nothing to do but wait.

Andy reached down to her side. Her shirt was soaked with blood. Her fingers found a tiny hole in the material.

Then the tip of her finger found another hole in her skin.

She had been shot.

August 2, 1986

14

Jane felt the ivory keys of the Steinway Concert Grand soften beneath the tips of her fingers. The stage lights warmed the right side of her body. She allowed herself a furtive glance at the audience, picked out a few of their faces under the lights.

Rhapsodic.

Carnegie had sold out within one day of the tickets going on sale. Over two thousand seats. Jane was the youngest woman ever to take center stage. The hall's acoustics were remarkable. The reverb poured like honey into her ears, bending and elongating each note. The Steinway gave Jane more than she had dared hope for; the key action was loose enough to bring a nuanced delicacy that bathed the room in an almost ethereal wave of sound. She felt like a wizard pulling off the most wondrous trick. Every keystroke was perfect. The orchestra was perfect. The audience was perfect. She lowered her gaze past the lights, taking in the front row.

Jasper, Annette, Andrew, Martin—
Nick.

He was clapping his hands. Grinning with pride.

Jane missed a note, then another, then she was playing along to the staccato of Nick's hands like she had not done since Martin first sat her down on the bench and told her to play. The noise sharpened as Nick's clapping amplified through the hall. Jane had to cover her ears. The music stopped. Nick's mouth twisted into a sneer. He kept clapping and clapping. Blood began to seep from his hands, down his arms, into his lap. He clapped harder. Louder. Blood splattered onto his white shirt, onto Andrew, her father, the stage.

Jane opened her eyes.

The room was dark. Confusion and fear mixed to bring her heart into her throat. Slowly, Jane's senses came back to her. She was lying in bed. She pulled away the afghan covering her body. She recognized the blue color.

The farmhouse.

She sat up so fast that she was almost knocked back by a wave of dizziness. She fumbled for the switch on the lamp.

A syringe and vial were on the table.

Morphine.

The syringe was still capped, but the bottle was almost empty.

Panicked, Jane checked her arms, legs, feet for needle marks.

Nothing, but what was she afraid of? That Nick had drugged her? That he had somehow infected her with Andrew's tainted blood?

Her hand went to her neck. Nick had strangled her. She could still remember those last moments in the bathroom as she desperately gasped for air. Her throat pulsed beneath her fingers. The skin was tender. Jane moved her hand lower. The round swell of her belly filled her palm. Slowly, she inched down farther and checked between her legs for the tell-tale spots of blood. When she pulled back her hand, it was clean. Relief nearly took her breath away.

Nick had not beaten another child out of her body.

This time, at least for this moment, they were safe.

Jane found her socks on the floor, tugged on her boots. She walked over to the large window across from the bed and drew back the curtains. Darkness. Her eyes picked out the silhouette of the van parked in front of the barn, but the other two cars were gone.

She listened to the house.

There were low voices, at least two people talking, on the far side of the house. Chopping sounds. Pots and pans clattering.

Jane leaned over to buckle her boots. She had a moment where she remembered doing the same thing days ago. Before they walked downstairs to speak with agents Barlow and Danberry. Before they had left in Jasper's Porsche without realizing that they would never go back. Before Nick had made Jane choose between him or her brother.

These anarchist groups think they're doing the right thing, right up until they end up in prison or flat on their backs in the morgue.

The door opened.

Jane didn't know who she expected to see. Certainly not Paula, who barked, "Wait in the living room."

"Where's Andrew?"

"He went for a run. Where the fuck do you think?" Paula stalked off, her footsteps like two hammers hitting the floor.

Jane knew she should look for Andrew, but she had to compose herself before she spoke with her brother. The last hours or days of his life should not be filled with recriminations.

She went across the hall to the bathroom. She used the toilet, praying that she did not feel the sharp pain, see the spots of blood.

Jane looked down at the bowl.

Nothing.

The tub drew her attention. She had not fully bathed in almost four days. Her skin felt waxen, but the thought of getting undressed and finding soap and locating towels was too much. She flushed the toilet. Her eyes avoided the mirror as she washed her hands, then her face, with warm water. She looked for a rag and wiped under her arms and between her legs. She felt another wave of relief when she saw there was still no blood.

Were you stupid enough to think I'd let you keep it?

Jane walked into the living room. She looked for a telephone, but there wasn't one. Calling Jasper was likely pointless, anyway. All of the family phone lines would be tapped. Even if Jasper

371

was inclined to help, his hands would be tied. Jane was completely on her own now.

She had made her choice.

From the sound of it, someone had rolled the TV into the kitchen. She blinked, and time shifted back. Nick was on his knees in front of the set, adjusting the volume, insisting they all watch their crimes being cataloged for the nation. The group had arrayed themselves around him like blades on a fan. Clara on the floor taking in the frenetic energy. Edwin solemn and watchful. Paula beaming at Nick like he was the second coming of Christ. Jane standing there, dazed from the news that Clara had given her.

Even then, Jane had stayed in the room rather than finding Andrew because she still did not want to let Nick down. None of them did. That was the biggest fear they all had—not that they would get caught, or die, or be thrown into prison for the rest of their lives, but that they would disappoint Nick.

She knew that now there would be a reckoning for her defiance. Nick had left her here with Paula for a reason.

Jane rested her hand on the swinging door to the kitchen and listened.

She heard a knife blade striking a cutting board. The murmur of a television program. Her own breathing.

She pushed open the door. The kitchen was small and cramped, the table wedged against the end of the laminate countertop. Still, it had its charms. The metal cabinets were painted a cheery yellow. The appliances were all new.

Andrew was sitting at the table.

Jane felt her heart stir at the sight of him. He was here. He was still alive, though the smile he gave her was weak.

He motioned for Jane to turn down the television. She twisted the knob. Her eyes stayed on his.

Did he know what Nick had done to Jane in the bathroom?

Paula said, "I told you to wait in there." She threw seasoning into a pot on the stove. "Hey, Dumb Bitch, I said—"

Jane gave her the finger as she sat down with her back to Paula.

Andrew chuckled. The metal box was open in front of him. Folders were spread out on the table. The tiny key was by his elbow. A large envelope was addressed to the *Los Angeles Times*. He was doing his part for Nick. Even at death's door, still the loyal trooper.

Jane worked to keep the sorrow out of her expression. Impossibly, he looked even more pale. His eyes could have been lined in red crayon. His lips were starting to turn blue. Every breath was like a saw grinding back and forth across a piece of wet wood. He should be resting comfortably in a hospital, not struggling to stay upright in a hard wooden chair.

She said, "You're dying."

"But you're not," he said. "Nick took the ELISA test last month. He's clean. You know he's terrified of needles. And the other way—he's never been into that."

Jane felt a cold sweat break out. The thought had not even crossed her mind, but now that it was there, she felt sickened by the realization that, even if Nick had been infected, he probably would've never told her. They would've kept making love and Jane would've kept growing their child and she would've not found out the truth until it came from a doctor's mouth.

Or a medical examiner's.

"You'll be okay," Andrew said. "I promise."

Now was not the time to call her brother a liar. "What about Ellis-Anne?"

"She's clean," Andrew said. "I told her to get tested as soon as . . ." He let his voice trail off. "She wanted to stay with me. Can you believe that? I couldn't let her do it. It wasn't fair. And we had all this going on, so . . ." His voice trailed off again in a long sigh. "Barlow, the FBI agent. He told me they talked to her. I know she must've been afraid. I regret—well, I regret a lot of things."

Jane did not want him to dwell on regrets. She reached for his hands. They felt heavy, weighted somehow by what was to come. His shirt collar was open. She could see the purplish lesions on his chest.

He couldn't stay here in this too-warm house with less than half a thimbleful of morphine. She wouldn't allow it.

"What is it?" he asked.

"I love you."

Andrew was never one to return the sentiment, but he squeezed her hands, smiled again, so that she knew he felt the same.

Paula mumbled, "Christ."

Jane turned to glare at her. She had started cutting up a tomato. The knife was dull. The skin tore like paper.

Paula asked, "You two into incest now?"

Jane turned back around.

Andrew told her, "I'm going to rest for a while. Okay?"

She nodded. They would stand a better chance of leaving if Andrew was not involved in the negotiation.

"Get a scarf," Paula said. "Keep your neck warm. It helps the cough."

Andrew raised a skeptical eyebrow at Jane as he tried to stand. He shrugged off her offer of help. "I'm not that far gone."

She watched him lurch toward the swinging door. His shirt was soaked with sweat. The back of his hair was damp. Jane turned away from the door only when it stopped swinging.

She took Andrew's seat parallel to Paula because she did not want her back to the woman. She looked down at the files on the table. These were the two things that Nick had valued most: Jasper's signature attesting to his part in the fraud. The Polaroids with their red rubber band.

Paula said, "I know what you're thinking, and you're not going anywhere."

Jane had thought that she was incapable of feeling any more emotions, but she had never abhorred Paula so much as she did in this moment. "I just want to take him to the hospital."

"And let the pigs know where we are?" Paula huffed out a laugh. "You might as well take off your fancy boots, 'cause you ain't goin' anywhere."

Jane turned away from her, clasped her hands together on the table.

"Hey, Dumb Bitch." Paula lifted up her shirt and showed Jane the handgun tucked into the waist of her jeans. "Don't get any ideas. I'd love to shoot six new holes into that asshole you call a face."

Jane looked at the clock on the wall. Ten in the evening. The Chicago team would already be in the city. Nick was on his way to New York. She had to find a way out of here.

She asked, "Where are Clara and Edwin?"

"Selden and Tucker are in position."

Edwin's apartment in the city. He was supposed to wait for phone calls in case anyone was arrested.

Jane said, "Northwestern can't be far from here. They're a teaching hospital. They'll know how to take care of—"

"Northwestern is straight down I-88, about forty-five minutes away, but it might as well be on the moon because you're not fucking going anywhere and neither is he." Paula rested her hand on her hip. "Look, bitch, they can't do anything for him. You did your rich girl slumming at the AIDS ward. You know how this story ends. The prince doesn't ride again. Your brother is going to die. As in tonight. He's not going to see the sunrise."

Hearing her fears confirmed brought a lump into Jane's throat. "The doctors can make him comfortable."

"Nick left a vial of morphine for that."

"It's almost empty."

"That's all we could find on short notice, and we're lucky we could get that. It'll probably be enough, and if it's not—" She shrugged her shoulder. "Nothing we can do about it."

Jane thought again of Ben Mitchell, one of the first young men she'd met on the AIDS ward. He'd been desperate to go back to Wyoming to see his parents before he died. They had finally relented, and the last eight minutes of Ben's life had been spent in terror as he suffocated on his own fluids because the rural hospital staff were too frightened to stick a tube down his throat to help him breathe.

Jane knew the panic that came from not being able to breathe. Nick had strangled her before. Once during sex. Once the last time she was pregnant. Once a few hours ago, when he was threatening to kill her. No matter how many times it happened, there was no way to prepare for that terrifying sensation of not being able to pull air into your lungs. The way her heart felt like it was filling with blood. The searing pain from her muscles cramping. The burning in her lungs. The numbness in her hands and feet as the body gave up on everything but staying alive.

Jane could not let her brother experience that terror. Not for one minute, certainly not for eight.

She told Paula, "The doctors can knock him out so that he's unconscious for the worst of it."

"Maybe he wants to be conscious," she said. "Maybe he wants to feel it."

"You sound like Nick."

"I'll take that as a compliment."

"Don't," Jane said. "It's meant to make you think about what you're doing, because it's wrong. All of this is wrong."

"The concept of *right* and *wrong* are patriarchal constructs to control the populace."

Jane turned her head to look at the woman. "You can't be serious."

"You're too fucking blind to see it. At least now you are." Paula had picked up a knife. She chopped brutally at a bundle of carrots. "I heard you with him in the van. All that lovey-dovey bullshit, telling Nick how wonderful he is, how much you love him, how you believe in what we're doing, and then you get here and suddenly you're abandoning him."

"Did you hear him in the bathroom, strangling me into unconsciousness?"

"I could happily hear that every day for the rest of my life."

A piece of carrot landed on the floor beside Jane.

If Jane stood up, if she took one small step, she could close the distance between them. She could grab the knife from Paula's hand, wrench the gun from her waist.

And then what?

376

Could Jane kill her? There was a difference between despising someone and murdering them.

Paula said, "It happened before Berlin, right?" She motioned down at her own stomach with the knife. "I thought you were getting fat, but—" She blew out air between her lips. "No such luck."

Jane looked down at her stomach. She had been so nervous about telling people about the baby, but everyone seemed to have figured it out on their own.

Paula said, "You don't deserve to carry his child."

Jane watched the knife move up and down. Paula wasn't paying attention to Jane.

Stand up, take one step, grab the knife—

"If it was up to me, I'd cut it out of you." Paula pointed the blade at Jane. "Want me to?"

Jane tried to pretend that the threat had not sent an arrow into her heart. She had to think about her child. This wasn't just about Andrew. If she attacked Paula and failed, then she could lose her baby before she even had the chance to hold it.

"That's what I thought." Paula turned back to the carrots with a grin on her face.

Jane tucked her chin to her chest. She had never been good at confrontation. Her way was to remain silent and hope that the explosion would pass. That was what she had always done with her father. That's what she did with Nick.

She looked at the bundle of Polaroids on the table. The photo on top showed the deep gash in her leg. Jane touched her leg in that same spot now, feeling the ridge of the pink scar.

Bite mark.

She remembered clearly when the pictures had been taken. Jane and Nick were staying in Palm Springs while Jane's cuts and bruises healed. Nick had gone out for lunch and returned with the camera and instant film.

I'm sorry, my darling, I know you're hurting, but I've just had the best idea.

Back home, Andrew had been wavering about the plan. There

were good reasons. Andrew didn't want Laura Juneau to go to prison for attacking Martin with the red dye packs. He was especially conflicted about hurting Martin's pride. Despite the beatings and the disappointments and even the awful things that Nick had uncovered while working at Queller Healthcare, Andrew still had a sliver of love for their father.

Then, when they returned from Palm Springs, Nick had shown him the Polaroids.

Look at what your father did to your sister. We have to make him pay for this. Martin Queller has to pay for all of his sins.

Nick had assumed that Jane would play along, and why wouldn't she? Why wouldn't she keep from her brother the fact that it was Nick who had beaten her face, who had ripped open her skin with his teeth, who had pummeled her stomach until blood had poured from between her legs and their baby was gone?

Why wouldn't she?

Jane dropped the Polaroids into the metal box. She wiped her sweaty hands on her legs. She thought about sitting with Agent Danberry in the backyard. In less than a week, the cops had seen right through Nick.

He had everybody in his circle convinced he was smarter than he actually was. More clever than he was.

Paula said, "I used to be so jealous of you. Did you know that?"

Jane stacked the files and put them back in the box. "No shit."

"Yeah, well." Paula had moved on to chopping a potato. She was using a meat cleaver. "The first time I met you, I thought, 'What's that snooty bitch doing here? Why does she want to change shit when all the shit in the world benefits her?'"

Jane didn't have an answer anymore. She had hated her father. That's where it had started. Martin had raped her when she was a child, beaten her throughout her teenage years, terrorized her into her twenties, and Nick had given Jane a way to make it stop. Not for herself, but for other people. For Robert Juneau.

For Andrew. For all the other patients who had been hurt. Jane was not strong enough to pull away from Martin for her own sake, so Nick had contrived a plan to wrench Martin away from Jane.

She put her hand to her mouth. She wanted to laugh, because she had just now realized that Nick had done the same with Andrew, using the Polaroids to weaponize his anger on behalf of Jane.

They were like yo-yos he could snap back with a flick of his wrist.

Paula said, "Andy has everything, too, but he's so conflicted about it, you know? He struggles with it." She used her teeth to tear the plastic wrap around a bundle of celery. "You never seemed to struggle, but I guess that's the point with gals like you, right? All the right schools and the right clothes and the right hair. They Pygmalion your skinny white asses from birth so you don't ever seem to struggle with anything. You know what forks to use, and who painted what Mona Lisa and blah-dee-duh-blah. But underneath, you're just—" She clenched her hands into tight fists. "So fucking angry."

Jane had never thought of herself as angry, but she understood now that it had lived just beneath the fear all along. "Rage is a luxury."

"Rage is a fucking narcotic." Paula laughed as she attacked the celery with her knife. "That's why Nick is so good for me. He helped me turn my rage into power."

Jane felt her eyebrows go up. "You're babysitting his girlfriend while he's out planting bombs."

"Shut your fucking mouth." Paula threw the knife on the counter. "You think you're so fucking clever? You think you're better than me?" When Jane didn't answer, she demanded, "Look at me, Dumb Bitch. Say that to my face. Say you're better than me. I fucking dare you."

Jane turned sideways in the chair so that she was facing Paula. "Did Nick ever fuck you?"

Paula's jaw dropped. She was evidently thrown by the question.

379

Jane wasn't sure where it had come from, but now, she pressed on. "It's all right if he did. I'm pretty sure he fucked Clara." Jane laughed, because she could see it so clearly now. "He's always been drawn to fragile, famous women. And fragile, famous women are always drawn to guys like Nick."

"That's bullshit."

Jane found herself puzzled that the thought of Nick and Clara together elicited not even a flicker of jealousy. Why was Jane so okay with it? Why was all of her envy directed at Clara, who had somehow managed to get what she wanted out of Nick without losing herself completely?

Jane told Paula, "I bet he didn't fuck you." She could tell from Paula's pained expression that this was true. "It's not that he wouldn't fuck you if he needed to, but you're so brazenly desperate for any show of kindness. Not giving it to you was much more effective than giving it to you. Right? And it provides your drama with a villain—me—because I'm the only thing keeping him from being with you."

Paula's lower lip started to tremble. "Shut up."

"One of the FBI agents called it days ago. He said that Nick was just another con man running another cult so he could bed the pretty girls and play God with all the boys."

"I said shut your goddamn mouth." The bluster had gone out of her tone. She pressed her palms to the edge of the counter. Tears dripped down her cheeks. She kept shaking her head. "You don't know. You don't know anything about us."

Jane closed the lid on the metal box. There was a tiny handle on the side, too small for Andrew's hand, but Jane's fingers easily slid through the loop.

She stood up from the table.

Paula reached for the knife as she started to turn.

Jane took a step forward. She swung the box at Paula's head.

Pop.

Like a toy gun going off.

Paula's mouth dropped open.

The knife slipped from her hand.

She crumpled to the floor.

Jane leaned over Paula and found the steady pulse in her neck. She pressed open her eyelids. There was a milky white in her left eye, but the pupil in her right eye dilated in the harsh overhead light.

Jane pushed through the swinging door, the box tucked under her arm. She walked through the living room and down the hall. Andrew was sleeping in the bedroom. The morphine bottle was empty. She shook him, saying, "Andy. Andy, wake up."

He turned toward her voice, a glassy look in his eyes. "What is it?"

"Didn't you hear the phone?" Jane could only think of one lie that would move him. "Nick called. We have to get out of here."

"Where's—" He struggled to sit up. "Where's Paula?"

"She took off. There was another car parked on the road." Jane struggled to get him up. "I've got the box. We have to go, Andrew. Now. Nick said we had to get out."

He tried to stand. Jane had to lift him to his feet. He was so thin that holding him up was almost effortless.

He asked, "Where are we going?"

"We have to hurry." Jane almost dropped the metal box as she guided him down the hall, out the front door. The walk to the van seemed to take hours. She should've gagged Paula. Tied her up. How long before she woke up and started screaming? Would Andrew leave if he thought they were betraying Nick and the plan?

Jane couldn't risk it.

"Come on," she begged her brother. "Keep moving. You can sleep in the van, all right?"

"Yeah," was all he could manage between raspy breaths.

Jane had to drag him the last few yards. She leaned him against the van, her knee keeping his knees from bending, so that she could open the door. She was buckling him into the seat when she remembered—

The keys.

"Stay here."

Jane ran back to the house. She pushed through the door into the kitchen. Paula was on her hands and knees, head shaking like a dog.

Without thinking, Jane kicked her in the face.

Paula *oofed* out a sound, then collapsed flat to the floor.

Jane patted Paula's pockets until she found the keys. She was halfway to the van when she remembered the gun in Paula's waistband. She could go back and get it, but what was the point? It was better to leave than risk giving Paula another chance to stop them.

"Jay—" Andrew watched her climb behind the wheel. "How did . . . how did they find . . ."

"Selden," she told him. "Clara. She backed out. She changed her mind. Nick said we have to hurry." Jane threw the van into reverse. She pressed the gas pedal to the floor as she drove back up the driveway. She checked the rearview mirror. All she saw was dust. Her heart kept pounding into her throat as she drove down the winding roads outside the farm. It wasn't until they'd finally reached the interstate that Jane felt her breathing return to normal. She looked over at Andrew. His head was lolling to the side. She counted his arduous breaths, the painful in and out as he strained for air.

For the first time in almost two years, Jane felt at peace. An eerie calmness had taken over. This was the right thing to do. After giving herself over to Nick's insanity for so long, she was finally lucid again.

Jane had been to Northwestern Hospital once before. She was in the middle of a tour and suffering from an earache. Pechenikov had driven her to the emergency room. He had fussed around her, telling the nurses that Jane was the most important patient that would ever care for. Jane had rolled her eyes at the praise but been secretly pleased to be handled with such care. She had loved Pechenikov so much, not just because he was a teacher, but because he was a decent and loving man.

Which was likely why Nick had made Jane leave him.

Why did you give it up?

Because my boyfriend was jealous of a seventy-year-old homosexual.

An ambulance whizzed by on Jane's right. She followed it up the exit. She saw the Northwestern Memorial Hospital sign glowing in the distance.

"Jane?" The ambulance siren had woken Andrew. "What are you doing?"

"Nick told me to take you to the hospital." She pushed up the turn signal, waited for the light.

"Jane—" Andrew started coughing. He covered his mouth with both hands.

"I'm just doing what Nick told me to do," she lied. Her voice was shaking. She had to keep strong. They were so close. "He made me promise, Andrew. Do you want me to break my promise to Nick?"

"You don't—" he had to stop to catch his breath. "I know what you're—that Nick didn't—"

Jane looked at her brother. He reached out, his fingers gently touching her neck.

She glanced into the mirror, saw the bruises from Nick's hands strangling her. Andrew knew what had happened in the bathroom, that Jane had chosen to stay with him.

She realized now that Nick must have given Andrew the same ultimatum. Andrew had not driven to New York with Nick. He had stayed at the farmhouse with Jane.

She told her brother, "We're quite a pair, aren't we?"

He closed his eyes. "We can't," he said. "Our faces—on the news—the police."

"It doesn't matter." Jane mumbled a curse at the red light, then another at herself. The van was the only vehicle in sight. It was the middle of the night and she was obeying traffic laws.

She pressed the gas and blew through the light.

"Jane—" Andrew broke off for another coughing fit. "Y-you can't do this. They'll catch you."

Jane took another right, followed another blue sign with a white H on it.

"Please." He rubbed his face with his hands, something he used to do when he was a boy and things got too frustrating for him to handle.

Jane coasted through another red light. She was on autopilot now. Everything inside of her was numb again. She was a machine as much as the van, a mode of conveyance that would take her brother to the hospital so he could die peacefully in his sleep.

Andrew tried, "Please. Listen to—" Another coughing fit took hold. There was no rattle, just a straining noise, as if he was trying to suck air through a reed.

She said, "Try to save your breath."

"Jane," he repeated, his voice no more than a whisper. "If you leave me, you have to leave me. You can't let them catch you. You have to—" His words broke off into more coughing. He looked down at his hand. There was blood.

Jane swallowed back her grief. She was taking him to the hospital. They would put a tube down his throat to help him breathe. They would give him drugs to help him sleep. This was likely the last conversation they would ever have.

She told him, "I'm sorry, Andy. I love you."

His eyes were watering. Tears slid down his face. "I know that you love me. Even when you hated me, I know that you loved me."

"I never hated you."

"I forgive you, but—" He coughed. "Forgive me, too. Okay?"

Jane pushed the van to go faster. "There's nothing to forgive you for."

"I knew, Janey. I knew who he was. What he was. It's my—" he wheezed. "Fault. My fault. I'm so . . ."

Jane looked at him, but his eyes were closed. His head tilted back and forth with the motion of the van.

"Andrew?"

"I knew," he mumbled. "I knew."

She banked a hard left. Her heart shook at the sight of the NORTHWESTERN sign outside of the emergency room.

"Andy?" Jane panicked. She couldn't hear him breathing anymore. She held onto his hand. His flesh was like ice. "We're almost there, my darling. Just hang on."

His eyelids fluttered open. "Trade—" He choked a cough. "Trade him."

"Andy, don't try to speak." The hospital sign was getting closer. "We're almost there. Just hang on, my darling. Hang on for just a moment more."

"Trade all . . ." Andrew's eyelids fluttered again. His chin dropped to his chest. Only the whistling sound of air being sucked through his teeth told her that he was still alive.

The hospital.

Jane almost lost control of the wheel when the tires bumped over a curb. The van fishtailed. She somehow managed to screech to a halt in front of the entrance to the ER. Two orderlies were smoking on a nearby bench.

"Help!" Jane jumped out of the van. "Help my brother. Please!"

The men were already off the bench. One ran back into the hospital. The other opened the van door.

"He has—" Jane's voice caught. "He's infected with—"

"I gotcha." The man wrapped his arms around Andrew's shoulders as he helped him out of the van. "Come on, buddy. We're gonna take good care of you."

Jane's tears, long dried, started to flow again.

"You're all right," the man told Andrew. He sounded so kind that she wanted to fall to the ground and kiss his feet. He asked Andrew, "Can you walk? Let's go to this bench and—"

"Where—" Andrew was looking for Jane.

"I'm right here, my darling." She put her hand to his face. She pressed her lips to his forehead. His hand reached out. He was touching the round swell of her stomach.

"Trade . . ." he whispered, ". . . all of them."

The other orderly ran back through the door with a gurney.

The two men lifted Andrew off his feet. He was so light that they barely had to strain to get him onto the gurney. Andrew turned his head, looking for Jane.

He said, "I love you."

The men started to roll the gurney inside. Andrew kept his eyes on Jane for as long as he could.

The doors closed.

She watched through the glass as Andrew was rolled into the back of the emergency room. The double doors swung open. Nurses and doctors swarmed around him. The doors closed again, and he was gone.

They'll catch you.

Jane breathed in the cool night air. No one rushed out of the hospital with a gun, telling her to get down on the ground. None of the nurses were on the phone behind the desk.

She was safe. Andrew was being taken care of. She could leave now. No one knew where she was. No one could find her unless she wanted to be found.

Jane walked back to the van. She closed the passenger's side door. She climbed back behind the wheel. The engine was still running. She tried to remember everything Andrew had said. Moments before, she had been talking to her brother, and now Jane knew that she would never hear Andrew's voice ever again.

She put the car in gear.

Jane drove aimlessly, passing the marked parking spaces for the emergency room. Passing the parking deck for the hospital, for the university, for the shopping center at the end of the street.

Canada. The forger.

Jane could create a new life for herself and her child. The two hundred and fifty thousand dollars in cash was probably still in the back of the van. The small cooler. The Thermos of water. The box of Slim Jims. The blanket. The futon. Toronto was just over eight hours away. Skirt around the top of Indiana, through Michigan, then into Canada. That had been the plan after Nick's triumphant return from New York. They would stay in the farmhouse for a few weeks during the fallout from the bombings, then drive into Canada, buy more documents from the forger on East Kelly Street, and fly to Switzerland.

Nick had thought of everything.

A horn beeped behind Jane. She startled at the noise. She'd stopped in the middle of the road. Jane looked in the rearview mirror. The man behind her was waving his fist. She waved back an apology, pressing the gas pedal.

The angry driver passed her for no reason other than to prove that he could. Jane drove another few yards, but then she slowed the van and followed a sign toward a long-term parking garage. The temperature inside the van cooled as she spiraled down the ramp. She located a spot between two sedans on the lowest basement level. She backed into the space. She checked to make sure she wasn't being watched. No cameras on the walls. No two-way mirrors.

Nick's precious metal box was on the floor between the seats. Jane tucked it under her arm just as her brother always had. She crouched as she made her way into the back of the van. The padlock hung from the box that was bolted to the floor.

6-12-32.

They all knew the combination.

The cash was still there. The Thermos. The cooler. The box of Slim Jims.

Jane added Nick's box to the stash. She peeled off three hundred dollars, then closed the lid. She spun the lock. She got out of the van. She walked around to the back.

The steel bumper was hollow inside. Jane balanced the key on the rim. Then she walked back up the winding ramp. There was no after-hours parking attendant, just a stack of envelopes and a mail drop. Jane wrote down the space number for the van, then put the three hundred dollars in the envelope, enough for the van to park for one month.

Outside, she followed the cold breeze to Lake Michigan. Her thin blouse whipped in the wind. Jane could remember the first time she'd flown into Milwaukee to play at the Performing Arts

Center. She had thought the plane had overshot its mark and ended up at the Atlantic because, even from twenty thousand feet, she could not see the edge of the massive lake. Pechenikov had told her that you could take the entire island of Great Britain and put it in the lake without the edges touching the sides.

Jane was shaken by a deep and unwelcome sadness. Part of her had thought—had hoped—that one day, she would be able to go back. To performing. To Pechenikov. Not anymore. Her touring days were over. She would probably never fly in an airplane again. She would never tour again. Perform again.

She laughed at a sudden revelation.

The last notes she had played on the piano were the jumpy, glib opening bars to A-ha's "Take On Me."

The hospital's waiting room was packed. Jane became aware of how she must look. Her hair had not been washed in days. She had blood on her clothes. Her nose felt broken. Black bruises had come up around her neck. Probably the familiar pinprick dots of broken blood vessels riddled the whites of her eyes. She could see the questions in the nurses' eyes.

Battered woman? Junkie? Call girl?

Sister was the only title left to her. She found Andrew behind a curtain in the back of the emergency room. They had finally intubated him. Jane was glad that he could breathe, but she understood that she would never, ever hear his voice again. He would never tease her or make a joke about her weight or meet the baby that was growing inside of her.

The only thing that Jane could do for her brother now was hold his hand and listen to the monitor announce the ever-slowing beats of his heart. She held onto him while they wheeled him to the elevator, when they took him to his room in the ICU. She refused to leave his side even after the nurses told her that visitors were not allowed to stay more than twenty minutes at a time.

There were no windows in Andrew's room. The only glass was the window and sliding door that looked onto the nurses'

388

station. Jane had never had track of the time, so she didn't know how long it took for someone—a doctor, an orderly, a nurse—to recognize their faces. The tone of their voices changed. Then a lone policeman appeared outside the closed glass door. He didn't come inside. No one came into Andrew's small room but the ICU nurse, whose previously chatty demeanor was gone. Jane waited for an hour, then another hour, then she lost count. There were no agents from the CIA, NSA, Secret Service, FBI, Interpol. There was no one to stop Jane when she put her head beside Andrew's on the bed.

She put her lips to his ear. How many times had Nick done the same thing to her, put his mouth close, confided in Jane in such a way that made her believe they were the only two people who mattered in the world?

"I'm pregnant," she told her brother, the first time she had said the words aloud to anyone. "And I'm happy. I'm so happy, Andy, that I'm going to have a baby."

Andrew's eyes moved beneath his eyelids, but the nurse had told Jane not to read too much into it. He was in a coma. He would not wake up again. There was no way for Jane to know whether or not her brother knew she was there. But Jane knew she was there, and that was all that mattered.

I will never let anyone hurt you ever again.

"Jinx?"

Her older brother was standing in the doorway. Jane should have guessed that Jasper would eventually find his way here. Her big brother always swooped in to save her. She wanted to stand up and hug him, but she didn't have the strength to do more than slump into the chair. Jasper looked equally incapacitated as he closed the sliding glass door. The cop gave him a nod before walking across the hall to the nurses' station. It was the Air Force uniform, wrinkled but still impressive. Jasper obviously hadn't changed since she'd last seen him in the parlor of the Presidio Heights house.

He turned around, his mouth a clenched straight line. Jane felt sick with guilt. Jasper's skin was ashen. His hair was

389

cowlicked in the back. His tie was askew. He must have come straight from the airport after the four-hour flight from San Francisco.

Four hours in the air. Thirty hours in the van. Twelve hours to New York.

Nick had to be in Brooklyn by now.

Jasper asked, "Are you all right?"

Jane would have wept if she'd had any tears left. She held onto Andrew's hand and reached out to Jasper with the other. "I'm glad you're here."

He held her fingers for a moment before letting them go. He walked back a few steps. He leaned against the wall. She expected him to ask about her part in Martin's murder, but instead, he told Jane, "A bomb went off at the Chicago Mercantile Exchange."

The information sounded strange coming out of his mouth. They had planned it for so long, and now it had actually happened.

Jasper said, "At least one person's dead. Another was critically injured. The cops think they were trying to set the detonator when the bomb went off."

Spinner and Wyman.

He said, "That's the only reason the police aren't swarming all over you right now. Every guy with a badge or a uniform is over there trying to pick through the pieces in case there are more casualties."

Jane held tight to Andrew's hand. His face was slack, his skin the same color as the sheets. She said, "Jasper, Andy is—"

"I know about Andrew." Jasper's tone was flat, indecipherable. He had not once looked at Andrew since he'd walked into the room. "We have to talk. You and I."

Jane knew he was going to ask her about Martin. She looked at Andrew because she did not want to see the hope, then disappointment, then disgust, in Jasper's face.

He said, "Nick is a fraud. His name isn't even Nick."

Jane's head swiveled around.

"That FBI agent—Danberry—he told me that Nick's real name is Clayton Morrow. They identified him through the fingerprints in your bedroom."

Jane was without words.

"The real Nicholas Harp died of an overdose six years ago, his first day at Stanford. I've seen the death certificate. It was heroin."

The real Nicholas Harp?

"The real Nick's drug dealer, Clayton Morrow, assumed his identity. Do you understand what I'm saying, Jinx? Nick isn't really Nick. His real name is Clayton Morrow. He stole a dead man's identity. Maybe he even gave Harp the fatal overdose. Who knows what he's capable of?"

Stole a dead man's identity?

"Clayton Morrow grew up in Maryland. His father's a pilot with Eastern. His mother is the president of the PTA. He's got four younger brothers and a sister. The state police believe he murdered his girlfriend. Her neck was broken. She was beaten so badly they had to use dental films to identify her body."

Her neck was broken.

"Jinx, I need you to tell me you understand what I'm saying." Jasper had slid down the wall, rested his elbows on his knees, so he could be at her level. "The man you know as Nick lied to us. He lied to us all."

"But—" Jane struggled to make sense of what he'd said. "Agent Barlow told us all in the parlor that Nick's mother had sent him to California to live with his grandmother. That's the same story Nick told us."

"The real Nick's mother sent him out west." Jasper worked to keep the frustration out of his voice. "He knocked up a girl back home. They didn't want his life to be over. They sent him out here to live with his grandmother. That part was true, about the move, but the rest was just bullshit to make us feel sorry for him."

Jane had no more questions because none of this felt real. The prostitute mother. The abusive grandmother. The year of homelessness. The triumphant acceptance to Stanford.

Jasper said, "Don't you see that Clayton Morrow used just enough of the real Nick's story to make the lies he told us believable?" He waited, but Jane still had no words. "Do you hear what I'm saying, Jinx? Nick, or Clayton Morrow, or whoever he is, was a fraud. He lied to all of us. He was nothing but a drug dealer and a con man."

. . . just another con man running another cult so he could bed the pretty girls and play God with all the boys.

Jane felt a noise force its way out of her throat. Not grief, but laughter. She heard the sound bounce around the tiny room, so incongruous with the machines and pumps. She put her hand to her mouth. Tears streamed down her cheeks. Her stomach muscles cramped, she laughed so hard.

"Christ." Jasper stood back up. He was looking at her as if she had lost her mind. "Jinx, this is serious. You're going to go to prison if you don't make a deal."

Jane wiped her eyes. She looked at Andrew, so close to death that his flesh was nearly translucent. This was what he'd been trying to tell Jane in the van. The real Nick had been his assigned roommate at Stanford. She could easily see Nick persuading Andrew to play along, just as she could see Andrew doing whatever it took to befriend the dead man's drug dealer.

She wiped her eyes again. She held tight to Andrew's hand. None of it mattered. She forgave him everything, just as he had forgiven her.

"What is wrong with you?" Jasper asked. "You're laughing about the asshole who murdered our father."

Now he was finally getting to the point. She said, "Laura Juneau murdered our father."

"You think anybody in that fucking cult makes a move without his orders?" Jasper hissed out the words between clenched teeth. "This is serious, Jinx. Get yourself together. If you want to have anything like a normal life, you're going to have to turn your back on the troops."

Troops?

"They've already captured that idiot woman from San

392

Francisco. She stole a car and shot at a police officer." He loosened his tie as he paced the tiny room. "You have to talk before she does. They'll give a deal to the first person who squeals. If we're going to save your life, we have to act fast."

Jane watched her brother's nervous pacing. Sweat was pouring off of him. He looked agitated, which for anyone else would be a typical response. But Jasper's greatest gift was his ability to always keep his cool. Jane could count on one hand the number of times Jasper had really lost it.

For the first time in hours, she let go of Andrew's hand. She stood to tuck the blanket around him. She pressed her lips to his cool forehead. She wished for a moment that she could see into his mind, because he had clearly known so much more than her.

She told Jasper, "You called them troops."

Jasper stopped pacing. "What?"

"You were in the Air Force for fifteen years. You're still in the Reserves. You wouldn't dishonor that word by using it to describe the members of a cult." In her mind, Jane could see Nick clapping together his hands, preparing to deliver one of his rallying speeches. "That's what Nick calls us. His *troops*."

Jasper might have called her bluff, but he couldn't stop himself from nervously glancing at the cop across the hallway.

Jane said, "You knew about it. Oslo, at least."

He shook his head, but it made sense that Nick had found a way to pull him into their folly. Jasper had left the Air Force to run the company. Martin kept promising to step aside, but then the deadline would come and he would find another excuse to stay.

She said, "Tell me the truth, Jasper. I need to hear you say it."

"Stop talking." His voice was barely more than a whisper. He closed the space between them, his face inches from hers. "I'm trying to help you out of this."

"Did you give money?" Jane asked, because a lot of people had given money to the cause. Of all of them, only Jasper would personally benefit from Martin's public humiliation.

He said, "Why would I give that asshole money?"

Jasper's haughtiness gave him away. She had watched him use it as a weapon her entire life, but he had never, ever directed it toward Jane.

She told him, "Taking the company public would've been a lot more lucrative if Father was forced to resign. All of his essays and speeches about the Queller Correction made him too controversial."

Jasper's jaw worked. She could tell from his face that she was right.

"Nick was bribing you," Jane guessed. The stupid metal box with Nick's trophies. How smug he must have been when he told Jasper he'd stolen the forms right under his nose. "Tell me the truth, Jasper."

His eyes went back to the cop. The man was still across the hall talking to a nurse.

Jane said, "I'm on your side, whether you believe me or not. I never wanted you to get hurt. I only found out about the papers before everything went to hell."

Jasper cleared his throat. "What papers?"

She wanted to roll her eyes. There was no point to this game. "Nick stole the intervening reports with your signature on them. You verified billing for patients who were dead, like Robert Juneau, or ones who had already left the program. That's fraud. Nick had you dead to rights, and I know he used it to—"

Jasper's expression was almost comical in its astonishment. His eyebrows shot up. The whites of his eyes were completely visible. His mouth opened in a perfect circle.

"You didn't know?" Even as she asked the question, Jane knew the answer. Nick had double-crossed her brother. He hadn't been content to take his money. Jasper had to pay for snubbing Nick at the dinner table, looking down his nose, asking pointed questions about Nick's background, making it clear that he was not *one of us*.

"Christ." Jasper pressed his hands to the wall. His face had gone completely white. "I think I'm gonna be sick."

"I'm sorry, Jasper, but it's all right."

"I'll go to prison. I'll—"

"You won't go anywhere." Jane rubbed his back, tried to assuage his fears. "Jasper, I have the—"

"Please." He grabbed her arms, suddenly desperate. "You have to support me. Whatever Nick says, you have to—"

"Jasper I have—"

"Shut up, Jinx. Listen to me. We can say—we can—It was Andrew, all right?" He finally looked at their brother, dying only a few feet away. "We'll tell them it was all Andrew."

Jane concentrated on the pain from his fingers gouging into her skin.

"He forged my signature on the reports," Jasper decided. "He's done it before. He forged Father's signature on school forms, checks, credit card slips. There's a long history we can document. I know Father kept everything in his safe. I'm sure they—"

"No," Jane said, firmly enough to be heard. "I'm not going to let you do that to Andrew."

"He's dying, Jinx. What does it matter?"

"His legacy matters. His reputation."

"Are you fucking nuts?" Jasper shook her so hard her teeth clicked together. "Andrew's legacy is just like the rest of them— he was a faggot, and he's dying a faggot's death."

Jane tried to pull away, but Jasper held her in his grip.

"Do you know how many times I rescued him from yet another fag in the Tenderloin? How much cash I gave him so he could pay off whatever twink was threatening to go to Father?"

"Ellis-Anne—"

"Doesn't have AIDS because Andy could never get it up to screw her." Jasper finally let her go. He put his hand to his forehead. "Christ, Jinx, you never wondered why Nick would stick his tongue down your throat or grab your ass whenever Andrew was around? He was taunting him. We all saw it, even Mother."

395

Jane saw it now – more signs that she had missed. She laced her fingers through Andrew's again. She looked at his ravaged face. She had never noticed before, but his forehead had premature lines from his constant worrying.

Why had he never told Jane?

She wouldn't have stopped loving him. Maybe she would have loved him more, because suddenly, his lifetime of self-hatred and torture made sense.

She told Jasper, "It doesn't matter. I won't dishonor his death."

"Andy's the one who dishonored his death," Jasper said. "Don't you see he's getting exactly what he deserves? With any luck, all of them will."

Jane felt ice shoot through her veins. "How can you say that? He's still our brother."

"Think for a minute." Jasper had collected himself. He was back to trying to control everything. "Andy can finally be useful to both of us. You can tell the cops that he and Nick kidnapped you. Look at you—your nose is probably broken. Somebody tried to strangle the life out of you. Andy let it happen. He helped murder our father. He didn't care that people were going to die. He didn't try to stop it."

"We can't—"

"What's happening to him now is a Correction." Jasper invoked Martin Queller's theory as if it was suddenly gospel. "We have to accept that our brother is an abomination. He defied the natural order. He fell in love with Nick. He brought him into our house. You should've let Andy rot in the street. I should've let him hang in the basement. None of this would have happened without his disgusting perversion."

Jane could barely look at this man she had admired her entire life. She'd contorted herself to defend him. She had fought with Andrew to keep him out of harm's way.

Jasper said, "Save yourself, Jinx. Save me. We can still pull this family's name out of the gutter. In six months, maybe a year, we can take the company public. It won't be easy, but it will work if we stick together. Andrew's nothing more than a pus we have to drain from the Queller line."

Jane sank down onto Andrew's bed, her hand resting on his leg. She silently repeated Jasper's words, because in the future, if she ever wavered about never talking to her brother again, she wanted to remember in detail everything he had said.

She told him, "I have the paperwork, Jasper. All of it. I'll testify in front of any judge that it's your signature. I'll tell them that you knew about Oslo, and I'll tell them that you wanted to frame Andrew for everything."

Jasper stared at her. "How can you choose him over me?"

Jane was sick of men thinking they could give her ultimatums. "I've been standing here listening to you try to justify your crimes and talk about Andrew as if he's an aberration, but it's you I'm most ashamed of."

He huffed a disgusted laugh. "You're judging *me*?"

"You went along with Oslo because you wanted power and money and the private jets and another Porsche and the only way you could take control was to get Father out of the way. That makes you worse than all of us combined. At least we did it because it was something that we believed in. You did it for greed."

Jasper walked toward the door. Jane thought he was going to leave, but instead he closed the curtain across the glass. The cop lifted his chin to make sure everything was okay. Jasper waved him off again.

He turned around. He smoothed down his tie. He told Jane, "You don't understand how this works."

"Tell me."

"Everything you said is true. Father's academic bullshit was jeopardizing our valuation on the Stock Exchange. We were going to lose millions. Our investors wanted him to go, but he was refusing."

"So you thought the dye packs would do the trick."

"There's no trick to this, Jinx. These are very, very wealthy men we're dealing with. They will be very pissed off if they lose their money because of a spoiled little bitch who can't keep her mouth shut."

"I'm going to prison, Jasper." Hearing the words out loud didn't scare her as much as she thought they would. "I'm going to tell the FBI everything we did. I don't care about the collateral damage. The only way to atone for our atrocities is to stand up and tell the truth."

"Are you really so stupid that you think they can't kill us in prison?"

"They?"

"The investors." He looked at her as if she was a stubborn child to be dealt with. "I know too much. It's not just the fraud. You have no idea what kind of crooked shit Father was doing to inflate the numbers. I won't make it to lock-up, Jinx. They can't risk me making a deal to save my ass. They'll kill me, and then they'll kill you."

"They're wealthy men, not thugs."

"*We* are wealthy, Jinx. Look at what Father did to Robert Juneau. Look at what all three of us did to him." He lowered his voice. "Do you really think we're the only family in the world that is capable of conspiring to murder our enemies in cold blood?"

He was hovering over her.

Jane stood up to make him back away.

He said, "You will be signing your death warrant if you say one word against them." He jabbed his finger into her chest. "They'll chase you down and put a bullet in your head."

Jane's hand fluttered to her stomach.

Trade him.

"I'm not fucking around," Jasper said.

"Do you think I am? It's not just me I have to think about."

Jasper glanced down at her stomach. He had figured it out, too. "That's why you need to carefully consider what you're doing. They don't have daycare in prison."

Trade all of them.

He said, "These men, they've got long fucking memories. If you go against them—"

"What time is it?"

"What?"

She turned his hand so she could see his watch: 3:09 a.m. "Is this Chicago time?"

"You know I always change it when I land."

She dropped his hand. "You need to go home, Jasper. I never want to see you again."

He looked stunned.

"Live your corrupt life. Fuck over whoever you want. Keep your dangerous men happy, but remember I have those papers, and I can blow up your life, and their lives, anytime I please."

"Don't do this."

"What I do is no longer your business. I don't need you to save me. I'm saving myself."

He laughed, then he saw she was serious. "I hope you're right, Jinx, because if any of your shit blows back on me, I will not hesitate to tell them how to find you. You made your choice."

"You're damn right I did," Jane told him. "And if anybody comes looking for me, I'll use those papers to make sure you go down right beside me."

Jane pulled back the privacy curtain. She slid open the glass door.

The cop had already turned around. His hand was on his gun.

She told him, "Tell the FBI they've got less than three hours to offer me a deal or there's going to be a massive explosion in New York City."

August 26, 2018

15

Andy felt the tip of her finger slip through the hole in her skin.
She had been shot.

She leaned her head back against the wall. She sucked in air
through her teeth and tried not to pass out.

Edwin Van Wees was on the floor of his office. Broken glass
was scattered around his body. Pieces of paper. Blood. The
MacBook that Andy had used to find out about her mother.

Laura.

Andy reached out, her fingers brushing the edge of the burner
phone. The screen was cracked. She closed her eyes, concentrated
on listening. Was that her mother's voice? Was she still on the
phone?

A woman's scream came from the other side of the house.

Andy's heart stopped.

The second scream was louder, abruptly cut off by a loud
smack.

Andy clamped her jaw shut so she would not scream, too.

Clara.

Andy couldn't stay frozen this time. She had to do something.
Her legs shook as she tried to push herself up against the wall.
The pain almost ripped her open. She had to hunch over to stop
the cramping. Blood dribbled from the bullet hole in her side.
Andy's legs shook as she tried to move forward. This was her

fault. All of it. Laura had warned her to be careful and still, Andy had led them here.

They.

To kill Edwin. To kill Clara.

Andy's shoulder slid along the wall as she tried to find Clara, to give herself up, to stop this awful mess she had made. Her feet got caught up on the rug. Pain sliced into her side. Her head bumped against the photographs that lined the hallway. She had to stop to catch her breath. Her eyes kept going in and out of focus. She stared at the pictures on the wall. Different frames, different poses, some color, some black and white. Clara and Edwin with two women around Andy's age. A few snapshots of the women when they were younger, in high school, in kindergarten, and then—

Toddler Andy in the snow.

Andy felt numb as she stared at the image of her younger self.

Was it Edwin's hand she had been holding? The adjacent photo showed baby Andy sitting in Clara and Edwin's lap. Laura had cut Andy out of their lives and superimposed her onto the stock photo of the fake Randall grandparents.

"Nice, right?"

Andy turned her head. She had been expecting to find Mike, but it was a woman's voice. A woman she knew all too well.

Paula Kunde stood at the end of the hallway.

She pointed a familiar-looking revolver at Andy. "Thanks for leaving this for me in your car. Did you rub off the serial number, or was that Mommy?"

Andy didn't answer. She couldn't catch her breath.

"You're hyperventilating," Paula said. "Pick up the phone."

Andy turned her head. The burner phone was on the floor behind her. In the stillness, she could hear her mother wailing.

"Jesus." Paula stomped down the hall, scooped up the phone and held it to her ear. "Shut up, Dumb Bitch."

Laura didn't shut up. Her tinny voice was vibrating with rage.

Paula turned on the speakerphone.

". . . *touch a fucking hair on her*—"

"She's dying." Paula smiled at Laura's abrupt silence. She held the phone under Andy's chin. "Tell her, sweetheart."

Andy clutched her hand to her side. She could feel the blood seeping out of her.

"Andrea?" Laura said. "Please, talk to—"

"Mom . . ."

"Oh, my darling," Laura cried. "Are you okay?"

Andy broke down, a strangled cry coming from deep inside her body. "Mom—"

"What happened? Please—oh, God, please tell me you're okay!"

"I—" Andy didn't know if she could get the words out. "I was shot. She shot me in the—"

"That's enough." Paula raised the gun and Andy went silent. She told Laura, "You know what I want, Dumb Bitch."

"Edwin—"

"Is dead." Paula raised her eyebrows at Andy, as if this was a game.

"You stupid fucking idiot," Laura hissed. "He's the only one who knows—"

"Shut up with your bullshit," Paula said. "You know where it is. How much time do you need?"

"I can—" Laura stopped. "Two days."

"Sure, no problem." Paula grinned at Andy. "Maybe your kid will go into shock before she bleeds out."

"You fucking cunt."

Andy was rattled by the hateful words. She had never heard her mother like this.

Laura said, "I will slice open your fucking throat if you hurt my daughter. Do you understand me?"

"You dumb bitch," Paula said. "I'm hurting her right now."

Andy saw a flash.

Everything went black.

* * *

405

Andy was aware that something was wrong even before she opened her eyes. There was not a moment where it all came back to her, because she had never for a moment forgotten what had happened.

She had been shot. She was inside the trunk of a car. Her hands and feet were bound by some configuration of handcuffs. A towel was duct-taped around her waist to stanch the bleeding. The gag in her mouth had a rubber ball that made it hard for her to breathe because her nose was filled with blood from being pistol-whipped into unconsciousness.

As with everything else, Andy could recall the blows from the revolver. She hadn't really blacked out. She had felt more as if she'd been caught between the edge of sleep and wakefulness. When Andy was in art school, she had craved that stasis because it was where she found her best ideas. Her mind seemingly blank but still working through the various shades of black and white she would elicit from her pencil.

Did she have a concussion?

She should've been panicked, but the panic had gurgled back down like water circling a drain. An hour ago? Two hours? Now, her only overriding feeling was intense discomfort. Her lip was split. Her cheek felt bruised. Her eye was swollen. Her hands were numb. Her wrists had fallen asleep. If she lay the right way, if she kept her spine bent, if her breathing remained shallow, the burning in her side was manageable.

The guilt was another matter.

In her head, Andy kept playing back what happened inside the farmhouse, trying to identify the point at which everything had gone wrong. Edwin had told her to leave. Could Andy have left before the front of his shirt was ripped open by the bullets riddling his back?

She squeezed her eyes shut.

Click-click-click-click.

The revolver's cylinder spinning.

Andy tried to analyze Clara's two different screams, the startled quality of the first one, the *smack* that had cut off the second one. Not a hand slapping or a fist punching. Paula had struck Andy with the revolver. Had Clara suffered a similar fate? Had she awoken dazed in her own kitchen, walked down the hallway and found Edwin lying dead?

Or had she never opened her eyes again?

Andy cried out as the car hit a bump in the road.

Paula slowed for a turn. Andy felt the change in speed, the pull of gravity. The glow of the brake lights filled the darkness. Andy saw the stub of the emergency trunk release that Paula had cut off so that Andy could not escape.

They were in a rental car with Texas plates. Andy had seen as much when she'd been shoved into the trunk. Paula couldn't fly with the gun. She must have driven from Austin, the same as Andy, but Andy had been checking sporadically for Mike. Which meant that Paula had known exactly where Andy would eventually end up. She had played right into the bitch's hands.

Andy tasted bile in her throat.

Why hadn't she listened to her mother?

The car slowed again, but this time came to a full stop.

Paula had stopped once before. Twenty minutes ago? Thirty? Andy wasn't sure. She had tried to keep count, but her eyes kept closing and she'd end up having to jerk herself awake and start all over again.

Was she dying?

Her brain felt weirdly indifferent to everything that was happening. She was terrified, but her heart was not pounding, her hands were not sweating. She was hurting, but she wasn't hyperventilating or crying or begging for it to stop.

Was she in shock?

Andy heard the clicking of a turn signal.

The car wheels bumped onto a gravel road.

She tried not to remember all the horror movies that started with a car driving down a gravel road to a deserted campsite or an abandoned shack.

"*No.*" She said the word aloud into the darkness of the trunk. She would not let her panic ramp up again, because it would

407

only make her blind to any opportunities of escape. Andy was being held hostage. Laura had something that Paula wanted. Paula would not kill Andy until she got that thing.

Right?

The brakes whined as the car stopped again. This time, the engine turned off. The driver side door opened, then closed.

Andy waited for the trunk to open. She had gone through all kinds of scenarios in her head of what she was going to do when she saw Paula again, primary among them to raise her feet and kick the bitch in the face. The problem was, you needed stomach muscles to raise your feet, and Andy could barely breathe without feeling like a blow torch was blazing open her side.

She let her head rest on the floor of the trunk. She listened for sounds. All she could hear was the engine block cooling.

Click-click-click-click.

Like the cylinder spinning in the gun, but slower.

Andy started counting to give herself something to do. Being stuck in the Reliant, then Mike's truck, for so many hours had made her the type of person who said things out loud just to break the monotony.

"One," she mumbled. "Two . . . three . . ."

She was at nine hundred and eight-five when the trunk finally opened.

Andy blinked. It was dark outside, no moon in the sky. The only light came from the stairwell across from the open trunk. She had no idea where they were, except for another shitty motel in another shitty town.

"Look at me." Paula jammed the revolver underneath Andy's chin. "Don't fuck with me or I'll shoot you again. All right?"

Andy nodded.

Paula tucked the gun into the waist of her jeans. She worked the keys into the handcuffs. Andy groaned with relief when her arms and legs were finally released. She clawed at the ball gag. The pink leather straps snapped in the back. It looked like something from a *50 Shades of Grey* catalog.

Paula had the revolver out again. She glanced around the parking lot. "Get out and keep your mouth shut."

Andy tried to move, but the wound and her long confinement made it impossible.

"Christ." Paula jerked Andy up by her arm.

Andy could only roll, falling against the bumper and stumbling to the ground. There was so much pain in her body that she could not locate one source. Blood dribbled from her mouth. She had bitten her own tongue. Her feet were beset by pins and needles as the circulation returned.

"Stand up." Paula grabbed Andy's arm and pulled her to her feet.

Andy howled, bending over at the waist to stop the spasms.

"Stop whining," Paula said. "Put this on."

Andy recognized the white polo button-down from the blue Samsonite suitcase. Part of Laura's go-bag from the Carrollton storage unit.

"Hurry." Paula looked around the parking lot again as she helped Andy into the shirt. "If you're thinking about screaming, don't. I can't shoot you, but I can shoot anybody who tries to help you."

Andy started on the buttons. "What did you do to Clara?"

"Your second mommy?" She chuckled at Andy's expression. "She raised you for almost two years, her and Edwin. Did you know that?"

Andy was desperate not to give her a reaction. She kept her head down, watched her fingers work the buttons.

Had Edwin looked at her like her father because he was her father?

Paula said, "They wanted to keep you, but Jane took you for herself because that's the kind of selfish bitch she is." Paula was watching Andy carefully. "Seems like you're not surprised to hear that your mother's real name is Jane."

"Why did you kill Edwin?"

"Jesus, kid." She grabbed some handcuffs from the trunk. "Did you go through your entire life with a fish hook in your mouth?"

Andy mumbled, "Evidently."

Paula slammed the trunk shut. She picked up two plastic bags in one hand. The gun went into the waist of her jeans, but she kept her hand on the grip. "Move."

"Is Edwin—" Andy tried to think of a clever way of tricking her into admitting the truth, but her brain was incapable of any acrobatics. "Is he my father?"

"If he was your father, I would've already shot you in the chest and shit in the hole." She waved for Andy to get moving. "Up the stairs."

Andy found walking relatively easy, but climbing the stairs almost cut her in two. She kept her hand on her side, but there was no way to stop the feeling of a knife twisting her flesh. Each time she lifted her foot, she wanted to scream. Screaming would probably bring people out of their rooms, then Paula would shoot them, then Andy would have more than Edwin Van Wees and Clara Bellamy's deaths on her conscience.

"Left," Paula said.

Andy walked down a long, dark hallway. Shadows danced in front of her eyes. The nausea had returned. The dull pain had become sharp again. She had to put her hand to the wall so she would not trip or fall over. Why was she going along with everything like a lemming? Why didn't she scream in the parking lot? People didn't run out to help anymore. They would call the police, and then the police would—

"Here." Paula waved the keycard to open the door.

Andy entered the room ahead of her. The lights were already on. Two queen-sized beds, a television, a desk, small bistro table with two matching chairs. The bathroom was by the door. The curtains were closed on the window that probably looked out onto the parking lot.

Paula dropped the plastic grocery bags onto the table. Bottles of water. Fruit. Potato chips.

Andy sniffed. Blood rolled down her throat. She felt like the entire left side of her face was filled with hot water.

"All right." Paula's hand rested on the butt of the gun. "Go

410

ahead and holler if you want. This entire wing is empty, and anyway, this ain't the kind of hotel where people worry if they hear a gal begging for help."

Andy stared all of her hate into the woman.

Paula grinned, feeding off the rage. "If you need to piss, do it now. I won't offer again."

Andy tried to close the bathroom door, but Paula stopped her. She watched Andy labor to sit on the toilet without using her stomach muscles. A yelp slipped from Andy's lips as her ass hit the seat. She had to lean over her knees to keep the pain at bay. Normally, Andy's bladder was shy, but after so long in the car, she had no problem going.

Standing was another matter. Her knees started to straighten and then she was back on the toilet, groaning.

"Fucksakes." Paula yanked up Andy by the armpit. She zipped and buttoned Andy's jeans like she was three, then shoved her into the room. "Go sit down at the table."

Andy kept her back bent as she navigated her way into the rickety chair. The side of her body lit up like a bolt of lightning.

Paula shoved the chair underneath the table. "You need to do what I say when I say it."

"Fuck you." The words slipped out before Andy could stop them.

"Fuck you, too." Paula grabbed Andy's left arm. She clamped a handcuff on her wrist, then jerked her hand under the table and attached the cuff to the metal base.

Andy pulled at the restraint. The table rattled. She pressed her forehead to the top.

Why hadn't she gone to Idaho?

Paula said, "If your mother caught the first flight out, she won't be here for at least another two hours." She found an ibuprofen bottle in one of the bags. She used her teeth to rip off the safety seal. "How bad does it hurt?"

"Like I've been shot, you fucking psycho."

"Fair enough." Instead of being mad, Paula seemed delighted by Andy's anger. She put four gelcaps on the table. She opened one of the bottles of water. "Barbecue or regular?"

Andy stared at her.

Paula held up two bags of potato chips. "You have to eat something or you'll get a tummy ache from the pills."

Andy didn't know what to say but, "Barbecue."

Paula opened the bag with help from her teeth. She unwrapped two sandwiches. "Mustard and mayo?"

Andy nodded, watching the madwoman who'd shot and kidnapped her use a plastic knife to spread mayonnaise and mustard onto the bread of her turkey sandwich.

Why was this happening?

"Eat at least half." Paula slid over the sandwich and started adding mustard to her own. "I mean it, kid. Half. Then you can take the pills."

Andy picked it up, but she had an idiotic flash of the sandwich squirting out of the hole in her side. And then she remembered, "You're not supposed to eat before surgery."

Paula stared at her.

"The bullet. I mean, if—when—my mom gets here, and—"

"They won't operate. Easier to let the bullet stay inside. It's infection you should be worried about. That shit'll kill you." Paula turned on the television. She channeled around until she found Animal Planet, then muted the sound.

Pitbulls and Parolees.

"This is a good episode." Paula swiveled back around. She squirted mayonnaise onto her sandwich. "I wish they'd had this program at Danbury."

Andy watched her use the plastic knife to evenly spread the mayo across the bread.

This should've felt strange, but it didn't feel strange. Why would it? Andy had started the week by watching her mother kill a kid, then Andy had murdered a gun for hire, then she was on the run and kicking a thug in the balls and getting one, maybe two more people killed, so why wouldn't it feel natural to be handcuffed to a table, watching parolees try to reform abused animals with a psycho ex-con college professor?

Paula pressed the sandwich back together. She tugged at the

scarf around her neck, the same scarf she had been wearing two and a half days ago in Austin.

Andy said, "I thought you'd been suffocated."

Paula took a large bite. She spoke with her mouth full. "I'm getting a cold. You gotta keep your neck warm to stop the coughing."

Andy didn't bother to correct the asinine health advice. A cold explained Paula's raspy voice, but Andy said, "Your eye—"

"Your fucking mother." Food dropped from Paula's mouth, but she kept talking. "She whacked me in the head. They didn't do shit for me in jail. The left one went white, I got an infection in the right one. Still sensitive to light, so that's why I wear the sunglasses. Thanks to your mom, that's been my look for thirty-two years."

Interesting math.

Paula said, "What else you wanna know?"

Andy felt like she had nothing left to lose. She asked, "You sent the guy to Mom's house, right? To torture her?"

"Samuel Godfrey Beckett." Paula snorted, then coughed when the sandwich went down the wrong way. "Worth the money just for his stupid name. I thought for sure Jane would give it up. She's never been good at confrontation. Then again, she killed that kid in the diner. I about shit myself when I recognized her face on the news. *Fucking Laura Oliver.* Living on a goddamn beach while the rest of us rotted in jail."

Andy pressed her tongue to the roof of her mouth. The gun was still tucked into Paula's jeans, but her hands were occupied with eating. Could Andy push the table into Paula's gut, reach over with her free hand and grab the gun?

"What else, kid?"

Andy mentally walked herself through the motions. None of them worked out. Her handcuffed wrist was stretched too far under the table. She would end up impaling herself if she reached for the gun with her free hand.

"Come on." Paula bit off another chunk of sandwich. "Ask me all the questions you can't ask your mother."

413

Andy looked away. At the ugly floral bedspread. At the door almost twenty feet away. Paula was offering her everything, but after searching for so long, Andy didn't just want answers. She wanted an explanation, and that was something she could only get from her mother.

Paula looked for a napkin in the bag. "You turning shy on me?"

Andy did not want to, but she asked, "How will I know you're telling the truth?"

"I'm more honest than that whore you call a mother."

Andy chewed at the tip of her already sore tongue to keep from lashing out. "Who did you kill?"

"Some bitch who tried to stab me in prison. They couldn't prosecute me for Norway. Maplecroft wasn't my fault. Quarter was the one who snatched her. The other stuff wasn't on me." She stopped to chew. "I pleaded guilty to fleeing the scene of a crime. That got me six years, the bitch I shivved was self-defense, but they took me up to two dimes. Ask another question."

"How did you get your job at the university?"

"They were looking for a diversity hire and I lucked up with my sad sack reformed felon story. Ask another."

"Is Clara okay?"

"Ha, good try. How about this: why do I hate your dumb bitch of a mother?"

Andy waited, but Paula was waiting, too.

Andy made her tone as bored and disinterested as she could, asking, "Why do you hate my mother?"

"She turned on us. All of us except Edwin and Clara, but that was only because she wanted to control them." Paula waited for a reaction that Andy could not give her. "Jane was put into witness protection in exchange for her testimony. She got a sweetheart deal because the clock was literally ticking. We had another bomb ready to go, but her big fucking mouth stopped it all."

Andy searched Paula's expression for guile, but she saw none.

Witness protection.

Andy tried to wrap her brain around the information, to

414

figure out how it made her feel. Laura had lied to her, but Andy had become accustomed to the fact that her mother lied. Maybe what she was feeling was a slight sense of relief. All of this time, Andy had assumed that Laura was a criminal. And she was a criminal, but she had actually done something good by turning them all in.

Right?

Paula said, "The pigs still put her in prison for two years. They can do that, you know. Even with witness protection. And Jane did some heinous shit. We all did, but we did it for the cause. Jane did it because she was a spoiled bitch who got bored spending her daddy's money."

"QuellCorp," Andy said.

"Billions," Paula said. "All from the suffering and exploitation of the sick."

"So you're holding me ransom for money?"

"Hell no. I don't want her fucking blood money. This has nothing to do with QuellCorp. The family divested years ago. None of them have anything to do with it. Except raking in the dough from their stock options."

Andy wondered if that's where the cash came from in the Reliant. You had to pay taxes on stock gains, but if Laura was in witness protection, then everything would be above-board.

Right?

Paula said, "Jane never told you any of this?"

Andy didn't bother to confirm what the woman already knew.

"Did she tell you who your father is?"

Andy kept her mouth shut. She knew who her father was.

"Don't you want to know?"

Gordon was her father. He had raised her, taken care of her, put up with her maddening silences and indecision.

Paula gave a heavy, disappointed sigh. "Nicholas Harp. She never told you?"

Andy felt her curiosity rise, but not for the obvious reason. She recognized the name from the Wikipedia page. Harp had died of an overdose years before Andy was born.

415

She told Paula, "You're lying."

"No, I'm not. Nick is the leader of the Army of the Changing World. Everybody should know his name, but especially you."

"Wiki said that Clayton Morrow—"

"Nicholas Harp. That's your father's chosen name. Half of that bullshit on Wikipedia is lies. The other half is speculation." Paula leaned across the table, excited. "The Army of the Changing World stood for something. We really were going to change the world. Then your mother lost her nerve and it all turned into a shitshow."

Andy shook her head, because all they had done was kill people and terrorize the country. "That professor was murdered in San Francisco. Most of the people in your group are dead. Martin Queller was assassinated."

"You mean, your grandfather?"

Andy felt jarred. She had not had time to make the connection. *Martin Queller was her grandfather.*

He had been married to Annette Queller, her grandmother.

Which meant that Jasper Queller, the asshole billionaire, was her uncle.

Was Laura a billionaire, too?

"Finally putting it together, huh?" Paula tossed a stray piece of deli meat into her mouth. "Your father has been in prison for three decades because of Jane. She kept you away from him. You could've had a relationship, gotten to know who he is, but she denied you that honor."

Andy knew exactly who Clayton Morrow was, and she wanted nothing to do with him. He was not her father any more than Jerry Randall was. She had to believe that, because the alternative would have her curled into a ball on the floor.

"Come on." Paula wiped her mouth with the back of her hand. "Give me some more questions."

Andy thought through the last few days, the list of unknowns she had jotted down after meeting Paula. "What changed your mind back in Austin? One minute you were telling me to leave, the next minute you were telling me to look for Clara Bellamy."

Paula nodded, as if she approved of the question. "The pig whose nuts you marshmallowed. I figured you wouldn't have done that if you were working with your mother."

"What?"

"The pig. The US marshal."

Andy felt a flush work its way up her neck.

"You fucked up his shit. That bitch was lying on my front porch for an hour."

Andy leaned her head onto the table so that Paula couldn't see her face.

Mike.

The Marshal Service was in charge of administering the witness protection program. They could make all the driver's licenses they wanted because making new documents was part of their job—fake birth certificates and fake tax returns and even fake obituaries for a made-up guy named Jerry Randall.

Andy felt her bowels swirl.

Mike was Laura's handler. That's why he was at the hospital when she came out. Was that why he was following Andy? Was he trying to help her because she had unwittingly been in the program, too?

Had she taken out the only person who might be able to save them from this monster?

"Hey." Paula rapped her knuckles on the table. "More questions. Spit 'em out. We got nothing better to do."

Andy shook her head. She tried to put together Mike's involvement since the beginning. His truck in the Hazeltons' driveway with his rabbit's foot keychain. The magnetic signs he changed out with each new city.

The GPS tracker on the cooler.

Mike must have planted it while Andy was passed out in the Muscle Shoals motel. Then he'd gone across the street for a congratulatory beer and improvised when Andy walked through the door.

She had assumed that he was friends with the bartender, but guys like Mike made friends wherever they went.

417

"Hey," Paula repeated. "Focus on me, kid. If you're not going to keep me entertained, then I'm gonna truss you back up and watch my shows."

Andy had to shake her head to clear it. She lifted her chin up, rested it against her free hand. She didn't know what else to do but return to her list. "Why did you send me to find Clara?"

"Bitch refused to talk to me back when she had her marbles, and Edwin threatened to rat me to my P.O. I was hoping seeing you would trigger her memories. Then I could snatch you up and you could give me the information and happy ending for everybody. Except Edwin got in the way. But you know what? Fuck him for working Jane's deal to keep her out of prison for thirty years." Paula crammed a handful of chips into her mouth. "Your mother was part of a conspiracy to kill your grandfather. She watched Alexandra Maplecroft die. She was there when Quarter was shot in the heart. She helped drive the van to the farm. She was with us one hundred percent every step of the way."

"Until she wasn't," Andy said, because that was the part that she wanted to hold onto.

"Yeah, well, we took down the Chicago Mercantile before it was all over." She caught Andy's blank look. "That's where commodities are exchanged. Derivatives. You've heard of those? And Nick was on his way into Manhattan when they caught him trying to blow up the Stock Exchange. It would've been glorious."

Andy had watched along with everyone else planes hitting buildings and trucks mowing down pedestrians and all of the horrors in between. She knew that attacks like that were not glorious, just as she knew that no matter what these crazy groups tried to take down, it always got rebuilt—taller, stronger, better.

She asked Paula, "So why am I here? What do you want from my mom?"

"Took you long enough to get to that question," Paula said. "Jane has some papers your uncle Jasper signed."

Uncle Jasper.

Andy couldn't get used to having a family, though she wasn't sure the Quellers were a family that she wanted.

Paula said, "Nick's been up for parole six times in the last twelve years." She wadded up the potato chip bag and threw it toward the trash can. "Every single fucking time, Jasper Fucking Queller climbs up on his podium wearing his stupid Air Force insignia and American flag pin and starts whining about how Nick killed his father and infected his brother and made him lose his sister and wah-wah-wah."

"Infected his brother?"

"Nick had nothing to do with that. Your uncle was a fag. He died of AIDS."

Andy physically reeled from the invective.

Paula snorted. "Your generation and its fucking political correctness."

"Your generation and its fucking homophobia."

Paula snorted again. "Christ, if I'd known all it took to make your balls drop was to shoot you, I would've done you the favor back in Austin."

Andy closed her eyes for a second. She hated this brutal back and forth. "What's in the papers? Why are they so important?"

"Fraud." Paula raised her eyebrows, waiting for Andy to react. "Queller Healthcare was kicking patients out on the street, but still billing the state for their care."

Andy waited for more, but apparently, that was it. She asked, "And . . .?"

"What do you mean, *and* . . .?"

"I could go online right now and find dozens of videos showing poor people being kicked out of hospitals." Andy shrugged. "The hospitals just apologize and pay a fine. Sometimes they don't even do that. Nobody loses their job, except maybe the security guard who was following orders."

Paula was clearly thrown by her nonchalance. "It's still a crime."

"Okay."

"Do you ever watch the news or read a paper? Jasper Queller wants to be president."

Andy wasn't so sure that a fraud conviction would stop him. Paula was still fighting by 1980s rules, before spin doctors and crisis management teams had become part of the vernacular. All Jasper would have to do was go on an apology tour, cry a little, and he'd be more popular than before it all started.

Paula crossed her arms. She had a smug look on her face. "Trust me, Jasper will crumble at the first whiff of scandal. All he cares about is the Queller family reputation. We'll work him like a marionette."

Andy had to be missing something. She tried to work it out. "You saw my mom on TV. You hired a guy to torture her for the location of these documents, and now you're holding me ransom for them because you're going to blackmail Jasper into being silent so Clayton—Nick—will be paroled?"

"It's not rocket science, kid."

It wasn't even model rocket science.

How had her mother fallen in with these idiots?

Paula said, "I've got everything ready for Nick when he gets out. We'll get some art for the walls, find the right furniture. Nick has such a great eye. I wouldn't presume to choose those things without him."

Andy remembered the institutional blandness inside of Paula's house. Twenty years in prison, at least a decade on the outside, and she was still waiting for Clayton Morrow to tell her what to do.

She asked, "Did Nick put you up to this?" She remembered something Paula had said. "That's why you haven't killed me, right? Because I'm his daughter."

She grinned. "I guess you're not as stupid as you look."

Andy heard a cell phone vibrating.

Paula searched the bags and found the broken burner phone. She winked at Andy before answering. "What is it, Dumb Bitch?" Her eyebrows went up. "Porter Motel. I know you're familiar. Room 310."

Andy watched her close the phone. "She's on her way?"

420

"She's here. Guess she used some of those Queller billions to charter a flight." Paula stood up. She adjusted the gun in her waistband. "We're in Valparaiso, Indiana. I figured you'd want to see where you were born."

Andy had already chewed her tongue raw. She started on her cheek.

"Dumb Bitch was too good to be thrown into the general prison population. Edwin wrangled her a stay in the Porter County jail. She was in solitary the whole time, but so fucking what? Beats worrying some bitch is gonna shiv you in the back because you said her ass was big."

Andy's brain couldn't handle all the information at once. She said, "What about—"

Paula took off her scarf and shoved it deep into Andy's mouth.

"Sorry, kid, but I can't be distracted by your bullshit." She got on her knees and released the handcuff from the base of the table. "Put your right arm underneath."

Andy stretched both arms toward the base, and Paula ratcheted down the cuffs.

"Uhn," Andy tried. The scarf was shoved too far down her throat. She tried to work it out with her tongue.

"If your mom does what she's supposed to do, you'll be fine." Paula took a spool of clothesline out of the bag. She bound Andy's ankles to the chair leg. "Just in case you get any ideas."

Andy started to cough. The more she struggled to push out the scarf, the deeper it went.

"You know your dead uncle tried to hang himself with this stuff once?" She reached into the plastic bag again. She found a pair of scissors. She used her teeth to break them out of the packaging. "No, I guess you don't know. Left a scar on his neck, here—" she used the tip of the scissors to point to her neck, just below a smattering of dark moles.

Andy hoped she had skin cancer.

"Jasper saved him that time." Paula cut the end of the clothesline. "Andy was always needing saving. Weird that your mom calls you by his name."

Laura didn't like to call Andy by her dead brother's name. She winced every time she used anything other than Andrea.

Paula checked the handcuffs again, then the knots, to make sure they were secure. "All right. I'm gonna pee." She stuck the scissors into her back pocket. "Don't do anything stupid."

Andy waited until the bathroom door shut, then she looked for something stupid to do. The burner phone was still on the table. Her hands were out of the question, but maybe she could use her head. She tried to inch the chair forward but the burning was so intense that vomit spilled up her throat.

The scarf pushed it back down.

Fuck.

Andy let her eyes scan the room from floor to ceiling. Ice bucket and plastic cups on the desk under the TV. Water bottles. Trash can. Andy wrapped her fingers around the base of the table. She tested the weight as much as she could. Too heavy. And also, she had a bullet inside her body. Even if she managed to bite back the pain and lift the table, she would fall flat on her face because her ankles were tied to the chair.

The toilet flushed. The sink faucet ran. Paula came out with a towel in her hands. She tossed it onto the desk. Instead of addressing Andy, she sat down on the edge of the bed and watched television.

Andy let her forehead rest on the table. She closed her eyes. She felt a groan vibrate inside of her throat. It was too much. All of it was just too damn much.

Mike was a US marshal.

Her mother was in the witness protection program.

Her birth father was a murderous cult leader.

Edwin Van Wees was dead.

Clara Bellamy—

Andy could still clearly hear the *smack* that had cut off Clara's scream.

The *click-click-click-click* of the revolver's cylinder.

The ballerina and the lawyer had taken care of Andy for the

422

first two years of her life, and she had not remembered one detail about them.

There was a sound in the hallway.

Andy's heart jumped. She raised her head.

Two knocks rattled the door, then there was a pause, then another knock.

Paula snorted. "Your mom thinks she's being sneaky getting here sooner than she said." She turned off the TV. She pressed her finger to her lips as if Andy was capable of anything but silence.

The revolver was in Paula's hand by the time she opened the door.

Mom.

Andy started to cry. She couldn't help it. The relief was so overwhelming that she felt like her heart was going to explode.

Their eyes met.

Laura shook her head once, but Andy didn't know why.

Don't do anything?

This is the end?

Paula jammed the gun in Laura's face. "Move it. Hurry."

Laura leaned heavily on an aluminum cane as she walked into the room. Her coat was wrapped around her shoulders. Her face was drawn. She looked frail, like a woman twice her age. She asked Andy, "Are you okay?"

Andy nodded, alarmed by her mother's fragile appearance. She'd had almost a week to recover from her injuries. Was she sick again? Did she get an infection from the wound in her leg, the knife cut in her hand?

"Where are they?" Paula pressed the muzzle of the gun to the back of Laura's head. "The files. Where are they?"

Laura kept her gaze locked with Andy's. It was like a laser beam between them. Andy could remember the same look passing between them when the nurses were wheeling Laura into surgery, off to radiation therapy, into the chemo ward.

This was her mother. This woman, this stranger, had always been Andy's mother.

423

"Come on," Paula said. "Where—"

Laura shrugged her right shoulder, letting the coat slip to the floor. Her left arm was in a sling instead of strapped to her waist. A packet of file folders was tucked inside. The splint from the hospital was gone. She was wearing an Ace bandage that ballooned around her hand. Her swollen fingers curled from the opening like a cat's tongue.

Paula snatched away the files and opened them on the desk under the TV. The gun stayed trained on Laura while she thumbed through the pages. Paula's head swiveled back and forth like she was afraid Laura would pounce. "Is this all of them?"

"It's enough." Laura still would not look away from Andy. *What was she trying to say?*

"Spread your legs." Paula roughly patted down Laura with her hands, clapping up and down her body. "Take off the sling."

Laura didn't move.

"Now," Paula said, an edge to her voice that Andy had never heard before.

Was Paula afraid? Was the fearless bitch really scared of Laura?

"Take it off," Paula repeated. Her body was tense. She was shifting her weight back and forth between her feet. "Now, Dumb Bitch."

Laura sighed as she rested the cane against the bed. She reached up to her neck. She found the Velcro closure and carefully pulled away the sling. She held her wrapped hand away from her body. "I'm not wearing a wire."

Paula lifted Laura's shirt, ran her finger around the waistband. Laura's eyes found Andy. She shook her head again, just once. *Why?*

Paula said, "Sit on the bed."

"You have what you asked for." Laura's voice was calm, almost cold. "Let us go and no one else will get hurt."

Paula jammed the gun into Laura's face. "You're the only one who's going to get hurt."

Laura nodded at Andy, as if this was exactly what she had expected. She finally looked at Paula. "I'll stay. Let her go."

424

No! The word got caught in Andy's throat. She worked furiously to spit out the scarf. *No!*

"Sit down." Paula shoved her mother back onto the bed. There was no way for Laura to catch herself with one arm. She fell on her side. Andy watched her mother's expression contort in pain.

Anger seized Andy like a fever. She started groaning, snorting, making every noise she could manage.

Paula kicked away the aluminum cane. "Your daughter's going to watch you die."

Laura said nothing.

"Take this." Paula tossed the spool of clothesline at Laura.

She caught it with one hand. Her eyes went to Andy. Then she looked back at Paula.

What? Andy wanted to scream. *What am I supposed to do?*

Laura held up the spool. "Is this supposed to make me feel sad?"

"It's supposed to tie you up like a pig so I can gut you."

Gut you?

Andy started pulling at the handcuffs. She pressed her chest into the edge of the table. The pain was almost unbearable, but she had to do something.

"Penny, stop this." Laura slid toward the edge of the bed. "Nick wouldn't want—"

"What the fuck do you know about what Nick wants?" Paula gripped the gun with both hands. She was shaking with fury. "You fucking cold bitch."

"I was his lover for six years. I gave birth to his child." Laura's feet went flat to the ground. "Do you think he'd want his daughter to witness her mother's brutal murder?"

"I should just shoot you," Paula said. "Do you see my eye? Do you see what you did to me?"

"I'm actually quite proud of that."

Paula swung the gun into Laura's face.

Smack.

Andy felt her stomach clench as Laura struggled to stay upright.

425

Paula raised the gun again.

Andy squeezed her eyes closed, but she heard the horrible crunching sound of metal hitting bone. She was back at the farmhouse. Edwin was dead. Clara had screamed her first scream, then—

Click-click-click-click.

The cylinder spinning in the revolver.

Andy's eyes opened.

"Fucking bitch." Paula struck Laura across the face again. The skin had opened. Her mouth was bleeding.

Mom! Andy's yell came out like a grunt. *Mom!*

"It's gonna get worse," Paula told Andy. "Pace yourself."

Mom! Andy yelled. She looked at Laura, then looked at the gun, then looked back at Laura.

Think about it!

Why was Paula threatening to gut her? Why hadn't she shot Clara at the farmhouse? Why wasn't she shooting Laura and Andy right now?

The clicking back at the farmhouse was the sound of Paula checking to see if all of the cartridges in the revolver were spent.

She didn't have any bullets left in the gun.

Mom! Andy shook the chair so hard that fresh blood oozed out of her side. The table bumped into her chest. She twisted her wrists, trying to hold up her hands so that Laura could see them.

Look! Andy groaned, straining her vocal cords, begging her mother for attention.

Laura took another blow from the gun. Her head rolled to the side. She was dazed from the beating.

Mom! Andy shook the table harder. Her wrists were raw. She waved her hands, furiously trying to get Laura's attention.

"Come on, kid," Paula said. "All you're gonna do is knock yourself over."

Andy grunted, shaking her hands in the air so hard that the cuffs cut into her skin.

Look!

With painful slowness, Laura's eyes finally focused on Andy's hands.

Four fingers raised on the left. One finger raised on the right.

The same number of fingers Laura had shown Jonah Helsinger at the diner.

It's why you haven't pulled the trigger yet. There's only one bullet left.

While Laura watched, Andy raised the thumb of her left hand.

Six fingers.

Six bullets.

The gun was empty.

Laura sat up on the bed.

Paula was thrown by her sudden recovery from the beating, which was exactly what Laura needed.

She grabbed the gun with her right hand. Her left hand cork-screwed through the air, punching Paula square in the throat.

Everything stopped.

Neither woman moved.

Laura's fist was pressed to the front of Paula's neck.

Paula's hand was wrapped around Laura's arm.

A clock was ticking somewhere in the room.

Andy heard a gurgling sound.

Laura wrested away her injured hand.

A ribbon of red sagged into the collar of Paula's shirt. Her throat had been sliced open, the skin gaping in a crescent-shaped wound.

Blood dripped from the razorblade Laura held between her fingers.

I will slice open your fucking throat if you hurt my daughter.

That was why Laura wasn't wearing the splint. She needed her fingers free so that she could hold onto the blade and punch it into Paula's neck.

Paula coughed a spray of blood. She was shaking—not from fear this time, but from white hot fury.

Laura leaned in. She whispered something into Paula's ear.

Rage flickered like a candle in her eyes. Paula coughed again. Her lips trembled. Her fingers. Her eyelids.

Andy pressed her forehead down to the table.

She found herself feeling detached from the carnage. She wasn't shocked by sudden violence anymore. She finally understood the serenity on her mother's face when she had killed Jonah Helsinger.

She had seen it all before.

ONE MONTH LATER

I felt a cleaving in my Mind—
As if my Brain had split—
I tried to match it—Seam by Seam—
But could not make them fit.

The thought behind, I strove to join
Unto the thought before—
But Sequence ravelled out of Sound
Like Balls—upon a Floor.

                        —Emily Dickinson

EPILOGUE

Laura Oliver sat on a wooden bench outside the Federal Corrections Institute in Maryland. The complex resembled a large high school. The adjacent satellite facility was more akin to a boys' summer camp. Minimum security, mostly white-collar criminals who'd skimmed from hedge funds or forgotten to pay decades of taxes. There were tennis and basketball courts and two running tracks. The perimeter fence felt cursory. The guard towers were sparse. Many of the inmates were allowed to leave during the day to work at the nearby factories.

Given the seriousness of his crimes, Nick didn't belong here, but he had always been good at inserting himself into places he did not belong. He'd been convicted of manslaughter for killing Alexandra Maplecroft, and conspiracy to use a weapon of mass destruction for the New York piece of the plan. The jury had decided not only to spare Nick's life, but to give him the possibility of parole. Which was likely how he had wrangled his transfer to Club Fed. The worst thing that inmates had to worry about inside the blue-roofed pods spoking out from the main building was boredom.

Laura knew all about the boredom of incarceration, but not of the rarefied kind that Nick was experiencing. Per her plea deal, her two-year sentence had been spent in solitary confinement. At first, Laura had thought she would go mad. She had wailed and cried and even fashioned a keyboard on the frame of the bed, playing notes that only she could hear. Then, as her pregnancy had progressed, Laura had been overcome with exhaustion. When she wasn't sleeping, she was reading. When she wasn't reading, she was waiting for mealtimes or staring up at the ceiling having conversations with Andrew that she would've never had with him in person.

I can be strong. I can change this. I can get away.

She was mourning the loss of her brothers; Andrew to death, Jasper to his own greed. She was mourning the loss of Nick, because she had loved him for six years and felt the absence of that love as she would the loss of a limb. Then Andrea was born, and she was mourning the loss of her infant daughter.

Laura had been allowed to hold Andy only once before Edwin and Clara had taken her away. Of all the things that Laura had lost in her life, missing the first eighteen months of Andy's life was the one wound that would never heal.

Laura found a tissue in her pocket. She wiped her eyes. She turned her head, and there was Andy walking toward the bench. Her beautiful daughter was holding her shoulders straight, head high. Being on the road had changed Andy in ways that Laura could not quite get used to. She had worried for so long that her daughter had inherited all of her weakness, but now Laura saw that she'd passed on her resilience, too.

"You were right." Andy sat down on the bench beside her. "Those toilets were disgusting."

Laura wrapped her arm around Andy's shoulders. She kissed the side of her head even as Andy pulled away.

"Mom."

Laura relished the normalcy of her annoyed tone. Andy had been bristling about the over-protectiveness since she'd been released from the hospital. She had no idea how much Laura was holding back. Given the choice, she would have gladly pulled her grown daughter into her lap and read her a story.

Now that Andy knew the truth—at least the part of the truth

that Laura was willing to share—she was constantly asking Laura for stories.

Andy said, "I talked to Clara's daughters yesterday. They've found a place for her that specializes in people with Alzheimer's. A nice place, not, like, a nursing home but more like a community. They say she hasn't been asking about Edwin as much."

Laura rubbed Andy's shoulder, swallowing back her jealousy. "That's good. I'm glad."

Andy said, "I'm nervous. Are you nervous?"

Laura shook her head, but she wasn't sure. "It's nice to be out of the splint." She flexed her hand. "My daughter is safe and healthy. My ex-husband is speaking to me again. I think, in the scheme of things, I've got more to be happy about than not."

"Wow, that's some class-A misdirection."

Laura gave a surprised laugh, startled that the things Andy used to say inside of her head were finally coming out of her mouth. "Maybe I'm a little nervous. He was my first love."

"He beat the shit out of you. That's not love."

The Polaroids.

Andy had been the first person to whom Laura had told the truth about who'd beaten her. "You're right, sweetheart. It wasn't love. Not at the end."

Andy smoothed together her lips. She seemed to vacillate between wanting to know everything about her birth father and not wanting to know anything at all. "What was it like? The last time you saw him?"

Laura didn't have to think very hard to summon her memories of being on the witness stand. "I was terrified. He acted as his own lawyer, so he had a right to question me in open court." Nick had always thought he was so much smarter than everyone else. "It went on for six days. The judge kept asking me to speak up because I could hardly do more than whisper. I felt so powerless. And then I looked at the jury, and I realized that they weren't buying his act. That's the thing with con men—it takes time. They study you and figure out what's missing inside of you, then they make you feel like they're the only one who can fill the hole."

Andy asked, "What was missing inside of you?"

Laura pursed her lips. She had decided to spare Andy the details of Martin's sexual abuse. On good days, she was even able to persuade herself that she was holding back for Andy's sake rather than her own. "I had just turned seventeen when Andrew brought Nick home. I'd spent most of my life alone in front of a piano. I only got a few hours at school and then I was with a tutor and then . . ." Her voice trailed off. "I was so desperate to be noticed." She shrugged. "It sounds ludicrous, looking back on it now, but that's all it took for me to get hooked. He noticed me."

"Is that where you went when you disappeared on weekends?" Andy had moved away from Nick again. "Like when you went to the Tubman Museum and brought me back the snowglobe?"

"I was meeting with my WitSec handler. Witness security."

"I know what WitSec means." Andy rolled her eyes. She considered herself an expert on the criminal justice system since she'd been on the lam.

Laura smiled as she stroked back her hair. "I was on parole for fifteen years. My original handler was much more laid-back about the whole thing than Mike, but I still had to check in."

"I guess you don't like Mike?"

"He doesn't trust me because I'm a criminal and I don't trust him because he's a cop."

Andy kicked at the ground with the toe of her shoe. She was clearly still trying to reconcile Laura's sordid past with the woman she had always known as her mother. Or maybe she was trying to make peace with her own crimes.

"You can't tell Mike what happened," Laura reminded her. "We're damn lucky he hasn't figured it out."

Andy nodded, but still said nothing. She no longer seemed to feel guilty about killing the man they had all started calling Hoodie, but like Laura, she struggled to forgive herself for her part in jeopardizing Gordon's safety.

The night Andy had fled the house, Laura had sat on the

floor of her office, Hoodie's dead body a few feet away, and waited for the police to bust down the door and arrest her.

Instead, she'd heard men screaming on her front lawn.

Laura had opened the door to find Mike lying flat on the ground. Half a dozen cops were pointing their guns at his prone body. He'd been knocked out, likely by Hoodie. Which served him right for lurking around her front yard. If Laura had wanted the US Marshals Service involved in the Jonah Helsinger affair, she would've called Mike herself.

Then again, she shouldn't be too hard on him, considering Mike was the only reason that Laura had not been arrested that night.

Andy's text had been fairly nondescript:

419 Seaborne Ave armed man imminent danger pls hurry

If Laura was adept at anything, it was subterfuge. She'd told the cops she'd panicked when she saw a man outside her window, that she'd had no idea it was Mike, that she had no idea who'd hit him, and she had no idea why they wanted to come into the house but she knew she had the legal right to refuse them entry.

The only reason they had believed her was because Mike was too dazed to call bullshit. The ambulance had taken him to the hospital. Laura had waited until sun-up to call Gordon. They had waited until sundown to take the body from the house and put it in the river.

This was the transgression Andy could not get past. Killing Hoodie had been self-defense. Gordon's involvement in covering up her crime was more complicated.

Laura tried to assuage her guilt. "Darling, your father has no regrets. He's told you that over and over again. What he did was wrong, but it was for the right reason."

"He could get into trouble."

"He won't if we all keep our mouths shut. You have to remember that Mike wasn't following you around to keep you safe. He was trying to see what you were up to because he thought that I was breaking the law." Laura held onto Andy's

435

hand. "We'll be fine if we all stick together. Trust me on this. I know how to get away with a crime."

Andy glanced up at her, then looked away. Her silences had meaning now. They were no longer a symptom of her indecision. They were usually followed by a difficult question.

Laura held her breath and waited.

This was the moment when Andy would finally ask about Paula. Why Laura had killed her instead of grabbing the empty gun. What she'd whispered in Paula's ear as she was dying. Why she had told Andy to tell the police that she was unconscious when Paula had died.

Andy said, "There was only one suitcase in the storage unit."

Laura let out the breath. Her brain took a moment to dial back the anxiety and find the correct response. "Do you think that's the only storage unit?"

Andy raised her eyebrows. "Is the money from your family?"

"It's from the safe houses, the vans. I wouldn't take Queller money."

"Paula said the same thing."

Laura held her breath again.

Andy said, "Isn't it all blood money?"

"Yes." Laura had told herself that the stash money was different; she had justified keeping it because she was terrified Jasper would come after her. The make-up bag hidden inside the couch. The storage units. The fake IDs she had bought off the same forger in Toronto who had worked on Alexandra Maplecroft's credentials. All of her machinations had been done in case Jasper figured out where she was.

And all of her fears had been misplaced, because Andy was right.

Jasper clearly did not give a shit about the fraudulent paperwork. The statute of limitations on the fraud had run out years ago, and his public apology tour had actually raised his numbers in the early presidential polls.

Andy kept stubbing the toe of her shoe into the ground. "Why did you give it up?"

Laura almost laughed, because she had not been asked the question in such a long time that her first thought was, *Give up what?*

She said, "The short answer is Nick, but it's more complicated than that."

"We've got time for the long answer."

Laura didn't think there were that many hours left in her lifetime, but she tried, "When you play classical, you're playing the exact notes as written. You have to practice incessantly because you'll lose your dynamics—that's basically how you express the notes. Even a few days away, you can feel the dexterity leaving your fingers. Keeping it takes a lot of time. Time away from other things."

"Like Nick."

"Like Nick," Laura confirmed. "He never came out and told me to quit, but he kept making comments about the other things we could be doing together. So, when I gave up the classical part of my career, I thought I was making the decision for myself, but really, he was the one who put it into my head."

"And then you played jazz?"

Laura felt herself smiling. She had adored jazz. Even now she couldn't listen to it because the loss was too painful. "Jazz isn't about the notes, it's about the melodic expression. Less practice, more emotion. With classical, there's a wall between you and the audience. With jazz, it's a shared journey. Afterward, you don't want to leave the stage. And from a technical perspective, it's a completely different touch."

"Touch?"

"The way you press the keys; the velocity, the depth; it's hard to put into words, but it's really your essence as a performer. I loved being part of something so vibrant. If I had known what it was like to play jazz, I never would've gone the classical route. And Nick saw that, even before I did."

"So he talked you into giving that up, too?"

"It was my choice," Laura said, because that was the truth. Everything had been her choice. "Then I was in the studio, and

I found a way to love that, and Nick started making noises again and—" She shrugged. "He narrows your life. That's what men like Nick do. They pull you away from everything you love so that they are the only thing you focus on." Laura felt the need to add, "If you let them."

Andy's attention had strayed. Mike Falcone was getting out of his car. He was wearing a suit and tie. A grin split his handsome face as he approached them. Laura tried to ignore the way Andy perked up. Mike was charming and self-deprecating and everything about him set Laura's teeth on edge.

Charisma.

When he got close enough, Andy said, "What a coincidence."

He pointed to his ear. "Sorry, can't hear you. One of my testicles is still lodged in my ear canal."

Andy laughed, and Laura felt her stomach tense.

He said, "Beautiful day to visit a whackjob."

"You're selling yourself short," Andy teased. There was an easy grin on her face that Laura had never seen. "How are your three older sisters?"

"That part was true."

"And that thing about your dad?"

"Also true," he said. "You wanna explain how you ended up at Paula Kunde's house? She's at the top of your mom's no-fly list."

Laura felt Andy stiffen beside her. Her own nerves were rattled every time she thought about Andy eavesdropping on her conversation with Hoodie. Laura would never forgive herself for inadvertently sending her daughter into the lions' den.

Still, Andy held her own, just shrugging at Mike's question.

He tried, "What about those bricks of cash in your back pockets? Put quite a damper on the mood."

Andy smiled, shrugging again.

Laura waited, but there was nothing more except the weight of sexual tension.

Mike asked Laura, "Nervous?"

"Why would I be?"

He shrugged. "Just an average day where you meet a guy you sent to prison for the rest of his life."

"He sent himself to prison. You people are the jackasses who keep letting him go in front of the parole board."

"It takes a village." Mike pointed to the pink scar on his temple where he'd been hit in the head. "You ever figure out who knocked me out in your front yard?"

"How do you know it wasn't me?"

Laura smiled because he smiled.

He gave a slight bow of surrender, indicating the prison. "After you, ladies."

They walked ahead of Mike toward the visitors' entrance. Laura looked up at the tall building with bars over reinforced glass in the windows. Nick was inside. He was waiting for her. Laura felt a sudden shakiness after days of certainty. Could she do this?

Did she have a choice?

Her shoulders tensed as they were buzzed through the front doors. The guard who met them was massive, taller than Mike, his belly jutting past his black leather belt. His shoes squeaked as he led them through security. They stored their purses and phones in metal lockers, then he led them down a long corridor.

Laura fought a shudder. The walls felt like they were closing in. Every time a door or gate slammed shut, her stomach clenched. She had only been confined for two years, but the thought of being trapped alone in a cell again brought on a cold sweat.

Or was she thinking about Nick?

Andy slipped her hand into Laura's as they reached the end of the corridor. They followed the guard into a small, airless room. Monitors showed feeds from all of the cameras. Six guards sat with headphones on, eavesdropping on inmate conversations inside the visitors' room.

"Marshal?" There was a man standing with his back to the wall. Unlike the others, he was wearing a suit and tie. He shook Mike's hand. "Marshal Rosenfeld."

439

"Marshal Falcone," Mike said. "This is my witness. Her daughter."

Rosenfeld nodded to each of them as he pulled a small plastic case out of his pocket. "These go in your ears. They'll transmit back to the station over there where we will record everything that's said between you and the inmate."

Laura frowned at the plastic earbuds in the case. "They look like hearing aids."

"That's by design." Rosenfeld took the listening devices and placed them in her open hand. "Your words will be picked up through the vibrations in your jawbone. In order for us to pick up Clayton Morrow, he needs to be close. There's a lot of ambient noise in the visitation room. All the inmates know how to work the dead zones. If you want to get him on tape, you need to be no more than three feet away."

"That won't be a problem." Laura was more concerned with vanity. She did not want Nick to think she was an old woman who needed hearing aids.

Rosenfeld said, "If you feel threatened, or like you can't do it, just say the phrase, 'I would like a Coke.' There's a machine in there. He won't notice anything's off. We'll tell the closest guard to step in, but if Morrow somehow has a shiv or a weapon—"

"I'm not worried about that. He would only use his hands."

Andy gave an audible gulp.

"I'll be fine, sweetheart. It's just a conversation." Laura pushed the plastic buds into her ears. They felt like pebbles. She asked Rosenfeld, "What does he need to say, exactly? What's incriminating?"

"Anything that gives ownership to Paula Evans-Kunde's actions. Like, if Morrow says he sent her to the farm, that's enough. He doesn't have to say he sent her to kill anybody, or kidnap your daughter. That's the beauty of conspiracy. All you have to do is get him on tape taking credit for her actions."

The old Nick gladly took credit for everything, but Laura had absolutely no idea whether or not the present-day Nick had learned his lesson. "All I can do is try."

440

"Good to go." One of the guards raised his thumb into the air. "The sound is coming through perfect."

Rosenfeld gave him a thumbs-up in response. He asked Laura, "Ready?"

Laura felt a lump in her throat. She smiled at Andy. "I'm good."

Mike said, "Gotta say, it makes us all a little bit nervous, having you in the same room with this guy."

Laura knew he was trying to lighten the mood. "We'll try not to blow anything up."

Andy guffawed.

Mike said, "I'll walk you as far as the door. You still okay with Andy hearing all this?"

"Of course." Laura squeezed Andy's hand, though uncertainty nagged at her thoughts. She was worried that Nick would somehow sway Andy to his side. She was worried for her own sanity, because he had pulled her back in hundreds of times, but she had only managed to escape once.

"You're gonna do great, Mom." Andy grinned, and the gesture was so reminiscent of Nick that Laura felt her breath catch. "I'll be here when it's over. Okay?"

All Laura could do was nod.

Mike stepped back so that Laura could follow the guard down yet another long corridor. He kept his distance, but she could hear his heavy footsteps behind her. Laura touched her fingers to the wall to stop herself from wringing her hands together. She felt butterflies in her stomach.

She had taken a month to prepare for this, and now that she was here, she found herself terrifyingly unprepared.

"How's she doing?" Mike said, obviously trying to distract her again. "Andy. How's she doing?"

"She's perfect," Laura said, which was not that much of an exaggeration. "The surgeon got out most of the bullet. There won't be any lasting damage." Mike hadn't been asking about her physical recovery, but Laura wasn't going to talk about personal things with a man who had so openly flirted with her daughter.

"She's found an apartment in town. I think she might go back to college."

"She should try the Marshals Service. She was a damn good detective out there on the road."

Laura gave him a sharp look. "I would lock her in the basement before I let my daughter become a pig."

He laughed. "She's ridiculously adorable."

Laura had forgotten the earbuds. He was talking for Andy's benefit. She opened her mouth to cut him down to size, but any pithy comment Laura might have made was drowned out by the buzz of distant conversations.

Her throat tightened. Laura still remembered what a visitation room sounded like.

The guard worked his key in the lock.

"Ma'am." Mike gave her a salute, then walked back toward the monitoring room.

Laura gritted her teeth as the guard opened the door. She walked through. He closed the door, then looked for a key to the next one.

She could not help but start to wring together her hands. This was what she remembered most from her time in jail: a series of locked doors and gates, none of which she could open on her own.

Laura looked up at the ceiling. She gritted her teeth even harder. She was back in the courtroom with Nick. She was on the stand, wringing her hands, trying not to look into his eyes because she knew if she allowed herself that one weakness, she would crumble and it would all be over.

Trade him.

The guard opened the door. The conversations grew louder. She heard children laughing. Ping-pong balls hitting paddles. She touched the plastic earbuds, making sure they hadn't fallen out. Why was she so damn nervous? She wiped her hands on her jeans as she stood at the locked gate, the last barrier between her and Nick.

Everything felt wrong.

She wanted to rewind her day to this morning and start all over again. She had refused to dress up for the occasion, but now she found herself picking apart her choice of a simple black sweater and blue jeans. She should've worn heels. She should've dyed the gray out of her hair. She should've paid more attention to her make-up. She should've turned around and left, but then the gate was open and she was going around a corner and she saw him.

Nick was sitting at one of the tables in the back of the room. He lifted his chin by way of greeting.

Laura pretended not to notice, pretended that her heart was not trembling, her bones were not vibrating inside of her body.

She was here for Andrew, because his dying wish had to mean something.

She was here for Andrea, because her life had finally found purpose.

She was here for herself, because she wanted Nick to know that she had finally gotten away.

Laura caught flashes of movement as she walked through the large, open space. Fathers in khaki uniforms lifting babies into the air. Couples talking quietly and holding hands. A few lawyers speaking in hushed tones. Children playing in a roped-off corner. Two ping-pong tables manned by happy-looking teenagers. Cameras mounted every ten feet, microphones jutting from the ceiling, guards standing by the doors, the Coke machine, the emergency exit.

Nick was sitting only a few yards away. Laura looked past him, still unprepared for eye contact. Her heart jumped at the sight of the upright piano on the back wall. The Baldwin Hamilton School Model in walnut satin. The fallboard was missing. The keys were worn. She imagined that it was rarely tuned. She was so taken by the sight of the piano that she almost walked past Nick.

"Jinx?" He had his hands clasped together on the table. Improbably, he looked exactly the same as she remembered. Not in the courtroom, not when Laura was passing out in the bathroom at the farmhouse, but downstairs in the shed. Alexandra Maplecroft was still alive. None of the bombs had gone off yet. Nick was unbuttoning his navy peacoat as he kissed her on the cheek.

Switzerland.

"Should I call you Clayton?" she asked, still unable to look at him.

He indicated the seat across the table. "My darling, you may call me anything you like."

Laura almost gasped, ashamed that the smooth sound of his voice could still touch her. She took the seat. Her eyes measured the space between them, judging that they were well within the three feet required. She clasped her hands together on the table. For only a moment, she allowed herself the pleasure of looking at his face.

Still beautiful.

A little lined, but not much. His energy was the constant, as if a spring was wound tight inside of him.

Charisma.

"Is it Laura now?" Nick grinned. He had always basked under close scrutiny. "After our hero from Oslo?"

"It was random," she lied, looking past him, first at the wall, then at the piano. "Witness security doesn't let you set your own terms. You either go along or you don't."

He shook his head, as if the details didn't interest him. "You look the same."

Laura's fingers went nervously to her gray hair.

"Don't be ashamed, my love. It suits you. But then, you always did everything so gracefully."

She finally looked him in the eye.

The flecks of gold in his irises were a pattern as familiar as the stars. His long eyelashes. The flicker of curiosity mixed with awe, as if Laura was the most interesting person he had ever met.

He said, "There's my girl."

Laura struggled against the thrilling shock of his attention, that inexplicable rush of *need*. She could so easily fall into his vortex again. She could be seventeen years old, her heart floating out of her chest like a hot-air balloon.

Laura broke off first, looking behind him at the piano.

She reminded herself that, just down the corridor, Andy was in that small, dark room listening to everything they said. Mike, too. Marshal Rosenfeld. The six guards with their headphones and monitors.

Laura was not a lonely teenaged girl anymore. She was fifty-five years old. She was a mother, a cancer survivor, a businesswoman.

That was her life.

Not Nick.

She cleared her throat. "You look the same, too."

"Not much stress around here. Everything gets planned for me. I just have to show up. Still—" He turned his head to the side, looking at her ear. "Age is a cruel punishment for youth."

Laura touched the earbud. The lie came easily enough. "All those years of concerts finally caught up with me."

He carefully studied her expression. "Yes, I've heard about that. Something to do with the nerve cells."

"Hair cells inside the middle ear." She knew he was testing her. "They translate the sounds into electrical signals that activate the nerves. That is, if they're not destroyed by too much loud music."

He seemed to accept the explanation. "Tell me, my love. How have you been?"

"I'm good. And you?"

"Well, I'm in prison. Did you not hear about what happened?"

"I think I saw something in the news."

He leaned over the table.

Laura reeled back as if from a snake.

Nick grinned, the glow in his eyes sparking into flames. "I was just trying to get a look at the damage."

She held up her left hand so that Nick could see the scar where Jonah Helsinger's knife had gone through.

He said, "Pulled a Maplecroft, did you? A bit more successfully than the poor old gal could manage."

"I'd rather not joke about the woman you killed."

His laugh was almost jubilant. "Manslaughter, but yes, I get your point."

Laura gripped her hands under the table, physically forcing herself to take back control. "I assume you saw the diner video."

"Yes. And our daughter. She's so lovely, Jinx. Reminds me of you."

Her heart lurched into a violent pounding. Andy was listening. What would she make of the compliment? Could she still see that Nick was a monster? Or were these verbal volleys somehow normalizing him?

She asked, "Did you hear about Paula?"

"Paula?" He shook his head. "Doesn't ring a bell."

Laura was wringing her hands again. She made herself stop—again.

She said, "Penny."

"Ah, yes. Dear Penny. Such a loyal soldier. She always had it out for you, didn't she? I guess no matter how glowing the personality, there are always detractors."

"She hated me."

"She did." He shrugged. "A bit jealous, I think. But why bring up the old days when we were having so much fun?"

Laura fumbled for words. She couldn't keep doing this. She had come here for a reason and that reason was slipping through her fingers. "I'm a speech pathologist."

"I know."

"I work with patients who—" She had to stop to swallow. "I wanted to help people. After what we did. And when I was in jail, the only book I had was this textbook on speech—"

Nick interrupted her with a loud groan. "You know, it's sad, Jinxie. We used to have so much to talk about, but you've changed. You're so . . ." He seemed to look for the right word. "Suburban."

Laura laughed, because Nick had clearly wanted her to do

446

the opposite. "I *am* suburban. I wanted my daughter to have a normal life."

She waited for him to correct her about who Andy belonged to, but Nick said, "Sounds fascinating."

"It is, actually."

"Married a black fella, too. How cosmopolitan of you."

Black fella.

About a million years ago, Agent Danberry had used the same words to describe Donald DeFreeze.

Nick said, "You got a divorce. What happened, Jinx? Did he cheat on you? Did you cheat on him? You always had a wandering eye."

"I didn't know what I had," she said, keenly aware of her audience in the distant room. "I thought that being in love meant being on pins and needles all of the time. Passion and fury and arguing and making up."

"But it's not?"

She shook her head, because she had learned at least one thing from Gordon. "It's taking out the trash and saving up for vacations. Making sure the school forms are signed. Remembering to bring home milk."

"Is that really how you feel, Jinx Queller? You don't miss the excitement? The thrill? The fucking the shit out of each other?"

Laura tried to keep the blush off her face. "Love doesn't keep you in a constant state of turmoil. It gives you peace."

He pressed his forehead to the table and pretended to snore.

She laughed, though she didn't want to.

Nick opened one eye, smiled up at her. "I've missed that sound."

Laura looked over his shoulder at the piano.

"I heard you had breast cancer."

She shook her head. She wasn't going to talk to him about that.

He said, "I can remember what it felt like to put my mouth on your breasts. The way you used to moan and squirm when

I licked between your legs. Do you ever think about that, Jinx? How good we were together?"

Laura stared at him. She wasn't worried about Andy anymore. Nick's fatal flaw had reared its ugly head. He always overplayed his hand.

She asked, "How do you live with it?"

He raised an eyebrow. She had piqued his interest again.

"The guilt?" she asked. "For killing people. For putting it all into motion."

"*People?*" he asked, because the jury had been divided over his part in the Chicago bombing. "You tell me, darling. Jonah Helsinger? Was that his name?" He waited for Laura to nod. "Ripped out his throat, though they blur that part on TV."

She chewed the inside of her cheek.

"How do you live with it? How do you feel about murdering that boy?"

Laura let a tiny part of her brain think about what she had done. It was hard—for so long she had managed to face each day by discarding the day before. "Do you remember the look on Laura Juneau's face? When we were in Oslo?"

Nick nodded, and she marveled at the fact that he was the only person left alive with whom she could talk about one of the most pivotal moments of her life.

Laura said, "She seemed almost at peace when she pulled the trigger. Both times. I remember wondering how she did it. How she had turned off her humanity. But I think what happened was that she turned it on. Does that make sense? She was completely at peace with what she was doing. That's why she looked so serene."

He raised his eyebrow again, and this time she knew that he was waiting for her to get to the point.

"I kept saying I didn't want to see the video from the diner, but then I finally broke down and watched, and the look on my face was the exact same as Laura's. Don't you think?"

"Yes," Nick said. "I noticed that, too."

"I'll do anything I can to protect my daughter. Anything."

"Poor Penny found that out the hard way."

He raised his eyebrows, waiting.

Laura left the bait on the line, though if she thought about it hard enough, she could feel Paula's hot blood dripping down her hand.

She asked, "Have you seen Jasper on the news?"

Nick chuckled. "His grand apology tour. You know, it's cruel to say, but I'm quite enjoying the fact that he got very, very fat."

Laura kept her expression neutral.

"I suppose there's been some kind of family reunion? A replenishment of the bank accounts from the Queller coffers?"

Laura didn't answer.

"I will tell you, it's been a pleasure seeing Major Jasper in person every fucking time my parole comes up. He's so eloquent when he explains how my actions caused him to lose his entire family."

"He was always good at public speaking."

"Gets that from Martin, I suppose," Nick said. "I was very surprised when Jasper went liberal. He could barely tolerate Andrew's addiction, but when he found out he was a raving queer—" Nick made a slicing motion across his neck. "Oh, dear, is that too close to Penny?"

Laura felt her mouth go dry. Her guard had slipped just enough for him to wound her.

Nick said, "Poor, desperate Andrew. Did you give him a good death? Was it worth your choice, Jinx?"

"We laughed at you," she told Nick, because she knew that was the easiest way to wound him. "Because of the envelopes. Do you remember those? The ones you said were going to be mailed to all the FBI field offices and all the major newspapers?"

Nick's jaw tightened.

"Andrew laughed when I mentioned them. For good reason. You were never good with follow-through, and that's too bad, because if you had kept your word, Jasper would've been in prison a long time ago, and you would've been on parole picking out furniture with Penny."

"Furniture?" Nick said.

"I saw your letters with Penny."

Nick raised an eyebrow.

The warden and the marshals who screened his mail had been clueless because they didn't know the code.

Laura did.

Nick had made them all memorize the code.

She said, "You were still stringing her along. Telling her that you would be together if only you could find a way to get out of here."

He shrugged. "Idle chatter. I didn't think she'd actually do anything. She was always a bit crazy."

Mike had said that a jury would see it the same way. Even writing in code, Nick was still careful.

It's only paranoia if you're wrong.

Laura said, "When it all started to happen, I never once thought it was you." She had to be careful about Hoodie because Mike would have questions, but she wanted Nick to know, "You never even crossed my mind."

It was Nick's turn to look at the room over Laura's shoulder.

She told him, "I thought it was Jasper, that he had seen me in the diner video, and he was coming after me." Laura paused, again choosing her words carefully. "When I heard Penny's voice on the phone at the farmhouse, I was shocked."

Nick was always good at ignoring what he didn't like. He leaned his elbows on the table, rested his chin in his hands. "Tell me about the gun, Jinx."

She hesitated, anxiously shifting gears. "What gun?"

"The revolver Laura Juneau found taped to the back of the toilet and used to murder your father." He winked at her. "How did it get to Oslo?"

Laura glanced around the room. At the cameras mounted on the walls, the microphones jutting down from the ceiling, the guards standing sentry. She felt her nerves rattle.

Nick said, "We're just having a conversation, my love. What do you have to worry about? Is someone listening?"

Laura smoothed together her lips. The table next to them had emptied. All she could hear were the constant pops of the ping-pong ball bouncing across the table.

"My darling?" Nick said. "Is our visit over so soon?" He reached out his hands to her. "We're allowed to touch in here."

Laura stared at his hands. Like his face, they were almost suspended in time.

"Jane?"

Without thinking, she was reaching across the table, lacing her fingers through his. The connection was instantaneous, a plug sliding into an outlet. Her heart lifted. She wanted to cry as she felt that familiar magnetic energy flowing through her body.

That Nick could so easily unravel her was devastating.

"Tell me." He leaned across the table. His face was close to hers. The visitation room faded away. She was in the kitchen again reading a magazine. He walked in, wordlessly kissed her, then backed away.

Nick said, "If you keep your voice low, they can't hear."

"Can't hear what?"

"Where did you get the gun, Jane? The one Laura Juneau used to murder your father. That wasn't from me. I didn't know about it until I saw her pull it out of the bag."

Laura shifted her gaze to the piano behind him. She had not played for Andy yet. First her injured hand, then her anxiety, had stopped her.

"Darling," Nick whispered. "Tell me about the revolver."

Laura pulled her attention away from the piano. She looked down at their intertwined fingers. Her hands looked old, the creases more pronounced. She had arthritis in her fingers. The scar from Jonah Helsinger's hunting knife was still red and angry. Nick's skin felt as soft as it had always been. She remembered what his hands had felt like on her body. The gentle way he had stroked her. The intimate, lingering touches at the curve of her back. He had been the first man who had ever made love to her. He had touched Laura in a way that no one had ever touched her before or since.

451

"Tell me," he said.

She had no choice but to give him what he wanted. Very softly, she said, "I bought the gun in Berlin for eighty marks."

He smiled.

"I—" Laura's throat tightened around the hoarse whisper. She could almost smell the cigarette smoke from the underground bar that Nick had sent her to. The bikers licking their lips. Jeering at her. Touching her. "I took a flight out of East Berlin because the security was lax. I brought the gun to Oslo. I put it in a paper bag. I taped it to the back of the tank for Laura Juneau to find."

Nick smiled. "The old girl didn't hesitate, did she? It was magnificent."

"Did you send Penny to find Jasper's papers?" Nick tried to pull away, but she held onto his hands. "You wanted the paperwork from the metal box. You thought you could leverage your parole. You sent Penny to get it."

Nick's grin told her he was bored with this game. He slipped his hands from hers. He crossed his arms over his chest.

Still, Laura tried, "Did you know what Penny was doing? Did you know she was going to kidnap my daughter? Try to murder me?" She waited, but Nick said nothing. "Penny killed Edwin. She beat Clara so badly that her cheekbone was broken. Are you okay with that, Nick? Is that what you wanted her to do?"

He turned his head. He brushed imaginary lint off his pants.

Laura felt her stomach drop. She knew the look Nick got on his face when he was finished with someone. Her plan hadn't worked. The marshals. The earbuds. Andy waiting down the hall. Everything had gone to hell because she had pushed him too hard.

Was it on purpose?

Had Laura sabotaged everything because Nick's power over her was still too strong?

She stared at the piano, longing, aching, yearning, for a way to make this work.

Nick asked, "Do you still play?"

452

Laura's heart flipped inside of her chest, but she kept her gaze on the piano.

"You keep staring at it." He turned around to look for himself. "Do you still play?"

"I wasn't allowed." A nerve twitched in her eyelid as she tried not to give herself away. "Someone might recognize my sound, and then—"

"The gig is up—literally." He grinned at the pun. "Did you know, my love, that I've been taking piano lessons?"

"Really?" Laura imbued the word with sarcasm, but underneath, she could barely breathe.

He said, "It was collecting dust in the rec room for years, but then some fool started a petition to move it in here for the children, and of course everyone signed on *for the children.*" He rolled his eyes. "You can't imagine how painful it is, hearing three-year-olds peck out 'Chopsticks.'"

She took a quick breath so she could say, "Play something for me."

"Oh, no, Jinxie. That's not where this is going." He stood up. He motioned for the guard's attention and pointed to the piano. "My friend here wants to play, if that's all right?"

The guard shrugged, but Laura shook her head. "No, I don't. I won't."

"Oh, my darling. You know I hate it when you refuse me."

His tone was joking in that way that wasn't joking. Laura felt the old fear start to stir. Part of her would always be that terrified girl who had passed out in the bathroom.

He said, "I want to hear you play again, Jinx. I made you give it up once. Can't I make you pick it back up again?"

Her hands quivered in her lap. "I haven't played since—since Oslo."

"Please." He could still say the word without it sounding like a request.

"I don't—"

Nick walked around to her side of the table. Laura didn't flinch this time. He wrapped his fingers lightly around her arm and gently pulled. "It's the least you can do for me. I promise I won't ask for anything else."

Laura let him pull her up to standing. She reluctantly walked toward the piano. Her nerves were shot through with adrenaline. She was suddenly terrified.

Her daughter was listening.

"Come now, don't be shy." Nick had blocked the guard's view. He pushed her down on the bench so hard that she felt a jarring in her tailbone. "Play for me, Jinx."

Laura's eyes had closed of their own accord. She felt her stomach clench. The ball of fear that had lain dormant for so long began to stir.

"Jane." He dug his fingers into her shoulders. "I said play something for me."

She forced open her eyes. She looked at the keys. Nick was standing close, but not pressing against her. It was his fingers biting into her shoulders that fully awakened her old fear.

"Now," he said.

Laura raised her hands. She gently placed her fingers on the keys but did not press them. The plastic veneer was worn. Strips of wood showed like splinters.

"Something jaunty," Nick told her. "Quickly, before I get bored."

She wasn't going to warm up for him. She didn't know if there was any value in trying. She considered playing something specifically for Andy—one of those awful bubblegum bands that she loved. Her daughter had spent hours watching old Jinx Queller videos on YouTube, listening to bootlegs. Laura didn't have anything classical left in her fingers. Then she remembered that smoky bar in Oslo, her conversation with Laura Juneau, and it came to her that things should end up where they had started.

She took a deep breath.

She walked the bass line with her left hand, playing the notes that were so familiar in her head. She vamped on the E minor, then A, then back to E minor, then down to D, then the triplet

454

punches on the C before hitting the refrain in the major key, G to D, then C, B7 and back to the vamp on E minor.

In her head, she heard the song coming together—Ray Manzerek mastering the schizophrenic bass and piano parts. Robby Krieger's guitar. John Densmore coming in on the drums, finally, Jim Morrison singing—

Love me two times, baby . . .

"Fantastic," Nick raised his voice to be heard over the music.

Love me two times, girl . . .

Laura let her eyes close again. She fell into the bouncy triplets. The tempo was too fast. She didn't care. There was a swelling in her heart. This had been her first true love, not Nick. Just to play again was a gift. She didn't care that her fingers were old and clumsy, that she lagged the *fermate*. She was back in Oslo. She was tapping out the beat on the bar. Laura Juneau had seen the chameleon inside of Jane Queller, had been the first person to really appreciate the part of her that was constantly adapting.

If you can't play the music people appreciate, then you play the music that they love.

"My darling."

Nick's mouth was at Laura's ear.

She tried not to shudder. She had known it would come to this. She had felt him hovering at her ear so often, first during their six years together, then in her dreams, then in her nightmares. She had prayed if she could only get him to the piano, he wouldn't be able to resist.

"Jane." His thumb stroked the side of her neck. He thought the piano was canceling out his voice. "Are you still afraid of being suffocated?"

Laura squeezed her eyes closed. She tapped her foot to keep the beat, heightened the pitch of her fingers. It was simple, really. That was the beauty of the song. It was almost like a ping-pong match, the same notes being volleyed back and forth.

"I remember you saying that about Andrew—that being suffocated felt like a bag was being tied around your head. For twenty seconds, was it?"

He was taking credit for sending Hoodie. Laura hummed with the song, hoping the vibrations in her jawbone would cancel out Mike's recording.

Yeah, my knees got weak . . .

"Were you scared?" Nick asked.

She shook her head, hitting the damper pedal to bring out the vibration in the strings.

Last me all through the week . . .

Nick said, "This is all your fault, my love. Can't you see that?"

Laura stopped humming. She knew the rhythm of Nick's threats as well as the notes of the song.

"It's your fault I had to send Penny to the farmhouse."

The feel of his mouth on her ear was like sandpaper, but she did not pull away.

"If you had just given me what I wanted, Edwin would be alive, Clara wouldn't have been hurt, Andrea would've been safe. It's all on you, my love, because you wouldn't listen to me."

Conspiracy.

Laura kept playing even as she felt the air begin to seep from the balloon in her heart. He'd confessed to sending Paula. They had him on the recording back in the dark little room. Nick's days at Club Fed were over.

But he wasn't finished.

His lips brushed the tip of her ear. "I'm going to give you another choice, my darling. I need our daughter to speak on my behalf. To tell the parole board that she wants her daddy to come home. Can you make her do that?"

He pressed his thumb against her carotid artery, the same as he'd done when he'd strangled her into unconsciousness.

"Or do I have to force you to make another choice? Not Andrew this time, but your precious Andrea. It'd be awful if you lost her after all of this. I don't want to hurt our child, but I will."

Terroristic threats. Intimidation. Extortion.

Laura kept playing, because Nick never knew when to quit.

"I told you I would scorch the earth to get you back, my darling. I don't care how many people I have to send, or how many people die. You still belong to me, Jinx Queller. Every part of you belongs to me."

He waited for her reaction, his thumb pressed to her pulse for the tell-tale sign of panic.

She wasn't panicked. She was elated. She was playing music again. Her daughter was listening. Laura could've stopped right now—Nick had given them enough—but she was not going to deny herself the pleasure of finishing what she had started. Up to the A, then back to the E minor, down to the D, then she was hitting the triplets on the C again and she was at the Hollywood Bowl. She was at Carnegie. Tivoli. Musikverein. Hansa Tonstudio. She was holding her baby. She was loving Gordon. She was pushing him away. She was struggling with cancer. She was sending Andrea away. She was watching her daughter finally grow into a vibrant, interesting young woman. And she was holding onto her, because Laura was never going to give up another thing that she loved for this loathsome man.

One for tomorrow . . . one just for today . . .

She had hummed the words to the song in her jail cell. Tapped it out on her imaginary bed frame keyboard the same way she had tapped it on the bar top for Laura Juneau. Even now with Nick still playing the devil on her shoulder, Laura allowed herself the joy of playing the song right up until the final, sharp staccato brought her to the abrupt end—

I'm goin' away.

Laura's hands floated to her lap. She kept her head bowed.

There was the usual dramatic pause and then—

Clapping. Cheering. Feet stamping the floor.

"Fantastic," Nick shouted. He was basking in the glow of the applause, as if it was meant entirely for him. "That's my girl, ladies and gentlemen."

Laura stood up, shrugging off his hand. She walked past Nick, past the picnic tables and the children's play area, but then she

457

realized that this was truly the last time she would ever see the man who called himself Nicholas Harp again.

She turned around. She looked him in the eye. She told him, "I'm not damaged anymore."

There was a stray clap before the room went silent.

"Darling?" Nick's smile held a sharp warning.

"I'm not hurt," she told him. "I healed myself. My daughter healed me—*my* daughter. My husband healed me. My life without you healed me."

He chuckled. "All right, Jinxie. Run along now. You've got a decision to make."

"No." She said the word with the same determination she had expressed three decades ago in the farmhouse. "I will never choose you. No matter what the other option is. I don't choose you."

His teeth were clenched. She could feel his rage winding up.

She told him, "I'm magnificent."

He chuckled again, but he was not really laughing.

"I am magnificent," she repeated, her fists clenched at her side. "I'm magnificent because I am so uniquely me." Laura pressed her hand to her heart. "I am talented. And I am beautiful. I am amazing. And I found my way, Nick. And it was the right way because it was the path that I set out for myself."

Nick crossed his arms. She was embarrassing him. "We'll talk about this later."

"We'll talk about it in hell."

Laura turned around. She walked around the corner, stood at the locked gate. Her hands shook as she waited for the guard to find his key. The vibrations moved up her arms, into her torso, inside her chest. Her teeth had started to chatter by the time the gate swung open.

Laura walked through. Then there was another door. Another key.

Her teeth were clicking like marbles. She looked through the window. Mike was standing between the two locked doors. He looked worried.

He should be worried.

Laura felt a wave of nausea as she realized what had just happened. Nick had threatened Andy. He had told her to choose. Laura had made her choice. It was all happening again.

I don't want to hurt our child, but I will.

The door opened.

She told Mike, "He threatened my daughter. If he comes after us—"

"We'll take care of it."

"No," she told him. "I'll take care of it. Do you understand me?"

"Whoa." Mike held up his hands. "Do me a favor and call me first. Like you could've called me before you went to that hotel room. Or when you were in a shoot-out at the mall. Or—"

"Just keep him away from my family." Laura got a burning sensation in her spine that told her to be careful. Mike was a cop. She had been held blameless for Paula's death, but Laura of all people knew the government could always find a way to fuck you if they wanted.

"He'll be in a SuperMax," Mike said. "He won't be writing letters or getting visitors. He'll get one shower a week, maybe an hour of daylight, if he's lucky."

Laura took out the earbuds. She dropped them into Mike's hand. The burst of adrenaline was tapering off. Her fingers were steady. Her heart wasn't quivering like a cat's whisker anymore. She had done what she'd come here to do. It was over. She never had to see Nick again.

Not unless she chose to.

Mike said, "I gotta admit, I thought you had a screw loose when you told me to figure out a way to get that piano moved."

Laura knew she had to stay in his good graces. "The petition was a clever trick."

"Marshal School 101: you can get an inmate to do anything for potato chips." Mike was preening, his chest puffed out. He clearly loved the game. "The way you kept looking at the piano like a kid staring at a bag of candy. You really worked him."

Laura saw Andy through the window in the door. She looked older now, more like a woman than a girl. Her brow was creased. She was worried.

Laura told Mike, "I will do whatever it takes to keep my daughter safe."

"I can name a couple of corpses who found that out the hard way."

She turned to look at him. "Keep that in mind if you ever consider asking her out on a date."

The door opened.

"Mom—" Andy rushed into Laura's arms.

"I'm fine." Laura willed it to be true. "Just a little shaken."

"She was great." Mike winked at Laura, as if they were in this together. "She worked him like Tyson. The boxer, not the chicken."

Andy grinned.

Laura looked away. She could not abide seeing pieces of Nick in her child.

She told Mike, "I need to get out of here."

He waved for the guard. Laura almost tripped over the man's shoes as they exited back through security. She waited for Andy to get her purse out of the locker, her phone and keys.

"I've been thinking about something," Mike said, because he was incapable of being silent. "The old Nickster didn't know you already confessed to transporting the gun to Oslo, right? That's why you got two years in the slammer. The judge sealed that part of your immunity agreement. He didn't want to exacerbate international tensions. If the Germans found out an American smuggled a gun from West to East for the purposes of murder, there would've been hell to pay."

Laura took her purse from Andy. She checked to make sure her wallet was inside.

Mike said, "So, when you told Nick that stuff about the gun, he thought you were implicating yourself. But you weren't."

Laura said, "Thank you, Michael, for narrating back to me exactly what just happened." She shook his hand. "We've got it from here. I know you have a lot of work to do."

"Sure. I thought I'd scrapbook through some of my feelings, maybe open a pinot." He winked at Laura as he held out his hand to Andy. "Always a pleasure, beautiful."

Laura wasn't going to watch her daughter flirt with a pig. She followed the guard to the last set of doors. Finally, blissfully, she was outside, where there were no more locks and bars.

Laura took a deep breath of fresh air, holding it in her lungs until they felt like they might burst. The bright sunlight brought tears into her eyes. She wanted to be on the beach drinking tea, reading a book and watching her daughter play in the waves.

Andy looped her hand through Laura's arm. "Ready?"

"Will you drive?"

"You hate when I drive. It makes you nervous."

"You can get used to anything." Laura climbed into the car. Her leg was still sore from the shrapnel in the diner. She looked up at the prison. There were no windows on this side of the building, but part of her could not shake the feeling that Nick was watching.

In truth, she'd had that feeling for over thirty years.

Andy backed out of the parking space. She drove through the gate. Laura didn't let herself relax until they were finally on the highway. Andy's driving had improved on her interminable road trip. Laura only gasped every twenty minutes instead of every ten.

Laura said, "That part about loving Gordon, I meant it. He was the best thing that ever happened to me. Other than you. And I didn't know what I had."

Andy nodded, but the little girl who prayed for her parents to get back together was gone.

Laura asked, "Are you all right, sweetheart? Was it okay hearing his voice, or—"

"Mom." Andy checked the mirror before passing a slow-moving

461

truck. She leaned her elbow on the door. She pressed her fingers against the side of her head.

Laura watched the trees blur past. Pieces of her conversation with Nick kept coming into her mind, but she would not let herself dwell on what was said. If there was one thing Laura had learned, it was that she had to keep moving forward. If she ever stopped, Nick would catch up with her.

Andy said, "You talk like him." When Laura didn't answer, she said, "He calls you darling and my love, just like you call me."

"I don't talk like him. He talks like my mother." She stroked back Andy's hair so she could see her face. "Those were the words she used with me. They always made me feel loved. I wasn't going to let Nick keep me from using the same words with you."

"'She always knew where the tops to her Tupperware were,'" Andy quoted, one of the few things Laura could come up with to capture the essence of her mother.

Now, she told Andy, "It's more like she knew which china set was from the Queller side and where the Logan silverware was cast and all the other unimportant things she felt gave her control over her life." Laura said something that she'd only recently realized was the truth: "My mother was as much a victim of my father as the rest of us."

"She was an adult."

"She wasn't raised to be an adult. She was raised to be a rich man's wife."

Andy seemed to mull over the distinction. Laura thought she was finished asking questions, but then she said, "What did you say to Paula when she was dying?"

Laura had dreaded being asked about Paula for so long that she needed a moment to prepare. "Why are you asking now? It's been over a month."

Andy's shoulder went up in a shrug. Instead of going into one of her protracted silences, she said, "I wasn't sure you would tell me the truth."

Laura didn't acknowledge the point, which she proved by

462

saying, "It was a variation of what I told Nick. That I would see her in hell."

"Really?"

"Yes." Laura wasn't sure why her last words to Paula made it on the long list of pieces of herself that she still kept hidden from Andy. Perhaps she did not want to test the boundaries of her daughter's newfound moral ambiguity. Telling a crazy woman with a razorblade lodged in her throat *Nick is never going to fuck you now* seemed jealous and petty.

Which was probably why Laura had said it.

She asked Andy, "Does what I did to Paula bother you?"

Andy shrugged again. "She was a bad person. I mean—I guess you could break it down and say that she was still a human being and maybe there was another way to do it, but it's easy to say that when it's not your own life in danger."

Your life, Laura wanted to say, because she had known when she hid the razorblade inside her bandaged hand that she was going to kill Paula Evans for hurting her daughter.

Andy asked, "Back in the prison, when you were walking away, why didn't you tell him about the earbuds? That everything he said in your ear was recorded? Like, a final *fuck you*."

"I said what I needed to say," Laura told her, though with Nick, she was never sure of herself. It felt so good to say those things to his face. Now that she was away from him, she had doubts.

The yo-yo snapping back again.

Andy seemed content to end the conversation there. She turned on the radio. She scanned the stations.

Laura asked, "Did you like the song I played?"

"I guess. It's kind of old."

Laura put her hand to her heart, wounded. "I'll learn something else. Name it."

"How about 'Filthy'?"

"How about something that's actually music?"

Andy rolled her eyes. She punched at the buttons on the tuner, likely searching for a sound that had the depth of cotton candy. "I'm sorry about your brother."

463

Laura closed her eyes against the sudden tears.

"You did right by him," Andy said. "You stood up for him. That took a lot."

Laura found a tissue and dried her eyes. She still couldn't come to terms with what had happened. "I never left his side. Even when we were negotiating the deal with the FBI."

Andy stopped fiddling with the radio.

Laura said, "Andrew died about ten minutes after the plea agreement was signed. It was very peaceful. I was holding his hand. I got to say goodbye to him."

Andy sniffed back tears. She had always been sensitive to Laura's moods. "He stayed around long enough to make sure you were going to be okay."

She stroked Andy's hair behind her ear again. "That's what I like to think."

Andy wiped her eyes. She left the radio alone as she drove down the near-empty interstate. She was clearly thinking about something, but just as clearly content to keep her thoughts to herself.

Laura rested her head back against the seat. She watched the trees blur by. She tried to enjoy the comfortable silence. Not a night had gone by since Andy had returned home without Laura waking up in a cold sweat. She wasn't suffering post-traumatic stress or worrying about Andy's safety. She had been terrified of seeing Nick again. That the trick with the piano and the earbuds would not work. That he would not walk into the open trap. That she would walk blindly into one of his.

She hated him too much.

That was the problem.

You didn't hate someone unless part of you still loved them. From the beginning, the two extremes had always been laced into their DNA.

For six years, even while she'd loved him, part of Laura had hated Nick in that childish way that you hate something you can't control. He was headstrong, and stupid, and handsome, which gave him cover for a hell of a lot of the mistakes he

464

continually made—the same mistakes, over and over again, because why try new ones when the old ones worked so well in his favor?

He was charming, too. That was the problem. He would charm her. He would make her furious. Then he would charm her back again so that she did not know if Nick was the snake or if she was the snake and Nick was the handler.

The yo-yo snapping back into the palm of his hand.

So Nick sailed along on his charm, and his fury, and he hurt people, and he found new things that interested him more, and the old things were left broken in his wake.

Jane had been one of those broken, discarded things. Nick had sent her away to Berlin because he was tired of her. At first, she had enjoyed her freedom, but then she had panicked that he might not want her back. She had begged and pleaded with him and done everything she could think of to get his attention.

Then Oslo had happened.

Then her father was dead and Laura Juneau was dead and then, quite suddenly, Nick's charm had stopped working. A trolley car off the tracks. A train without a conductor. The mistakes could not be forgiven, and eventually, the second same mistake would not be overlooked, and the third same mistake had dire consequences that had ended with Alexandra Maplecroft's life being taken, a death sentence being passed on Andrew, then—almost—resulted in the loss of another life, her life, in the farmhouse bathroom.

Inexplicably, Laura had still loved him. Perhaps loved him even more.

Nick had let her live—that was what she kept telling herself while she went mad inside of her jail cell. He had left Paula at the farmhouse to guard her. He had planned to come back for her. To take her to their much-dreamed-of little flat in Switzerland, a country that had no extradition treaty with the US.

Which had given her a delirious kind of hope.

Andrew was dead and Jasper was gone and Laura had stared up at the jailhouse ceiling, tears running down her face, her neck still throbbing, her bruises still healing, her belly swelling with his child, and desperately loved him.

Clayton Morrow. Nicholas Harp. In her misery, she did not care.

Why was she so stupid?

How could she still love someone who had tried to destroy her?

When Laura had been with Nick—and she was decidedly with him during his long fall from grace—they had raged against the system that had so irrevocably exploited Andrew, and Robert Juneau, and Paula Evans, and William Johnson, and Clara Bellamy, and all the other members who eventually comprised their little army: The group homes. The emergency departments. The loony bin. The mental hospital. The squalor. The staff who neglected their patients. The orderlies who ratcheted tight the straightjackets. The nurses who looked the other way. The doctors who doled out the pills. The urine on the floor. The feces on the walls. The inmates, the fellow prisoners, taunting, wanting, beating, biting.

The spark of rage, not the injustice, was what had excited Nick the most. The novelty of a new cause. The chance to annihilate. The dangerous game. The threat of violence. The promise of fame. Their names in lights. Their righteous deeds on the tongues of schoolchildren who were taught the lessons of change.

A penny, a nickel, a dime, a quarter, a dollar bill . . .

In the end, their deeds became part of the public record, but not in the way Nick had promised. Jane Queller's sworn testimony laid out the plan from concept to demise. The training. The rehearsals. The drills. Jane had forgotten who'd first had the idea, but as with everything else, the plan had spread from Nick to all of them, a raging wildfire that would, in the end, consume every single one of their lives.

What Jane had kept hidden, the one sin that she could never confess to, was that she had ignited that first spark.

Dye packs.

That was what they had all agreed would be in the paper

bag. This was the Oslo plan: That Martin Queller would be stained with the proverbial blood of his victims on the world stage. Paula's cell had infiltrated the manufacturer outside of Chicago. Nick had given the packs to Jane when she had arrived in Oslo.

As soon as he was gone, Jane had thrown them into the trash.

It had all started with a joke—not a joke on Jane's part, but a joke made by Laura Juneau. Andrew had relayed it in one of his coded letters to Berlin:

Poor Laura told me that she would just as soon find a gun in the bag as a dye pack. She has a recurring fantasy of killing Father with a revolver like the one her husband used to murder their children, then turning the gun on herself.

No one, not even Andrew, had known that Jane had decided to take the joke seriously. She'd bought the revolver off a German biker in the dive bar, the same dive bar that Nick had sent her to when she'd first arrived in Berlin. The one where Jane was afraid that she would be gang-raped. The one that she had stayed at for exactly one hour because Nick had told her he would know if she left a minute sooner.

For over a week, Jane had left the gun on the counter of her studio apartment, hoping it would be stolen. She had decided not to take it to Oslo, and then she had taken it to Oslo. She had decided to leave it in her hotel room, and then she had taken it from her room. And then she was carrying it in a brown paper bag to the ladies room. And then she was taping it behind the toilet tank like a scene from *The Godfather*. And then she was sitting on the front row, watching her father pontificate on stage, praying to God that Laura Juneau would not follow through on her fantasy.

And also praying that she would.

Nick had always been drawn to new and exciting things. Nothing bored him more than the predictable. Jane had hated her father, but she had been motivated by much more than vengeance. She was desperate to have Nick's attention, to prove that she belonged by his side. She had desperately hoped that the violent shock of helping Laura Juneau commit murder would make Nick love her again.

And it had worked. But then it hadn't.

And Jane was crushed by guilt. But then Nick had talked her out of it.

And Jane persuaded herself that it all would've happened the same way without the gun.

But then she wondered . . .

Which was the typical pattern of their six years together. The push and pull. The vortex. The yo-yo. The rollercoaster. She worshipped him. She despised him. He was her weakness. He was her destroyer. Her ultimate all or none. There were so many ways to describe that tiny piece of herself that Nick could always nudge into insanity.

Laura had only ever been able to pull herself back for the sake of other people.

First for Andrew, then for Andrea.

That was the real reason she had gone to the prison today: not to punish Nick, but to push him away. To keep him locked up so that she could be free.

Laura had always believed—vehemently, with great conviction—that the only way to change the world was to destroy it.

Acknowledgments

Thanks very much to my editor, Kate Elton, and my team at Victoria Sanders and Associates, including but not limited to Victoria Sanders, Diane Dickensheid, Bernadette Baker-Baughman and Jessica Spivey. There are so many folks at HarperCollins International and Morrow who should be thanked: Liate Stehlik, Heidi Richter-Ginger, Kaitlin Harri, Chantal Restivo-Alessi, Samantha Hagerbaumer and Julianna Wojcik. Also a big hats off to all the fantastic divisions I visited last year and the folks I got to spend time with in Miami. I also want to include Eric Rayman on the team roster—thank you for all you do.

Writing this book took me down many different research paths, some of which did not end up being incorporated into the book, but I have a list of folks who were crucial to helping me capture certain moods and feelings. My good friend and fellow author Sara Blaedel put me in contact with Anne Mette Goddokken and Elisabeth Alminde for some Norwegian background. Another fantastic author and friend, Regula Venske, spoke to me about Germany; I so regret that only one percent of our fascinating conversation in Düsseldorf made it into the narrative. Elise Diffie gave me some help with cultural touchstones. I am very grateful to both Brandon Bush and Martin Kearns for offering insight into the life of a professional pianist.

A very heartfelt thank you goes to Sal Towse and Burt Kendall, my dear friends and resident San Francisco experts.

Sarah Ives and Lisa Palazzolo won the "have your name appear in the next book" contests. Adam Humphrey, I hope you're enjoying all the winning.

To my daddy—thank you so much for taking care of me while I'm in the throes of writing and trying to navigate life. Best for last to DA, my heart, for being nobody, too.

Can't wait for the next book from
internationally-bestselling author, Karin Slaughter?

Read on for a sneak peek of *The Last Widow*,
coming June 2019 . . .

PART ONE

Sunday, July 7, 2019

PROLOGUE

Michelle Spivey jogged through the back of the store, frantically scanning each aisle for her daughter, panicked thoughts circling her brain: *How did I lose sight of her I am a horrible mother my baby was kidnapped by a pedophile or a human trafficker should I flag store security or call the police or—*

Ashley.

Michelle stopped so abruptly that her shoe snicked against the floor. She took a sharp breath, trying to force her heart back into a normal rhythm. Her daughter was not being sold into slavery. She was at the make-up counter trying on samples.

The relief started to dissipate as the panic burned off.

Her eleven-year-old daughter.

At the make-up counter.

After they had told Ashley that she could not under any circumstances wear make-up until her twelfth birthday, and then it would only be blush and lip gloss, no matter what her friends were doing, end of story.

Michelle pressed her hand to her chest. She slowly walked up the aisle, giving herself time to transition into a reasoned and logical person.

Ashley's back was to Michelle as she examined lipstick shades. She twisted the tubes with an expert flick of her wrist because of course when she was with her friends, Ashley tried on all

475

their make-up and they practiced on each other because that was what girls did.

Some girls, at least. Michelle had never felt that pull toward primping. She could still recall her own mother's screeching tone when Michelle had refused to shave her legs: *You'll never be able to wear pantyhose!*

Michelle's response: *Thank God!*

That was years ago. Her mother was long gone. Michelle was a grown woman with her own child and like every woman, she had vowed not to make her mother's mistakes.

Had she over-corrected?

Were her general tomboyish tendencies punishing her daughter? Was Ashley really old enough to wear make-up, but because Michelle had no interest in eyeliners and bronzers and whatever else it was that Ashley watched for endless hours on YouTube, she was depriving her daughter of a certain type of girl's passage into womanhood?

Michelle had done the research on juvenile milestones. Eleven was an important age, a so-called benchmark year, the point at which children had attained roughly 50 percent of the power. You had to start negotiating rather than simply ordering them around. Which was very well-reasoned in the abstract but in practice was terrifying.

"Oh!" Ashley saw her mother and frantically jammed the lipstick into the display. "I was—"

"It's all right." Michelle stroked back her daughter's long hair. So many bottles of shampoo in the shower, and conditioner, and soaps and moisturizers when Michelle's only beauty routine involved sweat-proof sunscreen.

"Sorry." Ashley wiped at the smear of lip gloss on her mouth.

"It's pretty," Michelle tried.

"Really?" Ashley beamed at her in a way that tugged every string of Michelle's heart. "Did you see this?" She meant the lip gloss display. "They have one that's tinted, so it's supposed to last longer. But this one has cherry flavoring, and Hailey says b—"

Silently, Michelle filled in the words, *boys like it more*.

The assorted Hemsworths on Ashley's bedroom walls had not gone unnoticed.

Michelle asked, "Which do you like most?"

"Well . . ." Ashley shrugged, but there was not much an eleven-year-old did not have an opinion on. "I guess the tinted type lasts longer, right?"

Michelle offered, "That makes sense."

Ashley was still weighing the two items. "The cherry kind of tastes like chemicals? Like, I always chew—I mean, if I wore it, I would probably chew it off because it would irritate me?"

Michelle nodded, biting back the polemic raging inside her: *You are beautiful, you are smart, you are so funny and talented and you should only do things that make you happy because that's what attracts the worthy boys who think that the happy, secure girls are the interesting ones.*

Instead, she told Ashley, "Pick the one you like and I'll give you an advance on your allowance."

"Mom!" She screamed so loudly that people looked up. The dancing that followed was more Tigger than Shakira. "Are you serious? You guys said—"

You guys. Michelle gave an inward groan. How to explain this sudden turnabout when they had agreed that Ashley would not wear make-up until she was twelve?

It's only lip gloss!

She'll be twelve in five months!

I know we agreed not until her actual birthday but you let her have that iPhone!

That would be the trick. Turn it around and make it about the iPhone, because Michelle had purely by fate been the one who'd died on that particular hill.

Michelle told her daughter, "I'll handle the boss. Just lip gloss, though. Nothing else. Pick the one that makes you happy."

And it did make her happy. So happy that Michelle felt herself smiling at the woman in the checkout line, who surely understood that the glittery tube of candy pink Sassafras Yo Ass! was

477

not for the thirty-nine-year-old woman in running shorts with her sweaty hair scooped into a baseball cap.

"This—" Ashley was so gleeful she could barely speak. "This is so great, Mom. I love you so much, and I'll be responsible. So responsible."

Michelle's smile must have shown the early stages of rigor mortis as she started to load up their purchases into cloth bags.

The iPhone. She had to make it about the iPhone, because they had agreed about that, too, but then all of Ashley's friends had shown up at summer camp with one and the *No absolutely not* had turned into *I couldn't let her be the only kid without one* while Michelle was away at a conference.

Ashley happily scooped up the bags and headed for the exit. Her iPhone was already out. Her thumb slid across the screen as she alerted her friends to the lip gloss, likely predicting that in a week's time, she'd be sporting blue eyeshadow and doing that curve thing at the edges of her eyes that made girls look like cats.

Michelle felt herself start to catastrophize.

Ashley could get conjunctivitis or sties or blepharitis from sharing eye make-up. Herpes simplex virus or hep C from lip gloss and lip liner, not to mention she could scratch her cornea with a mascara wand. Didn't some lipsticks contain heavy metals and lead? Staph, strep, E. coli. What the hell had Michelle been thinking? She could be poisoning her own daughter. There were hundreds of thousands of proven studies about surface contaminants as opposed to the relative handfuls positing the indirect correlation between brain tumors and cell phones.

Up ahead, Ashley laughed. Her friends were texting back. She swung the bags wildly as she crossed the parking lot. She was eleven, not twelve, and twelve was still terribly young, wasn't it? Because make-up sent a signal. It telegraphed an interest in being interested in, which was a horribly non-feminist thing to say but this was the real world and her daughter was still a baby who knew nothing about rebuffing unwanted attention.

Michelle silently shook her head. Such a slippery slope. From lip gloss to MRSA to Phyllis Schlafly. She had to lock down her wild thoughts so that by the time she got home, she could present a reasoned explanation for buying Ashley make-up when they had made a solemn, parental vow not to.

As they had with the iPhone.

She reached into her purse to find her keys. It was dark outside. The overhead lights weren't enough, or maybe she needed her glasses because she was getting old—was already old enough to have a daughter who wanted to send signals to boys. She could be a grandmother in a few years' time. The thought made her stomach somersault into a vat of anxiety. Why hadn't she bought wine?

She glanced up to make sure Ashley hadn't bumped into a car or fallen off a cliff while she was texting.

Michelle felt her mouth drop open.

A van slid to a stop beside her daughter.

The side door rolled open.

A man jumped out.

Michelle gripped her keys. She bolted into a full-out run, cutting the distance between herself and her daughter.

She started to scream, but it was too late.

Ashley had run off, just like they had taught her to do.

Which was fine, because the man did not want Ashley.

He wanted Michelle.

ONE MONTH LATER

Sunday, August 4, 2019

1

Sara Linton leaned back in her chair, mumbling a soft, "Yes, Mama." She wondered if there would ever come a point in time when she was too old to be taken over her mother's knee.

"Don't give me that placating tone." The miasma of Cathy's anger hung above the kitchen table as she angrily snapped a pile of green beans over a newspaper. "You're not like your sister. You don't flit around. There was Steve in high school, then Mason for reasons I still can't comprehend, then Jeffrey." She glanced up over her glasses. "If you've settled on Will, then settle on him."

Sara waited for her Aunt Bella to fill in a few missing men, but Bella just played with the string of pearls around her neck as she sipped her iced tea.

Cathy continued, "Your father and I have been married for nearly forty years."

Sara tried, "I never said—"

Bella made a sound somewhere between a cough and a cat sneezing.

Sara didn't heed the warning. "Mom, Will's divorce was just finalized. I'm still trying to get a handle on my new job. We're enjoying our lives. You should be happy for us."

Cathy snapped a bean like she was snapping a neck. "It was bad enough that you were seeing him while he was still married."

Sara took a deep breath and held it in her lungs.

She looked at the clock on the stove.

1:37 p.m.

It felt like midnight and she hadn't even had lunch yet.

She slowly exhaled, concentrating on the wonderful odors filling the kitchen. This was why she had given up her Sunday afternoon: Fried chicken cooling on the counter. Cherry cobbler baking in the oven. Butter melting into the pan of cornbread on the stove. Biscuits, field peas, black-eyed peas, sweet potato soufflé, chocolate cake, pecan pie and ice cream thick enough to break a spoon.

Six hours a day in the gym for the next week would not undo the damage she was about to do to her body, yet Sara's only fear was that she'd forget to take home any leftovers.

Cathy snapped another bean, pulling Sara out of her reverie.

Ice tinkled in Bella's glass.

Sara listened for the lawn mower in the backyard. For reasons she couldn't comprehend, Will had volunteered to serve as a weekend landscaper to her aunt. The thought of him accidentally overhearing any part of this conversation made her skin vibrate like a tuning fork.

"Sara." Cathy took an audible breath before picking up where she'd left off: "You're practically living with him now. His things are in your closet. His shaving stuff, all his toiletries, are in the bathroom."

"Oh, honey." Bella patted Sara's hand. "Never share a bathroom with a man."

Cathy shook her head. "This will kill your father."

Eddie wouldn't die, but he would not be happy in the same way that he was never happy with any of the men who wanted to date his daughters.

Which was the reason Sara was keeping their relationship to herself.

At least part of the reason.

She tried to gain the upper hand, "You know, Mother, you just admitted to snooping around my house. I have a right to privacy."

484

Bella tsked. "Oh, baby, it's so sweet that you really think that."

Sara tried again, "Will and I know what we're doing. We're not giddy teenagers passing notes in the hall. We like spending time together. That's all that matters."

Cathy grunted, but Sara was not stupid enough to mistake the ensuing silence for acquiescence.

Bella said, "Well, I'm the expert here. I've been married five times, and—"

"Six," Cathy interrupted.

"Sister, you know that was annulled. What I'm saying is, let the child figure out what she wants on her own."

"I'm not telling her what to do. I'm giving her advice. If she's not serious about Will, then she needs to move on and find a man she's serious about. She's too logical for casual relationships."

"'It's better to be without logic than without feeling.'"

"I would hardly consider Charlotte Brontë an expert on my daughter's emotional well-being."

Sara rubbed her temples, trying to stave off a headache. Her stomach grumbled but lunch wouldn't be served until two, which didn't matter because if she kept having this conversation, one or maybe all three of them were going to die in this kitchen.

Bella asked, "Sugar, did you see this story?"

Sara looked up.

"Don't you think she killed her wife because she's having an affair? I mean, one of them is having an affair, so the wife killed the affair-haver." She winked at Sara. "This was what the conservatives were worried about. Gay marriage has rendered pronouns immaterial."

Sara was having a hard time tracking until she realized that Bella was pointing to an article in the newspaper. Michelle Spivey had been abducted from a shopping center parking lot four weeks ago. She was a scientist with the Centers for Disease Control, which meant that the FBI had taken over the investigation. The photo in the paper was from Michelle's driver's license. It showed an attractive woman in her late thirties with a spark in her eye that even the crappy camera at the DMV had managed to capture.

Bella asked, "Have you been following the story?"

Sara shook her head. Unwanted tears welled into her eyes. Her husband had been killed five years ago. The only thing she could think of that would be worse than losing someone she loved was never knowing whether or not that person was truly gone.

Bella said, "I'm going with murder for hire. That's what usually turns out to be the case. The wife traded up for a newer model and had to get rid of the old one."

Sara should've dropped it because Cathy was clearly getting worked up. But, because Cathy was clearly getting worked up, Sara told Bella, "I dunno. Her daughter was there when it happened. She saw her mother being dragged into a van. It's probably naive to say this, but I don't think her other mother would do something like that to their child."

"Fred Tokars had his wife shot in front of his kids."

"That was for the life insurance, I think? Plus, wasn't his business shady, and there was some mob connection?"

"And he was a man. Don't women tend to kill with their hands?"

"For the love of God." Cathy finally broke. "Could we please not talk about murder on the Lord's day? And Sister, you of all people should not be discussing cheating spouses."

Bella rattled the ice in her empty glass. "Wouldn't a mojito be nice in this heat?"

Cathy clapped her hands together, finished with the green beans. She told Bella, "You're not helping."

"Oh, Sister, one should never look to Bella for help."

Sara waited for Cathy to turn her back before she wiped her eyes. Bella hadn't missed her sudden tears, which meant that as soon as Sara had left the kitchen, they would both be talking about the fact that she had been on the verge of crying because— why? Sara was at a loss to explain her weepiness. Lately, anything

486

from a sad commercial to a love song on the radio could set her off.

She picked up the newspaper and pretended to read the story. There were no updates on Michelle's disappearance. A month was too long. Even her wife had stopped pleading for her safe return and was begging whoever had taken Michelle to please just let them know where they could find the body.

Sara sniffed. Her nose had started running. She didn't reach for a paper napkin from the pile. She used the back of her hand.

She didn't know Michelle Spivey, but last year she had briefly met her wife, Theresa Lee, at an Emory Medical School alumni mixer. Lee was an orthopedist and professor at Emory. Michelle was an epidemiologist at the CDC. According to the article, the two were married in 2015, which likely meant they'd tied the knot as soon as they were legally able. They had been together for fifteen years before that. Sara assumed that after two decades, they'd figured out the two most common causes of divorce: the acceptable temperature setting for the thermostat and what level of criminal act it was to pretend you didn't know the dishwasher was ready to be emptied.

Then again, she was not the marriage expert in the room.

"Sara?" Cathy had her back to the counter, arms crossed. "I'm just going to be blunt."

Bella chuckled. "Give it a try."

"It's okay to move on," Cathy said. "Make a new life for yourself with Will. If you're truly happy, then be truly happy. Otherwise, what the hell are you waiting for?"

Sara carefully folded the newspaper. Her eyes returned to the clock.

1:43 p.m.

Bella said, "I did like Jeffrey, rest his soul. He had that swagger. But Will is so sweet. And he does love you, honey." She patted Sara's hand. "He really does."

Sara chewed her lip. Her Sunday afternoon was not going to turn into an impromptu therapy session. She didn't need to work out her feelings. She was caught in the reverse problem of every

487

romantic comedy's first act: she had already fallen in love with Will, but she wasn't sure how to love him.

Will's social awkwardness she could deal with, but his inability to communicate had nearly been the end of them. Not just once or twice, but several times. Initially, Sara had persuaded herself he was trying to show his best side. That was normal. She had let six months pass before she'd worn her real pajamas to bed.

Then a year had gone by and he was still keeping things to himself. Stupid things that didn't matter, like not calling to tell her that he was going to have to work late, that his basketball game was running long, that his bike had broken down halfway into his ride, that he'd volunteered his weekend to help a friend move. He always looked shocked when she was mad at him for not communicating these things. She wasn't trying to keep track of him. She was trying to figure out what to order for dinner.

As annoying as those interactions were, there were other things that really mattered. Will didn't lie so much as find clever ways to not tell her the truth—whether it had to do with a dangerous work situation or some awful detail about his child-hood or, worse, a recent atrocity committed by his nasty, narcissistic bitch of an ex-wife.

Logically, Sara understood the genesis of Will's behavior. He had spent his childhood in the foster care system, where, if he wasn't being neglected, he was being abused. His ex-wife had weaponized his emotions against him. He had never really been in a healthy relationship. There were some truly heinous skeletons lurking in his past. Maybe Will felt like he was protecting Sara. Maybe he felt like he was protecting himself. The point was that she had no fucking idea which one it was because he wouldn't acknowledge the problem existed.

"Sara, honey," Bella said. "I meant to tell you—the other day, I was thinking about when you lived here back when you were in school. Do you remember that, sugar?"

Sara smiled at the memory of her college years, but then the edges of her lips started to give when she caught the look that was exchanged between her aunt and mother.

A hammer was about to drop.

They had lured her here with the promise of fried chicken.

Bella said, "Baby, I'm gonna be honest. This old place is too much house for your sweet Aunt Bella to handle. What do you think of moving back in?"

Sara laughed, but then she saw that her aunt was serious.

Bella said, "Y'all could fix up the place, make it your own."

Sara felt her mouth moving, but she had no words.

"Honey." Bella held on to Sara's hand. "I always meant to leave it to you in my will, but my accountant says the tax situation would be better if I transferred it to you now through a trust. I've already put down a deposit on a condo downtown. You and Will can move in by Christmas. That foyer takes a twenty-foot tree, and there's plenty of room for—"

Sara experienced a momentary loss of hearing.

She had always loved the grand old Georgian, which was built just before the Great Depression. Six bedrooms, five bathrooms, a two-bedroom carriage house, a tricked-out garden shed, three acres of grounds in one of the state's most affluent zip codes. A ten-minute drive would take you downtown. A ten-minute stroll would have you at the center of the Emory University campus. The neighborhood was one of the last commissions Frederick Law Olmstead took before his death, and parks and trees blended beautifully into the Fernbank Forest.

It was an enticing offer until the numbers started scrolling through her head.

Bella hadn't replaced anything since the 1980s. Central heating and air. Plumbing. Electrical. Plaster repairs. New windows. New roof. New gutters. Wrangling with the historical Society over minute architectural details. Not to mention the time they would lose because Will would want to do all the work himself and Sara's scant free evenings and long, lazy weekends would turn into arguments about paint colors and money.

Money.

That was the real obstacle. Sara had a lot more money than Will. The same had been true of her marriage. She would never forget the look on Jeffrey's face the first time he'd seen the balance in her trading account. Sara had actually heard the squeaking groan of his testicles retracting into his body. It had taken a hell of a lot of suction to get them back out again.

Bella was saying, "And of course I can help with any taxes, but—"

"Thank you." Sara tried to dive in. "That's very generous, but—"

"It could be a wedding present." Cathy smiled sweetly as she sat down at the table. "Wouldn't that be lovely?"

Sara shook her head, but not at her mother. What was wrong with her? Why was she worrying about Will's reaction? She had no idea how much money he had. He paid cash for everything. Whether this was because he didn't believe in credit cards or because his credit was screwed up was another conversation that they were not having.

"What was that?" Bella had her head tilted to the side. "Did y'all hear something? Like firecrackers? Or something?"

Cathy ignored her. "You and Will can make this your home. And your sister can take the apartment over the garage."

Sara saw the hammer make its final blow. Her mother wasn't merely trying to control Sara's life. She wanted to throw in Tessa for good measure.

Sara said, "I don't think Tess wants to live over another garage."

Bella asked, "Isn't she living in a mud hut now?"

"Sissy, hush." Cathy asked Sara, "Have you talked to Tessa about moving home?"

"Not really," Sara lied. Her baby sister's marriage was falling apart. She Skyped with her at least twice a day, even though Tessa was living in South Africa. "Mama, you have to let this go. This isn't the 1950s. I can pay my own bills. My retirement is taken care of. I don't need to be legally bound to a man. I can take care of myself."

Cathy's expression lowered the temperature in the room. "If that's what you think marriage is, then I have nothing else to say on the matter." She pushed herself up from the table and returned to the stove. "Tell Will to wash up for dinner."

Sara closed her eyes so that she wouldn't roll them.

She stood up and left the kitchen.

Her footsteps echoed through the cavernous living room as she skirted the periphery of the ancient Oriental rug. She stopped at the first set of French doors. She pressed her forehead against the glass. Will was happily pushing the lawnmower into the shed. The yard looked spectacular. He had even trimmed the boxwoods into neat rectangles. The edging showed a surgical precision.

What would he say to a 2.5 million-dollar fixer-upper?

Sara wasn't even sure she wanted such a huge responsibility. She had spent the first few years of her marriage remodeling her tiny craftsman bungalow with Jeffrey. Sara keenly recalled the physical exhaustion from stripping wallpaper and painting stair spindles and the excruciating agony of knowing that she could just write a check and let someone else do it, but her husband was a stubborn, stubborn man.

Her husband.

That was the third rail her mother had been reaching for in the kitchen: Did Sara love Will the same way she had loved Jeffrey, and if she did, why wasn't she marrying him, and if she didn't, why was she wasting her time?

All good questions, but Sara found herself caught in a Scarlett O'Hara loop of promising herself that she would think about it tomorrow.

She shouldered open the door and was met by a wall of heat. Thick humidity made the air feel like it was sweating. Still, she reached up and took the band out of her hair. The added layer on the back of her neck was like a heated oven mitt. Except for the smell of fresh grass, she might as well be walking into a steam room. She trudged up the hill. Her sneakers slipped on some loose rocks. Bugs swarmed around her face. She swatted at them as she walked toward what Bella called the shed but was actually a converted barn with a blue stone floor and space for two horses and a carriage.

491

The door was open. Will stood in the middle of the room. His palms were pressed to the top of the workbench as he stared out the window. There was a stillness to him that made Sara wonder if she should interrupt. Something had been bothering him for the last two months. She could feel it edging into almost every part of their lives. She had asked him about it. She had given him space to think about it. She had tried to fuck it out of him. He kept insisting that he was fine, but then she'd catch him doing what he was doing now: staring out a window with a pained expression on his face.

Sara cleared her throat.

Will turned around. He'd changed shirts, but the heat had already plastered the material to his chest. Pieces of grass were stuck to his muscular legs. He was long and lean and the smile that he gave Sara momentarily made her forget every single problem she had with him.

He asked, "Is it time for lunch?"

She looked at her watch. "It's one forty-six. We have exactly fourteen minutes of calm before the storm."

His smile turned into a grin. "Have you seen the shed? I mean, really seen it?"

Sara thought it was pretty much a shed, but Will was clearly excited.

He pointed to a partitioned area in the corner. "There's a urinal over there. An actual, working urinal. How cool is that?"

"Awesome," she muttered in a non-awesome way.

"Look how sturdy these beams are." Will was six-four, tall enough to grab the beam and do a few pull-ups. "And look over here. This TV is old, but it still works. And there's a full refrigerator and microwave over here where I guess the horses used to live."

She felt her lips curve into a smile. He was such a city boy he didn't know that it was called a stall.

"And the couch is kind of musty, but it's really comfortable." He bounced onto the torn leather couch, pulling her down beside him. "It's great in here, right?"

492

Sara coughed at the swirling dust. She tried not to connect the stack of her uncle's old *Playboys* to the creaking couch.

Will asked, "Can we move in? I'm only halfway kidding."

Sara bit her lip. She didn't want him to be kidding. She wanted him to tell her what he wanted.

"Look, a guitar." He picked up the instrument and adjusted the tension on the strings. A few strums later and he was making recognizable sounds. And then he turned it into a song.

Sara felt the quick thrill of surprise that always came with finding out something new about him.

Will hummed the opening lines of Bruce Springsteen's "I'm on Fire".

He stopped playing. "That's kind of gross, right? 'Hey little girl is your daddy home?'"

"How about 'Girl, You'll Be a Woman Soon'? Or 'Don't Stand So Close to Me'? Or the opening line to 'Sara Smile'?"

"Damn." He plucked at the guitar strings. "Hall and Oates, too?"

"Panic! At the Disco has a better version." Sara watched his long fingers work the strings. She loved his hands. "When did you learn to play?"

"High school. Self-taught." Will gave her a sheepish look. "Think of every stupid thing a sixteen-year-old boy would do to impress a sixteen-year-old girl and I know how to do it."

She laughed, because it wasn't hard to imagine. "Did you have a fade?"

"Duh." He kept strumming the guitar. "I did the Pee-wee Herman voice. I could flip a skateboard. Knew all the words to 'Thriller'. You should've seen me in my acid-washed jeans and Nember's Only jacket."

"Nember?"

"Dollar Store brand. I didn't say I was a millionaire." He looked up from the guitar, clearly enjoying her amusement. But then he nodded toward her head, asking, "What's going on up there?"

Sara felt her earlier weepiness return. Love overwhelmed her.

493

He was so tuned into her feelings. She so desperately wanted him to accept that it was natural for her to be tuned into his.

Will put down the guitar. He reached up to her face, used his thumb to rub the worry out of her brow. "That's better."

Sara kissed him. Really kissed him. This part was always easy. She ran her fingers through his sweaty hair. Will kissed her neck, then lower. Sara arched into him. She closed her eyes and let his mouth and hands smooth away all of her doubts.

They only stopped because the couch gave a sudden, violent shudder.

Sara asked, "What the hell was that?"

Will didn't trot out the obvious joke about his ability to make the earth move. He looked under the couch. He stood up, checking the beams overhead, rapping his knuckles on the petrified wood. "Remember that earthquake in Alabama a few years back? That felt the same, but stronger."

Sara straightened her clothes. "The country club does fireworks displays. Maybe they're testing out a new show?"

"In broad daylight?" Will looked dubious. He found his phone on the workbench. "There aren't any alerts." He scrolled through his messages, then made a call. Then another. Then he tried a third number. Sara waited, expectant, but Will ended up shaking his head. He held up the phone so she could hear the recorded message saying that all circuits were busy.

She noted the time in the corner of the screen.

1:51 p.m.

She told Will, "Emory has an emergency siren. It goes off when there's a natural disast—"

Boom!

The earth gave another violent shake. Sara had to steady herself against the couch before she could follow Will into the backyard.

He was looking up at the sky. A plume of dark smoke curled up behind the tree line. Sara was intimately familiar with the Emory University campus.

Fifteen thousand students.

494

Six thousand faculty and staff members.

Two ground-shaking explosions.

"Let's go." Will jogged toward the car. He was a special agent with the Georgia Bureau of Investigation. Sara was a doctor. There was no need to have a discussion about what they should do.

"Sara!" Cathy called from the back door. "Did you hear that?"

"It's coming from Emory." Sara ran into the house to find her car keys. She felt her thoughts spinning into dread. The urban campus sprawled over six hundred acres. The Emory University Hospital. Egleston Children's Hospital. The Centers for Disease Control. The National Public Health Institute. The Yerkes National Primate Research Center. The Winship Cancer Institute. Government labs. Pathogens. Viruses. Terrorist attack? School shooter? Lone gunman?

"Could it be the bank?" Cathy asked. "There were those bank robbers who tried to blow up the jail."

Martin Novak. Sara knew there was an important meeting taking place downtown, but the prisoner was stashed in a safe house well outside of the city.

Bella said, "Whatever it is, it's not on the news yet." She had turned on the kitchen television. "I've got Buddy's old shotgun around here somewhere."

Sara found her key fob in her purse. "Stay inside." She grabbed her mother's hand, squeezed it tight. "Call Daddy and Tessa and let them know you're okay."

She put her hair up as she walked toward the door. She froze before she reached it.

They had all frozen in place.

The deep, mournful wail of the emergency siren filled the air.

THE
LAST WIDOW

Karin Slaughter

THE
LAST
WIDOW

It begins with an abduction.

The routine of a family shopping trip is shattered when Michelle Spivey
is snatched as she leaves the mall with her young daughter. The police search
for her, her partner pleads for her release, but in the end...they find nothing.
It's as if she disappeared into thin air.

A month later, on a sleepy Sunday afternoon,

medical examiner Sara Linton is at lunch with her boyfriend Will Trent,
an agent with the Georgia Bureau of Investigation. But the serenity of
the summer's day is broken by the wail of sirens.

Sara and Will are trained to help in an emergency.

Their jobs - their vocations - mean that they run *towards* a crisis, not away
from it. But on this one terrible day that instinct betrays them both.
Within hours the situation has spiralled out of control; Sara is taken prisoner;
Will is forced undercover. And the fallout will lead them into the Appalachian
mountains, to the terrible truth about what really happened to Michelle,
and to a remote compound where a radical group has murder in mind...

PENGUIN BOOKS

BULLY FOR BRONTOSAURUS

'Professor Gould is unquestion⸺ ⸺t writer on science in English today ... H' ⸺ us through the byways of the fossil record a⸺ ⸺arative anatomy to bring us back time and again ⸺ ourselves, illuminated by this new and deeper knowled⸺' – *Independent*

'There is no scientist today whose books I look forward to reading with greater anticipation of enjoyment and enlightenment than Stephen Jay Gould' – Martin Gardner

'**Stephen Jay Gould, winner of the Science Book Prize for *Wonderful Life*, turns his attention here to forgotten, misunderstood or neglected scientists of the past, to revealing controversies, matters of art and politics, and discusses them with civilized intelligence and wit**' – *Observer*

'Reliably thrilling, fresh and delightful ... His style rests on his intellectual confidence ... He never sounds awkward or false: neither patrician nor populist' – *New Statesman & Society*

'**His art is not guile. It bubbles up from a laudable eagerness to enthuse non-scientists. Gould is an immensely popular science writer – probably the best-known Darwinian expert in America**' – *Daily Telegraph*

Stephen Jay Gould grew up in New York City. He graduated from Antioch College and received his Ph.D. from Columbia University in 1967. Since then he has been Professor of Geology and Zoology at Harvard University. He considers himself primarily a palaeontologist and an evolutionary biologist, though he teaches geology and the history of science as well. A frequent and popular speaker on the sciences, his published work includes *Ontogeny and Phylogeny*, a scholarly study of the theory of recapitulation; *The Mismeasure of Man*, winner of the National Book Critics' Circle Award for 1982 and reissued with new material in 1997; his popular collection of essays, *Ever Since Darwin: Reflections in Natural History* (1978), which received great acclaim and of which the *New Scientist* wrote 'unreservedly, they are brilliant'; *The Panda's Thumb: More Reflections in Natural History*, which won the 1981 American Book Award for Science; *Hen's Teeth and Horse's Toes: Further Reflections in Natural History* (1983); *The Flamingo's Smile* (1985); *Time's Arrow, Time's Cycle* (1987); *An Urchin in the Storm* (1988); *Wonderful Life*, winner of the Science Book Prize for 1991; *Bully for Brontosaurus* (1991); *Eight Little Piggies* (1993); *Dinosaur in a Haystack* (1996); *Life's Grandeur* (1996); and *Questioning the Millennium* (1997). Most of his books are published by Penguin.

This book is to be returned on or before the last date stamped below.

508

LIBREX

PENGUIN BOOKS

Published by the Penguin Group
Penguin Books Ltd, 27 Wrights Lane, London W8 5TZ, England
Penguin Putnam Inc., 375 Hudson Street, New York, New York 10014, USA
Penguin Books Australia Ltd, Ringwood, Victoria, Australia
Penguin Books Canada Ltd, 10 Alcorn Avenue, Toronto, Ontario, Canada M4V 3B2
Penguin Books (NZ) Ltd, 182–190 Wairau Road, Auckland 10, New Zealand

Penguin Books Ltd, Registered Offices: Harmondsworth, Middlesex, England

First published in Great Britain by Hutchinson Radius,
an imprint of Random Century Ltd, 1991
Published in Penguin Books 1992
10 9 8

Printed in England by Clays Ltd, St Ives plc

Pleni sunt coeli
et terra
gloria eius.

Hosanna in excelsis.

Contents

10 | PLANETS AS PERSONS

Prologue

IN FRANCE, they call this genre *vulgarisation*—but the implications are entirely positive. In America, we call it "popular (or pop) writing" and its practitioners are dubbed "science writers" even if, like me, they are working scientists who love to share the power and beauty of their field with people in other professions.

In France (and throughout Europe), *vulgarisation* ranks within the highest traditions of humanism, and also enjoys an ancient pedigree—from St. Francis communing with animals to Galileo choosing to write his two great works in Italian, as dialogues between professor and students, and not in the formal Latin of churches and universities. In America, for reasons that I do not understand (and that are truly perverse), such writing for non-scientists lies immured in deprecations—"adulteration," "simplification," "distortion for effect," "grandstanding," "whiz-bang." I do not deny that many American works deserve these designations—but poor and self-serving items, even in vast majority, do not invalidate a genre. "Romance" fiction has not banished love as a subject for great novelists.

I deeply deplore the equation of popular writing with pap and distortion for two main reasons. First, such a designation imposes a crushing professional burden on scientists (particularly young scientists without tenure) who might like to try their hand at this expansive style. Second, it denigrates the intelligence of millions of Americans eager for intellectual stimulation without patronization. If we writers assume a crushing mean of mediocrity and incomprehension, then not only do we have contempt

11

for our neighbors, but we also extinguish the light of excellence. The "perceptive and intelligent" layperson is no myth. They exist in millions—a low percentage of Americans perhaps, but a high absolute number with influence beyond their proportion in the population. I know this in the most direct possible way—by thousands of letters received from nonprofessionals during my twenty years of writing these essays, and particularly from the large number written by people in their eighties and nineties, and still striving, as intensely as ever, to grasp nature's richness and add to a lifetime of understanding.

We must all pledge ourselves to recovering accessible science as an honorable intellectual tradition. The rules are simple: no compromises with conceptual richness; no bypassing of ambiguity or ignorance; removal of jargon, of course, but no dumbing down of ideas (any conceptual complexity can be conveyed in ordinary English). Several of us are pursuing this style of writing in America today. And we enjoy success if we do it well. Thus, our primary task lies in public relations: We must be vigorous in identifying what we are and are not, uncompromising in our claims to the humanistic lineages of St. Francis and Galileo, not to the sound bites and photo ops in current ideologies of persuasion—the ultimate in another grand old American tradition (the dark side of anti-intellectualism, and not without a whiff of appeal to the unthinking emotionalism that can be a harbinger of fascism).

Humanistic natural history comes in two basic lineages. I call them Franciscan and Galilean in the light of my earlier discussion. Franciscan writing is nature poetry—an exaltation of organic beauty by corresponding choice of words and phrase. Its lineage runs from St. Francis to Thoreau on Walden Pond, W. H. Hudson on the English downs, to Loren Eiseley in our generation. Galilean composition delights in nature's intellectual puzzles and our quest for explanation and understanding. Galileans do not deny the visceral beauty, but take greater delight in the joy of causal comprehension and its powerful theme of unification. The Galilean (or rationalist) lineage has roots more ancient than its eponym—from Aristotle dissecting squid to Galileo reversing the heavens, to T. H. Huxley inverting our natural place, to P. B. Medawar dissecting the follies of our generation.

I love good Franciscan writing but regard myself as a fervent, unrepentant, pure Galilean—and for two major reasons. First, I would be an embarrassing flop in the Franciscan trade. Poetic writing is the most dangerous of all genres because failures are so conspicuous, usually as the most ludicrous form of purple prose (see James Joyce's parody, cited in Chapter 17). Cobblers should stick to their lasts and rationalists to their measured style. Second, Wordsworth was right. The child is father to the man. My youthful "splendor in the grass" was the bustle and buildings of New York. My adult joys have been walks in cities, amidst stunning human diversity of behavior and architecture—from the Quirinal to the Piazza Navona at dusk, from the Georgian New Town to the medieval Old Town of Edinburgh at dawn—more than excursions in the woods. I am not insensible to natural beauty, but my emotional joys center on the improbable yet sometimes wondrous works of that tiny and accidental evolutionary twig called *Homo sapiens.* And I find, among these works, nothing more noble than the history of our struggle to understand nature—a majestic entity of such vast spatial and temporal scope that she cannot care much for a little mammalian afterthought with a curious evolutionary invention, even if that invention has, for the first time in some four billion years of life on earth, produced recursion as a creature reflects back upon its own production and evolution. Thus, I love nature primarily for the puzzles and intellectual delights that she offers to the first organ capable of such curious contemplation.

Franciscans may seek a poetic oneness with nature, but we Galilean rationalists have a program of unification as well—nature made mind and mind now returns the favor by trying to comprehend the source of production.

This is the fifth volume of collected essays from my monthly series, "This View of Life," now approaching two hundred items over eighteen years in *Natural History* magazine (the others, in order, are *Ever Since Darwin, The Panda's Thumb, Hen's Teeth and Horse's Toes,* and *The Flamingo's Smile*). The themes may be familiar (with a good dollop of novelty, I trust), but the items are mostly new (and God has never left his dwelling place in the details).

Against a potential charge of redundancy, may I advance the immodest assertion that this volume is the best of the five. I think that I have become a better writer by monthly practice (I sometimes wish that all copies of *Ever Since Darwin* would self-destruct), and I have given myself more latitude of selection and choice in this volume. (The previous four volumes discarded only a turkey or two and then published all available items in three years of essays. This volume, covering six years of writing, presents the best, or rather the most integrated, thirty-five pieces from more than sixty choices.)

These essays, while centered on the enduring themes of evolution and the innumerable, instructive oddities of nature (frogs that use their stomachs as brood pouches, the gigantic eggs of Kiwis, an ant with a single chromosome), also record the specific passage of six years since the fourth volume. I have marked the successful completion of a sixty-year battle against creationism (since the Scopes trial of 1925) in our resounding Supreme Court victory of 1987 (see essays under "Scopes to Scalia"), the bicentennial of the French revolution (in an essay on Lavoisier, most prominent scientific victim of the Reign of Terror), and the magnificent completion of our greatest technical triumph in *Voyager*'s fly-by and photography of Uranus and Neptune (Essays 34 and 35). I also record, as I must, our current distresses and failures—the sorry state of science education (approached, as is my wont, not tendentiously, abstractly, and head-on, but through byways that sneak up on generality—fox terriers and textbook copying, or subversion of dinomania for intellectual benefit), and a sad epilogue on the extinction, between first writing and this republication, of the stomach-brooding frog.

Yet I confess that my personal favorites usually treat less immediate, even obscure, subjects—especially when correction of the errors that confined them to ridicule or obscurity retells their stories as relevant and instructive today. Thus, I write about Abbot Thayer's theory that flamingos are red to hide them from predators in the sunset, Petrus Camper's real intent (criteria for art) in establishing a measure later used by scientific racists, the admirable side of William Jennings Bryan and the racist nonsense in the text that John Scopes used to teach evolution, the actual (and much more interesting) story behind the heroic, cardboard version of the Huxley-Wilberforce debate of 1860.

For what it's worth, my own favorite is Essay 21 on N. S. Shaler and William James (I won't reveal my vote for the worst essays—especially since they have been shredded in my mental refuse bin and will not be included in these volumes). At least Essay 21 best illustrates my favorite method of beginning with something small and curious and then working outward and onward by a network of lateral connections. I found the fearful letter of Shaler to Agassiz in a drawer almost twenty years ago. I always knew that I would find a use for it someday—but I had no inkling of the proper context. A new biography of Shaler led me to explore his relationship with Agassiz. I then discovered the extent of Shaler's uncritical (and lifelong) fealty by reading his technical papers. At this point, luck intervened. One of my undergraduate advisees told me that William James, as a Harvard undergraduate, had sailed with Agassiz to Brazil on the master's penultimate voyage. I knew that Shaler and James had been friendly colleagues and intellectual adversaries—and now I had full connectivity in their shared link to Agassiz. But would anything interesting emerge from all these ties? Again, good fortune smiled. James had been critical of Agassiz right from the start—and in the very intellectual arena (contingency versus design in the history of life) that would host their later disagreements as distinguished senior professors. I then found a truly amazing letter from James to Shaler offering the most concise and insightful rebuttal I have ever read to the common misconception—as current today as when James and Shaler argued—that the improbability of our evolution indicates divine intent in our origin. James's document—also a brilliant statement on the general nature of probability—provided a climax of modern relevance for a story that began with an obscure note lying undiscovered in a drawer for more than a hundred years. Moreover, James's argument allowed me to resolve the dilemma of the museum janitor, Mr. Eli Grant, potential victim of Shaler's cowardly note—so the essay ends by using James's great generality to solve the little mystery of its beginning, a more satisfactory closure (I think) than the disembodied abstraction of James's brilliance.

Finally, and now thrice lucky, I received two years later a fascinating letter from Jimmy Carter presenting a theological alternative to the view of contingency and improbability in human evolution advanced in my last book, *Wonderful Life.* Carter's argument, though more subtle and cogent than Shaler's, follows the same logic—and James's rebuttal has never been bettered or more apropos. And so, by presidential proclamation, I had an epilogue that proved the modern relevance of Shaler's traditionalism versus James's probing.

Some people have seen me as a polymath, but I insist that I am a tradesman. I admit to a broad range of explicit detail, but all are chosen to illustrate the common subjects of evolutionary change and the nature of history. And I trust that this restricted focus grants coherence and integration to an overtly disparate range of topics. The bullet that hit George Canning in the ass really is a vehicle for discussing the same historical contingency that rules evolution. My sweet little story about nostalgia at the thirtieth reunion of my All-City high school chorus is meant to be a general statement (bittersweet in its failure to resolve a cardinal dichotomy) about the nature of excellence. The essay on Joe DiMaggio's hitting streak is a disquisition on probability and pattern in historical sequences; another on the beginnings of baseball explores creation versus evolution as primal stories for the origin of any object or institution. And Essay 32, the only bit I have ever been moved to write about my bout with cancer, is not a confessional in the personal mode, but a general statistical argument about the nature of variation in populations—the central topic of all evolutionary biology.

A final thought on Franciscans and Galileans in the light of our environmental concerns as a tattered planet approaches the millennium (by human reckoning—as nature, dealing in billions, can only chuckle). Franciscans engage the glory of nature by direct communion. Yet nature is so massively indifferent to us and our suffering. Perhaps this indifference, this majesty of years in uncaring billions (before we made a belated appearance), marks her true glory. Omar Khayyám's old quatrain grasped this fundamental truth (though he should have described his Eastern hotel, his metaphor for the earth, as grand rather than battered):

> Think, in this battered caravanserai
> Whose portals are alternate night and day,
> How sultan after sultan with his pomp
> Abode his destined hour, and went his way.

The true beauty of nature is her amplitude; she exists neither for nor because of us, and possesses a staying power that all our nuclear arsenals cannot threaten (much as we can easily destroy our puny selves).

The hubris that got us into trouble in the first place, and that environmentalists seek to avoid as the very definition of their (I should say our) movement, often creeps back in an unsuspected (and therefore potentially dangerous) form in two tenets frequently advanced by "green" movements: (1) that we live on a fragile planet subject to permanent ruin by human malfeasance; (2) that humans must act as stewards of this fragility in order to save our planet.

We should be so powerful! (Read this sentence with my New York accent as a derisive statement about our false sense of might, not as a literal statement of desire.) For all our mental and technological wizardry, I doubt that we can do much to derail the earth's history in any permanent sense by the proper planetary time scale of millions of years. Nothing within our power can come close to conditions and catastrophes that the earth has often passed through and beyond. The worst scenario of global warming under greenhouse models yields an earth substantially cooler than many happy and prosperous times of a prehuman past. The megatonnage of the extraterrestrial impact that probably triggered the late Cretaceous mass extinction has been estimated at 10,000 times greater than all the nuclear bombs now stockpiled on earth. And this extinction, wiping out some 50 percent of marine species, was paltry compared to the granddaddy of all—the Permian event some 225 million years ago that might have dispatched up to 95 percent of species. Yet the earth recovered from these superhuman shocks, and produced some interesting evolutionary novelties as a result (consider the potential for mammalian domination, including human emergence, following the removal of dinosaurs).

But recovery and restabilization occur at planetary, not human, time scales—that is, millions of years after the disturbing event. At this scale, we are powerless to harm; the planet will take care of itself, our puny foolishnesses notwithstanding. But this time scale, though natural for planetary history, is not appropriate in our legitimately parochial concern for our own species, and the current planetary configurations that now support us. For these planetary instants—our millennia—we do hold power to impose immense suffering (I suspect that the Permian catastrophe was decidedly unpleasant for the nineteen of twenty species that didn't survive).

We certainly cannot wipe out bacteria (they have been the modal organisms on earth right from the start, and probably shall be until the sun explodes); I doubt that we can wreak much permanent havoc upon insects as a whole (whatever our power to destroy local populations and species). But we can surely eliminate our fragile selves—and our well-buffered earth might then breathe a metaphorical sigh of relief at the ultimate failure of an interesting but dangerous experiment in consciousness. Global warming is worrisome because it will flood our cities (built so often at sea level as ports and harbors), and alter our agricultural patterns to the severe detriment of millions. Nuclear war is an ultimate calamity for the pain and death of billions, and the genetic maiming of millions in future generations.

Our planet is not fragile at its own time scale, and we, pitiful latecomers in the last microsecond of our planetary year, are stewards of nothing in the long run. Yet no political movement is more vital and timely than modern environmentalism—because we must save ourselves (and our neighbor species) from our own immediate folly. We hear so much talk about an environmental ethic. Many proposals embody the abstract majesty of a Kantian categorical imperative. Yet I think that we need something far more grubby and practical. We need a version of the most useful and ancient moral principle of all—the precept developed in one form or another by nearly every culture because it acts, in its legitimate appeal to self-interest, as a doctrine of stability based upon mutual respect. No one has ever improved upon the golden rule. If we execute such a compact with our planet, pledging to cherish the earth as we would wish to be treated ourselves, she may relent and allow us to muddle through. Such a limited goal may strike some readers as cynical or blinkered. But remember that, to an evolutionary biologist, persistence is the ultimate reward. And human brainpower, for reasons quite unrelated to its evolutionary origin, has the damnedest capacity to discover the most fascinating things, and think the most peculiar thoughts. So why not keep this interesting experiment around, at least for another planetary second or two?

1 | History in Evolution

1 | George Canning's Left Buttock and the Origin of Species

      I KNOW the connection between Charles Darwin and Abraham Lincoln. They conveniently contrived to enter the world on the same day, February 12, 1809, thus providing forgetful humanity with a mnemonic for ordering history. (Thanks also to John Adams and Thomas Jefferson for dying on the same momentous day, July 4, 1826, exactly fifty years after our nation's official birthdate.)

But what is the connection between Charles Darwin and Andrew Jackson? What can an English gentleman who mastered the abstractions of science hold in common with Old Hickory, who inaugurated the legend (later exploited by Lincoln) of the backwoodsman with little formal education fighting his way to the White House? (Jackson was born on the western frontier of the Carolinas in 1767, but later set up shop in the pioneer territory of Nashville.) This more difficult question requires a long string of connections more worthy of Rube Goldberg than of logical necessity. But let's have a try, in nine easy steps.

1. Andy Jackson, as a result of his military exploits in and around the ill-fated War of 1812, became a national figure, and ultimately, on this basis, a presidential contender. In a conflict conspicuously lacking in good news, Jackson provided much solace by winning the Battle of New Orleans, our only major victory on land after so many defeats and stalemates. With help from the privateer Jean Lafitte (who was then pardoned by President Madison but soon resumed his old ways), Jackson decisively defeated the British forces on January 8, 1815, and compelled their withdrawal from Louisiana. Cynics often point out, perhaps ungener-

ously, that Jackson's victory occurred more than two weeks after the war had officially ended, but no one had heard the news down in the bayous because the treaty had been signed in Ghent and word then traveled no faster than ship.

2. When we were about to withdraw from Vietnam and acknowledge (at least privately) that the United States had lost the war, some supporters of that venture (I was not among them) drew comfort from recalling that, patriotic cant aside, this was not our first military defeat. Polite traditions depict the War of 1812 as a draw, but let's face it, basically we lost—at least in terms of the larger goal espoused by hawks of that era: the annexation of Canada, at least in part. But we did manage to conserve both territory and face, an important boon to America's future and a crucial ingredient in Jackson's growing reputation. Washington, so humiliated just a few months before when British troops burned the White House and the Capitol, rejoiced in two items of news, received in early 1815 in reverse order of their actual occurrence: Jackson's victory at New Orleans, and the favorable terms of the Treaty of Ghent, signed on December 24, 1814.

3. The Treaty of Ghent restored all national boundaries to their positions before the war; thus, we could claim that we had lost not an inch of territory, even though expansion into Canada had been the not-so-hidden aim of the war's promoters. The treaty provided for commissions of arbitration to settle other points of dispute between the United States and Canada; all remaining controversies were negotiated peacefully under these provisions, including the establishment of our unfortified boundary, the elimination of naval forces from the Great Lakes, and the settlement of the Saint Lawrence boundary. Thomas Boylston Adams, descendant of John Quincy Adams (who negotiated and signed the treaty), recently wrote of that exemplary document (in his wonderful column "History Looks Ahead," appearing twice a month in the *Boston Globe*): "The treaty . . . ended a war that never should have been begun. Yet its consummation was unbounded good. The peace then confirmed . . . has never been broken. Its bounty has been the cheerful coexistence of two friendly nations divided by nothing more tangible than an invisible line that runs for 3,000 miles undefended by armed men or armaments."

4. If the war had not ended, fortunately for us, on such an upbeat, Andy Jackson's belated victory at New Orleans might

have emerged as a bitter joke rather than a symbol of (at least muted) success—and Jackson, deprived of status as a military hero, might never have become president. But why did Britain, in a fit of statesmanship, agree to such a conciliatory treaty, when they held the upper hand militarily? The reasons are complex and based, in part, on expediency (the coalition that had exiled Napoleon to Elba was coming apart, and more troops might soon be needed in Europe). But much credit must also go to the policies of Britain's remarkable foreign secretary, Robert Stewart, Viscount Castlereagh. In a secret dispatch sent to the British minister in Washington in 1817, Castlereagh set out his basic policy for negotiation, a stance that had guided the restructuring of Europe at the Congress of Vienna, following the final defeat of Napoleon: "The avowed and true policy of Great Britain in the existing State of the World is to secure if possible, for all states a long interval of repose."

Three years earlier, Castlereagh had put flesh on these brave words by helping to break the deadlock at Ghent and facilitate a peace treaty that did not take all that Britain could have demanded, thereby leaving the United States with both pride and flexibility for a future and deeper peace with Britain. Negotiations had gone badly at Ghent; anger and stalemate ruled. Then, on his way to Vienna, Castlereagh stopped for two days in Ghent, where, in secret meetings with his negotiators, he advocated conciliation and helped to break the deadlock.

5. We must thank the fortunate tides of history that Castlereagh, rather than his counterpart and rival, the hawkish and uncompromising George Canning, was presiding over Britain's foreign affairs in 1814. (And so you see, dear reader, we are finally getting to Mr. Canning's rear end, as promised in the title.) The vagaries of a key incident in 1809 led to this favorable outcome. Canning, then foreign secretary, had been pushing for Castlereagh's ouster as secretary of war. Castlereagh had sent a British expedition against Napoleon's naval base at Antwerp, but nature had intervened (through no fault of Castlereagh's), and the troops were boxed in on the island of Walcheren, dying in droves of typhoid fever. Canning used this disaster to press his advantage.

Meanwhile (this does get complicated), the prime minister, the duke of Portland, suffered a paralytic stroke and eventually had to resign. In the various reshufflings and explanations that follow such an event, Perceval, the new prime minister, showed Castlereagh some of Canning's incriminating letters. Castlereagh did not challenge Canning's right to lobby for his removal, but he exploded in fury at Canning's apparent secrecy in machination. Canning, for his part (and not without justice), replied that he had urged open confrontation of the issue, but that higher-ups (including the king) had imposed secrecy, hoping to paper over the affair and somehow preserve the obvious talents of both men in government.

Castlereagh, to say the least, was not satisfied and, in the happily abandoned custom of his age, insisted upon a duel. The two men and their seconds met on Putney Heath at 6 A.M. on September 21. They fired a first round to no effect, but Castlereagh insisted on a second, of much greater import. Castlereagh was spared the fate of Alexander Hamilton by inches, as Canning's bullet removed a button from his coat but missed his person. Canning was not so fortunate; though more embarrassed than seriously injured, he took Castlereagh's second bullet in his left buttock. (Historians have tended to euphemism at this point. The latest biography of Castlereagh holds that Canning got it "through the fleshy part of the thigh," but I have it on good authority that Canning was shot in the ass.) In any case, both men subsequently resigned.

As the world turns and passions cool, both Canning and Castlereagh eventually returned to power. Canning achieved his burning ambition (cause of his machinations against Castlereagh) to become prime minister, if only briefly, in 1827. Castlereagh came back in Canning's old job of foreign secretary, where he assured the Treaty of Ghent and presided for Britain at the Congress of Vienna.

6. Suppose Canning had fired more accurately and killed Castlereagh on the spot? Canning, or another of his hawkish persuasion, might have imposed stiffer terms upon the United States and deprived Andy Jackson of his hero's role. More important for our tale, Castlereagh would have been denied the opportunity to die as he actually did, by his own hand, in 1822. Castlereagh had suffered all his life from periods of acute and debilitating "melancholy" and would, today, almost surely be diagnosed as a severe manic depressive. Attacked by the likes of Lord Byron, Shelley,

and Thomas Moore for his foreign policies, and suffering from both overwork and parliamentary reverses, Castlereagh became unreasonably suspicious and downright paranoid. He thought that he was being blackmailed for supposed acts of homosexuality (neither the blackmail nor the sexual orientation has ever been proved). His two closest friends, King George IV and the duke of Wellington, failed to grasp the seriousness of his illness and did not secure adequate protection or treatment. On August 12, 1822, though his wife (fearing the worst) had removed all knives and razors from his vicinity, Castlereagh rushed into his dressing room, seized a small knife that had been overlooked, and slit his throat.

7. Yes, we are getting to Darwin, but it takes a while. Point seven is a simple statement of genealogy: Lord Castlereagh's sister was the mother of Robert FitzRoy, captain of HMS *Beagle* and host to Charles Darwin on a five-year voyage that bred the greatest revolution in the history of biology.

8. Robert FitzRoy took command of the *Beagle* at age twenty-three, after the previous captain had suffered a mental breakdown and shot himself. FitzRoy was a brilliant and ambitious man. He had been instructed to take the *Beagle* on a surveying voyage of the South American coast. But FitzRoy's own plans extended far beyond a simple mapping trip, for he hoped to set a new standard of scientific observation on a much broader scale. To accomplish his aim, he needed more manpower than the Admiralty was willing to supply. As a person of wealth, he decided to take some extra passengers at his own expense, to beef up the *Beagle's* scientific mettle.

A popular scientific myth holds that Darwin sailed on the *Beagle* as official ship's naturalist. This is not true. The official naturalist was the ship's surgeon, Robert McKormick. Darwin, who disliked McKormick and did eventually succeed him as naturalist (after the disgruntled McKormick "invalided out," to use the euphemism of his time), originally sailed as a supernumerary passenger at FitzRoy's discretion.

Why, then, did FitzRoy tap Darwin? The obvious answer—that Darwin was a promising young scientist who could aid FitzRoy's plans for improved observation—may be partly true, but does not get to the heart of FitzRoy's reasons. First of all, Darwin may have possessed abundant intellectual promise, but he had no scientific credentials when he sailed on the *Beagle*—a long-standing interest in natural history and bug collecting to be sure, but neither a degree in science nor an intention to enter the profession (he was preparing for the ministry at the time).

FitzRoy took Darwin along primarily for a much different, and personal, reason. As an aristocratic captain, and following the naval customs of his time, FitzRoy could have no social contact with officers or crew during long months at sea. He dined alone and conversed with his men only in an official manner. FitzRoy understood the psychological toll that such enforced solitude could impose, and he remembered the fate of the *Beagle*'s previous skipper. He decided on a course of action that others had followed in similar circumstances: He decided to take along, at his own expense, a supernumerary passenger to serve, in large part, as a mealtime companion for conversation. He therefore advertised discreetly among his friends for a young man of appropriate social status who could act as both social companion and scientific aid. Charles Darwin, son of a wealthy physician and grandson of the great scholar Erasmus Darwin, fitted the job description admirably.

But most captains did not show such solicitude for their own mental health. Why did FitzRoy so dread the rigors of solitude? We cannot know for sure, but the answer seems to lie, in good part, with the suicide of his uncle, Lord Castlereagh. FitzRoy, by Darwin's own account, was fearful of a presumed hereditary predisposition to madness, an anxiety that he embodied in the suicide of his famous uncle, whom he so much resembled in looks as well as temperament. Moreover, FitzRoy's fears proved well founded, for he did break down and temporarily relinquish his command in Valparaiso during a period of overwork and tension. On November 8, 1834, Darwin wrote to his sister Catherine: "We have had some strange proceedings on board the *Beagle* . . . Capt. FitzRoy has for the last two months, been working *extremely* hard and at the same time constantly annoyed. . . . This was accompanied by a morbid depression of spirits, and a loss of all decision and resolution. The Captain was afraid that his mind was becoming deranged (being aware of his hereditary predisposition). . . . He invalided and Wickham was appointed to the command."

Late in life, and with some hindsight, Darwin mused on the character of Captain FitzRoy in his autobiography:

FitzRoy's character was a singular one, with many very noble features: he was devoted to his duty, generous to a fault, bold, determined, indomitably energetic, and an ardent friend to all under his sway. . . . He was a handsome man, strikingly like a gentleman, with highly courteous manners, which resembled those of his maternal uncle, the famous Lord Castlereagh. . . . FitzRoy's temper was a most unfortunate one. This was shown not only by passion but by fits of long-continued moroseness. . . . He was also somewhat suspicious and occasionally in very low spirits, on one occasion bordering on insanity. He was extremely kind to me, but was a man very difficult to live with on the intimate terms which necessarily followed from our messing by ourselves in the same cabin. [Darwin does mean "eating," and we find no sexual innuendo either here or anywhere else in their relationship.]

I am struck by the similarity, according to Darwin's description, between FitzRoy and his uncle, Lord Castlereagh, not only in physical characteristics and social training, but especially in the chronicle of a mental history so strongly implying a lifelong pattern of severe manic depression. In other words, I think that FitzRoy was correct in his self-diagnosis of a tendency to hereditary mental illness. Castlereagh's dramatic example had served him well as a warning, and his decision, so prompted, to take Darwin on the *Beagle* was history's reward.

But suppose Canning had killed Castlereagh, rather than just removing a button from his coat? Would FitzRoy have developed so clear a premonition about his own potential troubles without the terrible example of his beloved uncle's suicide during his most impressionable years (FitzRoy was seventeen when Castlereagh died)? Would Darwin have secured his crucial opportunity if Canning's bullet had been on the mark?

Tragically, FitzRoy's premonition eventually came to pass in almost eerie consonance with his own nightmare and memory of Castlereagh. FitzRoy's later career had its ups and downs. He suffered from several bouts of prolonged depression, accompanied by increasing suspicion and paranoia. In his last post, FitzRoy served as chief of the newly formed Meteorological Office and became a pioneer in weather forecasting. FitzRoy is much admired today for his cautious and excellent work in a most difficult field. But he encountered severe criticism during his own tenure, and for the obvious reason. Weathermen take enough flak today for incorrect predictions. Imagine the greater uncertainties more than a century ago. FitzRoy was stung by criticism of his imprecision. With a healthy mind, he would have parried the blows and come out fighting. But he sank into even deeper despair and eventually committed suicide by slitting his throat on April 20, 1865. Darwin mourned for his former friend (and more recent enemy of evolution), noting the fulfillment of the prophecy that had fostered his own career: "His end," Darwin wrote, "was a melancholy one, namely suicide, exactly like that of his uncle Ld. Castlereagh, whom he resembled closely in manner and appearance."

9. Finally, the other short and obvious statement: We must reject the self-serving historical myth that Darwin simply "saw" evolution in the raw when he broke free from the constraints of his culture and came face to face with nature all around the world. Darwin, in fact, did not become an evolutionist until he returned to England and struggled to make sense of what he had observed in the light of his own heritage: of Adam Smith, William Wordsworth, and Thomas Malthus, among others. Nonetheless, without the stimulus of the *Beagle*, I doubt that Darwin would have concerned himself with the origin of species or even entered the profession of science at all. Five years aboard the *Beagle* did serve as the sine qua non of Darwin's revolution in thought.

My chain of argument runs in two directions from George Canning's left buttock: on one branch, to Castlereagh's survival, his magnanimous approach to the face-saving Treaty of Ghent, the consequent good feeling that made the Battle of New Orleans a heroic conquest rather than a bitter joke, to Andrew Jackson's emergence as a military hero and national figure ripe for the presidency; on the other branch, to Castlereagh's survival and eventual death by his own hand, to the example thus provided to his similarly afflicted nephew Robert FitzRoy, to FitzRoy's consequent decision to take a social companion aboard the *Beagle*, to the choice of Darwin, to the greatest revolution in the history of biological thought. The duel on Putney Heath branches out in innumerable directions, but one leads to Jackson's presidency and the other to Darwin's discovery.

I don't want to push this style of argument too far, and this essay is meant primarily as comedy (however feeble the attempt). Anyone can set out a list of contrary proposals. Jackson was a tough customer and might have made his way to the top without a boost from New Orleans. Perhaps FitzRoy didn't need the drama of Castlereagh's death to focus a legitimate fear for his own sanity. Perhaps Darwin was so brilliant, so purposeful, and so destined that he needed no larger boost from nature than a beetle collection in an English parsonage.

No connections are certain (for we cannot perform the experiment of replication), but history presents, as its primary fascination, this feature of large and portentous movements arising from tiny quirks and circumstances that appear insignificant at the time but cascade into later, and unpredictable, prominence. The chain of events makes sense after the fact, but would never occur in the same way again if we could rerun the tape of time.

I do not, of course, claim that history contains nothing predictable. Many broad directions have an air of inevitability. A theory of evolution would have been formulated and accepted, almost surely in the mid-nineteenth century, if Charles Darwin had never been born, if only for the simple reason that evolution is true, and not so veiled from our sight (and insight) that discovery could long have tarried behind the historical passage of cultural barriers to perception.

But we are creatures of endless and detailed curiosity. We are not sufficiently enlightened by abstractions devoid of flesh and bones, idiosyncrasies and curiosities. We cannot be satisfied by concluding that a thrust of Western history, and a dollop of geographic separation, virtually guaranteed the eventual independence of the United States. We want to know about the tribulations at Valley Forge, the shape of the rude bridge that arched the flood at Concord, the reasons for crossing out "property" and substituting "pursuit of happiness" in Jefferson's great document. We care deeply about Darwin's encounter with Galápagos tortoises and his studies of earthworms, orchids, and coral reefs, even if a dozen other naturalists would have carried the day for evolution had Canning killed Castlereagh, FitzRoy sailed alone, and Darwin become a country parson. The details do not merely embellish an abstract tale moving in an inexorable way. The details are the story itself; the underlying predictability, if discernible at all, is too nebulous, too far in the background, and too devoid of hooks upon actual events to count as an explanation in any satisfying sense.

Darwin, that great beneficiary of a thousand chains of improbable circumstance, came to understand this principle and to grasp thereby the essence of history in its largest domain of geology and life. When America's great Christian naturalist Asa Gray told Darwin that he was prepared to accept the logic of natural selection but recoiled at the moral implications of a world without divine guidance, Darwin cited history as a resolution. Gray, in obvious distress, had posed the following argument: Science implies lawfulness; laws (like the principle of natural selection) are instituted by God to ensure his benevolent aims in the results of nature; the path of history, however full of apparent sorrow and death, must therefore include purpose. Darwin replied that laws surely exist and that, for all he knew, they might well embody a purpose legitimately labeled divine. But, Darwin continued, laws only regulate the broad outlines of history, "with the details, whether good or bad, left to the working out of what we may call chance." (Note Darwin's careful choice of words. He does not mean "random" in the sense of uncaused; he speaks of events so complex and contingent that they fall, by their unpredictability and unrepeatability, into the domain of "what we may *call* chance.")

But where shall we place the boundary between lawlike events and contingent details? Darwin presses Gray further. If God be just, Darwin holds, you could not claim that the improbable death of a man by lightning or the birth of a child with serious mental handicaps represents the general and inevitable way of our world (even though both events have demonstrable physical causes). And if you accept "what we may call chance" (the presence of this man under that tree at that moment) as an explanation for a death, then why not for a birth? And if for the birth of an individual, why not for the origin of a species? And if for the origin of a species, then why not for the evolution of *Homo sapiens* as well?

You can see where Darwin's chain of argument is leading: Human intelligence itself—the transcendent item that, above all else, supposedly reflected God's benevolence, the rule of law, and the necessary progress of history—might be a detail, and not the predictable outcome of first principles. I wouldn't push this argument to an absurd extreme. Consciousness in some form might lie in the realm of predictability, or at least reasonable probability. But we care about details. Consciousness in *human* form—by means of a brain plagued with inherent paths of illogic, and weighted down by odd and dysfunctional inheritances, in a body with two eyes, two legs, and a fleshy upper thigh—is a detail of history, an outcome of a million improbable events, never destined to repeat. We care about George Canning's sore behind because we sense, in the cascade of consequences, an analogy to our own tenuous existence. We revel in the details of history because they are the source of our being.

2 | Grimm's Greatest Tale

WITH THE POSSIBLE EXCEPTION of Eng and Chang, who had no choice, no famous brothers have ever been closer than Wilhelm and Jacob Grimm, who lived and worked together throughout their long and productive lives. Wilhelm (1786–1859) was the prime mover in collecting the *Kinder- und Hausmärchen* (fables for the home and for children) that have become a pillar and icon of our culture. (Can you even imagine a world without Rapunzel or Snow White?) Jacob, senior member of the partnership (1785–1863), maintained a primary interest in linguistics and the history of human speech. His *Deutsche Grammatik,* first published in 1819, became a cornerstone for documenting relationships among Indo-European languages. Late in their lives, after a principled resignation from the University of Göttingen (prompted by the king of Hanover's repeal of the 1833 constitution as too liberal), the brothers Grimm settled in Berlin where they began their last and greatest project, the *Deutsches Wörterbuch*—a gigantic German dictionary documenting the history, etymology, and use of every word contained in three centuries of literature from Luther to Goethe. Certain scholarly projects are, like medieval cathedrals, too vast for completion in the lifetimes of their architects. Wilhelm never got past *D;* Jacob lived to see the letter *F.*

Speaking in Calcutta, during the infancy of the British raj in 1786, the philologist William Jones first noted impressive similarities between Sanskrit and the classical languages of Greece and Rome (an Indian king, or raja, matches *rex,* his Latin counterpart). Jones's observation led to the recognition of a great Indo-European family of languages, now spread from the British Isles and Scandinavia to India, but clearly rooted in a single, ancient origin. Jones may have marked the basic similarity, but the brothers Grimm were among the first to codify regularities of change that underpin the diversification of the rootstock into its major subgroups (Romance languages, Germanic tongues, and so on). Grimm's law, you see, does not state that all frogs shall turn into princes by the story's end, but specifies the characteristic changes in consonants between Proto–Indo-European (as retained in Latin) and the Germanic languages. Thus, for example, Latin *p*'s become *f*'s in Germanic cognates (voiceless stops become voiceless fricatives in the jargon). The Latin *plēnum* becomes "full" (*voll*, pronounced "foll" in German); *piscis* becomes "fish" (*Fisch* in German); and *pēs* becomes "foot" (*Fuss* in German). (Since English is an amalgam of a Germanic stock with Latin-based imports from the Norman conquest, our language has added Latin cognates to Anglo-Saxon roots altered according to Grimm's law—*plenty, piscine,* and *podiatry.* We can even get both for the price of one in *plentiful.*)

I first learned about Grimm's law in a college course more than twenty-five years ago. Somehow, the idea that the compilers of Rapunzel and Rumpelstiltskin also gave the world a great scholarly principle in linguistics struck me as one of the sweetest little facts I ever learned—a statement, symbolic at least, about interdisciplinary study and the proper contact of high and vernacular culture. I have wanted to disgorge this tidbit for years and am delighted that this essay finally provided an opportunity.

A great dream of unification underlay the observations of Jones and the codification of systematic changes by Jacob Grimm. Nearly all the languages of Europe (with such fascinating exceptions as Basque, Hungarian, and Finnish) could be joined to a pathway that spread through Persia all the way to India via Sanskrit and its derivatives. An origin in the middle, somewhere in the Near East, seemed indicated, and such "fossil" Indo-European tongues as Hittite support this interpretation. Whether the languages were spread, as convention dictates, by conquering nomadic tribes on horseback or, as Colin Renfrew argues in his recent book (*Archaeology and Language,* 1987), more gently and passively by the advantages of agriculture, evidence points to a single source with a complex history of proliferation in many directions.

Might we extend the vision of unity even further? Could we link Indo-European with the Semitic (Hebrew, Arabic) languages of the so-called Afro-Asiatic stock; the Altaic languages of Tibet, Mongolia, Korea, and Japan; the Dravidian tongues of southern India; even to the native Amerindian languages of the New World? Could the linkages extend even further to the languages of southeastern Asia (Chinese, Thai, Malay, Tagalog), the Pacific Islands, Australia, and New Guinea, even (dare one dream) to the most different tongues of southern Africa, including the Khoisan family with its complex clicks and implosions?

Most scholars balk at the very thought of direct evidence for connections among these basic "linguistic phyla." The peoples were once united, of course, but the division and spread occurred so long ago (or so the usual argument goes) that no traces of linguistic similarity should be left according to standard views about rates of change in such volatile aspects of human culture. Yet a small group of scholars, including some prominent émigrés from the Soviet Union (where theories of linguistic unification are not so scorned), persists in arguing for such linkages, despite acrimonious rebuttal and dismissal from most Western colleagues. One heterodox view tries to link Indo-European with linguistic phyla of the Near East and northern Asia (from Semitic at the southwest, to Dravidian at the southeast, all the way to Japanese at the northeast) by reconstructing a hypothetical ancestral tongue called Nostratic (from the Latin *noster*, meaning "our"). An even more radical view holds that modern tongues still preserve enough traces of common ancestry to link Nostratic with the native languages of the Americas (all the way to South America via the Eskimo tongues, but excluding the puzzling Na-Dene languages of northwestern America).

The vision is beguiling, but I haven't the slightest idea whether any of these unorthodox notions has a prayer of success. I have no technical knowledge of linguistics, only a hobbyist's interest in language. But I can report, from my own evolutionary domain, that the usual biological argument, invoked a priori against the possibility of direct linkage among linguistic phyla, no longer applies. This conventional argument held that *Homo sapiens* arose and split (by geographical migration) into its racial lines far too long ago for any hope that ancestral linguistic similarities might be retained by modern speakers. (A stronger version held that various races of *Homo sapiens* arose separately and in parallel from different stocks of *Homo erectus*, thus putting the point of common linguistic ancestry even further back into a truly inaccessible past. Indeed, according to this view, the distant common ancestor of all modern people might not even have possessed language. Some linguistic phyla might have arisen as separate evolutionary inventions, scotching any hope for theories of unification.)

The latest biological evidence, mostly genetic but with some contribution from paleontology, strongly indicates a single and discrete African origin for *Homo sapiens* at a date much closer to the present than standard views would have dared to imagine—perhaps only 200,000 years ago or so, with all non-African diversity perhaps no more than 100,000 years old. Within this highly compressed framework of common ancestry, the notion that conservative linguistic elements might still link existing phyla no longer seems so absurd a priori. The idea is worth some serious testing, even if absolutely nothing positive eventually emerges.

This compression of the time scale also suggests possible success for a potentially powerful research program into the great question of historical linkages among modern peoples. Three major and entirely independent sources of evidence might be used to reconstruct the human family tree: (1) direct but limited evidence of fossil bones and artifacts by paleontology and archaeology; (2) indirect but copious data on degrees of genetic relationship among living peoples; (3) relative similarities and differences among languages, as discussed above. We might attempt to correlate these separate sources, searching for similarities in pattern. I am delighted to report some marked successes in this direction ("Reconstruction of Human Evolution: Bringing Together Genetic, Archaeological, and Linguistic Data," by L. L. Cavalli-Sforza, A. Piazza, P. Menozzi, and J. Mountain, *Proceedings of the National Academy of Sciencs*, 1988). The reconstruction of the human family tree—its branching order, its timing, and its geography—may be within our grasp. Since this tree is the basic datum of history, hardly anything in intellectual life could be more important.

Our recently developed ability to measure genetic distances for large numbers of protein or DNA sequences provides the keystone for resolving the human family tree. As I have argued many times, such genetic data take pride of place not because genes are "better" or "more fundamental" than data of morphology, geography, and language, but only because genetic data are so copious and so comparable. We all shared a common origin, and therefore a common genetics and morphology, as a single ancestral population some quarter of a million years ago. Since then, differences have accumulated as populations separated and diversified. As a rough guide, the more extensive the measured differences, the greater the time of separation. This correlation between extent of difference and time of separation becomes our chief tool for reconstructing the human family tree.

But this relationship is only rough and very imperfect. So many factors can distort and disrupt a strict correlation of time and difference. Similar features can evolve independently—black skin in Africans and Australians, for example, since these groups stand as far apart genealogically as any two peoples on earth. Rates of change need not be constant. Tiny populations, in particular, can undergo marked increases in rate, primarily by random forces of genetic drift. The best way to work past these difficulties lies in a "brute force" approach: The greater the quantity of measured differences, the greater the likelihood of a primary correlation between time and overall distance. Any single measure of distance may be impacted by a large suite of forces that can disrupt the correlation of time and difference—natural selection, convergence, rapid genetic drift in small populations. But time is the only common factor underlying all measures of difference; when two populations split, all potential measures of distance become free to diverge. Thus, the more independent measures of distance we compile, the more likely we are to recover the only common signal of diversification: time itself. Only genetic data (at least for now) can supply this required richness in number of comparisons.

Genetic data on human differences are flowing in from laboratories throughout the world, and this essay shall be obsolete before it hits the presses. Blood groups provided our first crude insights during the 1960s, and Cavalli-Sforza was a pioneer in these studies. When techniques of electrophoresis permitted us to survey routinely for variation in the enzymes and proteins coded directly by genes, then data on human differences began to accumulate in useful cascades. More recently, our ability to sequence DNA itself has given us even more immediate access to the sources of variation.

The methodologically proper and powerful brute force comparisons are, for the moment, best made by studying differing states and frequencies of genes as revealed in the amino acid sequences of enzymes and proteins. Cavalli-Sforza and colleagues used information from alleles (varying states of genes, as in tall versus short for Mendel's peas) to construct a tree for human populations least affected by extensive interbreeding. (Few human groups are entirely aboriginal, and most populations are interbred to various degrees, given the two most characteristic attributes of *Homo sapiens:* wanderlust and vigorous sexuality. Obviously, if we wish to reconstruct the order of diversified branching from a common point of origin, historically mixed populations will confuse our quest. The Cape Colored, living disproof from their own ancestors for the Afrikaner "ideal" of apartheid, would join Khoisan with Caucasian. One town in Brazil might well join everyone.)

Cavalli-Sforza's consensus tree, based on overall genetic distances among 120 alleles for 42 populations—probably the best we can do for now, based on the maximal amount of secure and consistent information—divides modern humans into seven major groups, as shown in the accompanying chart. Only branching order counts in assessing relative similarity, not the happenstance of alignment along the bottom of the chart. Africans are not closer to Caucasians than to Australians just because the two groups are adjacent; rather, Africans are equally far from all other peoples by virtue of their common branching point with the ancestor of all six additional groups. (Consider the diagram as a mobile, free to rotate about each vertical "string." We could turn around the entire array of Groups II to VII, placing Australians next to Africans and Caucasians at the far right, without altering the branching order.)

These seven basic groups, established solely on genetic distances, make excellent sense when we consider the geographic distribution of *Homo sapiens.* Humans presumably evolved in Africa, and the first great split separates Africans from all other groups—representing the initial migration of some *Homo sapiens*

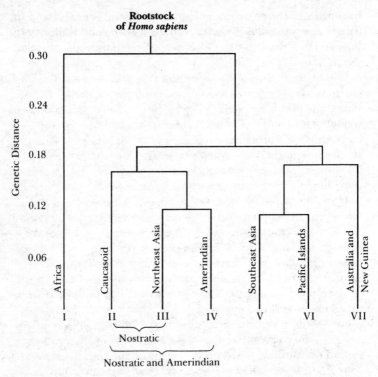

Cavalli-Sforza's consensus tree for the evolutionary relationships of human groups based on overall genetic distances. Postulated relationships among language families match this pattern remarkably well. See text for details. IROMIE WEERAMANTRY. COURTESY OF *NATURAL HISTORY*.

out of the mother continent. The next split separates the coherent region of the Pacific and Southeast Asia from the rest of the world. One group reached Australia and New Guinea, perhaps 40,000 years ago, forming the aboriginal populations of this region. A later division separated the Pacific island peoples (Group VI, including Polynesians, Micronesians, and Melanesians) from the southeastern Asiatics (Group V, including southern Chinese, Thai, Malayan, and Filipino).

Meanwhile, the second great branch divided to split the northern Oriental stocks from the Caucasians (Group II, including

Europeans, Semitic peoples of southwest Asia, Iranians, and Indians). A second division separated the Native American peoples (Group IV) from the northeast Asian family (Group III, including the Uralic peoples who left Hungarian, Finnish, and Estonian as their non–Indo-European calling cards from invasions into Caucasian territories, and the Altaic peoples of Mongolia, Korea, and Japan).

This good and sensible order indicates that genetic data are not betraying our efforts to reconstruct the human family tree. But Cavalli-Sforza and colleagues go further toward the great promise of extending this correlation between genes and geography to the other great sources of independent information—the geological and linguistic records.

I find the linguistic correlations more exciting than anything else in the work of Cavalli-Sforza and colleagues. Language is so volatile. Conquerors can impose their language as well as their will. Tongues interpenetrate and merge with an explosive ease not granted to genes or morphology. Look at English; look at any of us. I, for example, live in America, the indigenous home of very different people. I speak English, and consider the cathedral of Chârtres the world's most beautiful building. But my grandparents spoke Hungarian, a non–Indo-European language. And, along with Disraeli, my more distant ancestors were priests in the Temple of Solomon when the physical forebears of the original English people still lived as "brutal savages in an unknown island." One might have anticipated very little correlation between language and the tree of human ancestry.

Yet the mapping of linguistic upon genetic tree is remarkable in its degree of overlap. Exceptions exist, of course, and for the reasons mentioned above. Ethiopians speak an Afro-Asiatic language (in the phylum of Hebrew and Arabic), but belong to the maximally distant African group by genes. The Tibetan language links with Chinese in Group V, although the Tibetan people belong with northeast Asians in Group III. But Tibetans migrated from the steppes north of China, and Ethiopians have maintained primary contact and admixture with Semitic speakers for millennia. The correlations, however, are striking. Each genetic group also defines either a single linguistic phylum or a few closely related phyla. The Pacific island languages, with their mellifluous vowels and nearly nonexistent consonants, define

Group VI almost as well as the genetic distances. The Indo-European languages set the borders of Caucasian affinity, while the other major tongues of Caucasian peoples (Afro-Asiatic of the Semitic group) belong to a related linguistic phylum.

I am especially intrigued that the heterodox hypotheses for linkages among linguistic phyla, and for potential reconstructions of human languages even closer to the original tongue, follow the genetic connections so faithfully. Nostratic would link Groups II and III. The even more heterodox connection of Nostratic with Amerindian tongues would include Group IV as well. Note that Groups II to IV form a coherent limb of the human family tree. The Tower of Babel may emerge as a strikingly accurate metaphor. We probably did once speak the same language, and we did diversify into incomprehension as we spread over the face of the earth. But this original tongue was not an optimal construction given by a miracle to all people. Our original linguistic unity is only historical happenstance, not crafted perfection. We were once a small group of Africans, and the mother tongue is whatever these folks said to each other, not the Holy Grail.

This research has great importance for the obvious and most joyously legitimate parochial reason—our intense fascination with ourselves and the details of our history. We really do care that our species arose closer to 250,000 than to 2 million years ago, that Basque is the odd man out of European languages, and that the peopling of the Americas is not mysterious for its supposed "delay," but part of a regular process of expansion from an African center, and basically "on time" after all.

But I also sense a deeper importance in this remarkable correlation among all major criteria for reconstructing our family tree. This high correspondence can only mean that a great deal of human diversity, far more than we ever dared hope, achieves a remarkably simple explanation in history itself. If you know when a group split off and where it spread, you have the basic outline (in most cases) of its relationships with others. The primary signature of time and history is not effaced, or even strongly overlain in most cases, by immediate adaptation to prevailing circumstances or by recent episodes of conquest and amalgamation. We remain the children of our past—and we might even be able to pool our differences and to extract from inferred pathways of change a blurred portrait of our ultimate parents.

The path is tortuous and hard to trace, as the sister of the seven ravens learned when she went from the sun to the moon to the glass mountain in search of her brothers. History is also a hard taskmaster, for she covers her paths by erasing so much evidence from her records—as Hansel and Gretel discovered when birds ate their Ariadne's thread of bread crumbs. Yet the potential rewards are great, for we may recover the original state so hidden by our later changes—the prince behind the frog or the king that became the bear companion of Snow White and Rose Red. And the criteria that may lead to success are many and varied—not only the obvious data of genes and fossils but also the clues of language. For we must never doubt the power of names, as Rumpelstiltskin learned to his sorrow.

3 | The Creation Myths of Cooperstown

YOU MAY EITHER LOOK upon the bright side and say that hope springs eternal or, taking the cynic's part, you may mark P.T. Barnum as an astute psychologist for his proclamation that suckers are born every minute. The end result is the same: You can, Honest Abe notwithstanding, fool most of the people all of the time. How else to explain the long and continuing compendium of hoaxes—from the medieval shroud of Turin to Edwardian Piltdown Man to an ultramodern array of flying saucers and astral powers—eagerly embraced for their consonance with our hopes or their resonance with our fears.

Some hoaxes make a sufficient mark upon history that their products acquire the very status initially claimed by fakery—legitimacy (although as an object of human or folkloric, rather than natural, history; I once held the bones of Piltdown Man and felt that I was handling an important item of Western culture).

The Cardiff Giant, the best American entry for the title of paleontological hoax turned into cultural history, now lies on display in a shed behind a barn at the Farmer's Museum in Cooperstown, New York. This gypsum man, more than ten feet tall, was "discovered" by workmen digging a well on a farm near Cardiff, New York, in October 1869. Eagerly embraced by a gullible public, and ardently displayed by its creators at fifty cents a pop, the Cardiff Giant caused quite a brouhaha around Syracuse, and then nationally, for the few months of its active life between exhumation and exposure.

The Cardiff Giant was the brainchild of George Hull, a cigar manufacturer (and general rogue) from Binghamton, New York.

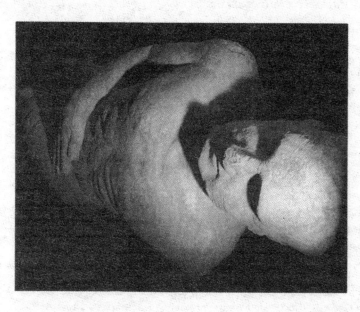

The Cardiff Giant as now on display in the Farmer's Museum in Cooperstown, New York. NEW YORK STATE HISTORICAL ASSOCIATION, COOPERSTOWN, NY.

A broadsheet from 1869 giving vital statistics of the Cardiff Giant. NEW YORK STATE HISTORICAL ASSOCIATION, COOPERSTOWN, NY.

He quarried a large block of gypsum from Fort Dodge, Iowa, and shipped it to Chicago, where two marble cutters fashioned the rough likeness of a naked man. Hull made some crude and minimal attempts to give his statue an aged appearance. He chipped off the carved hair and beard because experts told him that such items would not petrify. He drove darning needles into a wooden block and hammered the statue, hoping to simulate skin pores. Finally, he dumped a gallon of sulfuric acid all over his creation to simulate extended erosion. Hull then shipped his giant in a large box back to Cardiff.

Hull, as an accomplished rogue, sensed that his story could not hold for long and, in that venerable and alliterative motto, got out while the getting was good. He sold a three-quarter interest in the Cardiff Giant to a consortium of highly respectable businessmen, including two former mayors of Syracuse. These men raised the statue from its original pit on November 5 and carted it off to Syracuse for display.

The hoax held on for a few more weeks, and Cardiff Giant fever swept the land. Debate raged in newspapers and broadsheets between those who viewed the giant as a petrified fossil and those who regarded it as a statue wrought by an unknown and wondrous prehistoric race. But Hull had left too many tracks—at the gypsum quarries in Fort Dodge, at the carver's studio in Chicago, along the roadways to Cardiff (several people remembered seeing an awfully large box passing by on a cart). By December, Hull was ready to recant, but held his tongue a while longer. Three months later, the two Chicago sculptors came forward, and the Cardiff Giant's brief rendezvous with fame and fortune ended.

The common analogy of the Cardiff Giant with Piltdown Man works only to a point (both were frauds passed off as human fossils) and fails in one crucial respect. Piltdown was cleverly wrought and fooled professionals for forty years, while the Cardiff Giant was preposterous from the start. How could a man turn to solid gypsum, while preserving all his soft anatomy, from cheeks to toes to penis? Geologists and paleontologists never accepted Hull's statue. O. C. Marsh, later to achieve great fame as a discoverer of dinosaurs, echoed a professional consensus in his unambiguous pronouncement: "It is of very recent origin and a decided humbug."

Why, then, was the Cardiff Giant so popular, inspiring a wave of interest and discussion as high as any tide in the affairs of men during its short time in the sun? If the fraud had been well executed, we might attribute this great concern to the dexterity of the hoaxers (just as we grant grudging attention to a few of the most accomplished art fakers for their skills as copyists). But since the Cardiff Giant was so crudely done, we can only attribute its fame to the deep issue, the raw nerve, touched by the subject of its fakery—human origins. Link an absurd concoction to a noble and mysterious subject and you may prevail, at least for a while. My opening reference to P.T. Barnum was not meant sarcastically; he was one of the great practical psychologists of the nineteenth century—and his motto applies with special force to the Cardiff Giant: "No humbug is great without truth at bottom." (Barnum made a copy of the Cardiff Giant and exhibited it in New York City. His mastery of hype and publicity assured that his model far outdrew the "real" fake when the original went on display at a rival establishment in the same city.)

For some reason (to be explored, but not resolved, in this essay), we are powerfully drawn to the subject of beginnings. We yearn to know about origins, and we readily construct myths when we do not have data (or we suppress data in favor of legend when a truth strikes us as too commonplace). The hankering after an origin myth has always been especially strong for the closest subject of all—the human race. But we extend the same psychic need to our accomplishments and institutions—and we have origin myths and stories for the beginning of hunting, of language, of art, of kindness, of war, of boxing, bow ties, and brassieres. Most of us know that the Great Seal of the United States pictures an eagle holding a ribbon reading *e pluribus unum.* Fewer would recognize the motto on the other side (check it out on the back of a dollar bill): *annuit coeptis*—"he smiles on our beginnings."

Cooperstown may house the Cardiff Giant, but the fame of this small village in central New York does not rest upon its celebrated namesake, author James Fenimore, or its lovely Lake Otsego or the Farmer's Museum. Cooperstown is "on the map" by virtue of a different origin myth—one more parochial but no less powerful for many Americans than the tales of human beginnings that gave life to the Cardiff Giant. Cooperstown is the sacred founding place in the official myth about the origin of baseball.

Origin myths, since they are so powerful, can engender enormous practical problems. Abner Doubleday, as we shall soon see, most emphatically did not invent baseball at Cooperstown in 1839 as the official tale proclaims; in fact, no one invented baseball at any moment or in any spot. Nonetheless, this creation myth made Cooperstown the official home of baseball, and the Hall of Fame, with its associated museum and library, set its roots in this small village, inconveniently located near nothing in the way of airports or accommodations. We all revel in bucolic imagery on the field of dreams, but what a hassle when tens of thousands line the roads, restaurants, and Port-a-potties during the annual Hall of Fame weekend, when new members are enshrined and two major league teams arrive to play an exhibition game at Abner Doubleday Field, a sweet little 10,000-seater in the middle of town. Put your compass point at Cooperstown, make your radius at Albany—and you'd better reserve a year in advance if you want any accommodation within the enormous resulting circle.

After a lifetime of curiosity, I finally got the opportunity to witness this annual version of forty students in a telephone booth or twenty circus clowns in a Volkswagen. Since Yaz (former Boston star Carl Yastrzemski to the uninitiated) was slated to receive baseball's Nobel in 1989, and his old team was playing in the Hall of Fame game, and since I'm a transplanted Bostonian (although still a New Yorker and not-so-secret Yankee fan at heart), Tom Heitz, chief of the wonderful baseball library at the Hall of Fame, kindly invited me to join the sardines in this most lovely of all cans.

The silliest and most tendentious of baseball writing tries to wrest profundity from the spectacle of grown men hitting a ball with a stick by suggesting linkages between the sport and deep issues of morality, parenthood, history, lost innocence, gentleness, and so on, seemingly *ad infinitum*. (The effort reeks of silliness because baseball is profound all by itself and needs no excuses; people who don't know this are not fans and are therefore unreachable anyway.) When people ask me how baseball imitates life, I can only respond with what the more genteel newspapers used to call a "barnyard epithet," but now, with growing bravery, usually render as "bullbleep." Nonetheless, baseball is a major item of our culture, and the sport does have a long and interesting history. Any item or institution with these two properties must generate a set of myths and stories (perhaps even some truths) about beginnings. And the subject of beginnings is the bread and butter of these essays on evolution in the broadest sense. I shall make no woolly analogies between baseball and life; this is an essay on the origins of baseball, with some musings on why beginnings of all sorts hold such fascination for us. (I thank

A.G. Spalding, promoter of the Doubleday creation myth. NATIONAL BASEBALL LIBRARY, COOPERSTOWN, NY.

Tom Heitz not only for the invitation to Cooperstown at its yearly acme but also for drawing the contrast between creation and evolution stories of baseball, and for supplying much useful information from his unparalleled storehouse.)

Stories about beginnings come in only two basic modes. An entity either has an explicit point of origin, a specific time and place of creation, or else it evolves and has no definable moment of entry into the world. Baseball provides an interesting example of this contrast because we know the answer and can judge received wisdom by the two chief criteria, often opposed, of external fact and internal hope. Baseball evolved from a plethora of previous stick-and-ball games. It has no true Cooperstown and no Doubleday. Yet we seem to prefer the alternative model of origin by a moment of creation—for then we can have heroes and sacred places. By contrasting the myth of Cooperstown with the fact of evolution, we can learn something about our cultural practices and their frequent disrespect for truth.

The official story about the beginning of baseball is a creation myth, and a review of the reasons and circumstances of its fabrication may give us insight into the cultural appeal of stories in this mode. A. G. Spalding, baseball's first great pitcher during his early career, later founded the sporting goods company that still bears his name and became one of the great commercial moguls of America's gilded age. As publisher of the annual *Spalding's Official Base Ball Guide,* he held maximal power in shaping both public and institutional opinion on all facets of baseball and its history. As the sport grew in popularity, and the pattern of two stable major leagues coalesced early in our century, Spalding and others felt the need for clarification (or merely for codification) of opinion on the hitherto unrecorded origin of an activity that truly merited its common designation as America's "national pastime."

In 1907, Spalding set up a blue ribbon committee to investigate and resolve the origin of baseball. The committee, chaired by A. G. Mills and including several prominent businessmen and two senators who had also served as presidents of the National League, took much testimony but found no smoking gun. Then, in July 1907, Spalding himself transmitted to the committee a letter from an Abner Graves, then a mining engineer in Denver, who reported that Abner Doubleday had, in 1839, interrupted a

Abner Doubleday, who fired the first Union volley at Fort Sumter, but who, in the words of one historian, didn't know a baseball from a kumquat. NATIONAL BASEBALL LIBRARY, COOPERSTOWN, NY.

marbles game behind the tailor's shop in Cooperstown, New York, to draw a diagram of a baseball field, explain the rules of the game, and designate the activity by its modern name of "base ball" (then spelled as two words).

Such "evidence" scarcely inspired universal confidence, but the commission came up with nothing better—and the Doubleday myth, as we shall soon see, was eminently functional. Therefore, in 1908, the Mills Commission reported its two chief findings: first, "that base ball had its origins in the United States"; and second, "that the first scheme for playing it, according to the best evidence available to date, was devised by Abner Doubleday, at Cooperstown, New York, in 1839." This "best evidence" consisted only of "a circumstantial statement by a reputable gentleman"—namely Grave's testimony as reported by Spalding himself.

Henry Chadwick, who knew that baseball had evolved from English stick-and-ball games. NATIONAL BASEBALL LIBRARY, COOPERSTOWN, NY.

When cited evidence is so laughably insufficient, one must seek motivations other than concern for truth. The key to underlying reasons stands in the first conclusion of Mills's committee: Hoopla and patriotism (cardboard version) decreed that a national pastime must have an indigenous origin. The idea that baseball had evolved from a wide variety of English stick-and-ball games—although true—did not suit the mythology of a phenomenon that had become so quintessentially American. In fact, Spalding had long been arguing, in an amiable fashion, with Henry Chadwick, another pioneer and entrepreneur of baseball's early years. Chadwick, born in England, had insisted for years that baseball had developed from the British stick-and-ball game called rounders; Spalding had vociferously advocated a purely American origin, citing the colonial game of "one old cat" as a distant precursor, but holding that baseball itself represented something so new and advanced that a pinpoint of origin—a creation myth—must be sought.

Chadwick considered the matter of no particular importance, arguing (with eminent justice) that an English origin did not "detract one iota from the merit of its now being unquestionably a thoroughly American field sport, and a game too, which is fully adapted to the American character." (I must say that I have grown quite fond of Mr. Chadwick, who certainly understood evolutionary change and its chief principle that historical origin need not match contemporary function.) Chadwick also viewed the committee's whitewash as a victory for his side. He labeled the Mills report as "a masterful piece of special pleading which lets my dear old friend Albert [Spalding] escape a bad defeat. The whole matter was a joke between Albert and myself."

We may accept the psychic need for an indigenous creation myth, but why Abner Doubleday, a man with no recorded tie to the game and who, in the words of Donald Honig, probably "didn't know a baseball from a kumquat"? I had wondered about this for years, but only ran into the answer serendipitously during a visit to Fort Sumter in the harbor of Charleston, South Carolina. There, an exhibit on the first skirmish of the Civil War points out that Abner Doubleday, as captain of the Union artillery, had personally sighted and given orders for firing the first responsive volley following the initial Confederate attack on the fort. Doubleday later commanded divisions at Antietam and Fredericksburg, became at least a minor hero at Gettysburg, and retired as a brevet major general. In fact, A. G. Mills, head of the commission, had served as part of an honor guard when Doubleday's body lay in state in New York City, following his death in 1893.

If you have to have an American hero, could anyone be better than the man who fired the first shot (in defense) of the Civil War? Needless to say, this point was not lost on the members of Mills's committee. Spalding, never one to mince words, wrote to the committee when submitting Graves's dubious testimony: "It certainly appeals to an American pride to have had the great national game of base ball created and named by a Major General in the United States Army." Mills then concluded in his report: "Perhaps in the years to come, in view of the hundreds of thousands of people who are devoted to baseball, and the millions who will be, Abner Doubleday's fame will rest evenly, if not quite as much, upon the fact that he was its inventor . . . as upon his brilliant and distinguished career as an officer in the Federal Army."

And so, spurred by a patently false creation myth, the Hall of Fame stands in the most incongruous and inappropriate locale of a charming little town in central New York. Incongruous and inappropriate, but somehow wonderful. Who needs another museum in the cultural maelstroms (and summer doldrums) of New York, Boston, or Washington? Why not a major museum in a beautiful and bucolic setting? And what could be more fitting than the spatial conjunction of two great American origin myths—the Cardiff Giant and the Doubleday Fable? Thus, I too am quite content to treat the myth gently, while honesty requires 'fessing up. The exhibit on Doubleday in the Hall of Fame Museum sets just the right tone in its caption: "In the hearts of those who love baseball, he is remembered as the lad in the pasture where the game was invented. Only cynics would need to know more." Only in the hearts; not in the minds.

Baseball evolved. Since the evidence is so clear (as epitomized below), we must ask why these facts have been so little appreciated for so long, and why a creation myth like the Doubleday story ever gained a foothold. Two major reasons have conspired: first, the positive block of our attraction to creation stories; second, the negative impediment of unfamiliar sources outside the usual purview of historians. English stick-and-ball games of the nineteenth century can be roughly classified into two categories along social lines. The upper and educated classes played cricket, and the history of this sport is copiously documented because literati write about their own interests and because the activities of men in power are well recorded (and constitute virtually all of history, in the schoolboy version). But the ordinary pastimes of rural and urban working people can be well nigh invisible in conventional sources of explicit commentary. Working people played a different kind of stick-and-ball game, existing in various forms and designated by many names, including "rounders" in western England, "feeder" in London, and "base ball" in southern England. For a large number of reasons, forming the essential difference between cricket and baseball, cricket matches can last up to several days (a batsman, for example, need not run after he hits the ball and need not expose himself to the possibility of being put out every time he makes contact). The leisure time of working people does not come in such generous gobs, and the lower-class stick-and-ball games could not run more than a few hours.

Several years ago, at the Victoria and Albert Museum in London, I learned an important lesson from an excellent exhibit on late nineteenth century history of the British music hall. This is my favorite period (Darwin's century, after all), and I consider myself tolerably well informed on cultural trends of the time. I can sing any line from any of the Gilbert and Sullivan operas (a largely middle-class entertainment), and I know the general drift of high cultural interests in literature and music. But the music hall provided a whole world of entertainment for millions, a realm with its heroes, its stars, its top-forty songs, its gaudy theaters—and I knew nothing, absolutely nothing, about this world. I felt chagrined, but my ignorance had an explanation beyond personal insensitivity (and the exhibit had been mounted explicitly to counteract the selective invisibility of certain important trends in history). The music hall was a chief entertainment of Victorian working classes, and the history of working people is often invisible in conventional written sources. This history must be rescued and reconstituted from different sorts of data; in this case, from posters, playbills, theater accounts, persistence of some songs in the oral tradition (most were never published as sheet music), recollections of old-timers who knew the person who knew the person. . . .

The early history of baseball—the stick-and-ball game of working people—presents the same problem of conventional invisibility, and the same promise of rescue by exploration of unusual sources. Work continues and intensifies as the history of sport becomes more and more academically respectable, but the broad outlines (and much fascinating detail) are now well established. As the upper classes played a codified and well-documented cricket, working people played a largely unrecorded and much more diversified set of stick-and-ball games ancestral to baseball. Many sources, including primers and boys' manuals, depict games recognizable as precursors to baseball well into the eighteenth century. Occasional references even spill over into high culture. In *Northanger Abbey,* written in 1798 or 1799, Jane Austen remarks: "It was not very wonderful that Catherine . . . should prefer cricket, base ball, riding on horseback, and running about the country, at the age of fourteen, to books." As this quotation illustrates, the name of the game is no more Doubleday's than the form of play.

These ancestral styles of baseball came to America with early settlers and were clearly well established by colonial times. But they were driven ever further underground by Puritan proscriptions of sport for adults. They survived largely as children's games and suffered the double invisibility of location among the poor and the young. But two major reasons brought these games into wider repute and led to a codification of standard forms quite close to modern baseball between the 1820s and the 1850s. First, a set of social reasons, from the decline of Puritanism to increased concern about health and hygiene in crowded cities, made sport an acceptable activity for adults. Second, middle-class and professional people began to take up these early forms of baseball, and this upward social drift inspired teams, leagues, written rules, uniforms, stadiums, guidebooks: in short, all the paraphernalia of conventional history.

I am not arguing that these early games could be called baseball with a few trivial differences (evolution means substantial change, after all), but only that they stand in a complex lineage, better designated a nexus, from which modern baseball emerged, eventually in a codified and canonical form. In those days before instant communication, every region had its own version, just as every set of outdoor steps in New York City generated a different form of stoopball in my youth, without threatening the basic identity of the game. These games, most commonly called town ball, differed from modern baseball in substantial ways. In the Massachusetts Game, a codification of the late 1850s drawn up by ball players in New England towns, four bases and three strikes identify the genus, but many specifics are strange by modern standards. The bases were made of wooden stakes projecting four feet from the ground. The batter (called the striker) stood between first and fourth base. Sides changed after a single out. One hundred runs (called tallies), not higher score after a specified number of innings, spelled victory. The field contained no

A.J. Cartwright, a most interesting point in the continuum of baseball's evolution. NATIONAL BASEBALL LIBRARY, COOPERSTOWN, NY.

foul lines, and balls hit in any direction were in play. Most important, runners were not tagged out, but rather dismissed by "plugging," that is, being hit with a thrown ball while running between bases. Consequently, since baseball has never been a game for masochists, balls were soft—little more than rags stuffed into leather covers—and could not be hit far. (Tom Heitz has put together a team of Cooperstown worthies to re-create town ball for interested parties and prospective opponents. Since few other groups are well schooled in this lost art, Tom's team hasn't been defeated in ages, if ever. "We are the New York Yankees of town ball," he told me. His team is called, quite appropriately in general but especially for this essay, the Cardiff Giants.)

Evolution is continual change, but not insensibly gradual transition; in any continuum, some points are always more interesting than others. The conventional nomination for most salient point in this particular continuum goes to Alexander Joy Cartwright, leader of a New York team that started to play in Lower Manhattan, eventually rented some changing rooms and a field in Hoboken (just a quick ferry ride across the Hudson), and finally drew up a set of rules in 1845, later known as the New York Game. Cartwright's version of town ball is much closer to modern baseball, and many clubs followed his rules—for standardization became ever more vital as the popularity of early baseball grew and opportunity for play between regions increased. In particular, Cartwright introduced two key innovations that shaped the disparate forms of town ball into a semblance of modern baseball. First, he eliminated plugging and introduced tagging in the modern sense; the ball could now be made harder, and hitting for distance became an option. Second, he introduced foul lines, again in the modern sense, as his batter stood at a home plate and had to hit the ball within lines defined from home through first and third bases. The game could now become a spectator sport because areas close to the field but out of action could, for the first time, be set aside for onlookers.

The New York Game may be the highlight of a continuum, but it provides no origin myth for baseball. Cartwright's rules were followed in various forms of town ball. His New York Game still included many curiosities by modern standards (twenty-one runs, called aces, won the game, and balls caught on one bounce were outs). Moreover, our modern version is an amalgam of the

New York Game plus other town-ball traditions, not Cartwright's baby grown up by itself. Several features of the Massachusetts Game entered the modern version in preference to Cartwright's rules. Balls had to be caught on the fly in Boston, and pitchers threw overhand, not underhand as in the New York Game (and in professional baseball until the 1880s).

Scientists often lament that so few people understand Darwin and the principles of biological evolution. But the problem goes deeper. Too few people are comfortable with evolutionary modes of explanation in any form. I do not know why we tend to think so fuzzily in this area, but one reason must reside in our social and psychic attraction to creation myths in preference to evolutionary stories—for creation myths, as noted before, identify heroes and sacred places, while evolutionary stories provide no palpable, particular object as a symbol for reverence, worship, or patriotism. Still, we must remember—and an intellectual's most persistent and nagging responsibility lies in making this simple point over and over again, however noxious and bothersome we render ourselves thereby—that truth and desire, fact and comfort, have no necessary, or even preferred, correlation (so rejoice when they do coincide).

To state the most obvious example in our current political turmoil: Human growth is a continuum, and no creation myth can define an instant for the origin of an individual life. Attempts by anti-abortionists to designate the moment of fertilization as the beginning of personhood make no sense in scientific terms (and also violate a long history of social definitions that traditionally focused on the quickening, or detected movement, of the fetus in the womb). I will admit—indeed, I emphasized as a key argument of this essay—that not all points on a continuum are equal. Fertilization is a more interesting moment than most, but it no more provides a clean definition of origin than the most intriguing moment of baseball's continuum—Cartwright's codification of the New York Game—defines the beginning of our national pastime. Baseball evolved and people grow; both are continua without definable points of origin. Probe too far back and you reach absurdity, for you will see Nolan Ryan on the hill when the first ape hit a bird with a stone, or you will define both masturbation and menstruation as murder—and who will then cast the first stone? Look for something in the middle, and you find nothing but continuity—always a meaningful "before," and always a more modern "after." (Please note that I am not stating an opinion on the vexatious question of abortion—an ethical issue that can only be decided in ethical terms. I only point out that one side has rooted its case in an argument from science that is not only entirely irrelevant to the proper realm of resolution but also happens to be flat-out false in trying to devise a creation myth within a continuum.)

And besides, why do we prefer creation myths to evolutionary stories? I find all the usual reasons hollow. Yes, heroes and shrines are all very well, but is there not grandeur in the sweep of continuity? Shall we revel in a story for all humanity that may include the sacred ball courts of the Aztecs, and perhaps, for all we know, a group of *Homo erectus* hitting rocks or skulls with a stick or a femur? Or shall we halt beside the mythical Abner Doubleday, standing behind the tailor's shop in Cooperstown, and say "behold the man"—thereby violating truth and, perhaps even worse, extinguishing both thought and wonder?

4 | The Panda's Thumb of Technology

THE BRIEF STORY of Jephthah and his daughter (Judg. 11:30–40) is, to my mind and heart, the saddest of all biblical tragedies. Jephthah makes an intemperate vow, yet all must abide by its consequences. He promises that if God grant him victory in a forthcoming battle, he will sacrifice by fire the first living thing that passes through his gate to greet him upon his return. Expecting (I suppose) a dog or a goat, he returns victorious to find his daughter, and only child, waiting to meet him "with timbrels and with dances."

Handel's last oratorio, *Jephtha*, treats this tale with great power (although his librettist couldn't bear the weight of the original and gave the story a happy ending, with angelic intervention to spare Jephthah's daughter at the price of her lifelong chastity). At the end of Part 2, while all still think that the terrible vow must be fulfilled, the chorus sings one of Handel's wonderful "philosophical" choruses. It begins with a frank account of the tragic circumstance:

> How dark, O Lord, are thy decrees! . . .
> No certain bliss, no solid peace,
> We mortals know on earth below.

Yet the last two lines, in a curious about-face, proclaim (with magnificent musical solidity as well):

> Yet on this maxim still obey:
> WHATEVER IS, IS RIGHT

This odd reversal, from frank acknowledgment to unreasonable acceptance, reflects one of the greatest biases ("hopes" I like to call them) that human thought imposes upon a world indifferent to our suffering. Humans are pattern-seeking animals. We must find cause and meaning in all events (quite apart from the probable reality that the universe both doesn't care much about us and often operates in a random manner). I call this bias "adaptationism"—the notion that everything must fit, must have a purpose, and in the strongest version, must be for the best.

The final line of Handel's chorus is, of course, a quote from Alexander Pope, the last statement of the first epistle of his *Essay on Man,* published twenty years before Handel's oratorio. Pope's text contains (in heroic couplets to boot) the most striking paean I know to the bias of adaptationism. In my favorite lines, Pope chastises those people who may be unsatisfied with the senses that nature bestowed upon us. We may wish for more acute vision, hearing, or smell, but consider the consequences.

If nature thunder'd in his op'ning ears
And stunn'd him with the music of the spheres
How would he wish that Heav'n had left him still
The whisp'ring zephyr, and the purling rill!

And my favorite couplet, on olfaction:

Or, quick effluvia darting thro' the brain,
Die of a rose in aromatic pain.

What we have is best for us—whatever is, is right.

By 1859, most educated people were prepared to accept evolution as the reason behind similarities and differences among organisms—thus accounting for Darwin's rapid conquest of the intellectual world. But they were decidedly not ready to acknowledge the radical implications of Darwin's proposed mechanism of change, natural selection, thus explaining the brouhaha that the *Origin of Species* provoked—and still elicits (at least before our courts and school boards).

Darwin's world is full of "terrible truths," two in particular. First, when things do fit and make sense (good design of organisms, harmony of ecosystems), they did not arise because the laws of nature entail such order as a primary effect. They are, rather, only epiphenomena, side consequences of the basic causal process at work in natural populations—the purely "self-ish" struggle among organisms for personal reproductive success. Second, the complex and curious pathways of history guarantee that most organisms and ecosystems cannot be designed optimally. Indeed, to make an even stronger statement, imperfections are the primary proofs that evolution has occurred, since optimal designs erase all signposts of history.

This principle of imperfection has been a major theme of my essays for several years. I call it the panda principle to honor my favorite example, the panda's false thumb. Pandas are the herbivorous descendants of carnivorous bears. Their true anatomical thumbs were, long ago during ancestral days of meat eating, irrevocably committed to the limited motion appropriate for this mode of life and universally evolved by mammalian Carnivora. When adaptation to a diet of bamboo required more flexibility in manipulation, pandas could not redesign their thumbs but had to make do with a makeshift substitute—an enlarged radial sesamoid bone of the wrist, the panda's false thumb. The sesamoid thumb is a clumsy, suboptimal structure, but it works. Pathways of history (commitment of the true thumb to other roles during an irreversible past) impose such jury-rigged solutions upon all creatures. History inheres in the imperfections of living organisms—and thus we know that modern creatures had a different past, converted by evolution to their current state.

We can accept this argument for organisms (we know, after all, about our own appendixes and aching backs). But is the panda principle more pervasive? Is it a general statement about all historical systems? Will it apply, for example, to the products of technology? We might deem this principle irrelevant to the manufactured objects of human ingenuity—and for good reason. After all, constraints of genealogy do not apply to steel, glass, and plastic. The panda cannot shuck its digits (and can only build its future upon an inherited ground plan), but we can abandon gas lamps for electricity and horse carriages for motor cars. Consider, for example, the difference between organic architecture and human buildings. Complex organic structures cannot be re-evolved following their loss; no snake will redevelop front legs. But the apostles of post-modern architecture, in reaction to the sterility of so many glass-box buildings of the international style, have juggled together all the classical forms of history in a cascading effort to rediscover the virtues of ornamentation. Thus, Philip Johnson could place a broken pediment atop a New York skyscraper and raise a medieval castle of plate glass in downtown Pittsburgh. Organisms cannot recruit the virtues of their lost pasts.

Yet I am not so sure that technology is exempt from the panda principle of history, for I am now sitting face to face with the best example of its application. Indeed, I am in most intimate (and striking) contact with this object—the typewriter keyboard.

I could type before I could write. My father was a court stenographer, and my mother is a typist. I learned proper eight-finger touch-typing when I was about nine years old and still endowed with small hands and weak, tiny pinky fingers. I was thus, from the first, in a particularly good position to appreciate the irrationality of placement for letters on the standard keyboard—called QWERTY by all aficionados in honor of the first six letters on the top letter row.

Clearly, QWERTY makes no sense (beyond the whiz and joy of typing QWERTY itself). More than 70 percent of English words can be typed with the letters DHIATENSOR, and these should be on the most accessible second, or home, row—as they were in a failed competitor to QWERTY introduced as early as 1893. But in QWERTY, the most common English letter, E, requires a reach to the top row, as do the vowels U, I, and O (with O struck by the weak fourth finger), while A remains in the home row but must be typed with the weakest finger of all (at least for the dexterous majority of right-handers)—the left pinky. (How I struggled with this as a boy. I just couldn't depress that key. I once tried to type the Declaration of Independence and ended up with: th t ll men re cre ted equ l.)

As a dramatic illustration of this irrationality, consider the accompanying photograph, the keyboard of an ancient Smith-Corona upright, identical with the one (my dad's original) that I use to type these essays (a magnificent machine—no breakdown in twenty years and a fluidity of motion unmatched by any manual typewriter since). After more than half a century of use, some of the most commonly struck keys have been worn right through the surface into the soft pad below (they weren't solid plastic in those days). Note that E, A, and S are worn in this way—but note also that all three are either not in the home row or are struck with the weak fourth and pinky fingers in QWERTY.

This claim is not just a conjecture based on idiosyncratic personal experience. Evidence clearly shows that QWERTY is drastically suboptimal. Competitors have abounded since the early days of typewriting, but none has supplanted or even dented the universal dominance of QWERTY for English typewriters. The best-known alternative, DSK, for Dvorak Simplified Keyboard, was introduced in 1932. Since then, virtually all records for speed typing have been held by DSK, not QWERTY, typists. During the 1940s, the U.S. Navy, ever mindful of efficiency, found that the increased speed of DSK would amortize the cost of retraining typists within ten days of full employment. (Mr. Dvorak was not Anton of the *New World Symphony,* but August, a professor of education at the University of Washington, who died disappointed in 1975. Dvorak was a disciple of Frank B. Gilbreth, pioneer of time and motion studies in industrial management.)

Since I have a special interest in typewriters (my affection for them dates to childhood days of splendor in the grass and glory in the flower), I have wanted to write such an essay for years. But I never had the data I needed until Paul A. David, Coe Professor of American Economic History at Stanford University, kindly sent me his fascinating article, "Understanding the Economics of QWERTY: The Necessity of History" (in *Economic History and the Modern Economist,* edited by W. N. Parker, New York, Basil Blackwell Inc., 1986, pp. 30–49). Virtually all the nonidiosyncratic data in this essay come from David's work, and I thank him for this opportunity to satiate an old desire.

The puzzle of QWERTY's dominance resides in two separate questions: Why did QWERTY ever arise in the first place? And why has QWERTY survived in the face of superior competitors?

My answers to these questions will invoke analogies to principles of evolutionary theory. Let me, then, state some ground rules for such a questionable enterprise. I am convinced that comparisons between biological evolution and human cultural or technological change have done vastly more harm than good—and examples abound of this most common of all intellectual traps. Biological evolution is a bad analogue for cultural change

A classic upright typewriter of World War I vintage. Brother to the machine that I use to write these essays.

Notice the patterns of wear for most frequently used keys, as illustrated by breakage through the surface after so many years of striking. In QWERTY, all the most common keys are either not in the home row, or are hit by weak fingers in the home row—thus illustrating the suboptimality of this standard arrangement.

A keyboard for a typewriter made in the 1880's, illustrating one of the many competing non-QWERTY arrangements so common at the time.

because the two systems are so different for three major reasons that could hardly be more fundamental.

First, cultural evolution can be faster by orders of magnitude than biological change at its maximal Darwinian rate—and questions of timing are of the essence in evolutionary arguments. Second, cultural evolution is direct and Lamarckian in form: The achievements of one generation are passed by education and publication directly to descendants, thus producing the great potential speed of cultural change. Biological evolution is indirect and Darwinian, as favorable traits do not descend to the next generation unless, by good fortune, they arise as products of genetic change. Third, the basic topologies of biological and cultural change are completely different. Biological evolution is a system of constant divergence without subsequent joining of branches. Lineages, once distinct, are separate forever. In human history, transmission across lineages is, perhaps, the major source of cultural change. Europeans learned about corn and potatoes from Native Americans and gave them smallpox in return.

So, when I compare the panda's thumb with a typewriter keyboard, I am not attempting to derive or explain technological change by biological principles. Rather, I ask if both systems might not record common, deeper principles of organization. Biological evolution is powered by natural selection, cultural evolution by a different set of principles that I understand but dimly. But both are systems of historical change. More general principles of structure must underlie all systems that proceed through history (perhaps I now only show my own bias for intelligibility in our complex world)—and I rather suspect that the panda principle of imperfection might reside among them.

My main point, in other words, is not that typewriters are like biological evolution (for such an argument would fall right into the nonsense of false analogy), but that both keyboards and the panda's thumb, as products of history, must be subject to some regularities governing the nature of temporal connections. As scientists, we must believe that general principles underlie structurally related systems that proceed by different overt rules. The proper unity lies not in false applications of these overt rules (like natural selection) to alien domains (like technological change), but in seeking the more general rules of structure and change themselves.

The Origin of QWERTY: True randomness has limited power to intrude itself into the forms of organisms. Small and unimportant changes, unrelated to the working integrity of a complex creature, may drift in and out of populations by a process akin to throwing dice. But intricate structures, involving the coordination of many separate parts, must arise for an active reason—since the bounds of mathematical probability for fortuitous association are soon exceeded as the number of working parts grows.

But if complex structures must arise for a reason, history may soon overtake the original purpose—and what was once a sensible solution becomes an oddity or imperfection in the altered context of a new future. Thus, the panda's true thumb permanently lost its ability to manipulate objects when carnivorous ancestors found a better use for this digit in the limited motions appropriate for creatures that run and claw. This altered thumb then becomes a constraint imposed by past history upon the panda's ability to adapt in an optimal way to its new context of herbivory. The panda's thumb, in short, becomes an emblem of its different past, a sign of history.

Similarly, QWERTY had an eminently sensible rationale in the early technology of typewriting but soon became a constraint upon faster typing as advances in construction erased the reason for QWERTY's origin. The key (pardon the pun) to QWERTY's origin lies in another historical vestige easily visible on the second row of letters. Note the sequence: DFGHJKL—a good stretch of the alphabet in order, with the vowels E and I removed. The original concept must have simply arrayed the letters in alphabetical order. Why were the two most common letters of this sequence removed from the most accessible home row? And why were other letters dispersed to odd positions?

Those who remember the foibles of manual typewriters (or, if as hidebound as yours truly, still use them) know that excessive speed or unevenness of stroke may cause two or more keys to jam near the striking point. You also know that if you don't reach in and pull the keys apart, any subsequent stroke will type a repetition of the key leading the jam—as any key subsequently struck will hit the back of the jammed keys and drive them closer to the striking point.

These problems were magnified in the crude technology of early machines—and too much speed became a hazard rather than a blessing, as key jams canceled the benefits of celerity. Thus, in the great human traditions of tinkering and pragmatism, keys were moved around to find a proper balance between speed and jamming. In other words—and here comes the epitome of the tale in a phrase—QWERTY arose in order to slow down the maximal speed of typing and prevent jamming of keys. Common letters were either allotted to weak fingers or dispersed to positions requiring a long stretch from the home row.

This basic story has gotten around, thanks to short takes in *Time* and other popular magazines, but the details are enlightening, and few people have the story straight. I have asked nine typists who knew this outline of QWERTY's origin and all (plus me for an even ten) had the same misconception. The old machines that imposed QWERTY were, we thought, of modern design—with keys in front typing a visible line on paper rolled around a platen. This leads to a minor puzzle: Key jams may be a pain in the butt, but you see them right away and can easily reach in and pull them apart. So why QWERTY?

As David points out, the prototype of QWERTY, a machine invented by C. L. Sholes in the 1860s, was quite different in form from modern typewriters. It had a flat paper carriage and did not roll paper right around the platen. Keys struck the paper invisibly from beneath, not patently from the front as in all modern typewriters. You could not view what you were typing unless you stopped to raise the carriage and inspect your product. Keys jammed frequently, but you could not see (and often did not feel) the aggregation. Thus, you might type a whole page of deathless prose and emerge only with a long string of E's.

Sholes filed for a patent in 1867 and spent the next six years in trial-and-error efforts to improve his machine. QWERTY emerged from this period of tinkering and compromise. As another added wrinkle (and fine illustration of history's odd quirks), R joined the top row as a last-minute entry, and for a somewhat capricious motive according to one common tale (perhaps apocryphal)—for salesmen could then impress potential buyers by smooth and rapid production of the brand name TYPE WRITER, all on one row. (Although I wonder how many sales were lost when TYPE EEEEEE appeared after a jam!)

The Survival of QWERTY: We can all accept this story of QWERTY's origin, but why did it persist after the introduction of the modern platen roller and front-stroke key? (The first typewriter with a fully visible printing point was introduced in 1890.) In fact, the situation is even more puzzling. I thought that alternatives to keystroke typing only became available with the IBM electric ball, but none other than Thomas Edison filed a patent for an electric print-wheel machine as early as 1872, and L. S. Crandall marketed a writing machine without typebars in 1879. (Crandall arranged his type on a cylindrical sleeve and made the sleeve revolve to the required letter before striking the printing point.)

The 1880s were boom years for the fledgling typewriter industry, a period when a hundred flowers bloomed and a hundred schools of thought contended. Alternatives to QWERTY were touted by several companies, and both the variety of printing designs (several without typebars) and the improvement of keystroke typewriters completely removed the original rationale for QWERTY. Yet during the 1890s, more and more companies made the switch to QWERTY, which became an industry standard by the early years of our century. And QWERTY has held on stubbornly, through the introduction of the IBM Selectric and the Hollerith punch card machine to that ultimate example of its nonnecessity, the microcomputer terminal.

To understand the survival (and domination to this day) of drastically suboptimal QWERTY, we must recognize two other commonplaces of history, as applicable to life in geological time as to technology over decades—contingency and incumbency. We call a historical event—the rise of mammals or the dominance of QWERTY—contingent when it occurs as the chancy result of a long string of unpredictable antecedents, rather than as a necessary outcome of nature's laws. Such contingent events often depend crucially upon choices from a distant past that seemed tiny and trivial at the time. Minor perturbations early in the game can nudge a process into a new pathway, with cascading consequences that produce an outcome vastly different from any alternative.

Incumbency also reinforces the stability of a pathway once the little quirks of early flexibility push a sequence into a firm channel. Suboptimal politicians often prevail nearly forever once they gain office and grab the reins of privilege, patronage, and visibility. Mammals waited 100 million years to become the dominant animals on land and only got a chance because dinosaurs succumbed during a mass extinction. If every typist in the world stopped using QWERTY tomorrow and began to learn Dvorak, we would all be winners, but who will bell the cat or start the ball rolling? (Choose your cliché, for they all record this evident truth.) Stasis is the norm for complex systems; change, when provoked at all, is usually rapid and episodic.

QWERTY's fortunate and improbable ascent to incumbency occurred by a concatenation of circumstances, each indecisive in itself, but all probably necessary for the eventual outcome. Remington had marketed the Sholes machine with its QWERTY keyboard, but this early tie with a major firm did not secure QWERTY's victory. Competition was tough, and no lead meant much with such small numbers in an expanding market. David estimates that only 5,000 or so QWERTY machines existed at the beginning of the 1880s.

The push to incumbency was complex and multifaceted, dependent more upon the software of teachers and promoters than upon the hardware of improving machines. Most early typists used idiosyncratic hunt-and-peck, few-fingered methods. In 1882, Ms. Longley, founder of the Shorthand and Typewriter Institute in Cincinnati, developed and began to teach the eight-finger typing that professionals use today. She happened to teach with a QWERTY keyboard, although many competing arrangements would have served her purposes as well. She also published a popular do-it-yourself pamphlet. At the same time, Remington began to set up schools for typewriting using (of course) its QWERTY standard. The QWERTY ball was rolling but this head start did not guarantee a place at the summit. Many other schools taught rival methods on different machines and might have gained an edge.

Then a crucial event in 1888 probably added the decisive increment to QWERTY's small advantage. Longley was challenged to prove the superiority of her eight-finger method by Louis Taub, another Cincinnati typing teacher, who worked with four fingers on a rival non-QWERTY keyboard with six rows, no shift action, and (therefore) separate keys for upper- and lowercase letters. As her champion, Longley engaged Frank E. McGurrin, an experienced QWERTY typist who had given himself a decisive advantage that, apparently, no one had utilized before. He had memorized the QWERTY keyboard and could therefore operate his machine as all competent typists do today—by what we now call touch-typing. McGurrin trounced Taub in a well-advertised and well-reported public competition.

In public perception, and (more important) in the eyes of those who ran typing schools and published typing manuals, QWERTY had proved its superiority. But no such victory had really occurred. The tie of McGurrin to QWERTY was fortuitous and a good break for Longley and for Remington. We shall never know why McGurrin won, but reasons quite independent of QWERTY cry out for recognition: touch-typing over hunt-and-peck, eight fingers over four fingers, the three-row letter board with a shift key versus the six-row board with two separate keys for each letter. An array of competitions that would have tested QWERTY were never held—QWERTY versus other arrangements of letters with both contestants using eight-finger touch-typing on a three-row keyboard, or McGurrin's method of eight-finger touch-typing on a non-QWERTY three-row keyboard versus Taub's procedure to see whether the QWERTY arrangement (as I doubt) or McGurrin's method (as I suspect) had secured his success.

In any case, the QWERTY steamroller now gained crucial momentum and prevailed early in our century. As touch-typing by QWERTY became the norm in America's typing schools, rival manufacturers (especially in a rapidly expanding market) could adapt their machines more easily than people could change their habits—and the industry settled upon the wrong standard.

If Sholes had not gained his tie to Remington, if the first typist who decided to memorize a keyboard had used a non-QWERTY design, if McGurrin had a bellyache or drank too much the night before, if Longley had not been so zealous, if a hundred other perfectly possible things had happened, then I might be typing this essay with more speed and much greater economy of finger motion.

But why fret over lost optimality. History always works this way. If Montcalm had won a battle on the Plains of Abraham, perhaps I would be typing *en français.* If a portion of the African jungles had not dried to savannas, I might still be an ape up a tree. If some comets had not struck the earth (if they did) some 60 million years ago, dinosaurs might still rule the land, and all mammals would be rat-sized creatures scurrying about in the dark corners of their world. If *Pikaia,* the only chordate of the Burgess Shale, had not survived the great sorting out of body plans after the Cambrian explosion, mammals might not exist at all. If multicellular creatures had never evolved after five-sixths of life's history had yielded nothing more complicated than an algal mat, the sun might explode a few billion years hence with no multicellular witness to the earth's destruction.

Compared with these weighty possibilities, my indenture to QWERTY seems a small price indeed for the rewards of history.

For if history were not so maddeningly quirky, we would not be here to enjoy it. Streamlined optimality contains no seeds for change. We need our odd little world, where QWERTY rules and the quick brown fox jumps over the lazy dog.*

Postscript

Since typing falls into the category of things that many, if not most of us, can do (like walking and chewing gum simultaneously) this essay elicited more commentary than most of my more obscure ramblings.

Some queried the central premises and logic. An interesting letter from Folsom Prison made a valid point in the tough humor of such institutions. (I receive many letters from prisoners and am always delighted by such reminders that, at least for many people, the quest for knowledge never abates, even in most uncongenial temporary domiciles):

> Some of us were left with a nagging question: If the hunt 'n peck method prevailed until around 1882, how could Sholes or his cohorts have "relegated common letters to weak fingers" when there were no weak fingers, just hunt 'n peck type fingers? At least none of the hunt 'n peck typing clerks or cops around here use the weak fingers. If you could find the time to answer this it would really be appreciated and could serve to reduce the likelihood of increased violence at Folsom between opposing QWERTY origin factions.

My correspondent is quite right, and I misspoke (I also trust that recent tension at Folsom had sources other than the great typewriter wars—yes, I did answer the letter promptly). Fortu-

---

*I must close with a pedantic footnote, lest nonaficionados be utterly perplexed by this ending. This quirky juxtaposition of uncongenial carnivores is said to be the shortest English sentence that contains all twenty-six letters. It is, as such, *de rigueur* in all manuals that teach typing.

nately, my hypothesis is secure against my own carelessness—for Sholes needed simply to separate frequently struck keys to avoid jamming. The finger used to strike mattered little (I also rather suspect that many people were experimenting with many-fingered typing before the full four-fingered methods became canonical).

But the vast bulk of correspondence, more than 80 percent, took issue with my throwaway and tangential last line—thanks to our long-standing and happy fascination with words and word games. I gave the conventional typist's sentence as being the shortest phrase using all letters:

The quick brown fox jumps over the lazy dog.

I have since learned that sentences containing all letters of the alphabet are called "pangrams," and that the quest for the shortest represents at least a minor industry, with much effort spent, and opposing factions with strong passions. Many readers suggested, as a well-known alternative with three fewer letters (32 versus 35),

Pack my box with five dozen liquor jugs.

Zoological enthusiasts and prohibitionists then retort that the fox-dog classic can still tie by dropping the first article and becoming only slightly less grammatical:

Quick brown fox jumps over the lazy dog.

But Ted Leather wins this limited derby for shortest sensible pangram with the 31-stroke

Jackdaws love my big sphinx of quartz.

We now enter the world of arcana. Can shorter pangrams be made? Can the ultimate 26-letter sentence be constructed? This quest has so far stymied all wordsmiths. Using common words only, we can get down to 28 (but only by the slightly dishonorable route of using proper names):

Waltz, nymph, for quick jigs vex Bud.

And to 27, with some archaic orthography:

Frowzy things plumb vex'd Jack Q.

But for the ultimate of 26, we either use initials in abundance (which doesn't seem quite fair),

J. Q. Schwartz flung V. D. Pike my box,

or we avoid names and initials, but employ such unfamiliar and marginally admissable words that an equal feeling of dissatisfaction arises,

Zing! Vext cwm fly jabs Kurd qoph.

A *cwm* is a mountain hollow in Wales, while *qoph,* the nineteenth letter of the Hebrew alphabet, has been drawn (and has attracted the ire of an immigrant fly) by a member of an Iranian minority. Sounds awfully improbable.

My favorite proposal for a 26-letter pangram requires an entire story for comprehension (thanks to Dan Lufkin of Hood College):

During World War I, Lawrence's Arab Legion was operating on the southern flank of the Ottoman Empire. Hampered by artillery fire from across a river, Lawrence asked for a volunteer to cross the river at night and locate the enemy guns. An Egyptian soldier stepped forward. The man was assigned to Lawrence's headquarters [G.H.Q. for "general headquarters"—this becomes important later] and had a reputation for bringing bad luck. But Lawrence decided to send him. The mission was successful and the soldier appeared, at dawn the next morning, at a remote sentry post near the river, dripping wet, shivering, and clad in nothing but his underwear and native regimental headgear. The sentry wired to Lawrence for instructions, and he replied:

Warm plucky G.H.Q. jinx, fez to B.V.D.'s.

A free copy of this and all my subsequent books to anyone who can construct a 26-letter pangram with common words only and no proper names.

2 | Dinomania

5 | Bully for Brontosaurus

QUESTION: What do Catherine the Great, Attila the Hun, and Bozo the Clown have in common? Answer: They all have the same middle name.

Question: What do San Marino, Tannu Tuva, and Monaco have in common? Answer: They all realized that they could print pretty pieces of perforated paper, call them stamps, and sell them at remarkable prices to philatelists throughout the world. (Did these items ever bear any relationship to postage or utility? Does anyone own a canceled stamp from Tannu Tuva?) Some differences, however, must be admitted. Although San Marino (a tiny principality within Italy) and Tannu Tuva (a former state adjacent to Mongolia but now annexed to the Soviet Union) may rely on stamps for a significant fraction of their GNP, Monaco, as we all know, has another considerable source of outside income—the casino of Monte Carlo (nurtured by all the hype and elegance of the Grimaldis—Prince Rainier, Grace Kelly, and all that).

So completely do we identify Monaco with Monte Carlo that we can scarcely imagine any other activity, particularly something productive, taking place in this little land of fantasy and fractured finances.

Nonetheless, people are born, work, and die in Monaco. And this tiny nation boasts, among other amenities, a fine station for oceanographic research. This combination of science and hostelry makes Monaco an excellent place for large professional meetings. In 1913, Monaco hosted the International Zoological Congress, the largest of all meetings within my clan. This 1913 gathering adopted the important Article 79, or "plenary powers decision," stating that "when stability of nomenclature is threatened in an individual case, the strict application of the Code may under specified conditions be suspended by the International Commission on Zoological Nomenclature."

Now I will not blame any reader for puzzlement over the last paragraph. The topic—rules for giving scientific names to organisms—is easy enough to infer. But why should we be concerned with such legalistic arcana? Bear with me. We shall detour around the coils of *Boa constrictor,* meet the International Code of Zoological Nomenclature head-on, and finally arrive at a hot issue now generating much passion and acrimony at the heart of our greatest contemporary fad. You may deny all concern for rules of taxonomy, our last domain of active Latin (now that Catholicism has embraced the vernacular), but millions of Americans are now het up about the proper name of *Brontosaurus,* the canonical dinosaur. And you can't grasp the name of the beast without engaging the beastly rules of naming.

Nonprofessionals often bridle at the complex Latin titles used by naturalists as official designations for organisms. Latin is a historical legacy from the foundation of modern taxonomy in the mid-eighteenth century—a precomputer age when Romespeak was the only language shared by scientists throughout the world. The names may seem cumbersome, now that most of us pass our youthful years before a television set, rather than declaiming *hic-haec-hoc* and *amo-amas-amat.* But the principle remains sound. Effective communication demands that organisms have official names, uniformly recognized in all countries, while a world of changing concepts and increasing knowledge requires that rules of naming foster maximal stability and minimal disruption.

New species are discovered every day; old names must often change as we correct past errors and add new information. If every change of concept demanded a redesignation of all names and a reordering of all categories, natural history would devolve into chaos. Our communications would fail as species, the basic units of all our discourse, would have no recognized labels. All past literature would be a tangle of changing designations, and we could not read without a concordance longer than the twenty volumes of the *Oxford English Dictionary.*

The rules for naming animals are codified in the *International Code of Zoological Nomenclature,* as adopted and continually revised by the International Union of Biological Sciences (plant people have a different code based on similar principles). The latest edition (1985), bound in bright red, runs to 338 pages. I will not attempt to summarize the contents, but only state the primary goal: to promote maximal stability as new knowledge demands revision.

Consider the most prevalent problem demanding a solution in the service of stability: When a single species has been given two or more names, how do we decide which to validate and which to reject? This common situation can arise for several reasons: Two scientists, each unaware of the other's work, may name the same animal; or a single scientist, mistaking a variable species for two or more separate entities, may give more than one name to members of the same species. A simple and commonsensical approach might attempt to resolve all such disputes with a principle of priority—let the oldest name prevail. In practice, such "obvious" solutions rarely work. The history of taxonomy since Linnaeus has featured three sequential approaches to this classic problem.

1. *Appropriateness.* Modern nomenclature dates from the publication, in 1758, of the tenth edition of Linnaeus's *Systema Naturae.* In principle, Linnaeus endorsed the rule of priority. In practice, he and most of his immediate successors commonly changed names for reasons, often idiosyncratic, of supposed "appropriateness." If the literal Latin of an original name ceased to be an accurate descriptor, new names were often devised. (For example, a species originally named *floridensis* to denote a restricted geographic domain might be renamed *americanus* if it later spread throughout the country.)

Some unscrupulous taxonomists used appropriateness as a thinly veiled tactic to place their own stamp upon species by raiding rather than by scientific effort. A profession supposedly dedicated to expanding knowledge about things began to founder into a quagmire of arguments about names. In the light of such human foibles, appropriateness could not work as a primary criterion for taxonomic names.

2. *Priority.* The near anarchy of appropriateness provoked a chorus of demands for reform and codification. The British Association for the Advancement of Science finally appointed a committee to formulate a set of official rules for nomenclature. The Strickland Committee, obedient to the age-old principle that

periods of permissiveness lead to stretches of law 'n' order (before the cycle swings round again), reported in 1842 with a "strict construction" that must have brought joy to all Robert Borks of the day. Priority in publication shall be absolutely and uncompromisingly enforced. No ifs, ands, buts, quibbles, or exceptions.

This decision may have ended the anarchy of capricious change, but it introduced another impediment, perhaps even worse, based on the exaltation of incompetence. When new species are introduced by respected scientists, in widely read publications with clear descriptions and good illustrations, people take notice and the names pass into general use. But when Ignatz Doofus publishes a new name with a crummy drawing and a few lines of telegraphic and muddled description in the *Proceedings of the Philomathematical Society of Pfennighalbpfennig* (circulation 533), it passes into well-deserved oblivion. Unfortunately, under the Strickland Code of strict priority, Herr Doofus's name, if published first, becomes the official moniker of the species—so long as Doofus didn't break any rule in writing his report. The competence and usefulness of his work have no bearing on the decision. The resulting situation is perversely curious. What other field defines its major activity by the work of the least skilled? As Charles Michener, our greatest taxonomist of bees, once wrote: "In other sciences the work of incompetents is merely ignored; in taxonomy, because of priority, it is preserved."

If the Sterling/Doofus ratio were high, priority might pose few problems in practice. Unfortunately, the domain of Doofuses forms a veritable army, issuing cannonade after cannonade of publications filled with new names destined for oblivion but technically constituted in correct form. Since every profession has its petty legalists, its boosters of tidiness and procedure over content, natural history sank into a mire of unproductive pedantry that, in Ernst Mayr's words, "deflected taxonomists from biological research into bibliographic archeology." Legions of technocrats delighted in searching obscure and forgotten publications for an earlier name that could displace some long-accepted and stable usage. Acrimonious arguments proliferated, for Doofus's inadequate descriptions rarely permitted an unambiguous identification of his earlier name with any well-defined species. Thus, a rule introduced to establish stability against capricious change for appropriateness sowed even greater disruption by forcing the abandonment of accepted names for forgotten predecessors.

3. *Plenary Powers.* The abuses of Herr Doofus and his ilk induced a virtual rebellion among natural historians. A poll of Scandinavian zoologists, taken in 1911, yielded 2 in favor and 120 opposed to strict priority. All intelligent administrators know that the key to a humane and successful bureaucracy lies in creative use of the word *ordinarily.* Strict rules of procedure are ordinarily inviolable—unless a damned good reason for disobedience arises, and then flexibility permits humane and rational exceptions. The Plenary Powers Rule, adopted in Monaco in 1913 to stem the revolt against strict priority, is a codification of the estimable principle of *ordinarily.* It provided, as quoted early in this essay, that the first designation shall prevail, unless a later name has been so widely accepted that its suppression in favor of a forgotten predecessor would sow confusion and instability.

Such exceptions to strict priority cannot be asserted by individuals but must be officially granted by the International Commission of Zoological Nomenclature, acting under its plenary powers. The procedure is somewhat cumbersome and demands a certain investment of time and paperwork, but the plenary powers rule has served us well and has finally achieved stability by locating the fulcrum between strict priority and proper exception. To suppress an earlier name under the plenary powers, a taxonomist must submit a formal application and justification to the International Commission (a body of some thirty professional zoologists). The commission then publishes the case, invites commentary from taxonomists throughout the world, considers the initial appeal with all elicited support and rebuttal, and makes a decision by majority vote.

The system has worked well, as two cases may illustrate. The protozoan species *Tetrahymena pyriforme* has long been a staple for biological research, particularly on the physiology of single-celled organisms. John Corliss counted more than 1,500 papers published over a 27-year span—all using this name. However, at least ten technically valid names, entirely forgotten and unused, predate the first publication of *Tetrahymena.* No purpose would be served by resurrecting any of these earlier designations and suppressing the universally accepted *Tetrahymena*. Corliss's petition to the commission was accepted without protest, and *Tetrahymena* has been officially accepted under the plenary powers.

One of my favorite names recently had a much closer brush with official extinction. The generic names of many animals are the same as their common designation: the gorilla is *Gorilla;* the rat, *Rattus.* But I know only one case of a vernacular name identical with both generic *and* specific parts of the technical Latin. The boa constrictor is (but almost wasn't) *Boa constrictor,* and it would be a damned shame if we lost this lovely consonance. Nevertheless, in 1976, *Boa constrictor* barely survived one of the closest contests ever brought before the commission, as thirteen members voted to suppress this grand name in favor of *Boa canina,* while fifteen noble nays stood firm and saved the day. The details are numerous and not relevant to this essay. Briefly, in the founding document of 1758, Linnaeus placed nine species in his genus *Boa,* including *canina* and *constrictor.* As later zoologists divided Linnaeus's overly broad concept of *Boa* into several genera, a key question inevitably arose: Which of Linnaeus's original species should become the "type" (or name bearer) for the restricted version of *Boa,* and which should be assigned to other genera? Many professional herpetologists had accepted *canina* as the best name bearer (and assigned *constrictor* to another genus); but a world of both technical and common usage, from textbooks to zoo labels to horror films, recognized *Boa constrictor.* The commission narrowly opted, in a tight squeeze (sorry, I couldn't resist that one), for the name we all know and love. Ernst Mayr, in casting his decisive vote, cited the virtue of stability in validating common usage—the basis for the plenary powers decision in the first place:

> I think here is clearly a case where stability is best served by following usage in the general zoological literature. I have asked numerous zoologists "what species does the genus *Boa* call to your mind?" and they all said immediately *"constrictor."* . . . Making *constrictor* the type of *Boa* will remove all ambiguity from the literature.

These debates often strike nonprofessionals as a bit ridiculous—a sign, perhaps, that taxonomy is more wordplay than science. After all, science studies the external world (through the dark glass of our prejudices and perceptions to be sure). Questions of first publication versus common usage raise no issues about the animals "out there," and only concern human conventions for naming. But this is the point, not the problem. These are debates about names, not things—and the arbitrary criteria of human decision-making, not boundaries imposed by the external world, apply to our resolutions. The aim of these debates (although not always, alas, the outcome) is to cut through the verbiage, reach a stable and practical decision, and move on to the world of things.

Which leads—did you think that I had forgotten my opening paragraph?—back to philately. The United States government, jumping on the greatest bandwagon since the hula hoop, recently issued four striking stamps bearing pictures of dinosaurs—and labeled *Tyrannosaurus, Stegosaurus, Pteranodon,* and *Brontosaurus.*

Thrusting itself, with all the zeal of a convert, into the heart of commercial hype, the U.S. Post Office seems committed to shedding its image for stodginess in one fell, crass swoop. Its small brochure, announcing October as "national stamp collecting month," manages to sponsor a contest, establish a tie-in both with T-shirts and a videocassette for *The Land Before Time,* and offer a dinosaur "discovery kit" (a $9.95 value for just $3.95; "Valid while supplies last. Better hurry!"). You will, in this context, probably not be surprised to learn that the stamps were officially launched on October 1, 1989, in Orlando, Florida, at Disney World.

Amidst this maelstrom of marketing, the Post Office also engendered quite a brouhaha about the supposed subject of one stamp—a debate given such prominence in the press that much of the public (at least judging from my voluminous mail) now thinks that an issue of great scientific importance has been raised to the detriment and shame of an institution otherwise making a worthy step to modernity. (We must leave this question for another time, but I confess great uneasiness about such approbation. I appreciate the argument that T-shirts and videos heighten awareness and expose aspects of science to millions of kids otherwise unreached. I understand why many will accept the forceful spigot of hype, accompanied by the watering-down of content—all in the interest of extending contact. But the argument works only if, having made contact, we can then woo these kids to a deeper intellectual interest and commitment. Unfortunately, we are often all too ready to compromise. We hear the blandishments: Dumb it down; hype it up. But go too far and you cannot turn back; you lose your own soul by dripping degrees. The space for wooing disappears down the maw of commercialism. Too many wise people, from Shakespeare to my grandmother, have said that dignity is the only bit of our being that cannot be put up for sale.)

This growing controversy even reached the august editorial pages of the *New York Times* (October 11, 1989), and their description serves as a fine epitome of the supposed mess:

> The Postal Service has taken heavy flak for mislabeling its new 25-cent dinosaur stamp, a drawing of a pair of dinosaurs captioned *"Brontosaurus."* Furious purists point out that the "brontosaurus" is now properly called "apatosaurus." They accuse the stamp's authors of fostering scientific illiteracy, and want the stamps recalled.

Brontosaurus versus *Apatosaurus.* Which is right? How important is this issue? How does it rank amidst a host of other controversies surrounding this and other dinosaurs: What head belongs on this dinosaur (whether it be called *Brontosaurus* or *Apatosaurus*); were these large dinosaurs warm-blooded; why did they become extinct? The press often does a good job of reporting basic facts of a dispute, but fails miserably in supplying the context that would allow a judgment about importance. I have tried, in the first part of this essay, to supply the necessary context for grasping *Brontosaurus* versus *Apatosaurus.* I regret to report, and shall now document, that the issue could hardly be more trivial—for the dispute is only about names, not about things. The empirical question was settled to everyone's satisfaction in 1903. To understand the argument about names, we must know the rules of taxonomy and something about the history of debate on the principle of priority. But the exposure of context for *Brontosaurus* versus *Apatosaurus* does provide an interesting story in itself and does raise important issues about the public presentation of science—and thus do I hope to snatch victory (or at least interest) from the jaws of defeat (or triviality).

Brontosaurus versus *Apatosaurus* is a direct legacy of the most celebrated feud in the history of vertebrate paleontology—Cope versus Marsh. As E. D. Cope and O. C. Marsh vied for the glory of finding spectacular dinosaurs and mammals in the American West, they fell into a pattern of rush and superficiality born of their intense competition and mutual dislike. Both wanted to bag as many names as possible, so they published too quickly, often with inadequate descriptions, careless study, and poor illustrations. In this unseemly rush, they frequently gave names to fragmentary material that could not be well characterized and sometimes described the same creature twice by failing to make proper distinctions among the fragments. (For a good history of this issue, see D. S. Berman and J. S. McIntosh, 1978. These authors point out that both Cope and Marsh often described and officially named a species when only a few bones had been excavated and most of the skeleton remained in the ground.)

In 1877, in a typically rushed note, O. C. Marsh named and described *Apatosaurus ajax* in two paragraphs without illustrations ("Notice of New Dinosaurian Reptiles from the Jurassic Formation," *American Journal of Science,* 1877). Although he noted that this "gigantic dinosaur . . . is represented in the Yale Museum by a nearly complete skeleton in excellent preservation," Marsh described only the vertebral column. In 1879, he published another page of information and presented the first sketchy illustrations—of pelvis, shoulder blade, and a few vertebrae ("Principal Characters of American Jurassic Dinosaurs, Part II," *American Journal of Science,* 1879). He also took this opportunity to pour some vitriol upon Mr. Cope, claiming that Cope had misnamed and misdescribed several forms in his haste. "Conclusions based on such work," Marsh asserts, "will naturally be received with distrust by anatomists."

In another 1879 article, Marsh introduced the genus *Brontosaurus,* with two paragraphs (even shorter than those initially devoted to *Apatosaurus*), no illustrations, and just a few comments on the pelvis and vertebrae. He did estimate the length of his new beast at seventy to eighty feet, in comparison with some fifty feet for *Apatosaurus* ("Notice of New Jurassic Reptiles," *American Journal of Science,* 1879).

Marsh considered *Apatosaurus* and *Brontosaurus* as distinct but

Marsh's famous illustration of the complete skeleton of *Brontosaurus*.
FROM THE SIXTEENTH ANNUAL REPORT OF THE U.S. GEOLOGICAL SURVEY,
1895. NEG. NO. 328654. COURTESY DEPARTMENT OF LIBRARY SERVICES, AMERI-
CAN MUSEUM OF NATURAL HISTORY.

closely related genera within the larger family of sauropod dinosaurs. *Brontosaurus* soon became everyone's typical sauropod—
indeed *the* canonical herbivorous dinosaur of popular consciousness, from the Sinclair logo to Walt Disney's *Fantasia*— for
a simple and obvious reason. Marsh's *Brontosaurus* skeleton, from
the most famous of all dinosaur localities at Como Bluff Quarry
10, Wyoming, remains to this day "one of the most complete
sauropod skeletons ever found" (quoted from Berman and McIntosh, cited previously). Marsh mounted the skeleton at Yale and
often published his spectacular reconstruction of the entire animal. (*Apatosaurus,* meanwhile, remained a pelvis and some vertebrae.) In his great summary work, *The Dinosaurs of North America*,
Marsh wrote (1896): "The best-known genus of the Atlanto-
sauridae is *Brontosaurus,* described by the writer in 1879, the type
specimen being a nearly entire skeleton, by far the most complete
of any of the Sauropoda yet discovered." *Brontosaurus* also became the source of the old stereotype, now so strongly challenged, of slow, stupid, lumbering dinosaurs. Marsh wrote in

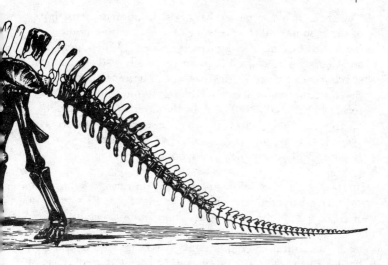

1883, when presenting his full reconstruction of *Brontosaurus* for the first time:

> A careful estimate of the size of *Brontosaurus,* as here restored, shows that when living the animal must have weighed more than twenty tons. The very small head and brain, and slender neural cord, indicate a stupid, slow-moving reptile. The beast was wholly without offensive or defensive weapons, or dermal armature. In habits, *Brontosaurus* was more or less amphibious, and its food was probably aquatic plants or other succulent vegetation.

In 1903, Elmer Riggs of the Field Museum in Chicago restudied Marsh's sauropods. Paleontologists had realized by then that Marsh had been overgenerous in his designation of species (a "splitter" in our jargon), and that many of his names would have to be consolidated. When Riggs restudied *Apatosaurus* and *Brontosaurus,* he recognized them as two versions of the same creature, with *Apatosaurus* as a more juvenile specimen. No big deal; it happens all the time. Riggs rolled the two genera into one in a single paragraph:

The genus *Brontosaurus* was based chiefly upon the structure of the scapula and the presence of five vertebrae in the sacrum. After examining the type specimens of these genera, and making a careful study of the unusually well-preserved specimen described in this paper, the writer is convinced that the Apatosaur specimen is merely a young animal of the form represented in the adult by the Brontosaur specimen. . . . In view of these facts the two genera may be regarded as synonymous. As the term *"Apatosaurus"* has priority, *"Brontosaurus"* will be regarded as a synonym.

In 1903, ten years before the plenary powers decision, strict priority ruled in zoological nomenclature. Thus, Riggs had no choice but to sink the later name, *Brontosaurus,* once he had decided that Marsh's earlier name, *Apatosaurus,* represented the same animal. But then I rather doubt that Riggs would have gone to bat for *Brontosaurus* even if he could have submitted a case on its behalf. After all, *Brontosaurus* was not yet an icon of pop culture in 1903—no Sinclair logo, no Alley-Oop, no *Fantasia,* no *Land Before Time.* Neither name had captured public or scientific fancy, and Riggs probably didn't lament the demise of *Brontosaurus.*

No one has ever seriously challenged Riggs's conclusion, and professionals have always accepted his synonymy. But Publication 82 of the "Geological Series of the Field Columbian Museum" for 1903—the reference for Riggs's article—never gained much popular currency. The name *Brontosaurus,* still affixed to skeletons in museums thoughout the world, still perpetuated in countless popular and semi-technical books about nature, never lost its luster, despite its technical limbo. Anyone could have applied to the commission for suppression of *Apatosaurus* under the plenary powers in recognition of the widespread popularity and stability of *Brontosaurus.* I suspect that such an application would have succeeded. But no one bothered, and a good name remains in limbo. (I also wish that someone had fought for suppression of the unattractive and inappropriate name *Hyracotherium* in favor of the lovely but later *Eohippus,* also coined by Marsh. But again, no one did.)

I'm afraid there's not much more to this story—not nearly the issue hyped by your newspapers as the Great Stamp Flap. No argument of fact arises at all, just a question of names, settled in

1903, but never transferred to a general culture that continues to learn and favor the technically invalid name *Brontosaurus*. But the story does illustrate something troubling about the presentation of science in popular media. The world of *USA Today* is a realm of instant fact and no analysis. Hundreds of bits come at us in pieces never lasting more than a few seconds—for the dumb-downers tell us that average Americans can't assimilate anything more complex or pay attention to anything longer.

This oddly "democratic" procedure makes all bits equal—the cat who fell off a roof in Topeka (and lived) gets the same space as the Soviet withdrawal from Afghanistan. Equality is a magnificent system for human rights and morality in general, but not for the evaluation of information. We are bombarded with too much in our inordinately complex world; if we cannot sort the trivial from the profound, we are lost in terminal overload. The criteria for sorting must involve context and theory—the larger perspective that a good education provides.

In the current dinosaur craze without context, all bits are mined for their superficial news value as items in themselves—a lamentable tendency abetted by the "trivial pursuit" one-upman-ship that confers status on people who know (and flaunt) the most bits. (If you play this dangerous game in real life, remember that ignorance of context is the surest mark of a phony. If you approach me in wild lament, claiming that our postal service has mocked the deepest truth of paleontology, I will know that you have only skimmed the surface of my field.)

Consider the four items mentioned earlier in this essay. They are often presented in *USA Today* style as equal factoids. But with a context to sort the trivial from the profound, we may recognize some as statements about words, others as entries to the most general questions we can ask about the history of life. *Apatosaurus* versus *Brontosaurus* is a legalistic quibble about words and rules of naming. Leave the Post Office alone. They take enough flak (much justified of course) as it is. The proper head for *Apatosaurus* is an interesting empirical issue, but of little moment beyond the sauropods. Marsh found no skull associated with either his *Apatosaurus* or his *Brontosaurus* skeleton. He guessed wrong and mounted the head of another sauropod genus called *Camarosaurus*. *Apatosaurus* actually bore a head much more like that of the different genus *Diplodocus*. The head issue (*Camarosaurus*-like versus *Diplodocus*-like) and the name issue (*Apatosaurus* versus *Brontosaurus*) are entirely separate questions, although the press has confused and conflated them.

The question of warm-bloodedness (quite unresolved at the moment) is more general still, as it affects our basic concepts of dinosaur physiology and efficiency. The issue of extinction is the broadest of all—for basic patterns of life's history are set by differential survival of groups through episodes of mass dying. We are here today, arguing about empty issues like *Apatosaurus* versus *Brontosaurus,* because mammals got through the great Cretaceous extinction, while dinosaurs did not.

I hate to be a shill for the Post Office, but I think that they made the right decision this time. Responding to the great *Apatosaurus* flap, Postal Bulletin Number 21744 proclaimed: "Although now recognized by the scientific community as *Apatosaurus,* the name *Brontosaurus* was used for the stamp because it is more familiar to the general population. Similarly, the term "dinosaur" has been used generically to describe all the animals, even though the *Pteranodon* was a flying reptile." Touché and right on; no one bitched about *Pteranodon,* and that's a real error.

The Post Office has been more right than the complainers, for Uncle Sam has worked in the spirit of the plenary powers rule. Names fixed in popular usage may be validated even if older designations have technical priority. But now . . . Oh Lord, why didn't I see it before! Now I suddenly grasp the secret thread behind this overt debate! It's a plot, a dastardly plot sponsored by the apatophiles—that covert society long dedicated to gaining support for Marsh's original name against a potential appeal to the plenary powers. They never had a prayer before. Whatever noise they made, whatever assassinations they attempted, they could never get anyone to pay attention, never disturb the tranquillity and general acceptance of *Brontosaurus.* But now that the Post Office has officially adopted *Brontosaurus,* they have found their opening. Now enough people know about *Apatosaurus* for the first time. Now an appeal to the plenary powers would not lead to the validation of *Brontosaurus,* for *Apatosaurus* has gained precious currency. They have won; we brontophiles have been defeated.

Apatosaurus means "deceptive lizard"; *Brontosaurus* means "thunder lizard"—a far, far better name (but appropriateness, alas, as we have seen, counts for nothing). They have deceived us; we brontophiles have been outmaneuvered. Oh well, graciousness in defeat before all (every bit as important as dignity, if not an aspect thereof). I retreat, not with a bang of thunder, but with a whimper of hope that rectification may someday arise from the ashes of my stamp album.

6 | The Dinosaur Rip-off

WE LOVE occasional reversals of established order, both to defuse the tension of inequity and to infuse a bit of variety into our lives. Consider the medieval feast of fools (where slaves could be masters, in jest and only for a moment), Sadie Hawkins Day, and the genre of quiz that supplies the answer and asks a contestant to reconstruct the question. I begin this essay in such a spirit by giving my answer to a question that has surpassed all others (except, perhaps, "Where is human evolution going?") in my catalogue of inquiries from people who love natural history. My answer, unfortunately, must be: "Damned if I know"—which won't help you much in trying to guess the question. So I'll reveal the question without further ado: "What's behind the great dinosaur mania that's been sweeping the country during the past few years?"

Readers will scarcely need my words to document the phenomenon, for we are all surrounded by dinosaur tote bags, lunch boxes, pens and pencils, underpants, ties, and T-shirts that say "bossosaurus" or "secretaryosaurus," as the case may be. You can buy dinosaur-egg soap to encourage your kids to take a bath, a rocking stegosaurus for indoor recreation (a mere 800 bucks from F.A.O. Schwarz), a brontosaurus bank to encourage thrift, or a dinosaur growth chart to hang on the wall and measure your tyke's progress toward the N.B.A. In Key West, where dinosaurs have edged out flamingos as icons of kitsch, I even saw dinosaur toilet paper with a different creature on each perforated segment—providing quite a sense of power, I suppose, when used for its customary purpose. (This reminded me of the best attempt

I ever encountered for defusing the Irish situation. I once stayed in a small motel in Eire where the bathrooms had two rolls of toilet paper—one green, the other orange.)

I offer no definitive answer to the cause of this mania, but I can at least document a fact strongly relevant to the solution. Perhaps dinosaur mania is intrinsic and endemic, a necessary and permanent fact of life (once the fossils had been discovered and properly characterized); perhaps dinosaurs act as the trigger for a deep Jungian archetype of the soul; perhaps they rank as incarnations of primal fears and fascinations, programmed into our brains as the dragons of Eden. But these highfalutin suggestions cannot suffice for the simple reason that dinosaurs have been well documented throughout our century, while few people granted them more than passing notice before the recent craze hit.

I can testify to the previous status of dinosaurs among the arcana of our culture, for I was a kiddie dinosaur nut in the late 1940s when nobody gave a damn. I fell in love with the great skeletons at the American Museum of Natural History and then, with all the passion of youth, sought collateral material with thoroughness and avidity. I would pounce on any reinforcement of my greatest interest—a Sinclair Oil logo or a hokey concrete tyrannosaur bestriding (like a colossus) Hole 15 at the local miniature golf course. There sure wasn't much to find—a few overpriced brass figures and a book or two by Roy Chapman Andrews and Ned Colbert, all hard to get anywhere outside the Museum shop. Representations in pop culture were equally scarce, ranging little beyond King Kong versus the pteranodon and Alley Oop riding a brontosaurus.

One story will indicate both the frustration of a young adept in a world of ignorance and the depth of that ignorance itself. At age nine or so, in the Catskills at one of those innumerable summer camps with an Indian name, I got into a furious argument with a bunkmate over the old issue of whether humans and dinosaurs ever inhabited the earth together. We agreed—bad, bad mistake—to abide by the judgment of the first adult claiming to know the answer, and we bet the camp currency, a chocolate bar, on the outcome. We asked all the counselors and staff, but none had ever heard of a brontosaurus. At parents' weekend, his came and mine didn't. We asked his father, who assured us that of course dinosaurs and people lived together; just look at Alley Oop. I paid—and seethed—and still seethe. This could not happen today. Anyone—a few "scientific creationists" excepted—would both know the answer and give you the latest rundown on theories for the extinction of dinosaurs.*

All this I tell for humor, but a part of the story isn't so funny. Kiddie culture can be cruel and fiercely anti-intellectual. I survived because I wasn't hopeless at punchball, and I won some respect for my knowledge of baseball stats. But any kid with a passionate interest in science was a wonk, a square, a dweeb, a doofus, or a geek (I don't remember what word held sway at the time, but one item in that particular litany of cruelty is always in vogue). I was taunted by many classmates as peculiar. I was called "fossil face" on the playground. It hurt.

I once asked my colleague Shep White, a leading child psychologist, why kids were so interested in dinosaurs. He gave an answer both elegant and succinct: "Big, fierce, and extinct." I love this response, but it can't resolve the question that prompted this essay. Dinosaurs were also big, fierce, and extinct twenty years ago, but few kids or adults gave a damn about them. And so I return to the original question: What started the current dinosaur craze?

The optimistic answer for any intellectual must be that public taste follows scientific discovery. The past twenty years have been a heyday for new findings and fundamental revisions in our view of dinosaurs. The drab, lumbering, slow-witted, inefficient beasts of old interpretations have been replaced with smooth, sleek, colorful, well-oiled, and at least adequately intelligent revised versions. The changes have been most significant in three subjects: anatomy, behavior, and extinction. All three have provided a more congenial and more interesting perspective on dinosaurs. For anatomy, a herd of brontosauruses charging through the desert inspires more awe than a few behemoths so encumbered by their own weight that they must live in ponds. For behavior, the images of the newly christened *Maiasauria*, the good mother liz-

---

*I was too optimistic. Never overestimate the depth of our anti-intellectual traditions! A week after I published this essay, results of a comprehensive survey showed that about 30 percent of American adults accept the probable contemporaneity of humans and dinosaurs. Still, our times are better than before. Seventy percent of that camp could have answered our inquiry before parental arrival.

ard, brooding her young, or a herd of migrating ornithopods, with vulnerable juveniles in the center and strong adults at the peripheries, inspire more sympathy than a dumb stegosaur laying her eggs and immediately abandoning them by instinct and ignorance. For extinction, crashing comets and global dust clouds surely inspire more attention than gradually changing sea levels or solar outputs.

I wish that I could locate the current craze in these exciting intellectual developments. But a moment's thought must convince anyone that this good reason cannot provide the right answer. Dinosaurs might not have been quite so jazzy and sexy twenty years ago, but the brontosaurs weren't any smaller back then, the tyrannosaurs were just as fierce, and the whole clan was every bit as extinct (my camp friend's father notwithstanding). You may accept or reject Shep White's three categories, but choose any alternate criteria and dinosaurs surely had the capacity to inspire a craze at any time—twenty years ago as well as today. (At least two mini-crazes of earlier years—in England after Waterhouse Hawkins displayed his life-sized models at the Crystal Palace in the 1850s, and in America after Sinclair promoted a dinosaur exhibit at the New York World's Fair in 1939—illustrate this permanent potential.) We must conclude, I think, that dinosaurs have never lacked the seeds of appeal, that the missing ingredient must be adequate publicity, and that the key to "why now?" resides in promotion, not new knowledge.

I must therefore assume that the solution lies in that great and dubious driving force of American society—marketing. At some definable point, some smart entrepreneur recognized an enormous and largely unexploited potential for profit. What craze is any different? Did goldfish reach an optimal size and tastiness for swallowing in the early 1940s? Did a breakthrough in yo-yo technology spawn the great passion that swept the streets of New York in my youth? Did hula hoops fit some particular social niche and need uniquely confined to a few months during the 1950s?

I don't doubt that a few more general factors may form part of the story. Perhaps the initial entrepreneurs developed their own interest and insight by reading about new discoveries. Perhaps the vast expansion of museum gift shops—a dubious trend (in my view), with more to lament in skewed priorities than to praise in heightened availability of worthy paraphernalia—gave an essential boost in providing an initial arena for sales. Still, most crazes get started for odd and unpredictable reasons and then propagate by a kind of mass intoxication and social conformity. If I am right in arguing that the current dinosaur craze could have occurred long ago and owes both its origin and initial spread to a marketing opportunity seized by a few diligent entrepreneurs (with later diffusion by odd mechanisms of crowd psychology that engender chain reactions beyond a critical mass), then the source of this phenomenon may not be a social trend or a new discovery, but the cleverness of a person or persons unknown (with a product or products unrecognized). As this craze is no minor item in twentieth-century American cultural history, I would love to identify the instigators and the insights. If anyone knows, please tell me.

I do confess to some cynical dubiety about the inundation of kiddie culture with dinosaurs in every cute, furry, and profitable venue that any marketing agent can devise. I don't, of course, advocate a return to the ignorance and unavailability of information during my youth, but a dinosaur on every T-shirt and milk carton does foreclose any sense of mystery or joy of discovery—and certain forms of marketing do inexorably lead to trivialization. Interest in dinosaurs becomes one of those ephemeral episodes—somewhere between policeman and fireman—in the canonical sequence of childhood interests. Something to burn brightly in its appointed season and then, all too often, to die—utterly and without memory.

As intellectuals, we acknowledge and accept a minority status in our culture (since hope, virtue, and reality rarely coincide). We therefore know that we must seize our advantages by noting popular trends and trying to divert some of their energy into rivulets that might benefit learning and education. The dinosaur craze should be a blessing for us, since the source material is a rip-off of our efforts—the labor of paleontologists, the great skeletons mounted in our museums. Indeed, we have done well—damned well, as things go. Lurking in and around the book covers and shopping bags are a pretty fair number of mighty good books, films, puzzles, games, and other items of—dare I say it—decent intellectual and educational content.

It is now time to segue, via a respectable transition, into the second part of this essay. (But before we do, and while I'm throwing out requests for enlightenment, can anyone tell me how this fairly obscure Italian term from my musical education managed its recent entry into trendy American speech?*)

We all acknowledge the sorry state of primary and secondary education in America, both by contrast with the successes of other nations and by any absolute standard of educational need in an increasingly complex world. We also recognize that the crisis is particularly acute for the teaching of science. Well, being of an optimistic nature, I survey the dinosaur craze and wonder why science suffers so badly within our schools. The dinosaur craze has generated, amidst a supersaurus-sized pile of kitsch and crap, a remarkable range of worthy material that kids seem to like and use. Kids love science so long as fine teaching and good material grace the presentation. If the dinosaur craze of pop culture has been adequately subverted for educational ends, why can't we capitalize on this benevolent spin-off? Why can't we sustain the interest, rather than letting it wither like the flower of grass, as soon as a child moves on to his next stage? Why can't we infuse some of this excitement into our schools and use it to boost and expand interest in all of science? Think of the aggregate mental power vested in 10 million five-year-olds, each with an average of twenty monstrous Latin dinosaur names committed to memory with the effortless joy and awesome talent of human beings at the height of their powers for rote learning. Can't we transfer this skill to all the other domains—arithmetic, spelling, and foreign languages, in particular—that benefit so greatly from rote learning in primary school years? (Let no adult disparage the value of rote because we lose both the ability and the joy in later years.)

Why is the teaching of science in such trouble in our nation's public schools? Why is the shortage of science teachers so desperate that hundreds of high schools have dropped physics entirely, while about half of all science courses still on the books are now being taught by people without formal training in science? To understand this lamentable situation, we must first dispel the silly and hurtful myth that science is simply too hard for preadults. (Supporters of this excuse argue that we succeeded in the

---

*See the postscript to this essay for an interesting reaction to this appeal.

past only because science was much simpler before the great explosion of modern knowledge.)

This claim cannot be sustained for two basic reasons. First, science uses and requires no special mental equipment beyond the scope of a standard school curriculum. The subject matter may be different but the cerebral tools are common to all learning. Science probes the factual state of the world; religion and ethics deal with moral reasoning; art and literature treat aesthetic and social judgment.

Second, we may put aside all abstract arguments and rely on the empirical fact that other nations have had great success in science education. If their kids can handle the material, so can ours, with proper motivation and instruction. Korea has made great strides in education, particularly in mathematics and the physical sciences. And if you attempt to take refuge in the cruel and fallacious argument that Orientals are genetically built to excel in such subjects, I simply point out that European nations, filled with people more like most of us, have been just as successful. The sciences are well taught and appreciated in the Soviet Union, for example, where the major popular bookstores on Leninsky Prospekt are stocked with technical books both browsed and purchased in large numbers. Moreover, we proved the point to ourselves in the late 1950s, when the Soviet Sputnik inspired cold war fears of Russian technological takeover, and we responded, for once, with adequate cash, expertise, and enthusiasm, by launching a major effort to improve secondary education in science. But that effort, begun for the wrong reasons, soon petered out into renewed mediocrity (graced, as always, with pinpoints of excellence here and there, whenever a great teacher and adequate resources coincide).

We live in a profoundly nonintellectual culture, made all the worse by a passive hedonism abetted by the spread of wealth and its dissipation into countless electronic devices that impart the latest in entertainment and supposed information—all in short (and loud) doses of "easy listening." The kiddie culture, or playground, version of this nonintellectualism can be even more strident and more one-dimensional, but the fault must lie entirely with adults—for our kids are only enhancing a role model read all too clearly.

I'm beginning to sound like an aging Miniver Cheevy, or like the chief reprobate on Ko-Ko's little list "of society offenders who might well be underground"—and he means dead and buried, not romantically in opposition: "the idiot who praises with enthusiastic tone, all centuries but this and every country but his own." I want to make an opposite and curiously optimistic point about our current mores: We are a profoundly nonintellectural culture, but we are not committed to this attitude; in fact, we are scarcely committed to anything. We may be the most labile culture in all history, capable of rapid and massive shifts of prevailing opinions, all imposed from above by concerted media effort. Passivity and nonintellectual judgment are the greatest spurs to such lability. Everything comes to us in fifteen-second sound bites and photo opportunities. All possibility for ambiguity—the most precious trait of any adequate analysis—is erased. He wins who looks best or shouts loudest. We are so fearful of making judgments ourselves that we must wait until the TV commentators have spoken before deciding whether Bush or Dukakis won the debate.

We are therefore maximally subject to imposition from above. Nonetheless, this dangerous trait can be subverted for good. A few years ago, in the wake of an unparalleled media blitz, drugs rose from insignificance to a strong number one on the list of serious American problems in that most mercurial court of public opinion as revealed by polling. Surely we can provoke the same immediate recognition for poor education. Talk about "wasted minds." Which cause would you pick as the greater enemy, quantitatively speaking, in America: crack or lousy education abetted by conformity and peer pressure in an anti-intellectual culture?

We live in a capitalist economy, and I have no particular objection to honorable self-interest. We cannot hope to make the needed, drastic improvement in primary and secondary education without a dramatic restructuring of salaries. In my opinion, you cannot pay a good teacher enough money to recompense the value of talent applied to the education of young children. I teach an hour or two a day to tolerably well-behaved near-adults—and come home exhausted. By what possible argument are my services worth more in salary than those of a secondary-school teacher with six classes a day, little prestige, less support, massive problems of discipline, and a fundamental role in shaping minds. (In comparison, I only tinker with intellects already largely formed.) Why are salaries so low, and attendant prestige so limited, for the most important job in America? How can our priorities be so skewed that when we wish to raise the status of science teachers, we take the media route and try to place a member of the profession into orbit (with disastrous consequences, as it happened), rather than boosting salaries on earth? (The crisis in science teaching stems directly from this crucial issue of compensation. Science graduates can begin in a variety of industrial jobs at twice the salary of almost any teaching position; potential teachers in the arts and humanities often lack these well-paid alternatives and enter the public schools *faute de mieux.*)

We are now at a crux of opportunity, and the situation may not persist if we fail to exploit it. If I were king, I would believe Gorbachev, realize that the cold war is a happenstance of history—not a necessary and permanent state of world politics—make some agreements, slash the military budget, and use just a fraction of the savings to double the salary of every teacher in American public schools. I suspect that a shift in prestige, and the consequent attractiveness of teaching to those with excellence and talent, would follow.

I don't regard these suggestions as pipe dreams, but having been born before yesterday, I don't expect their immediate implementation either. I also acknowledge, of course, that reforms are not imposed from above without vast and coordinated efforts of lobbying and pressuring from below. Thus, as we work toward a larger and more coordinated solution, and as a small contribution to the people's lobby, could we not immediately subvert more of the dinosaur craze from crass commercialism to educational value?

Dinosaur names can become the model for rote learning. Dinosaur facts and figures can inspire visceral interest and lead to greater wonder about science. Dinosaur theories and reconstructions can illustrate the rudiments of scientific reasoning. But I'd like to end with a more modest suggestion. Nothing makes me sadder than the peer pressure that enforces conformity and erases wonder. Countless Americans have been permanently deprived of the joys of singing because a thoughtless teacher once told them not to sing, but only to mouth the words at the school assembly because they were "off-key." Once told, twice shy and perpetually fearful. Countless others had the light of intellectual wonder extinguished because a thoughtless and swaggering fellow student called them nerds on the playground. Don't point to the obsessives—I was one—who will persist and succeed despite these petty cruelties of youth. For each of us, a hundred are lost—more timid and fearful, but just as capable. We must rage against the dying of the light—and although Dylan Thomas spoke of bodily death in his famous line, we may also apply his words to the extinction of wonder in the mind, by pressures of conformity in an anti-intellectual culture.

The *New York Times,* in an article on science education in Korea, interviewed a nine-year-old girl and inquired after her personal hero. She replied: Stephen Hawking. Believe me, I have absolutely nothing against Larry Bird or Michael Jordan, but wouldn't it be lovely if even one American kid in 10,000 gave such an answer. The article went on to say that science whizzes are class heroes in Korean schools, not isolated and ostracized dweebs.

English wars may have been won on the playing fields of Eton, but American careers in science are destroyed on the playgrounds of Shady Oaks Elementary School. Can we not invoke dinosaur power to alleviate these unspoken tragedies? Can't dinosaurs be the great levelers and integrators—the joint passion of the class rowdy and the class intellectual? I will know that we are on our way when the kid who names *Chasmosaurus* as his personal hero also earns the epithet of Mr. Cool.

Postscript

I had never made an explicit request of readers before, but I was really curious and couldn't find the answer in my etymological books. Hence, my little parenthetical inquiry about *segue:* "Can anyone tell me how this fairly obscure Italian term from my musical education managed its recent entry into trendy American speech?" The question bugged me because two of my students, innocent alas (as most are these days) of classical music, use *segue* all the time, and I longed to know where they found it. Both simply considered *segue* as Ur-English when I asked, perhaps the very next word spoken by our ultimate forefather after his introductory, palindromic "Madam I'm Adam" (as in "segue into the garden with me, won't you").

I am profoundly touched and gratified. The responses came in waves and even yielded, I believe, an interesting resolution. (These letters also produced the salutary effect of reminding me how lamentably ignorant I am about a key element of American culture—pop music and its spin-offs.) I've always said to myself that I write these essays primarily for personal learning; this claim has now passed its own test.

One set of letters (more than two dozen) came from people in their twenties and thirties who had been (or in a case or two, still are) radio deejays for rock stations (a temporary job on a college radio station for most). They all report that *segue* is a standard term for the delicate task (once rather difficult in the days of records and turntables) of making an absolutely smooth transition, without any silence in between or words to cover the change, from one song to the next.

I was quite happy to accept this solution, but I then began to receive letters from old-timers in the radio and film business—all pointing to uses in the 1920s and 1930s (and identifying the lingo of rock deejays as a later transfer). David Emil wrote of his work in television during the mid-1960s:

> The word was in usage as a noun and verb when I worked in the television production industry. . . . It was common for television producers to use the phrase to refer to connections between segments of television shows. . . . Interestingly, although I read a large number of scripts at this time, I never saw the word in writing or knew how it was spelled until the mid-1970s when I came across the word in a more traditional usage.

Bryant Mather, former curator of minerals at the Field Museum in Chicago, sent me an old mimeographed script of his sole appearance on radio—an NBC science show of 1940 entitled *How Do You Know,* and produced "as a public service feature by the Field Museum of Natural History in cooperation with the University Broadcasting Council."

The script, which uses *segue* to describe all transitions between scenes in a dramatization of the history of the Orloff diamond, reminds us by its stereotyping and barely concealed racism (despite the academic credentials of its origin) that some improvements have been made in our attitudes toward human diversity. In one scene, for example, the diamond is bought by Isaacs, described as "a Jewish merchant." His hectoring wife, called "Mama" by Mr. Isaacs, keeps pestering: "Buy it, Isaacs—you hear me—buy it." Isaacs later sells to a shifty Persian, who cheats him by placing lead coins under the surface of gold in his treasure bag. Isaacs, discovering the trick, laments: "Counterfeit—lead—oi, oi, oi—Mama—we are ruined—we are ruined." (Shades of Shylock—my ducats, my daughter.) The script's next line reads "segue to music suggestive of Amsterdam or busy port."

Page Gilman made the earliest link to radio and traced a most sensible transition (dare I say segue) between musical and modern media usages. I will accept his statement as our best resolution to date:

> I think you may find that a bridge between the classical music to which you refer and today's disk jockey use would be the many years of network radio. I began in 1927 and even the earliest scripts would occasionally use "segue" because we had a big staff of professional *working* musicians—people who worked (in those days) in restaurants, theaters (especially), and now radio. Today you'll find a real corps of such folks only in New York and L.A. . . . You'll find me corroborated a little by Pauline Kael of the *New Yorker,* who remembers Horace Heidt's orchestra at the Golden Gate Theater in San Francisco. That was the time when I was dating one of the Downey Sisters in the same orchestra. [May I also report the confirmation of my beloved 92-year-old Uncle Mordie of Rochester, New York, who relished his 1920s daily job in a movie orchestra, playing with the Wurlitzer during the silents and between shows—and never liked nearly as much his forty-year subsequent stint as lead violist in the Rochester Symphony.] I wonder if Bruce Springsteen ever heard of "segue." On such uncultured times have working musicians fallen.

This tracing of origins does not solve the more immediate problem of recent infiltration into general trendy speech. But perhaps this is not even an issue in our media-centered world, where any jargon of the industry stands poised to break out. Among many suggestions for this end of the tale, several readers report that Johnny Carson has prominently used *segue* during the past few years—and I doubt that we would need much more to effect a general spread.

Finally, on my more general inquiry into the sources of our current dinomania, I can't even begin to chronicle the interesting suggestions for fear of composing another book. Just one wistful observation for now. Last year, riding a bus down Haight Street in San Francisco, I approached the junction with Ashbury eager to see what businesses now occupied the former symbolic and actual center of American counterculture. Would you believe that just three or four stores down from the junction itself stands one of those stores that peddles nothing but reptilian parapher-nalia and always seems to bear the now-clichéd name "Dino-store." What did Tennyson say in the *Idylls of the King?*

> The old order changeth, yielding
>   place to new;
> And God fulfills himself in
>   many ways,
> Lest one good custom should corrupt
>   the world.

3 | Adaptation

7 | Of Kiwi Eggs and the Liberty Bell

LIKE OZYMANDIAS, once king of kings but now two legs of a broken statue in Percy Shelley's desert, the great façade of Union Station in Washington, D.C., stands forlorn (but ready to front for a bevy of yuppie emporia now under construction), while Amtrak now operates from a dingy outpost at the side.* Six statues, portraying the greatest of human arts and inventions, grace its parapet. Electricity holds a bar of lightning; his inscription proclaims: "Carrier of light and power. Devourer of time and space. . . . Greatest servant of man. . . . Thou hast put all things under his feet."

Yet I will cast my vote for the Polynesian double canoe, constructed entirely with stone adzes, as the greatest invention for devouring time and space in all human history. These vessels provided sufficient stability for long sea voyages. The Polynesian people, without compass or sextant, but with unparalleled understanding of stars, waves, and currents, navigated these canoes to colonize the greatest emptiness of our earth, the "Polynesian triangle," stretching from New Zealand to Hawaii to Easter Island at its vertices. Polynesians sailed forth into the open Pacific more than a thousand years before Western navigators dared to leave

---

*It is so good and pleasant, in our world of woe and destruction, to report some good news for a change. Union Station has since reopened with a triumphant and vibrant remodeling that fully respects the spirit and architecture of the original. Trains now depart from the heart of this great station, and a renaissance of rational public transportation, with elements of grand style at the termini, may not be a pipe dream.

the coastline of Africa and make a beeline across open water from the Guinea coast to the Cape of Good Hope.

New Zealand, southwestern outpost of Polynesian migrations, is so isolated that not a single mammal (other than bats and seals with their obvious means of transport) managed to intrude. New Zealand was a world of birds, dominated by several species (thirteen to twenty-two by various taxonomic reckonings) of large, flightless moas. Only *Aepyornis,* the extinct elephant bird of Madagascar, ever surpassed the largest moa, *Dinornis maximus,* in weight. Ornithologist Dean Amadon estimated the average weight of *D. maximus* at 520 pounds (although some recent revisions nearly double this bulk), compared with about 220 pounds for ostriches, the largest living birds.

We must cast aside the myths of noble non-Westerners living in ecological harmony with their potential quarries. The ancestors of New Zealand's Maori people based a culture on hunting moas, but soon made short work of them, both by direct removal and by burning of habitat to clear areas for agriculture. Who could resist a 500-pound chicken?

Only one species of New Zealand ratite has survived. (Ratites are a closely related group of flightless ground birds, including moas, African ostriches, South American rheas, and Australian–New Guinean emus and cassowaries. Flying birds have a keeled breastbone, providing sufficient area for attachment of massive flight muscles. The breastbones of ratites lack a keel, and their name honors that most venerable of unkeeled vessels, the raft, or *ratis* in Latin.) We know this curious creature more as an icon on tins of shoe polish or as the moniker for New Zealand's human inhabitants—the kiwi, only hen-sized, but related most closely to moas among birds.

Three species of kiwis inhabit New Zealand today, all members of the genus *Apteryx* (literally, wingless). Kiwis lack an external tail, and their vestigial wings are entirely hidden beneath a curious plumage—shaggy, more like fur than feathers, and similar in structure to the juvenile down of most other birds. (Maori artisans used kiwi feathers to make the beautiful cloaks once worn by chiefs; but the small, secretive, and widely ranging nocturnal kiwis managed to escape the fate of their larger moa relatives.)

The furry bodies, with even contours unbroken by tail or wings, are mounted on stout legs—giving the impression of a double blob (small head and larger body) on sticks. Kiwis eat seeds, berries, and other parts of plants, but they favor earthworms. Their long, thin bills probe the soil continually, suggesting the oddly reversed perspective of a stick leading a blind man. This stick, however, is richly endowed as a sensory device, particularly as an organ of smell. The bill, uniquely among birds, bears long external nostrils, while the olfactory bulb of kiwi brains is second largest among birds relative to size of the forebrain. A peculiar creature indeed.

But the greatest of kiwi oddities centers upon reproduction. Females are larger than males. They lay one to three eggs and may incubate them for a while, but they leave the nest soon thereafter, relegating to males the primary task of incubation, a long seventy to eighty-four days. Males sit athwart the egg, body at a slight angle and bill stretched out along the ground. Females may return occasionally with food, but males must usually fend for

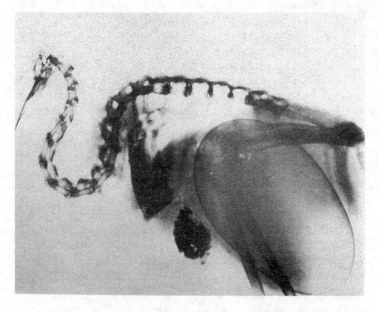

An amazing and famous photo of a female kiwi one day before laying its enormous egg. COURTESY OF THE OTOROHANGA ZOOLOGICAL SOCIETY, NEW ZEALAND.

themselves, covering both eggs and nest entrance with debris and going forth to forage once or twice on most nights.

The kiwi egg is a wonder to behold, and the subject of this essay. It is, by far, the largest of all bird eggs relative to body size. The three species of kiwis just about span the range of domestic poultry: the largest about the size of Rhode Island Reds; the smallest similar to bantams—say five pounds as a rough average (pretty meaningless, given the diversity of species, but setting the general domain). The eggs range to 25 percent of the female's body weight—quite a feat when you consider that she often lays two, and sometimes three, in a clutch, spacing them about thirty-three days apart. A famous X-ray photo of kiwi and egg taken at the kiwi sanctuary of Otorohanga, New Zealand, tells the tale more dramatically than any words I could produce. The egg is so large that females must waddle, legs spread far apart, for several days before laying, as the egg passes down the oviduct toward the cloaca. The incubation patch of male kiwis extends from the top of the chest all the way down to the cloaca—in other words, they need almost all their body to cover the egg.

A study of the general relationship between egg size and body size among birds shows that average birds of kiwi dimensions lay eggs weighing from 55 to 100 grams (as do domestic hens). Eggs of the brown kiwi weigh between 400 and 435 grams (about a pound). Put another way, an egg of this size would be expected from a twenty-eight-pound bird, but brown kiwis are about six times as small.

The obvious question, of course, is why? Evolutionary biologists have a traditional approach to riddles of this sort. They seek some benefit for the feature in question, then argue that natural selection has worked to build these advantages into the animal's way of life. The greatest triumphs of this method center upon odd structures that seem to make no sense or (like the kiwi egg) appear, prima facie, to be out of proportion and probably harmful. After all, anyone can see that a bird's wing (although not a kiwi's) is well designed for flight, so reference to natural selection teaches you little about adaptation that you didn't already know. Thus, the test cases of textbooks are apparently harmful structures that, on closer examination, confer crucial benefits upon organisms in their Darwinian struggle for reproductive success.

This general strategy of research suggests that if you can find out what a structure is good for, you will possess the major ingredient for understanding why it is so big, so colorful, so peculiarly shaped. Kiwi eggs should illustrate this basic method. They seem to be too big, but if we can discover how their large size benefits kiwis, we shall understand why natural selection favored large eggs. Readers who have followed my essays for some time will realize that I wouldn't be writing about this subject if I didn't think that this style of Darwinian reasoning embodied a crucial flaw.

The flaw lies not with the claim of utility. I regard it as proved that kiwis benefit from the unusually large size of their eggs—and for the most obvious reason. Large eggs yield large and well-developed chicks that can fend for themselves with a minimum of parental care after hatching. Kiwi eggs are not only large; they are also the most nutritious of all bird eggs for a reason beyond their maximal bulk: they contain a higher percentage of yolk than any other egg. Brian Reid and G. R. Williams report that kiwi eggs may contain 61 percent yolk and 39 percent albumin (or white). By comparison, eggs of other so-called precocial species (with downy young hatching in an active, advanced, and open-eyed state) contain 35 to 45 percent yolk, while eggs of altricial species (with helpless, blind, and naked hatchlings) carry only 13 to 28 percent yolk.

The lifestyle of kiwi hatchlings demonstrates the benefits of their large, yolky eggs. Kiwis are born fully feathered and usually receive no food from their parents. Before hatching, they consume the unused portion of their massive yolk reserve and do not feed (but live off these egg-based supplies) for their first seventy-two to eighty-four hours alfresco. Newly hatched brown kiwi chicks are often unable to stand because their abdomens are so distended with this reserve of yolk. They rest on the ground, legs splayed out to the side, and only take a first few clumsy steps when they are some sixty hours old. A chick does not leave its burrow until the fifth to ninth day when, accompanied by father, it sallies forth to feed sparingly.

Kiwis thus spend their first two weeks largely living off the yolk supply that their immense egg has provided. After ten to fourteen days, the kiwi chick may weigh one-third less than at hatching—a fasting marked by absorption of ingested yolk from the egg. Brian Reid studied a chick that died a few hours after hatching. Almost half its weight consisted of food reserves—112 grams of yolk and 43 grams of body fat in a 319-gram hatchling. Another chick, killed outside its burrow five to six days after hatching, weighed 281 grams and still held almost 54 grams of enclosed yolk.

I am satisfied that kiwis do very well by and with their large eggs. But can we conclude that the outsized egg was built by natural selection in the light of these benefits? This assumption—the easy slide from current function to reason for origin—is, to my mind, the most serious and widespread fallacy of my profession, for this false inference supports hundreds of conventional tales about pathways of evolution. I like to identify this error of reasoning with a phrase that ought to become a motto: *Current utility may not be equated with historical origin,* or, when you demonstrate that something works well, you have not solved the problem of how, when, or why it arose.

I propose a simple reason for labeling an automatic inference from current utility to historical origin as fallacious: Good function has an alternative interpretation. A structure now useful may have been built by natural selection for its current purpose (I do not deny that the inference often holds), but the structure may also have developed for another reason (or for no particular functional reason at all) and then been co-opted for its present use. The giraffe's neck either got long in order to feed on succulent leaves atop acacia trees or it elongated for a different reason (perhaps unrelated to any adaptation of feeding), and giraffes then discovered that, by virtue of their new height, they could reach some delicious morsels. The simple good fit of form to function—long neck to top leaves—permits, in itself, no conclusion about why giraffes developed long necks. Since Voltaire understood the foibles of human reason so well, he allowed the venerable Dr. Pangloss to illustrate this fallacy in a solemn pronouncement:

Things cannot be other than they are. . . . Everything is made for the best purpose. Our noses were made to carry spectacles, so we have spectacles. Legs were clearly intended for breeches, and we wear them.

This error of sliding too easily between current use and historical origin is by no means a problem for Darwinian biologists alone, although our faults have been most prominent and unexamined. This procedure of false inference pervades all fields that try to infer history from our present world. My favorite current example is a particularly ludicrous interpretation of the so-called anthropic principle in cosmology. Many physicists have pointed out—and I fully accept their analysis—that life on earth fits intricately with physical laws regulating the universe, in the sense that were various laws even slightly different, molecules of the proper composition and planets with the right properties could never have arisen—and we would not be here. From this analysis, a few thinkers have drawn the wildly invalid inference that human evolution is therefore prefigured in the ancient design of the cosmos—that the universe, in Freeman Dyson's words, must have known we were coming. But the current fit of human life to physical laws permits no conclusion about the reasons and mechanisms of our origin. Since we are here, we have to fit; we wouldn't be here if we didn't—though something else would, probably proclaiming, with all the hubris that a diproton might muster, that the cosmos must have been created with its later appearance in mind. (Diprotons are a prominent candidate for the highest bit of chemistry in another conceivable universe.)

But back to kiwi eggs. Most literature has fallen into the fallacy of equating current use with historical origin, and has defined the problem as explaining why the kiwi's egg should have been actively enlarged from an ancestor with an egg more suited to the expectations of its body size. Yet University of Arizona biologist William A. Calder III, author of several excellent studies on kiwi energetics (see 1978, 1979, and 1984 in the bibliography), has proposed an opposite interpretation that strikes me as much more likely (though I think he has missed two or three good arguments for its support, and I shall try to supply them here).

The alternative interpretation holds that kiwis are phyletic dwarfs, evolved from a lineage of much larger birds. Since these large ancestors laid big eggs appropriate to their body size, kiwis just never (or only slightly) reduced the size of their eggs as their bodies decreased greatly in bulk. In other words, kiwi eggs never became unusually large; kiwi bodies got small—and these statements are not equivalent, just as we know that an obese man is not short for his weight, despite the old jest.

(Such a hypothesis is not anti-adaptationist in the sense that maintenance of a large egg as size decreases—and in the face of energetic and biochemical costs imposed by such a whopping contribution to the next generation—may well require a direct boost from natural selection to prevent an otherwise advantageous decrease more in keeping with life at Colonel Sanders's favorite size. Still, there is a world of difference between retaining something you already have, and first developed for other reasons [in this case simple appropriateness for large body size], and actively evolving such a unique and cumbersome structure for some special benefit.)

Calder's interpretation might seem forced or farfetched but for the outstanding fact of taxonomy and biogeography cited as the introduction to this essay. Moas are the closest cousins of kiwis, and most moas were very large birds. "Is the kiwi perhaps a shrunken moa?" Calder asks. Unfortunately, all moa fossils lie in rocks of a geological yesterday, and kiwi fossils are entirely unknown—so we have no direct evidence about the size of ancestral kiwis. Still, I believe that all the inferential data support Calder's alternative hypothesis for the great size of kiwi eggs—a "structural" or "historical" explanation if you will, not a conventional account based on natural selection for immediate advantages.

Although the best argument for viewing kiwis as much smaller than their ancestors must be the large size of their closest moa cousins, Calder has also developed a quirky and intriguing speculation to support the dwarfed status of kiwis. (I hasten to point out that neither of these arguments amounts to more than a reasonable conjecture. All evidence can be interpreted in other ways. Both moas and kiwis, for example, might have evolved from a kiwi-sized common ancestor, with moas enlarging later. Still, since the kiwi is the smallest of all ratites—a runt among ostriches, rheas, emus, and cassowaries—its decrease seems more probable than moa increase. But we will not know until we have direct evidence of fossil ancestry.)

Calder notes that in many respects, some rather curious, kiwis have adopted forms and lifestyles generally associated with mammals, not birds. Kiwis, for example, are unique among birds in retaining ovaries on both sides (the right ovary degenerates in all other birds)—and eggs alternate between sides, as in mammals. The seventy- to eighty-four-day incubation period matches the eighty-day pregnancy expected for a mammal of kiwi body size, not the forty-four days predicted for birds of this weight. Calder continues: "When one adds to this list, the kiwi's burrow habit, its furlike body feathers, and its nocturnal foraging highly dependent on its sense of smell, the evidence for convergence seems overpowering." Of course, this conjunction of traits could be fortuitous and each might mean something quite unmammalian to a kiwi, but the argument does gain strength when we remember that no terrestrial mammals reached New Zealand, and that the success of many introduced species indicates a hospitable environment for any creature that could exploit a mammalian way of life.

You will be wondering what these similarities with mammals could possibly mean for my key claim that kiwis are probably descendants of much larger birds. After all, mammals are superior, noble, and large. But they aren't. The original and quintessential mammalian way of life (still exploited by a majority of species) is secretive, furtive, nocturnal, smell-oriented in a non-visual world—and, above all, small. Remember that for two-thirds of their geological history, all mammals were little creatures living in the interstices of a world ruled by dinosaurs. If a large bird converged upon a basically mammalian lifestyle in the absence of "proper" inhabitants as a result of geographic isolation, *decrease* in size would probably be a first and best step.

Perhaps I have convinced you that kiwis probably decreased in size during their evolution. But why should this dwarfing help to explain their large eggs? Why didn't egg size just keep pace with body size as kiwis scaled down? We now come to the strong evidence of the case.

The study of changes in form and proportion as organisms increase or decrease in size is called allometry. It has been a popular and fruitful subject in evolutionary research since Julian Huxley's pioneering work of the 1920s. One of Huxley's own classic studies (*Journal of the Linnaean Society of London,* 1927) bore the title: "On the Relation between Egg-weight and Body-weight in Birds." Huxley found that if you plot one point for each species on the hummingbird-to-moa curve for egg weight versus body weight, relative egg size decreases in an even and predictable way. The eggs of large birds, he found, are absolutely larger, but relatively smaller in proportion to body weight, than those of small birds.

Huxley's work has since been extended several times with more voluminous and consistent data. In the two best studies that I know, Samuel Brody (in his masterful compendium, *Bioenergetics and Growth*, 1945) calculated a slope of 0.73, while H. Rahn, C. V. Paganelli, and A. Ar (1975), with even more data from some 800 species, derived a similar value of 0.67. This means that as birds increase in body weight, egg weight enlarges only about two-thirds as fast. Conversely, as birds decrease in size, egg weight diminishes more slowly—so little birds have relatively heavy eggs.

This promising datum will not, however, explain the kiwi's out-sized egg, for the two-thirds slope represents the general standard for all birds. Kiwi eggs are huge compared with the *expected* egg weight for a bird of kiwi body weight along this standard curve.

But the literature of allometry has also yielded a generality that will, I think, explain the kiwi's massive egg. The two-thirds slope of the egg weight/body weight curve represents a type of allometry technically called interspecific scaling—that is, you plot one point for each species in a related group of organisms and attempt to establish the characteristic change of proportion along a gradient of increasing size. (These curves are popularly called mouse-to-elephant for relationships among mammals—hence my designation hummingbird-to-moa for birds.) Allometricians have established hundreds of interspecific curves for birds and mammals.

Another kind of allometry is called intraspecific scaling. Here you plot one point for each individual among adults of varying body weights within a single species—the Tom Thumb–to–Manute Bol curve for human males, if you will. Since the similarity of these technical terms—interspecific and intraspecific—is so confusing, I shall call them, instead, among-species (for mouse-to-elephant) and within-species (for Thumb-to-Bol).

As an important generality in allometric studies, within-species curves usually have a substantially lower slope than among-species curves for the same property. For example (and in our best-studied case), the mouse-to-elephant curve for brain weight versus body weight in mammals has a slope of about two-thirds (as does the egg weight/body weight curve for birds). But the within-species curve from small to large adults of a single species, while varying from one group to another, almost always has a much lower slope in the range of 0.2 to 0.4. In other words, while brains increase about two-thirds as fast as bodies among species (implying that large mammals have relatively small brains), brains only increase about one-fifth to two-fifths as fast as bodies when we move from small to large adults within a single mammalian species.

Such a regularity, if it applied to egg weight as well, could resolve the kiwi paradox—if kiwis evolved from larger ancestors. Suppose that kiwi forebears start at moa size. By the humming-bird-to-moa among-species standard, egg size should decrease along the two-thirds slope. But suppose that natural selection is operating to favor small adults within a population. If the within-species curve for egg weight had a slope much lower than two-thirds, then size decrease by continued selection of small adults might produce a new species with outsized eggs well above the two-thirds slope, and therefore well above the expected weight for a bird of this reduced size. (Quantitative arguments like this are always easier to grasp by picture than by words—and a glance at the accompanying graph should resolve any confusion.)

But what is the expected within-species relationship for egg weight? Is the shape of the curve low, as for brain weight, thus affirming my conjecture? I reached for my well-worn copy of Brody's unparalleled compendium and found that for adults of domestic fowl, egg weight increases not two-thirds as fast, but only 15 percent as fast as body weight! (Brody uses this fact to argue that small hens are usually better than large, so long as egg production remains the same—for egg size diminishes very little with a large decrease in body mass, and the small loss in egg volume is more than compensated by large decreases in feeding costs.)

The same argument might apply to kiwis. As a poultryman might choose small hens for minimal decrease in egg size with maximal decline in body weight, natural selection for smaller adults might markedly decrease the average body weight within a species with very little accompanying reduction in egg weight.

I believe that this general argument, applied to kiwis, may be

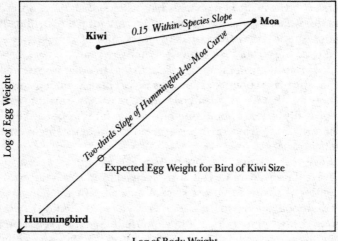

Proposed allometric explanation for the large egg of the kiwi. The kiwi probably evolved from a much larger bird by backing down the very shallow within-species slope (upper line). Most birds arrange themselves on the standard hummingbird-to-moa curve with its steeper slope (lower line). Therefore, a kiwi has a much heavier egg than predicted for a bird of its body size. BEN GAMIT. ADAPTED FROM JOE LEMONNIER. COURTESY OF *NATURAL HISTORY.*

defended on three strong grounds. First, as stated above, a general finding in allometric studies teaches us that within-species slopes for adults of one species are usually much lower than among-species slopes along mouse-to-elephant curves. Thus, any evolution of decreasing size along the within-species curve should produce a dwarfed descendant with more of the particular item being measured than an average nondwarfed species at the same body weight. Second, we have actual data, for domestic poultry at least, indicating that the within-species curve does have a substantially lower slope than the hummingbird-to-moa curve for our crucial measure of egg weight.

Third, I have studied many cases of dwarfism, and I believe we can state as a general phenomenon—rooted in the first point above—that decline in body size often far outstrips decrease in many particular features. Dwarfs, in several respects, always seem to have much more of certain body parts than related non-dwarfed species of the same body size. For example, I once studied tooth size in three species of dwarfed hippos (two fossil and the modern Liberian pygmy)—and found their molar teeth substantially larger, for each of three separate evolutionary events, than expected values for related hoofed mammals at their body size (*American Zoologist*, 1975).

In another example, the talapoin, a dwarfed relative of the rhesus monkey, has the largest relative brain weight among monkeys. Since within-species brain curves have substantially lower slopes than the two-thirds value for the marmoset-to-baboon curve, evolution to smaller size by backing down the within-species curve would yield a dwarf with a far larger brain than an ordinary monkey at the same body size.

Put all this together and a resolution fairly jumps at you for kiwis. Their enormous eggs require no special explanation if kiwis have evolved by marked decrease in size. Kiwi eggs exhibit the weight expected for backing down the within-species curve if natural selection operates only to decrease body size and no other factor intervenes to favor an active reduction in egg size—as we might anticipate in New Zealand, this easy land of no natural predators, where a female might waddle without fear as an enormous egg distends her abdomen during passage down the oviduct.

In this interpretation, if you ask me why kiwi eggs are so large, I reply, "Because kiwis are dwarfed descendants of larger birds, and just followed ordinary principles of scaling in their evolution." This answer differs sharply from the conventional form of evolutionary explanation: "Because these big eggs are good for something now, and natural selection favored them."

My answer will also strike many people as deeply unsatisfactory. It provides a reason rooted in history, pure and simple (with a bit of scaling theory thrown in)—kiwis are as they are because their ancestors were as they were. Don't we want answers that invoke general laws of nature rather than particular contingencies of history?

I would reply that my resolution is quite satisfactory, that evolutionary arguments are often properly resolved by such historical statements, and that we would do well to understand this important and neglected principle of reasoning—for we might save ourselves many a stumble in trying to apply preferred, but inappropriate, styles of explanation to situations encountered again and again in our daily lives.

To cite just one example where I learned, to my deep chagrin, that a peculiarity of history, rather than a harmonious generality, resolved an old personal puzzle: I had been troubled for a long time by something I didn't understand in the inscription on the Liberty Bell—not losing any sleep to be sure, but troubled nonetheless, for little things count. This national symbol bears, like most bells, an appropriate quotation: "Proclaim liberty throughout all the land unto all the inhabitants thereof" (Lev. 25:10). But the bell also says, "Pass and Stow." I assumed that this line must also be a quotation, fit to the purpose of the bell (as selection fits the features of organisms to their needs)—part of the general harmony and chosen plan. I pondered these cryptic words quite a bit because I didn't recognize the source. I consulted Bartlett's and found nothing. I constructed various possibilities: This too will pass, as we stow courage for the coming conflict; oh ye who pass by, remember, they prosper that stow and do not waste; pass the grass and stow the dough. Finally I asked the attendant on duty in Philadelphia. Of course, I should have figured it out, but I was too busy trying to make intrinsic sense of the inscription. The bell was cast by Messrs. John Pass and John Stow. Pass and Stow is a statement about the particular history of the bell; nothing more.

My odd juxtapositions sometimes cause consternation; some readers might view this particular comparison as outright sacrilege. Some may claim that the only conceivable similarity between kiwi eggs and the Liberty Bell is that both are cracked, but I reply that they stand united in owing their peculiarity and meaning to pathways of history.

The Liberty Bell on display in Philadelphia, advertising its makers, Mr. Pass and Mr. Stow. THE BETTMANN ARCHIVE.

8 | Male Nipples and Clitoral Ripples*

THE MARQUIS DE CONDORCET, enthusiast of the French Revolution but not radical enough for the Jacobins—and therefore forced into hiding from a government that had decreed, and would eventually precipitate, his death—wrote in 1793 that "the perfectibility of man is really boundless. . . . It has no other limit than the duration of the globe where nature has set us." As Dickens so aptly remarked, "It was the best of times, it was the worst of times."

The very next year, as Condorcet lay dying in prison, a famous voice from across the channel published another paean to progress in a world that many judged on the brink of ruin. This treatise, called *Zoonomia, or the Laws of Organic Life,* was written by Erasmus Darwin, grandfather of Charles.

Zoonomia is primarily a dissertation on the mechanisms of human physiology. Yet, in the anachronistic tradition that judges biological works by their attitude to the great watershed of evolution, established by grandson Charles in 1859, *Zoonomia* owes its modern reputation to a few fleeting passages that look upon organic transmutation with favor.

---

*The proper and most accurate title of this piece should be "Tits and Clits"—but such a label would be misread as sexist because people would not recognize the reference point as *male* tits. My wife, a master at titles, suggested this alternative. (During the short heyday of that most unnecessary of all commercially touted products—vaginal deodorants—she wanted to market a male counterpart to be known as "cocksure.") *Natural History* magazine, published by a group of fine but slightly overcautious folks, first brought out this essay under their imposed title: "Freudian Slip." Not terrible; but not really descriptive either.

The evolutionary passages of *Zoonomia* occur in Item 8, Part 4, of Section 39, entitled, "Of Generation," Erasmus Darwin's thoughts on reproduction and embryology. He viewed embryology as a tale of continuous progress to greater size and complexity. Since his evolutionary speculations are strictly analogous to his concept of embryology, organic transformation also follows a single pathway to more and better:

> Would it be too bold to imagine that in the great length of time, since the earth began to exist . . . all warm-blooded animals have arisen from one living filament . . . possessing the faculty of continuing to improve by its own inherent activity, and of delivering down those improvements by generation to its posterity, world without end?

As the last sentence states, Erasmus Darwin's proposed mechanism of evolution lay in the inheritance of *useful* characters acquired by organisms during their lifetimes. This false theory of heredity has passed through later history under the label of Lamarckism, but the citation by Erasmus (a contemporary of Lamarck) illustrates the extent of this misnomer. Inheritance of acquired characters was the standard folk wisdom of the time, used by Lamarck to be sure, but by no means original or distinctive with him. For Erasmus, this mechanism of evolution required a concept of pervasive utility. New structures arose only when needed and by direct organic striving for an evident purpose. Erasmus discusses adaptations in three great categories: reproduction, protection and defense, and food. Of the last, he writes:

> All . . . seem to have been gradually produced during many generations by the perpetual endeavor of the creatures to supply the want of food, and to have been delivered to their posterity with constant improvement of them for the purposes required.

In this long section, Erasmus considers only one potential exception to the principle of pervasive utility: "the breasts and teats of all male quadrupeds, to which no use can be now assigned." He also suggests two exits from this potential dilemma: first, that male nipples are vestiges of a previous utility if, as Plato had suggested, "mankind with all other animals were originally hermaphrodites during the infancy of the world, and were in process of time separated into male and female"; and second, that some males may lactate and therefore help to feed their babies (in the absence of any direct evidence, Erasmus cites the milky-colored feeding fluids, produced in the crops of both male and female pigeons, as a possible analogue).

The tenacity of anomalies through centuries of changing beliefs can be truly astounding. As a consequence of writing these essays for so many years, I receive hundreds of letters from readers puzzled about one or another apparent oddity of nature. With so large a sample, I have obtained a pretty good feel for the issues and particulars of evolution that pose conundrums for well-informed nonscientific readers. I have been fascinated (and, I confess, surprised) over the years to discover that no single item has evoked more puzzlement than the very issue that Erasmus Darwin chose as a primary challenge to his concept of pervasive utility—male nipples. I have received more than a dozen requests to explain how evolution could possibly produce such a useless structure.

Consider my latest example from a troubled librarian. "I have a question that no one can answer for me, and I don't know where or how to look up the answer. Why do men have nipples? . . . This question nags at me whenever I see a man's bare chest!"

I was fascinated to note that her two suggestions paralleled exactly the explanations floated by Erasmus Darwin. First, she reports, she asked a doctor. "He told me that men in primitive societies used to nurse babies." Finding this incredible, she tried Darwin's first proposal for nipples as a vestige of previous utility: "Can you tell me—was there once only one sex?"

If you are committed—as Erasmus was, and as a distressingly common version of "pop," or "cardboard," Darwinism still is—to a principle of pervasive utility for all parts of all creatures, then male nipples do raise an insoluble dilemma, hence (I assume) my voluminous correspondence. But as with so many persistent puzzles, the resolution does not lie in more research within an established framework but rather in identifying the framework itself as a flawed view of life.

Suppose we begin from a different point of view, focusing on rules of growth and development. The external differences be-tween male and female develop gradually from an early embryo so generalized that its sex cannot be easily determined. The clito-ris and penis are one and the same organ, identical in early form, but later enlarged in male fetuses through the action of testoster-one. Similarly, the labia majora of women and the scrotal sacs of men are the same structure, indistinguishable in young embryos, but later enlarged, folded over, and fused along the midline in male fetuses.

I do not doubt that the large size and sensitivity of the female breast should count as an adaptation in mammals, but the smaller male version needs no adaptive explanation at all. Males and females are not separate entities, shaped independently by natu-ral selection. Both sexes are variants upon a single ground plan, elaborated in later embryology. Male mammals have nipples be-cause females need them—and the embryonic pathway to their development builds precursors in all mammalian fetuses, enlarg-ing the breasts later in females but leaving them small (and with-out evident function) in males.

In a similar case that illuminates the general principle, the panda develops a highly functional false "thumb" from the radial sesamoid bone of its wrist. Interestingly, the corresponding bone of the foot, the tibial sesamoid, is also enlarged in the same man-ner (but not nearly so much), although increase of the tibial sesa-moid has no apparent function.

As D. Dwight Davis argued in his great monograph on the giant panda (1964), evolution works on growth fields. Radial and tibial sesamoids are homologous structures, probably affected in con-cert by the same genetic factors. If natural selection operates for an enlarged radial sesamoid, a bigger tibial sesamoid will proba-bly "come along for the ride." Davis drew a profound message from this case: Organisms are integral and constrained struc-tures, "pushing back" against the force of selection to channel changes along permitted paths; complex animals are not a disso-ciable collection of independent, optimal parts. Davis wrote that "the effect seen in the sympathetic enlargement of the tibial sesa-moid . . . strongly suggests that a very simple mechanism, per-haps involving a single factor, lies behind the hypertrophy of the radial sesamoid."

In my view of life, akin to Davis's concept of constraint and integration, male nipples are an expectation based on pathways of sexual differentiation in mammalian embryology.

At this point, readers might demur with the most crushing of all rejoinders: "Who cares?" Why worry about little items that ride piggyback on primary adaptations? Let's concentrate on the important thing—the adaptive value of the female breast—and leave aside the insignificant male ornament that arises as its consequence. Adaptations are preeminent; their side effects are nooks and crannies of organic design, meaningless bits and pieces. This argument is, I think, the standard position of strict Darwinian adaptationists.

I could defend the importance of structural nonadaptation with a long and abstruse general argument (I have done so in several technical papers). Let me proceed instead by the most compelling route I know by presenting a second example based on human sexuality, a case entirely comparable in concept with the origin of male nipples but differing in importance for human culture—a case, moreover, where the bias of utility has brought needless pain and anxiety into the lives of millions (where, indeed, one might argue that Freudian traditions have provided a manifestly false but potent weapon, however unintentional, for the subjugation of women). Consider the anatomical site of orgasm in human females.

As women have known since the dawn of our time, the primary site for stimulation to orgasm centers upon the clitoris. The revolution unleashed by the Kinsey report of 1953 has, by now, made this information available to men who, for whatever reason, had not figured it out for themselves by the more obvious routes of experience and sensitivity.

The data are unambiguous. Consider only the three most widely read of extensive surveys—the Kinsey report of 1953, Masters and Johnson's book of 1966, and *The Hite Report* of 1976. In his study of genital anatomy, Kinsey reports that the female clitoris is as richly supplied with sensory nerves as the male penis—and therefore as capable of excitation. The walls of the vagina, on the other hand, "are devoid of end organs of touch and are quite insensitive when they are gently stroked or lightly pressed. For most individuals the insensitivity extends to every part of the vagina."

The data on masturbation are particularly convincing. Kinsey reports from his sample of 8,000 women that 84 percent of individuals who have ever masturbated depend "primarily on labial and/or clitoral techniques." *The Hite Report* on 3,000 individuals found that 79 percent of women who masturbate do so by directly stimulating the clitoris and surrounding vulva, while only 1.5 percent use vaginal entry.

The data on intercourse affirm this pattern. Shere Hite reports a frequency of orgasm with intercourse at 30 percent and often attained only with simultaneous stimulation of the clitoris by hand. She concludes: *"not* to have orgasm from intercourse is the experience of the majority of women." Masters and Johnson only included women who experienced orgasm with intercourse in their study. But they concluded that all orgasms are identical in physiology and clitoral in origin. These findings led Hite to comment that human copulation "sounds more like a Rube Goldberg scheme than a reliable way to orgasm. . . . Intercourse was never meant to stimulate women to orgasm." As Kinsey had said earlier with his characteristic economy and candor: "The techniques of masturbation and of petting are more specifically calculated to effect orgasm than the techniques of coitus itself."

This conclusion should be utterly unsurprising—once we grasp the proper role and limitation of adaptationist argument in evolutionary biology. I don't believe in the mystery style of writing essays: build up suspense but save the resolution until the end—for then readers miss the significance of details along the way for want of proper context. The reason for a clitoral site of orgasm is simple—and exactly comparable with the nonpuzzle of male nipples. The clitoris is the homologue of the penis—it is the same organ, endowed with the same anatomical organization and capacity of response.

Anatomy, physiology, and observed responses all agree. Why then do we identify an issue at all? Why, in particular, does the existence of clitoral orgasm seem so problematic? Why, for example, did Freud label clitoral orgasm as infantile and define feminine maturity as the shifting to an unattainable vaginal site?

Part of the reason, of course, must reside in simple male vanity. We (and I mean those of my sex, not the vague editorial pronoun) simply cannot abide the idea—though it flows from obvious biology—that a woman's sexual pleasure might not arise most reliably as a direct result of our own coital efforts. But the issue extends further. Clitoral orgasm is a paradox not only for the traditions of Darwinian biology but also for the bias of utility that underlies all functionally based theories of evolution (including Lamarck's and Darwin's) and, in addition, the much older tradition of natural theology that saw God's handiwork in the exquisite fit of organic form to function.

Consider the paradox of clitoral orgasm in any world of strict functionalism (I present a Darwinian version, but parallel arguments can be made for the entire range of functionalist thinking, from Paley's natural theology to Cuvier's creationism): Evolution arises from a struggle among organisms for differential reproductive success. Sexual pleasure, in short, must evolve as a stimulus for reproduction.

This formulation works for men since the peak of sexual excitement occurs during ejaculation—a primary and direct adjunct of intercourse. For men, maximal pleasure is linked with the greatest possibility of fathering offspring. In this perspective, the sexual pleasure of women should also be centered upon the act that causes impregnation—on intercourse itself. But how can our world be functional and Darwinian if the site of orgasm is divorced from the place of intercourse? How can sexual pleasure be so separated from its functional significance in the Darwinian game of life? (For the most divergent, but equally functionalist, view of some conservative Christians, sex was made by God to foster procreation; any use in any other context is blasphemy.)

Elisabeth Lloyd, a philosopher of science at Berkeley, has just completed a critical study of explanations recently proposed by evolutionary biologists for the origin and significance of female orgasm. Nearly all these proposals follow the lamentable tradition of speculative storytelling in the a priori adaptationist mode. In all the recent Darwinian literature, I believe that Donald Symons is the only scientist who presented what I consider the proper answer—that female orgasm is not an adaptation at all. (See his book, *The Evolution of Human Sexuality*, 1979.)

Many of these scientists don't even know the simple facts of the matter; they assume that female orgasms are triggered by intercourse and draw the obvious Darwinian conclusion. A second

group recognizes the supposed paradox of nonassociation between orgasm and intercourse and then proposes another sort of
adaptive explanation, usually based on maintenance of their pair
bond by fostering close relationships through sexual pleasure.
Desmond Morris (*The Naked Ape*, 1969), the most widely read
promoter of this view, writes that female orgasm evolved for its
role in promoting the pair bond by "the immense behavioral
reward it brings to the act of sexual cooperation with the mated
partner." Perhaps no popular speculation has been more androcentric than George Pugh's (*Biological Origin of Human Values*,
1977), who speaks about "the development of a female orgasm,
which makes it easier for a female to be satisfied by one male, and
which also operates psychologically to produce a stronger emotional bond in the female." Or Eibl-Eibesfeldt, who argues
(1975) that the evolution of female orgasm "increases her readi-
ness to submit and, in addition, strengthens her emotional bond
to the partner."

This popular speculation about pair bonding usually rests
upon an additional biological assumption—almost surely false—
that capacity for female orgasm is an especially human trait. Yet
Symons shows, in his admirable review of the literature, that
whereas most female mammals do not experience orgasm during
ordinary copulation, prolonged clitoral stimulation—either ar-
tificially in the laboratory (however unpleasant a context from the
human point of view) or in nature by rubbing against another
animal (often a female)—does produce orgasm in a wide range of
mammals, including many primates. Symons concludes that "orgasm is most parsimoniously interpreted as a potential all female
mammals possess."

Adaptive stories for female orgasm run the full gamut—leaving
only the assumption of adaptation itself unquestioned. Sarah
Hrdy (1981), for example, has taken up the cudgels against an-
drocentrism in evolutionary speculation, not by branding the entire enterprise as bankrupt, but by showing that she can tell just
as good an adaptive story from a female-centered point of view.
She argues—turning the old pair-bond theory on its head—that
the dissociation between orgasm and intercourse is an adaptation
for promiscuous behavior, permitting females to enlist the support of several males to prevent any one from harming her ba-

bies. (In many species, a male that displaces a female's previous partner may kill her offspring, presumably to foster his own reproductive success by immediate remating.)

Indeed, no one surpasses Hrdy in commitment to the adaptationist assumption that orgasm must have evolved for Darwinian utility in promoting reproductive success. Chosen language so often gives away an underlying bias; note Hrdy's equation of nonadaptation both with despair in general and with the denigration of women's sexuality in particular.

> Are we to assume, then, that [the clitoris] is irrelevant? . . . It would be safer to suspect that, like most organs . . . it serves a purpose, or once did. . . . The lack of obvious purpose has left the way open for both orgasm, and female sexuality in general, to be dismissed as "nonadaptive."

But why are adaptationist arguments "safer," and why is nonadaptation a "dismissal"? I do not feel degraded because my nipples are concomitants of a general pattern in human development and not a sign that ancestors of my sex once lactated. In fact, I find this nonadaptationist explanation particularly fascinating, both because it teaches me something important about structural rules of development and because it counters a pervasive and constraining bias that has harmed evolutionary biology by restricting the range of permitted hypotheses. Why should the dissociation of orgasm from intercourse degrade women when it merely records a basic (if unappreciated) fact of human anatomy that happens to unite both sexes as variations of a common pattern in development? (Such an argument would only hold if adaptations were "good" and all other aspects of anatomy "irrelevant." I, for one, am quite attached to all my body parts and do not make such invidious rankings and distinctions among them.)

I could go on but will stop here for the obvious reason that this discussion, however amusing, might be deemed devoid of social importance. After all, these biologists may be enjoying themselves and promoting their view of life, but isn't all this strictly *entre nous?* I mean, after all, who cares about speculative ideas if they impose no palpable harm upon people's lives? But unfortunately, the history of psychology shows that one of the most influential theories of our century—a notion that had a direct and deeply negative effect upon millions of women—rested upon the false assumption that clitoral orgasm cannot be the natural way of a mature female. I speak, of course, about Sigmund Freud's theory of transfer from clitoral to vaginal orgasm.

In Freud's landmark and most influential book *Three Essays on the Theory of Sexuality* (1905, but first published in complete form in 1915), the third essay on "transformations of puberty" argues that "the leading erotogenic zone in female children is located at the clitoris." He also, as a scientist originally trained in anatomy, knows the reason—that the clitoris "is homologous to the masculine genital zone of the glans penis."

Freud continues: "All my experience concerning masturbation in little girls has related to the clitoris and not the regions of the external genitalia that are important in later sexual functioning." So far so good; Freud recognizes the phenomenon, knows its anatomical basis, and should therefore identify clitoral orgasm as a proper biological expression of female sexuality. Not at all, for Freud then describes a supposed transformation in puberty that defines the sexuality of mature women.

Puberty enhances the libido of boys but produces an opposite effect in girls—"a fresh wave of repression." Later, sexuality resumes in a new way. Freud writes:

> When at last the sexual act is permitted and the clitoris itself becomes excited, it still retains a function: the task, namely, of transmitting the excitation to the adjacent female sexual parts, just as—to use a simile—pine shavings can be kindled in order to set a log of harder wood on fire.

Thus, we encounter Freud's famous theory of female sexual maturity as a transfer from clitoral to vaginal orgasm:

> When erotogenic susceptibility to stimulation has been successfully transferred by a woman from the clitoris to the vaginal orifice, it implies that she has adopted a new leading zone for the purposes of her later sexual activity.

This dogma of transfer from clitoral to vaginal orgasm became a shibboleth of pop culture during the heady days of pervasive

Freudianism. It shaped the expectations (and therefore the frustration and often misery) of millions of educated and "enlightened" women told by a brigade of psychoanalysts and by hundreds of articles in magazines and "marriage manuals" that they must make this biologically impossible transition as a definition of maturity.

Freud's unbiological theory did further harm in two additional ways. First, Freud did not define frigidity only as an inability to perform sexually or as inefficacy in performance, but proposed as his primary definition a failure to produce this key transfer from clitoris to vagina. Thus, a woman who greatly enjoys sex, but only by clitoral stimulation, is frigid by Freud's terminology. "This anaesthesia," Freud writes, "may become permanent if the clitoridal zone refuses to abandon its excitability."

Second, Freud attributed a supposedly greater incidence of neurosis and hysteria in women to the difficulty of this transfer—for men simply retain their sexual zone intact from childhood, while women must undergo the hazardous switch from clitoris to vagina. Freud continues:

> The fact that women change their leading erotogenic zone in this way, together with the wave of repression at puberty . . . are the chief determinants of the greater proneness of women to neurosis and especially to hysteria. These determinants, therefore, are intimately related to the essence of femininity.

In short, Freud's error may be encapsulated by stating that he defined the ordinary biology of female sexuality as an aberration based on failure to abandon an infantile tendency.

The sources of Freud's peculiar theory are complex and involve many issues not treated in this essay (in particular his androcentric biases in interpreting the act of intercourse from a man's point of view and in defining both clitoral and penile stimulation in childhood as a fundamentally masculine form of sexuality that must be shunned by a mature woman). But another important source resides in the perspective underlying all the fanciful theories that I have discussed throughout this essay, from male nipples as sources of milk to clitoral orgasm as a clever invention to cement pair bonds—the bias of utility, or the exclusive commitment to functionalist explanations.

The more I read Kinsey, the more he wins my respect for his humane sensibility, and for his simple courage. (His 1953 report on *Sexual Behavior in the Human Female* appeared during the height of McCarthyism in America and led to a withdrawal of funding for his research and the effective end, during his lifetime, of his programs—see the essay "Of Wasps and WASPs" in my previous book, *The Flamingo's Smile.*) Kinsey was a measured man. He wrote in a dry and clinical fashion (probably more for reasons of necessity than inclinations of temperament). Yet, every once in a while, his passion spills forth and his rage erupts in a single, well-controlled phrase. Nowhere does Kinsey express more agitation than in his commentary on Freud's theory of the shift from clitoral to vaginal orgasm.

Kinsey locates his discussion of Freud in the proper context—in his section on sexual anatomy (Chapter 14, "Anatomy of Sexual Response and Orgasm"). He reports the hard data on adult masturbation and on the continuing clitoral site of orgasm in mature women. He locates the reason for clitoral orgasm not in any speculative theory about function but in the basic structure of sexual anatomy.

> In any consideration of the functions of the adult genitalia, and especially of their liability to sensory stimulation, it is important and imperative that one take into account the homologous origins of the structures in the two sexes.

Kinsey then provides a long and beautifully clear discussion of anatomical homologies, particularly the key unity of penis and clitoris. He concludes that "the vaginal walls are quite insensitive in the great majority of females. . . . There is no evidence that the vagina is ever the sole source of arousal, or even the primary source of erotic arousal in any female." Kinsey has now laid the foundation for a swift demolition of Freud's hurtful theory. He cites (in a long footnote, for his text is not contentious) a compendium of psychoanalytical proclamations from the Freudian heyday of the 1920s to 1940s. Consider just three items on his list:

1. (from 1936): "If this transition [from clitoris to vagina] is not successful, then the woman cannot experience satisfaction in the sexual act. . . . The first and decisive requisite of a normal orgasm is vaginal sensitivity."

2. (again from 1936): "The sole criterion of frigidity is the absence of the vaginal orgasm."

3. (from 1927): "In frigidity the pleasurable sensation is as a rule situated in the clitoris and the vaginal zone has none."

Kinsey's sole paragraph of evaluation ranks as the finest dismissal by understatement (and by incisive phrase at the end) that I have ever read.

> This question is one of considerable importance because much of the literature and many of the clinicians, including psychoanalysts and some of the clinical psychologists and marriage counselors, have expended considerable effort trying to teach their patients to transfer "clitoral responses" into "vaginal responses." Some hundreds of women in our own study and many thousands of the patients of certain clinicians have consequently been much disturbed by their failure to accomplish this biological impossibility.

I then must ask myself, why could Kinsey be so direct and sensible in 1953, while virtually all evolutionary discussion of female orgasm during the past twenty years has been not only biologically erroneous but also obtuse and purely speculative? I'm sorry to convert this essay into something of a broken record in contentious repetition, but the same point pervades the discussion all the way from Erasmus Darwin on male nipples to Sarah Hrdy on clitoral orgasm. The fault lies in a severely restrictive (and often false) functionalist view of life. Most functionalists have not misinterpreted male nipples, for their unobtrusive existence poses no challenge. But clitoral orgasm is too central to the essence of life for any explanation that does not focus upon the role of sexuality in reproductive success. And yet the obvious, nonadaptive structural alternative stares us in the face as the most elementary fact of sexual anatomy—the homology of penis and clitoris.

Kinsey's ability to cut through this morass right to the core of the strong developmental argument has interesting roots. Kinsey began his career by devoting twenty years to the taxonomy of gall-forming wasps. He pursued this work in the 1920s and 1930s before American evolutionary biology congealed around Darwinian functionalism. In Kinsey's day, many (probably most) taxonomists accepted the nonadaptive nature of much small-scale geographic variability within species. Kinsey followed this structuralist tradition and never absorbed the bias of utility. He was therefore able to grasp the meaning of this elemental fact of homology between penis and clitoris—a fact that stares everyone in the face, but becomes invisible if the bias of utility be strong enough.

I well remember something that Francis Crick said to me many years ago, when my own functionalist biases were strong. He remarked, in response to an adaptive story I had invented with alacrity and agility to explain the meaning of repetitive DNA: "Why do you evolutionists always try to identify the value of something before you know how it is made?" At the time, I dismissed this comment as the unthinking response of a hidebound molecular reductionist who did not understand that evolutionists must always seek the "why" as well as the "how"—the final as well as the efficient causes of structures.

Now, having wrestled with the question of adaptation for many years, I understand the wisdom of Crick's remark. If all structures had a "why" framed in terms of adaptation, then my original dismissal would be justified for we would know that "whys" exist whether or not we had elucidated the "how." But I am now convinced that many structures (including male nipples and clitoral orgasm) have no direct adaptational "why." And we discover this by studying pathways of genetics and development—or, as Crick so rightly said to me, by first understanding how a structure is built. In other words, we must first establish "how" in order to know whether or not we should be asking "why" at all.

I began with Charles Darwin's grandpa Erasmus and end with his namesake, Desiderius Erasmus, the greatest of all Renaissance scholars. Of more than 3,000 proverbs from antiquity collected in his *Adagia* of 1508, perhaps two are best known and wonderfully apt for the point of this essay (which is not a diatribe against adaptation but a plea for expansion by alternative hypotheses and for fruitful competition and synthesis between functional and structural perspectives). First a comment on limitations of outlook: "No one is injured save by himself." Second, probably the most famous of zoological metaphors about human temperament: "The fox has many tricks, and the hedgehog only one, but that is the best of all." Some have taken the hedgehog's part in this dichotomy, but I will cast my lot for a diversity of options—for our complex world may offer many paths to salvation, and the hounds of hell press continually upon us.

9 | Not Necessarily a Wing

FROM *Flesh Gordon* to *Alex in Wonderland*, title parodies have been a stock-in-trade of low comedy. We may not anticipate a tactical similarity between the mayhem of *Mad* magazine's movie reviews and the titles of major scientific works, yet two important nineteenth-century critiques of Darwin parodied his most famous phrases in their headings.

In 1887, E. D. Cope, the American paleontologist known best for his fossil feud with O. C. Marsh (see Essay 5) but a celebrated evolutionary theorist in his own right, published *The Origin of the Fittest*—a takeoff on Herbert Spencer's phrase, borrowed by Darwin as the epigram for natural selection: survival of the fittest. (Natural selection, Cope argued, could only preserve favorable traits that must arise in some other manner, unknown to Darwin. The fundamental issue of evolution cannot be the differential survival of adaptive traits, but their unexplained origin—hence the title parody.)

St. George Mivart (1817–1900), a fine British zoologist, tried to reconcile his unconventional views on religion and biology but ended his life in tragedy, rejected by both camps. At age seventeen, he abandoned his Anglican upbringing, became a Roman Catholic, and consequently (in a less tolerant age of state religion) lost his opportunity for training in natural history at Oxford or Cambridge. He became a lawyer but managed to carve out a distinguished career as an anatomist nonetheless. He embraced evolution and won firm support from the powerful T. H. Huxley, but his strongly expressed and idiosyncratic anti-Darwinian views led to his rejection by the biological establishment of Britain. He tried to unite his biology with his religion in a series of books and essays, and ended up excommunicated for his trouble six weeks before his death.

Cope and Mivart shared the same major criticism of Darwin—that natural selection could explain the preservation and increase of favored traits but not their origin. Mivart, however, went gunning for a higher target than Darwin's epigram. He shot for the title itself, naming his major book (1871) *On the Genesis of Species.* (Darwin, of course, had called his classic *On the Origin of Species.*)

Mivart's life may have ended in sadness and rejection thirty years later, but his *Genesis of Species* had a major impact in its time. Darwin himself offered strong, if grudging, praise and took Mivart far more seriously than any other critic, even adding a chapter to later editions of the *Origin of Species* primarily to counter Mivart's attack.

Mivart gathered, and illustrated "with admirable art and force" (Darwin's words), all objections to the theory of natural selection—"a formidable array" (Darwin's words again). Yet one particular theme, urged with special attention by Mivart, stood out as the centerpiece of his criticism. This argument continues to rank as the primary stumbling block among thoughtful and friendly scrutinizers of Darwinism today. No other criticism seems so troubling, so obviously and evidently "right" (against a Darwinian claim that seems intuitively paradoxical and improbable).

Mivart awarded this argument a separate chapter in his book, right after the introduction. He also gave it a name, remembered ever since. He called his objection "The Incompetency of 'Natural Selection' to Account for the Incipient Stages of Useful Structures." If this phrase sounds like a mouthful, consider the easy translation: We can readily understand how complex and fully developed structures work and how their maintenance and preservation may rely upon natural selection—a wing, an eye, the resemblance of a bittern to a branch or of an insect to a stick or dead leaf. But how do you get from nothing to such an elaborate something if evolution must proceed through a long sequence of intermediate stages, each favored by natural selection? You can't fly with 2 percent of a wing or gain much protection from an iota's similarity with a potentially concealing piece of vegetation.

How, in other words, can natural selection explain the incipient stages of structures that can only be used in much more elaborated form?

I take up this old subject for two reasons. First, I believe that Darwinism has, and has long had, an adequate and interesting resolution to Mivart's challenge (although we have obviously been mightily unsuccessful in getting it across). Second, a paper recently published in the technical journal *Evolution* has provided compelling experimental evidence for this resolution applied to its most famous case—the origin of wings.

The dilemma of wings—*the* standard illustration of Mivart's telling point about incipient stages—is set forth particularly well in a perceptive letter that I recently received from a reader, a medical doctor in California. He writes:

> How does evolutionary theory as understood by Darwin explain the emergence of items such as wings, since a small move toward a wing could hardly promote survival? I seem to be stuck with the idea that a significant quality of wing would have to spring forth all at once to have any survival value.

Interestingly, my reader's proposal that much or most of the wing must arise all at once (because incipient stages could have no adaptive value) follows Mivart's own resolution. Mivart first enunciated the general dilemma (1871, p. 23):

> Natural selection utterly fails to account for the conservation and development of the minute and rudimentary beginnings, the slight and infinitesimal commencements of structures, however useful those structures may afterwards become.

After fifty pages of illustration, he concludes: "Arguments may yet be advanced in favor of the view that new species have from time to time manifested themselves with suddenness, and by modifications appearing at once." Advocating this general solution for wings in particular, he concludes (p. 107): "It is difficult, then, to believe that the Avian limb was developed in any other way than by a comparatively sudden modification of a marked and important kind."

Darwin's theory is rooted in the proposition that natural selection acts as the primary creative force in evolutionary change. This creativity will be expressed only if the fortuitous variation forming the raw material of evolutionary change can be accumulated sequentially in tiny doses, with natural selection acting as the sieve of acceptance. If new species arise all at once in an occasional lucky gulp, then selection has no creative role. Selection, at best, becomes an executioner, eliminating the unfit following this burst of good fortune. Thus, Mivart's solution—bypassing incipient stages entirely in a grand evolutionary leap—has always been viewed, quite rightly, as an anti-Darwinian version of evolutionary theory.

Darwin well appreciated the force, and potentially devastating extent, of Mivart's critique about incipient stages. He counterattacked with gusto, invoking the standard example of wings and arguing that Mivart's solution of sudden change presented more problems than it solved—for how can we believe that so complex a structure as a wing, made of so many coordinated and co-adapted parts, could arise all at once:

> He who believes that some ancient form was transformed suddenly through an internal force or tendency into, for instance, one furnished with wings, will be . . . compelled to believe that many structures beautifully adapted to all the other parts of the same creature and to the surrounding conditions, have been suddenly produced; and of such complex and wonderful co-adaptations, he will not be able to assign a shadow of an explanation. . . . To admit all this is, as it seems to me, to enter into the realms of miracle, and to leave those of Science.

(This essay must now go in other directions but not without a small, tangential word in Mivart's defense. Mivart did appreciate the problem of complexity and coordination in sudden origins. He did not think that any old complex set of changes could arise all at once when needed—*that* would be tantamount to miracle. Most of Mivart's book studies the regularities of embryology and comparative anatomy to learn which kinds of complex changes might be possible as expressions and elaborations of developmental programs already present in ancestors. He advocates these changes as possible and eliminates others as fanciful.)

Darwin then faced his dilemma and developed the interestingly paradoxical resolution that has been orthodox ever since (but more poorly understood and appreciated than any other principle in evolutionary theory). If complexity precludes sudden origin, and the dilemma of incipient stages forbids gradual development in functional continuity, then how can we ever get from here to there? Darwin replies that we must reject an unnecessary hidden assumption in this argument—the notion of functional continuity. We will all freely grant that no creature can fly with 2 percent of a wing, but why must the incipient stages be used for flight? If incipient stages originally performed a different function suited to their small size and minimal development, natural selection might superintend their increase as adaptations for this original role until they reached a stage suitable for their current use. In other words, the problem of incipient stages disappears because these early steps were not inadequate wings but well-adapted something-elses. This principle of *functional change in structural continuity* represents Darwin's elegant solution to the dilemma of incipient stages.

Darwin, in a *beau geste* of argument, even thanked Mivart for characterizing the dilemma so well—all the better to grant Darwin a chance to elaborate his solution. Darwin writes: "A good opportunity has thus been afforded [by Mivart] for enlarging a little on gradations of structure, often associated with changed functions—an important subject, which was not treated at sufficient length in the former editions of this work." Darwin, who rarely added intensifiers to his prose, felt so strongly about this principle of functional shift that he wrote: "In considering transitions of organs, it is so important to bear in mind the probability of conversion from one function to another."

Darwin presented numerous examples in Chapters 5 and 7 of the final edition of the *Origin of Species*. He discussed organs that perform two functions, one primary, the other subsidiary, then relinquish the main use and elaborate the formerly inconspicuous operation. He then examined the flip side of this phenomenon—functions performed by two separate organs (fishes breathing with both lungs and gills). He argues that one organ may assume the entire function, leaving the other free for evolution to some other role (lungs for conversion to air bladders, for example, with respiration maintained entirely by gills). He does not, of course, neglect the classic example of wings, arguing that insects evolved their organs of flight from tracheae (or breathing organs—a minority theory today, but not without supporters). He writes: "It is therefore highly probable that in this great class organs which once served for respiration have been actually converted into organs of flight."

Darwin's critical theory of functional shift, usually (and most unfortunately) called the principle of "preadaptation,"* has been with us for a century. I believe that this principle has made so little headway not only because the basic formulation seems paradoxical and difficult, but mainly because we have so little firm, direct evidence for such functional shifts. Our technical literature contains many facile verbal arguments—little more than plausible "just-so" stories. The fossil record also presents some excellent examples of sequential development through intermediary stages that could not work as modern organs do—but we lack a rigorous mechanical analysis of function at the various stages.

Let us return, as we must, to the classic case of wings. *Archaeopteryx,* the first bird, is as pretty an intermediate as paleontology

---

*This dreadful name has made a difficult principle even harder to grasp and understand. Preadaptation seems to imply that the proto-wing, while doing something else in its incipient stages, knew where it was going—predestined for a later conversion to flight. Textbooks usually introduce the word and then quickly disclaim any odor of foreordination. (But a name is obviously ill-chosen if it cannot be used without denying its literal meaning.) Of course, by "preadaptation" we only mean that some structures are fortuitously suited to other roles if elaborated, not that they arise with a different future use in view—now there I go with the standard disclaimer. As another important limitation, preadaptation does not cover the important class of features that arise without functions (as developmental consequences of other primary adaptations, for example) but remain available for later co-optation. I suspect, for example, that many important functions of the human brain are co-opted consequences of building such a large computer for a limited set of adaptive uses. For these reasons, Elizabeth Vrba and I have proposed that the restrictive and confusing word "preadaptation" be dropped in favor of the more inclusive term "exaptation"—for any organ not evolved under natural selection for its current use—either because it performed a different function in ancestors (classical preadaptation) or because it represented a nonfunctional part available for later co-optation. See our technical article, "Exaptation: A Missing Term in the Science of Form," *Paleobiology,* 1981.

could ever hope to find—a complex mélange of reptilian and avian features. Scientists are still debating whether or not it could fly. If so, *Archaeopteryx* worked like the Wrights' biplane to a modern eagle's Concorde. But what did the undiscovered ancestors of *Archaeopteryx* do with wing rudiments that surely could not produce flight? Evolutionists have been invoking Darwin's principle of functional shift for more than 100 years, and the list of proposals is long. Proto-wings have been reconstructed as stabilizers, sexual attractors, or insect catchers. But the most popular hypothesis identifies thermoregulation as the original function of incipient stages that later evolved into feathered wings. Feathers are modified reptilian scales, and they work very well as insulating devices. Moreover, if birds evolved from dinosaurs (as most paleontologists now believe), they arose from a lineage particularly subject to problems with temperature control. *Archaeopteryx* is smaller than any dinosaur and probably arose from the tiniest of dinosaur lineages. Small animals, with high ratios of surface area to volume, lose heat rapidly and may require supplementary devices for thermoregulation. Most dinosaurs could probably keep warm enough just by being large. Surface area (length × length, or length squared) increases more slowly than volume (length × length × length, or length cubed) as objects grow. Since animals generate heat over their volumes and lose it through their surfaces, small animals (with their relatively large surface areas) have most trouble keeping warm.

There I go again—doing what I just criticized. I have presented a plausible story about thermoregulation as the original function of organs that later evolved into wings. But science is tested evidence, not tall tales. This lamentable mode of storytelling has been used to illustrate Darwin's principle of functional shift only *faute de mieux*—because we didn't have the goods so ardently desired. At least until recently, when my colleagues Joel G. Kingsolver and M. A. R. Koehl published the first hard evidence to support a shift from thermoregulation to flight as a scenario for the evolution of wings. They studied insects, not birds—but the same argument has long been favored for nature's smaller and far more abundant wings (see their article, "Aerodynamics, Thermoregulation, and the Evolution of Insect Wings: Differential Scaling and Evolutionary Change," in *Evolution*, 1985).

In preparing this essay, I spent several days reading the classical literature on the evolution of insect flight—and emerged with a deeper understanding of just how difficult Darwin's principle of functional shift can be, even for professionals. Most of the literature hasn't even made the first step of applying functional shift at all, not to mention the later reform of substituting direct evidence for verbal speculation. Most reconstructions are still trying to explain the incipient stages of insect wings as somehow involved in airborne performance from the start—not for flapping flight, of course, but still for some aspect of motion aloft rather than, as Darwin's principle would suggest, for some quite different function.

To appreciate the dilemma of such a position (so well grasped by Mivart more than 100 years ago), consider just one recent study (probably the best and most widely cited) and the logical quandaries that a claim of functional continuity entails. In 1964, J. W. Flower presented aerodynamic arguments for wings evolved from tiniest rudiment to elaborate final form in the interest of airborne motion. Flower argues, supporting an orthodox view, that wings evolved from tiny outgrowths of the body used for gliding prior to elaboration for sustained flight. But Flower recognizes that these incipient structures must themselves evolve from antecedents too small to function as gliding planes. What could these very first, slight outgrowths of the body be for? Ignoring Darwin's principle of functional shift, Flower searches for an aerodynamic meaning even at this very outset. He tries to test two suggestions: E. H. Hinton's argument that initial outgrowths served for "attitude control," permitting a falling insect to land in a suitable position for quick escape from predators; and a proposal of the great British entomologist Sir Vincent Wigglesworth (wonderful name for an insect man, I always thought) that such first stages might act as stabilizing or controlling devices during takeoff in small, passively aerial insects.

Flower proceeded by performing aerodynamic calculations on consequences of incipient wings for simple body shapes when dropped—and he quickly argued himself into an inextricable logical corner. He found, first of all, that tiny outgrowths might help, as Wigglesworth, Hinton, and others had suggested. But the argument foundered on another observation: The same advantages could be gained far more easily and effectively by another, readily available alternative route—evolution to small size (where increased surface/volume ratios retard falling and enhance the probability of takeoff). Flower then realized that he would have to specify a reasonably large body size for incipient wings to have any aerodynamic effect. But he then encountered another problem: At such sizes, legs work just as well as, if not better than, proto-wings for any suggested aerodynamic function. Flower admitted:

> The first conclusion to be drawn from these calculations is that the selective pressure in small insects is towards smaller insects, which would have no reason to evolve wings.

I would have stopped and searched elsewhere (in Darwin's principle of functional shift) at this point, but Flower bravely continued along an improbable path:

> The main conclusions, however, are that attitude control of insects would be by the use of legs or by very small changes in body shape [*i.e.*, by evolving small outgrowths, or proto-wings].

Flower, in short, never considered an alternative to his assumption of functional continuity based upon some aspect of aerial locomotion. He concluded:

> At first they [proto-wings] would affect attitude; later they could increase to a larger size and act as a true wing, providing lift in their own right. Eventually they could move, giving the insect greater maneuverability during descent, and finally they could "flap," achieving sustained flight.

As an alternative to such speculative reconstructions that work, in their own terms, only by uncomfortable special pleading, may I suggest Darwin's old principle of functional shift (preadaptation—ugh—for something else).

The physiological literature contains voluminous testimony to the thermodynamic efficiency of modern insect wings: in presenting, for example, a large surface area to the sun for quick heating (see B. Heinrich, 1981). If wings can perform this subsidiary function now, why not suspect thermoregulation as a primary role at the outset? M. M. Douglas (1981), for example, showed that, in *Colias* butterflies, only the basal one-third of the wing operates in thermoregulation—an area approximately equal to the thoracic lobes (proto-wings) of fossil insects considered ancestral to modern forms.

Douglas then cut down some *Colias* wings to the actual size of these fossil ancestral lobes and found that insects so bedecked showed a 55 percent greater increase in body temperature than bodies deprived of wings entirely. These manufactured proto-wings measured 5 by 3 millimeters on a body 15 millimeters long. Finally, Douglas determined that no further thermoregulatory advantage could be gained by wings longer than 10 millimeters on a 15-millimeter body.

Kingsolver and Koehl performed a host of elaborate and elegant experiments to support a thermoregulatory origin of insect proto-wings. As with so many examples of excellent science producing clear and interesting outcomes, the results can be summarized briefly and cleanly.

Kingsolver and Koehl begin by tabulating all the aerodynamic hypotheses usually presented in the literature as purely verbal speculations. They arrange these proposals of functional continuity (the explanations that do not follow Darwin's solution of Mivart's dilemma) into three basic categories: proto-wings for gliding (aerofoils for steady-state motion), for parachuting (slowing the rate of descent in a falling insect), and attitude stability (helping an insect to land right side up). They then transcended the purely verbal tradition by developing aerodynamic equations for exactly how proto-wings should help an insect under these three hypotheses of continuity in adaptation (increasing the lift/drag ratio as the major boost to gliding, increasing drag to slow the descent rate in parachuting, measuring the moment about the body axis produced by wings for the hypothesis of attitude stability).

They then constructed insect models made of wire, epoxy, and other appropriate materials to match the sizes and body shapes of flying and nonflying forms among early insect fossils. To these models, they attached wings (made of copper wire enclosing thin, plastic membranes) of various lengths and measured the actual aerodynamic effects for properties predicted by various hypotheses of functional continuity. The results of many experiments in wind tunnels are consistent and consonant: Aerodynamic benefits begin for wings above a certain size, and they increase as wings get larger. But at the small sizes of insect proto-wings, aerodynamic advantages are absent or insignificant and do not increase with growing wing length. These results are independent of body shape, wind velocity, presence or placement of legs, and mounting position of wings. In other words, large wings work well and larger wings work better—but small wings (at the undoubted sizes of Mivart's troubling incipient stages) provide no aerodynamic edge.

Kingsolver and Koehl then tested their models for thermoregulatory effects, constructing wings from two materials with different thermal conductivities (construction paper and aluminum foil) and measuring the increased temperature of bodies supplied with wings of various lengths versus wingless models. They achieved results symmetrically opposite to the aerodynamic experiments. For thermoregulation, wings work well at the smallest sizes, with benefits increasing as the wing grows. However, beyond a measured length, further increase of the wing confers no additional effect. Kingsolver and Koehl conclude:

> At any body size, there is a relative wing length above which there is no additional thermal effect, and below which there is no significant aerodynamic effect.

The accompanying chart illustrates these combined results. Note how the thermoregulatory effect of excess body temperature due to wings (solid line) increases rapidly at small wing sizes but not at all above an intermediate wing length. Conversely, the aerodynamic effect of lift/drag ratio does not increase at all until intermediate wing length, but grows rapidly thereafter.

We could not hope for a more elegant experimental confirmation of Darwin's solution to Mivart's challenge. Kingsolver and Koehl have actually measured the functional shift by showing that incipient wings aid thermoregulation but provide no aerodynamic benefit—while larger wings provide no further thermoregulatory oomph but initiate aerodynamic advantage and increase the benefits steadily thereafter. The crucial intermediate

The Evolution of Insect Wings

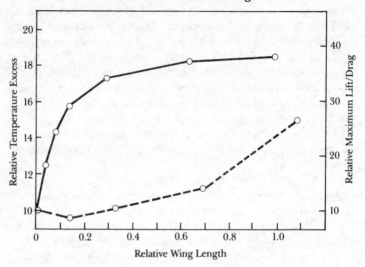

The thermoregulatory (upper curve) and aerodynamic (lower curve) advantages for increasing wing length in insects. Note that thermodynamic benefits accrue rapidly when the wing is very small (too small for flight), but scarcely increase at all for wings of larger size. Aerodynamic advantages, on the other hand, are insignificant for small size, but increase rapidly at larger wing dimensions, just as the thermodynamic benefits cease. BEN GAMIT. ADAPTED FROM JOE LEMONNIER. COURTESY OF *NATURAL HISTORY.*

wing length, where thermoregulatory gain ceases and aerodynamic benefits begin, represents a domain of functional shift, as aerodynamic advantages pick up the relay from waning thermoregulation to continue the evolutionary race to increasing wing size.

But what might push an insect across the transition? Why reach this crucial domain at all? If wings originally worked primarily for thermoregulation, why not just stop as the length of maximum benefit approached? Here, Kingsolver and Koehl present an interesting speculation based on another aspect of their data. They found that the domain of transition between thermal and aerial effects varied systematically with body size: The larger the body, the sooner the transition (in terms of relative wing length). For a body 2 centimeters long, the transition occurred with wings 40 to 60 percent of body length; but a 10-centimeter body switches to aerodynamic advantage at only 10 percent of body length.

Now suppose that incipient ancestral wings worked primarily for thermoregulation and had reached a stable, optimum size for greatest benefit. Natural selection would not favor larger wings and a transition to the available domain of aerodynamic advantage. But if body size increased for other reasons, an insect might reach the realm of aerial effects simply by growing larger, without any accompanying change of body shape or relative wing length.

We often think, naively, that size itself should make no profound difference. Why should just more of the same have any major effect beyond simple accumulation? Surely, any major improvement or alteration must require an extensive and explicit redesign, a complex reordering of parts with invention of new items.

Nature does not always match our faulty intuitions. Complex objects often display the interesting and paradoxical property of major effect for apparently trifling input. Internal complexity can translate a simple quantitative change into a wondrous alteration of quality. Perhaps that greatest and most effective of all evolutionary inventions, the origin of human consciousness, required little more than an increase of brain power to a level where internal connections became rich and varied enough to force this seminal transition. The story may be much more complex, but we have no proof that it must be.

Voltaire quipped that "God is always for the big battalions." More is not always better, but more can be very different.

4 | Fads and Fallacies

10 | The Case of the Creeping Fox Terrier Clone

WHEN ASTA the fox terrier exhumed the body of the Thin Man, his delightfully tipsy detective master, Nick Charles, exclaimed, "You're not a terrier; you're a police dog" (*The Thin Man*, MGM 1934 original with William Powell and Myrna Loy). May I now generalize for Asta's breed in the case of the telltale textbook.

The wisdom of our culture abounds with mottoes that instruct us to acknowledge the faults within ourselves before we criticize the failings of others. These words range from clichés about pots and kettles to various sayings of Jesus: "And why beholdest thou the mote that is in thy brother's eye, but perceivest not the beam that is in thine own eye?" (Luke 6:41); "He that is without sin among you, let him first cast a stone at her" (John 8:7). I shall follow this wisdom by exposing my own profession in trying to express what I find so desperately wrong about the basic tool of American teaching, the textbook.

In March 1987, I spent several hours in the exhibit hall of the National Science Teachers Association convention in Washington, D.C. There I made an informal, but reasonably complete, survey of evolution as treated (if at all) in major high-school science textbooks. I did find some evidence of adulteration, pussyfooting, and other forms of capitulation to creationist pressure. One book, *Life Science*, by L. K. Bierer, V. F. Liem, and E. P. Silberstein (Heath, 1987), in an accommodation that at least makes you laugh while you weep for lost integrity in education, qualifies every statement about the ages of fossils—usually in the most barbarous of English constructions, the passive infinitive.

155

We discover that trilobites are "believed to have lived 500–600 million years ago," while frozen mammoths are "thought to have roamed the tundra 22,000 years ago." But of one poor bird, we learn with terrible finality, "There are no more dodoes living today." Their extinction occurred within the bounds of biblical literalism and need not be hedged.

But I was surprised and pleased to note that most books contained material at reasonable length about evolution, and with no explicit signs of tampering to appease creationists. Sins imposed by others were minimal. But I then found the beam in our own eye and became, if anything, more distressed than by any capitulation to the yahoos. The problem does not lie in what others are doing to us, but in what we are doing to ourselves. In book after book, the evolution section is virtually cloned. Almost all authors treat the same topics, usually in the same sequence, and often with illustrations changed only enough to avoid suits for plagiarism. Obviously, authors of textbooks are copying material on a massive scale and passing along to students an ill-considered and virtually Xeroxed version with a rationale lost in the mists of time.

Just two months after making this depressing observation, I read Diane B. Paul's fascinating article "The Nine Lives of Discredited Data" (*The Sciences*, May 1987). Paul analyzed the sections on heritability of IQ from twenty-eight textbooks on introductory genetics published between 1978 and 1984. She paid particular attention to their treatment of Sir Cyril Burt's data on identical twins raised separately. We now know that these "studies" represent one of the most striking cases of fraud in twentieth-century science—for Burt invented both data and co-workers. His sad story had been well publicized, and all authors of texts published since 1978 surely knew that Burt's data had been discredited and could not be used. Several texts even included discussions of the Burt scandal as a warning about caution and scrutiny in science.

But Paul then found that nearly half these books continued to cite and use Burt's data, probably unconsciously. Of nineteen textbooks that devoted more than a paragraph to the subject of genetics and IQ, eleven based their conclusions about high heritability on a review article published in *Science* in 1963. This review featured a figure that ten of these textbooks reproduced either directly or in slightly altered and simplified form. This figure includes, as a prominent feature, the results of Sir Cyril Burt (not yet suspect in 1963). We must conclude that the authors of these texts either had not read the 1963 article carefully or had not consulted it at all. Paul infers (correctly, I am sure) that this carelessness arises because authors of textbooks copy from other texts and often do not read original sources. How else to explain the several books that discussed the Burt scandal explicitly and then, unbeknownst to their authors, used the same discredited data in a figure?

Paul argues that the increasing commercialization of textbooks has engendered this virtual cloning of contents. Textbook publishing is a big business, replete with market surveys, fancy art programs, and subsidiary materials in the form of slide sets, teachers' guides, even test-making and grading services. The actual text of the book can become secondary and standardized; any departure from a conventional set of topics could derail an entire industry of supporting materials. Teachers are also locked into a largely set curriculum based on this flood of accoutrements. Paul concludes: "Today's textbooks are thicker, slicker, more elaborate, and more expensive than they used to be. They are also more alike. Indeed, many are virtual clones, both stylistic and substantive, of a market leader."

The marketplace rules. Most publishing houses are now owned by conglomerates—CBS, Raytheon, and Coca-Cola among them—with managers who never raise their eyes from the financial bottom line, know little or nothing about books, and view the publishing arm of their diversified empire as but one more item for the ultimate balance. I received a dramatic reminder of this trend last week when I looked at the back cover of my score for Mozart's *Coronation Mass,* now under rehearsal in my chorus. It read: "Kalmus Score. Belwin Mills Publishing Company, distributed by Columbia Pictures Publication, a unit of the Coca-Cola Company." I don't say that Bill Cosby or Michael Jackson or whoever advertises the stuff doesn't like Mozart; I merely suspect that Don Giovanni can't be high on the executive agenda when the big boys must worry about such really important issues as whether or not to market Cherry Coke (a resounding "yes" vote from this old New York soda fountain junkie).

Paul quotes a leading industry analyst from the 1984 *Book Publishing Annual.* Future textbooks, the analyst argues, will have "more elaborate designs and greater use of color. . . . The ancillary packages will become more comprehensive. . . . New, more aggressive marketing plans will be needed just to maintain a company's position. The quality of marketing will make the difference." Do note the conspicuous absence of any mention whatsoever about the quality of the text itself.

Paul is obviously correct in arguing that this tendency to cloning has accelerated remarkably as concerns of the market overwhelm scholarly criteria in the composition of textbooks. But I believe that the basic tendency has always been present and has a human as well as a corporate face. Independent thought has always been more difficult than borrowing, and authors of textbooks have almost always taken the easier way out. Of course I have no objection to the similar recording of information by textbooks. No author can know all the byways of a profession, and all must therefore rely on written sources for areas not enlightened by personal expertise. I speak instead of the thoughtless, senseless, and often false copying of phrase, anecdote, style of argument, and sequence of topics that perpetuates itself by degraded repetition from text to text and thereby loses its anchor in nature.

I present an example that may seem tiny and peripheral in import. Nevertheless, and perhaps paradoxically, such cases provide our best evidence for thoughtless copying. When a truly important and well-known fact graces several texts in the same form, we cannot know whether it has been copied from previous sources or independently extracted from any expert's general knowledge. But when a quirky little senseless item attains the frequency of the proverbial bad penny, copying from text to text is the only reasonable interpretation. There is no other source. My method is no different from the standard technique of bibliographic scholars, who establish lineages of texts by tracing errors (particularly for documents spread by copyists before the invention of printing).

When textbooks choose to illustrate evolution with an example from the fossil record, they almost invariably trot out that greatest warhorse among case studies—the history of horses themselves (see the next essay in this section for fallacies of the usual tale). The standard story begins with an animal informally called *Eohippus* (the dawn horse), or more properly, *Hyracotherium*. Since evolutionary increase in size is a major component of the traditional tale, all texts report the diminutive stature of ancestral *Hyracotherium.* A few give actual estimates or measurements, but most rely upon a simile with some modern organism. For years, I have been much amused (and mildly bothered) that the great majority of texts report *Hyracotherium* as "like a fox-terrier" in size. I was jolted into action when I found myself writing the same line, and then stopped. "Wait a minute," said my inner voice, "beyond some vague memories of Asta last time I watched a Thin Man movie, I haven't the slightest idea what a fox terrier is. I can't believe that the community of textbook authors includes only dog fanciers—so if I don't know, I'll bet most of them don't either." Clearly, the classic line has been copied from text to text. Where did it begin? What has been its history? Is the statement even correct?

My immediate spur to action came from a most welcome and unexpected source. I published a parenthetical remark about the fox terrier issue (see Essay 11), ending with a serious point: "I also wonder what the textbook tradition of endless and thoughtless copying has done to retard the spread of original ideas."

I have, over the years, maintained a correspondence about our favorite common subject with Roger Angell of the *New Yorker,* who is, among other things, the greatest baseball writer ever. I assumed that his letter of early April would be a scouting report for the beginning of a new season. But I found that Roger Angell is a man of even more dimensions than I had realized; he is also a fox terrier fancier. He had read my parenthetical comment and wrote, "I am filled with excitement and trepidation at the prospect of writing you a letter about science instead of baseball."

Angell went on to suggest a fascinating and plausible explanation for the origin of the fox terrier simile (no excuse, of course, for its later cloning). Fox terriers were bred "to dig out foxes from their burrows, when a fox had gone to earth during a traditional British hunt." Apparently, generations of fox-hunting gentlemen selected fox terriers not only for their functional role in the hunt but also under a breeder's artifice to make them look as much like horses as possible. Angell continues, "The dogs rode up on the saddle during the hunt, and it was a pretty conceit for the owner-horseman to appear to put down a little simulacrum of a horse when the pack of hounds and the pink-coated throng had arrived at an earth where the animal was to do his work." He also pointed out that fox terriers tend to develop varied patches of color on a basically white coat and that a "saddle" along the back is "considered desirable and handsome." Thus, Angell proposed his solution: "Wouldn't it seem possible that some early horse geologist, in casting about for the right size animal to fit his cliché-to-be, might have settled, quite unconsciously, on a breed of dog that fitted the specifications in looks as well as size?"

This interesting conjecture led me to devise the following, loosely controlled experiment. I asked David Backus, my research assistant, to record every simile for *Hyracotherium* that he could find in the secondary literature of texts and popular books during more than a century since O. C. Marsh first recognized this animal as a "dawn horse." We would then use these patterns in attempting to locate original sources for favored similes in the primary literature of vertebrate paleontology. We consulted the books in my personal library as a sample, and compiled a total of eighty-six descriptions. The story turns out to be much more ascertainable and revealing than I had imagined.

The tradition of simile begins at the very beginning. Richard Owen, the great British anatomist and paleontologist, described the genus *Hyracotherium* in 1841. He did not recognize its relationship with horses (he considered this animal, as his chosen name implies, to be a possible relative of hyraxes, a small group of Afro-Asian mammals, the "coneys" of the Bible). In this original article, Owen likened his fossil to a hare in one passage and to something between a hog and a hyrax in another. Owen's simile plays no role in later history because other traditions of comparison had been long established before scientists realized that Owen's older discovery represented the same animal that Marsh later named *Eohippus*. (Hence, under the rules of taxonomy, Owen's inappropriate and uneuphonious name takes unfortunate precedence over Marsh's lovely *Eohippus*—see Essay 5 on the rules of naming.)

The modern story begins with Marsh's description of the earliest horses in 1874. Marsh pressed "go" on the simile machine by writing, "This species was about as large as a fox." He also described the larger descendant *Miohippus* as sheeplike in size.

Throughout the nineteenth century all sources that we have found (eight references, including such major figures as Joseph Le Conte, Archibald Geikie, and even Marsh's bitter enemy E. D.

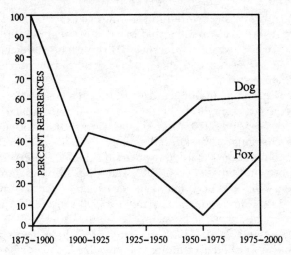

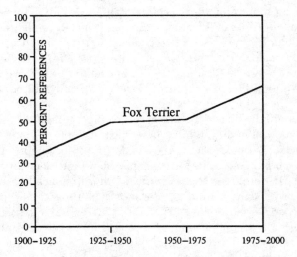

The rise to dominance of fox terriers as similes for the size of the earliest horses. Top graph: Increasing domination of dogs over foxes through time. Lower graph: Increase in percentage of fox terrier references among sources citing dogs as their simile. IROMIE WEERAMAN-TRY. COURTESY OF *NATURAL HISTORY*.

Cope) copy Marsh's favored simile—they all describe *Eohippus* as fox-sized. We are confident that Marsh's original description is the source because most references also repeat his statement that *Miohippus* is the size of a sheep. How, then, did fox terriers replace their prey?

The first decade of our century ushered in a mighty Darwinian competition among three alternatives and led to the final triumph of fox terriers. By 1910, three similes were battling for survival. Marsh's original fox suffered greatly from competition, but managed to retain a share of the market at about 25 percent (five of twenty citations between 1900 and 1925 in our sample)—a frequency that has been maintained ever since (see accompanying figure). Competition came from two stiff sources, however—both from the American Museum of Natural History in New York.

First, in 1903, W. D. Matthew, vertebrate paleontologist at the Museum, published his famous pamphlet *The Evolution of the Horse* (it remained in print for fifty years, and was still being sold at the Museum shop when I was a child). Matthew wrote: "The earliest known ancestors of the horse were small animals not larger than the domestic cat." Several secondary sources picked up Matthew's simile during this quarter century (also five of twenty references between 1900 and 1925), but felines have since faded (only one of fifteen references since 1975), and I do not know why.

Second, the three-way carnivorous competition of vulpine, feline, and canine began in earnest when man's best friend made his belated appearance in 1904 under the sponsorship of Matthew's boss, American Museum president and eminent vertebrate paleontologist Henry Fairfield Osborn. Remember that no nineteenth-century source (known to us) had advocated a canine simile, so Osborn's late entry suffered a temporal handicap. But Osborn was as commanding (and enigmatic) a figure as American natural history has ever produced (see Essay 29)—a powerful patrician in science and politics, imperious but kind, prolific and pompous, crusader for natural history and for other causes of opposite merit (Osborn wrote, for example, a glowing preface to the most influential tract of American scientific racism, *The Passing of the Great Race,* by his friend Madison Grant).

In the *Century Magazine* for November 1904, Osborn published a popular article, "The Evolution of the Horse in America."

(Given Osborn's almost obsessively prolific spate of publications, we would not be surprised if we have missed an earlier citation.) His first statement about *Eohippus* introduces the comparison that would later win the competition:

> We may imagine the earliest herds of horses in the Lower Eocene (*Eohippus,* or "dawn horse" stage) as resembling a lot of small fox-terriers in size. . . . As in the terrier, the wrist (knee) was near the ground, the hand was still short, terminating in four hoofs, with a part of the fifth toe (thumb) dangling at the side.

Osborn provides no rationale for his choice of breeds. Perhaps he simply carried Marsh's old fox comparison unconsciously in his head and chose the dog most similar in name to the former standard. Perhaps Roger Angell's conjecture is correct. Osborn certainly came from a social set that knew about fox hunting. Moreover, as the quotation indicates, Osborn extended the similarity of *Eohippus* and fox terrier beyond mere size to other horselike attributes of this canine breed (although, in other sources, Osborn treated the whippet as even more horselike, and even mounted a whippet's skeleton for an explicit comparison with *Eohippus*). Roger Angell described his fox terrier to me: "The back is long and straight, the tail is held jauntily upward like a trotter's, the nose is elongated and equine, and the forelegs are strikingly thin and straight. In motion, the dog comes down on these forelegs in a rapid and distinctive, stiff, flashy style, and the dog appears to walk on his tiptoes—on hooves, that is."

In any case, we can trace the steady rise to domination of dog similes in general, and fox terriers in particular, ever since. Dogs reached nearly 50 percent of citations (nine of twenty) between 1900 and 1925, but have now risen to 60 percent (nine of fifteen) since 1975. Meanwhile, the percentage of fox terrier citations among dog similes had also climbed steadily, from one-third (three of nine) between 1900 and 1925 to one-half (eight of sixteen) between 1925 and 1975, to two-thirds (six of nine) since 1975. Osborn's simile has been victorious.

Copying is the only credible source for these shifts of popularity—first from experts; then from other secondary sources. Shifts in fashion cannot be recording independent insights based on observation of specimens. *Eohippus* could not, by itself, say "fox" to every nineteenth-century observer and "dog" to most twentieth-century writers. Nor can I believe that two-thirds of all dog-inclined modern writers would independently say, "Aha, fox terrier" when contemplating the dawn horse. The breed is no longer so popular, and I suspect that most writers, like me, have only the vaguest impression about fox terriers when they copy the venerable simile.

In fact, we can trace the rise to dominance of fox terriers in our references. The first post-Osborn citation that we can find (Ernest Ingersoll, *The Life of Animals,* MacMillan, 1906) credits Osborn explicitly as author of the comparison with fox terriers. Thereafter, no one cites the original, and I assume that the process of text copying text had begun.

Two processes combined to secure the domination of fox terriers. First, experts began to line up behind Osborn's choice. The great vertebrate paleontologist W. B. Scott, for example, stood in loyal opposition in 1913, 1919, and 1929 when he cited both alternatives of fox and cat. But by 1937, he had switched: *"Hyracotherium* was a little animal about the size of a fox-terrier, but horse-like in all parts." Second, dogs became firmly ensconced in major textbooks. Both leading American geology textbooks of the early twentieth century (Chamberlin and Salisbury, 1909 edition, and Pirsson and Schuchert, 1924 edition) opt for canines, as does Hegner's zoology text (1912) and W. Maxwell Read's fine children's book (a mainstay of my youth) *The Earth for Sam* (1930 edition).

Fox terriers have only firmed up their position ever since. Experts cite this simile, as in A. S. Romer's leading text, *Vertebrate Paleontology* (3d edition, 1966): "'*Eohippus*' was a small form, some specimens no larger than a fox terrier." They have also entered the two leading high-school texts: (1) Otto and Towle (descendant of Moon, Mann, and Otto, the dominant text for most of the past fifty years): "This horse is called *Eohippus.* It had four toes and was about the size of a fox-terrier" (1977 edition); (2) the *Biological Sciences Curriculum Study, Blue Edition* (1968): "The fossil of a small four-toed animal about the size of a fox-terrier was found preserved in layers of rock." College texts also comply. W. T. Keeton, in his *Biological Science,* the Hertz of the profession, writes (1980 edition): "It was a small animal, only about the size of a fox-terrier." Baker and Allen's *The Study of Biology,* a strong Avis, agrees (1982 edition): "This small animal *Eohippus* was not much bigger than a fox-terrier."

You may care little for dawn horses or fox terriers and might feel that I have made much of nothing in this essay. But I cite the case of the creeping fox terrier clone not for itself, but rather as a particularly clear example of a pervasive and serious disease—the debasement of our textbooks, the basic tool of written education, by endless, thoughtless copying.

My younger son started high school last month. For a biology text, he is using the 4th edition of *Biology: Living Systems,* by R. F. Oram, with consultants P. J. Hummer and R. C. Smoot (Charles E. Merrill, 1983, but listed on the title page, following our modern reality of conglomeration, as a Bell and Howell Company). I was sad and angered to find several disgraceful passages of capitulation to creationist pressure. Page one of the chapter on evolution proclaims in a blue sidebar: "The theory of evolution is the most widely accepted scientific explanation of the origin of life and changes in living things. You may wish to investigate other theories." Similar invitations are not issued for any other well-established theory. Students are not told that "most folks accept gravitation, but you might want to check out levitation" or that "most people view the earth as a sphere, but you might want to consider the possibility of a plane." When the text reaches human history, it doesn't even grant majority status to our evolutionary consensus: "Humans are indeed unique, but because they are also organisms, many scientists believe that humans have an evolutionary history."

Yet, as I argued at the outset, I find these compromises to outside pressure, disgraceful though they be, less serious than the internal disease of cloning from text to text. There is virtually only one chapter on evolution in all high-school biology texts, copied and degraded, then copied and degraded again. My son's book is no exception. This chapter begins with a discussion of Lamarck and the inheritance of acquired characters. It then moves to Darwin and natural selection and follows this basic contrast with a picture of a giraffe and a disquisition of Lamarckian and Darwinian explanations for long necks. A bit later, we reach industrial melanism in moths and dawn horses of you-know-what size.

What is the point of all this? I could understand this development if Lamarckism were a folk notion that must be dispelled before introducing Darwin, or if Lamarck were a household name. But I will lay 100 to 1 that few high-school students have ever heard of Lamarck. Why begin teaching evolution by explicating a false theory that is causing no confusion? False notions are often wonderful tools in pedagogy, but not when they are unknown, are provoking no trouble, and make the grasp of an accepted theory more difficult. I would not teach more sophisticated college students this way; I simply can't believe that this sequence works in high school. I can only conclude that someone once wrote the material this way for a reason lost in the mists of time, and that authors of textbooks have been dutifully copying "Lamarck . . . Darwin . . . giraffe necks" ever since.

(The giraffe necks, by the way, make even less sense. This venerable example rests upon no data at all for the superiority of Darwinian explanation. Lamarck offered no evidence for his interpretation and only introduced the case in a few lines of speculation. We have no proof that the long neck evolved by natural selection for eating leaves at the tops of acacia trees. We only prefer this explanation because it matches current orthodoxy. Giraffes do munch the topmost leaves, and this habit obviously helps them to thrive, but who knows how or why their necks elongated? They may have lengthened for other reasons and then been fortuitously suited for acacia leaves.)

If textbook cloning represented the discovery of a true educational optimum, and its further honing and propagation, then I would not object. But all evidence—from my little story of fox terriers to the larger issue of a senseless but nearly universal sequence of Lamarck, Darwin, and giraffe necks—indicates that cloning bears an opposite and discouraging message. It is the easy way out, a substitute for thinking and striving to improve. Somehow I must believe—for it is essential to my notion of scholarship—that good teaching requires fresh thought and genuine excitement, and that rote copying can only indicate boredom and slipshod practice. A carelessly cloned work will not excite students, however pretty the pictures. As an antidote, we need only the most basic virtue of integrity—not only the usual, figurative meaning of honorable practice but the less familiar, literal definition of wholeness. We will not have great texts if authors cannot shape content but must serve a commercial master as one cog in an ultimately powerless consortium with other packagers.

To end with a simpler point amid all this tendentiousness and generality: Thoughtlessly cloned "eternal verities" are often false. The latest estimate I have seen for the body size of *Hyracotherium* (MacFadden, 1986), challenging previous reconstructions congenial with the standard simile of much smaller fox-terriers, cites a weight of some twenty-five kilograms, or fifty-five pounds.

Lassie come home!

11 | Life's Little Joke

I STILL DON'T UNDERSTAND why a raven is like a writing desk, but I do know what binds Hernando Cortés and Thomas Henry Huxley together.

On February 18, 1519, Cortés set sail for Mexico with about 600 men and, perhaps more important, 16 horses. Two years later, the Aztec capital of Tenochtitlán lay in ruins, and one of the world's great civilizations had perished.

Cortés's victory has always seemed puzzling, even to historians of an earlier age who did not doubt the intrinsic superiority of Spanish blood and Christian convictions. William H. Prescott, master of this tradition, continually emphasizes Cortés's diplomatic skill in making alliances to divide and conquer—and his good fortune in despoiling Mexico during a period of marked internal dissension among the Aztecs and their vassals. (Prescott published his *History of the Conquest of Mexico* in 1843; it remains among the most exciting and literate books ever written.)

Prescott also recognized Cortés's two "obvious advantages on the score of weapons"—one inanimate and one animate. A gun is formidable enough against an obsidian blade, but consider the additional impact of surprise when your opponent has never seen a firearm. Cortés's cavalry, a mere handful of horses and their riders, caused even more terror and despair, for the Aztecs, as Prescott wrote,

> had no large domesticated animals, and were unacquainted with any beast of burden. Their imaginations were bewildered when they beheld the strange apparition of the horse

and his rider moving in unison and obedient to one impulse, as if possessed of a common nature; and as they saw the terrible animal, with "his neck clothed in thunder," bearing down their squadrons and trampling them in the dust, no wonder they should have regarded him with the mysterious terror felt for a supernatural being.

On the same date, February 18, in 1870, Thomas Henry Huxley gave his annual address as president of the Geological Society of London and staked his celebrated claim that Darwin's ideal evidence for evolution had finally been uncovered in the fossil record of horses—a sequence of continuous transformation, properly arrayed in temporal order:

> It is easy to accumulate probabilities—hard to make out some particular case, in such a way that it will stand rigorous criticism. After much search, however, I think that such a case is to be made out in favor of the pedigree of horses.

Huxley delineated the famous trends to fewer toes and higher-crowned teeth that we all recognize in this enduring classic among evolutionary case histories. Huxley viewed this lineage as a European affair, proceeding from fully three-toed *Anchitherium,* to *Hipparion* with side toes "reduced to mere dew-claws [that] do not touch the ground," to modern *Equus,* where, "finally, the crowns of the grinding-teeth become longer. . . . The phalanges of the two outer toes in each foot disappear, their metacarpal and metatarsal bones being left as the 'splints.' "

In *Cat's Cradle,* Kurt Vonnegut speaks of the subtle ties that can bind people across worlds and centuries into aggregations forged by commonalities so strange that they must be meaningful. Cortés and Huxley must belong to the same karass (Vonnegut's excellent word for these associations)—for they both, on the same date, unfairly debased America with the noblest of animals. Huxley was wrong and Cortés, by consequence, was ever so lucky.

Horses evolved in America, through a continuity that extends unbroken across 60 million years. Several times during this history, different branches migrated to Europe, where Huxley arranged three (and later four) separate incursions as a false continuity. But horses then died in America at the dawn of human history in our hemisphere, leaving the last European migration as a source of recolonization by conquest. Huxley's error became Montezuma's sorrow, as an animal more American than Babe Ruth or apple pie came home to destroy her greatest civilization. (Montezuma's revenge would come later, and by another route.)

During our centennial year of 1876, Huxley visited America to deliver the principal address for the founding of Johns Hopkins University. He stopped first at Yale to consult the eminent paleontologist Othniel C. Marsh. Marsh, ever gracious, offered Huxley an architectural tour of the campus, but Huxley had come for a purpose and would not be delayed. He pointed to the buildings and said to Marsh: "Show me what you have got inside them; I can see plenty of bricks and mortar in my own country." Huxley was neither philistine nor troglodyte; he was simply eager to study some particular fossils: Marsh's collection of horses.

Two years earlier, Marsh had published his phylogeny of American horses and identified our continent as the center stage, while relegating Huxley's European sequence to a periphery of discontinuous migration. Marsh began with a veiled and modest criticism (*American Journal of Science*, 1874):

> Huxley has traced successfully the later genealogy of the horse through European extinct forms, but the line in America was probably a more direct one, and the record is more complete.

Later, he stated more baldly (p. 258): "The line of descent appears to have been direct, and the remains now known supply every important intermediate form."

Marsh had assembled an immense collection from the American West (prompted largely by a race for priority in his bitter feud with Edwin D. Cope—see Essay 5 for another consequence of this feud!). For every query, every objection that Huxley raised, Marsh produced a specimen. Leonard Huxley describes the scene in his biography of his father:

> At each inquiry, whether he had a specimen to illustrate such and such a point or to exemplify a transition from earlier and less specialized forms to later and more special-

ized ones, Professor Marsh would simply turn to his assistant and bid him fetch box number so and so, until Huxley turned upon him and said, "I believe you are a magician; whatever I want, you just conjure it up."

Years before, T. H. Huxley had coined a motto; now he meant to live by it: "Sit down before fact as a little child, be prepared to give up every preconceived notion." He capitulated to Marsh's theory of an American venue. Marsh, with growing pleasure and retreating modesty, reported his impression of personal triumph:

He [Huxley] then informed me that this was new to him, and that my facts demonstrated the evolution of the horse beyond question, and for the first time indicated the direct line of descent of an existing animal. With the generosity of true greatness, he gave up his own opinions in the face of new truth and took my conclusions.

A few days later, Huxley was, if anything, more convinced. He wrote to Marsh from Newport, his next stop: "The more I think of it the more clear it is that your great work is the settlement of the pedigree of the horse." But Huxley was scheduled to lecture on the evolution of horses less than a month later in New York. As he traveled about eastern America, Huxley rewrote his lecture from scratch. He also enlisted Marsh's aid in preparing a chart that would show the new evidence to his New York audience in pictorial form. Marsh responded with one of the most famous illustrations in the history of paleontology—the first pictorial pedigree of the horse.

Scholars are trained to analyze words. But primates are visual animals, and the key to concepts and their history often lies in iconography. Scientific illustrations are not frills or summaries; they are foci for modes of thought. The evolution of the horse—both in textbook charts and museum exhibits—has a standard iconography. Marsh began this traditional display in his illustration for Huxley. In so doing, he also initiated an error that captures pictorially the most common of all misconceptions about the shape and pattern of evolutionary change.

Errors in science are diverse enough to demand a taxonomy of

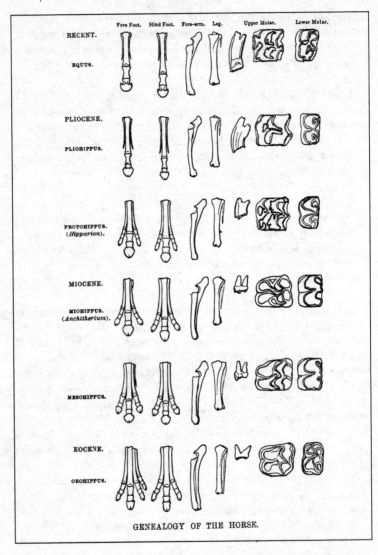

GENEALOGY OF THE HORSE.

The celebrated original figure drawn by O.C. Marsh for T.H. Huxley's New York lecture on the evolution of horses. This version appeared in an article by Marsh in the *American Journal of Science* for 1879. NEG. NO. 123823. COURTESY DEPARTMENT OF LIBRARY SERVICES, AMERICAN MUSEUM OF NATURAL HISTORY.

categories. Some make me angry, particularly those that arise from social prejudice, masquerade as objectively determined truth, and directly limit the lives of those caught in their thrall (scientific justifications for racism and sexism, as obvious examples). Others make me sad because honest effort ran headlong into unresolvable complexities of nature. Still others, as errors of logic that should not have occurred, bloat my already extended ego when I discover them. But I reserve a special place in perverse affection for a small class of precious ironies—errors that pass nature through a filter of expectation and reach a particular conclusion only because nature really works in precisely the opposite way. This result, I know, sounds both peculiar and unlikely, but bear with me for the premier example of life's little joke—as displayed in conventional iconography (and interpretation) for the most famous case study of all, the evolution of the horse.

In his original 1874 article, Marsh recognized the three trends that define our traditional view of old dobbin's genealogy: increase in size, decrease in the number of toes (with the hoof of modern horses made from a single digit, surrounded by two vestigial splints as remnants of side toes), and increase in the height and complexity of grinding teeth. (I am not treating the adaptive significance of these changes here, but wish to record the conventional explanation for the major environmental impetus behind trends in locomotion and dentition: a shift from browsing on lush lowland vegetation to grazing of newly evolved grasses upon drier plains. Tough grasses with less food value require considerably more dental effort.)

Marsh's famous chart, drawn for Huxley, depicts these trends as an ascending series—a ladder of uninterrupted progress toward one toe and tall, corrugated teeth (by scaling all his specimens to the same size, Marsh does not show the third "classic" trend toward increasing bulk).

We are all familiar with this traditional picture—the parade of horses from little eohippus (properly called *Hyracotherium*), with four toes in front and three behind, to Man o' War. (*Hyracotherium* is always described as "fox terrier" in size. Such traditions disturb and captivate me. I know nothing about fox terriers but have dutifully copied this description. I wonder who said it first, and why this simile has become so canonical. I also wonder what the textbook tradition of endless and thoughtless copying has done to retard the spread of original ideas.*)

In conventional charts and museum displays, the evolution of horses looks like a line of schoolchildren all pointed in one direction and arrayed in what my primary-school drill instructors called "size place" (also stratigraphic order in this case). The most familiar of all illustrations, first drawn early in the century for the American Museum of Natural History's pamphlet on the evolution of horses, by W. D. Matthew, but reproduced hundreds of times since then, shows the whole story: size, toes, and teeth arranged in a row by order of appearance in the fossil record. To cite just one example of this figure's influence, George W. Hunter reproduced Matthew's chart as the primary illustration of

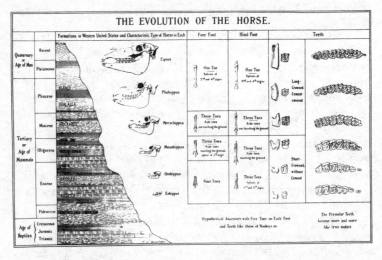

Most widely reproduced of all illustrations showing the evolution of horses as a ladder towards progress. Note increase in skull size, decrease in the number of toes, and increase in the height of teeth. The skulls are also arranged in stratigraphic order. W.D. Matthew used this illustration in several publications. This version comes from an article in the *Quarterly Review of Biology* for 1926. NEG. NO. 37969. COURTESY DEPARTMENT OF LIBRARY SERVICES, AMERICAN MUSEUM OF NATURAL HISTORY.

---

*This parenthetical comment inspired Roger Angell's letter and led directly to research and writing of the essay preceding this piece.

evolution in his high-school textbook of 1914, *A Civic Biology*. John Scopes assigned this book to his classes in Tennessee and was convicted for teaching its chapters on evolution, as William Jennings Bryan issued his last hurrah (see Essay 28): "No more repulsive doctrine was ever proclaimed by man . . . may heaven defend the youth of our land from [these] impious babblings."

But what is so wrong with these evolutionary ladders? Surely we can trace an unbroken continuity from *Hyracotherium* to modern horses. Yes, but continuity comes in many more potential modes than the lock step of the ladder. Evolutionary genealogies are copiously branching bushes—and the history of horses is more lush and labyrinthine than most. To be sure, *Hyracotherium* is the base of the trunk (as now known), and *Equus* is the surviving twig. We can, therefore, draw a pathway of connection from a common beginning to a lone result. But the lineage of modern horses is a twisted and tortuous excursion from one branch to another, a path more devious than the road marked by Ariadne's thread from the Minotaur at the center to the edge of our culture's most famous labyrinth. Most important, the path proceeds not by continuous transformation but by lateral stepping (with geological suddenness when punctuated equilibrium applies, as in this lineage, at least as read by yours truly, who must confess his bias as coauthor of the theory).

Each lateral step to a new species follows one path among several alternatives. Each extended lineage becomes a set of decisions at branching points—only one among hundreds of potential routes through the labyrinth of the bush. There is no central direction, no preferred exit to this maze—just a series of indirect pathways to every twig that ever graced the periphery of the bush.

As an example of distortions imposed by converting tortuous paths through bushes into directed ladders, consider the men associated with the two classical iconographies reproduced here. When Huxley made his formal capitulation to Marsh's interpretation in print (1880), he extended the ladder of horses as a metaphor for all vertebrates. Speaking of modern reptiles and teleost fishes, Huxley wrote (1880, p. 661): "They appear to me to be off the main line of evolution—to represent, as it were, side tracks starting from certain points of that line." But teleosts (modern bony fishes) are an enormously successful group. They stock the world's oceans, lakes, and rivers and maintain nearly 100 times as many species as primates (and more than all mammals combined). How can we call them "off the main line" just because we

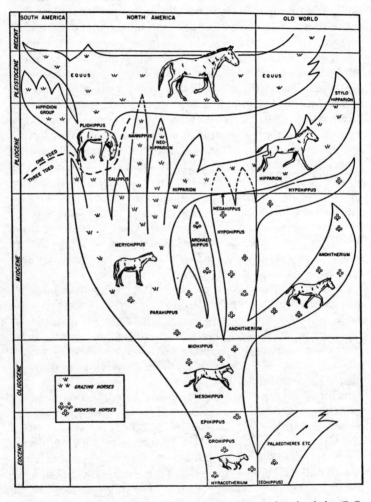

The evolution of horses depicted as at least a modest bush by G.G. Simpson in 1951. NEG. NO. 328907. COURTESY DEPARTMENT OF LIBRARY SERVICES, AMERICAN MUSEUM OF NATURAL HISTORY.

can trace our own pathway back to a common ancestry with theirs more than 300 million years ago?

W. D. Matthew slipped into an equally biased assessment of value because his designation of one pathway as a ladder forced an interpretation of all others as diversions. Matthew (1926, p. 164) designated his ladder as the "direct line of succession," but acknowledged that "there are also a number of side branches, more or less closely related." Three pages later, Matthew adds the opprobrium of near indecency to his previous charge of mere laterality, as he describes (p. 167) "a number of side branches leading up in a similar manner to aberrant specialized Equidae now extinct." But in what way are extinct lineages more specialized than a modern horse or in any sense more peculiar? Their historical death is the only possible rationale for a designation of aberrancy, but more than 99 percent of all species that ever lived are extinct—and disappearance cannot be the biological equivalent of a scarlet letter. We might as well call modern horses aberrant because, much to Montezuma's later sorrow, they became extinct in the land of their birth.

Yet we have recognized the bushiness of horse evolution from the very beginning. How else did Marsh forestall Huxley but by convincing him that his European "genealogy" of horses formed a stratigraphic sequence of discontinuous stages, falsely linking several side branches that had disappeared without issue?

As an example of bushiness, and a plug for the value of appropriate metaphors in general, consider the finest book on the evolution of horses ever written for popular audiences—G. G. Simpson's *Horses* (1951). Simpson redrew the genealogy of horses as a modest bush with no preferred main line. He also criticized the conceptual lock imposed by the bias of the ladder when he noted that modern one-toed horses are a side branch and extinct three-toed creatures the main line (if any center can be designated at all).

As nearly as there is a straight line in horse evolution, it culminated and ended with these animals [the three-toed anchitheres], which, like their ancestors, were multiple-toed browsers. From this point of view, it is the line leading to modern horses that was the side branch, even though it outlasted the straighter line of horse evolution [p. 130].

Yet Simpson, who held a lifelong commitment to the predominant role of evolution by transformational change within populations rather than by accumulation across numerous events of discrete, branching speciation, could not entirely let go of biases imposed by the metaphor of the ladder. In one revealing passage, he accepts bushiness, but bemoans the complexities thus introduced, as though they clouded evolution's essence of transformational change:

> *Miohippus* . . . intergraded with several different descendant groups. It is sad that this introduces possible confusion into the story, but there is not much point in criticizing nature for something that happened some millions of years ago. It would also be foolish to try to ignore the complications, which did occur and which are a very important part of the record.

But these "complications" are not a veil upon the essence of lineal descent; they are the primary stuff of evolution itself.

Moreover, Simpson restricted his bushiness as much as possible and retained linearity wherever he could avoid an inference of branching. In particular, he proposes the specific and testable hypothesis (see his illustration) that the early part of the record—the sequence of *Hyracotherium—Orohippus—Epihippus—Mesohippus—Miohippus—Hypohippus*—tells a story of linear descent, only later interrupted by copious branching among three-toed browsers: "The line from *Eohippus* to *Hypohippus,* for example, exemplifies a fairly continuous phyletic evolution" (p. 217). Simpson especially emphasizes the supposedly gradual and continuous transformation from *Mesohippus* to *Miohippus* near the top of this sequence:

> The more progressive horses of the middle Oligocene and all the horses of the late Oligocene are placed by convention in a separate genus, *Miohippus.* In fact *Mesohippus* and *Miohippus* intergrade so perfectly and the differences between them are so slight and variable that even experts find it difficult, at times nearly impossible, to distinguish them clearly.

The enormous expansion of collections since Simpson proposed this hypothesis has permitted a test by vertebrate paleontologists Don Prothero and Neil Shubin. Their results falsify Simpson's gradual and linear sequence for the early stages of horse evolution and introduce extensive bushiness into this last stronghold of the ladder.

Prothero and Shubin have made four major discoveries in the crucial segment of history that Simpson designated as the strongest case for a gradualistic sequence of lineal transformation—the transition from *Mesohippus* to *Miohippus*.

1. Previous experts were so convinced about the imperceptibly gradual transition between these two genera that they declared any search for distinguishing characters as vain, and arbitrarily drew the division between *Mesohippus* and *Miohippus* at a stratigraphic boundary. But far richer material available to Prothero and Shubin has permitted the identification of characters that cleanly distinguish the two genera. (Teeth are the hardest part of a vertebrate skeleton and the fossil record of mammals often contains little else. A technical course in the evolution of mammals is largely an exercise in the identification of teeth, and an old professional quip holds that mammalian evolution is the interbreeding of two sets of teeth to produce some slightly modified descendant choppers. *Miohippus* and *Mesohippus* do not have distinctive dentitions, and previous failure to find a clear separation should not surprise us. The new material is rich in skull and limb bones.) In particular, Prothero and Shubin found that *Miohippus* develops a distinctive articulation, absent in ancestral *Mesohippus*, between the enlarging third metatarsal (the foot bone of the digit that will become the entire hoof of modern horses) and the cuboid bone of the tarsus (ankle) above.

2. *Mesohippus* does not turn into *Miohippus* by insensible degrees of gradual transition. Rather, *Miohippus* arises by branching from a *Mesohippus* stock that continues to survive long afterward. The two genera overlap in time by at least 4 million years.

3. Each genus is itself a bush of several related species, not a rung on a ladder of progress. These species often lived and interacted in the same area at the same time (as different species of zebra do in Africa today). One set of strata in Wyoming, for example, has yielded three species of *Mesohippus* and two of *Miohippus,* all contemporaries.

4. The species of these bushes tend to arise with geological suddenness, and then to persist with little change for long periods. Evolutionary change occurs at the branch points themselves, and trends are not continuous marches up ladders, but concatenations of increments achieved at nodes of branching on evolutionary bushes. Of this phenomenon Prothero and Shubin write:

> There is no evidence of long-term changes within these well-defined species [of *Mesohippus* and *Miohippus*] through time. Instead, they are strikingly static through millions of years. Such stasis is apparent in most Neogene [later] horses as well, and in *Hyracotherium*. This is contrary to the widely-held myth about horse species as gradualistically-varying parts of a continuum, with no real distinctions between species. Throughout the history of horses, the species are well-marked and static over millions of years. At high resolution, the gradualistic picture of horse evolution becomes a complex bush of overlapping, closely related species.

Bushiness now pervades the entire phylogeny of horses.

We can appreciate this fundamental shift in iconography and meaning, but where is the "precious irony" that I promised? What is "life's little joke" of my title? Simply this. The model of the ladder is much more than merely wrong. It never could provide the promised illustration of evolution progressive and triumphant— for *it could only be applied to unsuccessful lineages.*

Bushes represent the proper topology of evolution. Ladders are false abstractions, made by running a steamroller over a labyrinthine pathway that hops from branch to branch through a phylogenetic bush. We cannot force a successful bush of evolution into a ladder because we may follow a thousand pathways through the maze of twigs, and we cannot find a criterion for preferring one route over another. Who ever heard of the evolutionary trend of rodents or of bats or of antelopes? Yet these are the greatest success stories in the history of mammals. Our proudest cases do not become our classic illustrations because we can draw no ladder of progress through a vigorous bush with hundreds of surviving twigs.

But consider the poor horses. Theirs was once a luxuriant bush, yet they barely survive today. Only one twig (the genus *Equus*, with horses, zebras, and asses) now carries all the heritage of a group that once dominated the history of hoofed mammals—and with fragility at that, for *Equus* died in the land of its birth and had to be salvaged from a stock that had migrated elsewhere. (In a larger sense, horses form one of three dwindling lines—tapirs and rhinos are the others—that now represent all the diversity of the formerly dominant order Perissodactyla, or odd-toed ungulates, among hoofed mammals. This mighty group once included the giant titanotheres, the clawed chalicotheres, and *Baluchitherium,* the largest land mammal that ever lived. It now hangs on as a remnant in a world increasingly dominated by the Artiodactyla, or even-toed ungulates—cows, deer, antelope, camels, hippos, giraffes, pigs, and their relatives.)

This is life's little joke. By imposing the model of the ladder upon the reality of bushes, we have guaranteed that our classic examples of evolutionary progress can only apply to unsuccessful lineages on the very brink of extermination—for we can linearize a bush only if it maintains but one surviving twig that we can falsely place at the summit of a ladder. I need hardly remind everybody that at least one other mammalian lineage, preeminent among all in our attention and concern, shares with horses the sorry state of reduction from a formerly luxuriant bush to a single surviving twig—the very property of extreme tenuousness that permits us to build a ladder reaching only to the heart of our own folly and hubris.

12 | The Chain of Reason versus the Chain of Thumbs

THE *Weekly World News*, most lurid entry in the dubious genre of shopping mall tabloids, shattered all previous records for implausibility with a recent headline: "Siamese Twins Make Themselves Pregnant." The story recounted the sad tale of a conjoined brother-sister pair from a remote Indian village (such folks never hail from Peoria, where their non-existence might be confirmed). They knew that their act was immoral, but after years of hoping in vain for ordinary partners, and in the depths of loneliness and frustration, they finally succumbed to an ever-present temptation. The story is heart-rending, but faces one major obstacle to belief: All Siamese twins are monozygotic, formed from a single fertilized egg that failed to split completely in the act of twinning. Thus, Siamese twins are either both male or both female.

I will, however, praise the good people at *Weekly World News* for one slight scruple. They did realize that they had created a problem with this ludicrous tale, and they did not shrink from the difficulty. The story acknowledged that, indeed, Siamese twins generally share the same sex, but held that this Indian pair had been formed, uniquely and differently, from two eggs that had fused! Usually, however, *Weekly World News* doesn't even bother with minimal cover-ups. Recently, for example, they ran a screaming headline about a monster from Mars, just sighted in a telescope and now on its way to earth. The accompanying photo of the monster showed a perfectly ordinary chambered nautilus (an odd-looking and unfamiliar creature to be sure). I mean, they didn't even bother to retouch the photo or to hide in any way their absurd transmogrification of a marine mollusk into an extraterrestrial marauder!

The sad moral of this tale lies not with the practices of *Weekly World News*, but with the nature of a readership that permits such a publication to prosper—for if *Weekly World News* could not rely, with complete confidence, on the ignorance of its consumers, the paper would be exposed and discredited. The Siamese twin story at least showed a modicum of respect for the credulity of readers; the tale of the Martian monster records utter contempt both for the consuming public and for truth in general.

We like to cite an old motto of our culture on the factual and ethical value of veracity: "And ye shall know the truth, and the truth shall make you free" (John 8:32). But ignorance has always prospered, serving the purposes of demagogues and profit-mongers. An overly optimistic account might try to link our increasing factual knowledge with the suppression of cruelties and abuses ranging from execution for witchcraft to human sacrifice for propitiating deities. But this hope cannot be sustained, for no century has exceeded our own in quantity of imposed cruelty (as "improvements" in the technology of genocide and warfare more than balance any overall gains in sensibility). Moreover, despite a great spread in the availability of education, the favored irrationalisms of the ages show no signs of abatement. Presidential calendars are still set by astrologers, while charlatans do a brisk business in necklaces made of colored glass masquerading as crystals that supposedly bathe believers in a salutary and intangible "energy." An astounding percentage of "educated" Americans think that the earth might be less than 10,000 years old, even while their own kids delight in dinosaurs at the local museum.

The champions of beleaguered rationalism—all heroes in my book—have been uncovering charlatans throughout the ages: from Elijah denouncing the prophets of Baal to Houdini exposing the tricks of mediums to James Randi on the trail of modern hoaxers and hucksters. Obviously, we have not won the war, but we have developed effective battle strategies—and would have triumphed long ago were our foe not able, like the Lernean Hydra, to grow several new heads every time we lop one off. Still, tales of past victories—including the story of this essay—are not only useful as spurs of encouragement; they also teach us effective methods of attack. For reason is timeless, and its application to unfamiliar contexts can be particularly instructive.

How many of us realize that we are invoking a verbal remnant of "the greatest vogue of the 1780s" (according to historian Robert Darnton) when we claim to be "mesmerized" by a wonderful concert or a beautiful sunset? Franz Anton Mesmer was a German physician who had acquired wealth through marriage to a well-endowed widow; connections by assiduous cultivation (Mozart,* a valued friend, had staged the first performance of his comic opera *Bastien und Bastienne* at Mesmer's private theater); and renown with a bizarre, if fascinating, theory of "animal magnetism" and its role in human health. In 1778, Mesmer transferred to Paris, then the most "open" and vibrant capital of Europe, a city embracing the odd mixture so often spawned by liberty—intellectual ferment of the highest order combined with quackery at its most abject: Voltaire among the fortune tellers; Benjamin Franklin surrounded by astrologers; Antoine Lavoisier amidst the spiritualists.

Mesmer, insofar as one can find coherence in his ideas at all, claimed that a single (and subtle) fluid pervaded the universe, uniting and connecting all bodies. We give different names to this fluid according to its various manifestations: gravity for planets in their courses; electricity in a thunderstorm; magnetism for navigation by compass. The same fluid flows through organisms and

---

*I thank Gerald A. Le Boff and Ernest F. Marmorek for informing me, after reading this essay at its initial publication, of another explicit link between Mozart (and his great librettist, DaPonte) and Mesmer. In *Cosi Fan Tutte,* the maid Despina, disguised as a physician, "cures" Ferrando and Guglielmo of their feigned illness by touching their foreheads with a large magnet and then gently stroking the length of their bodies. An orchestral tremolo recalls the curing mesmeric crisis, while Despina describes her magnet as:

> pietra Mesmerica
> ch'ebbe l'origine
> nell' Alemagna
> che poi si celebre
> lá in Francia fù.

—a mesmeric stone that had its origin in Germany and then was so famous in France (a fine epitome of Mesmer's tactic and its geographic history).

may be called animal magnetism. A blockage of this flow causes disease, and cure requires a reestablishment of the flux and a restoration of equilibrium. (Mesmer himself never went so far as to ascribe all bodily ills to blocked magnetism, but several disciples held this extreme view, and such a motto came to characterize the mesmeric movement: "There is only one illness and one healing.")

Cure of illness requires the intervention of an "adept," a person with unusually strong magnetism who can locate the "poles" of magnetic flow on the exterior of a human body and, by massaging these areas, break the blockage within to reestablish the normal flux. When working one on one, Mesmer would sit directly opposite his patient, establishing the proper contact and flow by holding the sufferer's knees within his own, touching fingers, and staring directly into her face (most patients were women, thus adding another dimension to charges of exploitation). Mesmer, by all accounts, was a most charismatic man—and we need no great psychological sophistication to suspect that he might have produced effects more by power of suggestion than by flow of any fluid.

In any case, the effects could be dramatic. Within a few minutes of mesmerizing, sensitive patients would fall into a characteristic "crisis" taken by Mesmer as proof of his method. Bodies would begin to shake, arms and legs move violently and involuntarily, teeth chatter loudly. Patients would grimace, groan, babble, scream, faint, and fall unconscious. Several repetitions of these treatments would reestablish magnetic equilibrium and produce cures. Mesmer carried sheaves of testimonials claiming recovery from a variety of complaints. Even his most determined critics did not deny all cures, but held that Mesmer had only relieved certain psychosomatic illnesses by the power of suggestion and had produced no physical effects with his putative universal fluid.

Mesmer's popularity required the development of methods for treating large numbers of patients simultaneously (such a procedure didn't hurt profits either), and Mesmer imposed high charges, in two senses, upon his mostly aristocratic crowd. Moreover, as a master of manipulation, Mesmer surely recognized the social value of treatment in groups—both the reinforcing effect of numerous crises and the simple value of conviviality in spread-

A patient falls into a Mesmeric crisis as the eponymous hero himself performs a cure. THE BETTMANN ARCHIVE.

ing any vogue as a joint social event and medical cure. Mesmer therefore began to magnetize inanimate objects and to use these charged bodies as instruments of unblocking and cure.

Many contemporary descriptions and drawings of Mesmer's sessions depict the same basic scene. Mesmer placed a large vat, called a *baquet,* in the center of a room. He then filled the *baquet* with "magnetized" water and, sometimes, a layer of iron filings as well. Some twenty thin metal rods protruded from the *baquet.* A patient would grab hold of a rod and apply it to the mesmeric poles of his body. To treat more than twenty, Mesmer would loop a rope from those who surrounded the *baquet* (and held the iron rods) to others in the room, taking care that the rope contained no knots, for such constrictions impeded the flux. Patients would then form a "mesmeric chain" by holding a neighbor's left thumb between their own right thumb and forefinger, while extending their own left thumb to the next patient down the line. By squeezing a neighbor's left thumb, magnetic impulses could be sent all the way down the chain.

Mesmer, whether consciously or not, surely exploited both the art and politics of psychosomatic healing. Everything in his curing room was carefully arranged to maximize results, efficiency, and profit. He installed mirrors to reflect the action and encourage mass response; he heightened the effect with music played on the ethereal tones of a glass harmonica, the instrument that Benjamin Franklin had developed; he employed assistants to carry convulsive patients into a "crisis room" lined with mattresses, lest they should hurt themselves in their frenzy. To avoid the charge of profitmongering among the rich alone, Mesmer provided a poor man's cure by magnetizing trees and inviting the indigent to take their relief gratis and alfresco.

I don't want to commit the worst historical error of wrenching a person from his own time and judging him by modern standards and categories. Thus, Franz Mesmer was not Uri Geller teleported to 1780. For one thing, historical records of Mesmer are scanty, and we do not even know whether he was a simple charlatan, purveying conscious fakery for fame and profit, or a sincere believer, deluded no less than his patients in mistaking the power of suggestion for the physical effects of an actual substance. For another, the lines between science and pseudoscience were not so clearly drawn in Mesmer's time. A strong group of rationalists was laboring to free science from speculation, system building, and untestable claims about universal harmonies. But their campaign also demonstrates that all-embracing and speculative systems were still viewed by many scholars as legitimate parts of science in the eighteenth century. Robert Darnton, who has written the best modern book on mesmerism, describes the French intellectual world of the 1780s (*Mesmerism and the End of the Enlightenment in France*, 1968):

They looked out on a world so different from our own that we can hardly perceive it; for our view is blocked by our own cosmologies assimilated, knowingly or not, from the scientists and philosophers of the 19th and 20th centuries. In the 18th century, the view of literate Frenchmen opened upon a splendid, baroque universe, where their gaze rode on waves of invisible fluid into realms of infinite speculation.

Still, whatever the differing boundaries and cultural assumptions, the fact remains that Mesmer based his system on specific claims about fluids, their modes of flow, and their role in causing and curing human disease—claims subject to test by the ordinary procedures of experimental science. The logic of argument has a universality that transcends culture, and late eighteenth century debunking differs in no substantial way from the modern efforts. Indeed, I write this essay because the most celebrated analysis of mesmerism, the report of the Royal Commission of 1784, is a masterpiece of the genre, an enduring testimony to the power and beauty of reason.

Mesmerism became such a craze in the 1780s that many institutions began to worry and retaliate. Conventional medicine, which offered so little in the way of effective treatment, was running scared. Empirical and experimental scientists viewed Mesmer as a throwback to the worst excesses of speculation. People in power feared the irrationalism, the potential for sexual license, the possibility that Mesmer's mass sessions might rupture boundaries between social classes. Moreover, Mesmer had many powerful friends in high circles, and his disturbing ideas might spread by export. (Mesmer counted Lafayette among his most ardent disciples. King Louis XVI asked Lafayette before he departed for America in 1784: "What will Washington think when he learns that you have become Mesmer's chief journeyman apothecary?" Lafayette did proselytize for Mesmer on our shores, although Thomas Jefferson actively opposed him. Lafayette even visited a group of Shakers, thinking that they had discovered a form of mesmerism in their religious dances.)

The mesmeric vogue became sufficiently serious that Louis XVI was persuaded to establish a Royal Commission in 1784 to evaluate the claims of animal magnetism. The commission was surely stacked against Mesmer, but it proceeded with scrupulous fairness and thoroughness. Never in history has such an extraordinary and luminous group been gathered together in the service of rational inquiry by the methods of experimental science. For this reason alone, the *Rapport des commissaires chargés par le roi de l'examen du magnétisme animal* (Report of the Commissioners Charged by the King to Examine Animal Magnetism) is a key document in the history of human reason. It should be rescued from its current obscurity, translated into all languages, and reprinted by organizations dedicated to the unmasking of quackery and the defense of rational thought.

The commissioners included several of France's leading physicians and scientists, but two names stand out: Benjamin Franklin and Antoine Lavoisier. (Franklin served as titular head of the commission, signed the report first, and designed and performed several of the experiments; Lavoisier was the commission's guiding spirit and probably wrote the final report.) The conjunction may strike some readers as odd, but no two men could have been more appropriate or more available. Franklin lived in Paris, as official representative of our newborn nation, from 1776 to 1785. American intellectuals sometimes underestimate Franklin's status, assuming perhaps that we revere him *faute de mieux* and for parochial reasons—and that he was really a pipsqueak and amateur among the big boys of Europe. Not at all. Franklin was a universally respected scholar and a great, world-class scientist in an age when nearly all practitioners were technically amateurs. As the world's leading expert on electricity—a supposed manifestation of Mesmer's universal fluid—Franklin was an obvious choice for the commission. His interest also extended to smaller details, in particular to Mesmer's use of the glass harmonica (Franklin's own invention) as an auxiliary in the precipitation of crises. As for Lavoisier, he ranks as one of the half-dozen greatest scientific geniuses of all time: He wrote with chilling clarity, and he thought with commanding rigor. If the membership contains any odd or ironic conjunction, I would point rather to the inclusion of Dr. Guillotin among the physicians—for Lavoisier would die, ten years later, under the knife that bore the good doctor's name (see Essay 24).

The experimental method is often oversold or promulgated as

the canonical, or even the only, mode of science. As a natural historian, I have often stressed and reported the different approaches used in explaining unique and complex historical events—aspects of the world that cannot be simulated in laboratories or predicted from laws of nature (see my book *Wonderful Life*, 1989). Moreover, the experimental method is fundamentally conservative, not innovative—a set of procedures for evaluating and testing ideas that originate in other ways. Yet, despite these caveats about nonexclusivity and limited range, the experimental method is a tool of unparalleled power in its appropriate (and large) domain.

Lavoisier, Franklin, and colleagues conclusively debunked Mesmer by applying the tools of their experimental craft, tried and true: standardization of complex situations to delineate possible causal factors, repetition of experiments with control and variation, and separation and independent testing of proposed causes. The mesmerists never recovered, and their leader and namesake soon hightailed it out of Paris for good, although he continued to live in adequate luxury, if with reduced fame and prestige, until 1815. Just a year after the commission's report, Thomas Jefferson, replacing Franklin as American representative in Paris, noted in his journal: "animal magnetism dead, ridiculed." (Jefferson was overly optimistic, for irrationalism born of hope never dies; still, the report of Franklin and Lavoisier was probably the key incident that turned the tide of opinion—a subtle fluid far more palpable and powerful than animal magnetism—against Mesmer.)

The commissioners began with a basic proposition to guide their testing: "Animal magnetism might well exist without being useful, but it cannot be useful if it doesn't exist." Yet, any attempt to affirm the existence of animal magnetism faced an intense and immediate frustration: The mesmerists insisted that their subtle fluid had no tangible or measurable attributes. Imagine the chagrin of a group of eminent physical scientists trying to test the existence of a fluid without physical properties! They wrote, with the barely concealed contempt that makes Lavoisier's report both a masterpiece of rhetoric and an exemplar of experimental method (the two are not inconsistent because fair and scrupulous procedures do not demand neutrality, but only strict adherence to the rules of the craft):

It didn't take the Commissioners long to recognize that this fluid escapes all sensation. It is not at all luminous and visible like electricity [the reference, of course, is to lightning before the days of "invisible" flow through modern wires]. Its action is not clearly evident, as the attraction of a magnet. It has no taste, no odor. It works without sound, and surrounds or penetrates you without warning you of its presence. If it exists in us and around us, it does so in an absolutely insensible manner. [All quotations from the commissioners' report are my translations from an original copy in Harvard's Houghton Library.]

The commissioners therefore recognized that they would have to test for the existence of animal magnetism through its effects, not its physical properties. This procedure suggested a focus either on cures or on the immediate (and dramatic) crises supposedly provoked by the flow of magnetism during Mesmer's sessions. The commissioners rejected a test of cures for three obvious and excellent reasons: Cures take too long and time was awasting as the mesmeric craze spread; cures can be caused by many factors, and the supposed effects of magnetism could not be separated from other reasons for recovery; nature, left to her own devices, relieves many ills without any human intervention. (Franklin wryly suspected that an unintended boost to nature lay at the root of Mesmer's successes. His fluid didn't exist, and his sessions produced no physical effect. But patients in his care stayed away from conventional physicians and therefore didn't take the ordinary pills and potions that undoubtedly did more harm than good and impeded natural recovery.) Mesmer, on the other hand, wanted to focus upon cures, and he refused to cooperate with the commission when they would not take his advice. The commission therefore worked in close collaboration with Mesmer's chief disciple, Charles Deslon, who attended the tests and attempted to magnetize objects and people. (Deslon's cooperation indicates that the chief mesmerists were not frauds, but misguided believers in their own system. Mesmer tried to dissociate himself from the commission's findings, arguing that Deslon was a blunderer unable to control the magnetic flux— but all to no avail, and the entire movement suffered from the exposé.)

The commissioners began by trying to magnetize themselves. Once a week, and then for three days in a row (to test a claim that such concentrated time boosted the efficiency of magnetism), they sat for two and a half hours around Deslon's *baquet* in his Paris curing room, faithfully following all the mesmeric rituals. Nobody felt a thing beyond boredom and discomfort. (I am, somehow, greatly taken by the image of these enormously talented and intensely skeptical men sitting around a *baquet,* presumably under their perukes, joined by a rope, each holding an iron rod, and "making from time to time," to quote Lavoisier, "the chain of thumbs." I can picture the scene, as Lavoisier says—Okay boys, ready? One, two, squeeze those thumbs now.)

The commissioners recognized that their own failure scarcely settled the issue, for none was seriously ill (despite Franklin's gout), and Mesmer's technique might only work on sick people with magnetic blockages. Moreover, they acknowledged that their own skepticism might be impeding a receptive state of mind. They therefore tested seven "common" people with assorted complaints and then, in a procedure tied to the social assumptions of the *ancien régime,* seven sufferers from the upper classes, reasoning that people of higher status would be less subject, by their refinement and general superiority, to the power of suggestion. The results supported power of suggestion as the cause of crises, rather than physical effects of a fluid. Only five of fourteen subjects noted any results, and only three—all from the lower classes—experienced anything severe enough to label as a crisis. "Those who belong to a more elevated class, endowed with more light, and more capable of recognizing their sensations, experienced nothing." Interestingly, two commoners who felt nothing—a child and a young retarded woman—might be judged less subject to the power of suggestion, but not less able to experience the flow of a fluid, if it existed.

These preliminaries brought the commissioners to the crux of their experiments. They had proceeded by progressive elimination and concentration on a key remaining issue. They had hoped to test for physical evidence of the fluid itself, but could not and chose instead to concentrate on its supposed effects. They had decided that immediate reactions rather than long-term cures must form the focus of experiments. They had tried the standard techniques on themselves, without result. They had given mesmerists the benefit of all doubt by using the same methods on people with illnesses and inclined to accept the mesmeric system—still without positive results. The investigation now came down to a single question, admirably suited for experimental resolution: The undoubted crises that mesmerists could induce might be caused by one of two factors (or perhaps both)—the psychological power of suggestion or the physical action of a fluid.

The experimental method demands that the two possible causes be separated in controlled situations. People must be subjected to the power of suggestion but not magnetized, and then magnetized but not subject to suggestion. These separations demanded a bit of honorable duplicity from the commissioners—for they needed to tell people that nonmagnetized objects were really full of mesmeric fluid (suggestion without physical cause), and then magnetize people without letting them know (physical cause without suggestion).

In a clever series of experiments, designed mainly by Lavoisier and carried out at Franklin's home in Passy, the commissioners made the necessary separations and achieved a result as clear as any in the history of debunking: Crises are caused by suggestion; not a shred of evidence exists for any fluid, and animal magnetism, as a physical force, must be firmly rejected.

For the separation of suggestion from magnetism, Franklin asked Deslon to magnetize one of five trees in his garden. A young man, certified by Deslon as particularly sensitive to magnetism, was led to embrace each tree in turn, but not told about the smoking gun. He reported increasing strength of magnetization in each successive tree and finally fell unconscious in a classic mesmeric crisis before the fourth tree. Only the fifth, however, had been magnetized by Deslon! Mesmerists rejected the result, arguing that all trees have some natural magnetization anyway, and that Deslon's presence in the garden might have enhanced the effect. But Lavoisier replied scornfully:

> But then, a person sensitive to magnetization would not be able to chance a walk in a garden without the risk of suffering convulsions, and such an assertion is therefore denied by ordinary, everyday experience.

Nevertheless, the commissioners persisted with several other experiments, all leading to the same conclusion—that suggestion without magnetism could easily produce full-scale mesmeric crises. They blindfolded a woman and told her that Deslon was in the room, filling her with magnetism. He was nowhere near, but the woman had a classic crisis. They then tested the patient without a blindfold, telling her that Deslon was in the next room directing the fluid at her. He was not, but she had a crisis. In both cases, the woman was not magnetized or even touched, but her crises were intense.

Lavoisier conducted another experiment at his home in the Arsenal (where he worked as Commissioner of Gunpowder, having helped America's revolution with matériel, as much as Lafayette had aided with men). Several porcelain cups were filled with water, one supposedly strongly magnetized. A particularly sensitive woman who, in anticipation, had already experienced a crisis in Lavoisier's antechamber, received each cup in turn. She began to quiver after touching the second cup and fell into a full crisis upon receiving the fourth. When she recovered and asked for a cup of water, the foxy Lavoisier finally passed her the magnetized liquid. This time, she not only held, but actually imbibed, although "she drank tranquilly and said that she felt relieved."

The commissioners then proceeded to the reverse test of magnetizing without unleashing the power of suggestion. They removed the door between two rooms at Franklin's home and replaced it with a paper partition (offering no bar at all, according to Deslon, to the flow of mesmeric fluid). They induced a young seamstress, a woman with particularly acute sensitivity to magnetism, to sit next to the partition. From the other side, but unknown to the seamstress, an adept magnetizer tried for half an hour to fill her with fluid and induce a crisis, but "during all this time, Miss B . . . made gay conversation; asked about her health, she freely answered that she felt very well." Yet, when the magnetizer entered the room, and his presence became known (while acting from an equal or greater distance), the seamstress began to convulse after three minutes and fell into a full crisis in twelve minutes.

The evident finding, after so many conclusive experiments—that no evidence exists for Mesmer's fluid and that all noted effects may be attributed to the power of imagination—seems almost anticlimactic, and the commissioners offered their result with clarity and brevity: "The practice of magnetization is the art of increasing the imagination by degrees." Lavoisier then ended the report with a brilliant analysis of the reasons for such frequent vogues of irrationalism throughout human history. He cited two major causes, or predisposing factors of the human mind and heart. First, our brains just don't seem to be well equipped for reasoning by probability. Fads find their most fertile ground in subjects, like the curing of disease, that require a separation of many potential causes and an assessment of probability in judging the value of a result:

> The art of concluding from experience and observation consists in evaluating probabilities, in estimating if they are high or numerous enough to constitute proof. This type of calculation is more complicated and more difficult than one might think. It demands a great sagacity generally above the power of common people. The success of charlatans, sorcerers, and alchemists—and all those who abuse public credulity—is founded on errors in this type of calculation.

I would alter only Lavoisier's patrician assumption that ordinary folks cannot master this mode of reasoning—and write instead that most people surely can but, thanks to poor education and lack of encouragement from general culture, do not. The end result is the same—riches for Las Vegas and disappointment for Pete Rose. But at least the modern view does not condemn us to a permanent and inevitable status as saps, dupes, and dunces.

Second, whatever our powers of abstract reasoning, we are also prisoners of our hopes. So long as life remains disappointing and cruel for so many people, we shall be prey to irrationalisms that promise relief. Lavoisier regarded his countrymen as more sophisticated than previous suckers of centuries past, but still victims of increasingly sly manipulators (nothing has changed today, as the Gellers and von Danikens remain one step ahead of their ever-gullible disciples):

> This theory [mesmerism] is presented today with the more imposing apparatus [I presume that Lavoisier means both ideas and contraptions] necessary in our more enlightened

century—but it is no less false. Man seizes, abandons, but then commits again the errors that flatter him.

Since hope is an ever-present temptress in a world of woe, mesmerism "attracts people by the two hopes that touch them the most: that of knowing the future and that of prolonging their days."

Lavoisier then drew an apt parallel between the communal crises of mesmeric sessions and the mass emotionalism so often exploited by demagogues and conquerors throughout history— *"l'enthousiasme du courage"* (enthusiasm of courage) or *"l'unité d'ivresse"* (unity of intoxication). Generals elicit this behavior by sounding drums and playing bugles; promoters by hiring a claque to begin and direct the applause after performances; demagogues by manipulating the mob.

Lavoisier's social theory offered no solution to the destructive force of irrationalism beyond a firm and continuing hegemony of the educated elite. (As my one criticism of the commissioners' report, Lavoisier and colleagues could see absolutely nothing salutary, in any conceivable form, in the strong emotionalism of a mesmeric crisis. They did not doubt the power of the psyche to cure, but as sons of the Enlightenment, children of the Age of Reason, they proclaimed that only a state of calm and cheerfulness could convey any emotional benefit to the afflicted. In this restriction, they missed an important theme of human complexity and failed to grasp the potential healing effect of many phenomena that call upon the wilder emotions—from speaking in tongues to catharsis in theatrical performance to aspects of Freudian psychoanalysis. In this sense, some Freudians view Mesmer as a worthy precursor with a key insight into human nature. I hesitate to confer such status upon a man who attained great wealth from something close to quackery—but I see the point.)

I envision no easy solution either, but I adopt a less pessimistic attitude than Lavoisier. Human nature is flexible enough to avert the baleful effects of intoxicated unity, and history shows that revolutionary enthusiasm need not devolve into hatred and mass murder. Consider Franklin and Lavoisier one last time. Our revolution remained in the rational hands of numerous Franklins, Jeffersons, and Washingtons; France descended from the Declaration of the Rights of Man into the Reign of Terror. (I do recognize the different situations, particularly the greater debt of hatred, based on longer and deeper oppression, necessarily discharged by the new rulers of France. Still, no inevitability attended the excesses fanned by mass emotionalism.) In other words:

> Antoine Lavoisier
> Lost his head
> Benjamin Franklin
> Died in bed.

From which, I think, we can only conclude that Mr. Franklin understood a thing or two when he remarked, speaking of his fellow patriots, but extended here to all devotees of reason, that we must either hang together or hang separately.

5 | Art and Science

13 | Madame Jeanette

THIRTY YEARS AGO, on April 30, 1958, to be exact, I sat with 250 students facing one of the most formidable men of our generation—Peter J. Wilhousky, director of music in the New York City schools and conductor of the New York All-City High School Chorus. As the warm, and primarily parental, applause receded at the concert's end, Wilhousky returned to the podium of Carnegie Hall, gestured for silence, and raised his baton to conduct the traditional encore, "Madame Jeanette." Halfway through, he turned and, without missing a beat (to invoke a cliché in its appropriate, literal sense), smiled to acknowledge the chorus alumni who stood at their seats or surrounded the podium, singing with their current counterparts. These former members seemed so ancient to me—though none had passed forty, for the chorus itself was then only twenty years old—and their solidarity moved me to a rare fit of tears at a time when teenage boys did not cry in public.

"Madame Jeanette" is a dangerous little piece, for it ventures so near the edge of cloying sentimentality. It tells the tale, in close four-part a cappella harmony, of a French widow who sits at her door by day and at her window by night. There she thinks only of her husband, killed so many years before on the battlefield of St. Pierre, and dreams of the day that they will be reunited at the cemetery of Père Lachaise. With 250 teenagers and sloppy conducting, "Madame Jeanette" becomes a maudlin and embarrassing tearfest. Wilhousky, ever the perfectionist, ever the rationalist, somehow steered to the right side of musicality, and ended each concert with integrity and control.

"Madame Jeanette" was our symbol of continuity. For a very insecure boy, singing second bass on the brink of manhood, "Madame Jeanette" offered another wonderful solace. It ends, for the basses, on a low D-flat, just about as far down the scale as any composer would dare ask a singer to venture. Yes, I knew even then that low did not mean masculine, or capable, or mature, or virile—but that fundament resonated with hope and possibility, even in pianissimo.

Len and I met at the bus stop every Saturday morning at 7:30, took the Q17 to 169th Street and the subway to Lexington Avenue, walked uptown along the line of the old Third Avenue El, and arrived at Julia Richman High School just in time for the 9 A.M. rehearsal.

We lived, thirty years ago, in an age of readier obedience, but I still marvel at the discipline that Wilhousky could maintain with his mixture of awe (inspired) and terror (promulgated). He forged our group of blacks from Harlem, Puerto Ricans from the great migration then in progress, Jews from Queens, and Italians from Staten Island into a responsive singing machine. He worked, in part, through intimidation by public ridicule. One day, he stopped the rehearsal and pointed to the tenor section, saying: "You, third row, fourth seat, stand up. You're singing flat. Ten years ago, Julius La Rosa sat in that same seat—and sang flat. And he's still singing flat." (Memory is a curious trickster. La Rosa, in a recent *New Yorker* profile, states that Wilhousky praised him in the same forum for singing so true to pitch. But I know what I heard. Or is the joke on me?) Each year, he cashiered a member or two for talking or giggling—in public, and with no hope of mercy or reinstatement.

But Peter Wilhousky had another side that inspired us all and conveyed the most important lesson of intellectual life. He was one of the finest choral conductors in America, yet he chose to spend every Saturday morning with high school kids. His only rule, tacit but pervasive, proclaimed: "No compromises." We could sing, with proper training and practice, as well as any group in America—nothing else would be tolerated or even conceptualized. Anything less would not be worth doing at all. I had encountered friendliness, grace, kindness, animation, clarity, and dedication among my teachers, but I had never even considered the notion that unqualified excellence could emerge from anything touched or made by students. The idea, however, is infectious. As I worked with Wilhousky, I slowly personalized the dream that excellence in one activity might be extended to become the pattern, or at least the goal, of an actual life.

Len phoned me a few months ago and suggested that we attend this year's concert, the thirtieth since our valedictory. I hesitated for two reasons. I feared that my memory of excellence would not be supported by reality, and I didn't relish the role of a graybeard from springs long past, standing and singing "Madame Jeanette" from the audience, should that peculiar tradition still be honored. But sentiment and curiosity prevailed, and we went.

Yes, Heraclitus, you cannot step twice into the same river. The raw material remains—talented kids of all colors, shapes, backgrounds. But the goal has been inverted. Wilhousky tried to mold all this diversity into the uncompromising, single standard of elite culture as expressed in the classical repertory for chorus and orchestra. In the auditorium of Julia Richman High School, before his arrival, we used to form small pickup groups to sing the latest rock-and-roll numbers. But when our sentinels spotted the maestro, they quickly spread the alarm and dead silence descended. Wilhousky claimed that rock-and-roll encouraged poor habits of voice and pitch, and he would expel anyone caught singing the stuff in his bailiwick.

Diversity has now triumphed, and the forbidden fruit of our era has become the entire first part of the program. The concert began with the All-City marching band, complete with drum major, baton twirlers, and flag carriers. Then the All-City jazz ensemble.

A full concert and two hours later, the orchestra and chorus finally received their turn. Not only has the number of ensembles expanded to respect the diversity of tastes and inclinations in our polyglot city, but each group has also retained a distinctive signature. Blacks predominate in the chorus; the string sections of the orchestra are overwhelmingly Asian. The chorus is now led by Edith Del Valle, a tall, stunning woman who heads the vocal department at Fiorello H. La Guardia High School of the Arts. (As a single sign of continuity, Anna Ext still coaches the sopranos, as she did in our day and has for thirty-two years. How can we convey adequate praise to a woman who has devoted so much, for so long, to a voluntary, weekend organization—except to say that our language contains no word more noble than "teacher"?)

The chorus still sings the same basic repertory—Randall Thompson's "Alleluia," Wilhousky's own arrangement of "The Battle Hymn of the Republic," some Bach and Beethoven, and an Irving Berlin medley for the season of his centennial.

How good are they, and how good were we? Was Wilhousky's insistence on full professionalism just a vain conceit? They sing by memory, and therefore (since eyes can be fixed on the conductor), with uncanny precision and unanimity. But I demur for two reasons. First, the sound, though lovely in raw quality, is so emotionless, as though text and style of composition have no influence upon interpretation. Perhaps we sang in the same manner. The soul of these classics may not be accessible before the legal age of drinking, driving, and voting.

But my second reservation troubles me more. The chorus is terribly unbalanced, with 129 women and only 31 men. The tenors are reduced to astringent shouting as the evening wears on. This cannot be by design, and can only mean that the chorus is not attracting anywhere near the requisite number of male applicants. Thirteen of the 31 men hail from the conductor's own specialty school, La Guardia High. Have they been pressed into desperate service? In our chorus, all sections were balanced. We clamored in our local high schools for the strictly limited right to audition, and fewer than half the applicants succeeded.

I mused upon these inadequacies as the evening wore on (and the tenors tired). The expanded diversity of bands and jazz is both exciting and a proper testimony to cultural pluralism. The relaxed attitude of performers contrasts pleasantly with the rigid formalism and nervousness of our era (I could have died in a spectacular backward plunge off the top riser of Carnegie Hall when I felt the chair's rearward creep, but didn't dare stop to fidget and readjust).

But has the evening's diversity and spontaneous joy pushed aside Wilhousky's uncompromising excellence? Can the two ideals, each so important in itself, coexist at all? And if not, whatever shall we do to keep alive that harsh vision of the best of the greatest?

But if I felt this single trouble amidst my pleasure, at least I wouldn't have to worry about "Madame Jeanette" in this new river. Surely, that tradition had evaporated, and I would not have to face brightness and acne from the depths of advancing middle age in the fifteenth row. After all, "Madame Jeanette" is a quiet classical piece for chorus alone—and the chorus no longer holds pride of place among the various ensembles.

I applauded warmly after the finale, pleasure only slightly tinged with a conceptual sort of sadness, and then turned to leave. But Edith Del Valle strode out from the wings and, with a presence fully equal to Wilhousky's, stepped onto the podium—to conduct "Madame Jeanette." Old members scurried to the front. Len and I looked at each other and, without exchanging a word, rose in unison.

No tears. We are both still terrified of Wilhousky's wrath, and his ghost surely stood on that stage, watching carefully for any sign of inattention or departure from pitch. This time, the chorus sang exquisitely, for "Madame Jeanette" succeeds by precision or fails by overinvolvement. The imbalance of sections does not affect such a quiet song, while its honest, but simple, sentimentality can be encompassed by the high-school soul.

Edith Del Valle, the black woman from La Guardia High, blended with her absolute opposite, the silver-haired Slavic aristocrat, Peter J. Wilhousky. The discipline and precision of her chorus—their species of excellence—had triumphed to convert the potentially maudlin into thoughtful dignity for tradition's sake. It was a pleasure to make music with her. If youth and age can produce such harmony, there must be hope for pluralism *and* excellence—but only if we can recover, and fully embrace, Wilhousky's dictum: No compromises.

I learned something else at this final celebration of continuity, something every bit as important to me, if only parochially: I can still hit that low D-flat. Father Lachaise may be beckoning, but "Madame Jeanette" and I are still hanging tough and young in our separate ways.

Postscript

This essay, which first appeared in the *New York Times Magazine*, unleashed a flood of reminiscence by correspondence, mostly from former chorus members and others who knew Peter Wil-housky. I was regaled with many sweet memories, particularly of our custom in jamming subway cars after leaving the rehearsals *en masse* and singing (generally to the keen surprise and enjoyment of passengers) until the accumulating departures of homebound choristers reduced our ranks to less than four-part harmony. But one theme, in its several guises, pervaded all the letters and rein-forced the serious, and decidedly nonsentimental, *raison d'être* of this essay—Wilhousky's commitment to excellence and its impact upon us. One woman wrote from a generation before mine:

> Mr. Wilhousky was my music teacher and mentor 55 years ago when I was a student at New Utrecht High in Brooklyn. We had an outstanding choir that won every competition in my four years at the school. How we adored and esteemed this wonderful man who by the way we were sure was a prince: so handsome and aristocratic. He was then, as well as you say later, a stickler for seriousness, discipline, and dedication to our work. He encouraged those of us with some talent to continue our studies and many of us did.

Another who sang in the chorus five years before me said:

> What memories you stirred for me, and brought forth some tears too. Only another choir member could share how spe-cial those rehearsals and concerts were. Just to be chosen to audition was an honor. . . . Madame Jeanette is turning around in my head now. I recall teaching the bass part to my kid brother so that we could sing. I've taught it to my hus-band and kids too. I was in awe of Peter J. Wilhousky. Disci-pline was never a problem in this group. How we loved to sing!

And from ten years after my watch:

> Today I am a professional singer in Philadelphia, having sung with umpteen college groups, choruses, community theaters, opera workshops, etc., but nothing will ever match that full-bodied enthusiastic blend of voices I remember now so well. My children poked gentle fun at me today as I

waxed enthusiastic over your story and they listened to INXS on their Walkmans as I hummed Madame Jeanette over and over again.

And finally, from a Wilhousky counterpart in Portland, Oregon: "The taste of excellence is the hook. The kids never forget—as you obviously have not."

This accumulated weight of testimony made me reassess the tone of the essay itself. I now think that I was a bit too ecumenically forgiving of the chorus's present insufficiencies. We probably were very good (if not quite so subtle and professional as clouds of memory suggest); in any case, the ideal of uncompromising excellence certainly pervaded our concepts and did pass down into our subsequent lives. I don't see how the present chorus can be engendering such an attitude with an appeal so feeble that male singers must be dredged up rather than turned away after dreaming, scheming, and begging for a chance (as we did). This is simply too great a loss for any gain in diversity or relaxation. Islands of excellence are too rare and precious in our world of mediocrity; any erosion and foundering is tragic.

Finally, for I really do not wish to end a sweet story on a sour note, may I report Julius La Rosa's version of his incident with Wilhousky. He writes in a letter of November 17, 1988, that the chorus was rehearsing "Begin the Beguine" (during his tenure in the late 1940s). Wilhousky wanted the men to sing with a cello-like tone. La Rosa writes:

> I swear to you, I can still see him holding an imaginary cello, his left hand on the neck, fingers pressing down on the strings and vibrating to achieve the desired tremolo. But we weren't getting it so he told us to stand up, *individually,* and sing the phrase. My turn. I sang it. He asked me to do it again, then exclaimed, "That's it!" And all I remember after that was walking back to the subway with Jeanette feeling seven feet tall.

La Rosa was also gracious enough to add: "And yes, though time does distort the memory, I wouldn't be surprised if I was flat the day he, Mr. Wilhousky, singled me out. I was terrified—and probably didn't take a good deep breath!!" (Actually, I don't doubt for a moment that both La Rosa's version and what I heard ten years later from Wilhousky are entirely accurate. We scarcely need *Rashomon* to teach us that rich events are remembered for different parts and different emphases—so that equally accurate, but partial versions yield almost contradictory impressions.)

And if La Rosa's reference to Jeanette (*not* Madame) puzzled you, let me close with his ultimate touché from earlier in his letter:

> All-City Chorus was an enchantment. . . . And lucky, too, I was 'cause I could walk from the subway along Third Avenue with Jeanette—Yes! Jeanette Caponegro, second alto—while you were stuck with Len!

14 | Red Wings in the Sunset

TEDDY ROOSEVELT borrowed an African proverb to construct his motto: Speak softly, but carry a big stick. In 1912, a critic turned Roosevelt's phrase against him, castigating the old Roughrider for trying to demolish an opponent by rhetoric alone: "Ridicule is a powerful weapon and the temptation to use it unsparingly is a strong one. . . . Even if we don't agree with him [Roosevelt's opponent], it is not necessary either to cut him into little pieces or to break every bone in his body with the 'big stick.' "

This criticism appeared in the midst of Roosevelt's presidential campaign (when he split the Republican party by trying to wrest the nomination from William Howard Taft, then formed his own Progressive, or Bull Moose, party to contest the election, thereby scattering the Republican vote and bringing victory to Democrat Woodrow Wilson). Surely, therefore, the statement must record one of Roosevelt's innumerable squabbles during a tough political year. It does not. Francis H. Allen published these words in an ornithological journal, *The Auk.* He was writing about flamingos.

When, as a cynical and posturing teenager, I visited Mount Rushmore, I gazed with some approval at the giant busts of Washington, Jefferson, and Lincoln, and then asked as so many others have—what in hell is Teddy Roosevelt doing up there? Never again shall I question his inclusion, for I have just discovered something sufficiently remarkable to warrant a sixty-foot stone likeness all by itself. In 1911, an ex-president of the United States, after seven exhausting years in office, and in the throes of preparing his political comeback, found time to write and publish a technical scientific article, more than one hundred pages long: "Revealing and Concealing Coloration in Birds and Mammals."

Roosevelt wrote his article to demolish a theory proposed by the artist-naturalist Abbott H. Thayer (and defended by Mr. Allen, who castigated Roosevelt for bringing the rough language of politics into a scientific debate). In 1896 Thayer, as I shall document in a moment, correctly elucidated the important principle of countershading (a common adaptation that confers near invisibility upon predators or prey). But he then followed a common path to perdition by slowly extending his valid theory to a doctrine of exclusivity. By 1909, Thayer was claiming that *all* animal colors, from the peacock's tail to the baboon's rump, worked primarily for concealment. As a backbreaking straw that sealed his fate and inspired Roosevelt's wrath, Thayer actually argued that natural selection made flamingos red, all the better to mimic the sunset. In the book that will stand forever as a monument to folly, to cockeyed genius, and to inspiration gone askew, Thayer stated in 1909 (in *Concealing-Coloration in the Animal Kingdom,* written largely by his son Gerald H. Thayer and published by Macmillan):

> These traditionally "showy" birds are, at their most critical moments, perfectly "obliterated" by their coloration. Conspicuous in most cases, when looked at from above, as man is apt to see them, they are wonderfully fitted for "vanishment" against the flushed, rich-colored skies of early morning and evening.

Roosevelt responded with characteristic vigor in his 1911 article:

> Among all the wild absurdities to which Mr. Thayer has committed himself, probably the wildest is his theory that flamingos are concealingly colored because their foes mistake them for sunsets. He has never studied flamingos in their haunts, he knows nothing personally of their habits or their enemies or their ways of avoiding their enemies . . . and certainly has never read anything to justify his suppositions; these suppositions represent nothing but pure guesswork, and even to call them guesswork is a little over-

conservative, for they come nearer to the obscure mental processes which are responsible for dreams.

Roosevelt's critique (and many others equally trenchant) sealed poor Thayer's fate. In 1896, Thayer had begun his campaign with praise, promise, and panache (his outdoor demonstrations of disappearing decoys became legendary). He faced the dawn of World War I in despair and dejection (though the war itself brought limited vindication as our armies used his valid ideas in theories of camouflage). He lamented to a friend that his avocation (defending his theory of concealing coloration) had sapped his career:

> Never . . . have I felt less a painter . . . I am like a man to whom is born, willy nilly, a child whose growth demanded his energies, he the while always dreaming that this growing offspring would soon go forth to seek his fortune and leave him to his profession, but the offspring again and again either unfolding some new faculties that must be nurtured and watched, or coming home and bursting into his parent's studio, bleeding and bruised by an insulted world, continued to need attention so that there was nothing for it but to lay down the brush and take him once more into one's lap.

I must end this preface to my essay with a confession. I have known about Thayer's "crazy" flamingo theory all my professional life—and for a particular reason. It is the standard example always used by professors in introductory courses to illustrate illogic and unreason, and dismissed in a sentence with the ultimate weapon of intellectual nastiness—ridicule that forecloses understanding. When I began my research for this essay, I thought that I would write about absurdity, another comment on unthinking adaptationism. But my reading unleashed a cascade of discovery, leading me to Roosevelt and, more importantly, to the real Abbott Thayer, shorn of his symbolic burden. The flamingo theory is, of course, absurd—that will not change. But how and why did Thayer get there from an excellent start that the standard dismissive anecdote, Thayer's unfortunate historical legacy, never acknowledges? The full story, if we try to understand Abbott Thayer aright, contains lessons that will more than compensate for laughter lost.

Who was Abbott Handerson Thayer anyway? I had always assumed, from the name alone, that he was an eccentric Yankee who used wealth and social postion to gain a hearing for his absurd ideas. I could find nothing about him in the several scientific books that cite the flamingo story. I was about to give up when I located his name in the *Encyclopedia Britannica*. I found, to my astonishment, that Abbott Thayer was one of the most famous painters of late nineteenth century America (and an old Yankee to be sure, but not of the wealthy line of Thayers—see the biography by Nelson G. White, *Abbott H. Thayer: Painter and Naturalist*). He specialized in ethereal women, crowned with suggestions of halos and accompanied by quintessentially innocent children. Art and science are both beset by fleeting tastes that wear poorly—far be it for me to judge. I had begun to uncover a human drama under the old pedagogical caricature.

But let us begin, as they say, at the beginning. Standard accounts of the adaptive value of animal colors use three categories to classify nature's useful patterns (no one has substantially improved upon the fine classic by Hugh B. Cott, *Adaptive Coloration in Animals,* 1940). According to Cott, adaptive colors and patterns may serve as (1) concealment (to shield an animal from predators or to hide the predator in nature's never-ending game); (2) advertisement, to scare potential predators (as in the prominent false eyespots of so many insects), to maintain territory or social position, or to announce sexual receptivity (as in baboon rump patches); and (3) disguise, as animals mimic unpalatable creatures to gain protection, or resemble an inanimate (and inedible) object (numerous leaf and stick insects, or a bittern, motionless and gazing skyward, lost amidst the reeds). Since disguise lies closer to advertisement than to concealment (a disguised animal does not try to look inconspicuous, but merely like something else), we can immediately appreciate Abbott Thayer's difficulty. He wanted to reduce all three categories to the single purpose of concealment—but fully two-thirds of all color patterns, in conventional accounts, serve the opposite function of increased visibility.

Abbott Thayer, a native of Boston, began his artistic career in the maelstrom of New York City but eventually retreated to a hermitlike existence in rural New Hampshire, where his old interests in natural history revived and deepened. As a committed Darwinian, he believed that all form and pattern must serve some crucial purpose in the unremitting struggle for existence. He also felt that, as a painter, he could interpret the colors of animals in ways and terms unknown to scientists. In 1896, Thayer published his first, landmark article in *The Auk:* "The Law Which Underlies Protective Coloration."

Of course, naturalists had recognized for centuries that many animals blend into their background and become virtually invisible—but scientists had not properly recognized how and why. They tended to think, naively (as I confess I did before my research for this essay), that protection emerged from simple matching between animal and background. But Thayer correctly identified the primary method of concealment as countershading—a device that makes creatures look flat. Animals must indeed share the right color and pattern with their background, but their ghostly disappearance records a loss of dimensionality, not just a matching of color.

In countershading, an animal's colors are precisely graded to counteract the effects of sunlight and shadow. Countershaded animals are darkest on top, where most sunlight falls, and lightest on the bottom (Thayer thereby identified the adaptive significance of light bellies—perhaps the most universal feature of animal coloration). The precise reversal between intensity of coloration and intensity of illumination neatly cancels out all shadow and produces a uniform color from top to bottom. As a result, the animal becomes flat, perfectly two-dimensional, and cannot be seen by observers who have, all their lives, perceived the substantiality of objects by shadow and shading. Artists have struggled for centuries to produce the illusion of depth and roundness on a flat canvas; nature has simply done the opposite—she shades in reverse in order to produce an illusion of flatness in a three-dimensional world.

Contrasting his novel principle of countershading with older ideas about mimicry, Thayer wrote in his original statement of 1896: "Mimicry makes an animal appear to be some other thing, whereas the newly discovered law makes him cease to appear to exist at all."

Thayer, intoxicated with the joy of discovery, attributed his success to his chosen profession and advanced a strong argument about the dangers of specialization and the particular value of "outsiders" to any field of study. He wrote in 1903: "Nature has evolved actual art on the bodies of animals, and only an artist can read it." And later, in his 1909 book, but now with the defensiveness and pugnacity that marked his retreat:

> The entire matter has been in the hands of the wrong custodians. . . . It properly belongs to the realm of pictorial art, and can be interpreted only by painters. For it deals wholly in optical illusion, and this is the very gist of a painter's life. He is born with a sense of it; and, from his cradle to his grave, his eyes, wherever they turn, are unceasingly at work on it—and his pictures live by it. What wonder, then, if it was for him alone to discover that the very art he practices is at full—beyond the most delicate precision of human powers—on almost all animals.

So far, so good. Thayer's first articles and outdoor demonstrations won praise from scientists. He began with relatively modest claims, arguing that he had elucidated the basis for a major principle of concealment but not denying that other patterns of color displayed quite different selective value. Initially, he accepted the other two traditional categories—revealing coloration and mimicry—though he always argued that concealment would gain a far bigger scope than previously admitted. In his most technical paper, published in the *Transactions of the Entomological Society of London* (1903), and introduced favorably by the great English Darwinian E. B. Poulton, Thayer wrote:

> Every possible form of advantageous adaptation must somewhere exist. . . . There must be unpalatability accompanied by warning coloration . . . and equally plain that there must be mimicry.

Indeed, Thayer sought ways to combine ideas of concealment with other categories that he would later deny. He supported, for example, the ingenious speculation of C. Hart Merriam that white rump patches are normally revealing, but that their true value lies in a deer's ability to "erase" the color at moments of danger—a deer "closes down" the patch by lowering its tail over the white blotch and then disappears, invisible, into the forest. In his 1909 book, however, Thayer explicitly repudiated this earlier interpretation and argued for pure concealment—the white patch as "sky mimicking" when seen from below.

Thayer's pathway from insight to ridicule followed a distressingly common route among intellectuals. Countershading for concealment, amidst a host of alternatives, was not enough. Thayer had to have it all. Little by little, plausibly at first, but grading slowly to red wings in the sunset, Thayer laid his battle plans (not an inappropriate metaphor for a father of camouflage). As article succeeded article, Thayer progressively invaded the categories of mimicry and revealing coloration to gain, or so he thought, more cases for concealment. Finally, nothing else remained: *All* patterns of color served to conceal. He wrote in his book: "All patterns and colors whatsoever of all animals that ever prey or are preyed upon are under certain normal circumstances obliterative."

Thayer made his first fateful step in his technical article of 1903. Here, he claimed a second major category of concealing coloration—what he called "ruptive" (we now call them "disruptive") bars, stripes, splotches, and other assorted markings. Disruptive markings make an animal "disappear" by a route different from countershading. They break an animal's coherent outline and produce an insubstantial array of curious and unrelated patches (this principle, more than countershading, became important in military camouflage). A zebra, Thayer argues, does not mimic the reeds in which it hides; rather, the stripes break the animal's outline into bars of light and darkness—and predators see no coherent prey at all.

Again, Thayer had proposed a good idea for some, even many, cases (though not for zebras, who rarely venture into fields of reeds). His 1903 article argues primarily that butterflies carry disruptive pictures of flowers and background scenery upon their wings: "The general aspect of each animal's environment," Thayer wrote, "is found painted upon his coat, in such a way as to minimize his visibility, by making the beholder think he sees *through* him."

But, amidst his good suggestions, Thayer had made his first overextended argument. Countershading could scarcely be mistaken for anything else and offered little scope for claiming too much. But the principle of "ruptive" concealment permitted enormous scope for encompassing other patterns that actually serve to reveal or mimic. Color patches and splotches—the classic domain of warning and revealing patterns (consider the peacock's tail)—could, for an overenthusiast like Thayer, become marks of disruptive concealment. Thus, to cite just one example of overstatement, Thayer argued in a 1909 article, adversarily entitled "An Arraignment of the Theories of Mimicry and Warning Colors," that white patches on a skunk's head mimic the sky when seen by mice from below:

> Such . . . victims as can see would certainly have much more chance to escape were not what would be a dark-looming predator's head converted, by its white sky-counterfeiting, into a deceptive imitation of mere sky.

Still, by 1903, Thayer was not yet ready to claim concealment for all colors. He admitted one category of obvious conspicuousness: "Only unshiny, bright monochrome is intrinsically a revealing coloration."

Now we can finally understand why Thayer was eventually driven to his absurd argument about flamingos and the sunset. (Divorced from the context of Thayer's own personal development, the idea sounds like simple disembodied craziness—as professors always present it for laughs in introductory classes.) Once Thayer decided to go for broke, and to claim that all color works for concealment, flamingos became his crucial test, his do-or-die attempt at exclusivity. As a last shackle before the final plunge, Thayer had admitted that stark monochromes—animals painted throughout with one showy color—were "intrinsically revealing." If he could now show that such monochromes also served for concealment, then his triumph would be complete. Flamingos occupied the center of his daring, not a curious diversion. He had to find a way to fade bright red into ethereal nothingness. Hence the sunset—his as well as the flamingo's.

So Thayer visited the West Indies, got down on his belly in the sulfurous muds, and looked at flamingos—not comfortably down from above (as he always accused lazy and uncritical zoologists of doing), but from the side as might a slithering anaconda or a hungry alligator. And he saw red wings fading into the sunset— the entire feeding flock became a pink cloud, a "sky-matching costume":

> These birds are largely nocturnal, so that the only sky bright enough to show any color upon them is the more or less rosy and golden one that surrounds them from sunset till dark and from dawn until soon after sunrise. They commonly feed in immense, open lagoons, wading in vast phalanxes, while the entire real sky above them and its reflected duplicate below them constitute either one vast hollow sphere of gold, rose, and salmon, or at least glow, on one side or the other, with these tones. Their whole plumage is a most exquisite duplicate of these scenes. . . . This flamingo, having at his feeding time so nearly only sunrise colors to match, wears, as he does, a wonderful imitation of them.

Thayer had finally gone too far and exasperated even his erstwhile supporters. His exaggerations—particularly his flamingos—now brought down a storm of criticism, including Roosevelt's hundred-page barrage. Critics pointed out Thayer's errors in every particular: Flamingos do not concentrate their feeding at dawn and dusk, but are active all day; anacondas and alligators do not inhabit the thin films of saline ponds that flamingos favor; flamingos eat by filtering tiny eyeless animals that cannot enjoy the visual pleasures of sunset.

Most sadly, Thayer's argument even failed in its own terms— and Thayer, who was overenthusiastic to a fault, but neither dishonest nor dishonorable, had to confess. Any object viewed *against* the fading light will appear dark, whatever its actual color. Thayer admitted this explicitly by painting a dark palm tree against the sunset in his infamous and fanciful painting of fading flamingos (reproduced here, for unfortunate practical reasons, in inappropriate black and white). Thus, he could only claim that flamingos looked like the sunset in the *opposite* side of the sky: red clouds of sunset in the west, red masses of flamingos in the east.

Would any animal be so confused by two "sunsets," with flamingos showing dark against the real McCoy? Thayer admitted in his 1909 book:

> Of course a flamingo seen against dawn or evening sky would look dark, like the palm in the lower left-hand figure, no matter what his colors were. The . . . right-hand figures, then, represent the lighted sides of flamingos at morning or evening, and show how closely these tend to reproduce the sky of this time of day; although always, of course, *in the*

White (top) and red (bottom) flamingos fade to invisibility against the sky at sunrise and sunset. From Thayer's 1909 book.

opposite quarter of the heavens [Thayer was good enough to underline his admission] from the sunset or dawn itself.

As a final, and feeble, parting salvo, Thayer added: "but the rosy hues very commonly suffuse both sides of the sky, so that . . . the flamingos' illuminated ruddy color very often has a true 'background' of illuminated ruddy sky."

Teddy Roosevelt was particularly perturbed. As an old big-game hunter, he knew that most of Thayer's "ruptive" patterns did not conceal quarries. How could Thayer have it both ways—how could a lion be concealed in the desert, a zebra amongst the reeds when, in fact, they share the same habitat, often to the zebra's fatal disadvantage? Thus, Roosevelt decided to counterattack and wrote his scientific *magnum opus* during some spare time amidst other chores. He saved his best invective for the poor flamingos. Writing on February 2, 1911, to University of California biologist Charles Kofoid, he stated:

> [Thayer's] book shows such a fantastic quality of mind on his part that it is a matter of very real surprise to me that any scientific observer . . . no matter how much credit he may give to Mr. Thayer for certain discoveries and theories, should fail to enter the most emphatic protest against the utter looseness and wildness of his theorizing. Think of being seriously required to consider the theory that flamingos are colored red so that fishes (or oysters for that matter—there is no absurdity of which Mr. Thayer could not be capable) would mistake them for the sunset!

The debate between Roosevelt and Thayer developed into an interesting discussion of scientific methodology, not merely some rhetorical sniping about specifics. To grasp Roosevelt's primarily methodological (and cogent) objections to Thayer's work, consider Thayer's most remarkable painting of all—the frontispiece to his 1909 book, showing a peacock obliterated in the foliage. Here, Thayer argues that every nuance of a peacock's coloration increases his concealment in a particular bit of habitat—the combined effect adding to invisibility. Given the usual interpretation of a peacock's color as revealing, and the gaudy impression that he makes both upon us and, one must assume, the peahen, Thayer's interpretation represents quite a departure from tradition and common sense:

> The peacock's splendor is the effect of a marvelous combination of "obliterative" designs, in forest-colors and patterns. . . . All imaginable forest-tones are to be found in this

A peacock in the woods, showing how, in at least one highly peculiar position, each "showy" feature can help blend the bird into invisibility. From Thayer's 1909 book. NEG. NO. 2A13238. COURTESY DEPARTMENT OF LIBRARY SERVICES, AMERICAN MUSEUM OF NATURAL HISTORY.

bird's costume; and they "melt" him into the scene to a degree past all human analysis.

Thayer then positions his bird so precisely that all features blend with surroundings. He paints the blue neck against a gap in the foliage, so that it may mimic "blue sky seen through the leaves." He matches the golden greens and browns of the back to forest tones. He depicts the white cheek patch as a "ruptive" hole that disaggregates the face. He paints the celebrated ocelli (eye-spots) of the tail feathers as leaf mimics. He also notes that ocelli are smallest and dimmest near the body, grading to larger and brighter toward the rear end: "They inevitably lead the eye away from the bird, till it finds itself straying amid the foliage beyond the tail's evanescent border." The spread tail, he claims, may impress the peahen, but it "looks also very much like a shrub bearing some kind of fruit or flower." Finally, he argues that the tail's coppery brown color represents perfectly "the bare ground and tree-trunks seen between the leaves."

What a tour de force, but what can we possibly make of such special pleading? Who would doubt that some conceivable habitat might conceal almost any animal? Note how precisely the peacock must choose his spot to receive the cryptic benefit that Thayer wishes to confer upon him. In particular, he must always place his shimmering blue neck in a gap amidst the foliage where it will vanish against a clear sky (but what does he do on a cloudy day, or in a bush so dense that no holes exist, as seen from all relevant directions at once?). Peacocks, in any case, live primarily in open fields. Their spreading display is a glory to behold—and the very opposite of invisible.

Thayer, of course, knew all this. He didn't claim (as his critics sometimes charged) that a habitat offering protection by conceal-ment must be the usual, or even a common, haunt of its invisible beneficiary. Thayer simply argued that such protection might be important at critical moments occurring only once or twice in an animal's lifetime—at crucial instants of impending death from a stalking predator.

But how could odd and improbable moments shape such com-plex and intricate patterns as the innumerable details of a pea-cock's design? With this question, we finally arrive at the key theoretical issue of this debate—the power of natural selection itself. In order to believe that complex designs might be constructed by such rare and momentary benefits as sunsets or particular positions in trees outside an animal's normal habitat, one must have an overarching faith in the power of natural selection. Selection must be so potent that even the rarest of benefits will eventually be engraved into the optimal designs of organisms. Thayer had this faith; Roosevelt, and most biologists then and since, did not. Thayer wrote in 1900: "Of course, to any one who feels the inevitability of natural selection, it is obvious that each organ or structural detail, and likewise each quality of organic forms, owes its existence to the sum of all its uses." Thayer then laid it on the line in stark epitome—patterns of color are built by natural selection, "pure, simple, and omnipotent."

Roosevelt and other acute critics correctly identified the central flaw in Thayer's science—not in his numerous factual errors, but in his methodology. Thayer found a hiding place for all his animals but with a method that made his theory untestable and therefore useless to science. Thayer insisted that he had proved his point simply by finding *any* spot that rendered an animal invisible. He didn't need to show that the creature usually frequented such a place or that the location formed part of a natural habitat at all. For the animal might seek its spot only in the rarest moments of need. But how then could we disprove any of Thayer's claims? We might work for years to show that an animal never entered its domain of invisibility, and Thayer would reply: Wait till tomorrow when urgent need arises. Scientists are trained to avoid such special pleading because it exerts a chilling and stupefying effect upon hypotheses, by rendering them invulnerable to test and potential disproof. Doing is the soul of science and we reject hypotheses that condemn us to impotence.

T. Barbour, former director of Harvard's Museum of Comparative Zoology (where I now sit composing this piece), and J. C. Phillips emphasized this point in reviewing Thayer's book in 1911:

Acquiescence in Mr. Thayer's views throws a pall over the entire subject of animal coloration. Investigation is discouraged; and we find jumbled together a great mass of fascinating and extremely complicated data, all simply ex-

plained by one dogmatic assertion. For we are asked to believe that an animal is protectively clothed whether he is like
his surroundings, or whether he is very unlike them (oblit-
eratively marked) or . . . if he falls between these two classes,
there is still plenty of space to receive him.

Teddy Roosevelt addressed the same issue with more vigor in a
letter to Thayer on March 19, 1912 (just imagine any presidential
candidate taking time out to pursue natural history more than a
month after the New Hampshire primary—oh, I know, campaigns
were shorter then):

There is in Africa a blue rump baboon. It is also true that
the Mediterranean Sea bounds one side of Africa. If you
should make a series of experiments tending to show that if
the blue rump baboon stood on its head by the Mediterranean you would mix up his rump and the Mediterranean,
you might be illustrating something in optics, but you
would not be illustrating anything that had any bearing
whatsoever on the part played by the coloration of the animal in actual life. . . . My dear Mr. Thayer, if you would face
facts, you might really help in elucidating some of the problems before me, but you can do nothing but mischief, and
not very much of that, when conducting such experiments.
. . . Your experiments are of no more real value than the
experiment of putting a raven in a coal scuttle, and then
claiming that he is concealed.

Contemporary (and later) accounts of Thayer's debacle rest
largely upon a red herring, concealed in more than the sunset,
that will not explain his failure and only reinforces a common and
harmful stereotype about the intrinsic differences among intellectual styles. In short, we are told that Abbott Thayer ultimately
failed because he possessed an artist's temperament—good for
an initial insight perhaps, but with no staying power for the hard
(and often dull) work of real science.

Such charges were often lodged against Thayer, and with undoubted rhetorical effect, but they represent a dangerous use of
ad hominem argument with anti-intellectual overtones. Thayer

may have laid himself open to such ridicule with a passionate temperament that he made no effort to control in a more formal age. John Jay Chapman, the acerbic essayist, wrote of Thayer (admittedly in a fit of pique when his wife, at his great displeasure, decided to study art in Thayer's studio):

> Thayer by the way, is a hipped egoist who paints three hours, has a headache, walks four hours—holds his own pulse, wants to save his sacred light for the world, cares for nobody, and has fits of dejection during which forty women hold his hand and tell him not to despair—for humanity's sake.

But is such passion the exclusive birthright of artists? I have known many scientists equally insufferable.

Thayer's scientific critics also raised the charge of artistic temperament. Roosevelt wrote, in a statement that might have attracted more attention in our litigious age: Thayer's misstatements "are due to the enthusiasm of a certain type of artistic temperament, an enthusiasm also known to certain types of scientific and business temperaments, and which when it manifests itself in business is sure to bring the owner into trouble as if he were guilty of deliberate misconduct." Barbour and Phillips argued that "Mr. Thayer, in his enthusiasm, has ignored or glossed over with an artistic haze. . . . This method of persuasion, while it does appeal to the public, is—there is no other word—simple charlatanry however unwitting." Barbour and Phillips then defended the cold light of dispassionate science in a bit of self-serving puffery:

> [Our statements] are simply the impressions made upon open-minded observers who have no axe to grind, and who have no reason to take sides on the question, one way or another. They have been written in a friendly spirit, and we hope they will be received in the same way.

Do friendly spirits ever accuse their opponents of "simple charlatanry"?

The charge of artistic temperament may be convenient and

effective, especially since it appeals to a common stereotype—but it won't wash. The facile interpretation that scientists wouldn't give Thayer a hearing because he was an "outsider" won't work either—for contemporary accounts belie such charges of territoriality and narrowness. Even though Thayer made such strong claims—quoted above—for scientists' incompetence in a domain accessible only to artists, naturalists welcomed his insights about countershading and enjoyed both his initial articles and his outdoor demonstrations. E. B. Poulton, one of England's greatest evolutionists, warmly supported Thayer and wrote introductions to his publications. Frank M. Chapman, great ornithologist and editor of *The Auk,* wrote in his *Autobiography of a Bird Lover:*

> As an editor, doubtless my most notable contributions to the Auk's pages were Abbott Thayer's classical papers on protective coloration. . . . I knew little of Thayer's eminence as an artist. It was the man himself who impressed me by the overwhelming force of his personality. He made direct and inescapable demands on one's attention. He was intensely vital and lived normally at heights which I reached only occasionally and then only for short periods.

Thayer's ultimate failure reflects a more universal tendency, distributed without reference to profession among all kinds of people. Nothing but habit and tradition separate the "two cultures" of humanities and science. The processes of thought and modes of reason are similar—so are the people. Only subject matter differs. Science may usually treat the world's empirical information; art may thrive on aesthetic judgment. But scientists also traffic in ideas and opinions, and artists surely respect fact.

The *idée fixe* is a common intellectual fault of all professions, not a characteristic failure of artists. I have often written about scientists as single-mindedly committed to absurd unities and false simplifications as Thayer was devoted to the exclusivity of concealing coloration in nature. Some are charming and a bit dotty—such as old Randolph Kirkpatrick, who thought that all rocks were made of single-celled nummulospheres (see Essay 22 in *The Panda's Thumb,* 1980). Others are devious and more than a bit dangerous—such as Cyril Burt, who fabricated data to prove that all intelligence resided in heredity (see my book *The Mismeasure of Man*).

Abbott Thayer had an *idée fixe;* he burned with desire to reduce a messy and complex world to one beautiful, simple principle of explanation. Such monistic schemes never work. History has built irreducible complexity and variety into the bounteous world of organisms. Diversity reigns at the superficial level of overt phenomena—animal colors serve many different functions. The unifying principles are deeper and more abstract—may I suggest evolution itself for starters.

Postscript

Abbott H. Thayer extended his flamingo theory ever further than I had realized. Historian of science Sharon Kingsland, who wrote an excellent technical article on "Abbott Thayer and the Protective Coloration Debate" in 1978 (and who therefore would have made my own work ever so much easier had I known of her prior efforts), sent me a 1911 note by Thayer triumphantly announcing a new genre of paintings with backgrounds made from the actual skins of animals supposedly concealed by their colors and markings. Thayer wrote, including flamingos of course:

> The public will soon be astonished when I show them a dawn picture made out of the entire skin of one of these birds [flamingos] simply "mosaicked" into the sky of a painting of one of their lagoons. I am now making such a picture. I have already nearly finished a picture of a Himalayan gorge made wholly of the skins of Monaul pheasants; and another one of a New Hampshire snow scene similarly done with magpies. Artists are positively amazed by both of them.

On a more practical and positive note, I learned from my correspondents that Thayer's views on concealment were far more important in the history of naval camouflage than I had realized or that the biological literature had recorded. I received two fascinating letters from Lewis R. Melson, USNR. He wrote:

> Many years ago, I was summarily ordered to assume the responsibility for directing the efforts of the U.S. Navy's Ship Concealment and Camouflage Division, relieving the genius who had guided this effort throughout World War II, Commander Dayton Reginald Evans Brown. Dayton had perfected the camouflage patterns employed on all naval ships and aircraft throughout the war. In his briefing of what I could expect in directing the continuation of his work, I found his theories and designs were based upon Abbott H. Thayer's earlier work in the field of concealment and camouflage. . . . Despite whatever everyone thought and thinks about Thayer's theories, both his "protective coloration" and "ruptive" designs were vital for concealing ships and aircraft.

Melson continued:

> All naval concealment and camouflage is designed for protection against the horizon in the case of shipping and either for concealment against a sea or sky background, again at long ranges, for aircraft. [Note from my essay how much of Thayer's work involved "disappearance" of an image seen against the sky or horizon.] Thayer's "protective coloration" designs were outstanding for aircraft, light undersides and dark above [as fish, seen from below by their predators, tend to display]. Ship concealment for temperate and tropical oceans employed the "protective coloration" designs, while "ruptive" or "disruptive" designs worked best against polar backgrounds.

Melson also taught me some history of camouflage during the two world wars. Despite our later and fruitful use in World War II, the U.S. Navy had originally rejected Thayer's proposal during World War I. However, Thayer had greater success in Britain, where his designs proved highly valuable during the First World War. Melson wrote:

Thayer's suggestions . . . called for very light colored ships using broken patterns of white and pale blue. The intent of this pattern was to blend the ship against the background at night and in overcast weather. In the high northern latitudes surrounding the British Isles with its frequent storms, fogs, and long periods of darkness, these patterns proved very successful. HMS *Broke* was the first ship so painted and it was rammed twice by sister ships of the Royal Navy, whose captains protested that they had been unable to see *Broke*.

Melson ended his letter with a fine affirmation of potential interaction between pure and applied science:

Thanks again for the article on Thayer. It will join my mementos of those heady days when we were able to contribute bits and pieces to the world of science and engineering.

15 | Petrus Camper's Angle

I REMEMBER WATCHING Toscanini, a little old man made even smaller on the tiny screen of our first television set. I understood nothing of classical music when I was nine, but Toscanini's intensity nearly moved me to tears—a man older than my grandfather and scarcely bigger than me, drawing such concerted sound from his players. I remember how he stepped off the podium after each piece and mopped his brow with a handkerchief.

Classical music had little currency in those days just before the long-playing record. In television's only other foray into this arcane world, we could watch the annual Christmas presentation of Menotti's opera *Amahl and the Night Visitors*. Amahl, the young cripple with a passion for embellishment, tells his mother that two kings are outside, requesting entry to their humble cottage. She chides him, laments his disinclination to speak truly, and sends him to the door again. Amahl returns to admit that, indeed, two kings do not stand outside. His mother rejoices, but Amahl proclaims: "There are three kings . . . and one of them is black."

I remembered this line when I started to visit art museums much later and soon realized that Menotti had been following an old tradition, not making a modern plea for racial harmony. One of the Magi is always depicted as a black man. This traditional iconography is not biblical, but a later interpretation. The gospel writers do not even specify the number of wise men who saw the star in the east and came to worship. Some early sources cite up to twelve, but the number soon stabilized at three. Later, this trio received names—Balthazar, Melchior, and Gaspar, first specified in a sixth-century mosaic in Ravenna—and then, symbolic interpretations. As these allegories moved from the specific to the general, the portrayal of one Magus as black stabilized. The three were first seen as kings of Arabia, Persia, and India, then (by the Venerable Bede, for example) as symbols for the three great continents of Africa, Europe, and Asia, and finally, as representatives of the three major human races: white, yellow, and black.

I was reminded of this iconographical tidbit recently as I read one of the classic works of physical anthropology—the historical beginning of scientific measurement of the human skull. Petrus Camper, Dutch anatomist and painter, was born in Leiden in 1722. He studied both art and science, then trained as a midwife before receiving his degree as a physician. (Men may be midwives. The name refers to a person, male or female, who stays with [*mit*, as in modern German] a woman [*wif*] during birth—so the female end of the etymology refers to the mother, not the attendant.) In 1755, he became a professor of anatomy in Amsterdam and spent the rest of his comfortable life alternating between his country home and his professional duties in Amsterdam and Groningen. Camper, who discovered the air spaces in bird bones and studied the hearing of fishes and the croaking of frogs, was revered as one of the great intellects of Europe during his own lifetime. The busy life that such attention brings, made even more hectic by the political career that he forged during his later years, left Camper little time to write and publish his scientific studies. At his death in 1789, he left his major work on the measurement of human anatomy in manuscript. His son published this posthumous document in 1791, both in the original Dutch and in French translation. (I read the French, an edition printed in Utrecht, presumably by typesetters who didn't know the language, and so full of errors that I almost decided it might be easier to learn Dutch and work from the other version.)

This work bears an extended title, both characteristic of the age and expressive of the contents: *Physical dissertation on the real differences that men of different countries and ages display in their facial traits; on the beauty that characterizes the statues and engraved stones of antiquity; followed by the proposition of a new method for drawing human heads with the greatest accuracy.* Camper's treatise is remembered today for one primary achievement—the definition of the so-called facial angle, the first widely accepted measurement for comparing the skulls of different races and nationalities.

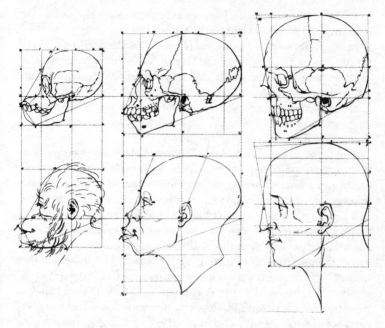

Illustration from Camper's original work showing increasing value for the facial angle of (left to right) an ape, an African, and a Grecian head. NEG. NO. 337249. COURTESY DEPARTMENT OF LIBRARY SERVICES, AMERICAN MUSEUM OF NATURAL HISTORY.

Camper's facial angle is the traditional beginning of craniometry, or the science of measuring human skulls, a major subdiscipline of physical anthropology.

The human skull may be divided into two basic components: the vault of the cranium itself and the face in front. Camper's facial angle sought to specify the relationship between these two parts. Camper first drew a line connecting the ear opening with the base of the nose (the so-called horizontal, or "h–k" on his illustration of an African head). He then constructed another line joining the most forward projection of the upper jaw (the bottom of the upper lip in living heads, usually the edge of the incisor teeth on skulls) with the most protruding point of the brow above the eyes ("h–n" on his African head), and called ever since the facial line. Camper then defined the facial angle as the intersection of the horizontal (his basis of reference) with the facial line (roughly, the forward slant of the face).

In a general way, the facial angle measures the relative flatness versus forward extension of the face. A low value means that the jaws extend far in front of the cranial vault, giving the entire skull a sloping appearance. A high value indicates a flat face with jaws projecting no farther forward than the brow itself. When a facial angle exceeds 90 degrees, the vault of the cranium projects farther forward than the underlying jaws.

The facial angle soon became the first widely accepted tool for quantitative comparison of human skulls. It spawned an immense literature, a host of proposals for slight improvements based on different criteria, and a bevy of instruments designed to measure this fundamental aspect of human life. Camper's angle became the first quantitative device for establishing invidious comparisons, based on inherent distinctions, among human races. The early craniometricians reported that African blacks possessed the lowest facial angles (farthest forward projection of the jaws), with Orientals in the middle, and Europeans on top, with facial angles sometimes approaching 90 degrees. Since apes had facial angles even lower than blacks, and since the facial angles for ancient statues of Greek deities exceeded those of all living Europeans, the smooth ascent from monkey to majesty seemed assured. Historian John S. Haller writes:

> The facial angle was the most extensively elaborated and artlessly abused criterion for racial somatology. . . . By 1860 the facial angle had become the most frequent means of explaining the graduation of species. Like the Chain of Being, the races of man consisted of an ordered hierarchy in which the Hottentot, the Kaffir, the Chinaman, and the Indian held a specific position in the order of life.

I had never read Camper's original definition of the facial angle or his own recommendations for its use and meaning. Neither had most of the nineteenth-century craniometricians who established the facial angle as a primary instrument of scientific racism (Camper's posthumous work has always been rare and difficult to obtain). I am no longer surprised when the study of a neglected original shows, as in this case, that later interpretations departed from an author's own intentions. Such stories cannot rank as news; they fall into the category of "dog bites man." And besides, maybe the later readings were correct and the initial proposal wrong—good insights for bad reasons are legion in the world of intellect.

The story of Camper's own interpretation of his facial angle is interesting for another reason. The archaeology of knowledge assumes greatest importance when it seeks new insights from our past. By cultural heritage and proven reliability, we approach problems in a set of stereotyped ways and often assume (following the cardinal sin of pride) that our modern conventions exhaust the domain of possible inquiry. We should study the past for the simplest of reasons—to increase our "sample size" in modes of thought, for we need all the help we can get. Camper's own rationale is instructive because it departs fundamentally from the sociology and a conceptual basis of modern scientific inquiry into human variability. We should recover and understand Camper's reasoning both to pay proper respect to a fine thinker and to expand our own sense of possibility.

Camper did not define the facial angle as a device for ranking races or nations by innate worth or intellect. He did not even approach the problem of human variability with motives that we would now recognize as scientific. In Camper's day, anthropology did not exist as a discipline; science had not been defined, either as a word or as a separate domain of knowledge. Scholars often worked simultaneously in areas now walled off into separate faculties of universities. Such "cross-disciplinary" work seemed neither odd nor prodigious to eighteenth-century thinkers.

Camper was a professor of anatomy and medicine, but he was also an accomplished artist, good enough to win admission to the Painter's Academy during a long visit to England (1748 to 1750). Camper defined his facial angle with the requisite precision of geometry and the quantitative preferences of science, but his motive lay in the domain of art. (He saw no contradiction, and neither should we.) We may now return to the issue of the black Magus and to Camper's own statement about his intentions.

Camper tells us right at the outset of his treatise that his desire to quantify human variation first arose in response to a minor annoyance with Western painting. He had studied the black

Magus in many classical paintings and noted that, while his color matched the hues of Africa, his face almost always displayed the features of European whites—a kind of Renaissance minstrel show with whites in blackface. (Since few Africans then lived in Europe, Camper reasoned that most artists had used white models, faithfully copying the facial features of a European and then painting the figure black.)

Camper wanted to prevent such errors by establishing a set of simple guidelines (lengths and angles) to define the chief characters of each human group. His treatise devotes more space to differences between old and young than to disparity among races or nations—for Camper was also distressed that the infant Jesus had often been drawn from an older model (no photographic surrogates to keep a baby's image still in Camper's day).

Yet Camper did not locate his immediate motive for the facial angle in descriptive anthropology of actual humans, but in a much loftier problem—no less than the definition of beauty itself. Like so many of his contemporaries, Camper believed that the cultures of ancient Greece and Rome had reached a height of refinement never since repeated and perhaps not even subject to recapture. (This is a difficult concept to grasp in the light of our later cultural preference for progress as a feature of technological history—old must mean inferior. But our forebears were not so encumbered, and ideas of a previous golden age, surpassing anything achieved since, had great power and attraction. The Renaissance [literally, rebirth] received its name from this conviction, and its heroes were trying, or so they thought, to recapture the knowledge and glory of antiquity, not to create novel improvements in art or architecture.)

Camper was obsessed with a particular issue arising from this reverence for antiquity. We can all agree, he states, that the great sculptors of ancient Greece achieved a beauty and nobility that we have not been able to match in our new art or often even to duplicate in simple attempts to copy ancient statues. One might take the easy route out of this dilemma and argue that Phidias and his brethren were just good copyists and that the people of ancient Greece surpassed all modern folk in beauty and proportion. But Camper had evidence against this proposition, for he noted that the few Greek attempts at actual portraiture (on coins, for example) showed people much like ourselves, warts and all.

Moreover, the Greeks had made no secret of their preference for idealization. Camper quotes Lysippus's desire "not to represent men as they are, but as they present themselves to our imagination." "The ideal of Antique Beauty," Camper writes, "does not exist in nature; it is purely a concept of the imagination."

But how shall we define this ideal of beauty? Camper traces the sorry attempts by poets, artists, and philosophers throughout the centuries. He notes that, in the absence of a firm criterion, each field has tried to fob off the definition by analogy—poets exemplify beauty by reference to art; artists by reference to poetry. Explicit attempts often foundered in nonsense, as in this example from 1584: "Beauty is only beautiful by its own beauty," a motto that inspired Camper's appropriate riposte, "Can there be a greater absurdity?"

And yet, Camper argues, we all agree about the beauty of certain objects, so some common criterion must exist. He writes:

> A beautiful starry sky pleases everyone. A sunrise, a calm sea, excites a sensation of pleasure in all people, and we all agree that these phenomena convey an impression of beauty.

Camper therefore decided to abandon the overarching attempts that had always devolved into nonsense and to concentrate instead on something specific that might be defined precisely—the human head.

Again he argues (incorrectly, I think, but I am explicating, not judging) that common standards exist and that, in particular, we all agree about the maximal beauty of Grecian statuary:

> We will not find a single person who does not regard the head of Apollo or Venus as possessing a superior Beauty, and who does not view these heads as infinitely superior to those of the most beautiful men and women [of our day].

Since the Greek achievement involved abstraction, not portraiture, some secret knowledge must have allowed them to improve the actual human form. Camper longed to recover their rule book. He did not doubt that the great sculptures of antiquity had proceeded by mathematical formulas, not simple intuition—for proportion and harmony, geometrically expressed, were hallmarks of Greek thought. Camper would, therefore, try to infer their physical rules of ratios and angles: "It is difficult to imitate the truly sublime beauty that characterizes Antiquity until we have discovered the true physical reasons on which it was founded."

Camper therefore devised an ingenious method of inference (also a good illustration of the primary counterintuitive principle that marks true excellence in science). When faced with a grand (but intractable) issue—like *the* definition of beauty—don't seek the ultimate, general solution; find a corner that can be defined precisely and, as our new cliché proclaims, go for it. He decided to draw, in profile and with great precision, a range of human heads spanning nations and ages. He would then characterize these heads by various angles and ratios, trying to establish simple gradations from what we regard as least to most pleasing. He would then extrapolate this gradient in the "more pleasing" direction to construct idealized heads that exaggerate those features regarded as most beautiful in actual people. Perhaps the Greeks had sculpted their deities in the same manner.

With this background, we can grasp Camper's own interpretation of the facial angle. Camper held that modern humans range from 70 degrees to somewhere between 80 and 90 degrees in this measure. He also made two other observations: first, that monkeys and other "brutes" maintained lower angles in proportion to their rank in the scale of nature (monkeys lower than apes, dogs lower than monkeys, and birds lower than dogs); second, that higher angles characterize smaller faces tucked below a more bulging cranium—a sign of mental nobility on the ancient theme of more is better.

Having established this range of improvement for living creatures, Camper extrapolated his facial angle in the favorable direction toward higher values. *Voilà.* He had found the secret. The beautiful skulls of antiquity had achieved their pleasing proportions by exaggerating the facial angle beyond values attained by real people. Camper could even define the distinctions that had eluded experts and made for such difficulty in attempts to copy and define. Romans, he found, preferred an angle of 95 degrees, but the ancient Greek sculptors all used 100 degrees as their

ideal—and this difference explains both our ease in distinguishing Greek originals from Roman copies and our aesthetic preference for Greek statuary. (Proportion, he also argued, is always a
balance between too little and too much. We cannot extrapolate
the facial angle forever. At values of more than 100 degrees, a
human skull begins to look displeasing and eventually monstrous—as in individuals afflicted with hydrocephalus. The peculiar genius of the Greeks, Camper argued, lay in their precise
understanding of the facial angle. The great Athenian sculptors
could push its value right to the edge, where maximal beauty
switches to deformity. The Romans had not been so brave, and
they paid the aesthetic price.)

Thus, Camper felt that he had broken the code of antiquity and
offered a precise definition of beauty (at least for the human
head): "What constitutes a beautiful face? I answer, a disposition
of traits such that the facial line makes an angle of 100 degrees
with the horizontal." Camper had defined an abstraction, but he
had worked by extrapolation from nature. He ended his treatise
with pride in this achievement: "I have tried to establish on the
foundation of Nature herself, the true character of Beauty in faces
and heads."

This context explains why the later use of facial angles for racist rankings represents such a departure from Camper's convictions and concerns. To be sure, two aspects of Camper's work
could be invoked to support these later interpretations, particularly in quotes taken out of context. First, he did, and without any
explicit justification, make aesthetic judgments about the relative
beauty of races—never doubting that Nordic Europeans must top
the scale objectively and never considering that other folks might
advocate different standards. "A Lapplander," he writes, "has
always been regarded, and without exception throughout the
world, as more ugly than a Persian or a Georgian." (One wonders
if anyone had ever sent a packet of questionnaires to the Scandinavian tundra; Camper, in any case at least, does not confine his
accusations of ugliness to non-Caucasians.)

Second, Camper did provide an ordering of human races by
facial angle—and in the usual direction of later racist rankings,
with Africans at the bottom, Orientals in the middle, and Europeans on top. He also did not fail to note that this ordering

placed Africans closest to apes and Europeans nearest to Greek gods. In discussing the observed range of facial angles (70 to 100 degrees in statues and actual heads), Camper notes that "It [this range] constitutes the entire gradation from the head of the Negro to the sublime beauty of the Greek of Antiquity." Extrapolating further, Camper writes:

> As the facial line moves back [for a small face tucked under bulging skull] I produce a head of Antiquity; as I bring it forward [for a larger, projecting face] I produce the head of a Negro. If I bring it still further forward, the head of a monkey results, more forward still, and I get a dog, and finally a woodcock; this, now, is the primary basis of my edifice.

(Our deprecations never cease. The French word for woodcock—*bécasse*—also refers to a stupid woman in modern French slang.)

I will not defend Camper's view of human variation any more than I would pillory Lincoln for racism or Darwin for sexism (though both are guilty by modern standards). Camper lived in a different world, and we cannot single him out for judgment when he idly repeats the commonplaces of his age (nor, in general, may we evaluate the past by the present, if we hope to understand our forebears).

Camper's comments on racial rankings are fleeting and stated *en passant*. He makes no major point of African distinctions except to suggest that artists might now render the black Magus correctly in painting the Epiphany. He does not harp upon differences among human groups and entirely avoids the favorite theme of all later writings in craniometric racism—finer scale distinctions between "inferior" and "superior" Europeans. His text contains not a whiff or hint of any suggestion that low facial angles imply anything about moral worth or intellect. He charges Africans with nothing but maximal departure from ideal beauty. Moreover, and most important, Camper's clearly stated views on the nature of human variability preclude, necessarily and a priori, any equation of difference with innate inferiority. This is the key point that later commentators have missed because we have lost Camper's world view and cannot interpret his text without recovering the larger structure of his ideas.

We now live in a Darwinian world of variation, shadings, and continuity. For us, variation among human groups is fundamental, both as an intrinsic property of nature and as a potential substratum for more substantial change. We see no difference in principle between variation within a species and established differences between species—for one can become the other via natural selection. Given this potential continuity, both kinds of variation may record an underlying and basically similar genetic inheritance. To us, therefore, linear rankings (like Camper's for the facial angle) quite properly smack of racism.

But Camper dwelt in the pre-Darwinian world of typology. Species were fixed and created entities. Differences among species recorded their fundamental natures. But variation within a species could only be viewed as a series of reversible "accidents" (departures from a species' essence) imposed by a variety of factors, including climate, food, habits, or direct manipulation. If all humans represented but a single species, then our variation could only be superficial and accidental in this Platonic sense. Physical differences could not be tokens of innate inferiority. (By "accidental," Camper and his contemporaries did not mean capricious or devoid of immediate import in heredity. They knew that black parents had black children. Rather, they argued that these traits, impressed into heredity by climate or food, had no fixed status and could be easily modified by new conditions of life. They were often wrong, of course, but that's not the point.)

Therefore, to understand Camper's views about human variability, we must first learn whether he regarded all humans as members of one species or as products of several separate creations (a popular position known at the time as polygeny). Camper recognized these terms of the argument and came down strongly and incisively for human unity as a single species (monogeny). In designating races by the technical term "variety," Camper used the jargon of his day to underscore his conviction that our differences are accidental and imposed departures from an essence shared by all; our races are not separated by differences fixed in heredity. "Blacks, mulattos, and whites are not diverse species of men, but only varieties of the human species. Our skin is constituted exactly like that of the colored nations; we are therefore only less black than they." We cannot even know, Camper adds, whether Adam and Eve were created white or black since transitions between superficial varieties can occur so easily (an attack on those who viewed blacks as degenerate and Adam and Eve as necessarily created in Caucasian perfection):

> Whether Adam and Eve were created white or black is an entirely indifferent issue without consequences, since the passage from white to black, considerable though it be, operates as easily as that from black to white.

Misinterpretation may be more common than accuracy, but a misreading precisely opposite to an author's true intent may still excite our interest for its sheer perversity. When, in order to grasp this inversion, we must stretch our minds and learn to understand some fossil systems of thinking, then we may convert a simple correction to a generality worthy of note. Poor Petrus Camper. He became the semiofficial grandpappy of the quantitative approach to scientific racism, yet his own concept of human variability precluded judgments about innate worth a priori. He developed a measure later used to make invidious distinctions among actual groups of people, but he pressed his own invention to the service of abstract beauty. He became a villain of science when he tried to establish criteria for art. Camper got a bad posthumous shake on earth; I only hope that he met the right deity on high (facial angle of 100 degrees, naturally), the God of Isaiah, who also equated beauty with number and proportion—he "who hath measured the waters in the hollow of his hand, and meted out heaven with the span."

16 | Literary Bias on the Slippery Slope

EVERY PROFESSION has its version: Some speak of "Sod's law"; others of "Murphy's law." The formulations vary, but all make the same point—if anything bad can happen, it will. Such universality of attribution can only arise for one reason—the principle is true (even though we know that it isn't).

The fieldworker's version is simply stated: You always find the most interesting specimens at the very last moment, just when you absolutely must leave. The effect of this phenomenon can easily be quantified. It operates weakly for localities near home and easily revisited and ever more strongly for distant and exotic regions requiring great effort and expense for future expeditions. Everyone has experienced this law of nature. I once spent two weeks on Great Abaco, visiting every nook and cranny of the island and assiduously proving that two supposed species of *Cerion* (my favorite land snail) really belonged to one variable group. On the last morning, as the plane began to load, we drove to the only unexamined place, an isolated corner of the island with the improbable name Hole-in-the-Wall. There we found hundreds of large white snails, members of the second species.

Each profession treasures a classic, or canonical, version of the basic story. The paleontological "standard," known to all my colleagues as a favorite campfire tale and anecdote for introductory classes, achieves its top billing by joining the most famous geologist of his era with the most important fossils of any time. The story, I have just discovered, is also entirely false (more than a bit embarrassing since I cited the usual version to begin an earlier essay in this series).

241

Charles Doolittle Walcott (1850–1927) was both the world's leading expert on Cambrian rocks and fossils (the crucial time for the initial flowering of multicellular life) and the most powerful scientific administrator in America. Walcott, who knew every president from Teddy Roosevelt to Calvin Coolidge, and who persuaded Andrew Carnegie to establish the Carnegie Institute of Washington, had little formal education and began his career as a fieldworker for the United States Geological Survey. He rose to chief, and resigned in 1907 to become secretary (their name for boss) of the Smithsonian Institution. Walcott had his finger, more accurately his fist, in every important scientific pot in Washington.

Walcott loved the Canadian Rockies and, continuing well into his seventies, spent nearly every summer in tents and on horseback, collecting fossils and indulging his favorite hobby of panoramic photography. In 1909, Walcott made his greatest discovery in Middle Cambrian rocks exposed on the western flank of the ridge connecting Mount Field and Mount Wapta in eastern British Columbia.

The fossil record is, almost exclusively, a tale told by the hard parts of organisms. Soft anatomy quickly disaggregates and decays, leaving bones and shells behind. For two basic reasons, we cannot gain an adequate appreciation for the full range of ancient life from these usual remains. First, most organisms contain no hard parts at all, and we miss them entirely. Second, hard parts, especially superficial coverings, often tell us very little about the animal within or underneath. What could you learn about the anatomy of a snail from the shell alone?

Paleontologists therefore treasure the exceedingly rare soft-bodied faunas occasionally preserved when a series of unusual circumstances coincide—rapid burial, oxygen-free environments devoid of bacteria or scavengers, and little subsequent disturbance of sediments.

Walcott's 1909 discovery—called the Burgess Shale—surpasses all others in significance because he found an exquisite fauna of soft-bodied organisms from the most crucial of all times. About 570 million years ago, virtually all modern phyla of animals made their first appearance in an episode called "the Cambrian explosion" to honor its geological rapidity. The Burgess

Shale dates from a time just afterward and offers our only insight into the true range of diversity generated by this most prolific of all evolutionary events.

Walcott, committed to a conventional view of slow and steady progress in increasing complexity and diversity, completely misinterpreted the Burgess animals. He shoehorned them all into modern groups, interpreting the entire fauna as a set of simpler precursors for later forms. A comprehensive restudy during the past twenty years has inverted Walcott's view and taught us the most surprising thing we know about the history of life: The fossils from this one small quarry in British Columbia exceed, in anatomical diversity, all modern organisms in the world's oceans today. Some fifteen to twenty Burgess creatures cannot be placed into any modern phylum and represent unique forms of life, failed experiments in metazoan design. Within known groups, the Burgess range far exceeds what prevails today. Taxonomists have described almost a million living species of arthropods, but all can be placed into three great groups—insects and their relatives, spiders and their kin, and crustaceans. In Walcott's single Canadian quarry, vastly fewer species include about twenty more basic anatomical designs! The history of life is a tale of decimation and later stabilization of few surviving anatomies, not a story of steady expansion and progress.

But this is another story for another time (see my book *Wonderful Life,* 1989). I provide this epitome only to emphasize the context for paleontology's classic instance of Sod's law. These are no ordinary fossils, and their discoverer was no ordinary man.

I can provide no better narration for the usual version than the basic source itself—the obituary notice for Walcott published by his longtime friend and former research assistant Charles Schuchert, professor of paleontology at Yale. (Schuchert was, by then, the most powerful paleontologist in America, and Yale became the leading center of training for academic paleontology. The same story is told far and wide in basically similar versions, but I suspect that Schuchert was the primary source for canonization and spread. I first learned the tale from my thesis adviser, Norman D. Newell. He heard it from his adviser, Carl Dunbar, also at Yale, who got it directly from Schuchert.) Schuchert wrote in 1928:

One of the most striking of Walcott's faunal discoveries came at the end of the field season of 1909, when Mrs. Walcott's horse slid in going down the trail and turned up a slab that at once attracted her husband's attention. Here was a great treasure—wholly strange Crustacea of Middle Cambrian time—but where in the mountain was the mother rock from which the slab had come? Snow was even then falling, and the solving of the riddle had to be left to another season, but next year the Walcotts were back again on Mount Wapta, and eventually the slab was traced to a layer of shale—later called the Burgess shale—3,000 feet above the town of Field, British Columbia, and 8,000 feet above the sea.

Stories are subject to a kind of natural selection. As they propagate in the retelling and mutate by embellishment, most eventually fall by the wayside to extinction from public consciousness. The few survivors hang tough because they speak to deeper themes that stir our souls or tickle our funnybones. The Burgess legend is a particularly good story because it moves from tension to resolution, and enfolds within its basically simple structure two of the greatest themes in conventional narration—serendipity and industry leading to its just reward. We would never have known about the Burgess if Mrs. Walcott's horse hadn't slipped going downslope on the very last day of the field season (as night descended and snow fell, to provide a dramatic backdrop of last-minute chanciness). So Walcott bides his time for a year in considerable anxiety. But he is a good geologist and knows how to find his quarry (literally in this case). He returns the next summer and finally locates the Burgess Shale by hard work and geological skill. He starts with the dislodged block and traces it patiently upslope until he finds the mother lode. Schuchert doesn't mention a time, but most versions state that Walcott spent a week or more trying to locate the source. Walcott's son Sidney, reminiscing sixty years later, wrote in 1971: "We worked our way up, trying to find the bed of rock from which our original find had been dislodged. A week later and some 750 feet higher we decided that we had found the site."

I can imagine two basic reasons for the survival and propagation of this canonical story. First, it is simply too good a tale to pass into oblivion. When both good luck and honest labor combine to produce victory, we all feel grateful to discover that fortune occasionally smiles, and uplifted to learn that effort brings reward. Second, the story might be true. And if dramatic and factual value actually coincide, then we have a real winner.

I had always grasped the drama and never doubted the veracity (the story is plausible, after all). But in 1988, while spending several days in the Walcott archives at the Smithsonian Institution, I discovered that all key points of the story are false. I found that some of my colleagues had also tracked down the smoking gun before me, for the relevant pages of Walcott's diary had been earmarked and photographed before.

Walcott, the great conservative administrator, left a precious gift to future historians by his assiduous recordkeeping. He never missed a day of writing in his diary. Even at the very worst moment of his life, July 11, 1911, he made the following, crisply factual entry about his wife: "Helena killed at Bridgeport Conn. by train being smashed up at 2:30 A.M. Did not hear of it until 3 P.M. Left for Bridgeport 5:35 P.M." (Walcott was meticulous, but please do not think him callous. Overcome with grief the next day, he wrote on July 12: "My love—my wife—my comrade for 24 years. I thank God I had her for that time. Her untimely fate I cannot now understand.")

Walcott's diary for the close of the 1909 field season neatly dismisses part one of the canonical tale. Walcott found the first soft-bodied fossils on Burgess ridge either on August 30 or 31. His entry for August 30 reads:

> Out collecting on the Stephen formation [the unit that includes what Walcott later called the Burgess Shale] all day. Found many interesting fossils on the west slope of the ridge between Mounts Field and Wapta [the right locality for the Burgess Shale]. Helena, Helen, Arthur, and Stuart [his wife, daughter, assistant, and son] came up with remainder of outfit at 4 P.M.

On the next day, they had clearly discovered a rich assemblage of soft-bodied fossils. Walcott's quick sketches (see figure) are so clear that I can identify the three genera he depicts—*Marrella* (upper left), the most common Burgess fossil and one of the

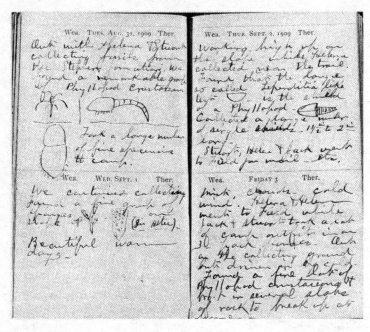

The smoking gun for exploding a Burgess Shale legend. Walcott's diary for the end of August and the beginning of September, 1909. He collected for an entire week in good weather. SMITHSONIAN INSTITUTION.

unique arthropods beyond the range of modern designs; *Waptia*, a bivalved arthropod (upper right); and the peculiar trilobite *Naraoia* (lower left). Walcott wrote: "Out with Helena and Stuart collecting fossils from the Stephen formation. We found a remarkable group of Phyllopod crustaceans. Took a large number of fine specimens to camp."

What about the horse slipping and the snow falling? If this incident occurred at all, we must mark the date as August 30, when Walcott's family came up the slope to meet him in the late afternoon. They might have turned up the slab as they descended for the night, returning the next morning to find the specimens that Walcott drew on August 31. This reconstruction gains some support from a letter that Walcott wrote to Marr (for whom he later named the "lace crab" *Marrella*) in October 1909:

When we were collecting from the Middle Cambrian, a stray slab of shale brought down by a snow slide showed a fine Phyllopod crustacean on a broken edge. Mrs. W. and I worked on that slab from 8 in the morning until 6 in the evening and took back with us the finest collection of Phyllopod crustaceans that I have ever seen.

(Phyllopod, or "leaf-footed," is an old name for marine arthropods with rows of lacy gills, often used for swimming, on one branch of their legs.)

Transformation can be subtle. A snow slide becomes a snowstorm, and the night before a happy day in the field becomes a forced and hurried end to an entire season. But far more important, Walcott's field season did not finish with the discoveries of August 30 and 31. The party remained on Burgess ridge until September 7! Walcott was thrilled by his discovery and collected with avidity every day thereafter. The diaries breathe not a single word about snow, and Walcott assiduously reported the weather in every entry. His happy week brought nothing but praise for Mother Nature. On September 1 he wrote: "Beautiful warm days."

Finally, I strongly suspect that Walcott located the source for his stray block during the last week of his 1909 field season—at least the basic area of outcrop, if not the very richest layers. On September 1, the day after he drew the three arthropods, Walcott wrote: "We continued collecting. Found a fine group of sponges on slope (*in situ*) [meaning undisturbed and in their original position]." Sponges, containing some hard parts, extend beyond the richest layers of soft-bodied preservation, but the best specimens come from the strata of the Burgess mother lode. On each subsequent day, Walcott found abundant soft-bodied specimens, and his descriptions do not read like the work of a man encountering a lucky stray block here and there. On September 2, he discovers that the supposed shell of an ostracode really houses the body of a Phyllopod: "Working high up on the slope while Helena collected near the trail. Found that the large so-called Leperditia-like test is the shield of a Phyllopod." The Burgess quarry is "high up on the slope," while stray blocks would slide down toward the trail.

On September 3, Walcott was even more successful: "Found a

fine lot of Phyllopod crustaceans and brought in several slabs of rock to break up at camp." In any event, he continued to collect, and put in a full day for his last hurrah on September 7: "With Stuart and Mr. Rutter went up on fossil beds. Out from 7 A.M. to 6:30 P.M. Our last day in camp for 1909."

If I am right about his discovery of the main beds in 1909, then the second part of the canonical tale—the week-long patient tracing of errant block to source in 1910—should be equally false. Walcott's diary for 1910 supports my interpretation. On July 10, champing at the bit, he hiked up to the Burgess Pass campground, but found the area too deep in snow for any excavations. Finally, on July 29, Walcott reports that his party set up "at Burgess Pass campground of 1909." On July 30, they climbed neighboring Mount Field and collected fossils. Walcott indicates that they made their first attempt to locate the Burgess beds on August 1:

> All out collecting the Burgess formation until 4 P.M. when a cold wind and rain drove us into camp. Measured section of the Burgess formation—420 feet thick. Sidney with me. Stuart with his mother and Helen puttering about camp.

("Measuring a section" is geological jargon for tracing the vertical sequence of strata and noting the rock types and fossils. If you wished to find the source of an errant block dislodged and tumbled below, you would measure the section above, trying to match your block to its most likely layer.)

I think that Charles and Sidney Walcott located the Burgess beds on this very first day, because Walcott writes for his next entry of August 2: "Out collecting with Helena, Stuart, and Sidney. We found a fine lot of 'lace crabs' and various odds and ends of things." "Lace crab" was Walcott's informal field term for *Marrella,* and *Marrella* is the marker of the mother lode—the most common animal in the Burgess Shale. If we wish to give the canonical tale all benefit of doubt, and argue that these lace crabs of August 2 came from dislodged blocks, we still cannot grant a week of strenuous effort for locating the mother lode, for Walcott writes just two days later on August 4: "Helena worked out a lot of Phyllopod crustaceans from 'Lace Crab layer.'" From then on, until the end of summer, they quarried the lace crab layer, now known as the Burgess Shale.

The canonical tale is more romantic and inspiring, but the plain factuality of the diary makes more sense. I have been to the Burgess ridge. The trail lies just a few hundred feet below the main Burgess beds. The slope is simple and steep, with strata well exposed. Tracing an errant block to its source should not have presented a major problem—for Walcott was more than a good geologist; he was a great geologist. He should have located the main beds right away, in 1909, since he had a week to work after first discovering soft-bodied fossils. He was not able to quarry in 1909—the only constraint imposed by limits of time. But he found many fine fossils and probably the main beds themselves. He knew just where to go in 1910 and set up shop in the right place as soon as the snows melted.

Memory is a fascinating trickster. Words and images have enormous power and can easily displace actual experience over the years. As an intriguing testimony to the power of legend, consider the late memories of Walcott's son Sidney. In 1971, more than sixty years after the events, Sidney wrote a short article for *Smithsonian*, "How I Found My Own Fossil." (The largest Burgess arthropod bears the name *Sidneyia inexpectans* in honor of his discovery.) Sidney must have heard the canonical tale over and over again across the many years (think of him enduring mounds of rubber chicken and endless repetitions of the anecdote in after-dinner speeches)—and his actual experience faded as the conventional myth took root.

Sidney's version includes the two main ingredients—serendipity in the chance discovery of a dislodged slab blocking the pathway of packhorses, and assiduous effort in the patient, week-long tracing of block to source. But Sidney places the packhorse incident on his watch in 1910, not on his mother's the previous year:

> Father suddenly told me to halt the packtrain. I signaled, and the horses started to browse at the side of the trail. Often on our summer camping trips I had seen Father throw stones and logs out of the trail to make the going a bit easier for the horses. So it was no surprise to see him upend a slab, worn white by the shoes of horses slipping on it for

years. He hit it a few times along its edge with his geological hammer and it split open. "Look Sidney," he called. I saw several extraordinary fossils on the rock surface. "Let's look further tomorrow. . . . We won't go to Field tonight." To our family, back in 1910, it seemed a miracle that Father's simple act of thoughtfulness for the comfort and safety of a few packhorses led to this discovery.

A lovely story, but absolutely nothing about it can be true. Sidney knew the canonical yarn about slabs and packhorses, but moved the tale a year forward. We cannot believe that slabs could have blocked paths for two years running, with fossils always on their upturned edges, especially since an unanticipated discovery in 1909 precludes a similar surprise the next year. Moreover, Sidney could not have remembered an actual incident of the first season, and then mixed up the years, because he wasn't there in 1909!

Sidney's second ingredient, his tale of a week-long search for the mother lode (cited previously in this essay), is equally false from the evidence of Walcott's diary, and similarly read into memory from the repetition of legend, not the recall of actual events.

Why am I bothering with all this detail? To be sure, truth has a certain moral edge over falsehood, but few people care much about corrections to stories they never heard about people they never knew. If the only lesson in this little reversal of Burgess orthodoxy exhorts us to be careful lest a tendency to embellish or romanticize stifle the weakly flickering flame of truth, then this essay is as banal as the sentence I just wrote. But I would defend my effort on two grounds. First, the Burgess animals happen to be the world's most important fossils, and the purely factual issues surrounding their discovery therefore demand more than the usual care and attention to accuracy. We might not challenge a family legend about Uncle Joe in the interests of domestic peace and benevolence, but we really would like to know how Jesus lived and died because different views have had such palpable effects upon billions of lives. Second, I believe that our tendencies to construct legends raise an issue far more interesting than watchdog warnings about eternal verity.

I would begin by asking why almost every canonical tale is false in the same way—a less interesting reality converted to a simple story with a message. Do we need these stories so badly because life isn't heroic or thrilling most of the time? Sean O'Casey said that the stage must be larger than life, and few poets or playwrights can succeed by fidelity to the commonplace. It takes the artistry of James Joyce to make a masterpiece from one day in the life of an ordinary man. Most of our existence is eating, sleeping, walking, and breathing. Even the life of a soldier, if expressed in real time, would be almost uninterrupted tedium—for an old motto identifies this profession as long periods of boredom interspersed with short moments of terror.

Astute scientists understand that political and cultural bias must impact their ideas, and they strive to recognize these inevitable influences. But we usually fail to acknowledge another source of error that might be called literary bias. So much of science proceeds by telling stories—and we are especially vulnerable to constraints of this medium because we so rarely recognize what we are doing. We think that we are reading nature by applying rules of logic and laws of matter to our observations. But we are often telling stories—in the good sense, but stories nonetheless. Consider the traditional scenarios of human evolution—tales of the hunt, of campfires, dark caves, rituals, and toolmaking, coming of age, struggle and death. How much is based on bones and artifacts and how much on the norms of literature?

If these reconstructions are stories, then they are bound by the rules of canonical legendmaking. And if we construct our stories to be *unlike* life—the main point of this essay—then our literary propensities are probably derailing our hope to understand the quotidian reality of our evolution. Stories only go in certain ways—and these paths do not conform to patterns of actual life.

This constraint does not apply only to something so clearly ripe for narration and close to home as "the rise of man from the apes" (to choose a storylike description that enfolds biases of gender and progress into its conventionality). Even the most distant and abstract subjects, like the formation of the universe or the principles of evolution, fall within the bounds of necessary narrative. Our images of evolution are caught in the web of tale telling. They involve progress, pageant; above all, ceaseless motion somewhere. Even revisionist stories that question ideas of gradual progress—the sort that I have been spinning for years in these essays—are tales of another kind about good fortune, unpredictability, and contingency (the kingdom lost for want of a horseshoe nail). But focus on almost any evolutionary moment, and nothing much is happening. Evolution, like soldiering and life itself, is daily repetition almost all the time. Evolutionary days may be generations, but as the Preacher said, one passeth away and another cometh, but the earth abideth forever. The fullness of time, of course, does provide a sufficient range for picking out rare moments of activity and linking them together into a story. But we must understand that nothing happens most of the time— and we don't because our stories don't admit this theme—if we hope to grasp the dynamics of evolutionary change. (This sentence may sound contradictory, but it isn't. To know the reasons for infrequent change, one must understand the ordinary rules of stability.) The Burgess Shale teaches us that, for the history of basic anatomical designs, almost everything happened in the geological moment just before, and almost nothing in more than 500 million years since.

Included in this "almost nothing," as a kind of geological afterthought of the last few million years, is the first development of self-conscious intelligence on this planet—an odd and unpredictable invention of a little twig on the mammalian evolutionary bush. Any definition of this uniqueness, embedded as it is in our possession of language, must involve our ability to frame the world as stories and to transmit these tales to others. If our propensity to grasp nature as story has distorted our perceptions, I shall accept this limit of mentality upon knowledge, for we receive in trade both the joys of literature and the core of our being.

6 | Down Under

17 | Glow, Big Glowworm

SMALL MISUNDERSTANDINGS are often a prod to insight or victory. For such a minor error with major consequences, Laurel and Hardy got into terminal trouble with the toymaster in *March of the Wooden Soldiers*—they got fired for building 100 soldiers six feet high, when Santa had ordered 600 at one foot. But the six-footers later saved Toyland from the invasion of Barnaby and his bogeymen.

In insects that undergo a complete metamorphosis, cells that will form adult tissues are already present in the bodies of larvae as isolated patches called imaginal disks. For many years, I regarded this term as one of the oddest in all biology—for I always read "imaginal" as "imaginary" and thought I was being told that this substrate of maturity really didn't exist at all.

When I learned the true origin of this term, I realized that I had not only misunderstood but had made an absolutely backward interpretation. I also discovered that my resolution had taught me something interesting—about ways of looking at the world, not about any facts of nature per se—and I therefore judged my former error as fruitful.

Linnaeus himself, father of taxonomy, named the stages of insect development. He designated the feeding stage that hatched from the egg as a larva (the caterpillar of a moth or the maggot of a housefly), and he called the sexually mature adult an imago, hence imaginal disk for precursors of adult tissues within the larva.

The etymologies of these terms provided my insight—a larva is a mask; an imago, the image or essential form of a species. Linnaeus, in other words, viewed the development of insects as progress toward fulfillment. The first stage is only preparatory; it hides the true and complete representation of a species. The final form embodies the essence of louseness, thripsness, or flyness. Imaginal disks, by both etymology and concept, are bits of higher reality lurking within initial imperfection—no sign of "let's pretend" here.

Most impediments to scientific understanding are conceptual locks, not factual lacks. Most difficult to dislodge are those biases that escape our scrutiny because they seem so obviously, even ineluctably, just. We know ourselves best and tend to view other creatures as mirrors of our own constitution and social arrangements. (Aristotle, and nearly two millennia of successors, designated the large bee that leads the swarm as a king.)

Few aspects of human existence are more basic than our life cycle of growth and development. For all the glories of childhood, we in the West have generally viewed our youngsters as undeveloped and imperfect adults—smaller, weaker, and more ignorant. Adulthood is a termination; childhood, an upward path. How natural, then, that we should also interpret the life cycles of other organisms as a linear path from imperfect potential to final realization—from the small, ill-formed creature that first develops from an egg to the large and complex fruition that produces the egg of the next generation.

How obvious, in particular, that insect larvae are imperfect juveniles and imagoes realized adults. Linnaeus's etymology embodies this traditional interpretation imposed from human life upon the development of insects. When we combine this dubious comparison of human and insect life cycles with our more general preference for viewing developmental sequences as ladders of progress (a prejudice that has hampered our understanding of evolution even more than our resolution of embryology), insect larvae seem doomed to easy dismissal by an aggregation of biases—etymological, conceptual, and parochial.

If we turn to two leading works of popular science, published five years after Darwin's *Origin of Species*—one on life cycles in general, the other on insects—we obtain a good sense of these traditional biases. A. de Quatrefages, great French student of that economic leader among insect larvae, the silkworm, wrote in

his *Metamorphosis of Man and the Lower Animals* (1864) that "larvae
. . . are always incomplete beings; they are true first sketches,
which are rendered more and more perfect at each developmental phase."

An Introduction to Entomology, by William Kirby, rector of Bar-
ham, and William Spence, wins first prize among British works of
popular science for celebrity, for longevity (its first edition appeared in 1815), and for prose in the most preciously purple
tradition of "nature writing," as satirized by example in James
Joyce's *Ulysses:* "Note the meanderings of some purling rill as it
babbles on its way, fanned by the gentlest zephyrs tho' quarrel-
ling with the stony obstacles, to the tumbling waters of Neptune's
blue domain. . . ." To which, Mr. Dedalus replies: "Agonizing
Christ, wouldn't it give you a heartburn on your arse." And for
which (among other things) *Ulysses* was once banned from the
United States as obscene—although I would sooner exclude that
purling rill than a heartburn on any part of the anatomy.

In their first post-Darwinian edition (1863), Kirby and Spence
make no bones about their preference for well-formed imagoes
and their distaste for grubby larvae (a redundancy for emphasis
of my point—grubs are larvae, and we owe this adjective to the
same prejudice):

> That active little fly, now an unbidden guest at your table,
> whose delicate palate selects your choicest viands, while ex-
> tending his proboscis to the margin of a drop of wine, and
> then gaily flying to take a more solid repast from a pear or
> peach; now gamboling with his comrades in the air, now
> gracefully currying his furled wings with his taper feet, was
> but the other day a disgusting grub, without wings, without
> legs, without eyes, wallowing, well pleased, in the midst of a
> mass of excrement.

The adult, they write, is called an imago "because, having laid
aside its mask [larva], and cast off its swaddling bands [the pupal
cocoon, or chrysalis], being no longer disguised [larva] or confined [pupa], or in any other respect imperfect, it is now become a
true representative or image of its species."

The burden of metaphor becomes immeasurably heavier for

larvae when Kirby and Spence then drag out that oldest of all insect analogies from an age of more pervasive Christianity—the life cycle of a butterfly to the passage of a soul from first life in the imperfect prison of a human body (larval caterpillar), to death and entombment (pupal chrysalis), to the winged freedom of resurrection (imago, or butterfly). This simile dates to the great Dutch biologist Jan Swammerdam, child of Cartesian rationalism but also, at heart, a religious mystic, who first discovered the rudimentary wings of butterflies, enfurled in late stages of larval caterpillars. Swammerdam wrote near the end of the seventeenth century: "This process is formed in so remarkable a manner in butterflies, that we see therein the resurrection painted before our eyes, and exemplified so as to be examined by our hands." Kirby and Spence then elaborated just a bit:

> To see a caterpillar crawling upon the earth sustained by the most ordinary kinds of food, which when . . . its appointed work being finished, passes into an intermediate state of seeming death, when it is wound up in a kind of shroud and encased in a coffin, and is most commonly buried under the earth . . . then, when called by the warmth of the solar beam, they burst from their sepulchres, cast off their raiments . . . come forth as a bride out of her chamber—to survey them, I say, arrayed in their nuptial glory, prepared to enjoy a new and more exalted condition of life, in which all their powers are developed, and they are arrived at the perfection of their nature . . . who that witnesses this interesting scene can help seeing in it a lively representation of man in his threefold state of existence. . . .The butterfly, the representative of the soul, is prepared in the larva for its future state of glory; . . . it will come to its state of repose in the pupa, which is its Hades; and at length, when it assumes the imago, break forth with new powers and beauty to its final glory and the reign of love.

But must we follow this tradition and view larvae as harbingers of better things? Must all life cycles be conceptualized as paths of progress leading to an adult form? Human adults control the world's media—and the restriction of this power to one stage of our life cycle imposes a myopic view. I would be happy to counter this prejudice (as many have) by emphasizing the creativity and specialness of human childhood, but this essay speaks for insects.

I will admit that our standard prejudice applies, in one sense, to creatures like ourselves. Our bodies do grow and transform in continuity. A human adult is an enlarged version of its own childhood; we grown-ups retain the same organs, reshaped a bit and often increased a great deal. (Many insects with simple life cycles, or so-called incomplete metamorphoses, also grow in continuity. This essay treats those insects that cycle through the classic stages of complete metamorphosis: egg, larva, pupa, and imago.)

But how can we apply this bias of the upward path to complex life cycles of other creatures? In what sense is the polyp of a cnidarian (the phylum of corals and their allies) more—or less—complete than the medusa that buds from its body? One stage feeds and grows; the other mates and lays eggs. They perform different and equally necessary functions. What else can one say? Insect larvae and imagoes perform the same division—larvae eat and imagoes reproduce. Moreover, larvae do not grow into imagoes by increase and complication of parts. Instead, larval tissues are sloughed off and destroyed during the pupal stage, while the imago largely develops from small aggregations of cells—the imaginal disks of this essay's beginning—that resided, but did not differentiate, within the larva. Degenerating larval tissues are often used as a culture medium for growth of the imago within the pupa. Larva and imago are different and discrete, not before and shadowy versus later and complete.

Even Kirby and Spence sensed this true distinction between objects equally well suited for feeding and reproduction, though they soon buried their insight in cascading metaphors about progress and resurrection:

> Were you . . . to compare the internal conformation of the caterpillar with that of the butterfly, you would witness changes even more extraordinary. In the former you would find some thousands of muscles, which in the latter are replaced by others of a form and structure entirely different. Nearly the whole body of the caterpillar is occupied by a capacious stomach. In the butterfly it has become converted into an almost imperceptible thread-like viscus; and the abdomen is now filled by two large packets of eggs.

If we break through the tyranny of our usual bias, to a different view of larvae and imagoes as separate and potentially equal devices for feeding and reproduction, many puzzles are immediately resolved. Each stage adapts in its own way, and depending upon ecology and environment, one might be emphasized, the other degraded to insignificance in our limited eyes. The "degraded" stage might be the imago as well as the larva—more likely, in fact, since feeding and growth can be rushed only so much, but mating, as poets proclaim, can be one enchanted evening. Thus, I used to feel sorry for the mayfly and its legendary one day of existence, but such brevity only haunts the imago, and longer-lived larvae also count in the total cycle of life. And what about the seventeen-year "locust" (actually a cicada)? Larvae don't lie around doing nothing during this dog's age, waiting patiently for their few days of visible glory. They have an active life underground, including long stretches of dormancy to be sure, but also active growth through numerous molts.

Thus, we find our best examples of an alternative and expansive view of life cycles among species that emphasize the size, length, and complexity of larval life at the apparent expense of imaginal domination—where, to borrow Butler's famous line with only minor change in context, a hen really does seem to be the egg's way of manufacturing another egg. I recently encountered a fine case during a visit to New Zealand—made all the more dramatic because human perceptions focus entirely upon the larva and ignore the imago.

After you leave the smoking and steaming, the boiling and puffing, the sulfurous stench of geysers, fumaroles, and mud pots around Rotorua, you arrive at the second best site on the standard tourist itinerary of the North Island—the glowworm grotto of Waitomo Cave. Here, in utter silence, you glide by boat into a spectacular underground planetarium, an amphitheater lit with thousands of green dots—each the illuminated rear end of a fly larva (not a worm at all). (I was dazzled by the effect because I found it so unlike the heavens. Stars are arrayed in the sky at random with respect to the earth's position. Hence, we view them as clumped into constellations. This may sound paradoxical, but my statement reflects a proper and unappreciated aspect of random distributions. Evenly spaced dots are well ordered for cause. Random arrays always include some clumping, just as we will flip several heads in a row quite often so long as we can make enough tosses—and our sky is not wanting for stars. The glowworms, on the other hand, are spaced more evenly because larvae compete with, and even eat, each other—and each constructs an exclusive territory. The glowworm grotto is an ordered heaven.)

These larval glowworms are profoundly modified members of the family Mycetophilidae, or fungus gnats. Imagoes of this species are unremarkable, but the larvae rank among the earth's most curious creatures. Two larval traits (and nothing imaginal) inspired the name for this peculiar species—*Arachnocampa luminosa,* honoring both the light and the silken nest that both houses the glowworm and traps its prey (for Arachne the weaver, namesake of spiders, or arachnids, as well). The imagoes of *Arachnocampa luminosa* are small and short-lived mating machines. The much larger and longer-lived larvae have evolved three complex and coordinated adaptations—carnivory, light, and webbing—that distinguish them from the simpler larval habits of ancestral fungus gnats: burrowing into mushrooms, munching all the way.

In a total life cycle (egg to egg) often lasting eleven months, *Arachnocampa luminosa* spends eight to nine months as a larval glowworm. Larvae molt four times and grow from 3- to 5-millimeter hatchlings to a final length of some 30 to 40 millimeters. (By contrast, imagoes are 12 to 16 millimeters in length, males slightly smaller than females, and live but one to four days, males usually longer than females.)

Carnivory is the focus of larval existence, the coordinating theme behind a life-style so different from the normal course of larval herbivory in fungus gnats. Consider the three principal ingredients:

Luminescence: The light organ of *A. luminosa* forms at the rear end of the larva from enlarged tips of four excretory tubes. These tubes carry a waste product that glows in the presence of luciferase, an enzyme also produced by the larva. This reaction requires a good supply of oxygen, and the four excretory tubes lie embedded in a dense network of respiratory tubules that both supply oxygen to fuel the reaction and then reflect and direct the light downward. This complex and specially evolved system functions to attract insects (mostly small midges) to the nest. Pupae and imagoes retain the ability to luminesce. The light of female pupae and adults attracts males, but the glow of adult males has no known function.

The Nest and Feeding Threads: From glands in its mouth, the glowworm exudes silk and mucus to construct a marvel of organic architecture. The young larva first builds the so-called nest—really more of a hollow tube or runway—some two to three times the length of its body. A network of fine silk threads suspends this nest from the cave's ceiling. The larva drops a curtain of closely spaced feeding threads from its nest. These "fishing lines" may number up to seventy per nest and may extend almost a foot in length (or ten times the span of the larva itself). Each line is studded along its entire length with evenly spaced, sticky droplets that catch intruding insects; the entire structure resembles, in miniature, a delicate curtain of glass beads. Since the slightest current of air can cause these lines to tangle, caves, culverts, ditches, and calm spaces amidst vegetation provide the limited habitats for *A. luminosa* in New Zealand.

Carnivory: Using its lighted rear end as a beacon, *A. luminosa* attracts prey to its feeding threads. Two posterior papillae contain sense organs that detect vibrations of ensnared prey. The larva then crawls partway down the proper line, leaving half to two-thirds of its rear in the nest, and hauls up both line and meal at a rate of some 2 millimeters per second.

The rest of the life cycle pales by comparison with this complexity of larval anatomy and behavior. The pupal stage lasts a bit less than two weeks and already records a marked reduction in size (15 to 18 millimeters for females, 12 to 14 for males). I have already noted the imago's decrease in body size and duration of life. Imaginal behavior also presents little in the way of diversity or complexity. Adult flies have no mouth and do not feed at all. We commit no great exaggeration by stating that they behave as unipurpose mating and egg-laying machines during their brief existence. Up to three males may congregate at a female pupa, awaiting her emergence. They jockey for positon and fight as the female fly begins to break through her encasement. As soon as the tip of her abdomen emerges, males (if present) begin to mate. Thus, females can be fertilized even before they break fully from the pupal case. Females may then live for less than a day (and no more than three), doing little more before they expire than finding an appropriate place for some 100 to 300 eggs, laid one at a time in clumps of 40 to 50. Males may live an additional day (up to four); with luck, they may find another female and do it again for posterity.

As a final and grisly irony, emphasizing larval dominance over the life cycle of *A. luminosa,* a rapacious glowworm will eat anything that touches its feeding threads. The much smaller imagoes often fly into the lines and end up as just another meal for their own children.*

Please do not draw from this essay the conclusion that larvae

---

*To throw in a tidbit for readers interested in the history of evolutionary theory, this tightly coordinated complex of larval adaptations so intrigued Richard Goldschmidt that he once wrote an entire article to argue that light, carnivory, and nest building could not have arisen by gradual piecemeal, since each makes no sense without the others—and that all, therefore, must have appeared at once as a fortuitous consequence of a large mutational change, a "hopeful monster," in his colorful terminology.

This proposal (published in English in *Revue Scientifique,* 1948) inspired a stern reaction from orthodox Darwinians. Although I have great sympathy for Goldschmidt's iconoclasm, he was, I think, clearly wrong in this case. As J. F. Jackson pointed out (1974), Goldschmidt made an error in the taxonomic assignment of *A. luminosa* among the Mycetophilidae. He ranked this species in the subfamily Bolitophilinae. All larvae of this group burrow into soft mushrooms, and none shows even incipient development of any among the three linked features that mark the unique form and behavior of *A. luminosa.* Hence, Goldschmidt argued for all or nothing.

But *A. luminosa* probably belongs in another subfamily, the Keroplatinae—and, unknown to Goldschmidt, several species within this group do display a series of plausible transitions. *Leptomorphus* catches and eats fungal spores trapped on a sheetlike nest slung below a mushroom. Some species of *Macrocera* and *Keroplatus* also build trap nets for fungal spores but will eat small arthropods that also become ensnared. Species of *Orfelia, Apemon,* and *Platyura* build webs of similar form but not associated with mushrooms—and they live exclusively on a diet of trapped insects. Finally, *Orfelia aeropiscator* (literally, air fisher) both builds a nest and hangs vertical feeding threads but does not possess a light.

These various "intermediates" are, of course, not ancestral to *A. luminosa.* Each represents a well-adapted species in its own right, not a transitional stage to the threefold association of New Zealand glowworms. But this array does show that each step in a plausible sequence of structurally intermediate stages can work as a successful organism. This style of argument follows Darwin's famous resolution for a potential evolutionary origin for the extraordinary complexity of the vertebrate eye. Darwin identified a series of structural intermediates, from simple light-sensitive dots to cameralike lens systems—not actual ancestors (for these are lost among nonpreservable eyes in a fossil record of hard parts) but plausible sequences disproving the "commonsense" notion that nothing in between is possible in principle.

are really more important than imagoes, either in *A. luminosa* or in general. I have tried to show that larvae must not be dismissed—as preparatory, undeveloped, or incomplete—by false analogy to a dubious (but socially favored) interpretation of human development. If any "higher reality" exists, we can only specify the life cycle itself. Larva and imago are but two stages of a totality—and you really can't have one without the other. Eggs need hens as much as hens need eggs.

I do try to show that child-adult is the wrong metaphor for understanding larva-imago. I have proceeded by discussing a case where larvae attract all our attention—literally as a source of beauty; structurally in greater size, length of life, and complexity of anatomy and behavior; and evolutionarily as focus of a major transformation from a simpler and very different ancestral style—while imagoes have scarcely modified their inherited form and behavior at all. But our proper emphasis on the larva of *A. luminosa* does not mark any superiority.

We need another metaphor to break the common interpretation that degrades larvae to a penumbra of insignificance. (How many of you include maggot in your concept of fly? And how many have ever considered the mayfly's longer larval life?) The facts of nature are what they are, but we can only view them through spectacles of our mind. Our mind works largely by metaphor and comparison, not always (or often) by relentless logic. When we are caught in conceptual traps, the best exit is often a change in metaphor—not because the new guideline will be truer to nature (for neither the old nor the new metaphor lies "out there" in the woods), but because we need a shift to more fruitful perspectives, and metaphor is often the best agent of conceptual transition.

If we wish to understand larvae as working items in their own right, we should replace the developmental metaphor of child-adult with an economic simile that recognizes the basic distinction in function between larvae and imagoes—larvae as machines built for feeding and imagoes as devices for reproduction. Fortunately, an obvious candidate presents itself on the very first page of the founding document itself—Adam Smith's *Wealth of Nations.* We find our superior metaphor in the title of Chapter 1, "On the Division of Labor," and in Smith's opening sentence:

The greatest improvement in the productive powers of labor, and the greater part of the skill, dexterity, and judgment with which it is anywhere directed, or applied, seem to have been the effects of the division of labor.

By allocating the different, sometimes contradictory, functions of feeding and reproduction to sequential phases of the life cycle, insects with complete metamorphosis have achieved a division of labor that permits a finer adaptive honing of each separate activity.

If you can dredge up old memories of your first college course in economics, you will remember that Adam Smith purposely chose a humble example to illustrate the division of labor—pin making. He identifies eighteen separate actions in drawing the wire, cutting, pointing, manufacture of the head, fastening head to shaft, and mounting the finished products in paper for sale. One man, he argues, could make fewer than twenty pins a day if he performed all these operations himself. But ten men, sharing the work by rigid division of labor, can manufacture about 48,000 pins a day. A human existence spent pointing pins or fashioning their heads or pushing them into paper may strike us as the height of tedium, but larvae of *A. luminosa* encounter no obvious psychic stress in a life fully devoted to gastronomy.

Hobbyists and professional entomologists will, no doubt, have recognized an unintended irony in Smith's selection of pin making to illustrate the division of labor. Pins are the primary stock-in-trade of any insect collector. They are used to fasten the dry and chitinous imagoes—but not the fat and juicy larvae—to collecting boards and boxes. Thus, the imagoes of *A. luminosa* may end their natural life caught in a larval web, but if they happen to fall into the clutches of a human collector, they will, instead, be transfixed by the very object that symbolizes their fall from conceptual dominance to proper partnership.

Postscript

Nothing brings greater pleasure to a scholar than utility in extension—the fruitfulness of a personal thought or idea when devel-

Stars

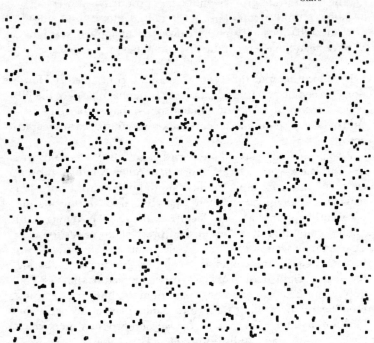

Output from Ed Purcell's computer program for arranging dots by the "stars," ABOVE (random), and the "worms," FACING PAGE (ordered by fields of inhibition around each dot), options. Note the curious psychological effect. Most of us would see order in the strings and clumps of the figure just above, and would interpret the figure on the opposite page, with its lack of apparent pattern, as random. In fact, the opposite is true, and our ordinary conceptions are faulty.

oped by colleagues beyond the point of one's own grasp. I make a tangential reference in this essay to a common paradox—the apparent pattern of random arrays versus the perceived absence of sensible order in truly rule-bound systems. This paradox arises because random systems are highly clumped, and we perceive clumps as determined order. I gave the example of the heavens—

Worms

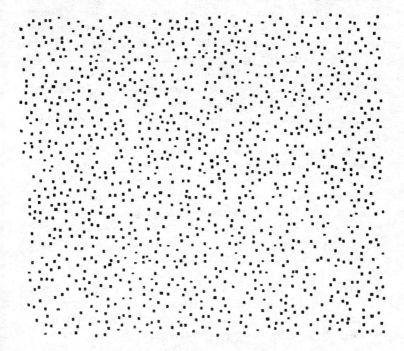

where we "see" constellations because stars are distributed at random relative to the earth's position. I contrasted our perception of heavenly order with the artificial "sky" of Waitomo Cave—where "stars" are the self-illuminated rear ends of fly larvae. Since these carnivorous larvae space themselves out in an ordered array (because they eat anything in their vicinity and therefore set up "zones of inhibition" around their own bodies), the Waitomo "sky" looks strange to us for its absence of clumping.

My favorite colleague, Ed Purcell (Nobel laureate in physics and sometime collaborator on baseball statistics), read this tangential comment and wrote a quick computer program to illustrate the effect. Into an array of square cells (144 units on the X-axis and 96 on the Y-axis for a total of 13,824 positions), Purcell placed either "stars" or "worms" by the following rules of randomness and order (following the heavens versus the fly larvae of Waitomo). In the stars option, squares are simply occupied at random (a random number generator spits out a figure between 1 and 13,824 and the appropriate square is inked in). In the worms option, the same generator spits out a number, but the appropriate square is inked in only if it and all surrounding squares are unoccupied (just as a worm sets up a zone of inhibition about itself). Thus, worm squares are spaced out by a principle of order; star squares are just filled in as the random numbers come up.

Now examine the patterns produced with 1,500 stars and worms (still less than 50 percent capacity for worms, since one in four squares could be occupied, and 3,456 potential worm holes therefore exist). By ordinary vernacular perception, we could swear that the "stars" program must be generating causal order, while the "worms" program, for apparent lack of pattern, seems to be placing the squares haphazardly. Of course, exactly the opposite is true. In his letter to me, Ed wrote:

> What interests me more in the random field of "stars" is the overpowering impression of "features" of one sort or another. It is hard to accept the fact that any perceived feature—be it string, clump, constellation, corridor, curved chain, lacuna—is a totally meaningless accident, having as its only cause the avidity for pattern of my eye and brain! Yet that is perfectly true in this case.

I don't know why our brains (by design or culture) equip us so poorly as probability calculators—but this nearly ubiquitous failure constitutes one of the chief, and often dangerous, dilemmas of both intellectual and everyday life (the essays of Section 9, particularly number 31 on Joe DiMaggio's hitting streak, discuss this subject at greater length). Ed Purcell adds, emphasizing the pervasiveness of misperception, even among people trained in probability:

> If you ask a physics student to take pen in hand and sketch a random pattern of 1,500 dots, I suspect the result will look more like the "worms" option than the "stars."

18 | To Be a Platypus

LONG AGO, garrulous old Polonius exalted brevity as the soul of wit, but later technology, rather than sweet reason, won his day and established verbal condensation as a form of art in itself. The telegram, sent for cash on the line and by the word, made brevity both elegant and economical—and the word *telegraphic* entered our language for a style that conveys bare essentials and nothing else.

The prize for transmitting most meaning with least verbosity must surely go to Sir Charles Napier, who subdued the Indian province of Sind and announced his triumph, via telegram to his superiors in London, with the minimal but fully adequate *"Peccavi."* This tale, in its own telegraphic way, speaks volumes about the social order and education of imperial Britain. In an age when all gentlemen studied Latin, and could scarcely rise in government service without a boost from the old boys of similar background in appropriate public schools, Napier never doubted that his superiors would remember the first-person past tense of the verb *peccare*—and would properly translate his message and pun: I have sinned.

The most famous telegram from my profession did not quite reach this admirable minimum, but it must receive honorable mention for conveying a great deal in few words. In 1884, W. H. Caldwell, a young Cambridge biologist, sent his celebrated telegram from Australia to a triumphant reading at the Annual Meeting of the British Association in Montreal. Caldwell wired: "Monotremes oviparous, ovum meroblastic."

This message may lack the ring of *peccavi* and might be viewed

269

by the uninitiated as pure mumbo jumbo. But all professional biologists could make the translation and recognize that Caldwell had solved a particularly stubborn and vexatious problem of natural history. In essence, his telegram said: The duckbilled platypus lays eggs.

(Each word of Caldwell's telegram needs some explication. Oviparous animals lay eggs, while viviparous creatures give birth to live young; ovoviviparous organisms form eggs within their bodies, and young hatch inside their mothers. Sorry for the jargon so early in the essay, but these distinctions become important later on. Monotremes are that most enigmatic group of mammals from the Australian region—including the spiny echidna, actually two separate genera of anteaters, and the duckbilled platypus, an inhabitant of streams and creeks. An ovum is an egg cell, and meroblastic refers to a mode of cleavage, or initial division into embryonic cells, after fertilization. Yolk, the egg's food supply, accumulates at one end of the ovum, called the vegetal pole. Cleavage begins at the other end, called the animal pole. If the egg is very yolky, the cleavage plane cannot penetrate and divide the vegetal end. Such an egg shows incomplete, or meroblastic, cleavage—division into discrete cells at the animal pole but little or no separation at the yolky end. Egg-laying land vertebrates, reptiles and birds, tend to produce yolky egg cells with meroblastic cleavage, while most mammals show complete, or holoblastic, cleavage. Therefore, in adding "ovum meroblastic" to "monotremes oviparous," Caldwell emphasized the reptilian character of these paradoxical mammals—not only do they lay eggs but the eggs are typically reptilian in their yolkiness.)

The platypus surely wins first prize in anybody's contest to identify the most curious mammal. Harry Burrell, author of the classic volume on this anomaly (*The Platypus: Its Discovery, Position, Form and Characteristics, Habits and Life History*, 1927), wrote: "Every writer upon the platypus begins with an expression of wonder. Never was there such a disconcerting animal!" (I guess I just broke tradition by starting with the sublime *Hamlet.*)

The platypus sports an unbeatable combination for strangeness: first, an odd habitat with curiously adapted form to match; second, the real reason for its special place in zoological history—its enigmatic mélange of reptilian (or birdlike), with obvious mammalian, characters. Ironically, the feature that first suggested premammalian affinity—the "duckbill" itself—supports no such meaning. The platypus's muzzle (the main theme of this column) is a purely mammalian adaptation to feeding in fresh waters, not a throwback to ancestral form—although the duckbill's formal name embodies this false interpretation: *Ornithorhynchus anatinus* (or the ducklike bird snout).

Chinese taxidermists had long fooled (and defrauded) European mariners with heads and trunks of monkeys stitched to the hind parts of fish—one prominent source for the persistence of mermaid legends. In this context, one can scarcely blame George Shaw for his caution in first describing the platypus (1799):

> Of all the Mammalia yet known it seems the most extraordinary in its conformation, exhibiting the perfect resemblance of the beak of a Duck engrafted on the head of a quadruped. So accurate is the similitude, that, at first view, it naturally excites the idea of some deceptive preparation.

But Shaw could find no stitches, and the skeleton was surely discrete and of one functional piece (the premaxillary bones of the upper jaw extend into the bill and provide its major support). Shaw concluded:

> On a subject so extraordinary as the present, a degree of scepticism is not only pardonable but laudable; and I ought perhaps to acknowledge that I almost doubt the testimony of my own eyes with respect to the structure of this animal's beak; yet must confess that I can perceive no appearance of any deceptive preparation . . . nor can the most accurate examination of expert anatomists discover any deception.

The frontal bill may have provoked most astonishment, but the rear end also provided numerous reasons for amazement. The platypus sported only one opening, the cloaca, for all excretory and reproductive business (as in reptiles, but not most mammals, with their multiplicity of orifices for birth and various forms of excretion; *Monotremata,* or "one-holed," the technical name for the platypus and allied echidna, honors this unmammalian feature).

Internally, the puzzle only increased. The oviducts did not

unite into a uterus, but extended separately into the cloacal tube. Moreover, as in birds, the right ovary had become rudimentary, and all egg cells formed in the left ovary. This configuration inevitably led to a most troubling hypothesis for biologists committed, as most were in these pre-Darwinian days, to the division of nature into unambiguous, static categories: no uterus, no internal space to form a placenta, a reproductive tract reptilian in form. All this suggested the unthinkable for a mammal—birth from eggs. The neighboring marsupials, with their pouches and tiny joeys, had already compromised the noble name of mammal. Would Australia also yield the ultimate embarrassment of fur from eggs?

As anatomists studied this creature early in the nineteenth century, the mystery only deepened. The platypus looked like a perfectly good mammal in all "standard" nonreproductive traits. It sported a full coat of hair and the defining anatomical signature of mammals—one bone, the dentary, in its lower jaw and three, the hammer, anvil, and stirrup, in its middle ear. (Reptiles have several jawbones and only one ear bone. Two reptilian jawbones became the hammer and anvil of the mammalian ear.) But pre-mammalian characters also extended beyond the reproductive system. In particular, the platypus grew an interclavicle bone in its shoulder girdle—a feature of reptiles shared by no placental mammal.

What could this curious mélange be, beyond a divine test of faith and patience? Debate centered on modes of reproduction, for eggs had not yet been found and Caldwell's telegram lay half a century in the future. All three possibilities boasted their vociferous and celebrated defenders—for no great biologist could avoid such a fascinating creature, and all leaders of natural history entered the fray. Meckel, the great German anatomist, and his French colleague Blainville predicted viviparity, argued that eggs would never be found, and accommodated the monotremes among ordinary mammals. E. Home, who first described the platypus in detail (1802), and the renowned English anatomist Richard Owen chose the middle pathway of ovoviviparity and argued that failure to find eggs indicated their dissolution within the female's body. But the early French evolutionists, Lamarck and Etienne Geoffroy Saint-Hilaire, insisted that anatomy could not lie and that the platypus must be oviparous. Eggs, they argued, would eventually be found.

Geoffroy, by the way, coined the name *monotreme* in an interesting publication that reveals as much about French social history as *peccavi* indicated for imperial Britain. This issue of the *Bulletin des sciences* is labeled *Thermidor, an 11 de la République*. With revolutionary fervor at its height, France broke all ties with the old order and started counting again from year one (1793). They also redivided the year into twelve equal months, and renamed the months to honor the seasons rather than old gods and emperors. Thus, Geoffroy christened the monotremes in a summer month (Thermidor) during the eleventh year (1803) of the Republic (see Essay 24 for more on the French revolutionary calendar).

Just one incident in the pre-Caldwell wars will indicate the intensity of nineteenth-century debate about platypuses and the relief at Caldwell's resolution. When the great naturalists delineated their positions and defined the battleground, mammary glands had not been found in the female platypus—an apparent argument for those, like Geoffroy, who tried to distance monotremes as far as possible from mammals. Then, in 1824, Meckel discovered mammary glands. But since platypuses never do anything by the book, these glands were peculiar enough to spur more debate rather than conciliation. The glands were enormous, extending nearly from the forelegs to the hind limbs—and they led to no common opening, for no nipples could be found. (We now know that the female excretes milk through numerous pores onto a portion of her ventral surface, where the baby platypus laps it up.) Geoffroy, committed to oviparity and unwilling to admit anything like a mammalian upbringing, counterattacked. Meckel's glands, he argued, were not mammary organs, but homologues of the odiferous flank glands of shrews, secreting substances for attraction of mates. When Meckel then extracted a milky substance from the mammary gland, Geoffroy admitted that the secretion must be food of some sort, but not milk. The glands, he now argued, are not mammary but a special feature of monotremes, used to secrete thin strands of mucus that thicken in water to provide food for young hatched from the undiscovered eggs.

Owen then counterattacked to support Meckel for three reasons: The glands are largest shortly after the inferred time of birth (though Geoffroy expected the same for mucus used in feeding). The female echidna, living in sand and unable to thicken mucus in water, possesses glands of the same form. Finally, Owen suspended the secretion in alcohol and obtained globules, like milk, not angular fragments, like mucus (an interesting commentary upon the rudimentary state of chemical analysis during the 1830s).

Geoffroy held firm—both to oviparity (correctly) and to the special status of feeding glands (incorrectly, for they are indeed mammary). In 1822, Geoffroy formally established the Monotremata as a fifth class of vertebrates, ranking equally with fishes, reptiles (then including amphibians), birds, and mammals. We may view Geoffroy as stubborn, and we certainly now regard the monotremes as mammals, however peculiar—but he presents a cogent and perceptive argument well worth our attention. Don't shoehorn monotremes into the class Mammalia to make everything neat and foreclose discussion, he pleads. Taxonomies are guides to action, not passive devices for ordering. Leave monotremes separate and in uncomfortable limbo—"which suggests the necessity of further examination [and] is far better than an assimilation to normality, founded on strained and mistaken relations, which invites indolence to believe and slumber" (letter to the Zoological Society of London, 1833).

Geoffroy also kept the flame of oviparity alive, arguing that the cloaca and reproductive tract bore no other interpretation: "Such as the organ is, such must be its function; the sexual apparatus of an oviparous animal can produce nothing but an egg." So Caldwell arrived in Australia in September 1883—and finally resolved the great debate, eighty years after its inception.

Caldwell, though barely a graduate, proceeded in the grand imperial style (he soon disappeared from biological view and became a successful businessman in Scotland). He employed 150 aboriginals and collected nearly 1,400 echidnas—quite a hecatomb for monotreme biology. On the subject of social insights, this time quite uncomfortable, Caldwell described his colonial style of collecting:

> The blacks were paid half-a-crown for every female, but the price of flour, tea, and sugar, which I sold to them, rose with

the supply of Echidna. The half-crowns were, therefore, always just sufficient to buy food enough to keep the lazy blacks hungry.

It was, of course, often done—but rarely said so boldly and without apology. In any case, Caldwell eventually found the eggs of the platypus (usually laid two at a time and easily overlooked at their small size of less than an inch in length).

Caldwell solved a specific mystery that had plagued zoology for nearly a century, but he only intensified the general problem. He had proved irrevocably that the platypus is a mélange, not available for unambiguous placement into any major group of vertebrates. Geoffroy had been right about the eggs; Meckel about the mammary glands.

The platypus has always suffered from false expectations based on human foibles. (This essay discusses the two stages of this false hoping, and then tries to rescue the poor platypus in its own terms.) During the half-century between its discovery and Darwin's *Origin of Species,* the platypus endured endless attempts to deny or mitigate its true mélange of characters associated with different groups of vertebrates. Nature needed clean categories established by divine wisdom. An animal could not both lay eggs and feed its young with milk from mammary glands. So Geoffroy insisted upon eggs and no milk; Meckel upon milk and live birth.

Caldwell's discovery coincided with the twenty-fifth anniversary of Darwin's *Origin.* By this time, evolution had made the idea of intermediacy (and mélanges of characters) acceptable, if not positively intriguing. Yet, freed of one burden, the platypus assumed another—this time imposed by evolution, the very idea that had just liberated this poor creature from uncongenial shoving into rigid categories. The platypus, in short, shouldered (with its interclavicle bone) the burden of primitiveness. It would be a mammal, to be sure—but an amoeba among the gods; a tawdry, pitiable little fellow weighted down with the reptilian mark of Cain.

Caldwell dispatched his epitome a century ago, but the platypus has never escaped. I have spent the last week as a nearly full-time reader of platypusology. With a few welcome exceptions (mostly among Australian biologists who know the creature intimately), nearly every article identifies something central about the platypus as undeveloped or inefficient relative to placental mammals—as if the undoubted presence of premammalian characters condemns each feature of the platypus to an unfinished, blundering state.

Before I refute the myth of primitiveness for the platypus in particular, I should discuss the general fallacy that equates early with inefficient and still underlies so much of our failure to understand evolution properly. The theme has circulated through these essays for years—ladders and bushes. But I try to provide a new twist here—the basic distinction between *early branching* and *undeveloped,* or *inefficient, structure.*

If evolution were a ladder toward progress, with reptiles on a rung below mammals, then I suppose that eggs and an interclavicle would identify platypuses as intrinsically wanting. But the Old Testament author of Proverbs, though speaking of wisdom rather than evolution, provided the proper metaphor, *etz chayim:* She is a *tree of life* to them who take hold upon her. Evolution proceeds by branching, and not (usually) by wholesale transformation and replacement. Although a lineage of reptiles did evolve into mammals, reptiles remain with us in all their glorious abundance of snakes, lizards, turtles, and crocodiles. Reptiles are doing just fine in their own way.

The presence of premammalian characters in platypuses does not brand them as inferior or inefficient. But these characters do convey a different and interesting message. They do signify an early branching of monotreme ancestors from the lineage leading to placental mammals. This lineage did not lose its reptilian characters all at once, but in the halting and piecemeal fashion so characteristic of evolutionary trends. A branch that split from this central lineage after the defining features of mammals had evolved (hair and an earful of previous jawbones, for example) might retain other premammalian characters (birth from eggs and an interclavicle) as a sign of early derivation, not a mark of backwardness.

The premammalian characters of the platypuses only identify the antiquity of their lineage as a separate branch of the mammalian tree. If anything, this very antiquity might give the platypus more scope (that is, more time) to become what it really is, in opposition to the myth of primitivity: a superbly engineered creature for a particular, and unusual, mode of life. The platypus is an elegant solution for mammalian life in streams—not a primitive relic of a bygone world. Old does not mean hidebound in a Darwinian world.

Once we shuck the false expectation of primitiveness, we can view the platypus more fruitfully as a bundle of adaptations. Within this appropriate theme of *good* design, we must make one further distinction between shared adaptations of all mammals and particular inventions of platypuses. The first category includes a coat of fur well adapted for protecting platypuses in the (often) cold water of their streams (the waterproof hair even traps a layer of air next to the skin, thus providing additional insulation). As further protection in cold water and on the same theme of inherited features, platypuses can regulate their body temperatures as well as most "higher" mammals, although the assumption of primitivity stalled the discovery of this capacity until 1973—before that, most biologists had argued that platypus temperatures plummeted in cold waters, requiring frequent returns to the burrow for warming up. (My information on the ecology of modern platypuses comes primarily from Tom Grant's excellent book, *The Platypus,* New South Wales University Press, 1984, and from conversations with Frank Carrick in Brisbane. Grant and Carrick are Australia's leading professional students of platypuses, and I thank them for their time and care.)

These features, shared by passive inheritance with other mammals, certainly benefit the platypus, but they provide no argument for my theme of direct adaptation—the replacement of restraining primitivity by a view of the platypus as actively evolving in its own interest. Many other features, however, including nearly everything that makes the platypus so distinctive, fall within the second category of special invention.

Platypuses are relatively small mammals (the largest known weighed just over five pounds and barely exceeded two feet from tip to tail). They construct burrows in the banks of creeks and rivers: long (up to sixty feet) for nesting; shorter for daily use. They spend most of their life in the water, searching for food (primarily insect larvae and other small invertebrates) by probing into bottom sediments with their bills.

The special adaptations of platypuses have fitted them in a subtle and intricate way for aquatic life. The streamlined body moves easily through water. The large, webbed forefeet propel the animal forward by alternate kicks, while the tail and partially webbed rear feet act as rudders and steering devices (in digging a burrow, the platypus anchors with its rear feet and excavates with its forelimbs). The bill works as a feeding structure par excellence, as I shall describe in a moment. Other features undoubtedly serve in the great Darwinian game of courtship, reproduction, and rearing—but we know rather little about this vital aspect of platypus life. As an example, males bear a sharp, hollow spur on their ankles, attached by a duct to a poison gland in their thighs. These spurs, presumably used in combat with competing males, grow large during the breeding season. In captivity, males have killed others with poison from their spurs, and many platypuses, both male and female, sport distinctive punctures when captured in the wild.

Yet even this long and impressive list of special devices has been commonly misrepresented as yet another aspect (or spin-off) of pervasive primitiveness. Burrell, in his classic volume (1927), actually argued that platypuses develop such complex adaptations because simple creatures can't rely upon the flexibility of intelligence and must develop special structures for each required action. Burrell wrote:

> Man . . . has escaped the need for specialization because his evolution has been projected outside himself into an evolution of tools and weapons. Other animals in need of tools and weapons must evolve them from their own bodily parts; we therefore frequently find a specialized adaptation to environmental needs grafted on to primitive simplicity of structure.

You can't win in such a world. You are either primitive prima facie or specialized as a result of lurking and implicit simplicity! From such a Catch-22, platypuses can only be rescued by new concepts, not additional observations.

As a supreme irony, and ultimate defense of adaptation versus ineptitude, the structure that built the myth of primitivity—the misnamed duckbill itself—represents the platypus's finest special invention. The platypus bill is not a homologue of any feature in birds. It is a novel structure, uniquely evolved by monotremes (the echidna carries a different version as its long and pointed snout). The bill is not simply a hard, inert horny structure. Soft skin covers the firm substrate, and this skin houses a remarkable array of sensory organs. In fact, and strange to tell, the platypus, when under water, shuts down all its other sensory systems and relies entirely upon its bill to locate obstacles and food. Flaps of skin cover tiny eyes and nonpinnate ears when a platypus dives, while a pair of valves closes off the nostrils under water.

E. Home, in the first monograph of platypus anatomy (1802), made an astute observation that correctly identified the bill as a complex and vital sensory organ. He dissected the cranial nerves and found almost rudimentary olfactory and optic members but a remarkably developed trigeminal, carrying information from the face to the brain. With great insight, Home compared the platypus bill to a human hand in function and subtlety. (Home never saw a live platypus and worked only by inference from anatomy.) He wrote:

> The olfactory nerves are small and so are the optic nerves; but the fifth pair which supplies the muscles of the face are uncommonly large. We should be led from this circumstance to believe, that the sensibility of the different parts of the bill is very great, and therefore it answers to the purpose of a hand, and is capable of nice discrimination in its feeling.

Then, in the same year that Caldwell discovered eggs, the English biologist E. B. Poulton found the primary sensory organs of the bill. He located numerous columns of epithelial cells, each underlain by a complex of neural transmitters. He called them "push rods," arguing by analogy with electrical bells that a sensory stimulus (a current of water or an object in bottom sediments) would depress the column and ignite the neural spark.

A set of elegant experiments in modern neurophysiology by R. C. Bohringer and M. J. Rowe (1977 and 1981) can only increase our appreciation for the fine-tuned adaptation of the platypus bill. They found Poulton's rods over the bill's entire surface, but four to six times more densely packed at the anterior border of the upper bill, where platypuses must first encounter obstacles and food items. They noted different kinds of nerve receptors under the rods, suggesting that platypuses can distinguish varying kinds of signals (perhaps static versus moving components or live versus dead food). Although individual rods may not provide sufficient information for tracing the direction of a stimulus, each rod maps to a definite location on the brain, strongly implying that the sequence of activation among an array of rods permits the platypus to identify the size and location of objects.

Neurophysiologists can locate areas of the brain responsible for activating definite parts of the body and draw a "map" of the body upon the brain itself. (These experiments proceed from either direction. Either one stimulates a body part and records the pattern of activity in a set of electrodes implanted into the brain, or one pulses a spot on the brain and determines the resulting motion of body parts.) We have no finer demonstrations of evolutionary adaptation than numerous brain maps that record the importance of specially developed organs by their unusually enlarged areas of representation upon the cortex. Thus, a raccoon's brain map displays an enormous domain for its forepaws, a pig's for its snout, a spider monkey's for its tail. Bohringer and Rowe have added the platypus to this informative array. A map of the platypus's cortex is mostly bill.

We have come a long way from the first prominent evolutionary interpretation ever presented for the platypus bill. In 1844, in the major pre-Darwinian defense of evolution written in English, Robert Chambers tried to derive a mammal from a bird in two great leaps, via the intermediate link of a duckbilled platypus. One step, Chambers wrote,

> would suffice in a goose to give its progeny the body of a rat, and produce the ornithorhynchus, or might give the progeny of an ornithorhynchus the mouth and feet of a true rodent, and thus complete at two stages the passage from the aves to the mammalia.

The platypus, having suffered such slings and arrows of outrageous fortune in imposed degradation by human hands, has cast its arms (and its bill) against a sea of troubles and vindicated itself. The whips and scorns of time shall heal. The oppressor's wrong, the proud man's contumely have been reversed by modern studies—enterprises of great pith and moment. The platypus is one honey of an adaptation.

19 | Bligh's Bounty

IN 1789, a British naval officer discovered some islands near Australia and lamented his inability to provide a good description:

> Being constantly wet, it was with the utmost difficulty I could open a book to write, and I am sensible that what I have done can only serve to point out where these lands are to be found again, and give the idea of their extent.

As he wrote these lines, Captain William Bligh was steering a longboat with eighteen loyal crew members into the annals of human heroism at sea—via his 4,000-mile journey to Timor, accomplished without loss of a single man, and following the seizure of his ship, *The Bounty,* in history's most famous mutiny.

Bligh may have been overbearing; he surely wins no awards for insight into human psychology. But history and Charles Laughton have not treated him fairly either. Bligh was committed, meticulous, and orderly to a fault—how else, in such peril, could he have bothered to describe some scattered pieces of new Pacific real estate.

Bligh's habit of close recording yielded other benefits, including one forgotten item to science. Obsessed by the failure of his *Bounty* mission to bring Tahitian breadfruit as food for West Indian slaves, Bligh returned to Tahiti aboard the *Providence* and successfully unloaded 1,200 trees at Port Royal, Jamaica, in 1793 (his ship was described as a floating forest). En route, he stopped in Australia and had an interesting meal.

George Tobin, one of Bligh's officers, described their quarry as

> a kind of sloth about the size of a roasting pig with a proboscis 2 or 3 inches in length. . . . On the back were short quills like those of the Porcupine. . . . The animal was roasted and found of a delicate flavor.

Bligh himself made a drawing of his creature before the banquet. The officers of the *Providence* had eaten an echidna, one of Australia's most unusual mammals—an egg-laying anteater closely related to the duckbilled platypus.

Bligh brought his drawing back to England. In 1802, it appeared as a figure (reproduced here) accompanying the first technical description of the echidna's anatomy by Everard Home in the *Philosophical Transactions of the Royal Society* (G. Shaw had published a preliminary and superficial description in 1792).

Home discovered the strange mix of reptilian and mammalian features that has inspired interest and puzzlement among biologists ever since. He also imposed upon the echidna, for the first time, the distinctive burden of primitivity that has continually hampered proper zoological understanding of all monotremes, the egg-laying mammals of Australia. Home described the echidna as not quite all there in mammalian terms, a lesser form stamped with features of lower groups:

> These characters distinguish [the echidna] in a very remarkable manner, from all other quadrupeds, giving this new tribe a resemblance in some respects to birds, in others to the Amphibia; so that it may be considered as an intermediate link between the classes of Mammalia, Aves, and Amphibia.

Unfortunately, Home could not study the organ that most clearly belies the myth of primitivity. "The brain," he wrote, "was not in a state to admit of particular examination." Home did have an opportunity to infer the echidna's anomalously large brain from the internal form of its skull, well drawn on the plate just preceding Bligh's figure (and also reproduced here). But Home said nothing about this potential challenge to his general interpretation.

Original drawing of an echidna by none other than
Captain Bligh of *Bounty* fame. NEG. NO. 337535. COUR-
TESY DEPARTMENT OF LIBRARY SERVICES, AMERICAN MU-
SEUM OF NATURAL HISTORY.

And so the burden of primitivity stuck tenaciously to echidnas,
and continues to hold fast in our supposedly more sophisticated
age. Some great zoologists have struggled against this convenient fallacy, most notably the early French evolutionist Etienne
Geoffroy Saint-Hilaire, who coined the name *Monotremata* (see

Essay 18) and labored unsuccessfully to establish the echidna and platypus as a new class of vertebrates, separate from both mammals and reptiles and not merely inferior to placentals. By his own manifesto, he chose his strategy explicitly to avoid the conceptual lock that assumptions of primitivity would clamp upon our understanding of monotremes. He wrote in 1827:

> What is defective, I repeat, is our manner of perception, our way of conceiving the organization of monotremes; that is, our determination, made a priori, to join them violently to mammals [by *violemment*, Geoffroy means, of course, "without any conceptual justification"], to place them in the same class and, after our disappointments and false judgments, then to make our unjust grievances heard, as when we speak of them as mammals essentially and necessarily outside the rules.

But Geoffroy's legitimate complaint, so eloquently expressed, did not prevail, and the myth of primitivity continues, despite its blatant flaw. As I argue in the preceding essay on platypuses, the myth of primitivity rests upon a logical confusion between early branching from the ancestors of placental mammals (the true meaning of reptilian characters retained by monotremes) and structural inferiority. Unless geological age of branching is a sure guide to level of anatomical organization—as it is not—egg laying and interclavicle bones do not brand platypuses and echidnas as inferior mammals.

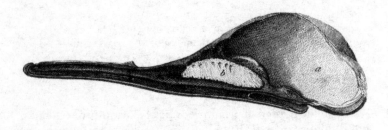

Everard Home's 1802 figure of an echidna's skull. The large size of the brain was apparent even then. NEG. NO. 337429. COURTESY DEPARTMENT OF LIBRARY SERVICES, AMERICAN MUSEUM OF NATURAL HISTORY.

Beyond this general defense, echidnas can provide ample specific evidence of their adequacy. They are, first of all, a clear success in ecological terms. Echidnas live all over the Australian continent (and extend into Papua-New Guinea), the only native mammal with such a wide range. Moreover, *the* echidna, as a single struggling relict, ranks with *the* rat and *the* monkey (those meaningless synecdoches of the psychological literature) as an absurd abstraction of nature's richness. Echidnas come as two species in two separate genera and with quite different habits. *Tachyglossus aculeatus* (the Australian form with Papuan extensions) rips apart ant and termite nests with its stout forelimbs and collects the inhabitants on its sticky tongue. The larger and longer-snouted *Zaglossus bruijni* of Papua-New Guinea lives on a nearly exclusive diet of earthworms. Moreover, three other species, including the "giant" echidna, *Zaglossus hacketti,* have been found as fossils in Australia. Echidnas are a successful and at least modestly varied group.

But echidnas hold a far more important ace in the hole as their ultimate defense against charges of primitivity. The same cultural biases that lead us to classify creatures as primitive or advanced have established the form and function of brains as our primary criterion of ranking. Echidnas have big and richly convoluted brains. Scientists have recognized this anomaly in the tale of primitivity for more than a century—and they have developed an array of arguments, indeed a set of traditions, for working around such an evident and disconcerting fact. Large brains undoubtedly serve echidnas well; but they also help to instruct us about an important issue in the practice of science—how do scientists treat factual anomalies? What do we do with evidence that challenges a comfortable view of nature's order?

The echidna's brain refutes the myth of primitivity with a double whammy—size and conformation. (I discuss only the Australian species, *Tachyglossus aculeatus;* its larger Papua-New Guinea relative, *Zaglossus,* remains virtually unknown to science—for basic information about echidnas, see the two books by M. Griffiths listed in the bibliography.) Since mammalian brains increase more slowly than body weight along the so-called mouse-to-elephant curve, we can use neither absolute nor relative brain weight as a criterion. (Big mammals have absolutely large brains as an uninteresting consequence of body size, while small mammals have relatively large brains because brains increase more slowly than bodies.) Biologists have therefore developed a standard criterion: measured brain weight relative to expected brain weight for an average mammal of *the same* body size. This ratio, dubbed EQ (or encephalization quotient) in amusing analogy with you know what, measures 1.0 for mammals right on the mouse-to-elephant curve, above 1.0 for brainier than average mammals, and less than 1.0 for brain weights below the norm.

To provide some feel for the range of EQ's, so-called basal insectivores—a selected stem group among the order traditionally ranked lowest among placental mammals—record a mean of 0.311. Adding advanced insectivores, the average rises to 0.443. Rodents, a perfectly respectable group (and dominant among mammals by sheer number), weigh in with a mean EQ of 0.652. (Primates and carnivores rank consistently above 1.0.) Monotremes are not, by this criterion, mental giants—their EQ's range from 0.50 to 0.75—but they rank way above the traditional primitives among placentals and right up there with rodents and other "respected" groups. Monotremes continue to shine by other standards of size as well. Some neurologists regard the ratio of brain to spinal cord as a promising measure of mental advance. Fish generally dip below 1:1 (spinal cord heavier than brain). We top-heavy humans tip the scale at 50:1; cats score 4:1. The "lowly" echidna waddles in front of tabby at approximately 6:1.

By conformation, rather than simple size alone, echidnas are even more impressive. The neocortex, the putative site of higher mental functions, occupies a larger percentage of total brain weight in supposedly advanced creatures. The neocortex of basal insectivores averages 13 percent of brain weight; the North American marsupial opossum records 22 percent. Echidnas score 43 percent (platypuses 48 percent), right up there with the prosimians (54 percent), basal group of the lordly primates. (All my figures for brain sizes come from H. J. Jerison, 1973, and P. Pirlot and J. Nelson, 1978.)

The neocortex of echidnas is not only expanded and nearly spherical as in primates; its surface is also richly convoluted in a series of deep folds and bumps (sulci and gyri), a traditional criterion of mental advance in mammals. (Curiously, by comparison, the platypus neocortex, while equally expanded and spherical, is almost completely smooth.)

Many famous nineteenth-century neuroanatomists studied monotreme brains, hoping to understand the basis of human mental triumph by examining its lowly origins. Echidnas provided an endless source of puzzlement and frustration. William Henry Flower dissected an echidna in 1865 and wrote of "this most remarkable brain, with its largely developed and richly convoluted hemispheres." He admitted: "It is difficult to see in many of the peculiarities of their brain even an approach in the direction of that of the bird." And Grafton Elliot Smith, the great Australian anatomist who later fell for Piltdown Man in such a big way, wrote with evident befuddlement in 1902:

> The most obtrusive feature of this brain is the relatively enormous development of the cerebral hemispheres. . . . In addition, the extent of the cortex is very considerably increased by numerous deep sulci. The meaning of this large neopallium is quite incomprehensible. The factors which the study of other mammalian brains has shown to be the determinants of the extent of the cortex fail completely to explain how it is that a small animal of the lowliest status in the mammalian series comes to possess this large cortical apparatus.

One might have anticipated that scientists, so enlightened by monotreme mentality, would simply abandon the myth of primitivity. But prompt submission to items of contrary evidence is not, despite another prominent myth (this time about scientific procedure), the usual response of scientists to nature's assaults upon traditional beliefs. Instead, most students of monotreme brains have recorded their surprise and then sought different criteria, again to affirm the myth of primitivity.

A favorite argument cites the absence in monotremes (and marsupials as well) of a corpus callosum—the bundle of fibers connecting the right and left hemispheres of "higher" mental processing in placental mammals. In a wonderful example of blatantly circular logic, A. A. Abbie, one of Australia's finest natural historians, wrote in a famous article of 1941 (commissures, to a neuroanatomist, are connecting bands of neural tissue, like the corpus callosum):

> Since in mammals cerebral evolution and with it any pro-
> gressive total evolution is reflected so closely in the state of
> the cerebral commissures it is clear that the taxonomic sig-
> nificance of these commissures far transcends that of any
> other physical character.

In other words, since we know (a priori) that monotremes are primitive, search for the character that affirms a lowly status (lack of a corpus callosum) and proclaim this character, ipso facto, more important than any other (size of brain, convolutions, or any other indication of monotreme adequacy). (I shall have more to say about commissures later on, but let me just mention for now that lack of a corpus callosum does not preclude communi-cation across the cerebral hemispheres. Monotremes possess at least two other commissures—the hippocampal and the ante-rior—capable of making connections, though by a route more circuitous than the pathway of the corpus callosum.)

This tradition of switching to another criterion continues in modern studies. In their 1978 article on monotreme brain sizes, for example, Pirlot and Nelson admit, after recording volumes and convolutions for echidnas: "It is very difficult to isolate crite-ria that clearly establish the 'primitiveness' of monotreme brains." But they seek and putatively find, though they honorably temper their good cheer with yet another admission of the puz-zling size of the monotreme neocortex:

> This cortex could be considered to be among the most
> primitive mammalian cortices on the basis of the low num-
> ber and low density of large, especially pyramidal neurons.
> It is surprising to find that a very high proportion of cortex
> is neocortex. This does not necessarily mean an advanced
> degree of progressiveness, although the two are usually re-
> lated.

The basic data on size and external conformation of echidna brains have been recorded (and viewed as troubling) for more than a century. More sophisticated information on neural fine structure and actual use of the cortical apparatus in learning has been gathered during the past twenty years—all affirming, again and again, the respectability of echidna intelligence.

In 1964, R. A. Lende published the first extensive map of localized sensory and motor areas on the echidna's cerebral cortex. (I discuss the general procedures of such study in the preceding essay on platypus brains. P. S. Ulinski, 1984, has recently confirmed and greatly extended Lende's work in a series of elegant experiments.) Lende discovered a surprising pattern of localization, basically mammalian in character but different from placental mappings. He identified separate areas for visual, auditory, and sensory control (the motor area overlapped the sensory region and extended forward to an additional section of the cortex), all demarcated one from the other by constant sulci (fissures of the cortex) and located together at the rear of the cortex.

Most surprisingly, these areas abut one another without any so-called association cortex in between. (Association cortex includes areas of the cerebral surface that do not control any specific sensory or motor function and may play a role in coordinating and integrating the basic inputs. For this reason, amount and position of association cortex have sometimes been advanced as criteria of "higher" mental function. But such negative definitions are troubling and should not be pushed too hard or far.) In any case, Lende identified a relatively enormous area of unspecified (perhaps association) cortex in front of his mapped sensory and motor areas. Lende concluded, in a statement oft-quoted against those who maintain the myth of primitivity:

> Ahead of the posteriorly situated sensory and motor areas established in this study there is relatively more "frontal cortex" than in any other mammal, including man, the function of which remains unexplained.

Other studies have tried to push the echidna brain to its practical limits by imposing upon these anteaters all the modern apparatus of mazes, levers, and food rewards so favored by the science of comparative psychology. Echidnas have performed remarkably well in all these studies, again confuting the persistent impression of stupidity still conveyed by textbooks, and even by the most "official" of all sources—the Australian Museum's *Complete*

Book of Australian Mammals, edited by R. Strahan (1983), which insists without evidence:

> In this last respect [brainpower], monotremes are inferior to typical placental mammals and, probably, to typical marsupials. The paucity of living monotremes may therefore be due to their being less bright, less adaptable in their behavior, than other mammals.

To cite just three studies among several of similar intent and conclusion:

1. Saunders, Chen, and Pridmore (1971) ran echidnas through a simple two-choice T-maze (down a central channel, then either right or left into a bin of food or a blank wall). They trained echidnas to move in one direction (location of the chow, of course), then switched the food box to the other arm of the T. In such studies of so-called habit-reversal learning, most fish never switch, birds learn very slowly, mammals rapidly. Echidnas showed quick improvement with a steady reduction in errors—and at typically mammalian rates. Half the experiments (seven of fifteen) on well-trained echidnas yielded the optimal performance of "one-trial reversal" (you switch the food box and the animal goes the wrong way—where the food used to be—the first time, then immediately cottons on and heads in the other direction, toward the chow, each time). Rats often show one-trial reversal learning, birds never.

2. Buchmann and Rhodes (1978) tested echidnas for their ability to learn positional (right or left) and visual-tactile (black and rough versus white and smooth) cues—with echidnas pushing the appropriate lever to gain their food reward. As an obvious testimony to mental adequacy, they report that "unsuccessful (unrewarded) responses were often associated with vigorous kicking at the operanda." Echidnas learned at a characteristic rate for placental mammals and also remembered well. One animal, retested a month later, performed immediate one-trial reversals.

Buchmann and Rhodes compared their echidnas with other animals tested in similar procedures. Crabs and goldfish did not show improvement (did not learn) over time. Echidnas displayed great variation in their speed of learning—one improved faster (and one slower) than rats; all echidnas performed better than cats. Take these results (and the reward for success as well) with a grain of salt because numbers are limited and procedures varied widely among studies—but still, the single best performer on the entire chart was an echidna.

Buchmann and Rhodes conclude: "There is no evidence that the performance of echidnas is inferior to eutherian [placental] or metatherian [marsupial] mammals." They end by ridiculing the "quaint, explicitly or tacitly-held views that echidnas are little more than animated pin-cushions, or, at the best, glorified reptiles."

3. Gates (1978) studied learning in visual discrimination (black versus white, and various complex patterns of vertical and horizontal striping). His results parallel the other studies—echidnas learned quickly, at typical mammalian rates. But he added an interesting twist that confutes the only serious, direct argument ever offered from brain anatomy for monotreme inferiority—the claim that absence of a corpus callosum precludes transfer between the cerebral hemispheres, thereby compromising "higher" mental functions.

Gates occluded one eye and taught echidnas to distinguish black from white panels with the other eye. They reached "criterion performance" in an average of 100 trials. He then uncovered the occluded eye, bandaged the one that had overseen the initial learning, and did the experiment again. If no information passes from one cerebral hemisphere to the other, then previous learning on one side of the brain should offer no help to the other, and the 100-trial average should persist. But echidnas only needed 40 trials to reach criterion with the second eye.

Gates conjectures that information is either passing across the other two commissures in the absence of a corpus callosum, or via the few optic fibers that do not cross to the other side of the brain. (In vertebrate visual systems, inputs from the right eye go to the left hemisphere of the brain, left eye to the right hemisphere; thus, each eye "informs" the opposite hemisphere. But about 1 percent of optic fibers do not cross over, and therefore map to their own hemisphere. These few fibers may sneak a little learning to the hemisphere dependent upon the occluded eye.) In addition, direct evidence of electrical stimulation has shown that inputs to one hemisphere can elicit responses in corresponding parts of the other hemisphere—information clearly gets across in the absence of a corpus callosum.

The solution to the paradox of such adequate intelligence in such a primitive mammal is stunningly simple. The premise—the myth of primitivity itself—is dead wrong. To say it one more, and one last, time: The reptilian features of monotremes only record their early branching from the ancestry of placental mammals— and time of branching is no measure of anatomical complexity or mental status.

Monotremes have evolved separately from placentals for a long time—more than enough for both groups to reach, by parallel evolution in independent lineages, advanced levels of mental functioning permitted by their basic, shared mammalian design. The primary evidence for parallel evolution has been staring us in the face for a century, forming part of the standard literature on echidnas, well featured even in primary documents that uphold the myth of primitivity. We know that the echidna's brain attained its large size by an independent route. The platypus has a smooth (if bulbous) brain. The echidna evolved complex ridges and folds on its cerebral surface as a special feature of its own lineage. These sulci and gyri cannot be identified (homologized) with the well-known convolutions of placental brains. The echidna brain is so different, by virtue of a separate evolution to large size, that its convolutions have been named by Greek letters to avoid any misplaced comparison with the different ridges and folds of placental brains. And Grafton Elliot Smith, the man most puzzled by echidna brains, did the naming—apparently without realizing that the very need for such separate designations provided the direct evidence that could refute the myth of primitivity.

In his eloquent plea for monotremes (1827), Geoffroy Saint-Hilaire wrote brilliantly about the subtle interplay of fact and theory in science. He recognized the power of theory to guide the discovery of fact and to set a context for fruitful interpretation. ("To limit our efforts to the simple practicalities of an ocular examination would be to condemn the activities of the mind.") But he also acknowledged the flip side of useful guidance, the extraordinary power of theory to restrict our vision, in particular to render "obvious" facts nearly invisible, by denying them a sensible context. ("At first useless, these facts had to remain un-perceived until the moment when the needs and progress of sci-ence provoked us to discover them.") Or as Warner Oland, the Swedish pseudo-Oriental Charlie Chan, once said in one of his most delightfully anachronistic pseudo-Confucian sayings (*Charlie Chan in Egypt*, 1935): "Theory like mist on eyeglasses. Obscure facts."

20 | Here Goes Nothing

GOLIATH PAID THE HIGHEST of prices to learn the most elementary of lessons—thou shalt not judge intrinsic quality by external appearance. When the giant first saw David, "he disdained him: for he was but a youth, and ruddy, and of a fair countenance" (1 Sam. 17:42). Saul had been similarly unimpressed when David presented himself as an opponent for Goliath and savior of Israel. Saul doubted out loud: "for thou art but a youth, and he a man of war from his youth" (1 Sam. 17:33). But David persuaded Saul by telling him that actions speak louder than appearances—for David, as a young shepherd, had rescued a lamb from a predatory lion: "I went out after him, and smote him, and delivered it out of his mouth" (1 Sam. 17:35).

This old tale presents a double entendre to introduce this essay—first as a preface to my opening story about a famous insight deceptively clothed in drab appearance; and second as a quirky lead to the body of this essay, a tale of animals that really do deliver from their mouths: *Rheobatrachus silus,* an Australian frog that swallows its fertilized eggs, broods tadpoles in its stomach, and gives birth to young frogs through its mouth.

Henry Walter Bates landed at Pará (now Belém), Brazil, near the mouth of the Amazon, in 1848. He arrived with Alfred Russel Wallace, who had suggested the trip to tropical jungles, arguing that a direct study of nature at her richest might elucidate the origin of species and also provide many fine specimens for sale. Wallace returned to England in 1852, but Bates remained for eleven years, collecting nearly 8,000 new species (mostly insects) and exploring the entire Amazon valley.

In 1863, Bates published his two-volume classic, perhaps the greatest work of nineteenth-century natural history and travel, *The Naturalist on the River Amazons.* But two years earlier, Bates had hidden his most exciting discovery in a technical paper with a disarmingly pedestrian title: "Contributions to an Insect Fauna of the Amazon Valley," published in the *Transactions of the Linnaean Society.* The reviewer of Bates's paper (*Natural History Reviews,* 1863, pp. 219–224) lauded Bates's insight but lamented the ill-chosen label: "From its unpretending and somewhat indefinite title," he wrote, "we fear [that Bates's work] may be overlooked in the ever-flowing rush of scientific literature." The reviewer therefore sought to rescue Bates from his own modesty by providing a bit of publicity for the discovery. Fortunately, he had sufficient oomph to give Bates a good send-off. The reviewer was Charles Darwin, and he added a section on Bates's insight to the last edition of the *Origin of Species.*

Bates had discovered and correctly explained the major style of protective mimicry in animals. In Batesian mimicry (for the phenomenon now bears his name), uncommon and tasty animals (the mimics) gain protection by evolving uncanny resemblance to abundant and foul-tasting creatures (the models) that predators learn to avoid. The viceroy butterfly is a dead ringer for the monarch, which, as a caterpillar, consumes enough noxious poisons from its favored plant foods to sicken any untutored bird. (Vomiting birds have become a cliché of natural history films. Once afflicted, twice shy, as the old saying goes. The tale may be more than twice told, but many cognoscenti do not realize that the viceroy's name memorializes its mimicry—for this butterfly is the surrogate, or vice-king, to the ruler, or monarch, itself.)

Darwin delighted in Bates's discovery because he viewed mimicry as such a fine demonstration of evolution in action. Creationism, Darwin consistently argued, cannot be disproved directly because it claims to explain everything. Creationism becomes impervious to test and, therefore, useless to science. Evolutionists must proceed by showing that any creationist explanation becomes a *reductio ad absurdum* by twists of illogic and special pleading required to preserve the idea of God's unalterable will in the face of evidence for historical change.

In his review of Bates's paper, Darwin emphasizes that creationists must explain the precision of duplicity by mimics as a simple act of divine construction—"they were thus clothed from the hour of their creation," he writes. Such a claim, Darwin then argues, is even worse than wrong because it stymies science by providing no possible test for truth or falsity—it is an argument "made at the expense of putting an effectual bar to all further inquiry." Darwin then presents his *reductio ad absurdum,* showing that any fair-minded person must view mimicry as a product of historical change.

Creationists had made a central distinction between true species, or entities created by God, and mere varieties, or products of small changes permitted within a created type (breeds of dogs or strains of wheat, for example). But Bates had shown that some mimics are true species and others only varieties of species that lack mimetic features in regions not inhabited by the model. Would God have created some mimics from the dust of the earth but allowed others to reach their precision by limited natural selection within the confines of a created type? Is it not more reasonable to propose that mimicking species began as varieties and then evolved further to become separate entities? And much worse for creationists: Bates had shown that some mimicking species resemble models that are only varieties. Would God have created a mimic from scratch to resemble another form that evolved (in strictly limited fashion) to its current state? God may work in strange ways, his wonders to perform—but would he really so tax our credulity? The historical explanation makes so much more sense.

But if mimicry became a source of delight for Darwin, it also presented a serious problem. We may easily grasp the necessity for a historical account. We may understand *how* the system works once all its elements develop, but *why* does this process of mimicry ever begin? What starts it off, and what propels it forward? Why, in Darwin's words, "to the perplexity of naturalists, has nature condescended to the tricks of the stage?" More specifically: Any butterfly mimic, in the rich faunas of the Amazon valley, shares its space with many potential models. Why does a mimic converge upon one particular model? We can understand how natural selection might perfect a resemblance already well established, but what begins the process along one of many potential pathways—especially since we can scarcely imagine that a 1 or 2 percent resemblance to a model provides much, if any, advantage for a mimic. This old dilemma in evolutionary theory even has a name in the jargon of my profession—the problem of the "incipient stages of useful structures." Darwin had a good answer for mimicry, and I will return to it after a long story about frogs—the central subject of this essay and another illustration of the same principle that Darwin established to resolve the dilemma of incipient stages.

We remember Darwin's *Beagle* voyage primarily for the big and spectacular animals that he discovered or studied: the fossil *Toxodon* and the giant Galápagos tortoises. But many small creatures, though less celebrated, brought enormous scientific reward—among them a Chilean frog appropriately named *Rhinoderma darwini*. Most frogs lay their eggs in water and then allow the tadpoles to make their own way, but many species have evolved various styles of parental care, and the range of these adaptations extols nature's unity in diversity.

In *R. darwini*, males ingest the fertilized eggs and brood them in the large throat pouches usually reserved for an earlier act of courtship—the incessant croaking that defines territory and attracts females. Up to fifteen young may fill the pouch, puffing out all along the father's ventral (lower) surface and compressing the vital organs above. G. B. Howes ended his classic account of this curious life-style (*Proceedings of the Zoological Society of London*, 1888) with a charming anthropomorphism. Previous students of *Rhinoderma*, he noted, had supposed that the male does not feed while carrying his young. But Howes dissected a brooding male and found its stomach full of beetles and flies and its large intestine clogged with "excreta like that of a normal individual." He concluded, with an almost palpable sigh of relief, "that this extraordinary paternal instinct does not lead up to that self-abnegation" postulated by previous authors.

But nature consistently frustrates our attempts to read intrinsic solicitude into her ways. In November 1973, two Australian scientists discovered a form of parental care that must preclude feeding, for these frogs brood their young in their stomachs and then give birth through their mouths. And we can scarcely imagine that a single organ acts as a nurturing uterus and a site of acid digestion at the same time.

Rheobatrachus silus, a small aquatic frog living under stones or in rock pools of shallow streams and rills in a small area of southeast

Queensland, was first discovered and described in 1973. Later that year, C. J. Corben and G. J. Ingram of Brisbane attempted to transfer a specimen from one aquarium to another. To their astonishment, it "rose to the surface of the water and, after compression of the lateral body muscles, propulsively ejected from the mouth six living tadpoles" (from the original description published by Corben, Ingram, and M. J. Tyler in 1974). They initially assumed, from their knowledge of *Rhinoderma,* that their brooder was a male rearing young in its throat pouch. Eighteen days later, they found a young frog swimming beside its parent; two days later, a further pair emerged unobserved in the night. At that point, they decided (as the euphemism goes) to "sacrifice" their golden goose. But the parent, when grasped, "ejected by propulsive vomiting eight juveniles in the space of no more than two seconds. Over the next few minutes a further five juveniles were ejected." They then dissected the parent and received their biggest surprise. The frog had no vocal sac. It was a female with "a very large, thin-walled, dilated stomach"—the obvious home of the next generation.

Natural birth had not yet been observed in *Rheobatrachus.* All young had either emerged unobserved or been vomited forth as a violent reaction after handling. The first young had greeted the outside world prematurely as tadpoles (since development clearly proceeds all the way to froghood in the mother's stomach, as later births demonstrated).

Art then frustrated nature, and a second observation also failed to resolve the mode of natural birth. In January 1978, a pregnant female was shipped express airfreight from Brisbane to Adelaide for observation. But the poor frog was—yes, you guessed it—"delayed" by an industrial dispute. The mother, still hanging on, eventually arrived surrounded by twenty-one dead young; a twenty-second frog remained in her stomach upon dissection. Finally, in 1979, K. R. McDonald and D. B. Carter successfully transported two pregnant females to Adelaide—and the great event was finally recorded. The first female, carefully set up for photography, frustrated all hopes by vomiting six juveniles "at great speed, flying upwards . . . for approximately one meter . . . a substantial distance relative to the body size of the female." But the second mother obliged. Of her twenty-six offspring, two appeared gently and, apparently, voluntarily. The mother "partially emerged from the water, shook her head, opened her mouth, and two babies actively struggled out." The photo of a fully formed baby frog, resting on its parent's tongue before birth, has already become a classic of natural history. This second female, about two inches long, weighed 11.62 grams after birth. Her twenty-six children weighed 7.66 grams, or 66 percent of her weight without them. An admirable effort indeed!

Rheobatrachus inspired great excitement among Australian scientists, and research groups in Adelaide and Brisbane have been studying this frog intensively, with all work admirably summarized and discussed in a volume edited by M. J. Tyler (1983). Rarely has such extensive and coordinated information been presented on a natural oddity, and we are grateful to these Australian scientists for bringing together their work in such a useful way.

This volume also presents enough detail (usually lacking in technical publications) to give nonscientists a feel for the actual procedures of research, warts and all (an appropriate metaphor for the subject). Glen Ingram's article on natural history, for example, enumerates all the day-to-day dilemmas that technical papers rarely mention: slippery bodies that elude capture; simple difficulties in seeing a small, shy frog that lives in inaccessible places (Ingram learned to identify *Rheobatrachus* by characteristic ripples made by its jump into water); rain, fog, and dampness; and regeneration that frustrates identification (ecologists must recognize individual animals in order to monitor size and movement of populations by mark-recapture techniques; amphibians and reptiles are traditionally marked by distinctive patterns of toe clipping, a painless and unobtrusive procedure, but *Rheobatrachus* frustrates tradition by regenerating its clipped toes, and Ingram could not reidentify his original captures). To this, we must add the usually unacknowledged bane of all natural history: boredom. You don't see your animals most of the time; so you wait and wait and wait (not always pleasant on the boggy banks of a stream in rainy season). Somehow, though, such plagues seem appropriate enough, given the subject. Frogs, after all, stand among the ten Mosaic originals: "I will smite all thy borders with frogs: And the river shall bring forth frogs abundantly, which shall go up and come into thine house, and into thy bedchambers, and upon thy bed . . . and into thine ovens, and into thy kneading troughs" (Exod. 8:2–3).

The biblical author of Exodus was, unfortunately, not describing *Rheobatrachus,* a rare animal indeed. Not a single *Rheobatrachus silus* has been seen in its natural habitat since 1981. A series of dry summers and late rains has restricted the range of this aquatic frog—and five years of no sitings must raise fears about extinction. Fortunately, a second species, named *R. vitellinus,* was discovered in January 1984, living in shallow sections of fast-flowing streams, about 500 miles north of the range of *R. silus.* This slightly larger version (up to three inches in length) also broods in its stomach; twenty-two baby frogs inhabited a pregnant female.

When discussed as a disembodied oddity (the problem with traditional writing in natural history), *Rheobatrachus* may pique our interest but not our intellect. Placed into a proper context among other objects of nature's diversity—the "comparative approach" so characteristic of evolutionary biology—gastric brooding in *Rheobatrachus* embodies a message of great theoretical interest. *Rheobatrachus,* in one sense, stands alone. No other vertebrate swallows its own fertilized eggs, converts its stomach into a brood pouch, and gives birth through its mouth. But in another sense, *Rheobatrachus* represents just one solution to a common problem among frogs.

In his review of parental care, R. W. McDiarmid argues that frogs display "the greatest array of reproductive modes found in any vertebrates" (see his article in G. M. Burghardt and M. Bekoff, 1978). Much inconclusive speculation has been devoted to reasons for the frequent and independent evolution of brooding (and other forms of parental care) in frogs—a profound departure, after all, from the usual amphibian habit of laying eggs in water and permitting the young to pass their early lives as unattended aquatic tadpoles. Several authors have suggested the following common denominator: In many habitats, and for a variety of reasons, life as a free-swimming tadpole may become sufficiently uninviting to impose strong evolutionary pressure for bypassing this stage and undergoing "direct development" from egg to completed frog. Brooding is an excellent strategy for direct development—since tadpole life may be spent in a brood pouch, and the bad old world need not be faced directly before froghood.

In any case, brooding has evolved often in frogs, and in an astonishing variety of modes. As a minimal encumbrance and modification, some frogs simply attach eggs to their exteriors. Males of the midwife toad *Alytes obstetricans* wrap strings of eggs about their legs and carry them in tow.

At the other extreme of modification, some frogs have evolved special brood pouches in unconventional places. The female *Gastrotheca riobambae,* an Ecuadorean frog from Andean valleys, develops a pouch on her back, with an opening near the rear and an internal extension nearly to her head. The male places fertilized eggs in her pouch, where they develop under the skin of her back for five to six weeks before emerging as late-stage tadpoles.

In another Australian frog, *Assa darlingtoni,* males develop pouches on their undersides, opening near their hind legs but extending forward to the front legs (see article by G. J. Ingram, M. Anstis, and C. J. Corben, 1975). Females lay their eggs among leaves. When they hatch, the male places himself in the middle of the mass and either coats himself with jelly from the spawn or, perhaps, secretes a slippery substance himself. The emerging tadpoles then perform a unique act of acrobatics among amphibians: they move in an ungainly fashion by bending their bodies, head toward tail, and then springing sideways and forward. In this inefficient manner, they migrate over the slippery body of their father and enter the brood pouch under their own steam. (I am almost tempted to say, given the Australian venue, that these creatures have been emboldened to perform in such unfroglike ways by watching too many surrounding marsupials, for the kangaroo's undeveloped, almost larval joey also must endure a slow and tortuous crawl to the parental pouch!)

In a kind of intermediate mode, some frogs brood their young internally but use structures already available for other purposes. I have already discussed *Rhinoderma,* the vocal-pouch brooder of Chile. Evolution seizes its opportunities. The male vocal pouch is roomy and available; in a context of strong pressure for brooding, some lineage will eventually overcome the behavioral obstacles and grasp this ready possibility. The eggs of *R. darwini* develop for twenty-three days before the tadpoles hatch. For the first twenty days, tadpoles grow within eggs exposed to the external environment. But tadpoles then begin to move, and this behavior apparently triggers a response from the male parent. He then takes the advanced eggs into his vocal pouch. They hatch there three days later and remain for fifty-two days until the end of metamorphosis, when the young emerge through their father's mouth as perfectly formed little froglets. In the related species *R. rufum,* muscular activity begins after eight days within the egg, and males keep the tadpoles in their vocal sacs for much shorter periods, finally expelling them, still in the tadpole stage, into water (see article by K. Busse, 1970).

In this context, *Rheobatrachus* is less an oddity than a fulfillment. Stomachs provide the only other large internal pouch with an egress of sufficient size. Some lineage of frogs was bound to exploit this possibility. But stomachs present a special problem not faced by vocal sacs or novel pouches of special construction— and we now encounter the key dilemma that will bring us back to mimicry in butterflies and the evolutionary problem of incipient stages. Stomachs are already doing something else—and that something is profoundly inimical to the care and protection of fragile young. Stomachs secrete acid and digest food—and eggs and tadpoles are, as they say down under, mighty good tucker.

In short, to turn a stomach into a brood pouch, something must turn off the secretion of hydrochloric acid and suppress the passage of eggs into the intestine. At a minimum, the brooding mother cannot eat during the weeks that she carries young in her stomach. This inhibition may arise automatically and present no special problem. Stomachs contain "stretch receptors" that tell an organism when to stop eating by imposing a feeling of satiety as the mechanical consequence of a full stomach. A batch of swallowed eggs will surely set off this reaction and suppress further eating.

But this fact scarcely solves our problem—for why doesn't the mother simply secrete her usual acid, digest the eggs, and relieve her feeling of satiety? What turns off the secretion of hydrochloric acid and the passage of eggs into the intestine?

Tyler and his colleagues immediately realized, when they discovered gastric brooding in *Rheobatrachus,* that suppression of stomach function formed the crux of their problem. "Clearly," they wrote, "the intact amphibian stomach is likely to be an alien environment for brooding." They began by studying the changes induced by brooding in the architecture of the stomach. They found that the secretory mucosa (the lining that produces acid) regresses while the musculature strengthens, thus converting the stomach into a strong and chemically inert pouch. Moreover, these changes are not "preparatory"—that is, they do not occur before a female swallows her eggs. Probably, then, something in the eggs or tadpoles themselves acts to suppress their own destruction and make a congenial place of their new home. The Australian researchers then set out to find the substance that suppresses acid secretion in the stomach—and they have apparently succeeded.

P. O'Brien and D. Shearman, in a series of ingenious experiments, concentrated water that had been in contact with developing *Rheobatrachus* embryos to test for a chemical substance that might suppress stomach function in the mothers. They dissected out the gastric mucosa (secreting surface) of the toad *Bufo marinus* (*Rheobatrachus* itself is too rare to sacrifice so many adult females for such an experiment) and kept it alive in vitro. They showed that this isolated mucosa can function normally to secrete stomach acids and that well-known chemical inhibitors will suppress the secretion. They then demonstrated that water in contact with *Rheobatrachus* tadpoles suppresses the mucosa, while water in contact with tadpoles of other species has no effect. Finally, they succeeded in isolating a chemical suppressor from the water—prostaglandin E_2. (The prostaglandins are hormonelike substances, named for their first discovery as secretions of the human prostate gland—though they form throughout the body and serve many functions.)

Thus, we may finally return to mimicry and the problem of incipient stages. I trust that some readers have been bothered by an apparent dilemma of illogic and reversed causality. The eggs of *Rheobatrachus* must contain the prostaglandin that suppresses secretion of gastric acid and allows the stomach to serve as an inert brood pouch. It's nice to know that eggs contain a substance for their own protection in a hostile environment. But in a world of history—not of created perfection—how can such a system arise? The ancestors of *Rheobatrachus* must have been conventional frogs, laying eggs for external development. At some point, a female *Rheobatrachus* must have swallowed its fertilized eggs (presumably taking them for food, not with the foresight of evolutionary innovation)—and the fortuitous presence of prostaglandin suppressed digestion and permitted the eggs to develop in their mother's stomach.

The key word is *fortuitous*. One cannot seriously believe that ancestral eggs actively evolved prostaglandin because they knew that, millions of years in the future, a mother would swallow them and they would then need some inhibitor of gastric secretion. The eggs must have contained prostaglandin for another reason or for no particular reason at all (perhaps just as a metabolic by-product of development). Prostaglandin provided a lucky break with respect to the later evolution of gastric brooding—a historical precondition fortuitously available at the right moment, a sine qua non evolved for other reasons and pressed into service to initiate a new evolutionary direction.

Darwin proposed the same explanation for the initiation of mimicry—as a general solution to the old problem of incipient stages. Mimicry works splendidly as a completed system, but what gets the process started along one potential pathway among many? Darwin argued that a mimicking butterfly must begin with a slight *and fortuitous* resemblance to its model. Without this leg up for initiation, the process of improvement to mimetic perfection cannot begin. But once an accidental, initial resemblance provides some slight edge, natural selection can improve the fit from imperfect beginnings.

Thus, Darwin noted with pleasure Bates's demonstration that mimicry always arose among butterflies more prone to vary than others that never evolve mimetic forms. This tendency to vary must be the precondition that establishes fortuitous initial resemblance to models in some cases. "It is necessary to suppose," Darwin wrote, that ancestral mimics "accidently resembled a member of another and protected group in a sufficient degree to afford some slight protection, this having given the basis for the subsequent acquisition of the most perfect resemblance." Ancestral mimics happened to resemble a model in some slight manner—and the evolutionary process could begin. The eggs of *Rheobatrachus* happened to contain a prostaglandin that inhibited gastric secretion—and their mother's stomach became a temporary home, not an engine of destruction.

New evolutionary directions must have such quirky beginnings based on the fortuitous presence of structures and possibilities evolved for other reasons. After all, in nature, as in human invention, one cannot prepare actively for the utterly unexpected. Gastric brooding must be an either-or, a quantum jump in evolutionary potential. As Tyler argues, what intermediary stage can one imagine? Many fishes (but no frogs) brood young in their mouths—while only males possess throat pouches, but only female *Rheobatrachus* broods in its stomach. Eggs can't develop halfway down the esophagus.

We glimpse in the story of *Rheobatrachus* a model for the introduction of creativity and new directions in evolution (not just a tale of growing bigger or smaller, fiercer or milder, by the everyday action of natural selection). Such new directions, as Darwin argued in resolving the problem of incipient stages, must be initiated by fortuitous prerequisites, thus imparting a quirky and unpredictable character to the history of life. These new directions may involve minimal changes at first—since the fortuitous prerequisites are already present, though not so utilized, in ancestors. A female *Rheobatrachus* swallowed its fertilized eggs, and a striking new behavior and mode of brooding arose at once by virtue of a chemical fortuitously present in eggs, and by the automatic action of stretch receptors in the stomach. Such minimal changes are pregnant with possibilities. Most probably lead nowhere beyond a few oddballs—as with *Rheobatrachus,* probably already well on its way to extinction.

But a few quirky new directions may become seeds of major innovations and floods of diversity in life's history. The first protoamphibian that crawled out of its pond has long been a favorite source of evolutionary cartoon humor. The captions are endless—from "see ya later as alligator" to "because the weather's better out here." But my favorite reads "here goes nothing." It doesn't happen often, but when nothing becomes something, the inherent power of evolution, normally an exquisitely conservative force, can break forth. Or, as Reginald Bunthorne proclaims in Gilbert and Sullivan's *Patience* (which evolution must have above all else): "Nature for restraint too mighty far, has burst the bonds of art—and here we are."

Postscript

It is my sad duty to report a change of state, between writing and republishing this essay, that has made its title eerily prophetic. *Rheobatrachus silus,* the stomach-brooding frog and star of this essay, has apparently become extinct. This species was discovered in 1973, living in fair abundance in a restricted region of southeast Queensland, Australia. In early 1990, the National Research Council (of the United States) convened a conference to discuss "unexplained losses of amphibian populations around the world" (as reported in *Science News,* March 3, 1990). Michael J. Tyler, member of the team that discovered stomach brooding in *Rheobatrachus,* reported that 100 specimens could easily be observed per night when the population maintained fair abundance during the mid-1970s. Naturalists have not found a single individual since 1981, and must now conclude that the species is extinct (for several years they hoped that they were merely observing a sharp and perhaps cyclical reduction in numbers). Even more sadly, this loss forms part of a disturbing and unexplained pattern in amphibian populations throughout the world. In Australia alone, 20 of 194 frog species have suffered serious local drops in population size during the past decade, and at least one other species has become extinct.

7 | Intellectual Biography

21 | In a Jumbled Drawer

AS MY SON GROWS, I have monitored the changing fashions in kiddie culture for words expressing deep admiration—what I called "cool" in my day, and my father designated "swell." The half-life seems to be about six months, as "excellent" (with curious lingering emphasis on the first syllable) gave way to "bad" (extended, like a sheep bleat, long enough to turn into its opposite), to "wicked," to "rad" (short for radical). The latest incumbent—"awesome"—possesses more staying power, and has been reigning for at least two years. My only objection, from the fuddy-duddy's corner, lies in kiddie criteria for discernment. Ethan's buddies require such a tiny extension beyond the ordinary to proclaim something "awesome"—just a little bit bigger, brighter, and, especially, louder will do. This or that is proclaimed awesome every second sentence—and we have a lost a wonderful English word.

Now let me tell you about awesome—the real thing, when adults still held possession of the concept. I collected fossils all my youthful life, or at least on those rare occasions of departure from the asphalt of New York City. I had amassed, by the end of college, five cartonsful, all ordered and labeled—and I was pretty proud of both quantity and quality. Then I got my present job as curator of fossil invertebrates at Harvard's Museum of Comparative Zoology. I came to Cambridge with my five cartons and discovered that my new stewardship extended to 15,000 drawers of fossils, including some of the world's finest and oldest specimens, brought from Europe by Louis Agassiz more than a century ago. I put the cartons in a back corner of my office twenty years ago this month. I have never opened them. Me with my five cartons facing those 15,000 drawers—that is awe.

But when awe subsides, ecstasy creeps in. For I had 15,000 drawers to open, each harboring a potential discovery or insight. Raise to the nth power any simile you ever heard for "as happy as"—a boy in a candy store, a pig in . . . well, you know what. I spent two weeks pulling out every last drawer, and I found a cornucopia of disparate objects that have fueled my aesthetic and intellectual pleasure ever since.

The fossils were sublime, but I found as much fascination in the odd paraphernalia of culture that, for various reasons, end up in museum drawers. Late eighteenth century apothecary boxes, thread cases from the mills of Lawrence, Victorian cigar boxes of gaudy Cuban design—all the better to house fossils. Tickets to Lowell Institute lecture series by Gray, Agassiz, and Lyell, invitations to a ball honoring Napoleon III, merchants' calling cards from Victorian Cincinnati—all the better (on their blank obverses) to label fossils. Pages from the Sears catalogue for 1903, snippets of nineteenth-century newspapers—all the better to wrap fossils. The most interesting news item, a headline from a Cincinnati paper for July 11, 1881, read "Garfield's Grit" and announced that the president, though severely wounded in the recent assassination attempt, "is now on the sunny side of life again," and would almost surely recover—the flip side to a happy Harry Truman holding that 1948 *Chicago Tribune* headline announcing Dewey's victory.

For my most interesting discovery, I opened a drawer late one night and found only a jumble of specimens inside. Someone had obviously overturned the drawer and dumped the contents. But the thick layer of dust identified the disordered pile as a very old jumble. Inside, I found the following note:

> This incident was the result of the carelessness of the Janitor Eli Grant who managed to overturn about half a dozen drawers of specimens by undertaking to move certain trays which he was not authorized to touch. The accident happened during my absence but I judge that it arose from an excess of zeal rather than from any recklessness. I have deemed it best to leave the specimens exactly as I found

them awaiting an opportunity to have them arranged by Mr. Hartt.

I developed an immediate dislike for this pusillanimous assistant—fingering the janitor, distancing himself even further from responsibility by assuring the boss that he hadn't been there at

The guilty note from N.S. Shaler, left in a drawer to forestall Agassiz's wrath.

the time, then feeling a bit guilty for placing Mr. Grant's job in jeopardy and praising him for zeal through the back door. I then looked at the date and signature—Cambridge, April 26, 1869, N. S. Shaler.

David lamented over Saul: "How are the mighty fallen." But one might look the other way in ontogeny and observe, "How meek are the mighty when young and subservient." Nathaniel Southgate Shaler became one of the greatest and most popular teachers in the history of Harvard University. He was a giant among late nineteenth century American naturalists. But in 1869, Shaler was just a junior professor without tenure, and his superior was the most powerful and imperious biologist in America— none other than Louis Agassiz himself. Obviously, Shaler had written that note in mortal fear of Agassiz's celebrated wrath. Equally obviously, Agassiz had never found out—for Shaler became professor of paleontology later that year, while a century of undisturbed dust still lies atop the jumbled specimens.

N. S. Shaler reaped the rewards of his unflinching loyalty to Agassiz. The path of devotion was not smooth. Agassiz was a transplanted European with an Old World sense of professorial authority. He told students what they would study, awarded degrees by oral examination and direct assessment of competence, and insisted upon personal approval for any publication based on material at his museum. He never failed in encouragement, warmth, and enthusiasm—and he was a beloved teacher. But he never relinquished one iota of authority. These attitudes might only have yielded a tightly run ship in times of intellectual quiescence, but Agassiz was captain on the most troubled waters of biological history. Agassiz opened his museum in 1859, the same year that Darwin published *The Origin of Species.* He gathered around himself the most promising, and therefore most independently minded, group of young zoologists in America, Shaler included. Inevitably, evolution became the chief subject of discussion. With equal inevitability, students flocked eagerly to this beacon of intellectual excitement and became enthusiastic converts. But Agassiz had built both a career and a coherent philosophy upon the creationist premise that species are ideas in God's mind, made incarnate by his hand in a world of material objects. Sooner shall a camel pass through the eye of a needle than the old lion and young wolf cubs shall dwell in harmony amidst such disagreement.

And so, inevitably once more, Agassiz's students revolted—against both his overweening authority and his old-fashioned ideas. In 1863, they formed what they called, in half-jest, a committee for the protection of American students from foreign-born professors. Agassiz, however, held all the cards in a hierarchical world, and he booted the rebels out, much to the benefit of American science, as they formed departments and centers at other great universities. Agassiz then staffed his museum with older and uncontroversial professionals, bringing peace and mediocrity once again to Harvard.

Of his truly excellent students, only Shaler remained loyal. And Shaler reaped his earthly reward. He received his bachelor of science in geology, *summa cum laude,* in July 1862. After a spell of service in the Civil War, fighting for the Union from his native Kentucky, Shaler returned to Harvard in 1864. Agassiz, describing Shaler as "the one of my American students whom I love the best," appointed him assistant in paleontology at the Museum of Comparative Zoology. In 1869, soon after he penned the guilty note that would lie unread for exactly 100 years (I found it in 1969), Shaler received his lifetime appointment as professor of geology, succeeding Agassiz (who continued to lecture in zoology until he died in 1873). There Shaler remained until his death in 1906, writing numerous treatises on everything from the geology of Martha's Vineyard to the nature of morality and immortality. He also became, by far, Harvard's most popular professor. His classes overflowed, and his students poured forth praise for his enthusiasm, his articulateness, and the comfort, optimism, and basic conventionality of his words, spoken to the elite at the height of America's gilded age. On the day of his funeral, flags in city buildings and student fraternities flew at half-mast, and many shops closed. Thirty years later, at the Harvard tercentenary of 1936, Shaler was named twelfth among the fifty people most important to the history of Harvard. To this day, his bust rests, with only fourteen others, including Franklin's, Longfellow's, and, of course, Agassiz's, in the faculty room of Bullfinch's University Hall (and you can take my word for it; I made a special field trip over there and counted).

Shaler's loyalty to Agassiz, and to comfortable convention in general, held as strongly in ideology as in practice. Shaler wrote these words of condolence to Agassiz's widow, Elizabeth Cary, founder of Radcliffe College, when Louis died in 1873: "He never was a greater teacher than now. He never was more truly at his chosen work. . . . While he lived I always felt myself a boy beside him." (See David N. Livingstone, *Nathaniel Southgate Shaler and the Culture of American Science,* University of Alabama Press, 1987, for the source of this quotation and an excellent account of Shaler's intellectual life.)

I don't think that Shaler, in his eulogy to Elizabeth, either erred or exaggerated in his chosen metaphor of subservience to Agassiz's vision. While Shaler remained subordinate, he followed Agassiz's intellectual lead, often with the epigone's habit of exaggerating his master's voice. Shaler's very first publication provides an interesting example ("Lateral Symmetry in Brachiopoda," 1861). Here Shaler supports both Agassiz's creationism and his zoological classification. Brachiopods, once a dominant group in the fossil record of marine invertebrates, are now a minor component of oceanic faunas. With their bivalved shells, they look superficially like clams, but their soft anatomy is entirely distinct, and they are now classified as a separate phylum. But Georges Cuvier, Agassiz's great mentor, had placed brachiopods with clams and snails in his phylum Mollusca—and Agassiz, whose loyalty to Cuvier matched any devotion of Shaler's, wished both to uphold Cuvier's classification and to use his concept of Mollusca as an argument against Darwin.

Shaler obliged in his first public performance. He affirmed Cuvier and Agassiz's inclusion of brachiopods in the Mollusca by claiming a bilateral symmetry of soft parts similar enough to the symmetry of such "standard" forms as clams and squids to justify a conclusion of common plan in design. But he then took a swipe at Darwin's reason for including separate groups in a single phylum by arguing that no evolutionary transition could possibly link adult brachiopod and clam. (Shaler was quite right about this, but not for his stated reason. You cannot transform a brachiopod into a clam, but then nature never did because brachiopods aren't mollusks and the two groups are entirely separate—contrary to Shaler's first conclusion.) The planes of bilateral symmetry are different for the two groups, Shaler argued correctly, and no transition could occur because any smooth intermediate would have to pass through a nonbilateral stage entirely inconsistent with molluscan design. Shaler wrote:

> Such a transition would require a series of forms, each of which must present a negation of that very principle of bilateral symmetry which we have found of so much importance. And must we not, therefore, conclude that the series which united these two orders is a series of thought, which is itself connected, though manifested by two structures which have no genetic relations.

Now if you're holding a nineteenth-century scorecard, and therefore know the players, only one man could be lurking behind this statement. Only one real Platonist of this ilk operated in America, only one leading biologist still willing to designate species as thoughts of a Creator, and taxonomic relationships as the interconnections within His mind—Louis Agassiz. Shaler, with the true zeal of the acolyte, even out-Agassized Agassiz in referring to the central character of bilateral symmetry as "the fundamental thought of the type" and then designating animal taxonomy as "a study of personified thought." Even Agassiz was not so explicit in specifying the attributes of his God.

When the winds of inevitability blew strongly enough, and when Shaler's own position became secure in the late 1860s, he finally embraced evolution, but ever so gently, and in a manner that would cause minimal offense to Agassiz and to any Brahmin member of the old Boston order. After Agassiz's death, Shaler continued to espouse a version of evolution with maximal loyalty to Agassiz's larger vision of natural harmony, and marked aversion to all Darwinian ideas of chanciness, contingency, unpredictability, opportunism, and quirkiness. He led the American Neo-Lamarckian school—a powerful group of anti-Darwinian evolutionists who held out for order, purpose, and progress in nature through the principle of inheritance for features acquired by the effort of organisms. Progress in mentality might be predictably ordained if some organisms strove for improvement during their lives and passed their achievements to their offspring. No waiting for the Darwinian chanciness of favorable environments and fortuitous variations.

Shaler's loyalty to Agassiz persisted right through this fundamental change from creationism to evolution. For example, though he could scarcely deny the common origin of all humans in the light of evolutionary theory, Shaler still advocated Agassiz's distinctive view (representing the "polygenist" school of pre-Darwinian anthropology) that human races are separate species, properly and necessarily kept apart both on public conveyances and in bedrooms. Shaler argued for an evolutionary separation of races so long ago that accumulated differences had become, for all practical purposes, permanent.

Practical purposes, in the genteel racism of patrician Boston, abetted by a slaveholding Kentucky ancestry, meant "using biology as an accomplice" (in Condorcet's words) to advocate a "nativist" social policy (where "natives" are not the truly indigenous American Indians, but the earliest immigrants from Protestant western and northern Europe). Shaler reserved his lowest opinion for black Americans, but invested his social energies in the Immigration Restriction League and its attempts to prevent dilution of American whites (read WASPs) by the great Catholic and Jewish unwashed of southern and eastern Europe.

One can hardly fathom the psychological and sociological complexities of racism, but the forced intellectual rationales are always intriguing and more accessible. Shaler's own defense merged his two chief interests in geography and zoology. He argued that we live in a world of sensible and optimal pattern, devoid of quirk or caprice. People differ because they have adapted by Lamarckian means to their local environments; our capacities are a map of our original homes—and we really shouldn't live elsewhere (hence the biological rectitude of restricting immigration). The languid tropics cannot inspire genius, and you cannot contemplate the Pythagorean absolute while trying to keep body and soul together in an igloo. Hence the tough, but tractable, lands of northern Europe yielded the best of humanity. Shaler wrote:

> Our continents and seas, cannot be considered as physical accidents in which, and on which, organic beings have found an ever-perilous resting place, but as great engines operating in a determined way to secure the advance of life.

Shaler then applied this cardinal belief in overarching order (against the Darwinian specter of unpredictable contingency) to the largest question of all—the meaning of human life as a proof of God's existence and benevolence. In so doing, he completed the evolutionary version of Agassiz's dearest principle—the infusion of sensible, progressive, divine order into the cosmos, with the elevation of "man" (and I think he really meant only half of us) to the pinnacle of God's intent. Shaler could not deny his generation's proof of evolution, and had departed from his master in this conviction, but he had been faithful in constructing a vision of evolution so mild that it left all cosmic comfort intact, thereby affirming the deepest principle of Agassiz's natural theology.

Shaler rooted his argument in a simple claim about probability. (Shaler often repeated this line of reasoning. My quotations come from his last and most widely read book—*The Individual: A Study of Life and Death,* 1901.) Human life is the end result of an evolutionary sequence stretching back into the immensity of time and including thousands of steps, each necessary as a link in the rising sequence:

> The possibility of man's development has rested on the successive institution of species in linked order. . . . If, in this succession of tens of thousands of species, living through a series of millions of years, any of these links of the human chain had been broken; if any one of the species had failed to give birth to its successor, the chance of the development of man would have been lost.

Human evolution, Shaler holds, would have been "unattainable without the guidance of a controlling power intent on the end." If one sequence alone could have engendered us, and if the world be ruled by Darwinian caprice and contingency, our appearance would have been "essentially impossible." For surely, one link would have failed, one step in ten thousand been aborted, thus ending forever the ascent toward consciousness. Only divine watchfulness and intent could have produced the human mind (not a direct finger in the pot, perhaps, but at least an intelligent construction of nature's laws with a desired end in view):

The facts connected with the organic approach to man afford what is perhaps the strongest argument, or at least the most condensed, in favor of the opinion that there is an intelligent principle in control of the universe.

Nathaniel Southgate Shaler was one of the most influential American intellectuals of his time. Today, he is unknown. I doubt that one in a hundred readers of this essay (geologists and Harvardians excepted) has ever heard of him. His biography rates thirteen lines in the *Encyclopaedia Britannica,* more than half devoted to a listing of book titles. Why has he faded, and what does his eclipse teach us about the power and permanence of human thought? We can, perhaps, best approach this question by considering one of Shaler's best friends, a man also influenced by Agassiz, but in a different way—William James. In their day, Shaler and James were peas in a pod of Harvard fame. Now Shaler is a memory for a few professionals, and James is one of America's great gifts to the history of human thought. Why the difference?

William James also came under Agassiz's spell during his student years. Agassiz decided to take six undergraduates along on his famous Thayer Expedition to Brazil (1866). They would help the trained scientists in collecting specimens and, in return, hear lectures from Agassiz on all aspects of natural history. William James, among the lucky six, certainly appreciated the value of Agassiz's formidable intellect and pedagogical skill. He wrote to his father: "I am getting a pretty valuable training from the Prof. who pitches into me right and left and makes me [own] up to a great many of my imperfections. This morning he said I was 'totally uneducated.' "

But James maintained his critical perspective, while Shaler became an acolyte and then an epigone. James wrote:

I have profited a great deal by hearing Agassiz talk, not so much by what he says, for never did a man utter a greater amount of humbug, but by learning the way of feeling of such a vast practical engine as he is. . . . I delight to be with him. I only saw his defects at first, but now his wonderful qualities throw them quite in the background. . . . I never saw a man work so hard.

Was James "smarter" than Shaler? Does their difference in renown today reflect some basic disparity in amount of intellectual power? This is a senseless question for many reasons. Intelligence is too complex and multifaceted a thing to reduce to any single dimension. What can we say? Both men had certain brilliance, but they used their skills differently. Shaler was content to follow Agassiz throughout his career, happy to employ his formidable intellect in constructing an elaborate rationale for contemporary preferences, never challenging the conservative assumptions of his class and culture. James questioned Agassiz from day one. James probed and wondered, reached and struggled every day of his life. Shaler built pretty buildings to house comfortable furniture. Intelligence or temperament; brains or guts? I don't know. But I do know that oblivion was one man's reward, enduring study and respect the other's.

As a dramatic illustration of the difference, consider James's critique of Shaler's "probability argument" for God's benevolence from the fact of human evolution. James read Shaler's *The Individual,* and wrote a very warm, though critical, letter to his dear friend. He praised "the gravity and dignity and peacefulness" of Shaler's thoughts, but singled out the probability argument for special rebuttal.

James points out that the actual result of evolution is the only sample we have. We cannot compute a "probability" or even speak in such terms. Any result in a sample of one would appear equally miraculous when you consider the vast range of alternative possibilities. But something had to happen. We may only talk of odds if we could return to the beginning, list a million possible outcomes, and then lay cold cash upon one possibility alone:

> We never know what ends may have been kept from realization, for the dead tell no tales. The surviving witness would in any case, and whatever he were, draw the conclusion that the universe was planned to make him and the like of him succeed, for it actually did so. But your argument that it is millions to one that it didn't do so by chance doesn't apply. It would apply if the witness had preexisted in an independent form and framed his scheme, and then the world had realized it. Such a coincidence would prove the world to have a kindred mind to his. But there has been no such

coincidence. The world has come but once, the witness is there after the fact and simply approves. . . . Where only one fact is in question, there is no relation of "probability" at all. [James's letter is reprinted, in full, in *The Autobiography of Nathaniel Southgate Shaler,* 1909.]

Old, bad arguments never die (they don't fade away either), particularly when they match our hopes. Shaler's false probability argument is still a favorite among those who yearn to find a cosmic rationale for human importance. And James's retort remains as brilliant and as valid today as when he first presented the case to Shaler. We could save ourselves from a lot of current nonsense if every devotee of the anthropic principle (strong version), every fan of Teilhard's noosphere, simply read and understood James's letter to Shaler.

James then continues with the ultimate Darwinian riposte to Shaler's doctrine of cosmic hope and importance. Human intellect is a thing of beauty—truly awesome. But our evolution need not record any more than a Darwinian concatenation of improbabilities:

> I think, therefore, that the excellence we have reached and now approve may be due to no general design, but merely to a succession of the short designs we actually know of, taking advantage of opportunity, and adding themselves together from point to point.

Which brings us back to Mr. Eli Grant. (I do hope, compassionate reader, that you have been worrying about this poor man's fate while I temporized in higher philosophical realms.) The young Shaler tried to cover his ass by exposing Grant's. Obviously, he succeeded, but what happened to the poor janitor, left to take the rap?

This story has a happy ending, based on two sources of evidence: one inferential, the other direct. Since Agassiz never found out, never saw the note, and since Mr. Hartt, like Godot, never arrived, we may assume that Grant's zealous accident eluded Agassiz's watchful eye. More directly, I am delighted to report that I found (in yet another drawer) a record book for the

Department of Invertebrate Paleontology in 1887. Mr. Eli Grant is still listed as janitor.

Was Mr. Grant meant to survive because he did? Does his tenure on the job indicate the workings of a benevolent and controlling mind? (Why not, for I can envisage 100 other scenarios, all plausible but less happy.) Or was Mr. Grant too small to fall under God's direct providence? But if so, by what hubris do we consider ourselves any bigger in a universe of such vastness? Such unprofitable, such unanswerable questions. Let us simply rejoice in the happy ending of a small tale, and give the last word to William James, still trying to set his friend Shaler straight:

> What if we did come where we are by chance, or by mere fact, with no one general design? What is gained, is gained, all the same. As to what may have been lost, who knows of it, in any case?

Postscript: A Letter from Jimmy Carter

I had heard many stories of Jimmy Carter's personal kindness, and I had long admired him as the most intellectual of presidents since Roosevelt (the competition has not been too fierce of late). But I was delighted and surprised (to the point of shock) when I received a call, late one afternoon, from a woman who said, in a strong southern accent: "Please hold the line; President Carter would like to speak with you." My first reaction, undoubtedly impolitic, was to blurt out: "President Carter who?" (I did think of Jimmy, but his tenure had ended nearly ten years ago and I didn't realize that certain titles, like diamonds and sainthood, are forever.) She replied with more than a hint of indignation: "Former president Jimmy Carter of the United States." I allowed that I would hold.

He came on the line a minute later. My first reaction was surprise that the voice sounded so much like that of our president from 1977 to 1980. My second reaction was to chastise myself for such incredible stupidity since it was, after all, Mr. Carter on the line—and people do tend to sound like themselves (even basically competent folks can be mighty dimwitted when flustered). My third reaction was to wonder why, in heaven's name, he was calling me. So I listened and soon found out. Carter said that he had read and enjoyed several of my books. He then read of my bout with cancer in the preface to *The Flamingo's Smile.* He wanted, in this light, to express his best wishes for my health but hesitated to call, lest I might be too ill to be disturbed. So he phoned my publishers, found out that my next book was in production, and that I had recovered. Feeling, therefore, that he would not be intruding, he had decided to call—simply to express his good wishes and his hopes for my continued good health.

What a lovely man, and what a gracious and kind act. I sent him, as a most inadequate expression of thanks, a copy of the book, *Wonderful Life,* when it appeared a few months later. Not long thereafter, I received a letter in reply:

> I had a chance to read *Wonderful Life* while traveling to Kenya, Sudan, and Ethiopia recently. Rosalynn and I were spending three weeks mediating between the Ethiopian government and the Eritrean People's Liberation Front. . . . You may or may not be familiar with the horrendous wars in those countries. Between negotiating sessions, I found your book to be thoroughly enjoyable—perhaps your best so far.

But Carter then voiced a major criticism, quite disabling if valid. I argue in *Wonderful Life* that human evolution would almost surely not occur again if we could rewind the tape of life back to the early history of multicellular animals (erasing what actually happened of course) and let it play again from an identical starting point (too many initial possibilities relative to later survivors, with no reason to think that survivors prevailed for reasons of superiority or any other version of predictability, and too much randomness and contingency in the pathways of life's later history). But Carter made a brilliant riposte to this central claim of my book.

Jimmy Carter, if I understand his religious attitudes properly, upholds an unconventional point of view among Christian intellectuals on the issue of relationships between God and nature. Most theologians (in agreement with most scientists) now argue that facts of nature represent a domain different from the realm of religious attitudes and beliefs, and that these two worlds of equal value interact rather little. But Jimmy Carter is a twentieth-century natural theologian—that is, he accepts the older argument, popular before Darwin, that the state of nature should provide material for inferring the existence and character of God. Nineteenth-century versions of natural theology, as embodied in Paley's classic work (1802) of the same name, tended to argue that God's nature and benevolence were manifest in the excellent design of organisms and the harmony of ecosystems—in other words, in natural goodness. Such an attitude would be hard to maintain in a century that knew two world wars, Hiroshima, and the Holocaust. If natural theology is to be advanced in our times, a new style of argument must be developed—one that acknowledges the misfits, horrors, and improbabilities, but sees God's action as manifest nonetheless. I think that Carter developed a brilliant twentieth-century version of natural theology by criticizing my book in the next paragraph of his letter:

> You seem to be straining mightily to prove that everything that has happened prior to an evolutionary screening period was just an accident, and that if the tape of life was replayed in countless different ways it is unlikely that cognitive creatures would have been created or evolved. It may be that when you raise "one chance in a million" to the 4th or 5th power there comes a time when pure "chance" can be questioned. I presume that you feel more at ease with the luck of 1 out of 10 to the 30th power than with the concept of a creator who/that has done some orchestrating.

In other words, Carter asks, can't the improbability of our evolution become so great that the very fact of its happening must indicate some divine intent? One chance in ten can be true chance, but the realization of one chance in many billion might indicate intent. What else could a twentieth-century natural theologian do but locate God in the realization of improbability, rather than in the ineffable beauty of design!

Carter's argument is fascinating but, I believe, wrong—and

wrong for the same reason that James invokes against Shaler (the central point of this essay). In fact, Carter's argument is Shaler's updated and more sophisticated. Shaler claimed that God must have superintended our evolution because the derailment or disruption of any of thousands of links in our evolutionary chain would have canceled the possibility of our eventual appearance. James replied that we cannot read God in contingencies of history because a probability cannot even be calculated for a singular occurrence known only after the fact (whereas probabilities could be attached to predictions made at the beginning of a sequence). James might as well have been answering Carter when he wrote to Shaler:

> But your argument that it is millions to one that it didn't do so by chance doesn't apply. It would apply if the witness had preexisted in an independent form and framed his scheme, and then the world had realized it. Such a coincidence would prove the world to have a kindred mind to his. But there has been no such coincidence. The world has come but once, the witness is there after the fact and simply approves. . . . Where only one fact is in question, there is no relation of "probability" at all.

Such is our intellectual heritage, such our continuity, that fine thinkers can speak to each other across the centuries.

22 | Kropotkin Was No Crackpot

IN LATE 1909, two great men corresponded across oceans, religions, generations, and races. Leo Tolstoy, sage of Christian nonviolence in his later years, wrote to the young Mohandas Gandhi, struggling for the rights of Indian settlers in South Africa:

> God helps our dear brothers and co-workers in the Transvaal. The same struggle of the tender against the harsh, of meekness and love against pride and violence, is every year making itself more and more felt here among us also.

A year later, wearied by domestic strife, and unable to endure the contradiction of life in Christian poverty on a prosperous estate run with unwelcome income from his great novels (written before his religious conversion and published by his wife), Tolstoy fled by train for parts unknown and a simpler end to his waning days. He wrote to his wife:

> My departure will distress you. I'm sorry about this, but do understand and believe that I couldn't do otherwise. My position in the house is becoming, or has become, unbearable. Apart from anything else, I can't live any longer in these conditions of luxury in which I have been living, and I'm doing what old men of my age commonly do: leaving this worldly life in order to live the last days of my life in peace and solitude.

The great novelist Leo Tolstoy, late in life. THE BETTMANN ARCHIVE.

But Tolstoy's final journey was both brief and unhappy. Less than a month later, cold and weary from numerous long rides on Russian trains in approaching winter, he contracted pneumonia and died at age eighty-two in the stationmaster's home at the railroad stop of Astapovo. Too weak to write, he dictated his last letter on November 1, 1910. Addressed to a son and daughter who did not share his views on Christian nonviolence, Tolstoy offered a last word of advice:

The views you have acquired about Darwinism, evolution, and the struggle for existence won't explain to you the meaning of your life and won't give you guidance in your actions, and a life without an explanation of its meaning and importance, and without the unfailing guidance that stems from it is a pitiful existence. Think about it. I say it, probably on the eve of my death, because I love you.

Tolstoy's complaint has been the most common of all indictments against Darwin, from the publication of the *Origin of Species* in 1859 to now. Darwinism, the charge contends, undermines morality by claiming that success in nature can only be measured by victory in bloody battle—the "struggle for existence" or "survival of the fittest" to cite Darwin's own choice of mottoes. If we wish "meekness and love" to triumph over "pride and violence" (as Tolstoy wrote to Gandhi), then we must repudiate Darwin's vision of nature's way—as Tolstoy stated in a final plea to his errant children.

This charge against Darwin is unfair for two reasons. First, nature (no matter how cruel in human terms) provides no basis for our moral values. (Evolution might, at most, help to explain why we have moral feelings, but nature can never decide for us whether any particular action is right or wrong.) Second, Darwin's "struggle for existence" is an abstract metaphor, not an explicit statement about bloody battle. Reproductive success, the criterion of natural selection, works in many modes: Victory in battle may be one pathway, but cooperation, symbiosis, and mutual aid may also secure success in other times and contexts. In a famous passage, Darwin explained his concept of evolutionary struggle (*Origin of Species,* 1859, pp. 62–63):

I use this term in a large and metaphorical sense including dependence of one being on another, and including (which is more important) not only the life of the individual, but success in leaving progeny. Two canine animals, in a time of dearth, may be truly said to struggle with each other which shall get food and live. But a plant on the edge of a desert is said to struggle for life against the drought. . . . As the mistletoe is disseminated by birds, its existence depends on birds; and it may metaphorically be said to struggle with other fruit-bearing plants, in order to tempt birds to devour and thus disseminate its seeds rather than those of other plants. In these several senses, which pass into each other, I use for convenience sake the general term of struggle for existence.

Yet, in another sense, Tolstoy's complaint is not entirely unfounded. Darwin did present an encompassing, metaphorical definition of struggle, but his actual examples certainly favored bloody battle—"Nature, red in tooth and claw," in a line from Tennyson so overquoted that it soon became a knee-jerk cliché for this view of life. Darwin based his theory of natural selection on the dismal view of Malthus that growth in population must outstrip food supply and lead to overt battle for dwindling resources. Moreover, Darwin maintained a limited but controlling view of ecology as a world stuffed full of competing species—so balanced and so crowded that a new form could only gain entry by literally pushing a former inhabitant out. Darwin expressed this view in a metaphor even more central to his general vision than the concept of struggle—the metaphor of the wedge. Nature, Darwin writes, is like a surface with 10,000 wedges hammered tightly in and filling all available space. A new species (represented as a wedge) can only gain entry into a community by driving itself into a tiny chink and forcing another wedge out. Success, in this vision, can only be achieved by direct takeover in overt competition.

Furthermore, Darwin's own chief disciple, Thomas Henry Huxley, advanced this "gladiatorial" view of natural selection (his word) in a series of famous essays about ethics. Huxley maintained that the predominance of bloody battle defined nature's way as nonmoral (not explicitly immoral, but surely unsuited as offering any guide to moral behavior).

From the point of view of the moralist the animal world is about on a level of a gladiator's show. The creatures are fairly well treated, and set to fight—whereby the strongest, the swiftest, and the cunningest live to fight another day. The spectator has no need to turn his thumbs down, as no quarter is given.

But Huxley then goes further. Any human society set up along these lines of nature will devolve into anarchy and misery—Hobbes's brutal world of *bellum omnium contra omnes* (where *bellum* means "war," not beauty): the war of all against all. Therefore, the chief purpose of society must lie in mitigation of the struggle that defines nature's pathway. Study natural selection and do the opposite in human society:

> But, in civilized society, the inevitable result of such obedience [to the law of bloody battle] is the re-establishment, in all its intensity, of that struggle for existence—the war of each against all—the mitigation or abolition of which was the chief end of social organization.

This apparent discordance between nature's way and any hope for human social decency has defined the major subject for debate about ethics and evolution ever since Darwin. Huxley's solution has won many supporters—nature is nasty and no guide to morality except, perhaps, as an indicator of what to avoid in human society. My own preference lies with a different solution based on taking Darwin's metaphorical view of struggle seriously (admittedly in the face of Darwin's own preference for gladiatorial examples)—nature is sometimes nasty, sometimes nice (really neither, since the human terms are so inappropriate). By presenting examples of all behaviors (under the metaphorical rubric of struggle), nature favors none and offers no guidelines. The facts of nature cannot provide moral guidance in any case.

But a third solution has been advocated by some thinkers who do wish to find a basis for morality in nature and evolution. Since few can detect much moral comfort in the gladiatorial interpretation, this third position must reformulate the way of nature. Darwin's words about the metaphorical character of struggle offer a promising starting point. One might argue that the gladiatorial examples have been over-sold and misrepresented as predominant. Perhaps cooperation and mutual aid are the more common results of struggle for existence. Perhaps communion rather than combat leads to greater reproductive success in most circumstances.

The most famous expression of this third solution may be

Petr Kropotkin, a bearded but gentle anarchist. THE
BETTMANN ARCHIVE.

found in *Mutual Aid*, published in 1902 by the Russian revolutionary anarchist Petr Kropotkin. (We must shed the old stereotype of anarchists as bearded bomb throwers furtively stalking
about city streets at night. Kropotkin was a genial man, almost
saintly according to some, who promoted a vision of small
communities setting their own standards by consensus for the
benefit of all, thereby eliminating the need for most functions of
a central government.) Kropotkin, a Russian nobleman, lived in
English exile for political reasons. He wrote *Mutual Aid* (in English) as a direct response to the essay of Huxley quoted above,
"The Struggle for Existence in Human Society," published in *The
Nineteenth Century*, in February 1888. Kropotkin responded to

Huxley with a series of articles, also printed in *The Nineteenth Century* and eventually collected together as the book *Mutual Aid*.

As the title suggests, Kropotkin argues, in his cardinal premise, that the struggle for existence usually leads to mutual aid rather than combat as the chief criterion of evolutionary success. Human society must therefore build upon our natural inclinations (not reverse them, as Huxley held) in formulating a moral order that will bring both peace and prosperity to our species. In a series of chapters, Kropotkin tries to illustrate continuity between natural selection for mutual aid among animals and the basis for success in increasingly progressive human social organization. His five sequential chapters address mutual aid among animals, among savages, among barbarians, in the medieval city, and amongst ourselves.

I confess that I have always viewed Kropotkin as daftly idiosyncratic, if undeniably well meaning. He is always so presented in standard courses on evolutionary biology—as one of those soft and woolly thinkers who let hope and sentimentality get in the way of analytic toughness and a willingness to accept nature as she is, warts and all. After all, he was a man of strange politics and unworkable ideals, wrenched from the context of his youth, a stranger in a strange land. Moreover, his portrayal of Darwin so matched his social ideals (mutual aid naturally given as a product of evolution without need for central authority) that one could only see personal hope rather than scientific accuracy in his accounts. Kropotkin has long been on my list of potential topics for an essay (if only because I wanted to read his book, and not merely mouth the textbook interpretation), but I never proceeded because I could find no larger context than the man himself. Kooky intellects are interesting as gossip, perhaps as psychology, but true idiosyncrasy provides the worst possible basis for generality.

But this situation changed for me in a flash when I read a very fine article in the latest issue of *Isis* (our leading professional journal in the history of science) by Daniel P. Todes: "Darwin's Malthusian Metaphor and Russian Evolutionary Thought, 1859–1917." I learned that the parochiality had been mine in my ignorance of Russian evolutionary thought, not Kropotkin's in his isolation in England. (I can read Russian, but only painfully, and with a dictionary—which means, for all practical purposes, that I can't read the language.) I knew that Darwin had become a hero of the Russian intelligentsia and had influenced academic life in Russia perhaps more than in any other country. But virtually none of this Russian work has ever been translated or even discussed in English literature. The ideas of this school are unknown to us; we do not even recognize the names of the major protagonists. I knew Kropotkin because he had published in English and lived in England, but I never understood that he represented a standard, well-developed Russian critique of Darwin, based on interesting reasons and coherent national traditions. Todes's article does not make Kropotkin more correct, but it does place his writing into a general context that demands our respect and produces substantial enlightenment. Kropotkin was part of a mainstream flowing in an unfamiliar direction, not an isolated little arroyo.

This Russian school of Darwinian critics, Todes argues, based its major premise upon a firm rejection of Malthus's claim that competition, in the gladiatorial mode, must dominate in an ever more crowded world, where population, growing geometrically, inevitably outstrips a food supply that can only increase arithmetically. Tolstoy, speaking for a consensus of his compatriots, branded Malthus as a "malicious mediocrity."

Todes finds a diverse set of reasons behind Russian hostility to Malthus. Political objections to the dog-eat-dog character of Western industrial competition arose from both ends of the Russian spectrum. Todes writes:

> Radicals, who hoped to build a socialist society, saw Malthusianism as a reactionary current in bourgeois political economy. Conservatives, who hoped to preserve the communal virtues of tsarist Russia, saw it as an expression of the "British national type."

But Todes identifies a far more interesting reason in the immediate experience of Russia's land and natural history. We all have a tendency to spin universal theories from a limited domain of surrounding circumstance. Many geneticists read the entire world of evolution in the confines of a laboratory bottle filled with fruit flies. My own increasing dubiousness about universal adaptation arises in large part, no doubt, because I study a peculiar snail that varies so widely and capriciously across an apparently unvarying environment, rather than a bird in flight or some other marvel of natural design.

Russia is an immense country, under-populated by any nineteenth-century measure of its agricultural potential. Russia is also, over most of its area, a harsh land, where competition is more likely to pit organism against environment (as in Darwin's metaphorical struggle of a plant at the desert's edge) than organism against organism in direct and bloody battle. How could any Russian, with a strong feel for his own countryside, see Malthus's principle of overpopulation as a foundation for evolutionary theory? Todes writes:

> It was foreign to their experience because, quite simply, Russia's huge land mass dwarfed its sparse population. For a Russian to see an inexorably increasing population inevitably straining potential supplies of food and space required quite a leap of imagination.

If these Russian critics could honestly tie their personal skepticism to the view from their own backyard, they could also recognize that Darwin's contrary enthusiasms might record the parochiality of his different surroundings, rather than a set of necessarily universal truths. Malthus makes a far better prophet in a crowded, industrial country professing an ideal of open competition in free markets. Moreover, the point has often been made that both Darwin and Alfred Russel Wallace independently developed the theory of natural selection after primary experience with natural history in the tropics. Both claimed inspiration from Malthus, again independently; but if fortune favors the prepared mind, then their tropical experience probably predisposed both men to read Malthus with resonance and approval. No other area on earth is so packed with species, and therefore so replete with competition of body against body. An Englishman who had learned the ways of nature in the tropics was almost bound to view evolution differently from a Russian nurtured on tales of the Siberian wasteland.

For example, N. I. Danilevsky, an expert on fisheries and population dynamics, published a large, two-volume critique of Darwinism in 1885. He identified struggle for personal gain as the credo of a distinctly British "national type," as contrasted with old Slavic values of collectivism. An English child, he writes, "boxes one on one, not in a group as we Russians like to spar." Danilevsky viewed Darwinian competition as "a purely English doctrine" founded upon a line of British thought stretching from Hobbes through Adam Smith to Malthus. Natural selection, he wrote, is rooted in "the war of all against all, now termed the struggle for existence—Hobbes' theory of politics; on competition—the economic theory of Adam Smith. . . . Malthus applied the very same principle to the problem of population. . . . Darwin extended both Malthus' partial theory and the general theory of the political economists to the organic world." (Quotes are from Todes's article.)

When we turn to Kropotkin's *Mutual Aid* in the light of Todes's discoveries about Russian evolutionary thought, we must reverse the traditional view and interpret this work as mainstream Russian criticism, not personal crankiness. The central logic of Kropotkin's argument is simple, straightforward, and largely cogent.

Kropotkin begins by acknowledging that struggle plays a central role in the lives of organisms and also provides the chief impetus for their evolution. But Kropotkin holds that struggle must not be viewed as a unitary phenomenon. It must be divided into two fundamentally different forms with contrary evolutionary meanings. We must recognize, first of all, the struggle of organism against organism for limited resources—the theme that Malthus imparted to Darwin and that Huxley described as gladiatorial. This form of direct struggle does lead to competition for personal benefit.

But a second form of struggle—the style that Darwin called metaphorical—pits organism against the harshness of surrounding physical environments, not against other members of the same species. Organisms must struggle to keep warm, to survive the sudden and unpredictable dangers of fire and storm, to persevere through harsh periods of drought, snow, or pestilence. These forms of struggle between organism and environment are best waged by cooperation among members of the same species—by mutual aid. If the struggle for existence pits two lions against one zebra, then we shall witness a feline battle and an equine carnage. But if lions are struggling jointly against the harshness of an inanimate environment, then fighting will not remove the common enemy—while cooperation may overcome a peril beyond the power of any single individual to surmount.

Kropotkin therefore created a dichotomy within the general notion of struggle—two forms with opposite import: (1) organism against organism of the same species for limited resources, leading to competition; and (2) organism against environment, leading to cooperation.

> No naturalist will doubt that the idea of a struggle for life carried on through organic nature is the greatest generalization of our century. Life *is* struggle; and in that struggle the fittest survive. But the answers to the questions "by which arms is the struggle chiefly carried on?" and "who are the fittest in the struggle?" will widely differ according to the importance given to the two different aspects of the struggle: the direct one, for food and safety among separate individuals, and the struggle which Darwin described as "metaphorical"—the struggle, very often collective, against adverse circumstances.

Darwin acknowledged that both forms existed, but his loyalty to Malthus and his vision of nature chock-full of species led him to emphasize the competitive aspect. Darwin's less sophisticated votaries then exalted the competitive view to near exclusivity, and heaped a social and moral meaning upon it as well.

> They came to conceive of the animal world as a world of perpetual struggle among half-starved individuals, thirsting for one another's blood. They made modern literature resound with the war-cry of *woe to the vanquished,* as if it were the last word of modern biology. They raised the "pitiless" struggle for personal advantages to the height of a biological principle which man must submit to as well, under the menace of otherwise succumbing in a world based upon mutual extermination.

Kropotkin did not deny the competitive form of struggle, but he argued that the cooperative style had been underemphasized and must balance or even predominate over competition in considering nature as a whole.

> There is an immense amount of warfare and extermination going on amidst various species; there is, at the same time, as much, or perhaps even more, of mutual support, mutual aid, and mutual defense. . . . Sociability is as much a law of nature as mutual struggle.

As Kropotkin cranked through his selected examples, and built up steam for his own preferences, he became more and more convinced that the cooperative style, leading to mutual aid, not only predominated in general but also characterized the most advanced creatures in any group—ants among insects, mammals among vertebrates. Mutual aid therefore becomes a more important principle than competition and slaughter:

> If we . . . ask Nature: "who are the fittest: those who are continually at war with each other, or those who support one another?" we at once see that those animals which acquire habits of mutual aid are undoubtedly the fittest. They have more chances to survive, and they attain, in their respective classes, the highest development of intelligence and bodily organization.

If we ask why Kropotkin favored cooperation while most nineteenth-century Darwinians advocated competition as the predominant result of struggle in nature, two major reasons stand out. The first seems less interesting, as obvious under the slightly cynical but utterly realistic principle that true believers tend to read their social preferences into nature. Kropotkin, the anarchist who yearned to replace laws of central government with consensus of local communities, certainly hoped to locate a deep preference for mutual aid in the innermost evolutionary marrow of our being. Let mutual aid pervade nature and human cooperation becomes a simple instance of the law of life.

> Neither the crushing powers of the centralized State nor the teachings of mutual hatred and pitiless struggle which

came, adorned with the attributes of science, from obliging philosophers and sociologists, could weed out the feeling of human solidarity, deeply lodged in men's understanding and heart, because it has been nurtured by all our preceding evolution.

But the second reason is more enlightening, as a welcome empirical input from Kropotkin's own experience as a naturalist and an affirmation of Todes's intriguing thesis that the usual flow from ideology to interpretation of nature may sometimes be reversed, and that landscape can color social preference. As a young man, long before his conversion to political radicalism, Kropotkin spent five years in Siberia (1862–1866) just after Darwin published the *Origin of Species.* He went as a military officer, but his commission served as a convenient cover for his yearning to study the geology, geography, and zoology of Russia's vast interior. There, in the polar opposite to Darwin's tropical experiences, he dwelled in the environment least conducive to Malthus's vision. He observed a sparsely populated world, swept with frequent catastrophes that threatened the few species able to find a place in such bleakness. As a potential disciple of Darwin, he looked for competition, but rarely found any. Instead, he continually observed the benefits of mutual aid in coping with an exterior harshness that threatened all alike and could not be overcome by the analogues of warfare and boxing.

Kropotkin, in short, had a personal and empirical reason to look with favor upon cooperation as a natural force. He chose this theme as the opening paragraph for *Mutual Aid:*

Two aspects of animal life impressed me most during the journeys which I made in my youth in Eastern Siberia and Northern Manchuria. One of them was the extreme severity of the struggle for existence which most species of animals have to carry on against an inclement Nature; the enormous destruction of life which periodically results from natural agencies; and the consequent paucity of life over the vast territory which fell under my observation. And the other was, that even in those few spots where animal life teemed in abundance, I failed to find—although I was eagerly looking for it—that bitter struggle for the means of existence among animals belonging to the same species, which was considered by most Darwinists (though not always by Darwin himself) as the dominant characteristic of struggle for life, and the main factor of evolution.

What can we make of Kropotkin's argument today, and that of the entire Russian school represented by him? Were they just victims of cultural hope and intellectual conservatism? I don't think so. In fact, I would hold that Kropotkin's basic argument is correct. Struggle does occur in many modes, and some lead to cooperation among members of a species as the best pathway to advantage for individuals. If Kropotkin overemphasized mutual aid, most Darwinians in Western Europe had exaggerated competition just as strongly. If Kropotkin drew inappropriate hope for social reform from his concept of nature, other Darwinians had erred just as firmly (and for motives that most of us would now decry) in justifying imperial conquest, racism, and oppression of industrial workers as the harsh outcome of natural selection in the competitive mode.

I would fault Kropotkin only in two ways—one technical, the other general. He did commit a common conceptual error in failing to recognize that natural selection is an argument about advantages to individual organisms, however they may struggle. The result of struggle for existence may be cooperation rather than competition, but mutual aid must benefit individual organisms in Darwin's world of explanation. Kropotkin sometimes speaks of mutual aid as selected for the benefit of entire populations or species—a concept foreign to classic Darwinian logic (where organisms work, albeit unconsciously, for their own benefit in terms of genes passed to future generations). But Kropotkin also (and often) recognized that selection for mutual aid directly benefits each individual in its own struggle for personal success. Thus, if Kropotkin did not grasp the full implication of Darwin's basic argument, he did include the orthodox solution as his primary justification for mutual aid.

More generally, I like to apply a somewhat cynical rule of thumb in judging arguments about nature that also have overt social implications: When such claims imbue nature with just those properties that make us feel good or fuel our prejudices, be doubly suspicious. I am especially wary of arguments that find kindness, mutuality, synergism, harmony—the very elements that we strive mightily, and so often unsuccessfully, to put into our own lives—intrinsically in nature. I see no evidence for Teilhard's noosphere, for Capra's California style of holism, for Sheldrake's morphic resonance. Gaia strikes me as a metaphor, not a mechanism. (Metaphors can be liberating and enlightening, but new scientific theories must supply new statements about causality. Gaia, to me, only seems to reformulate, in different terms, the basic conclusions long achieved by classically reductionist arguments of biogeochemical cycling theory.)

There are no shortcuts to moral insight. Nature is not intrinsically anything that can offer comfort or solace in human terms—if only because our species is such an insignificant latecomer in a world not constructed for us. So much the better. The answers to moral dilemmas are not lying out there, waiting to be discovered. They reside, like the kingdom of God, within us—the most difficult and inaccessible spot for any discovery or consensus.

23 | Fleeming Jenkin Revisited

THE EUROPEAN REVOLUTIONS of 1848 played a pivotal role in several famous lives. Karl Marx, exiled from Germany, published the last issue of his *Neue Rheinische Zeitung* in red, then moved to England, where he constructed *Das Kapital* in the reading room of the British Museum. The young Richard Wagner, espousing an idealistic socialism that he would later reject with vigor, manned the barricades of Dresden, then fled from Germany to avoid a warrant for his arrest and missed the premiere of *Lohengrin*.

Another man, destined for a lesser but secure reputation, experienced a touch of the same excitement. In February 1848, Henry Charles Fleeming Jenkin, a fourteen-year-old boy from Scotland, found himself in Paris surrounded by rebellion. He wrote to a friend in Edinburgh: "Now then, Frank, what do you think of it? I in a revolution and out all day. Just think, what fun!"

In 1867, the same Fleeming Jenkin would taste revolution of a different kind—this time as a transient participant, not a mere observer. In his much revised fifth edition of the *Origin of Species*, Charles Darwin made a substantial concession by admitting that favorable variations arising in single individuals could not spread through entire populations. (In retrospect, Darwin need not have conceded. He based his admission on a false view of heredity. In a Mendelian world, unknown to Darwin, such favorable variations can spread—see subsequent discussion in this essay. Nonetheless, Darwin's concession represents a small but celebrated incident in the history of evolutionary thought.) Darwin wrote:

340

I saw . . . that the preservation in a state of nature of any occasional deviation of structure . . . would be a rare event; and that, if preserved, it would generally be lost by subsequent intercrossing with ordinary individuals. Nevertheless, until reading an able and valuable article in the *North British Review* (1867), I did not appreciate how rarely single variations whether slight or strongly marked could be inherited.

Nearly every book in the history of evolution recounts the tale and refers to the author of this "able and valuable article" as "a Scottish engineer" or, more often, "an obscure Scottish engineer." The author was Fleeming (pronounced Flemming) Jenkin. Darwin, more explicit and vexed in private letters than in public texts, wrote to Joseph Hooker in 1869: "Fleeming Jenkin has given me much trouble. . . ."—and to Alfred Russel Wallace a few days later: "Fleeming Jenkin's arguments have convinced me."

All evolutionists recognize (and mispronounce by excessive literalism) Fleeming Jenkin as the man who forced an explicit, though unnecessary, concession from Darwin. But we know nothing about him and tend to assume that he rose from general obscurity for one small moment in our sun—a lamentable parochialism on our part.

My own career has included two fortuitous and peculiar intersections with Fleeming Jenkin—so I decided that I must write a column about him now, before a third encounter elevates coincidence to inescapable pattern. I was an undergraduate at Antioch College from 1958 to 1963. Antioch was (and is) a wonderful school in the finest American tradition of small liberal arts colleges. But it doesn't boast much in the way of library facilities for scholarship based on original sources. One day in 1960, I was browsing aimlessly through the stacks and found a crumbling run of the *North British Review* for the mid-nineteenth century. I recognized the name from Darwin's citation, and my heart skipped a beat as I hoped against hope that the volume for 1867 lay within the series. It did, and I then spent a more anxious minute convinced that I had the wrong title or that the issue for the right month would be missing. It wasn't. I found Jenkin's article and rushed to the pre-Xerox wet processor (anachronistically named smellox by a friend of mine several years later, in honor of the unpleasant chemical that left its signature even after drying). I fed dimes into the machine and soon had my precious copy of the original Fleeming Jenkin. What a prize I thought I had. I was sure that I possessed the only copy in the whole world. (Can you imagine what one peek at the Harvard library does to such naivete?) I have carried that copy with me ever since, assigning its properly Xeroxed offspring to classes now and again, but never dreaming that I would write anything about Jenkin.

Then, last month, I was browsing through a friend's Victorian literature collection, aimlessly running my eye along the titles of Robert Louis Stevenson's complete works. I found *Treasure Island, Kidnapped,* and all the other items of my old "Author's" card game. But my heart skipped another beat at the next title: *Memoir of Fleeming Jenkin.* The "obscure Scottish engineer" had achieved sufficient renown (in areas far from my own parish, where he only dabbled, however successfully) to win a full volume from Stevenson's pen. I kicked myself for sectarian assumptions in the granting of "importance," vowed to learn more about Jenkin (and to tell my fellow evolutionists), and raided the stacks of Widener Library, where I found several copies of Stevenson's memoir, amidst (no doubt) a liberal sprinkling of *North British Review*s for 1867 (which, *smelloci gratia,* I didn't need).

An interesting man, Fleeming Jenkin—and made all the more appealing by the strength of Stevenson's prose. Jenkin spent most of his life in Edinburgh, where he campaigned for the improvement of home sanitation, conducted some of Britain's first experiments with the phonograph, produced and directed amateur theatricals, hated golf (for a Scotsman, I suppose, about as bad as an American who barfs on apple pie), and became the first professor of engineering at the University of Edinburgh. Most important, he was a close friend and colleague of Lord Kelvin and spent most of his career designing and outfitting transoceanic cables with the great physicist.

Stevenson's book has a lovely, archaic charm. It describes a moral perfection that cannot be, and belongs to the genre of guiding homilies based on lives of the great. If Jenkin ever gazed at a woman other than his wife, if he ever raised his voice in anger or acted in even momentary pettiness, we are not told. Instead, we get glimpses of a simpler and formal world based on unquestioned certainties. In 1877, Jenkin writes to his absent wife about their son: "Frewen had to come up and sit in my room for company last night and I actually kissed him, a thing that has not occurred for years." The Captain, Jenkin's aged father, dies at age eighty-four but achieves solace in his last hour from a false report on the rescue of General "Chinese" Gordon at Khartoum: "He has been waiting with painful interest for news of Gordon and Khartoum; and by great good fortune, a false report reached him that the city was relieved, and the men of Sussex (his old neighbors) had been the first to enter. He sat up in bed and gave three cheers for the Sussex regiment."

Stevenson's memoir contains exactly one line on Jenkin's 1867 foray into evolutionary theory: "He had begun by this time to write. His paper on Darwin . . . had the merit of convincing on one point the philosopher himself." Evidently, Jenkin needed neither evolution nor the *North British Review* to merit Stevenson's extended attention. I felt a bit ashamed at my own previous parochialism. Do grocers know Thomas Jefferson (or was it Benjamin Franklin) only as the man who invented that thing that gets the cereal boxes down from the top shelf?

The backward reading of history has cruelly misserved many fine thinkers, Jenkin included. (Professionals refer to this unhappy tactic as "Whiggish history" in dubious memory of those Whig historians who evaluated predecessors exclusively by their adherence to ideals of Whig politics unknown in their own times.) Jenkin has suffered because commentators extract from his 1867 article just the one small point that provoked Darwin's concession—and then analyze his argument in modern terms by pointing out that a twentieth-century Darwin could stick to his Mendelian guns. No modern evolutionary biologist, to my knowledge, has ever considered Jenkin's treatise as a whole and appreciated its force, despite its errors in modern terms. I shall attempt this rescue but bow first to the constraints of history and discuss the point that secured Jenkin's slight renown in evolutionary circles.

Darwin and Jenkin accepted the usual notion of heredity prevalent in their times—a concept called blending inheritance. Under blending inheritance, the offspring of two parents tend to lie halfway between for inherited characters. Jenkin pointed out to Darwin, or so the usual and quite inadequate story goes, that blending inheritance would challenge natural selection because any favorable variant would be swamped out by back-breeding with the predominant parental forms. Jenkin's own example will make his argument clear. It also serves as a sad reminder of unquestioned racism in Victorian England—and as an indication that, for all our pressing problems, we have improved somewhat during the past century:

> Suppose a white man to have been wrecked on an island inhabited by negroes. . . . Suppose him to possess the physical strength, energy, and ability of a dominant white race . . . grant him every advantage which we can conceive a white to possess over the native. . . . Yet from all these admissions, there does not follow the conclusion that, after a limited or unlimited number of generations, the inhabitants of the island will be white. Our shipwrecked hero would probably become king; he would kill a great many blacks in the struggle for existence; he would have a great many wives and children, while many of his subjects would live and die as bachelors. . . . In the first generation there will be some dozens of intelligent young mulattoes, much superior in average intelligence to the negroes. We might expect the throne for some generations to be occupied by a more or less yellow king; but can any one believe that the whole island will gradually acquire a white, or even a yellow population . . . for if a very highly favored white cannot blanch a nation of negroes, it will hardly be contended that a comparatively dull mulatto has a good chance of producing a tawny tribe.

In other words, by blending inheritance, the offspring of the first generation will be only half white. Most of these mulattoes, since full blacks so greatly predominate (and following prohibitions against incest), will marry full blacks, and their offspring of the second generation will be one-quarter white. By the same argument, the proportion of white blood will dilute to one-eighth in the third generation and soon dwindle to oblivion, despite supposed advantages.

Darwin, or so the story goes, saw the strength of this argument and retreated in frustrated impotence toward the Lamarckian views that he had previously rejected. Whiggery then comes to the rescue. Inheritance is Mendelian, or "particulate," not blending (though Darwin died long before the rediscovery of Mendel's laws in 1900). Traits based on genetic mutations do not dilute; genes that determine such traits are entities or particles that do not degrade by mixing with genes of the other parent in offspring. Indeed, if recessive, a favorable trait will appear in *no* offspring of the first generation (in matings between the favored mutant and ordinary partners carrying the dominant gene). But the trait does not dilute to oblivion. In the second generation, one-quarter of the offspring between mixed parents will carry two doses of the advantageous recessive gene and will express the favored trait. Any subsequent matings between these double recessives will pass the favored trait to all offspring—and it can spread through the population if concentrated by natural selection. (Skin color and height seem to blend because they are determined by such a large number of particulate genes. The average effect may be a blend, yet the genes remain intact and subject to selection.)

But this usual story fails when we properly locate Jenkin's point about blending in the wider context of an argument that pervades the entire essay—and do not simply extract the item as a kernel deserving modern notice while discarding the rest as chaff. As historian Peter J. Vorzimmer notes in his excellent book, *Charles Darwin: The Years of Controversy* (1970), Jenkin presented his arguments about blending in discussing only one particular kind of variation—*single* favorable variants *substantially different* from parental forms.

Darwin was no fool. He had thought about variation as deeply as any man. His longest book, the two-volume *Variation of Animals and Plants Under Domestication* (1868), summarizes everything he and almost everyone else knew about the subject. Can we seriously believe that he had never thought about problems that blending posed for natural selection—that he needed a prod from an engineer to recognize the difficulty? As Vorzimmer shows, Darwin had pondered long and hard about problems provoked by blending. Jenkin did not introduce Darwin to this basic problem of inheritance; rather, he made a distinction between the kinds of variation that blending affects, and Darwin welcomed the argument because it reinforced and sharpened one of his favorite views. Darwin did not retreat before Jenkin's onslaught, but rather felt more secure in his preferred belief—hence his expressed gratitude to Jenkin and hence (I assume) Stevenson's single comment that Jenkin had convinced "on one point the philosopher himself." Stevenson, the novelist, understood. We have forgotten.

The real issue has been lost in a terminology understood in Darwin's time but no longer familiar. Let us return to Darwin's letter to Wallace, quoting the passage this time in full: "I always thought individual differences more important than single variations, but now I have come to the conclusion that they are of paramount importance, and in this I believe I agree with you. Fleeming Jenkin's arguments have convinced me."

In Darwin's time, "individual differences" referred to recurrent variations of small scale, while "single variations" identified unique changes of large scope and import—often called "sports." Debate had focused on whether small-scale and continuous, or occasional and larger, variations supplied the raw material for evolutionary change. Darwin, the quintessential continuationist of this or any other age, had long preferred recurrent small-scale changes but had continued to flirt (largely by weight of tradition) with larger sports. Now, the simple point of Jenkin's argument: Note that he speaks of *one* white man identified (in the racist tradition) as vastly superior to the natives—in other words, a single sport. Jenkin's famous blending argument refers only to single, marked variations—not to the continuous recurrent variations that Darwin preferred. By accepting Jenkin's view, Darwin could finally rid himself of a form of variation that he had never favored.

As for recurrent, small-scale variation (individual differences, in Darwin's terminology), blending posed no insurmountable problem, and Darwin had resolved the issue in his own mind long before reading Jenkin. A blending variation can still establish itself in a population under two conditions: first, if the favorable variation continues to arise anew so that any dilution by blending can be balanced by reappearances, thus keeping the trait visible to natural selection; second, if individuals bearing the favored trait can recognize each other and mate preferentially—a process known as assortative mating in evolutionary jargon. Assortative mating can arise for several reasons, including aesthetic preference for mates of one's own appearance and simple isolation of the favored variants from normal individuals. Darwin recognized both recurrent appearance and isolation as the primary reasons for natural selection's continued power in the face of blending.

With this background, we can finally exhume the real point and logic of Jenkin's essay—an issue still very much alive, and discussed (through all his factual errors) in a most interesting and perceptive way by Fleeming Jenkin. Jenkin's essay is a critique of Darwin's continuationist perspective—his distinctive claim, still maintained by the evolutionary orthodoxy—that all large-scale phenomena of evolution may be rendered by accumulating, through vast amounts of time, the tiny changes that we observe in modern populations. I call this conventional view the "extrapolationist" argument; I also share Jenkin's opinion (but for different reasons) that this traditional mode of thinking cannot explain all of evolution. I find it supremely ironic that the one small section of Jenkin's article *not* about Darwin's claim for continuity (his argument that single sports will be swamped by blending) has become the only part that we remember—and, to make matters worse, usually misinterpret. Such, however, is the usual fate of Whig heroes and villains.

A simple, almost pedantic, précis of Jenkin's argument should rescue his larger point. Jenkin's essay proceeds in four parts. The first, on limits of variation, admits that Darwin's favored style of recurrent, continuous variation does occur and can be manipulated by natural selection to change the average form of a species. But, Jenkin argues, such variations always fiddle in minor ways with parts already present; they cannot construct anything new. Thus, natural selection can make dogs big, small, blocky, or elongate—but cannot change a dog into something else. Jenkin expresses this argument in his powerful metaphor of the "sphere of variation." Natural selection may move the average form anywhere within the sphere, but not beyond its fixed limits:

> A given animal or plant appears to be contained, as it were, within a sphere of variation; one individual lies near one portion of the surface, another individual, of the same species, near another part of the surface; the average animal at the center.

Common experience, Jenkin affirms, supports his view. Artificial selection practiced by breeders proceeds rapidly at first but soon reaches frustrating limits. Jenkin writes of racehorses:

> Hundreds of skillful men are yearly breeding thousands of racers. Wealth and honor await the man who can breed one horse to run one part in five thousand faster than his fellows. As a matter of experience, have our racers improved in speed by one part in a thousand during the last twenty generations?

Darwin, Jenkin claims, maintains an unwarranted faith in the power of simple time to overcome these barriers:

> The difference between six years and six myriads, blending by a confused sense of immensity, leads men to say hastily that if six or sixty years can make a pouter out of a common pigeon, six myriads may change a pigeon to something like a thrush; but this seems no more accurate than to conclude that because we observe that a cannon-ball has traversed a mile in a minute, therefore in an hour it will be sixty miles off, and in the course of ages that it will reach the fixed stars.

Darwin might argue, Jenkin admits, that once a species reaches the limit of its glass sphere, time will eventually reconstitute this edge as a new center and produce a new sphere around the previously peripheral point. Jenkin also rejects this argument:

> The average or original race . . . will [in Darwin's view] spontaneously lose the tendency to relapse and acquire a tendency to vary outside the sphere. What is to produce this change? Time simply, apparently. . . . This seems rather like the idea that keeping a bar of iron hot or cold for a long time would leave it permanently hot or cold at the end of the period when the heating or cooling agent was withdrawn.

Jenkin's second section, on types of variation, begins by admitting Darwin's point that small-scale recurrent variations will not be destroyed by blending. But these are the very variations subject to strict limits by the previous argument about rigid spheres. What kind of variation might then induce the evolution of something substantially new? Single sports might seem promising, but these are the rare events that will be swamped by blending—and readers may now note the point that Jenkin himself wished to make with the only part of his argument that we remember. But perhaps some kinds of sports do not blend and do perpetuate their kind. Fine, Jenkin admits. Perhaps such creatures do occasionally arise and produce new species. But such a process is not Darwinian evolution, for Darwin insisted that natural selection acts as a creative force by gradually accumulating favorable variants. Indeed, would such a process be very different from what the vernacular calls "creation"?

The third part argues that even if Darwin could find (which he can't) some way to accumulate small-scale recurrent variations into something new, geology does not supply enough time for such a slow process. Here Jenkin relied on the false arguments of his dearest friend, Lord Kelvin, about the earth's relatively young age (see Essay 8, on Kelvin, in *The Flamingo's Smile*).

The last section presents a powerful (and I think entirely correct) argument about the difficulty of inferring historical pathways from current situations. Jenkin contends that nearly any current situation can arise via several historical routes; thus the situation by itself cannot specify the pathway. Jenkin points out that Darwin bases much of his argument upon the lack of definite boundaries in nature—the intergradation of species into species, or geographic region into region. Darwin's continuationism predicts just such an absence of boundaries since species are gradually and imperceptibly changed into their descendants, while a creator should leave gaps between his incarnated objects. But Jenkin argues that many natural items come as continua, yet clearly do not arise by a process of historical transformation. Arguing, as he does throughout, by metaphor and analogy, Jenkin writes:

> Legal difficulties furnish another illustration. Does a particular case fall within a particular statute? Is it ruled by this or that precedent? The number of statutes or groups is limited; the number of possible combinations of events almost unlimited.

Taken as an entirety, Jenkin's argument possesses a kind of relentless logic. The critique of Darwin's extrapolationism serves as its unifying theme. Part one argues that small-scale variation cannot extend beyond fixed limits. Part two claims that no style of variation can make something substantially new in a Darwinian world. Part three proposes that even if Darwin could find a way, geology does not permit enough time. Finally, part four holds that we cannot infer historical transformations from the admitted continua of nature.

I don't want to fall into a Whiggish pit and judge Jenkin by current standards (everything that has gone before in this essay adequately discharges, I hope, my dues to anti-Whiggery). But old arguments usually repay our close attention because we often stop discussing the fundamentals once an orthodoxy triumphs, and we need to consult the original debates in order to rediscover the largest issues—perhaps never really resolved but merely swept under a rug of concord. Much of Jenkin's argument fails today, for few things last a century in science. He was clearly wrong about blending in part two and about time in part three. But I believe that he was right about continua in part four and that we are still plagued by a tendency to make an almost automatic inference about history when we fail to find clear boundaries.

The first argument about limits of variation has also risen again in current debates about evolutionary processes. I don't accept Jenkin's metaphor of the sphere, because small quantitative changes can accumulate to qualitative effects or leaps (contrary to Jenkin's position), and because I accept Darwin's argument that new spheres can be reconstituted about previously peripheral points.

But neither (probably) is a species the kind of almost equipotential sphere that strict Darwinians envisaged—unconstrained and capable of rolling anywhere that natural selection pushes. Constraints imposed by genetics and development have emerged as a central topic in contemporary evolutionary debate—and Fleeming Jenkin did present an insight worth considering.

In short, Darwin's strictly extrapolationist vision may not describe large-scale evolution very well—small, local adaptations built in the refiner's fire of Darwinian competition among organisms struggling for reproductive success may not, by extension, explain trends that persist for millions of years or relays of changing diversity that mass extinctions produce. Jenkin, who presented the most logical dissection of Darwin's continuationist vision in 1867, does reach across a century to set us thinking, however superannuated his specific claims.

We may give the last word to Jenkin, via Robert Louis Stevenson. One day as a young man, Stevenson reports, Fleeming Jenkin argued bitterly with two young women about a pressing issue of Victorian hypermorality: Can a misdeed against moral codes ever be condoned, whatever the circumstances—stealing a knife to prevent a murder, for example? (Jenkin, to his credit, argued the affirmative.) As he left the house, his anger mellowed. He realized that even the most apparently peculiar belief deserves respect if argued honorably and if properly constructed upon a set of basic premises different from those usually cherished:

> From such passages-at-arms, many retire mortified and ruffled; but Fleeming had no sooner left the house than he fell into delighted admiration of the spirit of his adversaries. From that it was but a step to ask himself "what truth was sticking in their heads"; for even the falsest form of words (in Fleeming's life-long opinion) reposed upon some truth.

Postscript

My parochialism and ignorance in the case of Fleeming Jenkin were even deeper than I had realized. Having corrected the most blatant omission of failing to recognize the importance of his mainline career in engineering, I discovered, after publishing this essay, that I had also missed a tangential foray equal in importance to Jenkin's critique of Darwin. Several professors of economics wrote to inform me that Jenkin had made cogent contributions to the "dismal science" as well.

Robert B. Ekelund, Jr., of Auburn University, stated:

> Jenkin, an engineer by training, was the first English economist to draw and clearly understand supply and demand curves, the most familiar staple in all of economics. In two

amazing essays, published in 1868 and 1870, Jenkin developed demand and supply theory, applied it to labor markets, and introduced an innovative combination of stock and flow concepts for analyzing market fluctuations.

Christopher Bell of Davidson College then sent me an article from *Oxford Economics Papers* (Volume 15, 1963) by A. D. Brownlie and M. F. Lloyd Prichard entitled "Professor Fleeming Jenkin, 1833–1885, Pioneer in Engineering and Political Economy." This fascinating article cites the opinion of the great economist J. A. Schumpeter (1883–1950), who regarded Jenkin as "an economist of major importance, whose main papers . . . form an obvious stepping stone between J. S. Mill and Marshall."

In a time of great industrial strife, and considerable opposition to trade unionism, Jenkin used his quantitative analysis of supply and demand to defend, as practical and necessary, the rights of workers to form associations for collective bargaining. He wrote that "the total abolition of trade unions is out of the question as impolitic, undeserved, and impossible . . . [But] we must insist that the great power granted to the bodies of workmen shall be administered under stringent regulations."

Jenkin, scarcely a radical in politics, favored no massive redistribution of wealth, but only some minor tinkering for greater satisfaction and productivity of workers. He wrote: "Great inequality is necessary and desirable (observations seem to show that trade will extend faster with large profits and small wages than with small profits and large wages)." For, basically, Jenkin held firm to the ideals of the laissez-faire system so strongly identified with the intellectual history of his nation, particularly with Adam Smith in his own home city of Edinburgh. Jenkin wrote:

> We cannot deny that each man, acting rationally for his own advantage, will conduce to the good of all; and if the motive be not the highest, it is one which at least can always be counted on.

Yet Jenkin tempered the harshness of pure laissez-faire with a realization that the central argument, practically applied by people in power, almost always acted as a rationale for unfairness toward workers. He wrote:

> They [laborers] think it monstrous that one of two parties to a bargain should be told to shut his eyes and open his hands and take the wages fixed by Political Economy, which allegorical personage looks very like an employer on pay day.

A wonderful irony pervades all these themes, one that only an evolutionary biologist could fully identify and appreciate. Brownlie and Lloyd Prichard point out that Jenkin's economic writings were consigned to oblivion, largely because the two great opinion makers of later nineteenth-century English economics, Jevons and Marshall, "treated him shabbily to say the least." (Both Jevons and Marshall sensed that the "amateur" Jenkin had anticipated some of the "original" work that served as a basis of their own reputations. They therefore sought to disparage and discredit, and then to ignore, this gifted thinker, who did only limited work in economics and did not really threaten their turf, or even their prestige, in any large sense—an act, all too characteristic, alas, of conventional academic ungenerosity.)

Now, the irony: Jenkin was, basically, a proponent of the laissez-faire school. Darwin, as I have often argued in these essays, established his central theory of natural selection by importing the structure of Adam Smith's economic arguments into nature (with organisms struggling for individual reproductive success as the analogue of "each man, acting rationally for his own advantage" in Jenkin's quotation—and with organic progress and balance of nature arising as a result, just as "the good of all" supposedly emerges from concatenated selfishness in Adam Smith's system). How ironic then that Jenkin was belittled and disparaged for truly original work in the parent discipline of economics—but, thanks to Darwin's greater geniality and sense of fairness, honored and acknowledged for similarly cogent contributions to a field that had so benefited, just a little before (in 1859 when Darwin published the *Origin*), from generous consideration of economic theories.

24 | The Passion of Antoine Lavoisier

GALILEO AND LAVOISIER have more in common than their brilliance. Both men are focal points in a cardinal legend about the life of intellectuals—the conflict of lonely and revolutionary genius with state power. Both stories are apocryphal, however inspiring. Yet they only exaggerate, or encapsulate in the epitome of a bon mot, an essential theme in the history of thinking and its impact upon society.

Galileo, on his knees before the Inquisition, abjures his heretical belief that the earth revolves around a central sun. Yet, as he rises, brave Galileo, faithful to the highest truth of factuality, addresses a stage whisper to the world: *eppur se muove*—nevertheless, it does move. Lavoisier, before the revolutionary tribunal during the Reign of Terror in 1794, accepts the inevitable verdict of death, but asks for a week or two to finish some experiments. Coffinhal, the young judge who has sealed his doom, denies his request, stating, *La république n'a pas besoin de savants* (the Republic does not need scientists).

Coffinhal said no such thing, although the sentiments are not inconsistent with emotions unleashed in those frightening and all too frequent political episodes so well characterized by Marc Antony in his lamentation over Caesar: "O judgment! thou are fled to brutish beasts, And men have lost their reason." Lavoisier, who had been under arrest for months, was engaged in no experiments at the time. Moreover, as we shall see, the charges leading to his execution bore no relationship to his scientific work.

But if Coffinhal's chilling remark is apocryphal, the second most famous quotation surrounding the death of Lavoisier is ac-

DISCOURS

D'OUVERTURE ET DE CLÔTURE

D U

COURS DE ZOOLOGIE

Donné dans le Muséum national d'Histoire naturelle,
l'an IX de la République,

PAR LE.C^{en} LACEPÈDE,

Membre du Sénat, et de l'Institut national de France; l'un des
Professeurs du Muséum d'Histoire naturelle; membre de l'Institut
national de la République Cisalpine; de la société d'Arragon; de
celle des Curieux de la Nature, de Berlin; des sociétés d'Histoire
naturelle, des Pharmaciens, Philotechnique, Philomatique, et des
Observateurs de l'homme, de Paris; de celle d'Agriculture d'Agen;
de la société des Sciences et Arts de Montauban; du Lycée
d'Alencon, etc.

———

A PARIS;

CHEZ PLASSAN, IMPRIMEUR-LIBRAIRE:

———

L'AN IX DE LA REPUBLIQUE.

Title page for Lacépède's opening and closing addresses for the zoology course at the Natural History Museum in 1801–1802—but identified only as "year 9 of the Republic."

curate and well attested. The great mathematician Joseph Louis Lagrange, upon hearing the news about his friend's execution, remarked bitterly: "It took them only an instant to cut off that head, but France may not produce another like it in a century."

The French revolution had been born in hope and expansiveness. At the height of enthusiasm for new beginnings, the revolutionary government suppressed the old calendar, and started time all over again, with Year I beginning on September 22,

1792, at the founding of the French republic. The months would no longer bear names of Roman gods or emperors, but would record the natural passage of seasons—as in *brumaire* (foggy), *ventose* (windy), *germinal* (budding), and to replace parts of July and August, originally named for two despotic caesars, *thermidor.* Measures would be rationalized, decimalized, and based on earthly physics, with the meter defined as one ten-millionth of a quarter meridian from pole to equator. The metric system is our enduring legacy of this revolutionary spirit, and Lavoisier himself played a guiding role in devising the new weights and measures.

But initial optimism soon unraveled under the realities of internal dissension and external pressure. Governments tumbled one after the other, and Dr. Guillotin's machine, invented to make execution more humane, became a symbol of terror by sheer frequency of public use. Louis XVI was beheaded in January 1793 (Year I of the republic). Power shifted from the Girondins to the Montagnards, as the Terror reached its height and the war with Austria and Prussia continued. Finally, as so often happens, the architect of the terror, Robespierre himself, paid his visit to Dr. Guillotin's device, and the cycle played itself out. A few years later, in 1804, Napoleon was crowned as emperor, and the First Republic ended. Poor Lavoisier had been caught in the midst of the cycle, dying for his former role as tax collector on May 8, 1794, less than three months before the fall of Robespierre on July 27 (9 Thermidor, Year II).

Old ideals often persist in vestigial forms of address and writing, long after their disappearance in practice. I was reminded of this phenomenon when I acquired, a few months ago, a copy of the opening and closing addresses for the course in zoology at the Muséum d'Histoire naturelle of Paris for 1801–1802. The democratic fervor of the revolution had faded, and Napoleon had already staged his *coup d'état* of 18 Brumaire (November 9, 1799), emerging as emperor de facto, although not crowned until 1804. Nonetheless, the author of these addresses, who would soon resume his full name Bernard-Germain-Etienne de la Ville-sur-Illon, comte de Lacépède, is identified on the title page only as Cᵉⁿ Lacépède (for *citoyen,* or "citizen"—the democratic form adopted by the revolution to abolish all distinctions of address). The long list of honors and memberships, printed in small type below Lacépède's name, is almost a parody on the ancient forms; for instead of the old affiliations that always included "member of the royal academy of this or that" and "counsellor to the king or count of here or there," Lacépède's titles are rigorously egalitarian—including "one of the professors at the museum of natural history," and member of the society of pharmacists of Paris, and of agriculture of Agen. As for the year of publication, we have to know the history detailed above—for the publisher's date is given, at the bottom, only as "l'an IX de la République."

Lacépède was one of the great natural historians in the golden age of French zoology during the late eighteenth and early nineteenth centuries. His name may be overshadowed in retrospect by the illustrious quartet of Buffon, Lamarck, Geoffroy, and Cuvier, but Lacépède—who was chosen by Buffon to complete his life's work, the multivolumed *Histoire naturelle*—deserves a place with these men, for all were *citoyens* of comparable merit. Although Lacépède supported the revolution in its moderate first phases, his noble title bred suspicion and he went into internal exile during the Terror. But the fall of Robespierre prompted his return to Paris, where his former colleagues persuaded the government to establish a special chair for him at the Muséum, as zoologist for reptiles and fishes.

By tradition, the opening and closing addresses for the zoology course at the Muséum were published in pamphlet form each year. The opening address for Year IX, "Sur l'histoire des races ou principales variétés de l'espèce humaine" (On the history of races and principal varieties of the human species), is a typical statement of the liberality and optimism of Enlightenment thought. The races, we learn, may differ in current accomplishments, but all are capable of greater and equal achievement, and all can progress.

But the bloom of hope had been withered by the Terror. Progress, Lacépède asserts, is not guaranteed, but is possible only if untrammeled by the dark side of human venality. Memories of dire consequences for unpopular thoughts must have been fresh, for Lacépède cloaked his criticism of revolutionary excesses in careful speech and foreign attribution. Ostensibly, he was only describing the evils of the Indian caste system in a passage that must be read as a lament about the Reign of Terror:

Hypocritical ambition, . . . abusing the credibility of the multitude, has conserved the ferocity of the savage state in the midst of the virtues of civilization. . . . After having reigned by terror [*regné par la terreur*], submitting even monarchs to their authority, they reserved the domain of science and art to themselves [a reference, no doubt, to the suppression of the independent academies by the revolutionary government in 1793, when Lacépède lost his first post at the Muséum], and surrounded themselves with a veil of mystery that only they could lift.

At the end of his address, Lacépède returns to the familiar theme of political excesses and makes a point, by no means original of course, that I regard as the central structural tragedy in the working of any complex system, including organisms and social institutions—the crushing asymmetry between the need for slow and painstaking construction and the potential for almost instantaneous destruction:

Thus, the passage from the semisavage state to civilization occurs through a great number of insensible stages, and requires an immense amount of time. In moving slowly through these successive stages, man fights painfully against his habits; he also battles with nature as he climbs, with great effort, up the long and perilous path. But it is not the same with the loss of the civilized state; this is almost sudden. In this morbid fall, man is thrown down by all his ancient tendencies; he struggles no longer, he gives up, he does not battle obstacles, he abandons himself to the burdens that surround him. Centuries are needed to nurture the tree of science and make it grow, but one blow from the hatchet of destruction cuts it down.

The chilling final line, a gloss on Lagrange's famous statement about the death of Lavoisier, inspired me to write about the founder of modern chemistry, and to think a bit more about the tragic asymmetry of creation and destruction.

Antoine-Laurent Lavoisier, born in 1743, belonged to the nobility through a title purchased by his father (standard practice for boosting the royal treasury during the *ancien régime*). As a

Lavoisier and his wife as painted by the great artist David, who later became a fervent supporter of the revolution. THE METROPOLITAN MU-SEUM OF ART, PURCHASE, MR. AND MRS. CHARLES WRIGHTSMAN GIFT, 1977.

leading liberal and rationalist of the Enlightenment (a movement that attracted much of the nobility, including many wealthy intellectuals who had purchased their titles to rise from the bourgeoisie), Lavoisier fitted an astounding array of social and scientific services into a life cut short by the headsman at age fifty-one.

We know him best today as the chief founder of modern chemistry. The textbook one-liners describe him as the discoverer (or at least the namer) of oxygen, the man who (though anticipated by Henry Cavendish in England) recognized water as a compound of the gases hydrogen and oxygen, and who correctly described combustion, not as the liberation of a hypothetical substance called phlogiston, but as the combination of burning material with oxygen. But we can surely epitomize his contribution more accurately by stating that Lavoisier set the basis for modern chemistry by recognizing the nature of elements and compounds—by finally dethroning the ancient taxonomy of air, water, earth, and fire as indivisible elements; by identifying gas, liquid, and solid as states of aggregation for a single substance subjected to different degrees of heat; and by developing quantitative methods for defining and identifying true elements. Such a brief statement can only rank as a caricature of Lavoisier's scientific achievements, but this essay treats his other life in social service, and I must move on.

Lavoisier, no shrinking violet in the game of self-promotion, openly spoke of his new chemistry as "a revolution." He even published his major manifesto, *Traité élémentaire de chimie*, in 1789, starting date of the other revolution that would seal his fate.

Lavoisier, liberal child of the Enlightenment, was no opponent of the political revolution, at least in its early days. He supported the idea of a constitutional monarchy, and joined the most moderate of the revolutionary societies, the Club of '89. He served as an alternate delegate in the States General, took his turn as a *citoyen* at guard duty, and led several studies and commissions vital to the success of the revolution—including a long stint as *régisseur des poudres* (director of gunpowder, where his brilliant successes produced the best stock in Europe, thus providing substantial help in France's war against Austria and Prussia). He worked on financing the revolution by *assignats* (paper money backed largely by confiscated church lands), and he served on the commission of weights and measures that formulated the metric system. Lavoisier rendered these services to all governments, including the most radical, right to his death, even hoping at the end that his crucial work on weights and measures might save his life. Why, then, did Lavoisier end up in two pieces on the *place de la Révolution* (long ago renamed, in pleasant newspeak, *place de la Concorde*)?

The fateful move had been made in 1768, when Lavoisier joined the infamous Ferme Générale, or Tax Farm. If you regard the IRS as a less than benevolent institution, just consider taxation under the *ancien régime* and count your blessings. Taxation was regressive with a vengeance, as the nobility and clergy were entirely exempt, and poor people supplied the bulk of the royal treasury through tariffs on the movement of goods across provincial boundaries, fees for entering the city of Paris, and taxes on such goods as tobacco and salt. (The hated *gabelle,* or "salt tax," was applied at iniquitously differing rates from region to region, and was levied not on actual consumption but on presumed usage—thus, in effect, forcing each family to buy a certain quantity of taxed salt each year.)

Moreover, the government did not collect taxes directly. They set the rates and then leased (for six-year periods) the privilege of collecting taxes to a private finance company, the Ferme Générale. The Tax Farm operated for profit like any other private business. If they managed to collect more than the government levy, they kept the balance; if they failed to reach the quota, they took the loss. The system was not only oppressive in principle; it was also corrupt. Several shares in the Tax Farm were paid for no work as favors or bribes; many courtiers, even the king himself, were direct beneficiaries. Nonetheless, Lavoisier chose this enterprise for the primary investment of his family fortune, and he became, as members of the firm were called, a *fermier-général,* or "farmer-general."

(Incidentally, since I first read the sad story of Lavoisier some twenty-five years ago, I have been amused by the term farmer-general, for it conjures up a pleasantly rustic image of a country yokel, dressed in his Osh Kosh b'Gosh overalls, and chewing on a stalk of hay while trying to collect the *gabelle.* But I have just learned from the *Oxford English Dictionary* that my image is not only wrong, but entirely backward. A farm, defined as a piece of agricultural land, is a derivative term. In usage dating to Chaucer, a farm, from the medieval Latin *firma,* "fixed payment," is "a fixed yearly sum accepted from a person as a composition for taxes or other moneys which he is empowered to collect." By extension, to farm is to lease anything for a fixed rent. Since most leases applied to land, agricultural plots become "farms," with a first use in this sense traced only to the sixteenth century; the leasers of such land then became "farmers." Thus, our modern phrase "farming out" records the original use, and has no agricultural connotation. And Lavoisier was a farmer-general in the true sense, with no mitigating image of bucolic innocence.)

I do not understand why Lavoisier chose the Ferme Générale

for his investment, and then worked so assiduously in his role as tax farmer. He was surely among the most scrupulous and fair-minded of the farmers, and might be justifiably called a reformer. (He opposed the overwatering of tobacco, a monopoly product of the Ferme, and he did, at least in later years, advocate taxation upon all, including the radical idea that nobles might pay as well.) But he took his profits, and he provoked no extensive campaign for reform as the money rolled in. The standard biographies, all too hagiographical, tend to argue that he regarded the Ferme as an investment that would combine greatest safety and return with minimal expenditure of effort—all done to secure a maximum of time for his beloved scientific work. But I do not see how this explanation can hold. Lavoisier, with his characteristic energy, plunged into the work of the Ferme, traveling all over the country, for example, to inspect the tobacco industry. I rather suspect that Lavoisier, like many modern businessmen, simply jumped at a good and legal investment without asking too many ethical questions.

But the golden calf of one season becomes the shattered idol of another. The farmers-general were roundly hated, in part for genuine corruption and iniquity, in part because tax collectors are always scapegoated, especially when the national treasury is bankrupt and the people are starving. Lavoisier's position was particularly precarious. As a scheme to prevent the loss of taxes from widespread smuggling of goods into Paris, Lavoisier advocated the building of a wall around the city. Much to Lavoisier's distress, the project, financed largely (and involuntarily) through taxes levied upon the people of Paris, became something of a boondoggle, as millions were spent on fancy ornamental gates. Parisians blamed the wall for keeping in fetid air and spreading disease. The militant republican Jean-Paul Marat began a campaign of vilification against Lavoisier that only ended when Charlotte Corday stabbed him to death in his bath. Marat had written several works in science and had hoped for election to the Royal Academy, then run by Lavoisier. But Lavoisier had exposed the emptiness of Marat's work. Marat fumed, bided his time, and waited for the season when patriotism would become a good refuge for scoundrels. In January 1791, he launched his attack in *l'Ami du Peuple* (*The Friend of the People*):

I denounce you, Coryphaeus of charlatans, Sieur Lavoisier [coryphaeus, meaning highest, is the leader of the chorus in a classical Greek drama] Farmer-general, Commissioner of Gunpowders. . . . Just to think that this contemptible little man who enjoys an income of forty thousand livres has no other claim to fame than that of having put Paris in prison with a wall costing the poor thirty millions. . . . Would to heaven he had been strung up to the nearest lamppost.

The breaching of the wall by the citizens of Paris on July 12, 1789, was the prelude to the fall of the Bastille two days later.

Lavoisier began to worry very early in the cycle. Less than seven months after the fall of the Bastille, he wrote to his old friend Benjamin Franklin:

After telling you about what is happening in chemistry, it would be well to give you news of our Revolution. . . . Moderate-minded people, who have kept cool heads during the general excitement, think that events have carried us too far . . . we greatly regret your absence from France at this time; you would have been our guide and you would have marked out for us the limits beyond which we ought not to go.

But these limits were breached, just as Lavoisier's wall had fallen, and he could read the handwriting on the remnants. The Ferme Générale was suppressed in 1791, and Lavoisier played no further role in the complex sorting out of the farmers' accounts. He tried to keep his nose clean with socially useful work on weights and measures and public education. But time was running out for the farmers-general. The treasury was bankrupt, and many thought (quite incorrectly) that the iniquitously hoarded wealth of the farmers-general could replenish the nation. The farmers were too good a scapegoat to resist; they were arrested *en masse* in November 1793, commanded to put their accounts in order, and to reimburse the nation for any ill-gotten gains.

The presumed offenses of the farmers-general were not capital under revolutionary law, and they hoped initially to win their personal freedom, even though their wealth and possessions might be confiscated. But they had the misfortune to be in the wrong place (jail) at the worst time (as the Terror intensified).

Eventually, capital charges of counterrevolutionary activities were drummed up, and in a mock trial lasting only part of a day, the farmers-general were condemned to the guillotine.

Lavoisier's influential friends might have saved him, but none dared (or cared) to speak. The Terror was not so inexorable and efficient as tradition holds. Fourteen of the farmers-general managed to evade arrest, and one was saved by the intervention of Robespierre. Madame Lavoisier, who lived to a ripe old age, marrying and divorcing Count Rumford, and reestablishing one of the liveliest salons in Paris, never allowed any of these men over her doorstep again. One courageous (but uninfluential) group offered brave support in Lavoisier's last hours. A deputation from the Lycée des Arts came to the prison to honor Lavoisier and crown him with a wreath. We read in the minutes of that organization: "Brought to Lavoisier in irons, the consolation of friendship . . . to crown the head about to go under the ax."

It is a peculiar attribute of human courage that when no option remains but death, criteria of judgment shift to the manner of dying. Chronicles of the revolution are filled with stories about who died with dignity—and who went screaming to the knife. Antoine Lavoisier died well. He wrote a last letter to his cousin, in apparent calm, not without humor, and with an intellectual's faith in the supreme importance of mind.

> I have had a fairly long life, above all a very happy one, and I think that I shall be remembered with some regrets and perhaps leave some reputation behind me. What more could I ask? The events in which I am involved will probably save me from the troubles of old age. I shall die in full possession of my faculties.

Lavoisier's rehabilitation came almost as quickly as his death. In 1795, the Lycée des Arts held a first public memorial service, with Lagrange himself offering the eulogy and unveiling a bust of Lavoisier inscribed with the words: "Victim of tyranny, respected friend of the arts, he continues to live; through genius he still serves humanity." Lavoisier's spirit continued to inspire, but his head, once filled with great thoughts as numerous as the unwritten symphonies of Mozart, lay severed in a common grave.

Many people try to put a happy interpretation upon Lacépède's observation about the asymmetry of painstaking creation and instantaneous destruction. The collapse of systems, they argue, may be a prerequisite to any future episode of creativity—and the antidote, therefore, to stagnation. Taking the longest view, for example, mass extinctions do break up stable ecosystems and provoke episodes of novelty further down the evolutionary road. We would not be here today if the death of dinosaurs had not cleared some space for the burgeoning of mammals.

I have no objection to this argument in its proper temporal perspective. If you choose a telescope and wish to peer into an evolutionary future millions of years away, then a current episode of destruction may be read as an ultimate spur. But if you care for the here and now, which is (after all) the only time we feel and have, then massive extinction is only a sadness and an opportunity lost forever. I have heard people argue that our current wave of extinctions should not inspire concern because the earth will eventually recover, as so oft before, and perhaps with pleasant novelty. But what can a conjecture about ten million years from now possibly mean to our lives—especially since we have the power to blow up our planet long before then, and rather little prospect, in any case, of surviving so long ourselves (since few vertebrate species live for 10 million years).

The argument of the "long view" may be correct in some meaninglessly abstract sense, but it represents a fundamental mistake in categories and time scales. Our only legitimate long view extends to our children and our children's children's children—hundreds or a few thousands of years down the road. If we let the slaughter continue, they will share a bleak world with rats, dogs, cockroaches, pigeons, and mosquitoes. A potential recovery millions of years later has no meaning at our appropriate scale. Similarly, others could do the unfinished work of Lavoisier, if not so elegantly; and political revolution did spur science into some interesting channels. But how can this mitigate the tragedy of Lavoisier? He was one of the most brilliant men ever to grace our history, and he died at the height of his powers and health. He had work to do, and he was not guilty.

My title, "The Passion of Antoine Lavoisier," is a double entendre. The modern meaning of *passion,* "overmastering zeal or enthusiasm," is a latecomer. The word entered our language from the Latin verb for suffering, particularly for suffering physical pain. The Saint Matthew and Saint John Passions of J. S. Bach are musical dramas about the suffering of Jesus on the cross. This essay, therefore, focuses upon the final and literal passion of Lavoisier. (Anyone who has ever been disappointed in love—that is, nearly all of us—will understand the intimate connection between the two meanings of passion.)

But I also wanted to emphasize Lavoisier's passion in the modern meaning. For this supremely organized man—farmer-general; commissioner of gunpowder; wall builder; reformer of prisons, hospitals, and schools; legislative representative for the nobility of Blois; father of the metric system; servant on a hundred government committees—really had but one passion amidst this burden of activities for a thousand lifetimes. Lavoisier loved science more than anything else. He awoke at six in the morning and worked on science until eight, then again at night from seven until ten. He devoted one full day a week to scientific experiments and called it his *jour de bonheur* (day of happiness). The letters and reports of his last year are painful to read, for Lavoisier never abandoned his passion—his conviction that reason and science must guide any just and effective social order. But those who received his pleas, and held power over him, had heard the different drummer of despotism.

Lavoisier was right in the deepest, almost holy, way. His passion harnessed feeling to the service of reason; another kind of passion was the price. Reason cannot save us and can even persecute us in the wrong hands; but we have no hope of salvation without reason. The world is too complex, too intransigent; we cannot bend it to our simple will. Bernard Lacépède was probably thinking of Lavoisier when he wrote a closing flourish following his passage on the great asymmetry of slow creation and sudden destruction:

> Ah! Never forget that we can only stave off that fatal degradation if we unite the liberal arts, which embody the sacred fire of sensibility, with the sciences and the useful arts, without which the celestial light of reason will disappear.

The Republic needs scientists.

25 | The Godfather of Disaster

LEMUEL GULLIVER, marooned by pirates on a small Pacific island, lamented his apparently inevitable fate: "I considered how impossible it was to preserve my life, in so desolate a place; and how miserable my end must be." But then the floating island of Laputa appeared and he rode up on a chain to safety.

The Laputans, Gulliver soon discovered, were an odd lot, with an ethereal turn of mind well suited to their abode. Their thoughts, he noted, "are so taken up with intense speculation" that they can neither speak nor hear the words of others unless explicitly roused. Thus, each Laputan of status employs a "flapper" who gently strikes the ear or mouth of his master with an inflated bladder full of small pebbles whenever his lordship must either attend or answer.

The Laputans are not catholic in their distractions; only music and mathematics incite their unworldly concentration. Gulliver finds that their mathematical obsession extends to all spheres of life; he obtains for his first meal "a shoulder of mutton, cut into an equilateral triangle; a piece of beef into rhomboides; and a pudding into a cycloid."

But mathematics has its negative side, at least psychologically. The Laputans are not lost in a blissful reverie about the perfection of circles or the infinitude of pi. They are scared. Their calculations have taught them that "the earth very narrowly escaped a brush from the tail of the last comet . . . and that the next, which they have calculated for one and thirty years hence, will probably destroy [them]." The Laputans live in fear: "When they meet an acquaintance in the morning, the first question is about the sun's health; how he looked at his setting and rising, and what hopes they have to avoid the stroke of the approaching comet."

Jonathan Swift, as usual, was not writing abstract humor in reciting the Laputans' fear of comets. He was satirizing the influential theory of a political and religious enemy, William Whiston, handpicked successor to Isaac Newton as Lucasian Professor of Mathematics at Cambridge. In 1696, Whiston had published the first edition of a work destined for scientific immortality of the worst sort—as a primer of how not to proceed. Whiston called his treatise *A New Theory of the Earth from its Original to the Consummation of all Things, Wherein the Creation of the World in Six Days, the Universal Deluge, and the General Conflagration, as laid down in the Holy Scriptures, are shewn to be perfectly agreeable to Reason and Philosophy.*

Whiston has descended through history as the worst example of religious superstition viewed as an impediment to science. Whiston, we are told, was so wed to the few thousand years of Moses' chronology that he had to postulate absurd catastrophes via cometary collisions in order to encompass the earth's history in so short a time. This dismissal is no modern gloss but an old tradition in scientific rhetoric. Charles Lyell, conventional father of modernity in geological thought, poured contempt upon Whiston's extraterrestrial and catastrophic theories because they foreclosed proper attention to gradual, earth-based causes. Lyell wrote in 1830:

> [Whiston] retarded the progress of truth, diverting men from the investigation of the laws of sublunary nature, and inducing them to waste time in speculations on the power of comets to drag the waters of the ocean over the land—on the condensation of the vapors of their tails into water, and other matters equally edifying.

But Whiston did not only suffer the abuse of posthumous reputation; he became an object of ridicule in his own time as well (as Swift's satire indicates). His contemporary troubles did not stem from his cometary theory (which resembled several others of his day and did not strike fellow intellectuals as outré) but from his religious heterodoxies. Whiston's public support of the Arian heresy (a denial of the Trinity, and the consubstantiality of Christ with God the Father) led to dismissal from his Cambridge professorship (as Newton, his erstwhile champion, and a quieter, more measured exponent of the same heresy, remained conspicuously silent). Resettled in London, Whiston was tried twice for heresy and, though not formally convicted, lost most of his previous prestige and lived the rest of his long life (he died in 1752 at the age of eighty-four) as an independent intellectual, viewed as a prophet by some and as a crank by most. In the eighth plate of Hogarth's *The Rake's Progress,* set in the mental hospital of Bedlam, an inmate covers the wall with a sketch of Whiston's scheme for measuring longitude.

Despite continual rejection of Whiston, from his own time to ours, we must still grant him a major role in the history of science. The French historian Jacques Roger ended his article on Whiston (in the *Dictionary of Scientific Biography*) with these words:

> His writings were much disputed but also widely read throughout the eighteenth century, and not just in England. For example, Buffon, who summarized Whiston's theory in order to ridicule it, borrowed more from him than he was willing to admit. . . . It may be said that all the cosmogonies based on the impact of celestial bodies, including that of Jeans, owed something, directly or indirectly, to Whiston's inventions.

Moreover, we must not forget the early acclaim of his contemporaries. The greatest figure in all the history of science, Isaac Newton, personally chose Whiston as his successor. In my copy of Whiston's *New Theory* (the second edition of 1708), a Mr. Nathaniel Hancock, who bought the book in 1723, has inscribed on its title page, in a beautiful, flowing hand, the following judgment of Whiston and his book by John Locke:

> I have not heard any one of my acquaintance speak of it, but with great commendations (as I think it deserves). . . . He is one of those sort of writers that I always fancy should be most encouraged; I am always for the builders.

Comets were in the air in late seventeenth century Britain. In 1680, a great comet brightened the skies of Europe, followed two years later by a smaller object that sent Edmond Halley to the drawing boards of history and mathematics. Moreover, the seventeenth century had been a time of extraordinary change and tension in Britain—the execution of Charles I, Cromwell's Protectorate, the Restoration, and the Glorious Revolution to mention just a few of the tumultuous events of Whiston's age. These happenings fostered a revival of millennial thought—a scrutiny of the prophecies in Daniel and Revelation, leading to a conclusion that the end of this world lay in sight, and that the blessed millennium, or thousand-year reign of Christ, would soon begin. Since comets had long been viewed as harbingers or signals of great transitions and disasters (literally, "evil stars"), Whiston chose a propitious time to implicate comets as the prime movers of our planet's history.

Whiston's *New Theory* tried, above all, to establish a consistency between the two great sources of truth, as defined by his countrymen: the infallibility of Scripture and the mathematical beauty of the cosmos, so recently revealed by Newton. Whiston began his account of our planet's history by summarizing his method of inquiry in a single page, entitled *Postulata.* The first two statements illustrate his attempt to join Moses with Newton:

1. The obvious or literal sense of scripture is the true and real one, where no evident reason can be given to the contrary.

2. That which is clearly accountable in a natural way, is not, without reason, to be ascribed to a Miraculous Power.

Comets became Whiston's *deus ex machina* for rendering the cataclysmic events of Genesis with the forces of Newton's universe.

Consider Whiston's descriptions of the earth, from cradle to grave, with each of its five principal events tied to cometary causes:

1. *The Hexameron, or Moses' six days of creation.* Whiston prefaced the body of his work with a ninety-four-page "Discourse Concerning the Nature, Stile, and Extent of the Mosaick History of the Creation." Here, he attempts to preserve the literal sense of Scripture (first postulate above) in the light of Newton's nearly infinite universe. How could all this vastness be made in six days, and how could our earth, one tiny speck in one corner of the cosmos, be the focus of such infinitude? Whiston devotes his

preface to a single argument: Moses described the origin of the earth alone, not the entire universe; moreover, he tailored his words to describe not the abstract properties of nature's laws, but the visual appearance of events as an untutored observer might have witnessed them on the congealing surface of our planet. With these provisos, everything happened exactly as Genesis proclaims.

The earth began as a comet, and the chaos described in Genesis 1 ("and the earth was without form and void") represents the original swirling atmosphere. Whiston's contemporaries did not know the true size of comets, and many assumed, as he did, that comets might be of planetary dimensions, and therefore suitable for transformation into a planet. Whiston wrote:

> Tis very reasonable to believe, that a planet is a comet formed into a regular and lasting constitution, and placed at a proper distance from the sun . . . and a comet is a chaos, i.e., a planet unformed or in its primaeval state, placed in a very eccentrical [orbit].

To transform this comet, with its highly elliptical pathway, into a planet, God needs to render its orbit more nearly circular. The chaotic atmosphere will then clear and precipitate to form the solid surface of a planet. Whiston's attitude toward miracles (temporary suspension by God of his own natural laws) remained ambiguous. His second postulate stated a preference for natural explanations, but only when possible. He never did resolve whether the change in orbit that converted our cometary ancestor into the present earth had been a true miracle (accomplished by the immediate agency of God's own hand) or a natural event (the result of gravitational influences exerted by another body moving through the heavens according to Newton's laws). But since Newton's laws are God's laws, Whiston attached only limited importance to the distinction—for the transition from comet to planet occurred either by God's direct action or by laws that God had established in full knowledge of the later, desired result.

In any case, once the comet's orbit had been adjusted to its planetary pathway, the events of Genesis 1 would proceed naturally, as viewed by an observer on earth. The creation of light on the first day represents an initial clarification of a formerly opaque atmosphere (so that a brightness always present could finally be perceived). Similarly, the "creation" of the sun and moon records a further lightening of atmosphere.

> This fourth day is therefore the very time when . . . these heavenly bodies, which were in being before, but so as to be wholly strangers to a spectator on earth, were rendered visible.

Meanwhile, the products of this former atmosphere settled out by order of density into a series of concentric layers—solid at the center, water above, and a solid froth on top—to form the earth.

If all this activity still seems a bit much to compress into a mere six days, Whiston added an argument to increase our confidence. The original earth underwent no diurnal rotation on its axis but maintained a constant position as it revolved around the sun. The nearly equatorial Eden therefore experienced a year divided into halves: one of day; the second of night. Since we define a "day" as a single alternation of light and darkness, the days of Genesis 1 were all a year long—not a vast span for the work accomplished, but a big step in the right direction.

2. *The Fall, and expulsion of Adam and Eve from Eden.* The pristine earth stood bolt upright with no seasons, tides, or winds to disturb its primeval bliss. But "as soon as Man had sinned . . . and as God Almighty had pronounced a curse on the ground, and its production, presently the earth began a new and strange motion, and revolved from west to east on its own axis." This axis tilted to its present inclination of some 21 degrees, and the earth began its diurnal rotation, with days, nights, winds, and seasons. Whiston ascribed this change to a cometary collision:

> Now the only assignable cause is that of the impulse of a comet with little or no atmosphere, or of a central solid hitting obliquely upon the earth along some parts of its present equator.

3. *Noah's flood.* All the great works of this late seventeenth century vogue for "theories of the earth" (notably Burnet's *Sacred Theory of the Earth* and Woodward's *Essay Towards a Natural History of the Earth*) regarded an explanation of the Deluge as their cen-

tral test and focus. Events of the Creation were too distant and shrouded in mystery, phenomena of the coming millennium too tentative. But the Flood was a relatively recent incident, begun (or so Whiston deduced) precisely "on the 17th day of the 2nd month from the autumnal equinox . . . in the 2349th year before the Christian era." Any proper theory of the earth must, above all, render this cardinal and precisely specified event of a history remembered and recorded in the ancient chronicles.

The comet that unleashed the Flood did not strike the earth directly but passed close enough for two great effects that combined to produce the Deluge. First, the earth passed (for about two hours) directly through the "vaporous tail" of the comet, thus absorbing by gravity enough water to unleash forty days and nights of rain. Second, the tides generated by close passage of such an enormous body stretched the round earth into an oblate spheroid and eventually cracked the solid surface, allowing the underlying layer of water to rise and contribute to the great flood (Genesis, remember, speaks not only of rain from above, but also of upwelling from the "fountains of the deep").

(In a rather uncomfortable bit of special pleading, even in his own terms, Whiston argued that the cometary impact at the Fall had not unleashed a similar flood because this previous comet had no atmosphere. If we then ask why this earlier impact, more direct after all than the near miss that made the Flood, did not tear the surface and raise the waters from the abyss, Whiston responds that such a fracturing requires not only the gravitational force of the comet itself but also the pressing weight of waters from its tail.)

Above all, Whiston took delight in his cometary theory because it had resolved this cardinal event in our history as a consequence of nature's divinely appointed laws, and had thereby removed the need for a special, directly miraculous explanation:

> Whatever difficulties may hitherto have rendered this most noted catastrophe of the old world, that it was destroyed by waters, very hard, if not wholly inexplicable without an Omnipotent Power, and Miraculous Interposition: since the theory of comets, with their atmospheres and tails is discovered, they must vanish of their own accord. . . . We shall easily see that a deluge of waters is by no means an impossi-

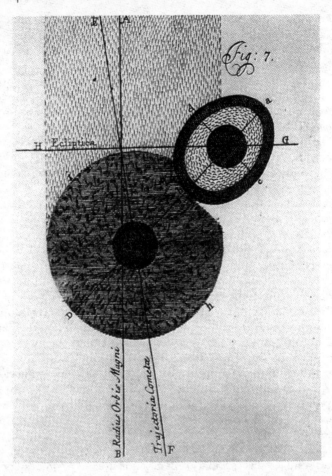

Cometary action as illustrated by Whiston in 1696. A passing comet (large object in the center) induces Noah's flood. The earth (upper right), entering the comet's tail, will receive its 40 days and nights of rain. The comet's gravity is stretching the earth into a spheroid. Under this gravitational tug, the earth's outer surface will soon crack, releasing water from below (the light, middle layer) to contribute to the deluge.

ble thing; and in particular that such an individual deluge
. . . which Moses describes, is no more so, but fully accountable that it might be, nay almost demonstrable that it really
was.

4. *The coming conflagration.* The prophetic books of Daniel and
Revelation speak of a worldwide fire that will destroy the current
earth, but in a purifying way that will usher in the millennium.
Whiston proposed (as the Laputans feared) that a comet would
instigate this conflagration for a set of coordinated reasons. This
comet would strip off the earth's cooling atmosphere, raise the
molten material at the earth's core, and contribute its own fiery
heat. Moreover, the passage of this comet would slow the earth's
rotation, thus initiating an orbit so elliptical that the point of
closest approach to the sun would be sufficient to ignite our
planet's surface. Thus, Whiston writes, "the theory of comets"
can provide "almost as commensurate and complete an account
of the future burning, as it already has done of the ancient drowning of the earth."

5. *The consummation.* As prophecy relates, the thousand-year
reign of Christ will terminate with a final battle between the just
and the forces of evil led by the giants Gog and Magog. Thereafter, the bodies of the just shall ascend to heaven, those of the
damned shall sink in the other direction—and the earth's appointed role shall be over. This time a comet shall make a direct
hit—no more glancing blows for diurnal rotation or near misses
for floods—and knock the earth either clear out of the solar system or into an orbit so elliptical that it will become, as it was in the
beginning, a comet.

Our conventional, modern reading of Whiston as an impediment to true science arises not only from the fatuous character of
this particular reconstruction but also, and primarily, from our
recognition that Whiston invoked the laws of nature only to validate a predetermined goal—the rendering of biblical history—
and not, as modern ideals proclaim, to chart with objectivity, and
without preconception, the workings of the universe. Consider,
for example, Whiston's reverie on how God established the laws
of nature so that a comet would instigate a flood just when human
wickedness deserved such a calamity.

That Omniscient Being, who foresaw when the degeneracy of human nature would be arrived at an unsufferable degree of wickedness . . . and when consequently his vengeance ought to fall upon them; predisposed and preadapted the orbits and motions of both the comet and the earth, so that at the very time, and only at that time, the former should pass close by the latter and bring that dreadful punishment upon them.

Yet such an assessment of Whiston seems singularly unfair and anachronistic. How can we justify a judgment of modern taxonomies that didn't exist in the seventeenth century? We dismiss Whiston because he violated ideals of science as we now define the term. But, in Whiston's time, science did not exist as a separate domain of inquiry; the word itself had not been coined. No matter how we may view such an enterprise today, Whiston's mixture of natural events and scriptural traditions defined a primary domain at the forefront of scholarship in his time. We have since defined Whiston's *New Theory* as a treatise in the history of science because we remain intrigued with his use of astronomical arguments but have largely lost both context for and interest in his exegesis of millennarian prophecy. But Whiston would not have accepted such a categorization; he would not even have recognized our concerns and divisions. He did not view his effort as a work of science, but as a treatise in an important contemporary tradition for using all domains of knowledge—revelations of Scripture, history of ancient chronicles, and knowledge of nature's laws—to reconstruct the story of human life on our planet. The *New Theory* contains—and by Whiston's explicit design—far more material on theological principles and biblical exegesis than on anything that would now pass muster as science.

Moreover, although Whiston later achieved a reputation as a crank in his own time, he wrote the *New Theory* at the height of his conventional acceptability. He showed the manuscript to Christopher Wren and won the hearty approval of this greatest among human architects. He then gave (and eventually dedicated) the work to Newton himself, and so impressed Mr. Numero Uno in our current pantheon of scientific heroes that he ended up as Newton's handpicked successor at Cambridge.

In fact, Whiston's arguments in the *New Theory* are neither marginal nor oracular, but preeminently Newtonian in both spirit and substance. In reading the *New Theory,* I was particularly struck by a feature of organization, a conceit really, that most commentators pass over. Whiston ordered his book in a manner that strikes us as peculiar (and ultimately quite repetitious). He presents the entire argument as though it could be laid out in a mathematical and logical framework, combining sure knowledge of nature's laws with clear strictures of a known history in order to deduce the necessity of cometary action as a primary cause.

Whiston begins with the page of *Postulata,* or general principles of explanation cited previously. He then lists eighty-five "lemmata," or secondary postulates derived directly from laws of nature. The third section discusses eleven "hypotheses"—not "tentative explanations" in the usual, modern sense of the word, but known facts of history assumed beforehand and used as terms in later deductions. Whiston then pretends that he can combine these lemmas and facts to deduce the proper explanation of our planet's history. The next section lists 101 "phaenomena," or particular facts that require explanation. The final chapter on "solutions" runs through these facts again to supply cometary (and other) explanations based on the lemmas and hypotheses. (Whiston then ends the book with four pages of "corollaries" extolling God's power and scriptural authority.)

I call this organization a conceit because it bears the form, but not the substance, of deductive necessity. The lemmas are not an impartial account of consequences from Newton's laws but a tailored list designed beforehand to yield the desired results. The hypotheses are not historical facts in the usual sense of verified, direct observations but inferences based on a style of biblical exegesis not universally followed even in Whiston's time. The solutions are not deductive necessities but possible readings that do not include other alternatives (even if one accepts the lemmas and hypotheses).

Still, we must not view Whiston's *New Theory* as a caricature of Newtonian methodology (if only from the direct evidence that Newton himself greatly admired the book). The Newton of our pantheon is a sanitized and modernized version of the man himself, as abstracted from his own time for the sake of glory, as Whiston has been for the sake of infamy. Newton's thinking combined the same interests in physics and prophecy, although an almost conspiratorial silence among scholars has, until recently, foreclosed discussion of Newton's voluminous religious writings, most of which remain unpublished. (James Force's excellent study, *William Whiston, Honest Newtonian,* 1985, should be consulted on this issue.) Newton and Whiston were soul mates, not master and jester. Whiston's perceived oddities arose directly from his Newtonian convictions and his attempt to use Newtonian methods (in both scientific and religious argument) to resolve the earth's history.

I have, over the years, written many essays to defend maligned figures in the traditional history of science. I usually proceed, as I have so far with Whiston, by trying to place an unfairly denigrated man into his own time and to analyze the power and interest of his arguments in their own terms. I have usually held that judgment by modern standards is the pitfall that led to our previous, arrogant dismissal—and that we should suppress our tendency to justify modern interest by current relevance.

Yet I would also hold that old arguments can retain a special meaning and importance for modern scientific debates. Some issues are so broad and general that they transcend all social contexts to emerge as guiding themes in scientific arguments across the centuries (see my book *Time's Arrow, Time's Cycle* for such a discussion about metaphors of linear and cyclical time in geology). In these situations, old versions can clarify and instruct our current research because they allow us to tease out the generality from its overlay of modern prejudices and to grasp the guiding power of a primary theme through its application to a past world that we can treat more abstractly, and without personal stake.

Whiston's basic argument about comets possesses this character of instructive generality. We must acknowledge, first of all, the overt and immediate fact that one of the most exciting items in contemporary science—the theory of mass extinction by extraterrestrial impact—calls upon the same agency (some versions even cite comets as the impacting bodies). Evidence continues to accumulate for the hypothesis that a large extraterrestrial object struck the earth some 65 million years ago and triggered, or at least greatly promoted, the late Cretaceous mass extinction (the sine qua non of our own existence, since the death of dinosaurs cleared ecological space for the evolution of large mammals). Intensive research is now under way to test the generality of this claim by searching for evidence of similar impacts during other episodes of mass extinction. We await the results with eager anticipation.

But theories of mass extinction do not provide the main reason why we should pay attention to Whiston today. After all, the similarities may be only superficial: Whiston made a conjecture to render millennarian prophecy; the modern theory has mustered some surprising facts to explain an ancient extinction. Guessing right for the wrong reason does not merit scientific immortality. No, I commend Whiston to modern attention for a different and more general cause—because the form and structure of his general argument embody a powerful abstraction that we need to grasp today in our search to understand the roles of stability, gradual change, and catastrophe in the sciences of history.

Whiston turned to comets for an interesting reason rooted in his Newtonian perspective, not capriciously as an easy way out for the salvation of Moses. Scientists who work with the data of history must, above all, develop general theories about how substantial change can occur in a universe governed by invariant natural laws. In Newton's (and Whiston's) world view, immanence and stability are the usual consequences of nature's laws: The cosmos does not age or progress anywhere. Therefore, if substantial changes did occur, they must be rendered by rapid and unusual events that, from time to time, interrupt the ordinary world of stable structure. In other words, Whiston's catastrophic theory of change arose primarily from his belief in the general stability of nature. Change must be an infrequent fracture or rupture. He wrote:

> We know no other natural causes that can produce any great and general changes in our sublunary world, but such bodies as can approach to the earth, or, in other words, but comets.

A major intellectual movement began about a century after Whiston wrote and has persisted to become the dominant ideology of our day. Whiston's notion of stability as the ordinary state of things yielded to the grand idea that change is intrinsic to the workings of nature. The poet Robert Burns wrote:

> Look abroad through nature's range
> Nature's mighty law is change.

This alternative idea of gradual and progressive change as inherent in nature's ways marked a major reform in scientific thinking and led to such powerful theories as Lyellian geology and Darwinian evolution. But this notion of slow, intrinsic alteration also established an unfortunate dogma that fostered an amnesia about other legitimate styles of change and often still leads us to restrict our hypotheses to one favored style falsely viewed as preferable (or even true) a priori. For example, the *New York Times* recently suggested that impact theories be disregarded on general principles:

> Terrestrial events, like volcanic activity or change in climate or sea level, are the most immediate possible cause of mass extinctions. Astronomers should leave to astrologers the task of seeking the causes of earthly events in the stars [editorial, April 2, 1985].

Perhaps they will now grant this paleontologist equal power of judgment over their next price increase.

The world is too complex for subsumption under any general theory of change. Whiston's model of stability, punctuated now and then by changes of great magnitude that induce new steady states, did not possess the generality that he or Newton supposed. But neither does Lyellian gradualism explain the entire course of our planet's history (and Lyell will have to eat his words about Whiston, just as the editors of the *Times* must now feast on theirs about the theory of mass extinction by extraterrestrial impact). Whiston's general style of argument—change as an interruption of usual stability—is on the ascendancy again as a worthy alternative to a way of thinking that has become too familiar, too automatic.

On the wall of Preservation Hall in New Orleans hangs a tattered and greasy sign, but the most incisive I have ever seen. It gives a price scale for requests by the audience to the aged men of the band who play jazz in the old style:

Traditional Requests	$1
Others	$2
The Saints	$5

Preservation Hall guards against too frequent repetition of the most familiar with the usual currency of our culture—currency itself. Scholars must seek other, more active tactics. We must have gadflies—and historical figures may do posthumous service—to remind us constantly that our usual preferences, channels, and biases are not inevitable modes of thought. I nominate William Whiston to the first rank of reminders as godfather to punctuational theories of change in geology.

Funny, isn't it? Whiston longed "to be in that number, when the Saints go marching in"; in fact, he wrote the *New Theory* largely to suggest that cometary impact would soon usher in this blessed millenium. Yet he is now a soul mate to those who wish to hear a different drummer.

8 | Evolution and Creation

26 | Knight Takes Bishop?

I HAVE NOT THE SLIGHTEST doubt that truth possesses inestimable moral value. In addition, as Mr. Nixon once found to his sorrow, truth represents the only way to keep a complex story straight, for no one can remember all the details of when he told what to whom unless his words have an anchor in actual occurrence.

> Oh, what a tangled web we weave,
> When first we practice to deceive!

Yet, for a scholar, there is nothing quite like falsehood. Lies are pinpoints—identifiable historical events that can be traced. Falsehoods also have motivations—points of departure for our ruminations on the human animal. Truth, on the other hand, simply happens. Its accurate report teaches us little beyond the event itself.

In this light, we should note with interest that the most famous story in all the hagiography of evolution is, if not false outright, at least grossly distorted by biased reconstruction long after the fact. I speak of Thomas Henry Huxley's legendary encounter with the bishop of Oxford, "Soapy Sam" Wilberforce, at the 1860 meeting of the British Association for the Advancement of Science, held in His Lordship's own see.

Darwin had published the *Origin of Species* in November 1859. Thus, when the British Association for the Advancement of Science met at Oxford in the summer of 1860, this greatest of all debates received its first prominent public airing. On Saturday,

June 30, more than 700 people wedged themselves into the largest room of Oxford's Zoological Museum to hear what was, by all accounts, a perfectly dreadful hour-long peroration by an American scholar, Dr. Draper, on the "intellectual development of Europe considered with reference to the views of Mr. Darwin." Leonard Huxley wrote, in *Life and Letters of Thomas Henry Huxley:*

> The room was crowded to suffocation. . . . The very windows by which the room was lighted down the length of its west side were packed with ladies, whose white handkerchiefs, waving and fluttering in the air at the end of the Bishop's speech, were an unforgettable factor in the acclamation of the crowd.

The throng, as Leonard Huxley notes, had not come to hear Dr. Draper drone on about Europe. Word had circulated widely that "Soapy Sam" Wilberforce, the silver-tongued bishop of Oxford, would attend with the avowed purpose of smashing Mr. Darwin in the discussion to follow Draper's paper.

The story of Wilberforce's oration and Huxley's rejoinder has been enshrined among the half-dozen greatest legends of science—surely equal to Newton beaned by an apple or Archimedes jumping from his bath and shouting "Eureka!" through the streets of Syracuse. We have read the tale from comic book to novel to scholarly tome. We have viewed the scene, courtesy of the BBC, in our living rooms. The story has an "official version" codified by Darwin's son Francis, published in his *Life and Letters of Charles Darwin,* and expanded in Leonard Huxley's biography of his father. This reconstruction has become canonical, copied from source to later source hundreds of times, and rarely altered even by jot or tittle. Consider just one of countless retellings, chosen as an average and faithful version (from Ruth Moore's *Charles Darwin,* Hutchinson, 1957):

> For half an hour the Bishop spoke savagely ridiculing Darwin and Huxley, and then he turned to Huxley, who sat with him on the platform. In tones icy with sarcasm he put his famous question: was it through his grandfather or his grandmother that he claimed descent from an ape? . . . At the Bishop's question, Huxley had clapped the knee of the

surprised scientist beside him and whispered: "The Lord hath delivered him into mine hands." . . . [Huxley] tore into the arguments Wilberforce had used. . . . Working himself up to his climax, he shouted that he would feel no shame in having an ape as an ancestor, but that he would be ashamed of a brilliant man who plunged into scientific questions of which he knew nothing. In effect, Huxley said that he would prefer an ape to the Bishop as an ancestor, and the crowd had no doubt of his meaning.

The room dissolved into an uproar. Men jumped to their feet, shouting at this direct insult to the clergy. Lady Brewster fainted. Admiral Fitzroy, the former Captain of the Beagle, waved a Bible aloft, shouting over the tumult that it, rather than the viper he had harbored in his ship, was the true and unimpeachable authority. . . .

The issue had been joined. From that hour on, the quarrel over the elemental issue that the world believed was involved, science versus religion, was to rage unabated.

We may list as the key, rarely challenged features of this official version the following claims:

1. Wilberforce directly bearded and taunted Huxley by pointedly asking, in sarcastic ridicule, whether he claimed descent from an ape on his grandfather's or grandmother's side.

2. Huxley, before rising to the challenge, mumbled his famous mock-ecclesiastical sarcasm about the Lord's aid in his coming rhetorical victory.

3. Huxley than responded to Wilberforce's arguments in loud, clear, and forceful tones.

4. Huxley ended his speech with a devastatingly effective parry to the bishop's taunt.

5. Although Huxley said only that he would prefer an ape to a man who used skills of oratory to obfuscate rather than to seek truth, many took him to mean (and some thought he had said) that he would prefer an ape to a bishop as an ancestor. (Huxley, late in life, disavowed this stronger version about apes and bishops. When Wilberforce's son included it in a biography of his father, Huxley protested and secured a revision.)

6. Huxley's riposte inspired an uproar. The meeting ended forthwith and in tumult.

7. Although Moore, to her credit, does not make this claim, we are usually told that Huxley had scored an unambiguous and decisive victory—a key incident in Darwin's triumph.

8. This debate focused the world's attention on the real and deep issue of Darwin's century—science versus religion. Huxley's victory was a pivotal moment in the battle for science and reason against superstition and dogma.

I have had a strong interest in this story ever since, as an assistant professor on sabbatical leave at Oxford in 1970, I occupied a dingy office in the back rooms of the Zoological Museum, now crammed with cabinets of fossils and subdivided into cubicles, but then the large and open room where Huxley and Wilberforce fell to blows. For six months, I sat next to a small brass plaque announcing that the great event had occurred on my very spot. I also felt strong discomfort about the official tale for two definite reasons. First, it is all too pat—the victor and the vanquished, good triumphing over evil, reason over superstition. So few heroic tales in the simplistic mode turn out to be true. Huxley was a brilliant orator, but why should Wilberforce have failed so miserably? Much as I dislike the man, he was no fool. He was as gifted an orator as Huxley and a dominant intellectual force among conservative Anglicans.

Second, I knew from preliminary browsings that the official tale was a reconstruction, made by Darwin's champions some quarter century after the fact. Amazingly enough (for all its later fame), no one bothered to record the event in any detail at the time itself. No stenographer was present. The two men exchanged words to be sure, but no one knows what they actually said, and the few sketchy reports of journalists and letter writers contain important gaps and contradictions. Ironically, the official version has been so widely accepted and unchallenged not because we know its truth by copious documentation, but rather because so little data exist for a potential challenge.

For years, this topic has been about number fifty in my list of one hundred or so potential essays (sorry folks, but, the Lord and editors willing, you may have me to kick around for some time to come). Yet for want of new data about my suspicions, it remained well back in my line of processing, until I received a letter from my friend and distinguished Darwin scholar Sam Schweber of Brandeis University. Schweber wrote: "I came across a letter from Balfour Stewart to David Forbes commenting on the BAAS meeting he just attended at which he witnessed the Huxley-Wilberforce debate. It is probably the most accurate statement of what transpired." I read Stewart's letter and sat bolt upright with attention and smiles. Stewart wrote, describing the scene along the usual lines, thus vouching for the basic outline:

> There was an animated discussion in a large room on Saturday last at Oxford on Darwin's theory where the Bishop of Oxford and Prof. Huxley fell to blows. . . . There was one good thing I cannot help mentioning. The Bishop said he had been informed that Prof. Huxley had said he didn't care whether his grandfather was an ape [*sic* for punctuation] now he [the bishop] would not like to go to the Zoological Gardens and find his father's father or his mother's mother in some antiquated ape. To which Prof. Huxley replied that he would rather have for his grandfather an honest ape low in the scale of being than a man of exalted intellect and high attainments who used his power to pervert the truth.

Colorful, though nothing new so far. But I put an ellipsis early in the quotation, and I should now like to restore the missing words. Stewart wrote: "I think the Bishop had the best of it." Score one big point for my long-held suspicions. Balfour Stewart was no benighted cleric, but a distinguished scientist, Fellow of the Royal Society, and director of the Kew Observatory. Balfour Stewart also thought that Wilberforce had won the debate!

This personal discovery sent me to the books (I thank my research assistant, Ned Young, for tracking down all the sources, no mean job for so many obscure bits and pieces). We gathered all the eyewitness accounts (damned few) and found a half dozen or so modern articles, mostly by literary scholars, on aspects of the debate. (See Janet Browne, 1978; Sheridan Gilley, 1981; J. R. Lucas, 1979. I especially commend Browne's detective work on Francis Darwin's construction of the official version, and Gilley's incisive and well-written account of the debate.) I confess disappointment in finding that Stewart's letter was no new discovery. Yet I remain surprised that its key value—the claim by an important scientist that Wilberforce had won—has received so little attention. So far as I know, Stewart's letter has never been quoted *in extenso,* and no reference gives it more than a passing sentence. But I was delighted to find that the falsity of the official version is common knowledge among a small group of scholars. All the more puzzling, then, that the standard, heroic account continues to hold sway.

What is so wrong with the official tale, as epitomized in my eight points above? We should begin by analyzing the very few eyewitness accounts recorded right after the event itself.

Turning to reports by journalists, we must first mark the outstanding negative evidence. In a nation with a lively press, and with traditions for full and detailed reporting (so hard to fathom from our age of television and breathless paragraphs for the least common denominator), the great debate stands out for its nonattention. *Punch,* Wilberforce's frequent and trenchant critic, ignored the exchange but wrote poem and parody aplenty on another famous repartee about evolution from the same meeting—Huxley versus Owen on the brains of humans and gorillas. The *Athenaeum,* in one of but two accounts (the other from *Jackson's Oxford Journal*), presents a straightforward report that, in its barest outline, already belies the standard version in two or three crucial respects. On July 7, the reporter notes Oxford's bucolic charms: "Since Friday, the air has been soft, the sky sunny. A sense of sudden summer has been felt in the meadows of Christ Church and in the gardens of St. John's; many a dreamer of dreams, tempted by the summer warmth . . . and stealing from section A or B [of the meeting] has consulted his ease and taken a boat." But we then learn of a contrast between fireworks inside and punting lazily downstream while taking one's *dolce far niente.*

> The Bishop of Oxford came out strongly against a theory which holds it possible that man may be descended from an ape. . . . But others—conspicuous among these, Prof. Huxley—have expressed their willingness to accept, for themselves, as well as for their friends and enemies, all actual truths, even the last humiliating truth of a pedigree not registered in the Herald's College. The dispute has at least made Oxford uncommonly lively during the week.

The next issue, July 14, devotes a full page of tiny type to Dr. Draper and his aftermath—the longest eyewitness account ever penned. The summary of Wilberforce's remarks indicates that his half-hour oration was not confined to gibe and rhetoric, but primarily presented a synopsis of the competent (if unoriginal) critique of the *Origin* that he later published in the *Quarterly Review*. The short paragraph allotted to Huxley's reply does not mention the famous repartee—an omission of no great import in a press that, however detailed, could be opaquely discreet. But the account of Huxley's words affirms what all letter writers (see below) also noted—that Huxley spoke briefly and presented no detailed refutation of the bishop's arguments. Instead, he focused his remarks on the logic of Darwin's argument, asserting that evolution was no mere speculation, but a theory supported by copious evidence even if the process of transmutation could not be directly observed.

By the standard account, chaos should now break out, FitzRoy should jump up raving, and Henslow should gavel the meeting closed. No such thing; the meeting went on. FitzRoy took the podium in his turn. Two other speakers followed. And then, the true climax—not entirely omitted in Francis Darwin's "official" version so many years later, but so relegated to a few lines of afterthought that the incident simply dropped out of most later accounts—leading to the popular impression that Huxley's riposte had ended the meeting. Henslow turned to Joseph Hooker, the botanist of Darwin's inner circle, and asked him "to state his view of the botanical aspect of the question."

The *Athenaeum* gave Hooker's remarks four times the coverage awarded to Huxley. It was Hooker who presented a detailed refutation of Wilberforce's specific arguments. It was Hooker who charged directly that the bishop had distorted and misunderstood Darwin's theory. We get some flavor of Hooker's force and effectiveness from a section of the *Athenaeum*'s report:

> In the first place, his Lordship, in his eloquent address, had as it appeared to him [Hooker], completely misunderstood Mr. Darwin's hypothesis: his Lordship intimated that this maintained the doctrine of the transmutation of existing species one into another, and had confounded this with that of the successive development of species by variation and natural selection. The first of these doctrines was so wholly opposed to the facts, reasonings and results of Mr. Darwin's

work, that he could not conceive how any one who had read it could make such a mistake—the whole book, indeed, being a protest against that doctrine.

Moreover, it was Hooker who presented the single most effective debating point against Wilberforce (according to several eyewitness accounts) by stating publicly that he had long opposed evolution but had been led to the probable truth of Darwin's claim by so many years of direct experience with the form and distribution of plants. The bishop did not respond, and Henslow closed the meeting after Hooker's successful speech.

When we turn to the few letters of eyewitnesses, we find the *Athenaeum* account affirmed, the official story further compromised, and some important information added—particularly on the exchange about apes and ancestors. We must note, first of all, that the three letters most commonly cited—those of Green, Fawcett, and Hooker himself—were all written by participants or strong partisans of Darwin's side. For example, future historian J. R. Green, source of the standard version for Huxley's actual words, began his account (to the geologist W. Boyd Dawkins) with a lovely Egyptian metaphor of fealty to Darwin:

> On Saturday morning I met Jenkins going to the Museum. We joined company, and he proposed going to Section D, the Zoology, etc. "to hear the Bishop of Oxford smash Darwin." "Smash Darwin! Smash the Pyramids," said I in great wrath. . . .

(These one-sided sources make Balfour Stewart's neglected letter all the more important—for he was the only uncommitted scientist who reported his impressions right after the debate.)

We may draw from these letters, I believe, three conclusions that further refute the official version. First, Huxley's words may have rung true, but his oratory was faulty. He was ill at ease (his great career as a public speaker lay in the future). He did not project; many in the audience did not hear what he said. Hooker wrote to Darwin on July 2:

> Well, Sam Oxon [short for *Oxoniensis*, Latin for "of Oxford," Wilberforce's ecclesiastical title] got up and spouted

for half an hour with inimitable spirit, ugliness and emptiness and unfairness. . . . Huxley answered admirably and
turned the tables, but he could not throw his voice over so
large an assembly, nor command the audience; and he did
not allude to Sam's weak points nor put the matter in a form
or way that carried the audience.

The chemist A. G. Vernon-Harcourt could not recall Huxley's
famous words many years later because he had not heard them
over the din. He wrote to Leonard Huxley: "As the point became
clear, there was a great burst of applause, which mostly drowned
the end of the sentence."

Second, for all the admitted success of Huxley's great moment,
Hooker surely made the more effective rebuttal—and the meeting ended with his upbeat. I hesitate to take Hooker's own account at face value, but he was so scrupulously modest and
self-effacing, and so willing to grant Huxley all the credit later on
as the official version congealed, that I think we may titrate the
adrenaline of his immediate joy with the modesty of his general
bearing and regard his account to Darwin as pretty accurate:

My blood boiled, I felt myself a dastard; now I saw my advantage; I swore to myself that I would smite that Amale-
kite, Sam, hip and thigh. . . . There and then I smashed him
amid rounds of applause. I hit him in the wind and then
proceeded to demonstrate in a few words: (1) that he could
never have read your book, and (2) that he was absolutely
ignorant of the rudiments of Bot [botanical] Science. I said
a few more on the subject of my own experience and conversion, . . . Sam was shut up—had not one word to say in
reply, and the meeting *was dissolved forthwith* [Hooker's ital-
ics].

Third, and most important, we do not really know what either
man said in the famous exchange about apes and ancestors. Huxley's retort is not in dispute. The eyewitness versions differ substantially in wording, but all agree in content. We might as well
cite Green's version, if only because it became canonical when
Huxley himself "approved" it for Francis Darwin's biography of
his father:

I asserted, and I repeat—that a man has no reason to be ashamed of having an ape for his grandfather. If there were an ancestor whom I should feel shame in recalling, it would rather be a *man,* a man of restless and versatile intellect, who, not content with an equivocal success in his own sphere of activity, plunges into scientific questions with which he has no real acquaintance, only to obscure them by an aimless rhetoric, and distract the attention of his hearers from the real points at issue by eloquent digressions and skilled appeals to religious prejudice.

Huxley later demurred only about the word "equivocal," asserting that he would not have besmirched the bishop's competence in matters of religion.

Huxley's own, though lesser-known version (in a brief letter written to his friend Dyster on September 9, 1860) puts the issue more succinctly, but to the same effect:

If then, said I, the question is put to me would I rather have a miserable ape for a grandfather or a man highly endowed by nature and possessed of great means of influence and yet who employs those faculties and that influence for the mere purpose of introducing ridicule into a grave scientific discussion—I unhesitatingly affirm my preference for the ape.

But what had Wilberforce said to incur Huxley's wrath? Quite astonishingly, on this pivotal point of the entire legend, we have nothing but a flurry of contradictory reports. No two accounts coincide. All mention apes and grandfathers, but beyond this anchor of agreement, we find almost every possible permutation of meaning.

We don't know, first of all, whether or not Wilberforce committed that most dubious imposition upon Victorian sensibilities by daring to mention *female* ancestry from apes—that is, did he add grandmothers or speak only of grandfathers? Several versions cite only the male parent, as in Green's letter: "He [Wilberforce] had been told that Professor Huxley had said that he didn't see that it mattered much to a man whether his grandfather was an ape or not. Let the learned professor speak for himself." Yet, I am inclined to the conclusion that Wilberforce must have said something about grandmothers. The distaff side of descent occurs in several versions, Balfour Stewart's neglected letter in particular (see earlier citation), by disinterested observers or partisans of Wilberforce. I can understand why opponents might have delighted in such an addition ("merely corroborative detail, intended to give artistic verisimilitude to an otherwise bald and unconvincing narrative," as Pooh-Bah liked to say). But why should sympathetic listeners remember such a detail if the bishop had not included it himself?

But, far more important, it seems most unlikely that the central claim of the official version can be true—namely, that Wilberforce taunted Huxley by asking him pointedly whether he could trace his personal ancestry from grandparents back to apes (made all the worse if the bishop really asked whether he could trace it on his mother's side). No contemporary account puts the taunt quite so baldly. The official version cites a letter from Lyell (who was not there) since the anonymous eyewitness (more on him later) who supplied Francis Darwin's account could not remember the exact words. Lyell wrote: "The Bishop asked whether Huxley was related by his grandfather's or grandmother's side to an ape." The other common version of this taunt was remembered by Isabel Sidgwick in 1898: "Then, turning to his antagonist with a smiling insolence, he begged to know, was it through his grandfather or his grandmother that he claimed his descent from a monkey?"

We will never know for sure, but the memories of Canon Farrar seem so firm and detailed, and ring so true to me, that I shall place my money on his version. Farrar was a liberal clergyman who once organized a meeting for Huxley to explain Darwinism to fellow men of the cloth. His memories, written in 1899 to Leonard Huxley, are admittedly forty years old, but his version makes sense of many puzzles and should be weighted well on that account—especially since he regarded Huxley as the victor and did not write to reconstruct history in the bishop's cause. Farrar wrote, taking the official version of Wilberforce's taunt to task:

> His words are quite misquoted by you (which your father refuted). They did not appear vulgar, nor insolent nor per-

sonal, but flippant. He had been talking of the perpetuity of species in birds [a correct memory since all agree that Wilberforce criticized Darwin on the breeds of pigeons in exactly this light]: and then denying *a fortiori* the derivation of the species Man from Ape, he rhetorically invoked the help of feeling: and said (I swear to the sense and form of the sentence, if not to the words) "If anyone were to be willing to trace his descent through an ape as his grandfather, would he be willing to trace his descent similarly on the side of his grandmother." It was (you see) the arousing of antipathy about degrading women to the Quadrumana [four-footed apes]. It was not to the point, but it was the purpose. It did not sound insolent, but unscientific and unworthy of the zoological argument which he had been sustaining. It was a bathos. Your father's reply . . . showed that there was a vulgarity as well as a folly in the Bishop's words; and the impression distinctly was, that the Bishop's party as they left the room, felt abashed; and recognized that the Bishop had forgotten to behave like a gentleman.

Farrar's analysis of Huxley's victory includes an interesting comment on Victorian sensibilities:

The victory of your father, was not the ironical dexterity shown by him, but the fact that he had got a victory in respect of manners and good breeding. You must remember that the whole audience was made up of gentlefolk, who were not prepared to endorse anything vulgar.

Finally, Farrar affirms the other major falsity of the official version by acknowledging the superiority of Hooker's reply:

The speech which really left its mark scientifically on the meeting, was the short one of Hooker. . . . I should say that to fair minds, the intellectual impression left by the discussion was that the Bishop had stated some facts about the perpetuity of species, but that no one had really contributed any valuable point to the opposite side except Hooker . . . but that your father had scored a victory over Bishop Wilberforce in the question of good manners.

And so, in summary, we may conclude that the heroic legend of the official version fails badly in two crucial points—our ignorance of Wilberforce's actual words and the near certainty that the forgotten Hooker made a better argument than Huxley. What, then, can we conclude, based on such poor evidence, about such a key event in the hagiography of science? Huxley did not debate Wilberforce at Oxford in 1860; rather, they both spoke, one after the other, in a prolonged discussion of Draper's paper. They had one short and wonderful exchange of rhetorical barbs on a totally nonintellectual point prompted by a whimsical remark, perhaps even a taunt, that Wilberforce made about apes and ancestry, though no one remembered precisely what he said. Huxley made a sharp and effective retort. Everyone enjoyed the incident immensely and recalled it in a variety of versions. Some thought Huxley had won the exchange; others credit Wilberforce. Huxley hardly dealt with Wilberforce's case against Darwin. Hooker, however, made an effective reply in Darwin's behalf, and the meeting ended.

All events before the codification of the official version support this ambiguous and unheroic account. In particular, Wilberforce seemed not a bit embarrassed by the incident. Disraeli spoke about it in his presence. Wilberforce reprinted his review of Darwin's *Origin,* the basis of his remarks that fateful day, in an 1874 collection of his works. His son recounted the tale with credit in Wilberforce's biography. Moreover, Darwin and Wilberforce remained on good terms. The ever genial Darwin wrote to Asa Gray that he found Wilberforce's review "uncommonly clever, not worth anything scientifically, but quizzes me in splendid style. I chuckled with laughter at myself." Wilberforce, told by the vicar of Downe about Darwin's reaction, said: "I am glad he takes it in this way. He is such a capital fellow."

Moreover, though I don't believe that self-justification provides much evidence for anything, we do have a short testimony from Wilberforce himself. He wrote to Sir Charles Anderson just three days after the event: "On Saturday Professor Henslow who presided over the Zoological Section called on me by name to address the Section on Darwin's Theory. So I could not escape and had quite a long fight with Huxley. I think I thoroughly beat him." This letter, now housed in the Bodleian Library of Oxford University, escaped all notice until 1978, when Josef L. Altholz cited it in the *Journal of the History of Medicine*. I would not exaggerate the importance of this document because it smacks of insincerity at least once—so why not in its last line as well? We know that 700 people crammed the Museum's largest room to witness the proceedings. They didn't come to hear Dr. Draper on the intellectual development of Europe. Wilberforce was on the dais, and if he didn't know that he would speak, how come everyone else did?

Why then, and how, did the official version so color this event as a primal victory for evolution? The answer largely lies with Huxley himself, who successfully promoted, in retrospect, a version that suited his purposes (and had probably, by then, displaced the actual event in his memory). Huxley, though not antireligious, was uncompromisingly and pugnaciously anticlerical. Moreover, he despised Wilberforce and his mellifluous sophistries. When Wilberforce died in 1873, from head injuries sustained in a fall from his horse, Huxley remarked (as the story goes): "For once, reality and his brains came into contact and the result was fatal."

Janet Browne has traced the construction of the official version in Francis Darwin's biography of his father. The story is told through an anonymous eyewitness, but Browne proves that Hooker himself wrote the account, volunteering for the task with direct purpose (writing to Francis): "Have you any account of the Oxford meeting? If not, I will, if you like, see what I can do towards vivifying it (and vivisecting the Bishop) for you." Hooker dredged his memory with pain and uncertainty. He had forgotten his letter to Darwin and admitted, "It is impossible to be sure of what one heard, or of impressions formed, after nearly thirty years of active life." And further, "I have been driven wild formulating it from memory." Huxley then vetted Hooker's account and the official story was set.

The tale was then twice embellished—first, in 1892, when Francis published a shorter biography of Charles Darwin, and Huxley contributed a letter, now remembering for the first time (more than thirty years later) his *sotto voce* crack, "The Lord hath delivered him into mine hands"; second, in 1900, when Leonard Huxley wrote the life of his father. Thus, dutiful sons presented the official version as constructed by a committee of two—the chief participants Huxley and Hooker—from memories colored by thirty years of battle. We can only agree with Sheridan Gilley, who writes:

> The standard account is a wholly one-sided effusion from the winning side, put together long after the event, uncritically copied from book to book, and shaped by the hagiographic conventions of the Victorian life and letters.

So much for correcting a moment of history. But why should we care today? Does the heroic version do any harm? And does its rectification have any meaning beyond our general preference for accuracy? Stories do not become primary legends simply because they tell rip-roaring narratives; they must stand as exemplars, particular representations of something deeper and far more general. The official version of Huxley versus Wilberforce is an archetype for a common belief about the nature of science and its history. The fame and meaning of the official version lie in this wider context. Yet this common belief is not only wrong (or at least seriously oversimplified) but ultimately harmful to science. Thus, in debunking the official version of Huxley versus Wilberforce, we might make a helpful correction for science itself.

Ruth Moore captured the general theme in her version of the standard account: "From that hour on, the quarrel over the elemental issue that the world believed was involved, science versus religion, was to rage unabated." The story has archetypal power because Huxley and Wilberforce, in the official version, are not mere men but symbols, or synecdoches, for a primal struggle: religion versus science, reaction versus enlightenment, dogma versus truth, darkness versus light.

All men have blind spots, however broad their vision. Thomas Henry Huxley was the most eloquent spokesman that evolution has ever known. But his extreme anticlericalism led him to an uncompromising view of organized religion as the enemy of science. Huxley could envision no allies among the official clergy. Conservatives like Wilberforce were enemies pure and simple; liberals lacked the guts to renounce what fact and logic had falsified, as they struggled to marry the irreconcilable findings of science with their supernatural vision. He wrote in 1887 of those "whose business seems to be to mix the black of dogma and the white of science into the neutral tint of what they call liberal theology." Huxley did view his century as a battleground between science and organized religion—and he took great pride in the many notches on his own gun.

This cardboard dichotomy seems favorable for science at first (and superficial) glance. It enshrines science as something pure and apart from the little quirks and dogmas of daily life. It exalts science as a disembodied method for discovering truth at all costs, while social institutions—religion in particular—hold fast to antiquated superstition. Comfort and social stability resist truth, and science must therefore fight a lonely battle for enlightenment. Its heroes, in bad times, are true martyrs—Bruno at the stake, Galileo before the Inquisition—or, in better times, merely irritated, as Huxley was, by ecclesiastical stupidity.

But no battle exists between science and religion—the two most separate spheres of human need. A titanic struggle occurs, always has, always will, between questioning and authority, free inquiry and frozen dogma—but the institutions representing these poles are not science and religion. These struggles occur *within* each field, not primarily across disciplines. The general ethic of science leads to greater openness, but we have our fossils, often in positions of great power. Organized religion, as an arm of state power so frequently in history, has tended to rigidity—but theologies have also spearheaded social revolution. Official religion has not opposed evolution as a monolith. Many prominent evolutionists have been devout, and many churchmen have placed evolution at the center of their personal theologies. Henry Ward Beecher, America's premier pulpiteer during Darwin's century, defended evolution as God's way in a striking commercial metaphor: "Design by wholesale is grander than design by retail"—better, that is, to ordain general laws of change than to make each species by separate fiat.

The struggle of free inquiry against authority is so central, so pervasive that we need all the help we can get from every side. Inquiring scientists must join hands with questioning theologians if we wish to preserve that most fragile of all reeds, liberty itself. If scientists lose their natural allies by casting entire institutions as enemies, and not seeking bonds with soul mates on other paths, then we only make a difficult struggle that much harder.

Huxley had not planned to enter that famous Oxford meeting.

He was still inexperienced in public debate, not yet Darwin's bull-dog. He wrote: "I did not mean to attend it—did not see the good of giving up peace and quietness to be episcopally pounded." But his friends prevailed upon him, and Huxley, savoring victory, left the meeting with pleasure and resolution:

> Hooker and I walked away from the meeting together, and I remember saying to him that this experience had changed my opinion as to the practical value of the art of public speaking, and that from that time forth I should carefully cultivate it, and try to leave off hating it.

So Huxley became the greatest popular spokesman for science in his century—as a direct result of his famous encounter with Wilberforce. He waded into the public arena and struggled for three decades to breach the boundaries between science and the daily life of ordinary people. And yet, ironically, his Manichean view of science and religion—abetted so strongly by the official version, his own construction in part, of the debate with Wilber-force—harmed his greatest hope by establishing boundaries to exclude natural allies and, ultimately, by encircling science as something apart from other human passions. We may, perhaps, read one last document of the great Oxford debate in a larger metaphorical context as a plea, above all, for solidarity among people of like minds and institutions of like purposes. Darwin to Hooker upon receiving his account of the debate: "Talk of fame, honor, pleasure, wealth, all are dirt compared with affection."

27 | Genesis and Geology

HERBERT HOOVER produced a fine translation, still in use, of Agricola's sixteenth-century Latin treatise on mining and geology. In the midst of his last presidential campaign, Teddy Roosevelt published a major monograph on the evolutionary significance of animal coloration (see Essay 14). Woodrow Wilson was no intellectual slouch, and John F. Kennedy did aptly remark to a group of Nobel laureates assembled at the White House that the building then contained more intellectual power than at any moment since the last time Thomas Jefferson dined there alone.

Still, when we seek a political past of intellectual eminence in the midst of current emptiness, we cannot do better than the helm of Victorian Britain. High ability may not have prevailed generally, as the wise Private Willis, guard to the House of Commons, reminds us in Gilbert and Sullivan's *Iolanthe:*

> When in that House M.P.'s divide,
> If they've a brain and cerebellum, too,
> They've got to leave that brain outside,
> And vote just as their leaders tell 'em to.
> But then the prospect of a lot
> Of dull M.P.'s in close proximity
> All thinking for themselves is what
> No man can face with equanimity.

But the men at the top—the Tory leader Benjamin Disraeli and his Liberal counterpart W. E. Gladstone—were formidable in many various ways. Disraeli maintained an active career as a respected romantic novelist, publishing the three-volume *Endymion* in 1880, at the height of his prestige and just a year before his death. Gladstone, a distinguished Greek scholar, wrote his three-volume *Studies on Homer and the Homeric Age* (1858) while temporarily out of office.

In 1885, following a series of setbacks including the death of General Gordon at Khartoum, Gladstone's government fell, and he resigned as prime minister. He did not immediately proceed to unwind with his generation's rum swizzle on a Caribbean beach (Chivas Regal on the links of Saint Andrews, perhaps). Instead, he occupied his enforced leisure by writing an article on the scientific truth of the book of Genesis—"Dawn of Creation and of Worship," published in *The Nineteenth Century,* in November 1885. Thomas Henry Huxley, who invented the word *agnostic* to describe his own feelings, read Gladstone's effort with disgust and wrote a response to initiate one of the most raucous, if forgotten, free-for-alls of late nineteenth century rhetoric. (Huxley disliked Gladstone and once described him as suffering from "severely copious chronic glossorrhoea.")

But why bring up a forgotten and musty argument, even if the protagonists were two of the most colorful and brilliant men of the nineteenth century? I do so because current events have brought their old subject—the correlation of Genesis with geology—to renewed attention.

Our legislative victory over "creation science" (Supreme Court in *Edwards* v. *Aguillard,* June 1987) ended an important chapter in American social history, one that stretched back to the Scopes trial of 1925. (Biblical literalism will never go away, so long as cash flows and unreason retains its popularity, but the legislative strategy of passing off dogma as creation science and forcing its instruction in classrooms has been defeated.) In this happy light, we are now free to ask the right question once again: In what *helpful* ways may science and religion coexist?

Ever since the Edwards decision, I have received a rash of well-meaning letters suggesting a resolution very much like Gladstone's. These letters begin by professing pleasure at the defeat of fundamentalism. Obviously, six days of creation and circa 6,000 years of biblical chronology will not encompass the earth's history. But, they continue, once we get past the nonsense of literalism, are we not now free to read Genesis 1 as factual in a more general sense? Of course the days of creation can't be twenty-four hours long. Of course the origin of light three days before the creation of the sun poses problems. But aren't the general order and story consistent with modern science, from the big bang to Darwinian theory? After all, plants come first in Genesis, then creatures of the sea, then land animals, and finally humans. Well, isn't this right? And, if so, then isn't Genesis true in the broad sense? And if true, especially since the scribes of Genesis could not have understood the geological evidence, must not the words be divinely inspired? This sequence of claims forms the core of Gladstone's article. Huxley's words therefore deserve a resurrection.

Huxley's rebuttal follows the argument that most intellectuals—scientists and theologians alike—make today. First, while the broadest brush of the Genesis sequence might be correct—plants first, people last—many details are dead wrong by the testimony of geological evidence from the fossil record. Second, this lack of correlation does not compromise the power and purpose of religion or its relationship with the sciences. Genesis is not a treatise on natural history.

Gladstone wrote his original article as a response to a book by Professor Alfred Réville of the Collège de France—*Prolegomena to the History of Religions* (1884). Gladstone fancied himself an expert on Homer, and he had labored for thirty years to show that common themes of the Bible and the most ancient Greek texts could be harmonized to expose the divine plan revealed by the earliest historical records of different cultures. Gladstone was most offended by Réville's dismissal of his Homeric claims, but his article focuses on the veracity of Genesis.

Gladstone did not advocate the literal truth of Genesis; science had foreclosed this possibility to any Victorian intellectual. He accepted, for example, the standard argument that the "days" of creation are metaphors for periods of undetermined length separating the major acts of a coherent sequence. But Gladstone then insisted that these major acts conform precisely to the order best specified by modern science—the cosmological events of the first four days (Genesis 1:1–19) to Laplace's "nebular hypothesis" for the origin of the sun and planets, and the biological events of "days" five and six (Genesis 1:20–31) to the geological record of fossils and Darwin's theory of evolution. He placed special emphasis on a fourfold sequence in the appearance of animals: the "water population" followed by the "air population" on the fifth day, and the "land population" and its "consummation in man" on the sixth day:

> And God said, Let the waters bring forth abundantly the moving creature that hath life, and fowl that may fly above the earth in the open firmament of heaven [Verse 20]. . . . And God said, Let the earth bring forth the living creature after its kind, cattle, and creeping thing, and beast of the earth after its kind; and it was so [Verse 24]. . . . And God said, Let us make man in our image [Verse 26].

Gladstone then caps his argument with the claim still echoed by modern reconcilers: This order, too good to be guessed by writers ignorant of geological evidence, must have been revealed by God to the scribes of Genesis:

> Then, I ask, how came . . . the author of the first chapter of Genesis to know that order, to possess knowledge which natural science has only within the present century for the first time dug out of the bowels of the earth? It is surely impossible to avoid the conclusion, first, that either this writer was gifted with faculties passing all human experience, or else his knowledge was divine.

In a closing flourish, Gladstone enlarged his critique in a manner sure to inspire Huxley's wrath. He professed himself satisfied as to the possibility of physical evolution, even by Darwin's mechanism. But the spirit, the soul, the "mind of man" must be divine in origin, thereby dwarfing to insignificance anything in the merely material world. Gladstone chided Darwin for reaching too far, for trying to render the ethereal realm by his crass and heartless mechanism. He ridiculed the idea "that natural selection and the survival of the fittest, all in the physical order, exhibit to us the great *arcanum* of creation, the sun and center of life, so that mind and spirit are dethroned from their old supremacy, are no longer sovereign by right, but may find somewhere by charity a place assigned them, as appendages, perhaps only as excrescences, of the material creation."

Ending on a note of deep sadness, Gladstone feared for our equanimity, our happiness, our political stability, our hopes for a moral order, should the festering sore of agnosticism undermine our assurance of God's existence and benevolence—"this belief, which has satisfied the doubts and wiped away the tears, and found guidance for the footsteps of so many a weary wanderer on earth, which among the best and greatest of our race has been so cherished by those who had it, and so longed and sought for by those who had it not." If science could now illustrate God by proving that he knew his stuff when he whispered into Moses' ear, then surely that sore could be healed.

Huxley, who had formally retired just a few months before, and who had forsworn future controversy of exactly this kind, responded with an article in the December issue of *The Nineteenth Century*—"The Interpreters of Genesis and the Interpreters of Nature." Obviously pleased with himself, and happy with his return to fighting form, he wrote to Herbert Spencer: "Do read my polishing off of the G.O.M. [Gladstone was known to friends and enemies alike as the "Grand Old Man"]. I am proud of it as a work of art, and as evidence that the volcano is not yet exhausted."

Huxley begins by ridiculing the very notion that harmonizing Genesis with geology has any hope of success or intellectual potential to illustrate anything meaningful. He places Gladstone among "those modern representatives of Sisyphus, the reconcilers of Genesis with science." (Sisyphus, king of Corinth, tried to cheat death and was punished in Hades with the eternal task of repeatedly rolling a large stone to the top of a hill, only to have it roll down again just as it reached the top.)

Huxley arranged his critique by citing four arguments against Gladstone's insistence that Genesis specified an accurate "fourfold order" of creation—water population, air population, land population, and man. Huxley wrote:

> If I know anything at all about the results attained by the natural sciences of our time, it is a demonstrated conclusion and established fact that the fourfold order given by Mr. Gladstone is not that in which the evidence at our disposal tends to show that the water, air and land populations of the

globe have made their appearance. . . . The facts which demolish his whole argument are of the commonest notoriety. [Huxley uses "notoriety" not in its current, pejorative meaning, but in the old sense of "easily and evidently known to all."]

He then presents his arguments in sequence:

1. Direct geological evidence shows that land animals arose before flying creatures. This reversal of biblical sequence holds whether we view the Genesis text as referring only to vertebrates (for terrestrial amphibians and reptiles long precede birds) or to all animals (for such terrestrial arthropods as scorpions arise before flying insects).

2. Even if we didn't know, or chose not to trust, the geological sequence, we could deduce on purely anatomical grounds that flying creatures must have evolved from preexisting terrestrial ancestors. Structures used in flight are derived modifications of terrestrial features:

> Every beginner in the study of animal morphology is aware that the organization of a bat, of a bird, or of a pterodactyle, presupposes that of a terrestrial quadruped, and that it is intelligible only as an extreme modification of the organization of a terrestrial mammal or reptile. In the same way, winged insects (if they are to be counted among the "air-population") presuppose insects which were wingless, and therefore as "creeping things," which were part of the land-population.

3. Whatever the order of first appearances, new species within all groups—water, air, and land dwellers—have continued to arise throughout subsequent time, whereas Genesis implies that God made *all* the sea creatures, then all the denizens of the air, and so on.

4. However we may wish to quibble about the order of animals, Gladstone should not so conveniently excise plants from his discussion. Genesis pushes their origin back to the third day, before the origin of any animal. But plants do not precede animals in the fossil record; and the terrestrial flowering plants specifically men-

tioned in Genesis (grass and fruit tree) arise very late, long after the first mammals.

Huxley then ends his essay with a powerful statement—every bit as relevant today as 100 years ago at its composition—on the proper domains and interactions of science and religion. Huxley expresses no antipathy for religion, properly conceived, and he criticizes scientists who overstep the boundaries and possibilities of their discipline as roundly as he condemns an antiquated and overextended role for the biblical text:

> The antagonism between science and religion, about which we hear so much, appears to me to be purely factitious, fabricated on the one hand by short-sighted religious people, who confound . . . theology with religion; and on the other by equally short-sighted scientific people who forget that science takes for its province only that which is susceptible of clear intellectual comprehension.

The moral precepts for our lives, Huxley argues, have been developed by great religious thinkers, and no one can improve on the Prophet Micah's statement: ". . . what doth the Lord require of thee, but to do justly, and to love mercy, and to walk humbly with thy God." Nothing that science might discover about the factual world could possibly challenge, or even contact, this sublime watchword for a proper life:

> But what extent of knowledge, what acuteness of scientific criticism, can touch this, if anyone possessed of knowledge or acuteness could be absurd enough to make the attempt? Will the progress of research prove that justice is worthless and mercy hateful? Will it ever soften the bitter contrast between our actions and our aspirations, or show us the bounds of the universe, and bid us say, "Go to, now we comprehend the infinite"?

Conflicts develop not because science and religion vie intrinsically, but when one domain tries to usurp the proper space of the other. In that case, a successful defense of home territory is not only noble per se, but a distinct benefit to honorable people in both camps:

The antagonism of science is not to religion, but to the heathen survivals and the bad philosophy under which religion herself is often well-nigh crushed. And, for my part, I trust that this antagonism will never cease, but that to the end of time true science will continue to fulfill one of her most beneficent functions, that of relieving men from the burden of false science which is imposed upon them in the name of religion.

Gladstone responded with a volley of rhetoric. He began from the empyrean heights, pointing out that after so many years of parliamentary life he was a tired (if still grand) old man, and didn't know if he could muster the energy for this sort of thing anymore—particularly for such a nettlesome and trivial opponent as the merely academic Huxley:

> As I have lived for more than half a century in an atmosphere of contention, my stock of controversial fire has perhaps become abnormally low; while Professor Huxley, who has been inhabiting the Elysian regions of science . . . may be enjoying all the freshness of an unjaded appetite.

(Much of the fun in reading through this debate lies not in the forcefulness of arguments or in the mastery of prose by both combatants, but in the sallying and posturing of two old gamecocks [Huxley was sixty, Gladstone seventy-six in 1885] pulling out every trick from the rhetorical bag—the musty and almost shameful, the tried and true, and even a novel flourish here and there.)

But once Gladstone got going, that old spark fanned quite a flame. His denunciations spanned the gamut. Huxley's words, on the one hand, were almost too trivial to merit concern—one listens "to his denunciations . . . as one listens to distant thunders, with a sort of sense that after all they will do no great harm." On the other hand, Huxley's attack could not be more dangerous. "I object," Gladstone writes, "to all these exaggerations . . . as savoring of the spirit of the Inquisition, and as restraints on literary freedom."

Yet, when Gladstone got down to business, he could muster only a feeble response to Huxley's particulars. He did effectively combat Huxley's one weak argument—the third charge that all groups continue to generate new species, whatever the sequence of their initial appearance. Genesis, Gladstone replies, only discusses the order of origin, not the patterns of subsequent history:

> If we arrange the schools of Greek philosophy in numerical order, according to the dates of their inception, we do not mean that one expired before another was founded. If the archaeologist describes to us as successive in time the ages of stone, bronze and iron, he certainly does not mean that no kinds of stone implement were invented after bronze began.

But Gladstone came to grief on his major claim—the veracity of the Genesis sequence: water population, air population, land population, and humans. So he took refuge in the oldest ploy of debate. He made an end run around his disproved argument and changed the terms of discussion. Genesis doesn't refer to all animals, but "only to the formation of the objects and creatures with which early man was conversant." Therefore, toss out all invertebrates (although I cannot believe that cockroaches had no foothold, even in the Garden of Eden) and redefine the sequence of water, air, land, and mentality as fish, bird, mammal, and man. At least this sequence matches the geological record. But every attempt at redefinition brings new problems. How can the land population of the sixth day—"every living thing that creepeth upon the earth"—refer to mammals alone and exclude the reptiles that not only arose long before birds but also provided the dinosaurian lineage of their ancestry. This problem backed Gladstone into a corner, and he responded with the weak rejoinder that reptiles are disgusting and degenerate things, destined only for our inattention (despite Eve and the serpent): "Reptiles are a family fallen from greatness; instead of stamping on a great period of life its leading character, they merely skulked upon the earth." Yet Gladstone sensed his difficulty and admitted that while reptiles didn't disprove his story, they certainly didn't help him either: "However this case may be regarded, of course I cannot draw from it any support to my general contention."

Huxley, smelling victory, moved in for the kill. He derided Gladstone's slithery argument about reptiles and continued to highlight the evident discrepancies of Genesis, read literally, with geology ("Mr. Gladstone and Genesis," *The Nineteenth Century*, 1896).

> However reprehensible, and indeed contemptible, terres-
> trial reptiles may be, the only question which appears to me
> to be relevant to my argument is whether these creatures
> are or are not comprised under the denomination of "ev-
> erything that creepeth upon the ground."

Contrasting the approved tactics of Parliament and science, Hux-ley obliquely suggested that Gladstone might emulate the wise cobbler and stick to his last. Invoking reptiles once again, he wrote:

> Still, the wretched creatures stand there, importunately de-
> manding notice; and, however different may be the practice
> in that contentious atmosphere with which Mr. Gladstone
> expresses and laments his familiarity, in the atmosphere of
> science it really is of no avail whatever to shut one's eyes to
> facts, or to try to bury them out of sight under a tumulus of
> rhetoric.

Gladstone's new sequence of fish, bird, mammal, and man per-forms no better than his first attempt in reconciling Genesis and geology. The entire enterprise, Huxley asserts, is misguided, wrong, and useless: "Natural science appears to me to decline to have anything to do with either [of Gladstone's two sequences]; they are as wrong in detail as they are mistaken in principle." Genesis is a great work of literature and morality, not a treatise on natural history:

> The Pentateuchal story of the creation is simply a myth [in
> the literary, not pejorative, sense of the term]. I suppose it
> to be a hypothesis respecting the origin of the universe
> which some ancient thinker found himself able to reconcile
> with his knowledge, or what he thought was knowledge, of

the nature of things, and therefore assumed to be true. As such, I hold it to be not merely an interesting but a venerable monument of a stage in the mental progress of mankind.

Gladstone, who was soon to enjoy a fourth stint as prime minister, did not respond. The controversy then flickered, shifting from the pages of *The Nineteenth Century* to the letters column of the *Times*. Then it died for a while, only to be reborn from time to time ever since.

I find something enormously ironical in this old battle, fought by Huxley and Gladstone a century ago and by much lesser lights even today. It doesn't matter a damn because Huxley was right in asserting that correspondence between Genesis and the fossil record holds no significance for religion or for science. Still, I think that Gladstone and most modern purveyors of his argument have missed the essence of the kind of myth that Genesis 1 represents. Nothing could possibly be more vain or intemperate than a trip on these waters by someone lacking even a rudder or a paddle in any domain of appropriate expertise. Still, I do feel that when read simply for its underlying metaphor, the story of Genesis 1 does contradict Gladstone's fundamental premise. Gladstone's effort rests upon the notion that Genesis 1 is a tale about *addition* and linear sequence—God makes this, then this, and then this in a sensible order. Since Gladstone also views evolution and geology as a similar story of progress by accretion, reconciliation becomes possible. Gladstone is quite explicit about this form of story:

> Evolution is, to me, a series with development. And like series in mathematics, whether arithmetical or geometrical, it establishes in things an unbroken progression; it places each thing . . . in a distinct relation to every other thing, and makes each a witness to all that have preceded it, a prophecy of all that are to follow it.

But I can't read Genesis 1 as a story about linear addition at all. I think that its essential theme rests upon a different metaphor—*differentiation* rather than accretion. God creates a chaotic and formless *totality* at first, and then proceeds to make divisions within—to precipitate islands of stability and growing complexity from the vast, encompassing potential of an initial state. Consider the sequence of "days."

On day one, God makes two primary and orthogonal divisions: He separates heaven from earth, and light from darkness. But each category only represents a diffuse potential, containing no differentiated complexity. The earth is "without form and void"; and no sun, moon, or stars yet concentrate the division of light from darkness. On the second day, God consolidates the separation of heaven and earth by creating the firmament and calling it heaven. The third day is then devoted to differentiating the chaotic earth into its stable parts—land and sea. Land then develops further by bringing forth plants. (Does this indicate that the writer of Genesis treated life under a taxonomy very different from ours? Did he see plants as essentially of the earth and animals as something separate? Would he have held that plants have closer affinity with soil than with animals?) The fourth day does for the firmament what the third day accomplished for earth: heaven differentiates and light becomes concentrated into two great bodies, the sun and moon.

The fifth and sixth days are devoted to the creation of animal life, but again the intended metaphor may be differentiation rather than linear addition. On the fifth day, the sea and then the air bring forth their intended complexity of living forms. On the sixth day, the land follows suit. The animals are not simply placed by God in their proper places. Rather, the places themselves "bring forth" or differentiate their appropriate inhabitants at the appointed times.

The final result is a candy box of intricately sculpted pieces, with varying degrees of complexity. But how did the box arise? Did the candy maker just add items piece by piece, according to a prefigured plan—Gladstone's model of linear addition? Or did he start with the equivalent of a tray of fudge, and then make smaller and smaller divisions with his knife, decorating each piece as he cut by sculpting wondrous forms from the potential inherent in the original material? I read the story in this second manner. And if differentiation be the more appropriate metaphor, then Genesis cannot be matching Gladstone's linear view of evolution. The two stories rest on different premises of organization—addition and differentiation.*

But does life's history really match either of these two stories? Addition and differentiation are not mutually exclusive truths inherent in nature. They are schemata of organization for human thought, two among a strictly limited number of ways that we have devised to tell stories about nature's patterns. Battles have been fought in their names many times before, sometimes strictly within biology. Consider, for example, the early nineteenth century struggle in German embryology between one of the greatest of all natural scientists, Karl Ernst von Baer, who viewed development as a process of differentiation from general forms to specific structures, and the *Naturphilosophen* (nature philosophers) with their romantic conviction that all developmental processes (including embryology) must proceed by linear addition of complexity as spirit struggles to incarnate itself in the highest, human form (see Chapter 2 of my book *Ontogeny and Phylogeny,* Harvard University Press, 1977).

My conclusion may sound unexciting, even wishy-washy, but I think that evolution just says yes to both metaphors for different parts of its full complexity. Yes, truly novel structures do arise in temporal order—first fins, then legs, then hair, then language—and additive models describe part of the story well. Yes, the coding rules of DNA have not changed, and all of life's history differentiates from a potential inherent from the first. Is the history of Western song a linear progression of styles or the construction of more and more castles for a kingdom fully specified in original blueprints by notes of the scale and rules of composition?

Finally, and most important, the bankruptcy of Gladstone's effort lies best exposed in this strictly limited number of deep metaphors available to our understanding. Gladstone was wrong in critical detail, as Huxley so gleefully proved. But what if he had been entirely right? What if the Genesis sequence had been generally accurate in its broad brush? Would such a correspondence

---

*After writing this essay, I visited the cathedral of San Marco in Venice, and was pleased to note that the early medieval mosaics of the great creation dome (in the south end of the narthex) picture the events of the first six days as an explicit sequence of divisions with differentiation.

mean that God had dictated the Torah word by word? Of course not. How many possible stories can we tell? How many can we devise beyond addition and differentiation? Simultaneous creation? Top down appearance? Some, perhaps, but not many. So what if the Genesis scribe wrote his beautiful myth in one of the few conceivable and sensible ways—and if later scientific discoveries then established some fortuitous correspondences with his tale? Bats didn't know about extinct pterodactyls, but they still evolved wings that work in similar ways. The strictures of flying don't permit many other designs—just as the limited pathways from something small and simple to something big and complex don't allow many alternatives in underlying metaphor. Genesis and geology happen not to correspond very well. But it wouldn't mean much if they did—for we would only learn something about the limits to our storytelling, not even the whisper of a lesson about the nature and meaning of life or God.

Genesis and geology are sublimely different. William Jennings Bryan used to dismiss geology by arguing that he was only interested in the rock of ages, not the age of rocks. But in our tough world—not cleft for us, and offering no comfortable place to hide—I think we had better pay mighty close attention to both.

28 | William Jennings Bryan's Last Campaign

    I HAVE SEVERAL REASONS for choosing to celebrate our legal victory over "creation science" by trying to understand with sympathy the man who forged this long and painful episode in American history—William Jennings Bryan. In June 1987, the Supreme Court voided the last creationist statute by a decisive 7–2 vote, and then wrote their decision in a manner so clear, so strong, and so general that even the most ardent fundamentalists must admit the defeat of their legislative strategy against evolution. In so doing, the Court ended William Jennings Bryan's last campaign, the cause that he began just after World War I as his final legacy, and the battle that took both his glory and his life in Dayton, Tennessee, when, humiliated by Clarence Darrow, he died just a few days after the Scopes trial in 1925.

My reasons range across the domain of Bryan's own character. I could invoke rhetorical and epigrammatic expressions, the kind that Bryan, as America's greatest orator, laced so abundantly into his speeches—Churchill's motto for World War II, for example: "In victory: magnanimity." But I know that my main reason is personal, even folksy, the kind of one-to-one motivation that Bryan, in his persona as the Great Commoner, would have applauded. Two years ago, a colleague sent me an ancient tape of Bryan's voice. I expected to hear the pious and polished shoutings of an old stump master, all snake oil and orotund sophistry. Instead, I heard the most uncanny and friendly sweetness, high pitched, direct, and apparently sincere. Surely this man could not simply be dismissed, as by H. L. Mencken, reporting the Scopes trial for the Baltimore *Sun:* as "a tinpot Pope in the Coca-Cola belt."

I wanted to understand a man who could speak with such warmth, yet talk such yahoo nonsense about evolution. I wanted, above all, to resolve a paradox that has always cried out for some answer rooted in Bryan's psyche. How could this man, America's greatest populist reformer, become, late in life, her arch reactionary?

For it was Bryan who, just one year beyond the minimum age of thirty-five, won the Democratic presidential nomination in 1896 with his populist rallying cry for abolition of the gold standard: "You shall not press down upon the brow of labor this crown of thorns. You shall not crucify mankind upon a cross of gold." Bryan who ran twice more, and lost in noble campaigns for reform, particularly for Philippine independence and against American imperialism. Bryan, the pacifist who resigned as Wilson's secretary of state because he sought a more rigid neutrality in the First World War. Bryan who stood at the forefront of most progressive victories in his time: women's suffrage, the direct election of senators, the graduated income tax (no one loves it, but can you think of a fairer way?). How could this man have then joined forces with the cult of biblical literalism in an effort to purge religion of all liberality, and to stifle the same free thought that he had advocated in so many other contexts?

This paradox still intrudes upon us because Bryan forged a living legacy, not merely an issue for the mists and niceties of history. For without Bryan, there never would have been anti-evolution laws, never a Scopes trial, never a resurgence in our day, never a decade of frustration and essays for yours truly, never a Supreme Court decision to end the issue. Every one of Bryan's progressive triumphs would have occurred without him. He fought mightily and helped powerfully, but women would be voting today and we would be paying income tax if he had never been born. But the legislative attempt to curb evolution was his baby, and he pursued it with all his legendary demoniac fury. No one else in the ill-organized fundamentalist movement had the inclination, and surely no one else had the legal skill or political clout. Ironically, fundamentalist legislation against evolution is the only truly distinctive and enduring brand that Bryan placed

William Jennings Bryan on the stump. Taken during the presidential campaign of 1896. THE BETTMANN ARCHIVE.

upon American history. It was Bryan's movement that finally bit the dust in Washington in June of 1987.

The paradox of shifting allegiance is a recurring theme in literature about Bryan. His biography in the *Encyclopaedia Britannica* holds that the Scopes trial "proved to be inconsistent with many progressive causes he had championed for so long." One prominent biographer located his own motivation in trying to discover "what had transformed Bryan from a crusader for social and economic reform to a champion of anachronistic rural evangelism, cheap moral panaceas, and Florida real estate" (L. W. Levine, 1965).

Two major resolutions have been proposed. The first, clearly the majority view, holds that Bryan's last battle was inconsistent with, even a nullification of, all the populist campaigning that had gone before. Who ever said that a man must maintain an unchanging ideology throughout adulthood; and what tale of human psychology could be more familiar than the transition from crusading firebrand to diehard reactionary. Most biographies treat the Scopes trial as an inconsistent embarrassment, a sad and unsettling end. The title to the last chapter of almost every book about Bryan features the word "retreat" or "decline."

The minority view, gaining ground in recent biographies and clearly correct in my judgment, holds that Bryan never transformed or retreated, and that he viewed his last battle against evolution as an extension of the populist thinking that had inspired his life's work (in addition to Levine, cited previously, see Paolo E. Coletta, 1969, and W. H. Smith, 1975).

Bryan always insisted that his campaign against evolution meshed with his other struggles. I believe that we should take him at his word. He once told a cartoonist how to depict the harmony of his life's work: "If you would be entirely accurate you should represent me as using a double-barreled shotgun, firing one barrel at the elephant as he tries to enter the treasury and another at Darwinism—the monkey—as he tries to enter the schoolroom." And he said to the Presbyterian General Assembly in 1923: "There has not been a reform for 25 years that I did not support. And I am now engaged in the biggest reform of my life. I am trying to save the Christian Church from those who are trying to destroy her faith."

But how can a move to ban the teaching of evolution in public schools be deemed progressive? How did Bryan link his previous efforts to this new strategy? The answers lie in the history of Bryan's changing attitudes toward evolution.

Bryan had passed through a period of skepticism in college. (According to one story, more than slightly embroidered no doubt, he wrote to Robert G. Ingersoll for ammunition but, upon receiving only a pat reply from his secretary, reverted immediately to orthodoxy.) Still, though Bryan never supported evolution, he did not place opposition high on his agenda; in fact, he evinced a positive generosity and pluralism toward Darwin. In "The Prince of Peace," a speech that ranked second only to the "Cross of Gold" for popularity and frequency of repetition, Bryan said:

> I do not carry the doctrine of evolution as far as some do; I am not yet convinced that man is a lineal descendant of the lower animals. I do not mean to find fault with you if you want to accept the theory. . . . While I do not accept the Darwinian theory I shall not quarrel with you about it.

(Bryan, who certainly got around, first delivered this speech in 1904, and described it in his collected writings as "a lecture delivered at many Chautauqua and religious gatherings in America, also in Canada, Mexico, Tokyo, Manila, Bombay, Cairo, and Jerusalem.")

He persisted in this attitude of laissez-faire until World War I, when a series of events and conclusions prompted his transition from toleration to a burning zeal for expurgation. His arguments did not form a logical sequence, and were dead wrong in key particulars; but who can doubt the passion of his feelings?

We must acknowledge, before explicating the reasons for his shift, that Bryan was no intellectual. Please don't misconstrue this statement. I am not trying to snipe from the depth of Harvard elitism, but to understand. Bryan's dearest friends said as much. Bryan used his first-rate mind in ways that are intensely puzzling to trained scholars—and we cannot grasp his reasons without mentioning this point. The "Prince of Peace" displays a profound ignorance in places, as when Bryan defended the idea of miracles by stating that we continually break the law of gravity: "Do we not suspend or overcome the law of gravitation every day? Every time we move a foot or lift a weight we temporarily overcome one of the most universal of natural laws and yet the world is not disturbed." (Since Bryan gave this address hundreds of times, I assume that people tried to explain to him the difference between laws and events, or reminded him that without gravity, our raised foot would go off into space. I must conclude that he didn't care because the line conveyed a certain rhetorical oomph.) He also explicitly defended the suppression of understanding in the service of moral good:

> If you ask me if I understand everything in the Bible, I answer no, but if we will try to live up to what we do understand, we will be kept so busy doing good that we will not have time to worry about the passages which we do not understand.

This attitude continually puzzled his friends and provided fodder for his enemies. One detractor wrote: "By much talking and little thinking his mentality ran dry." To the same effect, but with kindness, a friend and supporter wrote that Bryan was "almost unable to think in the sense in which you and I use that word. Vague ideas floated through his mind but did not unite to form any system or crystallize into a definite practical position."

Bryan's long-standing approach to evolution rested upon a threefold error. First, he made the common mistake of confusing the fact of evolution with the Darwinian explanation of its mechanism. He then misinterpreted natural selection as a martial theory of survival by battle and destruction of enemies. Finally, he made the logical error of arguing that Darwinism implied the moral virtuousness of such deathly struggle. He wrote in the *Prince of Peace* (1904):

> The Darwinian theory represents man as reaching his present perfection by the operation of the law of hate—the merciless law by which the strong crowd out and kill off the weak. If this is the law of our development then, if there is any logic that can bind the human mind, we shall turn backward toward the beast in proportion as we substitute the law of love. I prefer to believe that love rather than hatred is the law of development.

And to the sociologist E. A. Ross, he said in 1906 that "such a conception of man's origin would weaken the cause of democracy and strengthen class pride and the power of wealth." He persisted in this uneasiness until World War I, when two events galvanized him into frenzied action. First, he learned that the martial

view of Darwinism had been invoked by most German intellectuals and military leaders as a justification for war and future domination. Second, he feared the growth of skepticism at home,
particularly as a source of possible moral weakness in the face of
German militarism.

Bryan united his previous doubts with these new fears into a
campaign against evolution in the classroom. We may question
the quality of his argument, but we cannot deny that he rooted his
own justifications in his lifelong zeal for progressive causes. In
this crucial sense, his last hurrah does not nullify, but rather continues, all the applause that came before. Consider the three
principal foci of his campaign, and their links to his populist past:

1. For peace and compassion against militarism and murder. "I
learned," Bryan wrote, "that it was Darwinism that was at the
basis of that damnable doctrine that might makes right that had
spread over Germany."

2. For fairness and justice toward farmers and workers and
against exploitation for monopoly and profit. Darwinism, Bryan
argued, had convinced so many entrepreneurs about the virtue of
personal gain that government now had to protect the weak and
poor from an explosion of anti-Christian moral decay: "In the
United States," he wrote,

> pure-food laws have become necessary to keep manufactur-
> ers from poisoning their customers; child labor laws have
> become necessary to keep employers from dwarfing the
> bodies, minds and souls of children; anti-trust laws have
> become necessary to keep overgrown corporations from
> strangling smaller competitors, and we are still in a death
> grapple with profiteers and gamblers in farm products.

3. For absolute rule of majority opinion against imposing
elites. Christian belief still enjoyed widespread majority support
in America, but college education was eroding a consensus that
once ensured compassion within democracy. Bryan cited studies
showing that only 15 percent of college male freshmen harbored
doubts about God, but that 40 percent of graduates had become
skeptics. Darwinism, and its immoral principle of domination by a
selfish elite, had fueled this skepticism. Bryan railed against this

insidious undermining of morality by a minority of intellectuals, and he vowed to fight fire with fire. If they worked through the classroom, he would respond in kind and ban their doctrine from the public schools. The majority of Americans did not accept human evolution, and had a democratic right to proscribe its teaching.

Let me pass on this third point. Bryan's contention strikes at the heart of academic freedom, and I have often treated this subject in previous essays. Scientific questions cannot be decided by majority vote. I merely record that Bryan embedded his curious argument in his own concept of populism. "The taxpayers," he wrote,

> have a right to say what shall be taught . . . to direct or dismiss those whom they employ as teachers and school authorities. . . . The hand that writes the paycheck rules the school, and a teacher has no right to teach that which his employers object to.

But what of Bryan's first two arguments about the influence of Darwinism on militarism and domestic exploitation? We detect the touch of the Philistine in Bryan's claims, but I think we must also admit that he had identified something deeply troubling—and that the fault does lie partly with scientists and their acolytes.

Bryan often stated that two books had fueled his transition from laissez-faire to vigorous action: *Headquarters Nights,* by Vernon L. Kellogg (1917), and *The Science of Power,* by Benjamin Kidd (1918). I fault Harvard University for many things, but all are overbalanced by its greatest glory—its unparalleled resources. Half an hour after I needed these obscure books if I ever hoped to hold the key to Bryan's activities, I had extracted them from the depths of Widener Library. I found them every bit as riveting as Bryan had, and I came to understand his fears, even to agree in part (though not, of course, with his analysis or his remedies).

Vernon Kellogg was an entomologist and perhaps the leading teacher of evolution in America (he held a professorship at Stanford and wrote a major textbook, *Evolution and Animal Life,* with his mentor and Darwin's leading disciple in America, David Starr Jordan, ichthyologist and president of Stanford University). During the First World War, while America maintained official neutrality, Kellogg became a high official in the international, nonpartisan effort for Belgian relief, a cause officially "tolerated" by Germany. In this capacity, he was posted at the headquarters of the German Great General Staff, the only American on the premises. Night after night, he listened to dinner discussions and arguments, sometimes in the presence of the Kaiser himself, among Germany's highest military officers. *Headquarters Nights* is Kellogg's account of these exchanges. He arrived in Europe as a pacifist, but left committed to the destruction of German militarism by force.

Kellogg was appalled, above all, at the justification for war and German supremacy advanced by these officers, many of whom had been university professors before the war. They not only proposed an evolutionary rationale but advocated a particularly crude form of natural selection, defined as inexorable, bloody battle:

> Professor von Flussen is Neo-Darwinian, as are most German biologists and natural philosophers. The creed of the *Allmacht* ["all might" or omnipotence] of a natural selection based on violent and competitive struggle is the gospel of the German intellectuals; all else is illusion and anathema. . . . This struggle not only must go on, for that is the natural law, but it should go on so that this natural law may work out in its cruel, inevitable way the salvation of the human species. . . . That human group which is in the most advanced evolutionary stage . . . should win in the struggle for existence, and this struggle should occur precisely that the various types may be tested, and the best not only preserved, but put in position to impose its kind of social organization—its *Kultur*—on the others, or, alternatively, to destroy and replace them. This is the disheartening kind of argument that I faced at Headquarters. . . . Add the additional assumption that the Germans are the chosen race, and that German social and political organization the chosen type of human community life, and you have a wall of logic and conviction that you can break your head against but can never shatter—by headwork. You long for the muscles of Samson.

Kellogg, of course, found in this argument only "horrible academic casuistry and . . . conviction that the individual is nothing, the state everything." Bryan conflated a perverse interpretation with the thing itself and affirmed his worst fears about the polluting power of evolution.

Benjamin Kidd was an English commentator highly respected in both academic and lay circles. His book *Social Evolution* (1894) was translated into a dozen languages and as widely read as anything ever published on the implications of evolution. In *The Science of Power* (1918), his posthumous work, Kidd constructs a curious argument that, in a very different way from Kellogg's, also fueled Bryan's dread. Kidd, a philosophical idealist, believed that life must move toward progress by rejecting material struggle and individual benefit. Like the German militarists, but to excoriate rather than to praise, Kidd identified Darwinism with these impediments to progress. In a chapter entitled "The Great Pagan Retrogression," Kidd presented a summary of his entire thesis:

1. Darwin's doctrine of force rekindled the most dangerous of human tendencies—our pagan soul, previously (but imperfectly) suppressed for centuries by Christianity and its doctrines of love and renunciation:

> The hold which the theories of the *Origin of Species* obtained on the popular mind in the West is one of the most remarkable incidents in the history of human thought. . . . Everywhere throughout civilization an almost inconceivable influence was given to the doctrine of force as the basis of legal authority. . . .
>
> For centuries the Western pagan had struggled with the ideals of a religion of subordination and renunciation coming to him from the past. For centuries he had been bored almost beyond endurance with ideals of the world presented to him by the Churches of Christendom. . . . But here was a conception of life which stirred to its depths the inheritance in him from past epochs of time. . . . This was the world which the masters of force comprehended. The pagan heart of the West sang within itself again in atavistic joy.

2. In England and America, Darwinism's worst influence lay in its justification for industrial exploitation as an expression of natural selection ("social Darwinism" in its pure form):

> The prevailing social system, born as it had been in struggle, and resting as it did in the last resort on war and on the toil of an excluded proletariat, appeared to have become clothed with a new and final kind of authority.

3. In Germany, Darwin's doctrine became a justification for war:

> Darwin's theories came to be openly set out in political and military textbooks as the full justification for war and highly organized schemes of national policy in which the doctrine of force became the doctrine of Right.

4. Civilization can only advance by integration: The essence of Darwinism is division by force for individual advantage. Social progress demands the "subordination of the individual to the universal" via "the iron ethic of Renunciation."

5. Civilization can only be victorious by suppressing our pagan soul and its Darwinian justification:

> It is the psychic and spiritual forces governing the social integration in which the individual is being subordinated to the universal which have become the winning forces in evolution.

This characterization of evolution has been asserted in many contexts for nearly 150 years—by German militarists, by Kidd, by hosts of the vicious and the duped, the self-serving and the well-meaning. But it remains deeply and appallingly wrong for three basic reasons.

1. Evolution means only that all organisms are united by ties of genealogical descent. This definition says nothing about the mechanism of evolutionary change: In principle, externally directed upward striving might work as well as the caricatured straw man of bloody Darwinian battle to the death. The objections, then, are to Darwin's theory of natural selection, not to evolution itself.

2. Darwin's theory of natural selection is an abstract argument about a metaphorical "struggle" to leave more offspring in subsequent generations, not a statement about murder and mayhem. Direct elimination of competitors is one pathway to Darwinian advantage, but another might reside in cooperation through social ties within a species or by symbiosis between species. For every act of killing and division, natural selection can also favor cooperation and integration in other circumstances. Nineteenth-century interpreters did generally favor a martial view of selection, but to every militarist, we may counterpose a Prince Kropotkin (see Essay 22), urging that the "real" Darwinism be recognized as a doctrine of integration and "mutual aid."

3. Whatever Darwinism represents on the playing fields of nature (and by representing both murder and cooperation at different times, it upholds neither as nature's principal way), Darwinism implies nothing about moral conduct. We do not find our moral values in the actions of nature. One might argue, as Thomas Henry Huxley did in his famous essay "Evolution and Ethics," that Darwinism embodies a law of battle, and that human morality must be defined as the discovery of an opposite path. Or one might argue, as grandson Julian did, that Darwinism is a law of cooperation and that moral conduct should follow nature. If two such brilliant and committed Darwinians could come to such opposite opinions about evolution and ethics, I can only conclude that Darwinism offers no moral guidance.

But Bryan made this common threefold error and continually characterized evolution as a doctrine of battle and destruction of the weak, a dogma that undermined any decent morality and deserved banishment from the classroom. In a rhetorical flourish near the end of his "Last Evolution Argument," the final speech that he prepared with great energy, but never had an opportunity to present at the Scopes trial, Bryan proclaimed:

> Again force and love meet face to face, and the question "What shall I do with Jesus?" must be answered. A bloody, brutal doctrine—Evolution—demands, as the rabble did nineteen hundred years ago, that He be crucified.

I wish I could stop here with a snide comment on Bryan as yahoo and a ringing defense for science's proper interpretation of Darwinism. But I cannot, for Bryan was right in one crucial way. Lord only knows, he understood precious little about science, and he wins no medals for logic of argument. But when he said that Darwinism had been widely protrayed as a defense of war, domination, and domestic exploitation, he was right. Scientists would not be to blame for this if we had always maintained proper caution in interpretation and proper humility in resisting the extension of our findings into inappropriate domains. But many of these insidious and harmful misinterpretations had been promoted by scientists. Several of the German generals who traded arguments with Kellogg had been university professors of biology.

Just one example from a striking source. In his "Last Evolution Argument," Bryan charged that evolutionists had misused science to present moral opinions about the social order as though they represented facts of nature.

> By paralyzing the hope of reform, it discourages those who labor for the improvement of man's condition. . . . Its only program for man is scientific breeding, a system under which a few supposedly superior intellects, self-appointed, would direct the mating and the movements of the mass of mankind—an impossible system!

I cannot fault Bryan here. One of the saddest chapters in all the history of science involves the extensive misuse of data to support biological determinism, the claim that social inequalities based on race, sex, or class cannot be altered because they reflect the innate and inferior genetic endowments of the disadvantaged (see my book *The Mismeasure of Man*). It is bad enough when scientists misidentify their own social preferences as facts of nature in their technical writings and even worse when writers of textbooks, particularly for elementary- and high-school students, promulgate these (or any) social doctrines as the objective findings of science.

Two years ago, I obtained a copy of the book that John Scopes used to teach evolution to the children of Dayton, Tennessee—*A Civic Biology*, by George William Hunter (1914). Many writers have looked into this book to read the section on evolution that Scopes taught and Bryan quoted. But I found something disturbing in another chapter that has eluded previous commentators—an egregious claim that science holds the moral answer to questions about mental retardation, or social poverty so misinterpreted. Hunter discusses the infamous Jukes and Kallikaks, the "classic," and false, cases once offered as canonical examples of how bad heredity runs in families. Under the heading "Parasitism and Its Cost to Society—the Remedy," he writes:

> Hundreds of families such as those described above exist today, spreading disease, immorality and crime to all parts of this country. The cost to society of such families is very severe. Just as certain animals or plants become parasitic on other plants or animals, these families have become parasitic on society. They not only do harm to others by corrupting, stealing or spreading disease, but they are actually protected and cared for by the state out of public money. Largely for them the poorhouse and the asylum exist. They take from society, but they give nothing in return. They are true parasites.
>
> If such people were lower animals, we would probably kill them off to prevent them from spreading. Humanity will not allow this, but we do have the remedy of separating the sexes in asylums or other places and in various ways preventing intermarriage and the possibilities of perpetuating such a low and degenerate race.

Bryan had the wrong solution, but he had correctly identified a problem!

Science is a discipline, and disciplines are exacting. All maintain rules of conduct and self-policing. All gain strength, respect, and acceptance by working honorably within their bounds and knowing when transgression upon other realms counts as hubris or folly. Science, as a discipline, tries to understand the factual state of nature and to explain and coordinate these data into general theories. Science teaches us many wonderful and disturbing things—facts that need weighing when we try to develop standards of conduct and ponder the great questions of morals and aesthetics. But science cannot answer these questions alone and cannot dictate social policy.

Scientists have power by virtue of the respect commanded by

the discipline. We may therefore be sorely tempted to misuse that power in furthering a personal prejudice or social goal—why not provide that extra oomph by extending the umbrella of science over a personal preference in ethics or politics? But we cannot, lest we lose the very respect that tempted us in the first place.

If this plea sounds like the conservative and pessimistic retrenching of a man on the verge of middle age, I reply that I advocate this care and restraint in order to demonstrate the enormous power of science. We live with poets and politicians, preachers and philosophers. All have their ways of knowing, and all are valid in their proper domains. The world is too complex and interesting for one way to hold all the answers. Besides, highfalutin morality aside, if we continue to overextend the boundaries of science, folks like Bryan will nail us properly for their own insidious purposes.

We should give the last word to Vernon Kellogg, the great teacher who understood the principle of strength in limits, and who listened with horror to the ugliest misuses of Darwinism. Kellogg properly taught in his textbook (with David Starr Jordan) that Darwinism cannot provide moral answers:

> Some men who call themselves pessimists because they cannot read good into the operations of nature forget that they cannot read evil. In morals the law of competition no more justifies personal, official, or national selfishness or brutality than the law of gravitation justifies the shooting of a bird.

Kellogg also possessed the cardinal trait lacked both by Bryan and by many of his evolutionary adversaries: humility in the face of our profound ignorance about nature's ways, combined with that greatest of all scientific privileges, the joy of the struggle to know. In his greatest book, *Darwinism Today* (1907), Kellogg wrote:

> We are ignorant, terribly, immensely ignorant. And our work is, to learn. To observe, to experiment, to tabulate, to induce, to deduce. Biology was never a clearer or more inviting field for fascinating, joyful, hopeful work.

Amen, brother!

Postscript

As I was writing this essay, I learned of the untimely death from cancer (at age forty-seven) of Federal Judge William R. Overton of Arkansas. Judge Overton presided and wrote the decision in *McLean* v. *Arkansas* (January 5, 1982), the key episode that led to our final victory in the Supreme Court in June 1987. In this decision, he struck down the Arkansas law mandating equal time for "creation science." This precedent encouraged Judge Duplantier to strike down the similar Louisiana law by summary judgment (without trial). The Supreme Court then affirmed this summary judgment in their 1987 decision. (Since Arkansas and Louisiana had passed the only anti-evolution statutes in the country, these decisions close the issue.) Judge Overton's brilliant and beautifully crafted decision is the finest legal document ever written about this question—far surpassing anything that the Scopes trial generated, or any document arising from the two Supreme Court cases (*Epperson* v. *Arkansas* of 1968, striking down Scopes-era laws that banned evolution outright, and the 1987 decision banning the "equal time" strategy). Judge Overton's definitions of science are so cogent and clearly expressed that we can use his words as a model for our own proceedings. *Science,* the leading journal of American professional science, published Judge Overton's decision verbatim as a major article.

I was a witness in *McLean* v. *Arkansas* (see Essay 21 in *Hen's Teeth and Horse's Toes*). I never spoke to Judge Overton personally, and I spent only part of a day in his courtroom. Yet, when I fell ill with cancer the next year, I learned from several sources that Judge Overton had heard and had inquired about my health from mutual acquaintances, asking that his best wishes be conveyed to me. I mourn the passing of this brilliant and compassionate man, and I dedicate this essay to his memory.

29 | An Essay on a Pig Roast

ON INDEPENDENCE DAY, 1919, in Toledo, Ohio, Jack Dempsey won the heavyweight crown by knocking out Jess Willard in round three. (Willard, the six-foot six-inch wheat farmer from Kansas, was "the great white hope" who, four years earlier in Havana, had finally KO'd Jack Johnson, the first black heavyweight champ, and primary thorn in the side of racist America.) Dempsey ruled the ring for seven years, until Gene Tunney whipped him in 1926.

Yet during Dempsey's domination of pugilism in its active mode, some mighty impressive fighters were squaring away on other, less physical but equally contentious turfs. One prominent battle occurred entirely within Dempsey's reign, beginning with William Jennings Bryan's decision in 1920 to launch a nationwide legislative campaign against the teaching of evolution and culminating in the Scopes trial of 1925. The main bout may have pitted Bryan against Clarence Darrow at the trial itself, but a preliminary skirmish in 1922, before any state legislature had passed an anti-evolution law, had brought two equally formidable foes together—Bryan again, but this time against Henry Fairfield Osborn, head of the American Museum of Natural History. In some respects, the Bryan-Osborn confrontation was more dramatic than the famous main event three years later. One can hardly imagine two more powerful but more different men: the arrogant, patrician, archconservative Osborn versus the folksy "Great Commoner" from Nebraska. Moreover, while Darrow maintained a certain respect based on genuine affection for

432

Bryan (or at least for his earlier greatness), I detect nothing but pure venom and contempt from Osborn.

The enemy within, as the old saying goes, is always more dangerous than the enemy without. An atheist might have laughed at Bryan or merely felt bewildered. But Osborn was a dedicated theist and a great paleontologist who viewed evolution as the finest expression of God's intent. For Osborn, Bryan was perverting both science and the highest notion of divinity. (Darrow later selected Osborn as one of his potential witnesses in the Scopes trial not only because Osborn was so prominent, socially as well as scientifically, but primarily because trial strategy dictated that religiously devout evolutionists could blunt Bryan's attack on science as intrinsically godless.)

On February 26, 1922, Bryan published an article in the Sunday *New York Times* to further his legislative campaign against the teaching of evolution. Bryan, showing some grasp of the traditional parries against Darwin, but constantly confusing doubts about the mechanism of natural selection with arguments against the fact of evolution itself, rested his case upon a supposed lack of direct evidence for the claims of science:

> The real question is, Did God use evolution as His plan? If it could be shown that man, instead of being made in the image of God, is a development of beasts we would have to accept it, regardless of its effect, for truth is truth and must prevail. But when there is no proof we have a right to consider the effect of the acceptance of an unsupported hypothesis.

The *Times,* having performed its civic duty by granting Bryan a platform, promptly invited Osborn to prepare a reply for the following Sunday. Osborn's answer, published on March 5 and reissued as a slim volume by Charles Scribner's Sons under the title *Evolution and Religion,* integrated two arguments into a single thesis: The direct, primarily geological evidence for evolution is overwhelming, and evolution is not incompatible with religion in any case. As a motto for his approach, and a challenge to Bryan from a source accepted by both men as unimpeachable, Osborn cited a passage from Job (12:8): ". . . speak to the earth, and it shall teach thee." When, on the eve of the Scopes trial, Osborn expanded his essay into a longer attack on Bryan, he dedicated the new book to John Scopes and chose a biting parody of Job for his title—*The Earth Speaks to Bryan* (Charles Scribner's Sons, 1925).

When a man poses such a direct challenge to an adversary, nothing could possibly be more satisfying than a quick confirmation from an unanticipated source. On February 25, 1922, just the day before Bryan's *Times* article, Harold J. Cook, a rancher and consulting geologist, had written to Osborn:

> I have had here, for some little time, a molar tooth from the Upper, or Hipparion phase of the Snake Creek Beds, that very closely approaches the human type. . . . Inasmuch as you are particularly interested in this problem and, in collaboration with Dr. Gregory and others, are in the best position of anyone to accurately determine the relationships of this tooth, if it can be done, I will be glad to send it on to you, should you care to examine and study it.

In those bygone days of an efficient two-penny post, Osborn probably received this letter on the very morning following Bryan's diatribe or, at most, a day or two later. Osborn obtained the tooth itself on March 14, and, with his usual precision (and precisely within the ten-word limit for the basic rate), promptly telegraphed Cook: "Tooth just arrived safely. Looks very promising. Will report immediately." Later that day, Osborn wrote to Cook:

> The instant your package arrived, I sat down with the tooth, in my window, and I said to myself: "It looks one hundred per cent anthropoid." I then took the tooth into Dr. Matthew's room and we have been comparing it with all the books, all the casts and all the drawings, with the conclusion that it is the last right upper molar tooth of some higher Primate. . . . We may cool down tomorrow, but it looks to me as if the first anthropoid ape of America has been found.

But Osborn's enthusiasm only warmed as he studied the tooth and considered the implications. The human fossil record had improved sufficiently to become a source of strength, rather than an embarrassment, to evolutionists, with Cro-Magnon and Neanderthal in Europe (not to mention the fraudulent Piltdown, then considered genuine and strongly supported by Osborn) and *Pithecanthropus* (now called *Homo erectus*) in East Asia. But no fossils of higher apes or human ancestors had ever been found anywhere in the Americas. This absence, in itself, posed no special problem to evolutionists. Humans had evolved in Asia or Africa, and the Americas were an isolated world, accessible primarily by a difficult route of migration over the Bering land bridge. Indeed, to this day, ancient humans are unknown in the New World, and most anthropologists accept a date of 20,000 years or considerably less (probably more like 11,000) for the first peopling of our hemisphere. Moreover, since these first immigrants were members of our stock, *Homo sapiens*, no ancestral species have ever been found—and none probably ever will—in the Americas.

Still, an American anthropoid would certainly be a coup for Osborn's argument that the earth spoke to Bryan in the language of evolution, not to mention the salutary value of a local product for the enduring themes of hoopla, chauvinism, and flag-waving.

Therefore, Osborn's delight—and his confidence—in this highly worn and eroded molar tooth only increased. Within a week or two, he was ready to proclaim the first momentous discovery of a fossil higher primate, perhaps even a direct human ancestor, in America. He honored our hemisphere in choosing the name *Hesperopithecus*, or "ape of the western world." On April 25, less than two months after Bryan's attack, Osborn presented *Hesperopithecus* in two simultaneous papers with the same title and different content: one in the prestigious *Proceedings of the National Academy of Sciences;* the other, containing figures and technical descriptions, in the *Novitates of the American Museum of Natural History*—"*Hesperopithecus*, the First Anthropoid Primate Found in America."

Hesperopithecus was good enough news in the abstract, but Osborn particularly exulted in the uncannily happy coincidences of both time and place. Cook had probably written his letter at the very moment that the compositors were setting Bryan's oratory in type. Moreover, for the crowning irony, *Hesperopithecus* had been found in Nebraska—home state of the Great Commoner! If God had permitted a paleontologist to invent a fossil with maximal potential to embarrass Bryan, no one could have bettered *Hesperopithecus* for rhetorical impact. Needless to say, this preciously ironical situation was not lost on Osborn, who inserted the following gloat of triumph into his article for the staid *Proceedings*—about as incongruous in this forum as the erotic poetry of the Song of Songs between Ecclesiastes and Isaiah.

> It has been suggested humorously that the animal should be named *Bryopithecus* after the most distinguished Primate which the State of Nebraska has thus far produced. It is certainly singular that this discovery is announced within six weeks of the day (March 5, 1922) that the author advised William Jennings Bryan to consult a certain passage in the Book of Job, "Speak to the earth and it shall teach thee," and it is a remarkable coincidence that the first earth to speak on this subject is the sandy earth of the Middle Pliocene Snake Creek deposits of western Nebraska.

Old Robert Burns certainly knew his stuff when he lamented the frequent unraveling of the best laid plans of mice and men. Unless you browse in the marginal genre of creationist tracts, you will probably not have encountered *Hesperopithecus* in anything written during the past fifty years (except, perhaps, as a cautionary sentence in a textbook or a paragraph on abandoned hopes in a treatise on the history of science). The reign of *Hesperopithecus* was brief and contentious. In 1927, Osborn's colleague William King Gregory, the man identified in Cook's original letter as the best-qualified expert on primate teeth, threw in the towel with an article in *Science:* "*Hesperopithecus* Apparently not an Ape nor a Man." Expeditions sent out by Osborn in the summers of 1925 and 1926 to collect more material of *Hesperopithecus,* and to test the hypothesis of primate affinity, had amassed a large series to complement the original tooth. But this abundance also doomed Osborn's interpretation—for the worn and eroded *Hesperopithecus* tooth, when compared with others in better and more diagnostic condition, clearly belonged not to a primate but to the extinct peccary *Prosthennops.*

One can hardly blame modern creationists for making hay of this brief but interesting episode in paleontology. After all, they're only getting their fair licks at Osborn, who used the original interpretation to ridicule and lambaste their erstwhile champion Bryan. I don't think I have ever read a modern creationist tract that doesn't feature the tale of "Nebraska Man" in a feint from our remarkable record of genuine human fossils, and an attempted KO of evolution with the one-two punch of Piltdown and *Hesperopithecus*. I write this essay to argue that Nebraska man tells a precisely opposite tale, one that should give creationists pause (though I do admit the purely rhetorical value of a proclaimed primate ancestor later exposed as a fossil pig).

The story of *Hesperopithecus* was certainly embarrassing to Osborn and Gregory in a personal sense, but the sequence of discovery, announcement, testing, and refutation—all done with admirable dispatch, clarity, and honesty—shows science working at its very best. Science is a method for testing claims about the natural world, not an immutable compendium of absolute truths. The fundamentalists, by "knowing" the answers before they start, and then forcing nature into the straitjacket of their discredited preconceptions, lie outside the domain of science—or of any honest intellectual inquiry. The actual story of *Hesperopithecus* could teach creationists a great deal about science as properly practiced if they chose to listen, rather than to scan the surface for cheap shots in the service of debate pursued for immediate advantage, rather than interest in truth.

When we seek a textbook case for the proper operation of science, the correction of certain error offers far more promise than the establishment of probable truth. Confirmed hunches, of course, are more upbeat than discredited hypotheses. Since the worst traditions of "popular" writing falsely equate instruction with sweetness and light, our promotional literature abounds with insipid tales in the heroic mode, although tough stories of disappointment and loss give deeper insight into a methodology that the celebrated philosopher of science Karl Popper once labeled as "conjecture and refutation."

Therefore, I propose that we reexamine the case of Nebraska Man, not as an embarrassment to avoid in polite company, but as an exemplar complete with lessons and ample scope for the primary ingredient of catharsis and popular appeal—the opportunity to laugh at one's self. Consider the story as a chronological sequence of five episodes:

1. *Proposal.* Harold Cook's fossil tooth came from a deposit

about 10 million years old and filled with mammals of Asiatic ancestry. Since paleontologists of Osborn's generation believed that humans and most other higher primates had evolved in Asia, the inclusion of a fossil ape in a fauna filled with Asian migrants seemed entirely reasonable. Osborn wrote to Cook a month before publication:

> The animal is certainly a new genus of anthropoid ape, probably an animal which wandered over here from Asia with the large south Asiatic element which has recently been discovered in our fauna. . . . It is one of the greatest surprises in the history of American paleontology.

Osborn then announced the discovery of *Hesperopithecus* in three publications—technical accounts in the *American Museum Novitates* (April 25, 1922) and in the British journal *Nature* (August 26, 1922), and a shorter notice in the *Proceedings of the National Academy of Sciences* (August 1922, based on an oral report delivered in April).

2. *Proper doubt and statement of alternatives.* Despite all the hoopla and later recrimination, Osborn never identified *Hesperopithecus* as a human ancestor. The tooth had been heavily worn during life, obliterating the distinctive pattern of cusps and crown. Considering both this extensive wear and the further geological erosion of the tooth following the death of its bearer, Osborn knew that he could make no certain identification. He did not cast his net of uncertainty widely enough, however, for he labeled *Hesperopithecus* as an undoubted higher primate. But he remained agnostic about the crucial issue of closer affinity with the various ape branches or the human twig of the primate evolutionary tree.

Osborn described the tooth of *Hesperopithecus* as "a second or third upper molar of the right side of a new genus and species of anthropoid." Osborn did lean toward human affinity, based both on the advice of his colleague Gregory (see point three below) and, no doubt, on personal hope and preference: "On the whole, we think its nearest resemblances are with . . . men rather than with apes." But his formal description left this crucial question entirely open:

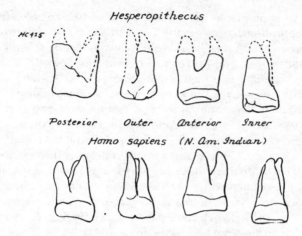

An illustration from Osborn's article of 1922, showing the strong similarity between worn teeth of *Hesperopithecus* and modern humans. NEG. NO. 2A17804. COURTESY DEPARTMENT OF LIBRARY SERVICES, AMERICAN MUSEUM OF NATURAL HISTORY.

The *Hesperopithecus* molar cannot be said to resemble any known type of human molar very closely. It is certainly not closely related to *Pithecanthropus erectus* in the structure of the molar crown. . . . It is therefore a new and independent type of Primate, and we must seek more material before we can determine its relationships.

3. *Encouragement of further study.* If Osborn had been grandstanding with evidence known to be worthless or indecipherable, he would have made his public point and then shut up after locking his useless or incriminating evidence away in a dark drawer in the back room of a large museum collection. Osborn proceeded in exactly the opposite way. He did everything possible to encourage further study and debate, hoping to resolve his own strong uncertainties. (Osborn, by the way, was probably the most pompous, self-assured S.O.B. in the history of American paleontology, a regal patrician secure in his birthright, rather than a scrappy, self-made man. He once published a book devoted en-

tirely to photographs of his medals and awards and to a list of his publications; as an excuse for such vanity, he claimed that he harbored only a selfless desire to inspire young scientists by illustrating the potential rewards of a fine profession. "Osborn stories" are still told by the score wherever vertebrate paleontologists congregate. And when a man's anecdotes outlive him by more than half a century, you know that he was larger than life. Thus, the real news about *Hesperopithecus* must be that, for once, Osborn was expressing genuine puzzlement and uncertainty.)

In any case, Osborn reached out to colleagues throughout the world. He made numerous casts of *Hesperopithecus* and sent them to twenty-six universities and museums in Europe and North America. As a result, he was flooded with alternative interpretations from the world's leading paleoanthropologists. He received sharp criticisms from both sides: from Arthur Smith Woodward, describer of Piltdown, who thought that *Hesperopithecus* was a bear (and I don't mean metaphorically), and from G. Elliot Smith, another "hero" of Piltdown, who became too enthusiastic about the humanity of Osborn's tooth, causing considerable later embarrassment and providing creationists with their "hook." Osborn tried to rein both sides in, beginning his *Nature* article with these words:

> Every discovery directly or indirectly relating to the prehistory of man attracts world-wide attention and is apt to be received either with too great optimism or with too great incredulity. One of my friends, Prof. G. Elliot Smith, has perhaps shown too great optimism in his most interesting newspaper and magazine articles on *Hesperopithecus,* while another of my friends, Dr. A. Smith Woodward, has shown too much incredulity.

Moreover, Osborn immediately enlisted his colleague W. K. Gregory, the acknowledged local expert on primate teeth, to prepare a more extensive study of *Hesperopithecus,* including a formal comparison of the tooth with molars of all great apes and human fossils. Gregory responded with two detailed, technical articles, both published in 1923 with the collaboration of Milo Hellman.

Gregory followed Osborn in caution and legitimate expression of doubt. He began his first article by dividing the characters of the tooth into three categories: those due to wear, to subsequent erosion, and to the genuine taxonomic uniqueness of *Hesperopithecus*. Since the first two categories, representing information lost, tended to overwhelm the last domain of diagnostic biology, Gregory could reach no conclusion beyond a basic placement among the higher primates:

> The type of *Hesperopithecus haroldcookii* represents a hitherto unknown form of higher primates. It combines characters seen in the molars of the chimpanzee, of *Pithecanthropus,* and of man, but, in view of the extremely worn and eroded state of the crown, it is hardly safe to affirm more than that *Hesperopithecus* was structurally related to all three.

In the second and longer article, Gregory and Hellman stuck their necks out a bit more—but in opposite directions. Hellman opted for the human side; Gregory for affinity with "the gorilla-chimpanzee group."

4. *Gathering of additional data.* Osborn knew, of course, that a worn and eroded tooth would never resolve the dilemma of *Hesperopithecus,* no matter how many casts were made or how many paleontologists peered down their microscopes. The answers lay in more data buried in the sands of Nebraska, and Osborn pledged, in his diatribe against Bryan, to make the earth speak further:

> What shall we do with the Nebraska tooth? Shall we destroy it because it jars our long preconceived notion that the family of manlike apes never reached the Western world, or shall we endeavor to interpret it, to discover its real relationship to the apes of Asia and of the more remote Africa. Or shall we continue our excavations, difficult and baffling as they are, in the confident hope, inspired by the admonition of Job, that if we keep on speaking to the earth we shall in time have a more audible and distinct reply [from *The Earth Speaks to Bryan,* p. 43].

To his professional audiences in *Nature,* Osborn made the same pledge with more detail: "We are this season renewing the search with great vigor and expect to run every shovelful of loose river sand which comprises the deposit through a sieve of mesh fine enough to arrest such small objects as these teeth."

Thus, in the summers of 1925 and 1926, Osborn sent a collecting expedition, led by Albert Thomson, to the Snake Creek beds of Nebraska. Several famous paleontologists visited the site and pitched in, including Barnum Brown, the great dinosaur collector; Othenio Abel of Vienna (a dark figure who vitiated the memory of his fine paleontological work by later activity in the Austrian Nazi party); and Osborn himself. They found abundant material to answer their doubts. The earth spoke both audibly and distinctly, but not in the tones that Osborn had anticipated.

5. *Retraction.* After all this buildup and detail, the denouement can only be described as brief, simple, and conclusive. The further expeditions were blessed with success. Abundant new specimens destroyed Osborn's dream for two reasons that could scarcely be challenged. First, the new specimens formed a series from teeth worn as profoundly as *Hesperopithecus* to others of the same species with crown and cusps intact. The diagnostic pattern of the unworn teeth proclaimed pig rather than primate. Second, the unworn teeth could not be distinguished from premolars firmly residing in a peccary's palate found during a previous expedition. Osborn, who was never praised for a charitable nature, simply shut up and never mentioned *Hesperopithecus* again in his numerous succeeding articles on human ancestry. He had enjoyed the glory, but he let Gregory take the heat in a forthright retraction published in *Science* (December 16, 1927):

> Among other material the expedition secured a series of specimens which have led the writer to doubt his former identification of the type as the upper molar of an extinct primate, and to suspect that the type specimen of *Hesperopithecus haroldcookii* may be an upper premolar of a species of *Prosthennops,* an extinct genus related to modern peccaries.

Why should the detractors of science still be drawing such mileage from this simple story of a hypothesis swiftly refuted by science working well? I would divide the reasons into red herrings and a smaller number of allowable points. The red herrings all center on rhetorical peculiarities that anyone skilled in debate could use to advantage. (Debate, remember, is an art form dedicated to the winning of arguments. Truth is one possible weapon, rarely the best, in such an enterprise.) Consider three good lines:

1. "How can you believe those evolutionists if they can make monkeys out of themselves by calling a pig a monkey?" As a trope of rhetoric, given the metaphorical status of pigs in our culture, the true affinity of *Hesperopithecus* became a blessing for creationists. What could possibly sound more foolish than the misidentification of a pig as a primate. My side might have been better off if *Hesperopithecus* had been, say, a deer or an antelope (both members of the order Artiodactyla, along with pigs, and therefore equally far from primates).

Yet anyone who has studied the dental anatomy of mammals knows immediately that this seemingly implausible mix-up of pig for primate is not only easy to understand but represents one of the classic and recurring confusions of the profession. The cheek teeth of pigs and humans are astonishingly and uncannily similar. (I well remember mixing them up more than once in my course on mammalian paleontology, long before I had ever heard the story of *Hesperopithecus.*) Unworn teeth can be told apart by details of the cusps, but isolated and abraded teeth of older animals are very difficult to distinguish. The *Hesperopithecus* tooth, worn so flat and nearly to the roots, was a prime candidate for just such a misidentification.

A wonderfully ironic footnote to this point was unearthed by John Wolf and James S. Mellett in an excellent article on Nebraska Man that served as the basis for my researches (see bibliography). In 1909, the genus *Prosthennops* was described by W. D. Matthew, Osborn's other paleontological colleague at the American Museum of Natural History, and—guess who—the same Harold Cook who would find *Hesperopithecus* ten years later. They explicitly warned their colleagues about the possible confusion of these peccary teeth with the dentition of primates:

> The anterior molars and premolars of this genus of peccaries show a startling resemblance to the teeth of Anthropoidea, and might well be mistaken for them by anyone not familiar with the dentition of Miocene peccaries.

2. "How can you believe those evolutionists if they can base an identification on a single worn tooth?" William Jennings Bryan,

the wily old lawyer, remarked: "These men would destroy the Bible on evidence that would not convict a habitual criminal of a misdemeanor."

My rejoinder may seem like a cavil, but it really isn't. Harold Cook did send but a single tooth to Osborn. (I do not know why he had not heeded his own previous warning of 1909. My guess would be that Cook played no part in writing the manuscript and that Matthew had been sole author of the statement. An old and admirable tradition grants joint authorship to amateur collectors who often find the material that professionals then exploit and describe. Matthew was the pro, Cook the experienced and sharp-eyed local collector.) Osborn sought comparative material in the Museum's collection of fossil mammals and located a very similar tooth found in the same geological strata in 1908. He added this second tooth to the sample and based the genus *Hesperopithecus* on both specimens. (This second tooth had been found by W. D. Matthew, and we must again raise the question of why Matthew didn't heed his own warning of 1909 about mixing up primates and peccaries. For Osborn showed both teeth to Matthew and won his assent for a probable primate identification. In his original description, Osborn wrote of this second tooth: "The specimen belonged to an aged animal and is so water-worn that Doctor Matthew, while inclined to regard it as a primate, did not venture to describe it.")

Thus the old canard about basing a human reconstruction on a single tooth is false. The sample of *Hesperopithecus* included two teeth from the start. You might say that two is only minimally better than one, and still so far from a whole animal that any conclusion must be risible. Not so. One of anything can be a mistake, an oddball, an isolated peculiarity; two, on the other hand, is the beginning of a pattern. Second specimens always provide a great increment of respect. The Piltdown fraud, for example, did not take hold until the forgers concocted a second specimen.

3. "How can you believe those evolutionists if they reconstruct an entire man—hair, skin, and all—from a single tooth?" On this issue, Osborn and Gregory were unjustly sandbagged by an over-zealous colleague. In England, G. Elliot Smith collaborated with the well-known scientific artist Amedee Forestier to produce a graphic reconstruction of a *Hesperopithecus* couple in a forest sur-

The infamous restoration of *Hesperopithecus* published in the *Illustrated London News* in 1922. NEG. NO. 2A17487. COURTESY DEPARTMENT OF LIBRARY SERVICES, AMERICAN MUSEUM OF NATURAL HISTORY.

rounded by other members of the Snake Creek fauna. Forestier, of course, could learn nothing from the tooth and actually based his reconstruction on the conventional rendering of *Pithecanthropus,* or Java man.

Forestier's figure is the one ridiculed and reproduced by creationists, and who can blame them? The attempt to reconstruct an entire creature from a single tooth is absolute folly—especially in this case when the authors of *Hesperopithecus* had declined to decide whether their creature was ape or human. Osborn had explicitly warned against such an attempt by pointing out how organs evolve at different rates, and how teeth of one type can be found in bodies of a different form. (Ironically, he cited Piltdown as an example of this phenomenon, arguing that, by teeth alone, the "man" would have been called an ape. How prescient in retrospect, since Piltdown is a fraud made of orangutan teeth and a human skull.)

Thus, Osborn explicitly repudiated the major debating point continually raised by modern creationists—the nonsense of reconstructing an entire creature from a single tooth. He said so obliquely and with gentle satire in his technical article for *Nature*, complaining that G. E. Smith had shown "too great optimism in his most interesting newspaper and magazine articles on *Hesperopithecus*." The *New York Times* reported a more direct quotation: "Such a drawing or 'reconstruction' would doubtless be only a figment of the imagination of no scientific value, and undoubtedly inaccurate."

Among the smaller number of allowable points, I can hardly blame creationists for gloating over the propaganda value of this story, especially since Osborn had so shamelessly used the original report to tweak Bryan. Tit for tat.

I can specify only one possibly legitimate point of criticism against Osborn and Gregory. Perhaps they were hasty. Perhaps they should have waited and not published so quickly. Perhaps they should have sent out their later expedition before committing anything to writing, for then the teeth would have been officially identified as peccaries first, last, and always. Perhaps they proceeded too rapidly because they couldn't resist such a nifty opportunity to score a rhetorical point at Bryan's expense. I am not bothered by the small sample of only two teeth. Single teeth, when well preserved, can be absolutely diagnostic of a broad taxonomic group. The argument for caution lay in the worn and eroded character of both premolars. Matthew had left the second tooth of 1908 in a museum drawer; why hadn't Osborn shown similar restraint?

But look at the case from a different angle. The resolution of *Hesperopithecus* may have been personally embarrassing for Osborn and Gregory, but the denouement was only invigorating and positive for the institution of science. A puzzle had been noted and swiftly solved, though not in the manner anticipated by the original authors. In fact, I would argue that Osborn's decision to publish, however poor his evidence and tentative his conclusions, was the most positive step he could have taken to secure a resolution. The published descriptions were properly cautious and noncommittal. They focused attention on the specimens, provided a series of good illustrations and measurements, provoked a rash of hypotheses for interpretation, and inspired the subsequent study and collection that soon resolved the issue. If Osborn had left the molar in a museum drawer, as Matthew had for the second tooth found in 1908, persistent anomaly would have been the only outcome. Conjecture and refutation is a chancy game with more losers than winners.

I have used the word *irony* too may times in this essay, for the story of *Hesperopithecus* is awash in this quintessential consequence of human foibles. But I must beg your indulgence for one last round. As their major pitch, modern fundamentalists argue that their brand of biblical literalism represents a genuine discipline called "scientific creationism." They use the case of Nebraska Man, in their rhetorical version, to bolster this claim, by arguing that conventional science is too foolish to merit the name and that the torch should pass to them.

As the greatest irony of all, they could use the story of *Hesperopithecus,* if they understood it properly, to advance their general argument. Instead, they focus on their usual ridicule and rhetoric, thereby showing their true stripes even more clearly. The real message of *Hesperopithecus* proclaims that science moves forward by admitting and correcting its errors. If creationists really wanted to ape the procedures of science, they would take this theme to heart. They would hold up their most ballyhooed, and now most thoroughly discredited, empirical claim—the coexistence of dinosaur and human footprints in the Paluxy Creek beds near Dallas—and publicly announce their error and its welcome correction. (The supposed human footprints turn out to be either random depressions in the hummocky limestone surface or partial dinosaur heel prints that vaguely resemble a human foot when the dinosaur toe strikes are not preserved.) But the world of creationists is too imbued with irrefutable dogma, and they don't seem able even to grasp enough about science to put up a good show in imitation.

I can hardly expect them to seek advice from me. May they, therefore, learn the virtue of admitting error from their favorite source of authority, a work so full of moral wisdom and intellectual value that such a theme of basic honesty must win special prominence. I remind my adversaries, in the wonderful mixed metaphors of Proverbs (25:11,14), that "a word fitly spoken is like apples of gold in pictures of silver. . . . Whoso boasteth himself of a false gift is like clouds and wind without rain."

30 | Justice Scalia's Misunderstanding

CHARLES LYELL, defending both his version of geology and his designation of James Hutton as its intellectual father, described Richard Kirwan as a man "who possessed much greater authority in the scientific world than he was entitled by his talents to enjoy."

Kirwan, chemist, mineralogist, and president of the Royal Academy of Dublin, did not incur Lyell's wrath for a mere scientific disagreement, but for saddling Hutton with the most serious indictment of all—atheism and impiety. Kirwan based his accusations on the unlikely charge that Hutton had placed the earth's origin beyond the domain of what science could consider or (in a stronger claim) had even denied that a point of origin could be inferred at all. Kirwan wrote in 1799:

> Recent experience has shown that the obscurity in which the philosophical knowledge of this [original] state has hitherto been involved, has proved too favorable to the structure of various systems of atheism or infidelity, as these have been in their turn to turbulence and immorality, not to endeavor to dispel it by all the lights which modern geological researches have struck out. Thus it will be found that geology naturally ripens . . . into religion, as this does into morality.

In our more secular age, we may fail to grasp the incendiary character of such a charge at the end of the eighteenth century, when intellectual respectability in Britain absolutely demanded an affirmation of religious fealty, and when fear of spreading revolution from France and America equated any departure from orthodoxy with encouragement of social anarchy. Calling someone an atheist in those best and worst of all times invited the same predictable reaction as asking Cyrano how many sparrows had perched up there or standing up in a Boston bar and announcing that DiMaggio was a better hitter than Williams.

Thus, Hutton's champions leaped to his defense, first his contemporary and Boswell, John Playfair, who wrote (in 1802) that

> such poisoned weapons as he [Kirwan] was preparing to use, are hardly ever allowable in scientific contest, as having a less direct tendency to overthrow the system, than to hurt the person of an adversary, and to wound, perhaps incurably, his mind, his reputation, or his peace.

Thirty years later, Charles Lyell was still fuming:

> We cannot estimate the malevolence of such a persecution, by the pain which similar insinuations might now inflict; for although charges of infidelity and atheism must always be odious, they were injurious in the extreme at that moment of political excitement [*Principles of Geology*, 1830].

(Indeed, Kirwan noted that his book had been ready for the printers in 1798 but had been delayed for a year by "the confusion arising from the rebellion then raging in Ireland"—the great Irish peasant revolt of 1798, squelched by Viscount Castlereagh, uncle of Darwin's Captain FitzRoy [see Essay 1 for much more on Castlereagh].)

Kirwan's accusation centered upon the last sentence of Hutton's *Theory of the Earth* (original version of 1788)—the most famous words ever written by a geologist (quoted in all textbooks, and often emblazoned on the coffee mugs and T-shirts of my colleagues):

> The result, therefore, of our present enquiry is, that we find no vestige of a beginning—no prospect of an end.

Kirwan interpreted both this motto, and Hutton's entire argument, as a claim for the earth's eternity (or at least as a statement of necessary agnosticism about the nature of its origin). But if the earth be eternal, then God did not make it. And if we need no God to fashion our planet, then do we need him at all? Even the weaker version of Hutton as agnostic about the earth's origin supported a charge of atheism in Kirwan's view—for if we cannot know that God made the earth at a certain time, then biblical authority is dethroned, and we must wallow in uncertainty about the one matter that demands our total confidence.

It is, I suppose, a testimony to human carelessness and to our tendency to substitute quips for analysis that so many key phrases, the mottoes of our social mythology, have standard interpretations quite contrary to their intended meanings. Kirwan's reading has prevailed. Most geologists still think that Hutton was advocating an earth of unlimited duration—though we now view such a claim as heroic rather than impious.

Yet Kirwan's charge was more than merely vicious—it was dead wrong. Moreover, in understanding why Kirwan erred (and why we still do), and in recovering what Hutton really meant, we illustrate perhaps the most important principle that we can state about science as a way of knowing. Our failure to grasp the principle underlies much public misperception about science. In particular, Justice Scalia's recent dissent in the Louisiana "creation science" case rests upon this error in discussing the character of evolutionary arguments. We all rejoiced when the Supreme Court ended a long episode in American history and voided the last law that would have forced teachers to "balance" instruction in evolution with fundamentalist biblical literalism masquerading under the oxymoron "creation science." I now add a tiny hurrah in postscript by pointing out that the dissenting argument rests, in large part, upon a misunderstanding of science.

Hutton replied to Kirwan's original attack by expanding his 1788 treatise into a cumbersome work, *The Theory of the Earth* (1795). With forty-page quotations in French and repetitive, involuted justifications, Hutton's new work condemned his theory to unreadability. Fortunately, his friend John Playfair, a mathematician and outstanding prose stylist, composed the most elegant pony ever written and published his *Illustrations of the Huttonian Theory of the Earth* in 1802. Playfair presents a two-part refutation for Kirwan's charge of atheism.

1. Hutton neither argued for the earth's eternity nor claimed

that we could say nothing about its origin. In his greatest contribution, Hutton tried to develop a cyclical theory for the history of the earth's surface, a notion to match the Newtonian vision of continuous planetary revolution about the sun. The materials of the earth's surface, he argued, passed through a cycle of perfect repetition in broad scale. Consider the three major stages. First, mountains erode and their products are accumulated as thick sequences of layered sediments in the ocean. Second, sediments consolidate and their weight melts the lower layers, forming magmas. Third, the pressure of these magmas forces the sediments up to form new mountains (with solidified magmas at their core), while the old, eroded continents become new ocean basins. The cycle then starts again as mountains (at the site of old oceans) shed their sediments into ocean basins (at the site of old continents). Land and sea change positions in an endless dance, but the earth itself remains fundamentally the same. Playfair writes:

> It is the peculiar excellence of this theory . . . that it makes the decay of one part subservient to the restoration of another, and gives stability to the whole, not by perpetuating individuals, but by reproducing them in succession.

We can easily grasp the revolutionary nature of this theory for concepts of time. Most previous geologies had envisioned an earth of short duration, moving in a single irreversible direction, as its original mountains eroded into the sea. By supplying a "concept of repair" in his view of magmas as uplifting forces, Hutton burst the strictures of time. No more did continents erode once into oblivion; they could form anew from the products of their own decay and the earth could cycle on and on.

This cyclical theory has engendered the false view that Hutton considered the earth eternal. True, the mechanics of the cycle provide no insight into beginnings or endings, for laws of the cycle can only produce a continuous repetition and therefore contain no notion of birth, death, or even of aging. But this conclusion only specifies that laws of nature's *present order* cannot specify beginnings or ends. Beginnings and ends may exist—in fact, Hutton considered a concept of starts and stops absolutely essential for any rational understanding—but we cannot learn anything about this vital subject from nature's present laws. Hutton, who was a devoted theist despite Kirwan's charge, argued that God had made a beginning, and would ordain an end, by summoning forces outside the current order of nature. For the stable period between, he had ordained laws that impart no directionality and therefore permit no insight into beginnings and ends.

Note how carefully Hutton chose the words of his celebrated motto. "No *vestige* of a beginning" because the earth has been through so many cycles since then that all traces of an original state have vanished. But the earth certainly had an original state. "No *prospect* of an end" because the current laws of nature provide no insight into a termination that must surely occur. Playfair describes Hutton's view of God:

> He may put an end, as he no doubt gave a beginning, to the present system, at some determinate period; but we may safely conclude, that this great catastrophe will not be brought about by any of the laws now existing, and that it is not indicated by any thing which we perceive.

2. Hutton did not view our inability to specify beginnings and ends as a baleful limitation of science but as a powerful affirmation of proper scientific methodology. Let theology deal with ultimate origins, and let science be the art of the empirically soluble.

The British tradition of speculative geology—from Burnet, Whiston, and Woodward in the late seventeenth century to Kirwan himself at the tail end of the eighteenth—had focused upon reconstructions of the earth's origin, primarily to justify the Mosaic narrative as scientifically plausible. Hutton argued that such attempts could not qualify as proper science, for they could only produce speculations about a distant past devoid of evidence to test any assertion (no vestige of a beginning). The subject of origins may be vital and fascinating, far more compelling than the humdrum of quotidian forces that drive the present cycle of uplift, erosion, deposition, and consolidation. But science is not speculation about unattainable ultimates; it is a way of knowing based upon laws now in operation and results subject to observation and inference. We acknowledge limits in order to proceed with power and confidence.

Hutton therefore attacked the old tradition of speculation about the earth's origin as an exercise in futile unprovability. Better to focus upon what we can know and test, leaving aside what the methods of science cannot touch, however fascinating the subject. Playfair stresses this theme more forcefully (and more often) than any other in his exposition of Hutton's theory. He regards Hutton's treatise as, above all, an elegant statement of proper scientific methodology—and he locates Hutton's wisdom primarily in his friend's decision to eschew the subject of ultimate origins and to focus on the earth's present operation. Playfair begins by criticizing the old manner of theorizing:

> The sole object of such theories has hitherto been, to explain the manner in which the present laws of the mineral kingdom were first established, or began to exist, without treating of the manner in which they now proceed.

He then evaluates this puerile strategy in one of his best prose flourishes:

> The absurdity of such an undertaking admits of no apology; and the smile which it might excite, if addressed merely to the fancy, gives place to indignation when it assumes the air of philosophic investigation.

Hutton, on the other hand, established the basis of a proper geological science by avoiding subjects "altogether beyond the limits of philosophical investigation." Hutton's explorations "never extended to the first origin of substances, but were confined entirely to their changes." Playfair elaborated:

> He has indeed no where treated of the first origin of any of the earths, or of any substance whatsoever, but only of the transformations which bodies have undergone since the present laws of nature were established. He considered this last as all that a science, built on experiment and observation, can possibly extend to; and willingly left, to more presumptuous inquirers, the task of carrying their reasonings beyond the boundaries of nature.

Finally, to Kirwan's charge that Hutton had limited science by his "evasion" of origins, Playfair responded that his friend had strengthened science by his positive program of studying what could be resolved:

> Instead of an *evasion,* therefore, any one who considers the subject fairly, will see, in Dr. Hutton's reasoning, nothing but the caution of a philosopher, who wisely confines his theory within the same limits by which nature has confined his experience and observation.

This all happened a long time ago, and in a context foreign to our concerns. But Hutton's methodological wisdom, and Playfair's eloquent warning, could not be more relevant today—for basic principles of empirical science have an underlying generality that transcends time. Practicing scientists have largely (but not always) imbibed Hutton's wisdom about restricting inquiry to questions that can be answered. But Kirwan's error of equating the best in science with the biggest questions about ultimate meanings continues to be the most common of popular misunderstandings.

I have written these monthly essays for nearly twenty years, and they have brought me an enormous correspondence from nonprofessionals about all aspects of science. From sheer volume, I obtain a pretty good sense of strengths and weaknesses in public perceptions. I have found that one common misconception surpasses all others. People will write, telling me that they have developed a revolutionary theory, one that will expand the boundaries of science. These theories, usually described in several pages of single-spaced typescript, are speculations about the deepest ultimate questions we can ask—what is the nature of life? the origin of the universe? the beginning of time?

But thoughts are cheap. Any person of intelligence can devise his half dozen before breakfast. Scientists can also spin out ideas about ultimates. We don't (or, rather, we confine them to our private thoughts) because we cannot devise ways to test them, to decide whether they are right or wrong. What good to science is a lovely idea that cannot, as a matter of principle, ever be affirmed or denied?

The following homily may seem paradoxical, but it embodies

Hutton's wisdom: The best science often proceeds by putting aside the overarching generality and focusing instead on a smaller question that can be reliably answered. In so doing, scientists show their intuitive feel for the fruitful, not their narrowness or paltriness of spirit. In this way we sneak up on big questions that only repel us if we try to engulf them in one fell speculation. Newton could not discover the nature of gravity, but he could devise a mathematics that unified the motion of a carriage with the revolution of the moon (and the drop of an apple). Darwin never tried to grasp the meaning of life (or even the manner of its origin on our planet), but he did develop a powerful theory to explain its manner of change through time. Hutton did not discover how our earth originated, but he developed some powerful and testable ideas about how it ticked. You might almost define a good scientist as a person with the horse sense to discern the largest answerable question—and to shun useless issues that sound grander.

Hutton's positive principle of restriction to the doable also defines the domain and procedures of evolutionary biology, my own discipline. Evolution is not the study of life's ultimate origin as a path toward discerning its deepest meaning. Evolution, in fact, is not the study of origins at all. Even the more restricted (and scientifically permissible) question of life's origin on our earth lies outside its domain. (This interesting problem, I suspect, falls primarily within the purview of chemistry and the physics of self-organizing systems.) Evolution studies the pathways and mechanisms of organic change following the origin of life. Not exactly a shabby subject either—what with such resolvable questions as "How, when, and where did humans evolve?"; "How do mass extinction, continental drift, competition among species, climatic change, and inherited constraints of form and development interact to influence the manner and rate of evolutionary change?"; and "How do the branches of life's tree fit together?" to mention just a few among thousands equally exciting.

In their recently aborted struggle to inject Genesis literalism into science classrooms, fundamentalist groups followed their usual opportunistic strategy of arguing two contradictory sides of a question when a supposed rhetorical advantage could be extracted from each. Their main pseudoargument held that Genesis literalism is not religion at all, but really an alternative form of science not acknowledged by professional biologists too hide-bound and dogmatic to appreciate the cutting edge of their own discipline. When we successfully pointed out that "creation science"—as an untestable set of dogmatic proposals—could not qualify as science by any standard definition, they turned around and shamelessly argued the other side. (They actually pulled off the neater trick of holding both positions simultaneously.) Now they argued that, yes indeed, creation science is religion, but evolution is equally religious.

To support this dubious claim, they tumbled (as a conscious trick of rhetoric, I suspect) right into Kirwan's error. They ignored what evolutionists actually do and misrepresented our science as the study of life's ultimate origin. They then pointed out, as Hutton had, that questions of ultimate origins are not resolvable by science. Thus, they claimed, creation science and evolution science are symmetrical—that is, equally religious. Creation science isn't science because it rests upon the untestable fashioning of life *ex nihilo* by God. Evolution science isn't science because it tries, as its major aim, to resolve the unresolvable and ultimate origin of life. But we do no such thing. We understand Hutton's wisdom—"he has nowhere treated of the first origin . . . of any substance . . . but only of the transformations which bodies have undergone. . . ."

Our legal battle with creationists started in the 1920s and reached an early climax with the conviction of John Scopes in 1925. After some quiescence, the conflict began in earnest again during the 1970s and has haunted us ever since. Finally, in June 1987, the Supreme Court ended this major chapter in American history with a decisive 7–2 vote, striking down the last creationist statute, the Louisiana equal time act, as a ruse to inject religion into science classrooms in violation of First Amendment guarantees for separation of church and state.

I don't mean to appear ungrateful, but we fallible humans are always seeking perfection in others. I couldn't help wondering how two justices could have ruled the other way. I may not be politically astute, but I am not totally naive either. I have read Justice Scalia's long dissent carefully, and I recognize that its main thrust lies in legal issues supporting the extreme judicial conservatism espoused by Scalia and the other dissenter, Chief

Justice Rehnquist. Nonetheless, though forming only part of his rationale, Scalia's argument relies crucially upon a false concept of science—Kirwan's error again. I regret to say that Justice Scalia does not understand the subject matter of evolutionary biology. He has simply adopted the creationists' definition and thereby repeated their willful mistake.

Justice Scalia writes, in his key statement on scientific evidence:

> The people of Louisiana, including those who are Christian fundamentalists, are quite entitled, as a secular matter, to have whatever scientific evidence there may be against evolution presented in their schools.

I simply don't see the point of this statement. Of course they are so entitled, and absolutely nothing prevents such a presentation, if evidence there be. The equal time law forces teaching of creation science, but nothing prevented it before, and nothing prevents it now. Teachers were, and still are, free to teach creation science. They don't because they recognize it as a ruse and a sham.

Scalia does acknowledge that the law would be unconstitutional if creation science is free of evidence—as it is—and if it merely restates the Book of Genesis—as it does:

> Perhaps what the Louisiana Legislature has done is unconstitutional because there is no such evidence, and the scheme they have established will amount to no more than a presentation of the Book of Genesis.

Scalia therefore admits that the issue is not merely legal and does hinge on a question of scientific fact. He then buys the creationist argument and denies that we have sufficient evidence to render this judgment of unconstitutionality. Continuing directly from the last statement, he writes:

> But we cannot say that on the evidence before us. . . . Infinitely less can we say (or should we say) that the scientific evidence for evolution is so conclusive that no one would be gullible enough to believe that there is any real scientific evidence to the contrary.

But this is exactly what I, and all scientists, do say. We are not blessed with absolute certainty about any fact of nature, but evolution is as well confirmed as anything we know—surely as well as the earth's shape and position (and we don't require equal time for flat-earthers and those who believe that our planet resides at the center of the universe). We have oodles to learn about how evolution happened, but we have adequate proof that living forms are connected by bonds of genealogical descent.

So I asked myself, how could Justice Scalia be so uninformed about the state of our basic knowledge? And then I remembered something peculiar that bothered me, but did not quite register, when I first read his dissent. I went back to his characterization of evolution and what did I find (repeated, by the way, more than a dozen times, so we know that the argument represents no one-time slip of his pen, but a consistent definition)?

Justice Scalia has defined evolution as the search for life's origin—and nothing more. He keeps speaking about "the current state of scientific evidence about the origin of life" when he means to designate evolution. He writes that "the legislature wanted to ensure that students would be free to decide for themselves how life began based upon a fair and balanced presentation of the scientific evidence." Never does he even hint that evolution might be the study of how life changes after it originates—the entire panoply of transformation from simple molecules to all modern, multicellular complexity.

Moreover, to make matters worse, Scalia doesn't even acknowledge the scientific side of the origin of life on earth. He argues that a creationist law might have a secular purpose so long as we can envisage a concept of creation not involving a personal God "who is the object of religious veneration." He then points out that many such concepts exist, stretching back to Aristotle's notion of an unmoved mover. In the oral argument before the Court, which I attended on December 10, 1986, Scalia pressed this point even more forcefully with counsel for our side. He sparred:

> What about Aristotle's view of a first cause, an unmoved mover? Would that be a creationist view? I don't think Aristotle considered himself as a theologian as opposed to a philosopher.

In fact, he probably considered himself a scientist. . . . Well, then, you could believe in a first cause, an unmoved mover, that may be impersonal, and has no obligation of obedience or veneration from men, and in fact, doesn't care what's happening to mankind. And believe in creation. [From the official transcript, and omitting the responses of our lawyer.]

Following this theme, Scalia presents his most confused statement in the written dissent:

Creation science, its proponents insist, no more must explain whence life came than evolution must explain whence came the inanimate materials from which it says life evolved. But even if that were not so, to posit a past creator is not to posit the eternal and personal God who is the object of religious veneration.

True indeed; one might be a creationist in some vernacular sense by maintaining a highly abstract and impersonal view of a creator. But Aristotle's unmoved mover is no more part of science than the Lord of Genesis. Science does not deal with questions of ultimate origins. We would object just as strongly if the Aristotelophiles of Delaware forced a law through the state legislature requiring that creation of each species *ex nihilo* by an unmoved mover be presented every time evolution is discussed in class. The difference lies only in historical circumstance, not the logic of argument. The unmoved mover doesn't pack much political punch; fundamentalism ranks among our most potent irrationalisms.

Consider also, indeed especially, Scalia's false concept of science. He equates creation and evolution because creationists can't explain life's beginning, while evolutionists can't resolve the ultimate origin of the inorganic components that later aggregated to life. But this inability is the very heart of creationist logic and the central reason why their doctrine is not science, while science's inability to specify the ultimate origin of matter is irrelevant because we are not trying to do any such thing. We know that we can't, and we don't even consider such a question as part of science.

We understand Hutton's wisdom. We do not search for unattainable ultimates. We define evolution, using Darwin's phrase, as "descent with modification" from prior living things. Our documentation of life's evolutionary tree records one of science's greatest triumphs, a profoundly liberating discovery on the oldest maxim that truth can make us free. We have made this discovery by recognizing what can be answered and what must be left alone. If Justice Scalia heeded our definitions and our practices, he would understand why creationism cannot qualify as science. He would also, by the way, sense the excitement of evolution and its evidence; no person of substance could be unmoved by something so interesting. Only Aristotle's creator may be so impassive.

Don Quixote recognized "no limits but the sky," but became thereby the literary embodiment of unattainable reverie. G. K. Chesterton understood that any discipline must define its borders of fruitfulness. He spoke for painting, but you may substitute any creative enterprise: "Art is limitation: the essence of every picture is the frame."

9 | Numbers and Probability

31 | The Streak of Streaks*

MY FATHER was a court stenographer. At his less than princely salary, we watched Yankee games from the bleachers or high in the third deck. But one of the judges had season tickets, so we occasionally sat in the lower boxes when hizzoner couldn't attend. One afternoon, while DiMaggio was going 0 for 4 against, of all people, the lowly St. Louis Browns, the great man fouled one in our direction. "Catch it, Dad," I screamed. "You never get them," he replied, but stuck up his hand like the Statue of Liberty—and the ball fell right in. I mailed it to DiMaggio, and, bless him, he actually sent the ball back, signed and in a box marked "insured." Insured, that is, to make me the envy of the neighborhood, and DiMaggio the model and hero of my life.

I met DiMaggio a few years ago on a small playing field at the Presidio of San Francisco. My son, wearing DiMaggio's old number 5 on his Little League jersey, accompanied me, exactly one generation after my father caught that ball. DiMaggio gave him a pointer or two on batting and then signed a baseball for him. One generation passeth away, and another generation cometh: But the earth abideth forever.

My son, uncoached by Dad, and given the chance that comes but once in a lifetime, asked DiMaggio as his only query about life

---

*This essay originally appeared in the *New York Review of Books* as a review of Michael Seidel's *Streak: Joe DiMaggio and the Summer of 1941* (New York: McGraw-Hill, 1988). I have excised the references to Seidel's book in order to forge a more general essay, but I thank him both for the impetus and for writing such a fine book.

463

and career: "Suppose you had walked every time up during one game of your 56-game hitting streak? Would the streak have been over?" DiMaggio replied that, under 1941 rules, the streak would have ended, but that this unfair statute has since been revised, and such a game would not count today.

My son's choice for a single question tells us something vital about the nature of legend. A man may labor for a professional lifetime, especially in sport or in battle, but posterity needs a single transcendant event to fix him in permanent memory. Every hero must be a Wellington on the right side of his personal Waterloo; generality of excellence is too diffuse. The unambiguous factuality of a single achievement is adamantine. Detractors can argue forever about the general tenor of your life and works, but they can never erase a great event.

In 1941, as I gestated in my mother's womb, Joe DiMaggio got at least one hit in each of 56 successive games. Most records are only incrementally superior to runners-up; Roger Maris hit 61 homers in 1961, but Babe Ruth hit 60 in 1927 and 59 in 1921, while Hank Greenberg (1938) and Jimmy Foxx (1932) both hit 58. But DiMaggio's 56-game hitting streak is ridiculously, almost unreachably far from all challengers (Wee Willie Keeler and Pete Rose, both with 44, come second). Among sabermetricians (a happy neologism based on an acronym for members of the Society for American Baseball Research, and referring to the statistical mavens of the sport)—a contentious lot not known for agreement about anything—we find virtual consensus that DiMaggio's 56-game hitting streak is the greatest accomplishment in the history of baseball, if not all modern sport.

The reasons for this respect are not far to seek. Single moments of unexpected supremacy—Johnny Vander Meer's back-to-back no-hitters in 1938, Don Larsen's perfect game in the 1956 World Series—can occur at any time to almost anybody, and have an irreducibly capricious character. Achievements of a full season—such as Maris's 61 homers in 1961 and Ted Williams's batting average of .406, also posted in 1941 and not equaled since—have a certain overall majesty, but they don't demand unfailing consistency every single day; you can slump for a while, so long as your average holds. But a streak must be absolutely exceptionless; you are not allowed a single day of subpar play, or even bad luck. You bat only four or five times in an average game. Sometimes two or three of these efforts yield walks, and you get only one or two shots at a hit. Moreover, as tension mounts and notice increases, your life becomes unbearable. Reporters dog your every step; fans are even more intrusive than usual (one stole DiMaggio's favorite bat right in the middle of his streak). You cannot make a single mistake.

Thus Joe DiMaggio's 56-game hitting streak is both the greatest factual achievement in the history of baseball and a principal icon of American mythology. What shall we do with such a central item of our cultural history?

Statistics and mythology may strike us as the most unlikely of bedfellows. How can we quantify Caruso or measure *Middlemarch*? *But if God could mete out heaven with the span (Isaiah 40:12), perhaps we can say something useful about hitting streaks. The statistics of "runs," defined as continuous series of good or bad results (including baseball's streaks and slumps), is a well-developed branch of the profession, and can yield clear—but wildly counterintuitive—results. (The fact that we find these conclusions so surprising is the key to appreciating DiMaggio's achievement, the point of this article, and the gateway to an important insight about the human mind.)*

Start with a phenomenon that nearly everyone both accepts and considers well understood—"hot hands" in basketball. Now and then, someone just gets hot, and can't be stopped. Basket after basket falls in—or out as with "cold hands," when a man can't buy a bucket for love or money (choose your cliché). The reason for this phenomenon is clear enough: It lies embodied in the maxim, "When you're hot, you're hot; and when you're not, you're not." You get that touch, build confidence; all nervousness fades, you find your rhythm; swish, swish, swish. Or you miss a few, get rattled, endure the booing, experience despair; hands start shaking and you realize that you shoulda stood in bed.

Everybody knows about hot hands. The only problem is that no such phenomenon exists. Stanford psychologist Amos Tversky studied every basket made by the Philadelphia 76ers for more than a season. He found, first of all, that the probability of making a second basket did not rise following a successful shot. Moreover, the number of "runs," or baskets in succession, was no greater than what a standard random, or coin-tossing, model would predict. (If the chance of making each basket is 0.5, for

466 | BULLY FOR BRONTOSAURUS

example, a reasonable value for good shooters, five hits in a row will occur, on average, once in 32 sequences—just as you can expect to toss five successive heads about once in 32 times, or 0.5^5.)

Of course Larry Bird, the great forward of the Boston Celtics, will have more sequences of five than Joe Airball—but not because he has greater will or gets in that magic rhythm more often. Larry has longer runs because his average success rate is so much higher, and random models predict more frequent and longer sequences. If Larry shoots field goals at 0.6 probability of success, he will get five in a row about once every 13 sequences (0.6^5). If Joe, by contrast, shoots only 0.3, he will get his five straight only about once in 412 times. In other words, we need no special explanation for the apparent pattern of long runs. There is no ineffable "causality of circumstance" (to coin a phrase), no definite reason born of the particulars that make for heroic myths—courage in the clinch, strength in adversity, etc. You only have to know a person's ordinary play in order to predict his sequences. (I rather suspect that we are convinced of the contrary not only because we need myths so badly, but also because we remember the successes and simply allow the failures to fade from memory. More on this later.) But how does this revisionist pessimism work for baseball?

My colleague Ed Purcell, Nobel laureate in physics but, for purposes of this subject, just another baseball fan, has done a comprehensive study of all baseball streak and slump records. His firm conclusion is easily and swiftly summarized. Nothing ever happened in baseball above and beyond the frequency predicted by coin-tossing models. The longest runs of wins or losses are as long as they should be, and occur about as often as they ought to. Even the hapless Orioles, at 0 and 21 to start the 1988 season, only fell victim to the laws of probability (and not to the vengeful God of racism, out to punish major league baseball's only black manager).*

But "treasure your exceptions," as the old motto goes. Pur-

---

*When I wrote this essay, Frank Robinson, the Baltimore skipper, was the only black man at the helm of a major league team. For more on the stats of Baltimore's slump, see my article "Winning and Losing: It's All in the Game," *Rotunda*, Spring 1989.

cell's rule has but one major exception, one sequence so many standard deviations above the expected distribution that it should never have occurred at all: Joe DiMaggio's 56-game hitting streak in 1941. The intuition of baseball aficionados has been vindicated. Purcell calculated that to make it likely (probability greater than 50 percent) that a run of even 50 games will occur once in the history of baseball up to now (and 56 is a lot more than 50 in this kind of league), baseball's rosters would have to include either four lifetime .400 batters or 52 lifetime .350 batters over careers of 1,000 games. In actuality, only three men have lifetime batting averages in excess of .350, and no one is anywhere near .400 (Ty Cobb at .367, Rogers Hornsby at .358, and Shoeless Joe Jackson at .356). DiMaggio's streak is the most extraordinary thing that ever happened in American sports. He sits on the shoulders of two bearers—mythology and science. For Joe DiMaggio accomplished what no other ballplayer has done. He beat the hardest taskmaster of all, a woman who makes Nolan Ryan's fastball look like a cantaloupe in slow motion—Lady Luck.

A larger issue lies behind basic documentation and simple appreciation. For we don't understand the truly special character of DiMaggio's record because we are so poorly equipped, whether by habits of culture or by our modes of cognition, to grasp the workings of random processes and patterning in nature.

Omar Khayyám, the old Persian tentmaker, understood the quandary of our lives (*Rubaiyat of Omar Khayyám*, Edward Fitzgerald, trans.):

> Into this Universe, and Why not knowing,
> Nor Whence, like Water willy-nilly flowing;
> And out of it, as Wind along the Waste,
> I know not Whither, willy-nilly blowing.

But we cannot bear it. We must have comforting answers. We see pattern, for pattern surely exists, even in a purely random world. (Only a highly nonrandom universe could possibly cancel out the clumping that we perceive as pattern. We think we see constellations because stars are dispersed at random in the heavens, and therefore clump in our sight—see Essay 17.) Our error lies not in the perception of pattern but in automatically imbuing pattern with meaning, especially with meaning that can bring us comfort, or dispel confusion. Again, Omar took the more honest approach:

> Ah, love! could you and I with Fate conspire
> To grasp this sorry Scheme of Things entire,
> Would not we shatter it to bits—and then
> Re-mould it nearer to the Heart's Desire!

We, instead, have tried to impose that "heart's desire" upon the actual earth and its largely random patterns (Alexander Pope, *Essay on Man,* end of Epistle 1):

> All Nature is but Art, unknown to thee;
> All Chance, Direction, which thou canst not see;
> All Discord, Harmony not understood:
> All partial Evil, universal Good.

Sorry to wax so poetic and tendentious about something that leads back to DiMaggio's hitting streak, but this broader setting forms the source of our misinterpretation. We believe in "hot hands" because we must impart meaning to a pattern—and we like meanings that tell stories about heroism, valor, and excellence. We believe that long streaks and slumps must have direct causes internal to the sequence itself, and we have no feel for the frequency and length of sequences in random data. Thus, while we understand that DiMaggio's hitting streak was the longest ever, we don't appreciate its truly special character because we view all the others as equally patterned by cause, only a little shorter. We distinguish DiMaggio's feat merely by quantity along a continuum of courage; we should, instead, view his 56-game hitting streak as a unique assault upon the otherwise unblemished record of Dame Probability.

Amos Tversky, who studied "hot hands," has performed, with Daniel Kahneman, a series of elegant psychological experiments. These long-term studies have provided our finest insight into "natural reasoning" and its curious departure from logical truth. To cite an example, they construct a fictional description of a young woman: "Linda is 31 years old, single, outspoken, and very bright. She majored in philosophy. As a student, she was deeply concerned with issues of discrimination and social justice, and also participated in anti-nuclear demonstrations." Subjects are then given a list of hypothetical statements about Linda: They must rank these in order of presumed likelihood, most to least probable. Tversky and Kahneman list eight statements, but five are a blind, and only three make up the true experiment:

Linda is active in the feminist movement;
Linda is a bank teller;
Linda is a bank teller and is active in the feminist movement.

Now it simply must be true that the third statement is least likely, since any conjunction has to be less probable than either of its parts considered separately. Everybody can understand this when the principle is explained explicitly and patiently. But all groups of subjects, sophisticated students who have pondered logic and probability as well as folks off the street corner, rank the last statement as more probable than the second. (I am particularly fond of this example because I know that the third statement is least probable, yet a little homunculus in my head continues to jump up and down, shouting at me—"but she can't just be a bank teller; read the description.")

Why do we so consistently make this simple logical error? Tversky and Kahneman argue, correctly I think, that our minds are not built (for whatever reason) to work by the rules of probability, though these rules clearly govern our universe. We do something else that usually serves us well, but fails in crucial instances: We "match to type." We abstract what we consider the "essence" of an entity, and then arrange our judgments by their degree of similarity to this assumed type. Since we are given a "type" for Linda that implies feminism, but definitely not a bank job, we rank any statement matching the type as more probable than another that only contains material contrary to the type. This propensity may help us to understand an entire range of human preferences, from Plato's theory of form to modern stereotyping of race or gender.

We might also understand the world better, and free ourselves of unseemly prejudice, if we properly grasped the workings of probability and its inexorable hold, through laws of logic, upon much of nature's pattern. "Matching to type" is one common error; failure to understand random patterning in streaks and slumps is another—hence Tversky's study of both the fictional Linda and the 76ers' baskets. Our failure to appreciate the uniqueness of DiMaggio's streak derives from the same unnatural and uncomfortable relationship that we maintain with probability. (If we knew Lady Luck better, Las Vegas might still be a roadstop in the desert.)

My favorite illustration of this basic misunderstanding, as applied to DiMaggio's hitting streak, appeared in a recent article by baseball writer John Holway, "A Little Help from His Friends," and subtitled "Hits or Hype in '41" (*Sports Heritage*, 1987). Holway points out that five of DiMaggio's successes were narrow escapes and lucky breaks. He received two benefits-of-the-doubt from official scorers on plays that might have been judged as errors. In each of two games, his only hit was a cheapie. In game 16, a ball dropped untouched in the outfield and had to be called a hit, even though the ball had been misjudged and could have been caught; in game 54, DiMaggio dribbled one down the third-base line, easily beating the throw because the third baseman, expecting the usual, was playing far back. The fifth incident is an oft-told tale, perhaps the most interesting story of the streak. In game 38, DiMaggio was 0 for 3 going into the last inning. Scheduled to bat fourth, he might have been denied a chance to hit at all. Johnny Sturm popped up to begin the inning, but Red Rolfe then walked. Slugger Tommy Henrich, up next, was suddenly swept with a premonitory fear: Suppose I ground into a double play and end the inning? An elegant solution immediately occurred to him: Why not bunt (an odd strategy for a power hitter). Henrich laid down a beauty; DiMaggio, up next, promptly drilled a double to left.

I enjoyed Holway's account, but his premise is entirely, almost preciously, wrong. First of all, none of the five incidents represents an egregious miscall. The two hits were less than elegant, but undoubtedly legitimate; the two boosts from official scorers were close calls on judgment plays, not gifts. As for Henrich, I can only repeat manager Joe McCarthy's comment when Tommy asked him for permission to bunt: "Yeah, that's a good idea." Not a terrible strategy either—to put a man into scoring position for an insurance run when you're up 3–1.

But these details do not touch the main point: Holway's premise is false because he accepts the conventional mythology about long sequences. He believes that streaks are unbroken runs of causal courage—so that any prolongation by hook-or-crook becomes an outrage against the deep meaning of the phenomenon. But extended sequences are not pure exercises in valor. Long streaks always are, and must be, a matter of extraordinary luck imposed upon great skill. Please don't make the vulgar mistake of thinking that Purcell or Tversky or I or anyone else would attribute a long streak to "just luck"—as though everyone's chances are exactly the same, and streaks represent nothing more than the lucky atom that kept moving in one direction. Long hitting streaks happen to the greatest players—Sisler, Keeler, DiMaggio, Rose—because their general chance of getting a hit is so much higher than average. Just as Joe Airball cannot match Larry Bird for runs of baskets, Joe's cousin Bill Ofer, with a lifetime batting average of .184, will never have a streak to match DiMaggio's with a lifetime average of .325. The statistics show something else, and something fascinating: There is no "causality of circumstance," no "extra" that the great can draw from the soul of their valor to extend a streak beyond the ordinary expectation of cointossing models for a series of unconnected events, each occurring with a characteristic probability for that particular player. Good players have higher characteristic probabilities, hence longer streaks.

Of course DiMaggio had a little luck during his streak. That's what streaks are all about. No long sequence has ever been entirely sustained in any other way (the Orioles almost won several of those 21 games). DiMaggio's remarkable achievement—its uniqueness, in the unvarnished literal sense of that word—lies in whatever he did to extend his success well beyond the reasonable expectations of random models that have governed every other streak or slump in the history of baseball.

Probability does pervade the universe—and in this sense, the old chestnut about baseball imitating life really has validity. The statistics of streaks and slumps, properly understood, do teach an important lesson about epistemology, and life in general. The history of a species, or any natural phenomenon that requires unbroken continuity in a world of trouble, works like a batting streak. All are games of a gambler playing with a limited stake against a house with infinite resources. The gambler must eventually go bust. His aim can only be to stick around as long as possible, to have some fun while he's at it, and, if he happens to be a moral agent as well, to worry about staying the course with honor. The best of us will try to live by a few simple rules: Do justly, love mercy, walk humbly with thy God, and never draw to an inside straight.

DiMaggio's hitting streak is the finest of legitimate legends because it embodies the essence of the battle that truly defines our lives. DiMaggio activated the greatest and most unattainable dream of all humanity, the hope and chimera of all sages and shamans: He cheated death, at least for a while.

32 | The Median Isn't the Message

MY LIFE HAS RECENTLY intersected, in a most personal way, two of Mark Twain's famous quips. One I shall defer to the end of this essay. The other (sometimes attributed to Disraeli) identifies three species of mendacity, each worse than the one before—lies, damned lies, and statistics.

Consider the standard example of stretching truth with numbers—a case quite relevant to my story. Statistics recognizes different measures of an "average," or central tendency. The *mean* represents our usual concept of an overall average—add up the items and divide them by the number of sharers (100 candy bars collected for five kids next Halloween will yield 20 for each in a fair world). The *median,* a different measure of central tendency, is the halfway point. If I line up five kids by height, the median child is shorter than two and taller than the other two (who might have trouble getting their mean share of the candy). A politician in power might say with pride, "The mean income of our citizens is $15,000 per year." The leader of the opposition might retort, "But half our citizens make less than $10,000 per year." Both are right, but neither cites a statistic with impassive objectivity. The first invokes a mean, the second a median. (Means are higher than medians in such cases because one millionaire may outweigh hundreds of poor people in setting a mean, but can balance only one mendicant in calculating a median.)

The larger issue that creates a common distrust or contempt for statistics is more troubling. Many people make an unfortunate and invalid separation between heart and mind, or feeling and intellect. In some contemporary traditions, abetted by attitudes

473

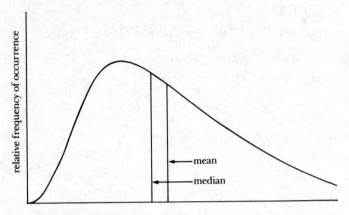

A right-skewed distribution showing that means must be higher than medians, and that the right side of the distribution extends out into a long tail. BEN GAMIT.

sterotypically centered upon Southern California, feelings are exalted as more "real" and the only proper basis for action, while intellect gets short shrift as a hang-up of outmoded elitism. Statistics, in this absurd dichotomy, often becomes the symbol of the enemy. As Hilaire Belloc wrote, "Statistics are the triumph of the quantitative method, and the quantitative method is the victory of sterility and death."

This is a personal story of statistics, properly interpreted, as profoundly nurturant and life-giving. It declares holy war on the downgrading of intellect by telling a small story to illustrate the utility of dry, academic knowledge about science. Heart and head are focal points of one body, one personality.

In July 1982, I learned that I was suffering from abdominal mesothelioma, a rare and serious cancer usually associated with exposure to asbestos. When I revived after surgery, I asked my first question of my doctor and chemotherapist: "What is the best technical literature about mesothelioma?" She replied, with a touch of diplomacy (the only departure she has ever made from direct frankness), that the medical literature contained nothing really worth reading.

Of course, trying to keep an intellectual away from literature works about as well as recommending chastity to *Homo sapiens*, the sexiest primate of all. As soon as I could walk, I made a bee-line for Harvard's Countway medical library and punched meso-thelioma into the computer's bibliographic search program. An hour later, surrounded by the latest literature on abdominal mesothelioma, I realized with a gulp why my doctor had offered that humane advice. The literature couldn't have been more bru-tally clear: Mesothelioma is incurable, with a median mortality of only eight months after discovery. I sat stunned for about fifteen minutes, then smiled and said to myself: So that's why they didn't give me anything to read. Then my mind started to work again, thank goodness.

If a little learning could ever be a dangerous thing, I had en-countered a classic example. Attitude clearly matters in fighting cancer. We don't know why (from my old-style materialistic per-spective, I suspect that mental states feed back upon the immune system). But match people with the same cancer for age, class, health, and socioeconomic status, and, in general, those with pos-itive attitudes, with a strong will and purpose for living, with com-mitment to struggle, and with an active response to aiding their own treatment and not just a passive acceptance of anything doc-tors say tend to live longer. A few months later I asked Sir Peter Medawar, my personal scientific guru and a Nobelist in immunol-ogy, what the best prescription for success against cancer might be. "A sanguine personality," he replied. Fortunately (since one can't reconstruct oneself at short notice and for a definite pur-pose), I am, if anything, even-tempered and confident in just this manner.

Hence the dilemma for humane doctors: Since attitude matters so critically, should such a somber conclusion be advertised, es-pecially since few people have sufficient understanding of statis-tics to evaluate what the statements really mean? From years of experience with the small-scale evolution of Bahamian land snails treated quantitatively, I have developed this technical knowl-edge—and I am convinced that it played a major role in saving my life. Knowledge is indeed power, as Francis Bacon proclaimed.

The problem may be briefly stated: What does "median mor-tality of eight months" signify in our vernacular? I suspect that most people, without training in statistics, would read such a statement as "I will probably be dead in eight months"—the very conclusion that must be avoided, both because this formulation is false, and because attitude matters so much.

I was not, of course, overjoyed, but I didn't read the statement in this vernacular way either. My technical training enjoined a different perspective on "eight months median mortality." The point may seem subtle, but the consequences can be profound. Moreover, this perspective embodies the distinctive way of thinking in my own field of evolutionary biology and natural history.

We still carry the historical baggage of a Platonic heritage that seeks sharp essences and definite boundaries. (Thus we hope to find an unambiguous "beginning of life" or "definition of death," although nature often comes to us as irreducible continua.) This Platonic heritage, with its emphasis on clear distinctions and separated immutable entities, leads us to view statistical measures of central tendency wrongly, indeed opposite to the appropriate interpretation in our actual world of variation, shadings, and continua. In short, we view means and medians as hard "realities," and the variation that permits their calculation as a set of transient and imperfect measurements of this hidden essence. If the median is the reality and variation around the median just a device for calculation, then "I will probably be dead in eight months" may pass as a reasonable interpretation.

But all evolutionary biologists know that variation itself is nature's only irreducible essence. Variation is the hard reality, not a set of imperfect measures for a central tendency. Means and medians are the abstractions. Therefore, I looked at the mesothelioma statistics quite differently—and not only because I am an optimist who tends to see the doughnut instead of the hole, but primarily because I know that variation itself is the reality. I had to place myself amidst the variation.

When I learned about the eight-month median, my first intellectual reaction was: Fine, half the people will live longer; now what are my chances of being in that half. I read for a furious and nervous hour and concluded, with relief: damned good. I possessed every one of the characteristics conferring a probability of longer life: I was young; my disease had been recognized in a relatively early stage; I would receive the nation's best medical treatment; I had the world to live for; I knew how to read the data properly and not despair.

Another technical point then added even more solace. I immediately recognized that the distribution of variation about the eight-month median would almost surely be what statisticians call "right skewed." (In a symmetrical distribution, the profile of variation to the left of the central tendency is a mirror image of variation to the right. Skewed distributions are asymmetrical, with variation stretching out more in one direction than the other—left skewed if extended to the left, right skewed if stretched out to the right.) The distribution of variation had to be right skewed, I reasoned. After all, the left of the distribution contains an irrevocable lower boundary of zero (since mesothelioma can only be identified at death or before). Thus, little space exists for the distribution's lower (or left) half—it must be scrunched up between zero and eight months. But the upper (or right) half can extend out for years and years, even if nobody ultimately survives. The distribution must be right skewed, and I needed to know how long the extended tail ran—for I had already concluded that my favorable profile made me a good candidate for the right half of the curve.

The distribution was, indeed, strongly right skewed, with a long tail (however small) that extended for several years above the eight-month median. I saw no reason why I shouldn't be in that small tail, and I breathed a very long sigh of relief. My technical knowledge had helped. I had read the graph correctly. I had asked the right question and found the answers. I had obtained, in all probability, that most precious of all possible gifts in the circumstances—substantial time. I didn't have to stop and immediately follow Isaiah's injunction to Hezekiah—set thine house in order: for thou shalt die, and not live. I would have time to think, to plan, and to fight.

One final point about statistical distributions. They apply only to a prescribed set of circumstances—in this case to survival with mesothelioma under conventional modes of treatment. If circumstances change, the distribution may alter. I was placed on an experimental protocol of treatment and, if fortune holds, will be in the first cohort of a new distribution with high median and a right tail extending to death by natural causes at advanced old age.*

---

*So far so good.

It has become, in my view, a bit too trendy to regard the acceptance of death as something tantamount to intrinsic dignity. Of course I agree with the preacher of Ecclesiastes that there is a time to love and a time to die—and when my skein runs out I hope to face the end calmly and in my own way. For most situations, however, I prefer the more martial view that death is the ultimate enemy—and I find nothing reproachable in those who rage mightily against the dying of the light.

The swords of battle are numerous, and none more effective than humor. My death was announced at a meeting of my colleagues in Scotland, and I almost experienced the delicious pleasure of reading my obituary penned by one of my best friends (the so-and-so got suspicious and checked; he too is a statistician, and didn't expect to find me so far out on the left tail). Still, the incident provided my first good laugh after the diagnosis. Just think, I almost got to repeat Mark Twain's most famous line of all: The reports of my death are greatly exaggerated.*

---

*Since writing this, my death has actually been reported in two European magazines, five years apart. *Fama volat* (and lasts a long time). I squawked very loudly both times and demanded a retraction; guess I just don't have Mr. Clemens's *savoir faire*.

33 | The Ant and the Plant

WHY DO WE CARE SO much about size and number? My friend Ralph Keyes, who tips the charts with me at five feet seven and a half inches, wrote an entire book about our obsession with this supposedly irrelevant subject—*The Height of Your Life*. He documented the extraordinary steps that short politicians and film stars often take to avoid discovery of their secret. (Ralph couldn't penetrate the subterfuges of Jimmy Carter's staff to discover the height of our shortest recent president, who is at least an inch or two taller than Ralph and me, and therefore at, or not far from, the American average.) The most amusing item in Ralph's book is an old publicity shot of a short Humphrey Bogart with two of his leading ladies, Lauren Bacall and Katharine Hepburn. They have just emerged from an airplane. Bogie is on the first step of the gangplank; the two women stand on the ground.

Why do we so stupidly equate more with better? Penises and automobiles, two objects frequently graded for size by foolish men, work just as well, and often more efficiently, at smaller than average lengths. Extremes in body size almost always entail tragic consequences (at least off the basketball court). Robert Wadlow, just shy of nine feet and the tallest human ever recorded, died at age twenty-two from infection caused by a faulty ankle brace needed for supplementary support since his legs could not adequately carry his body. Moving beyond the pathology of extreme individuals, entire species of unusually large body size generally have short geological lifetimes. I doubt that their problem lies in biomechanical inefficiency, as earlier theories of lumbering dino-

479

saurs held. Rather, large creatures tend to be anatomically specialized and form relatively small populations (fewer brontosauruses than boll weevils)—perhaps the two strongest detriments to extended survival in a world of large and capricious environmental fluctuation over time.

While most people do understand that large size does not guarantee long-term success, the myth of "more is better" still pervades our interpretations. I have, for example, noted with surprise, as I have monitored the impressions of students and correspondents for more than twenty years, how many people assume, as almost logically necessary a priori, that evolutionary "progress" and complexity should correlate with the amount of DNA in an organism's cell—the ultimate baseline for more is better. Not so. The very simplest creatures, including viruses at the low end, followed by bacteria and other prokaryotic organisms, do have relatively little DNA. But as soon as we reach multicellular life, based on eukaryotic cells with nuclei and chromosomes, the correlation breaks down completely. Mammals stand squarely in the middle of the pack, with 10^9–10^{10} nucleotides per haploid cell. The largest values, ranging to nearly 100 times more DNA than the most richly endowed mammals, belong to salamanders and to some flowering plants.

Many species of plants arise by polyploidy, or doubling of chromosome number. These doublings often run through several cycles among a group of closely related species, so the amount of DNA can increase greatly—and the high DNA content of some polyploid plants has never been much of a mystery. On the other hand, the extreme values for amphibians once puzzled zoologists sufficiently that they gave the phenomenon a name—"the C-value paradox." However, since the discovery that so little of the total DNA codes actively for enzymes and proteins, this hundredfold difference between some mammals and salamanders seems less troubling. Most DNA consists of repeated copies; much of it codes for nothing and may represent "junk" in terms of an organism's morphology. The hundredfold difference does not mean that salamanders have 100 times more active genes than mammals, for the disparity occurs chiefly in nonessential, or noncoding, regions. (We would still, of course, like to know why some groups accumulate more junk and more repetitions, but such differences do not merit special recognition as a formal paradox.)

This essay considers another expression of maximum and minimum, and another test of correlation between quantity and quality—numbers of chromosomes. We have voluminous data on average differences in number of chromosomes among groups of organisms, and some patterns surely emerge. Diptera (flies and their allies) tend to have few per cell; *Drosophila,* the great laboratory stalwart (and largely for this reason), harbors four pairs per diploid cell. Birds tend to have many. Instead of providing a compendium for these well-chronicled differences, I shall focus on the extreme cases of more and less among organisms. Extreme values may titillate our fancy, but they are also unusually instructive for recognizing and specifying generalities. Exceptions do prove rules. (The etymology of that cliché, usually mistaken for a reversed meaning, is not "prove" in the sense of verify, but "probe" in the sense of test or challenge. This definition, from the Latin *probare,* is not entirely archaic in English—consider printer's proof, or a proving ground for testing weapons.)

Until two years ago, the lowest number of chromosomes, a commandingly minimal one pair, had been found for only a single organism—a nematode worm, appropriately honored in its subspecific name as *Parascaris equorum univalens.* This minimal complement had been discovered long ago, in 1887, by Theodor Boveri, the greatest cytologist (student of cellular architecture) of the late nineteenth century. Boveri (1862–1915) was a great intellectual in the European tradition—a complex and fascinating man who lived for the laboratory, but who also played the piano and painted with professional competence. His short life was scarred by fits of depression, and he died in despondency as the First World War enveloped Europe. Of Boveri's many scientific discoveries, the two greatest centered on chromosomes. First, he established their individuality and shifted attention from the nucleus as a whole to chromosomes as the agent of inheritance (in years before the rediscovery of Mendel's laws). Second, he demonstrated the differential value of chromosomes. Before Boveri's experiments, many scientists had conjectured that each chromosome carried all the hereditary information, and that organisms with many chromosomes carried more copies of this totality. Boveri proved that each chromosome carried only part of the hereditary information (some of the genes, as we might say today), and that the full complement built the organism through a complex orchestration of development.

Boveri took great interest in his discovery of an organism that carried but one pair of chromosomes per cell—and therefore did place all its hereditary information into one package. But Boveri quickly discovered that *P. equorum univalens,* though no imposter in its claims to minimalism, was not entirely consistent either. Only the cells of the germ line, those destined to produce eggs and sperm by meiosis, kept all the hereditary material together in a single pair of chromosomes. In cells destined to form body tissues, this chromosome fractured several times during the first cleavage divisions of early embryology, leading to adult cells with up to seventy chromosomes!

Finally, in 1986, Australian zoologists Michael W. J. Crosland and Ross H. Crozier reported a remarkable new species within a closely related group of ants, previously united into the overextended species *Myrmecia pilosula* (see their article of 1988 cited in the bibliography). This name falsely amalgamates several distinct species sharing a similar body form, but carrying different numbers of chromosomes in their cells. Species with nine, ten, sixteen, twenty-four, thirty, thirty-one, and thirty-two pairs of chromosomes have been described. Obviously, this complex of forms has evolved some way of speciating in concert with substantial changes in chromosome number.

On February 24, 1985, on the Tidbinbilla Nature Reserve near Canberra, Crosland and Crozier collected a colony of winged males and females, plus a mated queen with pupae and more than 100 workers. All workers tested from this colony carried but a single pair of chromosomes in their cells—all of them, not just cells of a particular type. An unambiguous example of chromosomal minimalism had finally been discovered, almost exactly 100 years after Boveri found only one pair of chromosomes in the germ line cells of *Parascaris.*

But the story of *M. pilosula* is even better, deliciously so. If you were out searching for absolute minimalism, you would have to root for finding your single pair of chromosomes in an ant, bee, or wasp—for the following interesting reason: The Hymenoptera, and just a few other creatures, reproduce by an unusual genetic system called haplodiploidy. In most animals, all body cells contain chromosomes in pairs, and sex is determined by maternal and paternal contributions (or noncontributions in some cases) to a single pair. But haplodiploid organisms specify sex by a different route. Reproductive females usually store sperm, often for long periods. Genetic females (including the functionally neuter workers) arise from fertilized eggs, and therefore contain chromosomes in pairs. But males are produced when the queen fails to fertilize a developing egg with stored sperm (in most other animal groups unfertilized eggs are inviable). Thus, the cells of male ants, bees, and wasps do not carry chromosomes in pairs and bear only the single set inherited from their mother. These males have no father, and their cells contain only half the chromosomes of females—a condition called haploid, as opposed to the diploid, or paired, complement of their sisters. (The entire system therefore receives the name haplodiploid, or male-female in this case.)

Haplodiploidy implies, of course, that males of the Tidbinbilla colony of *M. pilosula* have a truly and absolutely minimal number of one chromosome per cell. Not even a single pair—just one. The only lower possibility is disappearance. Crosland and Crozier checked just to be sure. The males of their colony contained a single chromosome per cell.

If we have reached a limit in the search for less, the other extreme seems more open-ended. How many chromosomes can a cell contain and still undergo the orderly divisions of mitosis and meiosis? Can hundreds of chromosomes line up neatly along a mitotic spindle and divide precisely to place an equal complement into each daughter cell? At what point do things become so crowded that this most elegant of biological mechanisms breaks down?

Maximal numbers are most easily reached by polyploidy, or doubling of chromosomes. This process occurs in two basic modes with differing evolutionary significances. In autoploidy, a cell doubles its own complement, forming, initially at least, a cell with two sets of identical pairs. Thus, the new autoploid usually looks like its parent. Autoploidy is not a mechanism for rapid evolution of form, though the redundancy introduced by doubling does permit considerable evolutionary divergence afterward—as one member of the duplicated pair becomes free to change. On the other hand, alloploidy, the second mode of doubling, can produce viable hybrids between distant species and can serve as a mechanism for sudden and substantial changes in form. Hybrids, with different forms and numbers of maternal and paternal chromosomes, will usually be sterile because chromosomes have no partners for pairing before meiosis—the "reduction division" that produces sex cells with half the genetic information of body cells. But if the precursors of sex cells undergo polyploidy, then each chromosome will find a partner in the duplicated version of its own form.

Since polyploidy is so much more common in plants than animals, we should search for maximalism in our gardens, not our zoos. The numerical importance of polyploidy in plants can best be appreciated in a wonderful graph that I first encountered, when a graduate student, in Verne Grant's *The Origin of Adaptations*. This graph is a frequency distribution for chromosome pairs in monocot plants. For ten pairs of chromosomes and higher, without exception, all peaks are for even numbers of chromosome pairs.

At first inadequate sight, this pattern doesn't make sense in the deepest possible way. Biology is not numerology; its regularities do not take the form of such abstractions as "cleave to even numbers." Such a graph will not be satisfying until we figure out a biological mechanism that, as a side consequence and not because evens are better than odds per se, produces an imbalance of species with chromosomes in pairs of even numbers. The resolution is elegantly simple in this case. Polyploidy is very common in plants, and every number, odd or even, when doubled, yields an even number. The peaks therefore indicate the prevalence of polyploidy in plants. Estimates range as high as 50 percent for the number of angiosperm species produced by polyploidy.

Since polyploidy can continue in cycles—doubling followed by redoubling—chromosome numbers, like the pot in a poker game with table stakes, can rise alarmingly from small beginnings. The champions among all organisms are ferns in the family Ophioglossaceae. The genus *Ophioglossum* exhibits a basic number of 120 chromosome pairs, the lowest value among living species. (Such a high number must, itself, be derived from earlier incidents of polyploidy among species now extinct. The basic number for the entire family, 15 pairs, may have been the starting

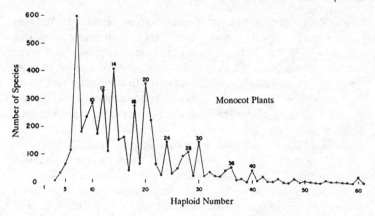

Frequency distribution for the number of chromosome pairs in monocot plants. Note that all peaks are for even numbers of chromosomes. This occurs because so many plant species are produced by polyploidy, or doubling of chromosome number, and a doubling of any number, odd or even, produces an even number. FROM VERNE GRANT, *THE ORIGIN OF ADAPTATIONS,* 1963.

point.) In any case, cycles of polyploidy have proceeded onward from this already large beginning of 120 pairs. The all-time champion, not only in *Ophioglossum,* but among all organisms, is *Ophioglossum reticulatum,* with about 630 pairs of chromosomes, or 1,260 per cell! (The total need not be an exact multiple of 120, because doubling may be imperfect, and secondary gains or losses for individual chromosomes are common.)

The very idea of a nucleus with 1,260 chromosomes, all obeying the rules of precise alignment and division as cells proliferate, inspired G. Ledyard Stebbins, our greatest living evolutionary botanist, to a rare emotion for a scientific paper—rapture (since Ledyard and I share a passion for Gilbert and Sullivan, I will write, for his sake, "modified rapture"—and he will know the reference and meaning): "At meiosis, these chromosomes pair regularly to form about 630 bivalents, a feat which to cytologists is as remarkable a wonder of nature as are the fantastic elaborations of form exhibited by orchids, insectivorous plants, and many animals" (see Stebbins, 1966, in the bibliography).

In fifteen years of writing these monthly essays, I have specialized in trying to draw general messages from particulars. But this time, I am stumped. I don't know what deep truth of nature emerges from the documentation of minimal and maximal chromosome numbers. Oh, I can cite some clichés and platitudes: Quantity is not quality; good things come in small packages. I can also state the obvious conclusion that inheritance and development do not depend primarily upon the number of distinct rods holding hereditary information—but this fact has been featured in textbooks of genetics for more than seventy years.

No, I think that every once in a while, we must simply let a fact stand by itself, for its own absolutely unvarnished fascination. Has your day not been brightened just a bit by learning that a plant can orchestrate the division of its cells by splitting 630 pairs of chromosomes with unerring accuracy—or that an ant, looking much like others, can gallivant about with an absolute minimum of one chromosome per cell? If so, I have earned my keep, and can go cultivate my garden. I think I'll try growing some ferns. Then I might take some colchicine, which often induces polyploidy, and maybe, just maybe. . . .

10 | Planets as Persons

Prologue

The *Voyager* expedition represents the greatest technological and intellectual triumph of our century. The fact that this tiny, relatively inexpensive machine could explore and photograph every outer planet except Pluto (but including Neptune, now the most distant planet, as Pluto temporarily moves closer to the sun on its eccentric orbit) is not only, as the cliché goes, a triumph of the human spirit (not to mention good old American tinkering and know-how), but also a living proof that billions of bucks, bureaucratic immuring, and hush-hush military spin-offs need not power our space program—and that knowledge and wonder really could be the main motivation and reward.

Such a triumph must be celebrated by any writer in natural history. I have chosen my own idiosyncratic mode. *Voyager*'s results convey many messages. These two essays, with their common theme, embody my reading of the main lesson from the standpoint of an evolutionary biologist: Planets are like organisms in that they have irreducible individuality and must therefore be explained by methods of historical analysis; they are not like molecules in a chemical equation. Planets therefore affirm the larger goal of unity among sciences by showing that methods of one approach (biological-historical) apply to cardinal objects of another mode often viewed as disparate or even opposed (physical-experimental).

34 | The Face of Miranda

WHEN MIRANDA, confined for all her conscious life on Prospero's magic island, saw a group of men for the first time, she exclaimed, "O, wonder! How many goodly creatures are there here! How beauteous mankind is! O brave new world, that has such people in't" (the source, of course, for Aldous Huxley's more sardonic citation). Now, almost 400 years after Miranda spoke through Shakespeare, we have returned the favor, gazed for the first time upon Miranda and found her every bit as wonderful—"so perfect and so peerless . . . she will outstrip all praise and make it halt behind her."

Prospero used all his magic to import his visitors by tempest. We have seen Miranda, the innermost large moon of Uranus, through the most stunning feat of technical precision in all our history. Ariel himself, Prospero's agent of magic (and also another moon of Uranus), would have been astounded. For we have sent a small probe hurtling though space for nine years, boosting it with the gravitational slings of both Jupiter and Saturn toward distant Uranus, there to transmit a signal across 2 billion miles and three light-hours, showing the face of Miranda with the same clarity that Prospero beheld when he gazed upon his daughter's beauty and exclaimed, "Thou didst smile, infused with a fortitude from heaven."

It is easy to wax poetic about this feat (especially with a little help from the Bard himself). *Voyager*'s data from Jupiter, Saturn, and now Uranus have supplied more scientific return for expended output than anything else that space exploration ever dared or dreamed. In the chorus of praise, however, we have not always recognized how much this new information has transcended the visually dazzling—how deeply our *ideas* about the formation and history of the solar system have been changed. This confluence of aesthetics and intellect must be celebrated above all—and I should like to record my delight by thoroughly repudiating an early essay in this series (March 1977) as an illustration both of our new understanding and of the vital generalization so obtained.

My story is the tale of an old and eminently reasonable hypothesis, proposed long ago and beautifully affirmed by the first explorations of other worlds—our moon, then Mercury, and finally Mars. Then, at the height of its triumph, the theory begins to unravel, first at the moons of Jupiter, then at the surface of Venus, and finally and irretrievably, in the face of Miranda.

The initial hypothesis sought to explain the surfaces (and inferred histories) of rocky planets and moons as simple consequences of their differences in size. Why, in particular, is the earth so different from the moon? Our moon is a dead world, covered with impact craters that have not eroded away since their formation, often billions of years ago. The earth, by contrast, is a dynamic world of relative smoothness.

This difference, we assume, is a result of historical divergence, not initial disparity. Billions of years ago, when the planets were young and our portion of space still abounded with debris not yet swept up in planets and moons, the earth must have been as intensely cratered as the moon. The current difference must therefore be a result of the moon's retention, and the earth's obliteration, of their early histories. Why the difference?

On earth, both internal and external "machines" recycle the landscape on a scale of millions of years. The atmosphere (external machine) generates agents of erosion—running water, wind, and ice—that quickly obliterate the topography of any crater. Yet even without rain and wind, the earth's internal activity of volcanism, earthquakes, and ultimately of plate tectonics itself would eventually disaggregate and erase any old topography. Surfaces do not last for billions of years on an active planet. But neither machine works on the moon. With no atmosphere, erosion proceeds (even in geological time) at a snail's pace. Likewise, the moon is a rigid body with a crust 600 miles thick. Moonquakes do not fracture the lunar surface and volcanoes do not rise from the tiny molten core.

The earth's activity and moon's silence are consequences of a single factor—size. Large bodies have much lower ratios of surface to volume than small bodies of the same shape, since surfaces (length × length) grow so much more slowly than volumes (length × length × length) as size increases. Our planet powers its two machines by low surface-to-volume ratios. The earth generates heat (by radioactivity) over its relatively large volume and then loses this heat through its relatively small surface—thus remaining hot and active enough to propel plate tectonics. The moon, by contrast, and by virtue of its higher surface-to-volume ratio, lost most of its internal heat long ago, and solidified nearly throughout. Likewise, the earth's large mass generates enough gravity to hold an atmosphere and power its external machine, while the moon lost any gases once produced.

As planetary exploration began, this "size-dependent" theory of planetary surfaces and their histories received its first tests and passed elegantly. The first photos of Mercury showed nothing but craters—as expected for a body about the same size as our moon.

Mars posed a clearer and more crucial test. As a planet about midway in size between the earth and moon, it should preserve some of its early topography, but also display the action of weak internal and external machines. The *Surveyor* flyby and *Viking* landings affirmed this prediction. The surface of Mars is about 50 percent cratered. The remaining areas show abundant signs of erosion, primarily by winds today (dune fields and etched boulders) and by running water in the past (now frozen), and internal churning more limited than on the earth. Most intriguing are signs of incipient (but unrealized) plate tectonics—as though the Martian crust remains pliant enough to fracture, but too rigid to move.

At this point in space exploration, I felt confident enough to write an essay extolling the size hypothesis as a sufficient and elegantly simple explanation of planetary surfaces and their histories. Contrasting the earth with the smaller bodies then known, I wrote (in March 1977) that "the difference arises from a disarmingly simple fact—*size itself, and nothing else:* the earth is a good deal larger than its neighbors."

The first test after my essay appeared would be *Voyager*'s photographic survey of the Galilean satellites of Jupiter—the four moon-sized rocky bodies that, by the size hypothesis, would surely be intensely cratered worlds, cold and dead. Thus, I waited with confidence as *Voyager* approached Io, the innermost moon of Jupiter. The first photos, distant and fuzzy, revealed some circular structures initially read as craters. Well and good. But the next day brought sharp photos, and evoked both wonder and surprise. The circles were not craters, but giant volcanoes, spewing forth lakes of sulfur. In fact, not a single crater could be found on Io, the most active satellite in the solar system. Yet, as a body smaller than our moon, Io should have been cold and cratered.

The explanation now offered for Io's intense activity had been predicted just a few days before the photos arrived. Io is so close to giant Jupiter that the interplay between Jupiter's gravitational tug and the reverse pull of the three other large satellites from the opposite side keeps the interior of Io fluid enough to resist rigidification.

As this information arrived, I could only stand by in awe and reflect that Io had been misnamed. The four Galilean satellites honor some of Jove's many lovers—an ecumenical assortment including his homosexual partner Ganymede; the nymph Callisto; and Europa, the mother of King Minos. Io, the fallen priestess, was changed to a heifer by jealous Hera, afflicted with a gadfly, and sent to roam Europe, where she forded (and indirectly named) the Bosporus (literally, the cow crossing) and finally emerged, human again, in Egypt. I thought that this innermost moon should be renamed Semele, to honor another lover who made the mistake of demanding that Jove appear to her in his true, rather than his disguised (and muted) human, form—and was immediately burned to a crisp!

Is the size hypothesis therefore wrong because Io violated its prediction? The principle of surfaces and volumes, as a basic law of physics and the geometry of space, is surely correct. Io does not challenge its validity, but only its scope. The size hypothesis does not merely claim that the surface-to-volume principle operates—for this we can scarcely doubt. The hypothesis insists, rather, that the surface-to-volume principle so dominates all other potential forces that we need invoke nothing further to understand the history and topography of rocky planetary surfaces. Io does not refute the principle. But Io does prove dramatically that other circumstances—in this case proximity to opposing gravitational sources—can so override the surface-to-volume rule that its predictions fail or, in this case (even worse), are diametrically refuted.

Planetary surfaces lie in the domain of complex historical sciences, where modes of explanation differ from the stereotypes of simple and well-controlled laboratory experiments. We are not trying to demonstrate the validity of physical laws. Rather, we must try to assess the relative importance of several complex and interacting forces. The validity of the surface-to-volume principle was never at issue, only its relative importance—and Io has challenged its domination.

We must therefore know, in order to judge the size hypothesis, whether Io is a lone exception in a singular circumstance or a general reminder that the surface-to-volume principle ranks as only one among many competing influences—and therefore not as *the* determinant of planetary surfaces and their history. The test will not center upon arguments about the laws of physics, but upon observations of other bodies, for we must establish, empirically, the relative importance of a hypothesis that worked until *Voyager* photographed Io.

Venus was the next candidate. Our sister planet, although closer to us than any other, had remained shrouded (literally) in mystery by its dense cover of clouds. But Russian and American probes have now mapped the Venusian surface with radio waves that can penetrate the clouds, as wavelengths in the visible spectrum cannot. Results are ambiguous and still under analysis, but proponents of the size hypothesis can scarcely react with unalloyed pleasure. Venus and Earth are just about the same size and Venus should, by the surface-to-volume hypothesis, be as active as our planet. Our sister world is, to be sure, no dead body. We have seen high mountains, giant rifts, and other signs of extensive tectonic activity. But Venus also seems to maintain too much old and cratered terrain for a body of its size, according to the principle of surfaces and volumes alone.

Scientists have advanced many explanations for the difference between Venus and Earth. Perhaps tidal forces generated by the moon's gravity keep Earth in its high state of geological flux. Venus has no satellite. Perhaps the high surface temperature of Venus, generated by a greenhouse effect under its dense cover of clouds, keeps the surface too pliable to form the thin and rigid plates that, in their constant motion, keep Earth's surface so active.

Voyager then moved toward Uranus and a final test. By this time, buffeted by Io and Venus, I was holding out little hope for the size hypothesis (and also wishing that the *Rubáiyát* had not spoken so truly about the moving finger, and that my publishers might deep-six all unsold copies of *The Panda's Thumb*, with its reprint of my original 1977 essay). In fact, anticipating final defeat for that elegantly simple proposal of earlier years, I actually managed to turn disappointment into a modest professorial coup. I have long believed that examinations have little intellectual value, existing only to fulfill, and ever so imperfectly at that, any large institution's need for assessment by number. Yet, for the first time, the moons of Uranus allowed me to ask an examination question with some intellectual interest and integrity.

I realized that the final examination for my large undergraduate course had been set for the morning of January 24, at the very hour that *Voyager* would be relaying photographs of Uranian moons to earth. I therefore predicted that Miranda, although the smallest of five major moons, would be most active among them, and asked the students to justify (or reject) such a speculation—though the conjecture itself is absurd under the size hypothesis with its evident prediction that Miranda, as the smallest moon with the highest surface-to-volume ratio, should be cratered and devoid of internal activity. I asked the students:

> As you take this exam, *Voyager 2* is sending back to Earth the first close-up pictures of Uranus and its moons. . . . On what basis might you predict that Miranda, although the smallest of these moons, is most likely to show some activity (volcanoes, for example) on its surface? We will probably know the answer before the exam ends!

(When I first wrote the exam in early January, I couldn't even provide my students with the moons' diameters, for they had not yet been measured precisely, though we knew that Miranda was smallest. Between writing and administering the exam, *Voyager* measured the diameters, and we rushed to the printers with an insert. Science, at its best, moves very quickly indeed.)

So I was ready for the final undoing of the size hypothesis, but not for the actual result of Miranda's countenance. The conjecture of my question turned out to be quite wrong. I had been thinking of Io and the gravity of a nearby giant planet. Since Miranda is closest to Uranus, I supposed that it might be lit with modern volcanoes. But no volcanoes are belching forth sulfur, or anything else, on Miranda. The actual observations, however, spoke even more strongly against the size hypothesis and its prediction of a cold, cratered world.

I had made one good prediction, probably for the wrong reason: Miranda is the most geologically active of Uranian moons, despite its small diameter of but 300 miles. (The moons of Uranus, outdoing even the mythic splendor of Jupiter's satellites, bear lovely Shakespearean names—in order from Uranus out: Miranda, Ariel, Umbriel, Titania, and Oberon. In addition, *Voyager* has discovered at least ten additional and much smaller moons between Miranda and the planet's surface.) The first photos of Miranda stunned and delighted the boys in Pasadena even more than her namesake had mesmerized Ferdinand on Prospero's island. Laurence Soderblom, speaking for the *Voyager* imaging team, exclaimed: "It's just mind boggling. . . . You name it, we have it. . . . Miranda is what you would get if you can imagine taking all the bizarre geological features in the solar system and putting them on one object." A brave new world, indeed. So much for the size hypothesis and its uniform blanket of craters.

Moreover, all the Uranian moons are surprisingly active (except for Umbriel, odd man out in more ways than one, as the only non-Shakespearean entry) in a gradient of increasing turmoil from the outermost king of *Midsummer Night* to the innermost daughter of the *Tempest.* "As you move closer to Uranus," Soderblom added, "we see an increasing ferocity, as though these bodies have been tectonically shuffled in a cataclysmic fashion."

I must save the details for another time, but for starters, the surface of Miranda is a jumble of frozen geological activity—long valleys, series of parallel grooves, and blocks of sunken crust. Most prominent, and also most notable for their lack of any clear counterpart on other worlds, are three structures that seem related in their formation. One has been dubbed a stack of pancakes, the second a chevron, and the third a racetrack. They are series of parallel grooves, or cracks, shaped to different forms according to their nicknames and full of evidence for massive slumping, rifting, and cliff making.

In short, Io failed the size hypothesis by its position too close to Jupiter. Venus may not conform by a particular history that left it moon free and cloud covered. Miranda has failed, we know not why, by showing signs of a frantic past when the hypothesis predicted a passive compendium of impacts. The physical principle invoked by the size hypothesis—the law of surfaces and volumes—is surely correct, but not potent enough to overwhelm other influences and lead to confident predictions by itself. As we learn more and more about the historical complexity of the heavens, we recognize that where you are (Io) and what you have been (Venus and Miranda) exert as much influence over a planet's surface as its size. After an initial success for our moon, Mercury, and Mars, the size hypothesis flunked all further tests.

The story of a theory's failure often strikes readers as sad and unsatisfying. Since science thrives on self-correction, we who practice this most challenging of human arts do not share such a feeling. We may be unhappy if a favored hypothesis loses or chagrined if theories that we proposed prove inadequate. But refutation almost always contains positive lessons that overwhelm disappointment, even when (as in this case) no new and comprehensive theory has yet filled the void. I chose this tale of failure for a particular reason, not only because Miranda excited me. I chose to confess my former errors because the replacement of a simple physical hypothesis with a recognition of history's greater complexity teaches an important lesson with great unifying power.

An unfortunate, but regrettably common, stereotype about science divides the profession into two domains of different status. We have, on the one hand, the "hard," or physical, sciences that deal in numerical precision, prediction, and experimentation. On the other hand, "soft" sciences that treat the complex objects of history in all their richness must trade these virtues for "mere" description without firm numbers in a confusing world where, at best, we can hope to explain what we cannot predict. The history

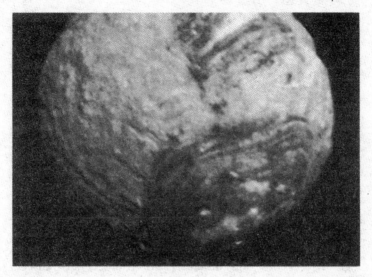

Voyager photograph of Miranda, showing fractured and reaggregated terrain. PHOTO COURTESY NASA/JPL.

of life embodies all the messiness of this second, and under-valued, style of science.

Throughout ten years of essays firmly rooted in this second style, I have tried to suggest by example that the sciences of history may be different from, but surely not worse than, the sciences of simpler physical objects. I have written about a hundred historical problems and their probable solutions, hoping to illustrate a methodology as powerful as any possessed by colleagues in other fields. I have tried to break down the barriers between these two styles of science by fostering mutual respect.

The story of planetary surfaces illustrates another path to the same goal of lowering barriers. The two styles are not divisible by discipline into the hard sciences of physical systems and the soft sciences of biological objects. All good scientists must use and appreciate both styles since large and adequate theories usually need to forage for insights in both physics and history. If we accepted the rigid dichotomy of hard and soft, we might argue that as physical bodies, planets should yield to predictive theories of the hard sciences. The size hypothesis represented this mode of explanation (and I was beguiled by it before I understood history better)—a simple law of physics to regulate a large class of complex objects. But we have learned, in its failure, that planets are more like organisms than billiard balls. They are intricate and singular bodies. Their individuality matters, and size alone will not explain planetary surfaces. We must know their particularities, their early histories, their present locations. Planets are physical bodies that require historical explanations. They break the false barrier between two styles of science by forcing the presumed methods of one upon the supposed objects of the other.

Finally, we should not lament that simple explanations have failed and that the "messy" uniqueness of each planet must be featured in any resolution. We might despair if the individuality of planets dashed all hope for general explanation. But the message of Io, Venus, and Miranda is not gridlock, but transcendence. We think that we understand Io, and we strive to fathom the moons of Uranus. Historical explanations are difficult, damned interesting, and eminently attainable by human cleverness. Whoever said that nature would be easy?

Prospero, after saving his foes from the tempest, asserts that he cannot relate the history of his life too simply, for " 'tis a chronicle of day by day, not a relation for a breakfast." The tale is long and intricate, but fascinating and resolvable. We can also know the richness of history in science. Proper explanation may require a tapestry of detail. Our stories may recall the subtle skills of Scheherazade rather than the crisp epitome of a segment in *Sixty Minutes,* but then who has ever been bored by Sinbad the Sailor or Aladdin's magic lamp?

35 | The Horn of Triton

THE ARGUMENTS of "iffy" history may range from the merely amusing to the horribly tragic. If Mickey Owen hadn't dropped that third strike, the Dodgers might have won the 1941 World Series. If Adolf Hitler had been killed in the Beer Hall Putsch, the alliances that led to World War II might not have formed, and we might not have lost our war fleet at Pearl Harbor just two months after Owen's miscue.

I don't think that we would be so fascinated by conjectures in this mode if we felt that anything could happen in history. Rather, we accept certain trends, certain predictabilities, even some near inevitabilities, particularly in war and technology, where numbers truly count. (I can't imagine any scenario leading to the victory of Grenada over the United States in our recent one-day conflict; nor can I conjecture how the citizens of Pompeii, without benefit of motorized transport, could have escaped a cloud of poisonous gases streaming down Mount Vesuvius at some forty miles per hour.) I suspect, in fact, that our fascination with iffy history arises largely from our awe at the ability of individuals to perturb, even greatly to alter, a process that seems to be moving in a definite direction for reasons above and beyond the power of mere mortals to deflect.

In opening *The Eighteenth Brumaire of Louis Bonaparte,* Karl Marx captured this essential property of history as a dynamic balance between the inexorability of forces and the power of individuals. He wrote, in one of the great one-liners of scholarship in the activist mode: "Men make their own history, but they do not make it just as they please." (Marx's title is, itself, a commentary

499

on the unique and the repetitive in history. The original Napoleon staged his *coup d'état* against the Directory on November 9–10, 1799, then called the eighteenth day of Brumaire, Year VIII, by the revolutionary calendar adopted in 1793 and used until Napoleon crowned himself emperor and returned to the old forms. But Marx's book traces the rise of Louis-Napoleon, nephew of the emperor, from the presidency of France following the revolution of 1848, through his own *coup d'état* of December 1851, to his crowning as Napoleon III. Marx seeks lessons from repetition, but continually stresses the individuality of each cycle, portraying the second in this case as a mockery of the first. His book begins with another great epigram, this time a two-liner, on the theme of repetition and individuality: "Hegel remarks somewhere that all facts and personages of great importance in world history occur, as it were, twice. He forgot to add the first time as tragedy, the second as farce.")

This essential tension between the influence of individuals and the power of predictable forces has been well appreciated by historians, but remains foreign to the thoughts and procedures of most scientists. We often define science (far too narrowly, I shall argue) as the study of nature's laws and their consequences. Individual objects have no power to shape general patterns in such a system. Walter the Water Molecule cannot freeze a pond, while Sarah the Silica Tetrahedron does not perturb the symmetry of quartz. Indeed, the very notion of Walter and Sarah only invites ridicule because laws of chemical behavior and crystal symmetry deny individuality to constituent units of larger structures. What else do we mean when we assert that hydrogen and oxygen make water or that silica tetrahedra sharing all their corner oxygen ions form quartz? (We could scarcely speak of a law if Ollie Oxygen willingly joined with Omar but refused to share with Oscar because they had a fight last Friday.) No actual quartz crystal has a perfect lattice of conjoined tetrahedra; all include additions and disruptions known as impurities or imperfections—but the very names given to these ingredients of individuality demonstrate that scientific content supposedly lies in the regularities, while uniquenesses of particular crystals fall into the domain of hobbyists and aestheticians.

(I don't mean to paint the world of science as a heartless place of perfect predictability under immutable laws. We permit a great deal of play and doubt under the guise of randomness. But randomness is equally hostile to the idea of individuality. In fact, classically random systems represent the ultimate denial of individuality. Coin-flipping and dice-throwing models rest upon the premise that each toss or each roll manifests the same probabilities: no special circumstances of time or place, no greater chance of a head if the last five tosses have been tails, or if you blow on the coin and say your mantra, or if Aunt Mary will die as a consequence of your failure to score—in other words, no individuality of particular trials. Individuality and randomness are opposing, not complementary, concepts. They both oppose the idea of clockwork determinism, but they do so in entirely different ways.)

Natural history does not share this consensus that individual units with particular legacies cannot shape the behavior and future state of entire systems. Our profession, although part of mainstream science since Aristotle, grants to individuals the potential for such a formative role. In this sense, we are truly historians by practice and we demonstrate the futility of disciplinary barriers between science and the humanities. We should be exploring our marked overlaps in explanatory procedures, not sniping at each other behind walls of definitional purity.

Natural history stands in the crossfire and should provoke a truce by reaching in both directions. Individual organisms can certainly set the local history of populations and may even shape the fate of species. Walter the Walrus and Sarah the Squirrel are friendly and congenial, rather than risible, concepts (and may be actual creatures at the municipal zoo). Two recent cases of extraordinary (although not particularly likable) individuals have led me to consider this theme and to grant more attention to the vagaries of one in my profession.

1. Jane Goodall's quarter century with the chimpanzees of Gombe will rank forever as one of the great achievements in scientific dedication combined with stunning results. With such unprecedented, long-term knowledge of daily history, Goodall can specify (and quantify) the major determinants of her population's fate. Contrary to our intuitions and expectations, the demography of the Gombe chimps has not been set primarily by daily rhythms of birth, feeding, sex, and death, but by three "rare events" (Goodall's words), all involving mayhem or misfortune: a

polio epidemic, a carnage of one sub-band by another, and the following tale of one peculiar individual.

With odd and unintended appropriateness as we shall see, for the word means "suffering," Goodall named one of the Gombe females Passion. Goodall met Passion in 1961 at the outset of her studies. In 1965, Passion gave birth to a daughter, Pom, and, as Goodall remarks (all quotes from *The Chimpanzees of Gombe,* Harvard University Press, 1986), "thereby gave us the opportunity to observe some extraordinarily inefficient and indifferent maternal behavior."

Nonetheless, Pom and Passion formed a "close, cooperative bond" as the daughter matured. In 1975, Passion began to kill and eat newborn babies of other females in her band. She could not easily wrest a baby from its mother and failed when acting solo, but Passion and Pom together formed an efficient killing duo. (Goodall observed three other "cannibalistic events" during nearly thirty years of work, all directed by males toward older chimps of other bands; Passion's depredations are the only recorded incidents of cannibalism within a band.) During a four-year period, Passion and Pom, in sight of observers, killed and ate three infants by seizing them from their mothers and biting through the skull bones (sorry, but nature isn't always pretty, and I hate euphemisms). They may have been responsible for the deaths of seven other infants. During this entire period, only one female successfully raised a baby. In studying Goodall's curves of Gombe demography, the depredations of Passion have as great an impact as any general force of climate or disease. Moreover, the effects are not confined to the short years of Passion's odd obsession (for reasons unknown, she stopped killing babies in 1977), but propagate well down the line. Since only one female was raising a baby in 1977, nearly all were in estrus, thus prompting a baby boomlet and sharp rise in population when Passion stopped her cannibalism.

Such observational work on the behavior of animals in their natural habitat requires a personal pledge to maximal noninterference. Passion taxed this principle to its absolute limit. Goodall told me that when Passion died "of an unknown wasting disease" in 1982, she (Jane, not Passion) watched with renewed faith in noninterference and some legitimate sense of moral retribution.

2. *Notornis,* the New Zealand ornithological journal, does not

show up in the scientific equivalent of the corner drug store; I was therefore delighted when Jared Diamond alerted me (via *Nature,* which does appear at our watering holes) to a fascinating article by Michael Taborsky entitled "Kiwis and Dog Predation: Observations in Waitangi State Forest" (see the bibliography). The Waitangi Forest houses the largest "known and counted" population of the brown kiwi *Apteryx australis*—some 800 to 1,000 birds. In June and July of 1987, Taborsky and colleagues tagged twenty-four birds with radio transmitters "so that their spacing and reproductive activities could be studied" (all quotations come from Taborsky's paper cited above).

On August 24, they found a dead female, evidently killed by a dog. Thus began a tale worthy of *The Hound of the Baskervilles.* By September 27, thirteen of the tagged birds had been killed. All showed extensive bruising, and most had defeathered areas; ten of the thirteen birds "were found partly covered or completely buried under leaf litter and soil." Scientists and forestry workers found ten more carcasses without transmitters, all killed and buried in the same way, and all dispatched during the same period.

It didn't take the sleuthing genius of Mr. Holmes to recognize that a single dog had wreaked this reign of terror. Distinctive footprints of the same form appeared by the carcasses, along with "dog droppings of one type and size." On September 30, a female German shepherd, wearing a collar but unregistered, was shot in the forest. Her "long claws suggested that she had not been on hard surfaces for some time, i.e., was probably living in the forest." The killings abruptly stopped. Taborsky tagged several more birds with transmitters, bringing the total to eighteen; all these birds survived to the end of the study on October 31.

This Rin Tin Tin of the Dark Side had killed more than half of the tagged birds in six weeks. As "there is no reason to believe that birds with transmitters were at greater risk than those without," the total killed may range to 500 of the 800 to 1,000 birds in the population. Lest this seem a staggering and unbelievable estimate, Taborsky provides the following eminently reasonable defenses. First, given the remote chance of finding a buried, untagged kiwi carcass, the ten actually located during the interval of killing must represent the tiny pinnacle of a large iceberg. Second, other evidence supports a dramatic fall in total population: Taborsky and colleagues noted a major drop in calling rates for these ordinarily noisy birds; a dog trained to find, but not to kill, kiwis could not locate a single live individual (although she found two carcasses) in a formerly well-inhabited section of the forest. Third, kiwis, having evolved without natural enemies and possessing no means of escape, could not be easier prey. Taborsky writes:

> Could a single dog really do so much damage? People working trained kiwi dogs at night know it is very easy indeed for a dog to spot and catch a kiwi. The birds are noisy when going through the bush and their smell is very strong and distinctive. When a kiwi calls, a dog can easily pick up the direction from more than 100 m away. With a kiwi density as high as it was in Waitangi Forest a dog could perhaps catch 10–15 kiwis a night, and the killing persisted for at least 6 weeks.

As to why a dog would kill so many animals "for sport," or at least not for food, who knows? We do, however, understand enough to brand as romantic twaddle the common litany that "man alone kills for sport, other animals only for food or in defense." The kiwi marauder of New Zealand may have set a new record for intensity of destruction, but she followed the killing pattern of many animals. In any case, she surely illustrated the power of individuals to alter the history of entire populations. Taborsky estimates that, given the extremely slow breeding of kiwis, "the population will probably need 10–20 years and a rigorous protection scheme to recover to previous densities."

These two stories may elicit both fascination and a *frisson,* but still strike some readers as unpersuasive regarding the role of individuals in science. To be sure, both Passion and the austral hell hound had a disturbing effect on their populations. But science is general pattern, not ephemeral perturbation. The Gombe chimps recovered in a few years, as a subsequent baby boom offset Passion's depredations. On the crucial issue of scale, individuals still don't set patterns in the fullness of time or the largeness of space. Predictability under nature's laws takes over at an amplitude of scale and a degree of generality meriting the name "science." I would offer three rebuttals to this argument.

First, scale is a relative concept. Who can set the boundary between perturbations in systems too small to matter and long-term patterns of appropriate generality? Human evolution is a tiny twig among millions on the tree of earthly evolution. But do all the generalities of anthropology therefore count only as details outside the more ample scope of true science? Earthly evolution may be only one story of life among unknown cosmic billions; are all the laws of biology therefore nothing but peculiarities of one insignificant example?

Second, small perturbations are not always reined in by laws of nature to bring systems back to a previous equilibrium. Perturbations, starting as tiny fluctuations wrought by individuals, can accumulate to profound and permanent alterations in much larger worlds. Much of the present fascination for chaos theory in mathematics stems from its attempt to model such agents of pattern, even in large systems operating under deterministic laws. The Gombe chimps may feel no long-term effect of Passion's cannibalism, but the Waitangi kiwis may never recover.

Third, some natural populations may be so small that individuality dominates over pattern even if a larger system might fall under predictable law. If I am flipping a coin 10,000 times in a row, with nothing staked on any particular toss, then an individual flip neither has much effect in itself nor influences the final outcome to any marked degree. But if I am flipping one coin once to start a football game, then a great deal rides on the unpredictability of an individual event. Some important populations in nature are closer in number to the single toss than to the long sequence. Yet we cannot deny them entry into the domain of science.

Consider the large, orbiting objects of our solar system—nine planets and a few score moons. The domain of celestial mechanics has long been viewed as the primal realm of lawfulness and predictability in science—the bailiwick of Newton and Kepler, Copernicus and Galileo, inverse square laws and eclipses charted to the second. We used to view the objects themselves, planets and moons, in much the same light—as regular bodies formed under a few determining conditions. Know composition, size, distance from the sun, and most of the rest follows.

As I write this essay, *Voyager 2* has just left the vicinity of Neptune and ventured beyond the planetary realm of our solar system—its "grand tour" complete after twelve years and the most colossal Baedecker in history: Jupiter, Saturn, Uranus, and Neptune. Scientists in charge have issued quite appropriate statements of humility, centered upon the surprises conveyed by stunning photographs of outer planets and their moons. I admit to the enormous mystery surrounding so many puzzling features—the whirling storms of Neptune, when the closer and larger Uranus appears so featureless; the diverse and complex terrain of Uranus's innermost moon, Miranda (see the preceding essay). But I do think that a generality has emerged from this confusing jumble of diverse results, so many still defying interpretation—a unifying principle usually missed in public reports because it falls outside the scope of stereotypical science.

I offer, as the most important lesson from *Voyager,* the principle of individuality for moons and planets. This contention should elicit no call for despair or surrender of science to the domain of narrative. We anticipated greater regularity, but have learned that the surfaces of planets and moons cannot be predicted from a few general rules. To understand planetary surfaces, we must learn the particular history of each body as an individual object—the story of collisions and catastrophes, more than steady accumulations; in other words, its unpredictable single jolts more than daily operations under nature's laws.

While *Voyager* recedes ever farther on its arc to the stars, we have made a conceptual full circle. When we launched *Voyager* in 1977, we mounted a copper disk on its side, with a stylus, cartridge, and instructions for playing. On this first celestial record, we placed the diversity of the earth's people. We sent greetings in fifty-five languages, and even added some whale song for ecumenical breadth. This babble of individuality was supposed to encounter, at least within our solar system, a regular set of worlds shaped by a few predictable forces. But the planets and moons have now spoken back to *Voyager* with all the riotous diversity of that unplayed record. The solar system is a domain of individuality by my third argument for small populations composed of distinctive objects. And science—that wonderfully diverse enterprise with methods attuned to resolve both the lawful millions and the unitary movers and shakers—has been made all the richer.

This is my third and last essay on *Voyager.* The first, which shall be my eternal incubus, praised the limited and lawful regularity that *Voyager* would presumably discover on planetary surfaces throughout the solar system. I argued, following the standard "line" at the time (but bowing to convention is never a good excuse), that simple rules of size and composition would set planetary surfaces. With sufficient density of rocky composition, size alone should reign. Small bodies, with their high ratios of surface to volume, are cold and dead—for they lose so much internal heat through their relatively large surface and are too small to hold an atmosphere. Hence, they experience no internal forces of volcanism and plate tectonics and no external forces of atmospheric erosion. In consequence, small planets and moons should be pristine worlds studded with ancient impact craters neither eroded nor recycled during billions of years. Large bodies, on the other hand, maintain atmospheres and internal heat machines. Their early craters should be obliterated, and their surfaces, like our earth's, should bear the marks of continuous, gentler action.

The first data from planetary probes followed these expectations splendidly. Small Mercury and smaller Phobos and Deimos (the moons of Mars) are intensely cratered, while Mars, at its intermediary size, showed a lovely mixture of ancient craters and regions more recently shaped by erosion and volcanic action. But then *Voyager* reached Jupiter and the story started to unravel in favor of individuality granted by distinctive histories for each object.

Io, Jupiter's innermost major moon, should have been dead and cratered at its size, but *Voyager* spotted large volcanoes spewing forth plumes of sulfur instead. Saturn's amazingly complex rings told a story of repeated collisions and dismemberments. Miranda, innermost moon of Uranus, delivered the *coup de grâce* to a dying theory. Miranda should be yet another placid body, taking its lumps in the form of craters and wearing the scars forever. Instead, *Voyager* photographed more signs of varied activity than any other body had displayed—a geological potpourri of features, suggesting that Miranda had been broken apart and reaggregated, perhaps more than once. Brave new world indeed.

I threw in the towel and wrote my second essay in the *mea culpa* mode (reprinted as the preceding essay). Now I cement my conversion. *Voyager* has just passed Neptune, last post of the grand tour, and fired a glorious parting shot for individuality. We knew that Triton, Neptune's largest moon, was odd in one important sense. All other bodies, planets around the sun and moons around the planets, revolve in the same direction—counterclockwise as you look down upon the plane of the solar system from above.* But Triton moves around Neptune in a clockwise direction. Still, at a size smaller than our moon, it should have been another of those dead and cratered worlds now mocked by the actual diversity of our solar system. Triton—and what a finale— is, if anything, even more diverse, active, and interesting than Miranda. *Voyager* photographed some craters, but also a complexly cracked and crumpled surface and, most unexpectedly of all, volcanoes, probably spewing forth nitrogen in streaks over the surface of Triton.

In short, too few bodies, too many possible histories. The planets and moons are not a repetitive suite, formed under a few simple laws of nature. They are individual bodies with complex histories. And their major features are set by unique events— mostly catastrophic—that shape their surfaces as Passion decimated the Gombe chimps or the austral hound wreaked havoc on the kiwis of Waitangi. Planets are like organisms, not water molecules; they have irreducible personalities built by history. They are objects in the domain of a grand enterprise—natural history—that unites both styles of science in its ancient and still felicitous name.

As *Voyager* has increased our knowledge, and at least for this paleontologist, integrated his two childhood loves of astronomy and fossils on the common ground of natural history, I cannot let this primary scientific triumph of our generation pass from our solar system (and these essays) without an additional comment in parting.

Knowledge and wonder are the dyad of our worthy lives as intellectual beings. *Voyager* did wonders for our knowledge, but

---

*Several Southern Hemisphere colleagues wrote to protest the indefensible parochialism of this image. The solar system has no natural "above" or "below." We think of the Northern Hemisphere as "above" only by cartographic convention in the Eurocentric tradition. I could have silently changed my restrictive image, but elected this correction by footnote since the illustration of such parochialism, however embarrassing, always serves to illustrate the power of unconscious bias and the need for continuous self-scrutiny.

performed just as mightily in the service of wonder—and the two elements are complementary, not independent or opposed. The thought fills me with awe—a mechanical contraption that could fit in the back of a pickup truck, traveling through space for twelve years, dodging around four giant bodies and their associated moons, and finally sending exquisite photos across more than four light-hours of space from the farthest planet in our solar system. (Pluto, although usually beyond Neptune, rides a highly eccentric orbit about the sun. It is now, and will be until 1999, within the orbit of Neptune and will not regain its status as outermost until the millennium. The point may seem a bit forced, but symbols matter and Neptune is now most distant. Moments and individualities count.)

The photos fill me with joy for their fierce beauty. To see the most distant moon with the detailed clarity of an object shot at ten palpable paces; the abstract swirling colors in Jupiter's great spot; the luminosity and order of Saturn's rings; the giant ripple-crater of Callisto, the cracks of Ganymede, the sulfur basins of Io, the craters of Mimas, the volcanoes of Triton. As *Voyager* passed Neptune, her programmers made a courtly and proper bow to aesthetics and took the most gorgeous picture of all, for beauty's sake—a photograph of Neptune as a large crescent, with Triton as a smaller crescent at its side. Two horns, proudly independent but locked in a common system. Future advertisers and poster makers may turn this exquisite object into a commercial cliché, but let it stand for now as a symbol for the fusion of knowledge and wonder.

Voyager has also served us well in literary allusions. Miranda is truly the "brave new world" of her most famous line. And Triton conjures all the glory and meaning of his most celebrated reference. You may have suppressed it, for forced memorization was a chore, but "The World Is Too Much with Us" remains a great poem (still assigned, I trust, by teachers). No one has ever matched Wordsworth in describing the wonder of childhood's enthusiasms—a wonder that we must strive to maintain through life's diminution of splendor in the grass and glory in the flower, for we are lost eternally when this light dies. So get to know Triton in his planetary form, but also remember him as Wordsworth's invocation to perpetual wonder:

. . . Great God! I'd rather be
A Pagan suckled in a creed outworn;
So might I, standing on this pleasant lea,
Have glimpses that would make me less forlorn;
Have sight of Proteus rising from the sea;
Or hear old Triton blow his wreathed horn.

The most elegant photograph of the *Voyager* mission—a symbol of both knowledge and wonder. The horns (crescents) of Neptune and Triton. PHOTO COURTESY NASA/J.P.L.

Bibliography

Altholz, Josef L. 1980. The Huxley-Wilberforce debate revisited. *Journal of the History of Medicine and Allied Science,* 35(3):313–316.

Baker, Jeffrey J.W., and Garland E. Allen. 1982. *The study of biology.* Reading, MA: Addison Wesley.

Barbour, T., and J.C. Phillips. 1911. Concealing coloration again. *The Auk,* 28(2):179–187.

Bates, Henry Walter. 1863. Contributions to an insect fauna of the Amazon Valley. *Transactions of the Linnaean Society.*

Bates, Henry Walter. 1876. *The naturalist on the river Amazons: A record of adventures, habits of animals, sketches of Brazilian and Indian life, and aspects of Nature under the equator, during eleven years of travel.* London: J. Murray.

Berman, D.S., and J.S. McIntosh. 1978. Skull and relationships of the Upper Jurassic sauropod *Apatosaurus. Bulletin of the Carnegie Museum of Natural History,* No. 8.

Bierer, L.K., V.F. Liem, and E.P. Silberstein. 1987. *Life Science.* Heath.

Bligh, W. 1792. *A voyage to the South Sea undertaken by command of his Majesty for the purpose of conveying the bread-fruit tree to the West Indies in his Majesty's ship the* Bounty, *commanded by Lt. W. Bligh, including an account of the mutiny on board the said ship.* London.

Bohringer, R.C. 1981. Cutaneous receptors in the bill of the platypus (*Ornithorhyncus anatinus*). *Australian Mammalogy* 4:93–105.

Bohringer, R.C., and M.J. Rowe. 1977. The organization of the sensory and motor areas of cerebral cortex in the platypus *Ornithorhynchus anatinus. Journal of Comparative Neurology,* 174(1): 1–14.

Borges, Jorge Luis. 1979. *The book of sand.* London: A. Lane.

Brody, Samuel. 1945. *Bioenergetics and growth: with special reference to the efficiency complex in domestic animals.* New York: Hefner.

Browne, Janet. 1978. The Charles Darwin–Joseph Hooker correspondence: An analysis of manuscript resources and their use in biography. *Journal of the Society for the Bibliography of Natural History,* 8:351–366.

Brownlie, A.D., and M.F. Lloyd Prichard. 1963. Professor Fleeming Jenkin, 1833–1885 pioneer in engineering and political economy. *Oxford Economic Papers,* NS, 15(3):204–216.

Burnet, Thomas. 1691. *Sacred theory of the earth.* London: R. Norton.

Burrell, Harry. 1927. *The platypus: Its discovery, position, form and characteristics, habits and life history.* Sydney: Angus and Robertson.

Bury, J.B. 1920. *The idea of progress: An inquiry into its origin and growth.* London: Macmillan and Co., Ltd.

Busse, K. 1970. Care of the young by male *Rhinodrma darwini. Copeia,* No. 2, p. 395.

Calder, A., III. 1978. The kiwi. *Scientific American,* July.

Calder, Wm. A., III. 1979. The kiwi and egg design: Evolution as a package deal. *Bioscience,* 29(8):461–467.

Calder, A., III. 1984. *Size, function and life history.* Cambridge, MA: Harvard University Press.

Caldwell, W.H. 1888. The embryology of Monotremata and Marsupialia. Part I. *Philosophical Transactions of the Royal Society of London* (B), 178:463–483.

Camper, Petrus. 1791. *Physical dissertation on the real differences that men of different countries and ages display in their facial traits; on the beauty that characterizes the statues and engraved stones of antiquity; followed by the proposition of a new method for drawing human heads with the greatest accuracy.* Utrecht: B. Wild & J. Altheer.

Cavalli-Sforza, L.L., A. Piazza, P. Mendozzi, and J. Mountain. 1988. Reconstruction of human evolution: Bringing together genetic, archaeological, and linguistic data. *Proceedings of the National Academy of Sciences,* August, pp. 6002–6006.

Chamberlin, T.C., and R. Salisbury. 1909. *College Geology* (American Science Series). New York: Henry Holt & Co.

Chambers, Robert. 1844. *Vestiges of the natural history of creation.* London: J. Churchill.

Chapman, Frank M. 1933. *Autobiography of a bird lover.* New York: D. Appleton-Century Co., Inc.

Coletta, Paolo E. 1969. *William Jennings Bryan:* Vol. 3, *Political Puritan.* University of Nebraska Press.

Cope, E.D. 1874. *The origin of the fittest, and the primary factors of organic evolution.* New York: Arno Press.

Corben, C.J., G.J. Ingram, and M.J. Tyler. 1974. Gastric brooding: Unique form of parental care in an Australian frog. *Science,* 186:946.

Cott, Hugh B. 1940. *Adaptive coloration in animals.* London: Methuen.

Crosland, M.J., and Ross H. Crozier. 1986. *Myrmecia pilosula,* an ant with only one pair of chromosomes. *Science,* 231:1278.

Darnton, Robert. 1968. *Mesmerism and the end of the Enlightenment in France.* Cambridge, MA: Harvard University Press.

Darwin, Charles. 1859. *On the origin of species by means of natural selection.* London: John Murray.

Darwin, Charles. 1863. Review of Bates's paper. *Natural History Reviews,* pp. 219–224.

Darwin, Charles. 1868. *Variation of animals and plants under domestication.* London: John Murray.

Darwin, Erasmus. 1794. *Zoonomia, or the laws of organic life.* London: J. Johnson.

Darwin, Francis. 1887. *The life and letters of Charles Darwin.* London: John Murray.

David, Paul A. 1986. Understanding the economics of QWERTY: The necessity of history. In W.N. Parker, ed., *Economic history and the modern economist,* pp. 30–49. New York: Basil Blackwell, Inc.

Davis, D.D. 1964. Monograph on the giant panda. Chicago: Field Museum of Natural History.

De Quatrefages, A. 1864. *Metamorphoses of man and the lower animals.* London: Robert Hardwicke, 192 Piccadilly.

Disraeli, Benjamin. 1880. *Endymion.*

Douglas, Matthew M. 1981. Thermoregulatory significance of

thoracic lobes in the evolution of insect wings. *Science,* 211:84–86.

Dyson, Freeman. 1981. *Disturbing the universe.* New York: Harper & Row.

Eibl-Eibesfeldt, I. 1975. *Krieg und Frieden aus der Sicht der Verhaltensforschung.* Munchen, Zurich: Piper.

Eldredge, N., and S.J. Gould. 1972. Punctuated equilibria: An alternative to phyletic gradualism. In T.J.M. Schopf, ed., *Models in paleobiology,* pp. 82–115. San Francisco: Freeman, Cooper and Co.

Erasmus, Desiderius. 1508. *Adagia.*

Flower, J.W. 1964. On the origin of flight in insects. *Journal of Insect Physiology,* 10:81–88.

Force, James. 1985. *William Whiston, honest Newtonian.* Cambridge, England: Cambridge University Press.

Freud, Sigmund. 1905–1915. Three essays on the theory of sexuality.

Gates, Richard G. 1978. Vision in the monotreme Echidna (*Tachyglossus aculeatus*). *Australian Zoologist,* 20(1):147–169.

Gilley, Sheridan. 1981. The Huxley-Wilberforce debate: A reconsideration. In K. Robbins, ed., *Religion and humanism,* Vol. 17, pp. 325–340.

Gilovich, T., R. Vallone, and A. Tversky. 1985. The hot hand in basketball: On the misperception of random sequences. *Cognitive Psychology,* 17:295–314.

Gladstone, W.E. 1858. *Studies on Homer and the Homeric Age.*

Gladstone, W.E. 1885. Dawn of creation and of worship. *The Nineteenth Century,* November.

Goldschmidt, R. 1940 (reprinted 1982 with introduction by S.J. Gould). *The material basis of evolution.* New Haven: Yale University Press.

Goldschmidt, R. 1948. Glowworms and evolution. *Révue Scientifique,* 86:607–612.

Goodall, Jane. 1986. *The chimpanzees of Gombe.* Cambridge, MA: Harvard University Press.

Gould, S.J. 1975. On the scaling of tooth size in mammals. *American Zoologist,* 15:351–362.

Gould, S.J. 1977. *Ontogeny and phylogeny.* Cambridge, MA: Harvard University Press.

Gould, S.J. 1980. *The panda's thumb.* New York: W.W. Norton.

Gould, S.J. 1981. *The mismeasure of man.* New York: W.W. Norton.

Gould, S.J. 1985. *The flamingo's smile.* New York: W.W. Norton.

Gould, S.J. 1985. Geoffroy and the homeobox. *Natural History,* November, pp. 22–23.

Gould, S.J. 1987. Bushes all the way down. *Natural History,* June, pp. 12–19.

Gould, S.J. 1987. *Time's arrow, time's cycle.* Cambridge, MA: Harvard University Press.

Gould, S.J. 1989. Winning and losing: It's all in the game. *Rotunda,* Spring 1989, pp. 25–33.

Gould, S.J., and Elisabeth S. Vrba. 1982. Exaptation—a missing term in the science of form. *Paleobiology,* 8(1):4–15.

Grant, Tom. 1984. *The Platypus.* New South Wales University Press.

Grant, Verne. 1963. *The origin of adaptations.* New York: Columbia University Press.

Gregory, William King. 1927. *Hesperopithecus* apparently not an ape nor a man. *Science,* 66:579–587.

Gregory, William King, and Milo Hellman. 1923. Notes on the type of *Hesperopithecus haroldcookii* Osborn. American Museum of Natural History *Novitates,* 53:1–16.

Gregory, William King, and Milo Hellman. 1923. Further notes on the molars of *Hesperopithecus* and of *Pithecanthropus. Bulletin of the American Museum of Natural History,* Vol. 48, Art. 13, pp. 509–526.

Griffiths, M. 1968. *Echidnas.* New York: Pergamon Press.

Griffiths, M. 1978. *The biology of monotremes.* San Diego/Orlando: Academic Press.

Haller, John S. 1971. *Outcasts from evolution.* University of Illinois Press.

Hegner, Robert W. 1912. *College zoology.* New York: Macmillan Co.

Heinrich, B. 1981. *Insect thermoregulation.* San Diego/Orlando: Academic Press.

Hite, Shere. 1976. *The Hite Report: A nationwide report on sexuality.* New York: Macmillan.

Holway, John. 1987. A little help from his friends. *Sports Heritage,* November/December.

518 | BIBLIOGRAPHY

Home, Everard. 1802. A description of the anatomy of the *Ornithorhynchus paradoxus*. *Philosophical Transactions of the Royal Society*, Part 1, No. 4, pp. 67–84.

Howes, G.B. 1888. Notes on the gular brood-pouch of *Rhinoderma darwini*. *Proceedings of the Zoological Society of London*, pp. 231–237.

Hrdy, Sarah. 1981. *The women that never evolved*. Cambridge, MA: Harvard University Press.

Hunter, George William. 1914. *A civic biology*. New York: American Book Company.

Hutton, J. 1788. Theory of the Earth. *Transactions of the Royal Society of Edinburgh*, 1:209–305.

Hutton, J. 1795. *The theory of the Earth*. Edinburgh: William Creech.

Huxley, Julian. 1927. On the relation between egg-weight and body-weight in birds. *Journal of the Linnaean Society of London*, 36:457–466.

Huxley, Leonard. 1906. *Life and letters of Thomas H. Huxley*. New York: Appleton.

Huxley, T. H. 1880. On the application of the laws of evolution to the arrangement of the Vertebrata, and more particularly of the Mammalia. *Proceedings of the Zoological Society of London*, No. 43, pp. 649–661.

Huxley, T. H. 1885. The interpreters of Genesis and the interpreters of Nature. *The Nineteenth Century*, December.

Huxley, T. H. 1888. The struggle for existence in human society. *The Nineteenth Century*, February.

Huxley, T. H. 1896. *Science and education*. New York: Appleton & Co.

Huxley, T. H. 1896. Mr. Gladstone and Genesis. *The Nineteenth Century*.

Huxley, T.H., and Julian Huxley. 1947. *Evolution and ethics*. London: Pilot Press.

Ingersoll, Ernest. 1906. *The life of animals*. New York: Macmillan.

Ingram, G.J., M. Anstis, and C.J. Corben. 1975. Observations on the Australian leptodactylid frog, *Assa darlingtoni*. *Herpetologia*, 31:425–429.

Jackson, J.F. 1974. Goldschmidt's dilemma resolved: Notes on the larval behavior of a new neotropical web-spinning Mycetophilid (Diptera). *American Midland Naturalist*, 92(1):240–245.

James, William. 1909. Letter quoted in *The autobiography of Nathaniel Southgate Shaler.* Boston: Houghton Mifflin.

Jenkin, F. 1867. Darwin and the origin of species. *North British Review,* June.

Jerison, H.J. 1973. *Evolution of the brain and intelligence.* San Diego/Orlando: Academic Press.

Jordan, David Starr, and Vernon L. Kellogg. 1900. *Animal life: A first book of zoology.* New York: D. Appleton & Co.

Kellogg, Vernon L. 1907. *Darwinism to-day.* London: G. Bell & Sons.

Kellogg, Vernon L. 1917. *Headquarters nights.* Boston.

Keyes, Ralph. 1980. *The height of your life.* Boston: Little, Brown.

Kidd, Benjamin. 1894. *Social evolution.* New York/London: Macmillan & Co.

Kidd, Benjamin. 1918. *The science of power.* New York.

Kingsland, S. 1978. Abbott Thayer and the protective coloration debate. *Journal of the History of Biology,* 11(2):223–244.

Kingsolver, J.G., and M.A.R. Koehl. 1985. Aerodynamics, thermoregulation, and the evolution of insect wings: Differential scaling and evolutionary change. *Evolution,* 39:488–504.

Kinsey, A.C. 1929. The gall wasp genus *Cynips:* A study in the origin of species. *Indiana University Studies,* Vol. 16.

Kinsey, A.C. 1936. The origin of higher categories in *Cynips. Indiana University Publications Science Series,* No. 4.

Kinsey, A.C., W.B. Pomeroy, C.E. Martin, and P.H. Gebhard. 1953. *Sexual behavior in the human female.* Philadelphia: W.B. Saunders.

Kirby, W., and W. Spence. 1863. *An introduction to entomology,* 7th ed. London: Longman, Green, Longman, Roberts & Green.

Kirwan, Richard. 1809. *Metaphysical essays.* London.

Kropotkin, P.A. 1902. *Mutual aid: A factor of evolution.* New York: McClure Phillips.

Lacépède, B.G.E. 1801 (1'an IX de la République). *Discours d'ouverture et de clôture du cours de zoologie donné dans le Muséum d'Histoire naturelle.* Paris: Plassan.

Lamarck, J.-B. 1809. *Philosophie zoologique.* Paris.

Lavoisier, A., B. Franklin et al. 1784. *Rapport des commissaires chargés par le roi de l'examen du magnétisme animal.* Paris: Imprimerie royale.

Lende, R.A. 1964. Representation in the cerebral cortex of a primitive mammal: Sensorimotor, visual and auditory fields in the Echidna (*Tachyglossus aculeatus*). *Journal of Neurophysiology*, 27:37–48.

Levine, L.W. 1965. *Defender of the faith: William Jennings Bryan, the last decade.* New York: Oxford University Press.

Linnaeus, C. 1758 (facsimile reprint 1956). *Systema naturae. Regnum animale.* London: British Museum (Natural History).

Livingstone, David N. 1987. *Nathaniel Southgate Shaler and the culture of American science.* University of Alabama Press.

Lovejoy, A.O. 1936. *The great chain of being.* Cambridge, MA: Harvard University Press.

Lucas, J.R. 1979. Wilberforce and Huxley: A legendary encounter. *The Historical Journal*, 22:313–330.

Lyell, Charles. 1830–1833. *Principles of geology, being an attempt to explain the former changes of the earth's surface by reference to causes now in operation.* London: John Murray.

MacFadden, B.J. 1986. Fossil horses from "Eohippus" (*Hyracotherium*) to *Equus:* Scaling, Cope's law, and the evolution of body size. *Paleobiology*, 12(4):355–369.

Marsh, O.C. 1874. Notice of new equine mammals from the Tertiary Formation. *American Journal of Science*, Series 3, Vol. 7, pp. 247–258.

Marsh, O.C. 1877. Notice of new dinosaurian reptiles from the Jurassic Formation. *American Journal of Science*, 14:514–516.

Marsh, O.C. 1879. Principal characters of American Jurassic dinosaurs, Part II. *American Journal of Science*, 17:86–92.

Marsh, O.C. 1879. Notice of new Jurassic reptiles. *American Journal of Science*, 18:501–505.

Marsh, O.C. 1883. Principal characters of American Jurassic Dinosaurs. Part VI: Restoration of *Brontosaurus. American Journal of Science*, Series 3, Vol. 26, pp. 81–85.

Marsh, O.C. 1896. *The dinosaurs of North America.* 16th Annual Report of the U.S. Geological Survey, Washington, D.C., Part 1, pp. 133–414.

Marshack, Alexander. 1985. *Hierarchical evolution of the human capacity: The Paleolithic evidence.* James Arthur Lecture on the evolution of the human brain. New York: American Museum of Natural History.

Masters, William H., and Virginia E. Johnson. 1966. *Human sexual response.* Boston: Little, Brown.

Matthew, W.D. 1903. *The evolution of the horse.* American Museum of Natural History pamphlet.

Matthew, W.D. 1926. The evolution of the horse: A record and its interpretation. *Quarterly Review of Biology,* 1(2):139–185.

Mayr, Ernst. 1982. *The growth of biological thought.* Cambridge, MA: Harvard University Press.

McDiarmid, R.W. 1978. Evolution of parental care in frogs. In G.M. Burghardt and M. Bekoff, eds., *The development of behavior: Comparative and evolutionary aspects.* New York: Garland Press.

Mivart, St. George J. 1871. *On the genesis of species.* New York: D. Appleton & Co.

Moore, Ruth. 1957. *Charles Darwin.* London: Hutchinson.

Morris, Desmond. 1969. *The naked ape.* New York: Dell Publishing Co.

Nisbet, R. 1980. *History of the idea of progress.* New York: Basil Books.

Osborn, Henry Fairfield. 1904. The evolution of the horse in America. *Century Magazine,* November.

Osborn, Henry Fairfield. 1921. Preface to Madison Grant's *The passing of the great race.* New York: C. Scribner's Sons.

Osborn, Henry Fairfield. 1922. *Evolution and religion.* New York: Charles Scribner's Sons.

Osborn, Henry Fairfield. 1922. *Hesperopithecus,* the first anthropoid Primate found in America. *American Museum of Natural History Novitates,* No. 37, pp. 1–5.

Osborn, Henry Fairfield. 1925. *The Earth speaks to Bryan.* New York: Charles Scribner's Sons.

Othar, L.K., and J. Rhodes. 1978. Instrumental learning in the Echidna (*Tachyglossus aculeatus setosus*). *Australian Zoologist,* 20(1): 131–145.

Otto, J.H., and A. Towle. 1977. *Modern biology.* New York: Holt, Rinehart & Winston.

Paul, Diane B. 1987. The nine lives of discredited data. *The Sciences,* May.

Pirlot, P., and J. Nelson. 1978. Volumetric analysis of monotreme brains. *Australian Zoologist,* 20(1):171–179.

Pirsson, L.V., and C. Schuchert. 1924. *Textbook of geology,* Part 2. New York: John Wiley & Sons, Inc.

Playfair, John. 1802. *Illustrations of the Huttonian theory of the Earth.* Edinburgh: William Creech.

Poulton, E.B. 1894. The structure of the bills and hairs of *Ornithorhynchus* with a discussion of the homologies and origin of mammalian hair. *Quarterly Journal of Microscopical Science*, 36: 143–199.

Prothero, D.R., and Neil Shubin. 1989. The evolution of Oligocene horses. In D.R. Prothero and R.M. Schoch, eds., *The evolution of perissodactyls*, pp. 142–175. Oxford: Oxford University Press.

Pugh, George E. 1977. *The biological origin of human values.* New York: Basic Books.

Rahn, H., C.G. Paganelli, and A. Ar. 1975. Relation of avian egg weight to body weight. *The Auk*, 92(4):750–765.

Read, W. Maxwell. 1930. *The Earth for Sam.* New York: Harcourt, Brace & Co.

Reid, B., and G.R. Williams. 1975. The kiwi. In G. Kuschel, ed., *Biogeography and ecology in New Zealand*, pp. 301–330. The Hague: D.W. Junk.

Renfrew, Colin. 1987. *Archaeology and language.* Cambridge, England: Cambridge University Press.

Réville, Alfred. 1881. *Prolegomenes de l'histoire des religions.* Paris: Fischbacher.

Riggs, Elmer. 1903. Structure and relationships of opisthocoelian dinosaurs. Part 1: *Apatosaurus. Geological Series of the Field Columbian Museum*, Publication 82, Vol. 2, No. 4, pp. 165–196.

Roger, J. 1976. "William Whiston," entry in the *Dictionary of Scientific Biography*, Vol. 14, pp. 295–296. New York: Charles Scribner's Sons.

Romer, A.S. 1966. *Vertebrate paleontology*, 3rd ed. Chicago: University of Chicago Press.

Roosevelt, Theodore. 1911. Revealing and concealing coloration in birds and mammals. *Bulletin of the American Museum of Natural History*, 30(8):119–231.

Sagan, Carl, and A. Druyan. 1985. *Comet.* New York: Random House.

Saint-Hilaire, Etienne Geoffroy. 1803. Extrait des observations anatomiques de M. Home, sur l'échidné. *Bulletin des Sciences par la Société philomathique*, an 11 de la République.

Saint-Hilaire, Etienne Geoffroy. 1827. Sur les appareils sexuels et urinaires de l'Ornithorhynque: *Mémoires du Muséum d'Histoire Naturelle.*

Schuchert, Charles. 1928. Charles Doolittle Walcott (1850–1927). *Proceedings of the American Academy of Arts and Sciences,* 62: 276–285.

Schweber, S.S. 1977. The origin of the *Origin* revisited. *Journal of the History of Biology,* 10:229–316.

Scott, W.B. 1913. *A history of land mammals in the Western Hemisphere.* New York: Macmillan.

Shaler, N.S. 1861. Lateral symmetry in Brachiopoda. *Proceedings of the Boston Society of Natural History,* 8:274–279.

Shaler, N.S. 1901. *The individual: A study of life and death.* New York: D. Appleton & Co.

Shaw, George. 1799. *The naturalist miscellany,* Plate 385.

Simpson, G.G. 1951. *Horses.* Oxford, England: Oxford University Press.

Smith, Grafton Elliot. 1902. On a peculiarity of the cerebral commissures in certain Marsupialia, not hitherto recognized as a distinctive feature of the Diprotodonta. *Proceedings of the Royal Society of London,* Vol. 70, No. 462, pp. 226–230.

Smith, W.H. 1975. *The social and religious thought of William Jennings Bryan.* Coronado Press.

Solecki, Ralph S. 1971. *Shanidar, the first flower people.* New York: Knopf.

Stanton, William. 1960. *The leopard's spots.* Chicago: University of Chicago Press.

Stebbins, G. Ledyard. 1966. Chromosomal variation and evolution. *Science,* 152:1463–1469.

Stevenson, R.L. 1887. *Papers literary, scientific, etc. by the late Fleeming Jenkin.* London: Longmans, Green & Co.

Strahan, R., ed. 1983. *Complete book of Australian mammals.* Sydney: Angus & Robertson.

Symons, Donald. 1979. *The evolution of human sexuality.* New York: Oxford University Press.

Taborsky, Michael. 1988. Kiwis and dog predation: Observations in Waitangi State Forest. *Notornis,* 35:197–202.

Thayer, Abbott H. 1896. The law which underlies protective coloration. *The Auk,* 13:124–129.

Thayer, Abbott H. 1900. Arguments against the banner mark theory. *The Auk,* 17(2):108–113.

Thayer, Abbott H. 1903. Protective coloration in its relation to mimicry, common warning colours, and sexual selection.

Transactions of the Entomological Society of London, Article 26, pp. 553–569.

Thayer, Abbott H. 1909. An arraignment of the theories of mimicry and warning colors. *Popular Science,* December.

Thayer, Abbott H. 1909. *Concealing-coloration in the animal kingdom.* New York: Macmillan.

Thayer, Abbott H. 1911. Concealing coloration. *The Auk,* 28: 146–148.

Todes, Daniel P. 1988. Darwin's Malthusian metaphor and Russian evolutionary thought, 1859–1917. *Isis,* 78:537–551.

Tyler, M.J. 1983. *The gastric brooding frog.* London/Canberra: Croom Helm.

Ulinski, Philip S. 1984. Thalamic projections to the somatosensory cortex of the Echidna (*Tachyglossus aculeatus*). *Journal of Comparative Neurology,* 229(2):153–170.

Vonnegut, Kurt. 1963. *Cat's cradle.* New York: Delacorte Press.

Vorzimmer, Peter J. 1970. *Charles Darwin: The years of controversy.* Temple University Press.

Walcott, Sidney. 1971. How I found my own fossil. *Smithsonian.*

Whiston, William. 1696. *A new theory of the Earth from its original to the consummation of all things, wherein the creation of the world in six days, the universal deluge, and the general conflagration, as laid down in the Holy Scriptures, are shewn to be perfectly agreeable to reason and philosophy.* London.

Whiston, William. 1708. *New theory,* 2d ed. London: B. Tooke.

White, Nelson G. 1951. *Abbott H. Thayer: Painter and naturalist.* Connecticut Printers.

Wilberforce, W. 1860. Review of "On the Origin of Species." *Quarterly Review,* 108:225–264.

Wolf, John, and J.S. Mellett. 1985. The role of "Nebraska Man" in the creation-evolution debate. *Creation/Evolution,* 5: 31–43.

Index

READ MORE IN PENGUIN

In every corner of the world, on every subject under the sun, Penguin represents quality and variety – the very best in publishing today.

For complete information about books available from Penguin – including Puffins, Penguin Classics and Arkana – and how to order them, write to us at the appropriate address below. Please note that for copyright reasons the selection of books varies from country to country.

In the United Kingdom: Please write to *Dept. EP, Penguin Books Ltd, Bath Road, Harmondsworth, West Drayton, Middlesex UB7 ODA*

In the United States: Please write to *Consumer Sales, Penguin Putnam Inc., P.O. Box 999, Dept. 17109, Bergenfield, New Jersey 07621-0120.* VISA and MasterCard holders call 1-800-253-6476 to order Penguin titles

In Canada: Please write to *Penguin Books Canada Ltd, 10 Alcorn Avenue, Suite 300, Toronto, Ontario M4V 3B2*

In Australia: Please write to *Penguin Books Australia Ltd, P.O. Box 257, Ringwood, Victoria 3134*

In New Zealand: Please write to *Penguin Books (NZ) Ltd, Private Bag 102902, North Shore Mail Centre, Auckland 10*

In India: Please write to *Penguin Books India Pvt Ltd, 210 Chiranjiv Tower, 43 Nehru Place, New Delhi 110 019*

In the Netherlands: Please write to *Penguin Books Netherlands bv, Postbus 3507, NL-1001 AH Amsterdam*

In Germany: Please write to *Penguin Books Deutschland GmbH, Metzlerstrasse 26, 60594 Frankfurt am Main*

In Spain: Please write to *Penguin Books S. A., Bravo Murillo 19, 1° B, 28015 Madrid*

In Italy: Please write to *Penguin Italia s.r.l., Via Benedetto Croce 2, 20094 Corsico, Milano*

In France: Please write to *Penguin France, Le Carré Wilson, 62 rue Benjamin Baillaud, 31500 Toulouse*

In Japan: Please write to *Penguin Books Japan Ltd, Kaneko Building, 2-3-25 Koraku, Bunkyo-Ku, Tokyo 112*

In South Africa: Please write to *Penguin Books South Africa (Pty) Ltd, Private Bag X14, Parkview, 2122 Johannesburg*

BY THE SAME AUTHOR

Eight Little Piggies

'A *tour de force* ... as both a respected scholar in his own field and a leading theorist of evolution, he packs a clout few science writers can match' – Derek Bickerton in *The New York Times Book Review*

Ever Since Darwin

Scientific insight and literary flair combine in Stephen Gould's fascinating collection of reflections concerning – among other subjects – the importance and relevance of Darwinism, the question of size in nature and the bizarre sex life of a mushroom maggot. 'A stimulating tour of new ideas in palaeontology, botany, geology and much else – a marvellous read' – *British Medical Journal*

The Panda's Thumb

'From the opening essay on the panda's thumb to an intriguing vignette on the Adactylithum mite which dies before it is born, the book provides a quirky and provocative exploration of the nature of evolution ... wonderfully entertaining' – *Sunday Telegraph*

Hen's Teeth and Horse's Toes

'No one knows more about Darwin and about evolution than Gould does. No one writes more clearly on these subjects' – Isaac Asimov

The Flamingo's Smile

'Gould's essays are remarkable, and not just for the scientific insights at their centre ... He veers about between the technical and the vernacular, the abstract and the concrete, the analytical and the auto-biographical ... extraordinary' – Patrick Wright in the *Guardian*

An Urchin in the Storm

In this dazzling set of review articles Gould ranges over almost the whole of modern science, providing a wealth of fresh insights into geology and evolution. Clear, incisive and beautifully written, the result will disappoint none of Gould's countless admirers.

BY THE SAME AUTHOR

Dinosaur in a Haystack

'An acknowledged master of the modern scientific essay . . . displaying a broad liberal mind, wit and impressive scholarship . . . And yes, the dinosaur *is* discovered at last in a "haystack", thus supporting a gripping theory about the last great extinction' – Max Wilkinson in the *Financial Times*

The Mismeasure of Man
Revised and Expanded Edition

With an extensive new introduction and additional essays, Stephen Jay Gould provides a brilliant riposte to those who would classify people according to their supposed genetic inheritance and reaffirms the Darwinian belief in the variety of human potential. 'This is a marvellous book . . . The history of these attempts to measure the intellectual and moral worth of individuals . . . turns out to be a detective story to rival most of Agatha Christie's' – *Sunday Times*

Wonderful Life
Winner of the 1991 Science Book Prize

'A masterpiece of analysis and imagination . . . It centres on a sensational discovery in the field of Palaeontology – the existence, in the Burgess Shale . . . of 530 million-year-old fossils unique in age, preservation and diversity . . . With skill and passion, Gould takes this mute collection of fossils and makes them speak to us. The result challenges some of our most cherished self-perceptions and urges a fundamental re-assessment of our place in the history of life on earth' – Michael Stewart in the *Sunday Times*

Time's Arrow, Time's Cycle

'Gould provides a fascinating, informally written excursion into the ways we conceptualize the past. He explores a central dichotomy between time's arrow (a unilinear Newtonian succession of unique events) and time's cycle (the recursive patterns that re-appear in a world that remains fundamentally unchanged) . . . Entertaining, sometimes annoying, highly personal, but never dull' – J.A. Secord in *The Times Higher Educational Supplement*